"What tales did you hear?"

Niklas shrugged. "Rumors that Pollard's been hunting down former mages. Several have disappeared and never returned. There were dark stories about men in black clothing ransacking the mage libraries and universities, carrying off sacks of items, and torching what was left." He grimaced. "Pollard seems to like setting fires. I'd heard the same about villages where he didn't get the information he was seeking." He snapped his fingers. "Went up in flames, and Raka take the survivors."

Outside, they heard a sudden crash. Horns sounded an alarm. Shouts and the sound of fighting filled the air. Niklas jumped to his feet, as did Blaine and the others. A guard appeared in the tent doorway.

"Sir, we're under attack."

"By whom?" Niklas had drawn his sword, and his eyes glinted with anger.

The guard looked as if he was struggling against his own fear. "*Talishte*, sir. We're being attacked by vampires."

Books by Gail Z. Martin

The Chronicles of the Necromancer
The Summoner
The Blood King
Dark Haven
Dark Lady's Chosen

The Fallen Kings Cycle
The Sworn
The Dread

The Ascendant Kingdoms Saga
Ice Forged
Reign of Ash
War of Shadows

REIGN OF ASH

BOOK TWO OF THE ASCENDANT KINGDOMS SAGA

WITHDRAWN

Gail Z. Martin

www.orbitbooks.net

Orbit
Hachette Book Group
237 Park Avenue, New York, NY 10017
HachetteBookGroup.com

First Edition: April 2014

Orbit is an imprint of Hachette Book Group, Inc. The Orbit name and logo are trademarks of Little, Brown Book Group Limited.

The Hachette Speakers Bureau provides a wide range of authors for speaking events. To find out more, go to www.hachettespeakersbureau.com or call (866) 376-6591.

The publisher is not responsible for websites (or their content) that are not owned by the publisher.

The characters and events in this book are fictitious. Any similarity to real persons, living or dead, is coincidental and not intended by the author.

Library of Congress Cataloging-in-Publication Data

Martin, Gail.
  Reign of ash / Gail Z. Martin. — First edition.
    pages cm. — (Ascendant kingdoms saga ; book 2)
  ISBN 978-0-316-09363-7 (trade pbk.)
  I. Title.
  PS3613.A77865R45 2014
  813'.6—dc23
                                        2013026299

10 9 8 7 6 5 4 3 2 1

RRD-C

Printed in the United States of America

To Larry, Kyrie, Chandler, and Cody, with all my love

CHAPTER ONE

W ATCH YOUR BACK!" BLAINE MCFADDEN BROUGHT his sword down hard on his opponent's blade, deflecting a killing blow.

Piran Rowse wheeled at the warning, muttering curses under his breath. Two dark-clad men were heading his way, swords at the ready. Piran ran toward them with a battle cry, a sword gripped in each hand, driving his enemies back with the sheer ferocity of his onslaught.

A force of at least twenty-five men, all dressed in black, had attacked them. Where their allegiance lay, Blaine could only guess. Why they had come was clear. Blaine had no doubt the fighters had been sent to track and kill them. To kill him.

Their battleground was the deserted barnyard of a ruined farm. Not far away, Dawe Killick caught his breath in the shelter of a tumbledown chicken coop that barely held his tall, rangy form. He dodged out to fire his crossbow, taking advantage of its reach to fell one of the dark-clad men.

Kestel Falke had grabbed the sword of one of the fallen attackers and pulled a dagger from the bandolier beneath her cloak. She circled one of the dead man's comrades warily, holding him at bay. From the top floor of the rickety barn, Verran Danning, expert thief and sometime musician, lobbed anything he could find at his opponents, striking one of the men in the head with a chunk of wood.

Four of the eleven guards they had brought with them were down, and while the remaining guards were fighting valiantly, Blaine knew the odds weren't in their favor. After narrowly escaping death the night before, it seemed a mockery to die so needlessly come sunrise.

Blaine's opponent came at him again, sword raised shoulder-high for a death strike. Blaine brought his own blade up inside the strike as he stepped aside, dodging the blow and managing to score a gash on his attacker's arm. At more than six feet tall with shoulders broadened from years of hard labor in the Velant prison colony, Lord Blaine McFadden could hold his own in a fight. Despite the cold late-autumn temperatures, the heat of the fight had plastered Blaine's long, chestnut brown hair against his head. His sea-blue eyes glinted with anger, focused on the man he intended to kill.

Blaine's body protested every jarring parry. Just the previous night, the wild magic he had sought to bind had nearly killed him, nearly killed all of them with its unharnessed power. They had lived through the assault, wearied and bloody, only to face a new danger. It had been sheer luck that the old tunnels had not collapsed around them, that they had been able to evade the dark-clad warriors, at least for a while. Not long enough.

"Who sent you?" Blaine shouted as his attacker came at him again, raining down a series of two-handed blows that nearly drove Blaine to his knees. Blaine knew he couldn't take much more—none of them could. Not after the toll the magic had taken last night. Their attackers were fresh to the fight. He'd traveled half the world to die here, in the middle of nowhere, without even coming close to achieving his task.

"Lord Pollard wants you dead," the black-clad man replied through gritted teeth. "Thought you'd have figured that out by now."

"Tell Lord Pollard he can—" Blaine's words died in his throat as an arrow zipped past him, narrowly missing his shoulder, and thudded into the rotted wood of the barn behind him.

"Incoming!" Dawe shouted, dragging a hand back through his straight, dark hair. He looked like a scarecrow, all angles and bones. "We've got new players." A hail of arrows fell, and several of the black-clad fighters went down, shot in the back. Kestel cried out as an arrow grazed her arm, but she kept on fighting, though blood colored the sleeve of her tunic.

"I think you and your men might want to run," Blaine said, a cold smile crossing his features. "Seems to me whoever's out there is aiming for your people, not mine."

For just an instant, Blaine took his eyes off his attacker to confirm the new threat. The yard was ringed with archers, all within bow range, but too far away from Blaine to make out any markings on their gray uniforms. *Sometimes the enemy of my enemy is my friend*, Blaine thought. *And other times, he's just a bigger, badder son of a bitch.*

Blaine's opponent spared no glance toward the archers. He came at Blaine ferociously, teeth bared and eyes wild. Blaine parried the first of the man's powerful strikes, but the second blow crashed down on his sword with enough force to numb his sword arm and send him staggering backward. The tip of his attacker's sword sliced into his right shoulder, and Blaine's sword fell from his numb hand. His enemy reared back, sword at chest height, to drive the point home, aiming for Blaine's heart.

An arrow sang through the air and Blaine's opponent stiffened, his face drawn in a ghastly mask of pain and fury. He lumbered forward, intent on his quarry, but the delay was just enough. Blaine dove for his sword, grasping it in his left hand, and lunged forward, ducking under his opponent's blade, expecting to feel the bite of steel against his neck at any moment. His sword plunged deep into the man's belly and his opponent fell forward, dropping his sword to the ground. Pinned under the man's body, Blaine felt hot blood seep over him as it poured from the dying man's wounds.

It took all of Blaine's waning strength to throw the man off, and more resolve still to make it as far as his knees before he saw that the battle had turned. Most of the black-clad fighters lay skewered by arrows, and the rest had run for their lives. Only six of his own guards remained standing, along with Dawe, Piran, Verran, and Kestel. But the soldiers who ringed the yard had not moved, nor had they lowered their bows.

"Surrender. Throw down your weapons. You can't win but you can die, and you surely will unless you drop your weapons now and raise your hands," a man's voice called from the line of archers.

Piran let out a barrage of creatively vulgar curses, but he let his swords fall. Dawe tossed his unloaded crossbow out into the open and emerged, his hands behind his head. Kestel dropped her sword and dagger, looking toward the archers with a baleful expression.

"You in the barn. Come out, or so help me Torven, we'll shoot the others," the voice called.

"Hold your fire! I'm coming down," Verran shouted, contempt thick in his voice.

"Let's stick to our story and see if they go for it," Blaine replied under his breath, just loud enough for his friends to hear.

"We mean you no harm," he called out to the archers. "We're tinkers and peddlers. We took shelter overnight and woke to find ourselves under attack. We'll be on our way, and no bother to you."

A half dozen men from the line of archers were moving toward them now, bows drawn and arrows at the ready. The archers still on the edge of the yard quashed any thoughts Blaine's group might have had of fighting their way free.

"You look well armed for tinkers," one of the archers replied. "Your bodyguards outnumber the rest of you," he said, with a nod to the Glenreith guards who, though wearing neither insignia nor rank, were conspicuous in their military appearance. "That's suspicious."

"These are dangerous times," Blaine replied. "We hired guards to protect us. We mean no harm. Just let us be on our way."

The leader looked as if he was considering Blaine's suggestion, then shook his head. "Not up to me. That's for the captain to say." He gestured, and more fighters joined him. "Get on your knees, and put your hands on top of your head. We'll see what the captain makes of you."

For a moment, Blaine feared from the expression on Piran's face that his friend might charge their captors. At a nod from Blaine, they knelt, hands on heads, and Blaine waited to feel a quarrel in the back.

More fighters moved forward, binding the captives' wrists

with strips of leather. One of the fighters moved to bind Blaine's wrists. He paused. "Sir," he called to the leader. "You should see this."

The leader walked over and frowned when he saw the brand on the inside of Blaine's left forearm, an "M" for murderer.

"You're a convict," the leader said, eyeing Blaine.

"I *was* a convict. Did my time in Velant. Earned my Ticket of Leave."

"Velant's up in Edgeland, at the top of the world," the leader said. "No one's supposed to come back from there."

"Just like there's *supposed* to be a king and magic's *supposed* to work," Blaine replied evenly. "Nothing's the way it's 'supposed' to be anymore."

"Got another one over here," the soldier said, lifting Dawe's arm to show the brand. Blaine sighed. He'd deserved his exile, but Dawe had been framed. And while the others bore no brands for their crimes, Verran for theft, Kestel for espionage, and Piran for court-martial-worthy insubordination, it wouldn't take too much for the fighter to figure out they were likely all 'escaped' convicts.

"Get on your feet," the leader said. "You can explain it to the captain. You're coming back to camp with us."

"What of our horses?" Blaine asked.

"We'll bring them," the leader replied. "If you can convince the captain to let you go, you can take them with you. If not," he said and shrugged, "we can put them to good use."

Blaine got to his feet, moving toward the barn's wide door. The others fell in behind him, while several of their captors moved to secure the horses and wagons.

"Who is your commander? What lord do you serve?" Blaine asked.

A bitter smile touched at the corners of the leader's mouth.

Now that Blaine got a good look at the man, he saw he was in his late teens or early twenties. The face was youthful, but there was a world-weariness in the man's eyes that seemed much older. "There are no lords left to serve," he replied. "No lords, no law, no liege. The war's over. Welcome to what's left."

The archers commandeered one of Blaine's group's wagons and horses and directed Blaine and the others to climb in. Two of the archers drove, while more archers walked beside the wagon.

"If I believed in the gods, I'd say now would be a good time to pray," muttered Piran.

"Our luck isn't looking good," Kestel replied with a sigh.

Piran snorted. "What? Just because wild magic ripped through some old, forgotten chamber and laid us all out flat as corpses, you think we're not ready for a good fight?" *Piran probably would be up for a brawl*, Blaine thought; at least, he had never shied away from one in the past. Shorter, stocky, with a bald head that Piran had kept shaved even in the bitter cold of the Edgeland wastes, Piran looked every bit the soldier he had been before his court-martial.

Blaine rubbed his temples, trying in vain to ease the throbbing headache that had begun the night before. When the warring kingdoms of Donderath and Meroven destroyed each other, the Continent also lost its control over magic. Without king, law, or magic, chaos followed. Tracking a series of clues that suggested magic might be restored, Blaine and his friends had made a failed attempt to harness the wild magic, an effort that had left several of their party, including Blaine, badly bruised and battered.

"Neither side was wearing any colors," Kestel murmured. "But this group has some kind of uniform, although it's hard to tell; they all look rather ragged." She paused. "I heard what the man you were fighting said about Lord Pollard. If the archers aren't Pollard's men, who do they belong to?"

Before her exile to the Velant prison colony in Edgeland, Kestel had been a sought-after courtesan, a spy in the court of King Merrill, and an assassin. Like the others, she'd followed Blaine back to Donderath on the scant hope that magic could be restored. Today, her red hair was bound up, and she wore a tunic, trews, and boots borrowed from Glenreith's guardhouse. Anyone who had seen her gowned and bejeweled for high court would have had difficulty recognizing Kestel as the same woman.

"Anyone else who wants to kill you, Mick, that you forgot to tell us about?" Verran asked, glancing nervously at the archers.

Blaine let out a long breath. "Not that I remember. But as you've seen, things aren't exactly the way they were when we shipped out."

"So we just sit here?" Piran's tone made his opinion clear.

Blaine rubbed his pounding forehead. Every muscle and joint ached as if he'd been beaten by the sheer, wild power of the magical backlash. "For now," he said.

They had tried to raise the magic at Mirdalur, a three-day ride from Blaine's family's manor at Glenreith. Geir, their vampire guide, had left them before dawn to find shelter from the daylight. Blaine and his friends, along with eleven of Glenreith's manor guards, had planned to sleep through the day and move out again once it was dark to avoid the bands of robbers and vagabonds that wandered the Donderath countryside.

"It's mid-afternoon, still daylight. That means this group is mortal," Kestel said. "That's one good thing."

Piran gave her a sidelong glance. "If that's the 'good' news, we're shit out of luck."

"I wish we knew who they were," Kestel said, bending closer to the gap in the wall for a better look. "They look like a bunch of vagrants but fight like a unit."

"I'm afraid we'll get an answer soon enough," Dawe Killick said, his head bowed and his face obscured by a hank of dark, lanky hair. Dawe was tall and slender, with a hawklike nose and piercing blue eyes. Despite the bonds on his wrists, Dawe's long-fingered hands clenched in frustration.

They rode for half a candlemark, away from the direction they had come. They were going north, as close as Blaine could reckon from the sun. Away from Mirdalur, and no closer to Glenreith. The odds weren't in their favor, despite the fact that Geir had escaped capture.

The wagon rolled into a camp of fighters, who regarded it with wary curiosity. Whoever's army the archers represented, it was a motley one. From what Blaine could see, only about half the men had tents, and those were stained and patched. Many had only the shelter of lean-tos or pieces of canvas held up by posts.

"How many do you figure are out there?" Kestel asked.

"Too many," Blaine replied.

The fighters' camp was as hard worn as the men themselves. A hodgepodge of moveable structures greeted them. Cook fires dotted the encampment, and in the rear, Blaine spotted mud-spattered horses and several wagons. No doubt the fighters would be glad to gain use of the horses and wagons his group had brought with them.

When they reached the outskirts of the camp, their Glenreith bodyguards were directed into two tents ringed with guards. Blaine, Kestel, Piran, Dawe, and Verran were ushered to a large tent in the center of the camp. By the tent's size,

Blaine guessed it to be the captain's, but if so, then the group's leader was an ascetic. A bedroll lay to one side, and a small brazier in the middle did little to drive out the late autumn chill. A soldier's satchel lay near the bedroll, and there was a small shrine to Charrot, Torven, and Esthrane at the foot of the bedding. Otherwise, the tent was empty.

"Wait here." The young man who seemed to be the leader of the archers spoke in low tones to two of the fighters, who remained by the tent's entrance. Then Blaine and his friends were left alone.

"Best odds we're going to have," Piran muttered. "Five against two."

"And more than two score on the other side of the doorway," Kestel replied in a whisper. "I knew you couldn't read, but I thought you could do figures," she added with a hint of a smile that softened her words.

Blaine sighed. "With luck, these men will see we've got no quarrel with them and let us go."

"I'd put the odds of that as slim to nil," Piran sighed. "If nothing else, they'll want the horses. And maybe Kestel."

Despite their situation, Kestel grinned. "Let 'em try," she replied, palming a dagger from somewhere on her body.

"Shh," Dawe warned as footsteps drew closer.

Muffled voices sounded outside the tent. One was the voice of the man who had brought them to the camp. The other voice, deeper and more mature, was muffled. The tent flap swung back and a tall man entered, flanked by two guards. The man was broad-shouldered, with short-cut, dark blonde hair. Several days' worth of stubble shadowed gaunt, high cheekbones. He wore a woolen coat over what might have been gray uniform pants, and his clothes looked as if he had been roughing it for quite some time.

"My officer says he's got a bunch of escaped convicts," the

man said, not bothering to look up as he entered. Then he lifted his head and stopped in his tracks, staring at Blaine.

"You're supposed to be dead," he breathed, and his face had gone pale as a ghost.

"So are you," Blaine responded, feeling as if he had been sucker punched. "Niklas?"

"Blaine McFadden died in Velant," the man repeated, his voice just above a whisper. "That's what we heard."

"Sorry to disappoint," Blaine replied. "Although several people did their damnedest to make that happen." He paused. "Aunt Judith said you'd died in the war."

A crooked grin spread across the man's face. "Sorry to disappoint," he echoed. "We were on the front lines, and it's been a damn long walk home." He sobered and turned to one of the guards. "Cut their bonds. Bring me some food, get a healer for them, and fetch whatever ale you can find."

"Sir?"

"Just do it, Lieutenant. I'll take my chances with them."

The soldier did as he was told. Blaine rubbed his wrists. "Does this mean we get our horses back?" he asked as the others looked between the two men, trying to figure out the sudden lurch in conversation.

Niklas laughed and stepped forward, extending a hand to Blaine and then folding him into a back-thumping embrace. "By Torven's horns, Blaine. I never thought I'd see you again."

"You know this bloke, Mick?" Piran asked warily.

Blaine nodded. "This is Niklas Theilsson. We grew up together. We've been friends for as long as I can remember."

Niklas gave Blaine a quizzical look. "You go by 'Mick' now?"

Blaine sighed. "I did in Velant. These are my mates from Edgeland."

The look in Niklas's blue eyes gave Blaine to guess the other was trying to put the pieces together. "Perhaps introductions are in order."

"We met in Velant and survived because we had each other's backs," Blaine started, a slight note of challenge in his voice as if he expected judgment from Niklas. When their host said nothing, Blaine continued. "Verran Danning is a master locksmith and sometime minstrel," he said, giving Verran's thieving a quick cleanup. "Dawe Killick was a silversmith. Kestel Falke was a courtesan and an assassin."

Kestel grinned. "It was the assassin part that got me my passage to Velant," she said, a flash of warning in her eyes.

"And finally, Piran Rowse—"

Niklas interrupted with a chuckle. "I know Piran by reputation," he said. "Your court-martial is still legendary."

Blaine and the others turned to look at Piran. "Was there more to the story than you let on, Piran dear?" Kestel asked in her sweetest voice.

Piran reddened. "Might have been. No more than Mick here forgetting to tell his mates he's a bleedin' lord."

Niklas swung an arm to indicate his nearly empty tent. "Please, have a seat. I think we have a lot to discuss."

Blaine nodded to the others, and they sat cross-legged on the ground. Niklas brought a low, folding table and set it in front of them, then joined them. An aide returned with a pitcher of ale, a cloth filled with hard bread, sausage, cheese, and a variety of battered, military-issue tin cups. A healer followed him.

"This is Ordel, my battle healer," Niklas said. "He'll patch up the damage from the fight." He turned to Ordel. "Blaine's an old friend, and these are friends of his. Can you take a look at their injuries?"

If Ordel thought it strange that Niklas's 'old friend' arrived bound and under guard, he made no comment. "Yes, sir," he replied and turned to Blaine. "Let's see the damage, and I'll do my best to have you patched up in time for supper," he said with a grin.

"Thank you," Blaine said, looking to both Niklas and Ordel. They were silent for the time it took Ordel to see to their wounds, and then the healer straightened and looked to Niklas.

"Nothing too serious," Ordel said. "They should be fine in a few days." Niklas nodded his thanks, and the healer ducked out of the tent.

"Eat," Niklas instructed, "because I have a feeling this isn't going to be a short conversation."

"Then fill us in," Blaine said, as he poured a cup of ale and passed the pitcher to the others. "We know Donderath lost the war. We know the magic is broken. But what led up to that— we don't know." He paused, fearful to ask the next question, yet knowing there was no way around it. "Before you start, I have to ask. Did Carr come back with you?"

Niklas suddenly looked tired, and his expression was grim. "Yes, Carr survived. Many of our soldiers didn't. Carr was lucky. He's out on extended patrol right now. I'll make sure the two of you have a chance to talk when he gets back."

Kestel laid a hand on Blaine's arm. "Carr's your younger brother, right?"

Blaine nodded. "He was just a kid when I was exiled."

Niklas sighed. "We were all a lot younger then. In so many ways, it was a completely different world." Niklas poured himself a cup of ale, and for a moment, he looked at a loss for words.

"There had been incidents along the border with Meroven for years," Niklas began. "I went into the army not long after you were sent away." Niklas glanced toward Blaine. "Even then, spies told us Edgar of Meroven was unstable, and that he was likely to try to expand his borders. One thing led to another, and soon, Donderath and Meroven had an open war. The other kingdoms were pulled in and before long, the entire Continent had chosen sides."

Niklas shook his head. "Casualties were terrible. I tried to keep Carr out of the war for as long as I could, but finally, I knew he'd sign up with someone else if I didn't take him. For your sake, I did my best to keep him as safe as possible."

"Thank you," Blaine murmured.

"After years of war, when it became clear that men alone wouldn't decide the outcome, the mages got involved." Niklas's eyes took on a haunted expression. "It was about a year ago. I thought I'd seen the worst carnage war had to offer, but the mages turned it into a bloodbath." He looked down for a few moments. "Still, the men on both sides never left their posts. I can only speak for my men, but when we saw what the Meroven mages could unleash, we feared what would befall our homeland if we could not hold the line."

Niklas looked toward them but his gaze seemed far away, and his expression was bleak. "One night, it all came to a head. On the ground, the sheer energy that crackled around us felt as if the gods were sparring, as if the world were coming to an end. And in a way, it did.

"A blast of magic more powerful than anything we had ever felt before swept over the battlefields, knocking down men as if they were bowling pins. Those who took the brunt of the force were killed instantly. Those of us lucky enough to be sheltered at that moment survived, but with injuries. The sky opened up and fire fell on us. The sky was filled with a green light, and wherever the light touched the ground, the land burned. It was the night of the Great Fire." Niklas's voice grew quiet, and he closed his eyes against the images in his memory.

"That night, whatever the mages did not only destroyed both armies, it destroyed the magic as well," Niklas went on. "Magic stopped working, at least the kind of magic men could control. Wild magic became a danger, with magical storms touching down without warning, destroying everything in their paths. Strange beasts out of nightmares started appearing. Men went mad.

"When I could gather what remained of my men, we started for home. The Great Fire had laid waste to Donderath. The manor houses were destroyed. When the magic 'died,' it took the little magics as well as the great ones. Buildings, dams, and fences held together with a bit of magic all collapsed. Healers couldn't use magic to heal. Farmers lost the magic to get rid of pests, so their crops failed. We never realized how many small magics we depended on until they stopped working."

Niklas met Blaine's gaze, and Blaine could see the grief in his friend's face. "We went to war to protect Donderath. We failed."

The group sat for a moment in silence as Niklas's story sank in. Finally, Niklas shook himself free of his memories. By now, Blaine and his friends had eaten their fill of the bread and cheese, and Blaine pushed food toward Niklas, refilling his cup with ale.

"That's quite a story," Blaine said, sobered by the account. "We knew bits of what happened, but not from the front lines."

"Something brought you back from the edge of the world, Blaine," Niklas replied, taking a sip of his ale. "I'd like very much to know what it was."

As briefly as he could, Blaine recounted how the death of magic on the Continent had affected even distant Edgeland. "Without the warden mages, Commander Prokief couldn't keep the convicts from rebelling, and the Velant prison fell," Blaine said. "Those of us who had earned our Tickets of Leave to become colonists realized that without supply ships from home, the colony wouldn't have enough food for the winter."

"How did you get a ship? And why did you, of anyone, come back?" Niklas pressed.

Blaine shrugged. "The ship was adrift and abandoned, and we towed her into Skalgerston Bay. We could take 500 people back with us, which was a burden off the colony. Those who wanted to return took their chances and made the trip."

Niklas fixed Blaine with a piercing gaze. "You still haven't answered me, Blaine. Why did you come back?"

Piran gave Blaine a warning glance, but Kestel nodded. Dawe shrugged. "Up to you, Mick," Dawe said.

Verran grinned. "You can tell him, but will he believe you?"

Blaine returned his gaze to where Niklas sat waiting. "It's a long story, but according to an ancient *talishte* and a very old mage's map, there's a chance that magic isn't gone forever." He paused, knowing that what he was about to say would strain the belief of even the best of friends. "Magic as we know it was harnessed four hundred years ago at Mirdalur when the king and the oldest nobles bound the wild power to their bidding. When the Meroven mages wiped out the Donderath nobility, they also broke the blood ties that bound the magic. All of the eldest heirs of the old Lords of the Blood are dead."

"Except one," Kestel said, with a meaningful look at Blaine.

Niklas met Blaine's gaze. "You're the last Lord of the Blood?"

"Apparently so."

"From what we've been told, as long as there is a living Lord of the Blood, it might be possible to harness the magic again," Kestel continued.

"That's why you returned?" Niklas asked, looking at Blaine as if he were suddenly a stranger.

"Told you he wouldn't believe you," Verran said.

Blaine looked down. "As crazy as it seems, yes."

"Only we tried it and nearly got ourselves all killed," Piran added. "So Mick wants to give it another go, because he can't leave well enough alone."

"The old records said the first lords harnessed the magic in a ritual at Mirdalur," Blaine said, with an exasperated look at Piran. "We tried going there, to see if my presence would reactivate the magic." He grimaced. "Piran's right. The wild magic nearly killed us."

"So that's it then?" Niklas asked. "There's no hope of bringing the magic back?"

"We're not sure," Kestel replied. "There are clues that it can be done—but we don't know quite how just yet." She hesitated. "There are some forces in Donderath that would be just as happy for the magic to stay dead."

Niklas frowned. "Forces?"

"Do you remember Vedran Pollard?" Blaine asked.

"Real son of a bitch," Niklas replied. "The only person I knew who was as mean as your father—maybe even worse."

"Yeah, that's Pollard. He's thrown in his lot with a vampire named Pentreath Reese."

Niklas whistled. "They're the ones who don't want to see magic return? Damn, Blaine. You sure know how to pick your enemies." He scowled. "That group my men fought, you think they were Pollard's men?"

Blaine nodded. "Yes. We had to dodge them the whole way to Mirdalur and then run for our lives when they nearly caught us there. Pollard also had his men camped outside Glenreith when we returned, trying to pressure Aunt Judith into an alliance."

Niklas made a rude noise. "You've got to be kidding." When he saw Blaine was serious, he shook his head. "For a man everyone thought was dead, you can still kick up a fuss."

"Somebody knew Blaine was alive," Kestel commented soberly. "Pollard sent an assassin to Velant to kill him."

All traces of humor drained from Niklas's expression. "Seriously? An assassin? So you think Pollard may know about this whole Lord of the Blood thing?"

"Looks that way," Blaine replied.

Niklas leaned forward. "Actually, this isn't the first I've heard of Pollard. We've seen his handiwork the whole way across Donderath."

Blaine frowned. "What do you mean?"

"We've never tangled with the black-clad men before, but only because we tried to stay out of their way. We have heard tales whenever we've stopped for provisions, and the stories aren't good." He rubbed the stubble on his chin. "Guess that's why, when my men saw them fighting your group and the odds looked uneven, they waded in."

"Believe me, we're grateful," Blaine said. "What tales did you hear?"

Niklas shrugged. "Rumors that Pollard's been hunting down former mages. Several have disappeared and never returned. There were dark stories about men in black clothing ransacking the mage libraries and universities, carrying off sacks of items, and torching what was left." He grimaced. "Pollard seems to like setting fires. I'd heard the same about villages where he didn't get the information he was seeking." He snapped his fingers. "Went up in flames, and Raka take the survivors."

Outside, they heard a sudden crash. Horns sounded an

alarm. Shouts and the sound of fighting filled the air. Niklas jumped to his feet, as did Blaine and the others. A guard appeared in the tent doorway.

"Sir, we're under attack."

"By whom?" Niklas had drawn his sword, and his eyes glinted with anger.

The guard looked as if he was struggling against his own fear. "*Talishte*, sir. We're being attacked by vampires."

CHAPTER TWO

I DON'T LIKE THIS." BEVIN CONNOR LOOKED AT the wooden coffin and shuddered. Before the Great Fire, Connor had been the assistant to the late Lord Garnoc, and the eyes and ears of Lanyon Penhallow, an ancient and powerful *talishte* lord. Now, pinned down by forces loyal to Pentreath Reese, Connor was debating whether Penhallow's proposed escape was preferable to remaining under siege.

"Do you have a better way out?" Penhallow asked. They stood in the caverns beneath the fortress of mercenary general Traher Voss, on the banks of a swiftly flowing subterranean river.

"You're already dead. You don't have to breathe," Connor replied testily.

Had Penhallow needed to draw breath, he might have sighed. Penhallow was a tall, lean-muscled man. Long brown hair framed an angular face and blue eyes. Though his features spoke of nobility, his body was as strong as an athlete's. And although he looked to be in his late thirties, Connor knew that Penhallow had existed for hundreds of years.

"We've been over this before, Bevin. The *kruvgaldur* bond

will let me put you into a deep trance. It'll slow your breathing and heartbeat, so you won't need much air for a short time. That's as long as we need to let the current take us out of the fortress and past the siege. By the time the boxes surface, Traher says we'll be in neutral territory."

"How does he know? Did he ever do this?"

"Not exactly," Traher Voss replied and cleared his throat. Voss was a portly man in his middle years, with a fringe of graying hair around his balding pate. Thick-necked and broad-shouldered, Voss looked like a career military man.

"But we have slipped materials out of the fortress when the king's guards were at the gate and the items were, shall we say, of questionable background," Voss went on. "We know the river comes back aboveground a few miles downstream, in a cave. Makes it unlikely someone happening by is going to notice when you bob back to the surface. It's far enough away that I doubt Reese's soldiers will be wandering around."

Connor spotted a second coffin a few yards away. "Who's that for?" he asked, glancing at Penhallow. "Are you going to be shut up in a box as well?"

Penhallow shook his head. "That's for Treven. He's supposed to meet us here, and he's late." Treven Lowrey, former mage and magic scholar, largely did as he pleased.

"How do you know it's wide enough in the underground passage? What if the box gets stuck? What if there's a second channel for the water and I end up gods-know-where?" Connor protested.

"When Traher suggested the idea, I had the same concerns," Penhallow replied. "So before I brought you down here, I navigated the course myself." He gave a slight smile, enough that the tips of his elongated eyeteeth were barely visible. "As you point out, I don't have to breathe."

"And?" Connor demanded, only slightly mollified.

Penhallow chuckled. "The passage is wide enough in most places," he answered. "Where it's not, I'll guide you. I'll travel the channel as I did before. If there were any trouble at all, I assure you, I could get you to safety."

Connor eyed the coffin again. The box had been weighted with enough rocks that it would sink below the water's surface, but it would not be heavy enough to come to rest on the bottom. It also looked as if it had been covered with pitch. "It's not the water," Connor muttered, and his blue eyes flashed. "I don't like being shut up in a box when I'm not dead yet."

"While we stand here talking, Reese's men are pounding the shit out of my walls," Voss grumbled. "And your friend McFadden is out there making a target of himself."

Connor winced at Voss's words. "All right," Connor said. "Let's do it before I have time to think about it." He paused and pushed a strand of dark blond hair out of his eyes. With a glance, he measured the coffin, glad that he was just average in height and build so that the box would not be too tight a fit. He repressed a shudder. At just twenty-two years old, he had hoped to wait a good long time before having a coffin fitted for him. "Will I sleep through it?"

Penhallow grimaced. "If I put you into a deep sleep and we have trouble on the other end of the passageway, I won't be able to wake you quickly enough. I can dull your senses, slow your breathing so the air lasts longer. You'll feel as if you've had too much wine, so that the voyage won't bother you quite so much."

Far over their heads, Connor knew that catapults continued their bombardment of the fortress. While Voss seemed confident that his fortifications could withstand the siege, Connor had felt nothing but cold dread with every pounding blow.

What's worse? Staying here and possibly being overrun and tortured or being put in a coffin and buried alive?

"Give me your arm," Penhallow said. Dutifully, Connor rolled up the sleeve on his left arm, revealing a series of small, white, pinpoint scars. Penhallow met his gaze for a moment, then pressed Connor's forearm to his mouth. Connor was used to the momentary pain of the bite as Penhallow's fangs pierced his skin. It was through the blood that Penhallow read his memories, gathered the intelligence Connor provided as a spy. And it was through the blood that Penhallow provided the *kruvgaldur*, or blood bond, that imparted his protection and a weak telepathic link.

"Don't fight it, Connor," Penhallow said quietly. "Let it take you."

It was instinct, not intention, that resisted the *talishte*'s compulsion. Penhallow had always been a kind master, asking for Connor's cooperation rather than wresting information from him by force. Now, Connor felt the full weight of Penhallow's power blurring his consciousness even as a primal part of him struggled to remain fully awake.

Penhallow lifted his mouth from the wound, and immediately, the skin began to heal. Connor's legs were unsteady, and both Penhallow and Voss reached to catch him as he wavered on his feet. Penhallow lifted him, showing no strain at hefting a grown man as easily as he might have picked up a sleepy child. He placed Connor into the coffin.

"I will never let you out of my sight in the river," Penhallow promised. "I won't allow any harm to come to you. Don't be afraid."

Groggy with the compulsion, Connor did not struggle as Penhallow lifted the lid of the coffin and fit it into place. He felt relaxed, as though he had drunk several bottles of wine. He recalled having been distressed over something but could not remember what. Distantly, Connor noticed glimmers of light around the coffin's lid, and some part of his mind seemed to think that wasn't a good idea.

The sharp smell of pitch filled the coffin. One by one, the glimmers of light disappeared, and Connor lay in total darkness. The coffin was just wide enough for his shoulders, and barely long enough for him to stretch out to his full length. A memory surfaced, something about how the joiner sometimes broke a corpse's legs to fit the box. Despite Penhallow's compulsion, Connor shuddered.

Inside the coffin, Connor jostled against the sides as Penhallow dragged the casket into the water. For a moment it seemed the casket might roll over, but before Connor could brace himself, the box righted. In the distance, he heard muffled voices, then felt the coffin sink until it touched the shallow bottom of the river's edge. Then he felt the current take him, and he heard the rush and roar of the river as loudly as if he bobbed beneath a waterfall.

The current grew swift, and the coffin yawed from side to side. Connor splayed out his arms and legs to brace himself within the narrow confines of the box. Yet his heartbeat did not spike with fear, and his breathing remained shallow and measured. He felt a curious sense of detachment, as if the journey were happening to someone else and he was only an observer.

With a crash, the box pivoted and the impact slammed Connor against the side of the coffin. The water sounded as if it might rip the box apart, and its force buffeted the box like a cork. Again and again it slammed against rock until Connor wondered whether the wood would hold. For a moment, the compulsion wavered, and Connor felt an instant of sheer panic.

I'm going to drown. Suffocate. Gods help me! Only then did he notice that the air in the coffin had grown stale and warm, and he drew in a great lungful, then felt his head spin.

The coffin lurched so hard that Connor was thrown to the side. His nose hit the wood and began to bleed freely. Terror overtook him, and Connor began to dig at the wood around him, tearing his fingernails, desperate to get out. Even the frigid cold of the underground river seemed better than the stifling confines of the sealed coffin.

The panic subsided as quickly as it came, and Connor felt a deep lethargy. He stopped scrabbling at the sides of his coffin, suddenly content to relax in its warm, dark solitude. Whatever had happened, the coffin was moving again, bobbing and swaying with the current. Soothed by the rocking motion, Connor's breathing slowed to the rhythm of deep sleep.

Gradually, the movement of the coffin slowed. The box ceased its rocking. Connor heard a grinding noise, and the coffin shuddered to a stop. Several sharp tugs jostled him within the confines of the box, starting his nose bleeding again. He heard a splintering noise, and suddenly, sweet, fresh, cold air swept in to fill his lungs.

"Connor."

The voice called to him from a far distance, at the very edge of hearing.

"Connor."

The voice seemed closer now. It was insistent, but without any threat of danger. Connor resisted. Honeyed warmth enfolded him, and he drifted, completely relaxed, at the verge of wakefulness.

"Wake now." The words were a command. The warmth melted away, and Connor came alert.

He lay in the wooden coffin. Its lid was open, and he saw at a glance that the cave roof above him was very different from the cavern where he had fallen asleep. Penhallow stood over him, dressed in dry clothing, although his long hair was wet. Penhallow extended a hand to Connor to help him sit up, and Connor realized the vampire's skin was even colder than usual.

"We're out," Penhallow said as Connor climbed out of the casket and wiped the blood from his face.

"Safe?"

Penhallow shrugged. "That's yet to be determined."

Connor gave a sharp glance toward the water. "What happened? There was a moment when it felt like the box was being smashed to bits."

Penhallow looked chagrined. "My apologies. The current took your coffin out of my grip for a moment and pinned it against the river wall. The compulsion may have slipped a bit as my concentration was elsewhere until I could get you free."

Connor frowned. "How do we know Reese's men aren't waiting for us at the cave mouth?"

"I've made a thorough scouting," Penhallow said. "It's safe... now," he replied. Connor glimpsed a few flecks of blood on Penhallow's shirt and wondered how many threats the vampire had eliminated.

A third man stood on the riverbank beside another opened casket. Treven Lowrey stood watching them, with a look on his face as if he were not quite sure his lunch would stay down. Lowrey's hard-angled features were more pinched-looking than usual, his wire-rimmed glasses were slightly askew, and his robes were wet at the hem.

"So Treven showed up after all?" Connor asked, struggling to remember whether Lowrey had been present when he had been placed in his own coffin.

"Kidnapped me, for all intents and purposes," Lowrey

grumbled, smoothing his long, gray hair where it had escaped from an untidy queue.

Penhallow chuckled. "You also claimed that Traher had 'kidnapped' you when he merely rescued you from Pollard's men. And now you think I've done the same. Honestly, Treven, aren't you a wee bit happy to be out of the siege?"

Lowrey glowered at him. "I'm not the least pleased about being packed up like a corpse. I don't like water. And you know the *kruvgaldur* always makes me nauseous."

Penhallow barely hid a smile. "I could take you back."

Lowrey cast a nervous glance toward his sodden casket. "That's all right. I'll make do." He reached into the coffin and took out a bulky knapsack. "I hope we don't have far to walk. I don't relish carrying these books."

"Books?" Connor questioned.

Lowrey gave him a piercing look over the rim of his glasses. "Vigus Quintrel's journal, and a few other items Penhallow and I agreed were too important to leave behind."

Penhallow reached into Connor's coffin and withdrew two swords, scabbards, and sword belts that had been stowed for the journey. "Best to be prepared," Penhallow added, handing one of the swords to Connor and belting on one of the weapons himself.

Penhallow lifted one of the coffins and drove a fist through the wooden bottom, a move Connor was sure would have badly broken a mortal's hand. After he had made a few more holes, he threw the coffin back into the water and watched it sink, then did the same with the second casket.

"What was that for?" Lowrey demanded.

Penhallow turned to look at Lowrey. "If anyone finds this cave, they won't have an easy answer on how we escaped. Let them figure it out for themselves."

"Where do we go, assuming there isn't an army outside

waiting for us?" Connor asked. "Blaine could already be at Mirdalur."

Penhallow nodded. "Been and gone, I'm afraid," he replied. "Geir's been doing his best to keep me informed, although the *kruvgaldur* link works imperfectly over distance. Despite my attempt to warn them, it seems they went to Mirdalur and the attempt failed."

Connor looked at him sharply. "Did they survive?"

Penhallow had begun walking toward the cave's entrance. "Yes, although it wasn't pleasant. I felt Geir's pain through the bond."

"And now?" Connor asked, falling into step beside him.

"The last sending from Geir was jumbled. There was a threat, and danger, but I couldn't clearly read it."

"So we're heading for Mirdalur? Or to Glenreith?" Connor scrambled to keep up with Penhallow's long strides.

"Neither," Penhallow replied. "We're going to Quillarth Castle—or what's left of it."

They had reached the cave's mouth. It was dark outside, and the evening was cold. Connor and Lowrey waited while Penhallow quickly scouted the area a second time.

Before long, Penhallow returned. "Voss was mistaken: Reese's men did know about this exit," Penhallow said, and Connor noted that even in the moonlight, the *talishte*'s pallor had faded. Connor had come to know that usually meant Penhallow had recently fed well. "I've eliminated the problem, but we'd best get moving before anyone finds the bodies."

"What do you mean, we're going to the castle?" Connor repeated in a whisper. He knew that he was quite loud enough for the *talishte*'s enhanced hearing. "What about Voss? Aren't you going to get reinforcements or something?"

Penhallow chuckled. "No, or at least not yet. Voss told me

he was quite prepared to sit out a siege. Blaine McFadden needs our help much more, and to provide that, we need more information. If there's anyone who knows how to bring back the magic, it's Vigus Quintrel. He's left a trail, and he left clues in your memory to help us track him down," Penhallow said, with a pointed look at Connor. "And I have a feeling we can pick up Quintrel's trail at the castle."

You mean Quintrel waylaid me, planted memories, and then made me forget—until I find the clues he's left for me, Connor thought ill-humoredly. For months, Connor had feared that the gaps in his memory meant he had somehow betrayed his master, only to learn later that Quintrel had tampered with his mind to assure that essential information would survive the Cataclysm.

Penhallow frowned. "What I don't understand is how Quintrel's magic continues to work on you, when other magic has vanished."

"It works because it wasn't magic—or at least, not all magic," Lowrey said. Connor and Penhallow looked at him.

"Explain," Penhallow said.

"It's possible to put a person into a trance and give him instructions—even instructions to be carried out later—without magic," Lowrey said. "Quintrel was fascinated with the topic. According to him, it's even possible to link the memories to a sight or sound that suddenly brings them back." He shook his head. "I don't claim to understand it, but Quintrel did."

He looked at Connor as if trying to peer into his thoughts. "That's the beauty of the 'buried treasure' spell. It speeds up the process and makes the memories clearer and stronger. After that, the magic isn't needed at all." He frowned. "It wouldn't matter now, since the suggestions he planted would still work—magic or not."

"It's not a perfect system," Connor mused. "Most of the time, the memories are fragments, just a sentence or two. If he was going to muck around in my mind, the least he could have done was made himself clear."

Lowrey chuckled. "It took a great deal of skill to leave you a trail of clues and the memories to unlock them," he said. "Especially since he doled out the memories so they would be triggered by an object or a place." He shook his head. "Maybe with all that going on, bits and pieces were all he could manage. And while they might be fragments, the clues he's left you have been valuable."

"Quintrel vanished months ago," Connor protested. "There's no telling where he is—or even whether he survived the Great Fire."

"He survived," Penhallow replied, tramping through the dry, tangled husks of the dead weeds that nearly obscured the area just beyond the cave opening. "In fact, I think Quintrel feared that something like the Great Fire might happen. Whether it was a premonition or just insight, I think he read the warning signals earlier than the rest of us and made plans accordingly. He wasn't the only one to vanish."

Lowrey tugged on the hem of his robe to free it from a bramble bush. "No, he wasn't," he affirmed. "There were disappearances for over a year before the Great Fire. It seemed random. All people with some tie to magic, but not all mages, and even those who were mages weren't particularly powerful. Researchers, historians, healers, people with a gift for creating elixirs or raising herbs for potions, and some people who didn't seem likely at all." From Lowrey's tone, Connor wondered if the scholar-mage felt slighted by not being among those chosen to vanish.

"Are you sure they all were spirited out by Quintrel?" Connor asked. "Maybe they had personal reasons for leaving. Or maybe they defected to Meroven when it started looking bad for our side."

Lowrey shrugged. "Perhaps. But it was wildly out of character for some of them. The vanishings were whispered about, and there was no shortage of theories."

"So why decide it was Quintrel?" Connor pressed.

Lowrey looked at him over his wire-rimmed glasses. "Because as far as I could tell, every one of them had some tie to Vigus Quintrel. It was the only thing they all had in common. When Quintrel himself disappeared, I was certain he was behind it."

"Ever think maybe he just killed them?" Connor replied, out of sorts as they slogged through a half-frozen, marshy area.

Penhallow chuckled, but Lowrey seemed to consider the possibility. "Doubtful," Lowrey said after a moment's reflection and shook his head. "Until he disappeared, Quintrel kept his position at the university in Castle Reach. Those who disappeared vanished from all over the kingdom."

"He could have hired assassins," Connor persisted, jerking his boot free where it broke through the ice crust and threatened to sink into the muddy marsh.

Lowrey glanced at Penhallow. "Is he always this suspicious?"

"He's spent most of his life at court, Treven," Penhallow replied. "A suspicious nature is required for survival." He paused. "Actually, I've considered all of the objections Connor raised. I've met Vigus on occasion. His magic was more than sufficient to land him an appointment to the king, but he managed to stay at the university instead. I read some of his research. It was excellent, but he wasn't named a dean. I had the distinct impression that Vigus intentionally deflected attention away from himself. At the time, I thought he was overly modest. Now, I wonder if he hadn't been planning something all along."

To Connor's relief, they saw no more sign of the soldiers who were besieging Voss's fortress, though they could hear the thud of catapults like distant thunder. They walked quite a distance in silence, keeping to the hedgerows along the road, alert for danger. Penhallow led them across the fields, and Connor was glad for the moonlight that helped him get his footing. As best he could tell, they were heading south, toward Castle Reach and the ruins of Quillarth Castle, though it would take more than a night's walk to get there.

Finally, Penhallow veered away from the road and headed down a long dirt lane rutted with carriage tracks. The road led to an old stone house. While not so grand or large as to be considered a manor, the house obviously belonged to someone of means. It was quite old, judging from both the height of the trees and mature plantings around it, and from the overgrowth of ivy that climbed its walls. Penhallow signaled for them to stop just as they reached the edge of the property.

"I thought we were going to Quillarth Castle," Connor protested in a hushed voice.

"We are."

"This isn't it."

Penhallow nodded. "No, it isn't. Audun Tormond lives here. And if I'm right, he may know something that could help us." He did not make any move to approach the house, and Connor looked around nervously.

"What now?" Connor whispered.

"We wait," Penhallow replied. "I want him to scent us, to realize we mean no threat."

Connor's throat tightened. "A *talishte*?"

Penhallow nodded and Connor searched his expression, hoping to find some clue as to the nature of Penhallow's relationship with this new vampire. He shot a nervous glance toward the old house. Despite Penhallow's calm assurance, Connor felt unwelcome. The house seemed forbidding, and Connor had to fight his instincts to approach the door.

The moonlight was bright enough that Connor could see the door swing partially open, revealing darkness inside. "We've been received," Penhallow murmured. "Let's go." He looked from Lowrey to Connor. "And let me do the talking."

Lowrey exchanged a glance with Connor that gave Connor to believe they were in agreement for the first time in their short acquaintance. They followed Penhallow at a respectful distance. Connor felt his heart pound. He took a deep breath, hoping to still his blood so that it did not call out attractively to their unknown host, in case he might be feeling hungry.

They stepped inside, and before Connor's eyes could adjust to the darkness, he heard the sound of rushing air and was lifted off his feet by a hand that clutched his throat hard enough that he feared it might snap his neck.

Within a heartbeat, a sword glinted in the moonlight, swinging with terrifying force, sinking deep into the arm that held Connor, and sending a shower of blood across Connor's face and chest. Shouting curses, Connor's attacker released him, and Connor sank to the floor, frozen by a mix of terror and sudden, overwhelming relief. Before he could take a second breath, Penhallow had interposed himself between Connor and the attacker. Lowrey sidestepped closer, so that he, too, was behind Penhallow.

"Why did you bring them here?" The voice was a deep growl. "I dislike the company of mortals."

"Both these men are under my protection." Penhallow's voice was as cold as the steel he held. "You're old enough in the Curse to feel that, Audun."

"You were always far too fond of mortals, Lanyon. Would you really challenge me, in my own home, on their account?"

"Yes, I would. Do I have your word that you will not harm these men—or cause them to come to harm?"

The silence seemed to last forever. "You have my word."

As Connor's eyes adjusted, he could make out the silhouette of the speaker. The man was shorter by a head than Connor, and narrower in the shoulders. He took a step that moved him into the moonlight. His features had the look of a man in his fourth decade, but his dark brown eyes looked much, much older and his face was gaunt. Their reluctant host was dressed like a nobleman at leisure, judging by the fit and quality of his waistcoat and breeches. Yet something was off, and then Connor realized that both the cut and the material were long out of fashion.

A rustling noise sounded in the darkness, and then a lantern illuminated the entranceway. Their host closed the door to the outside, and Connor's heart seemed to skip a beat as he heard the lock latch. "You might as well come into the parlor," the *talishte* said grudgingly. "I don't care to stand here all night."

Penhallow gave a nod to Connor and Lowrey to follow, then led the way. As Connor dragged a sleeve across his face to wipe away the blood, he noted that Penhallow maneuvered to keep himself between the two mortals and their host. While Connor appreciated the protection, the fact that Penhallow felt obliged to shield them did nothing to quiet his fears.

"Why have you come, Lanyon?" Audun asked.

"I'm looking for Vigus Quintrel," Penhallow replied.

Audun looked up sharply. "The mage? I assumed he burned in the Great Fire. What use do you have for a mage?" He glanced at both Connor and Lowrey, and his gaze lingered on Lowrey.

"Not just any mage," Penhallow corrected. "One particular mage. I need to find Quintrel."

"Magic doesn't work anymore, Lanyon." Audun's voice was clipped and his tone bordered on condescending. "Whatever Quintrel was before the Great Fire, he's nothing special now, if he's even still alive."

"I think Quintrel is alive," Penhallow replied. "And I think he might hold the key to checking Pentreath Reese's power."

At that, Audun's eyes sparked, and his face became animated for the first time, twisting in disgust. "Why do you even mention Reese's name in my presence? You know how I feel about him."

A tight smile touched the corners of Penhallow's mouth. "Yes, Audun. I know. That's why I thought you might help me. You, of all people, have an interest in seeing Reese brought to heel."

Audun's gaze flickered to Connor and Lowrey, who both sat silently, attempting to avoid notice. "Such things shouldn't be discussed in front of mortals."

"These two have already suffered much because of Reese."

"These mortals have suffered? And I'm to be impressed by that? You know what Reese has cost me, not in just one lifetime, but over centuries. And now you bring me mortals and ask for my pity?" Audun's features were taut with anger, and his long eyeteeth were prominent. As the *talishte*'s anger grew, Connor felt as if the air in the room became heavier, more oppressive, like power coalescing.

"I didn't come to ask for pity," Penhallow said sharply. "I came to ask for information. Reese intends to set himself up as a warlord now that there's no magic to challenge him. Restore the magic, and the odds against Reese's success improve dramatically." He leaned forward. "No one hates Reese as much as you do. That should make it an easy decision. Help us, hurt Reese."

Audun met Penhallow's gaze for a moment without moving, then finally looked away. "What do you want?"

"Show him the map and the disk, Connor," Penhallow said.

Reluctantly, Connor did as he was told, withdrawing a thin wooden box and an obsidian amulet from beneath his shirt. From the box he withdrew an old parchment map. He passed the map and the disk wordlessly to Penhallow, who held them out to Audun.

"This map came from the king's library in Quillarth Castle, the night of the Great Fire," Penhallow said as Audun studied it. "It's one of the four maps Archmage Valtyr created, and the only one Nadoren didn't steal from him. It marks places of strong and null magic on the Continent. At least one of the other three maps also survived and was taken all the way to Edgeland," Penhallow added. "That map marks similar places of magic and no-magic at the top of the world, but what's really interesting are the symbols. Can you make them out?"

Audun looked at Penhallow crossly. "I can make them out. I just can't read them."

"That's because it's a code," Lowrey snapped, ignoring Penhallow's order to remain silent. "Mages love riddles almost as much as magic. Valtyr tied the maps together with a code, and the disks hold the key."

Audun shrugged and handed the map back. "I only see one disk."

Penhallow nodded. "We have one. An associate of ours has another disk. Originally, there were thirteen disks, one for each of the Lords of the Blood."

Audun grew very still. "I haven't heard that term for a long time."

"Your maker was already *talishte* when the Lords of the Blood met at Mirdalur, wasn't he, Audun?" Penhallow said quietly.

Audun closed his eyes and flinched, as if in momentary pain. "Yes. He was already quite old then." He paused. "Sverre was not a Lord of the Blood."

"But he spoke of those times." Penhallow's comment was more statement than question. "He knew King Hougen. And he knew something of magic, too."

Audun nodded slowly, his eyes still closed, as if remembering the distant past. Finally, he opened his eyes, and his gaze bore the weight of ages. "My maker, Sverre, was a friend of King Hougen's. Because of that friendship, Sverre brought his brood to stand watch while Hougen and the Lords of the Blood attempted to bind the wild magic at Mirdalur. Kierken Vandholt was another *talishte* who was present, and he *was* one of the Lords of the Blood," Audun said with a look toward Penhallow. "That was before he became the Wraith Lord."

Audun turned the polished obsidian disk in his fingers, staring at it as if lost in its luster. "He spoke of disks like these, on the very few occasions when he spoke of that night at all. Each Lord of the Blood had a disk, artifacts that had been preserved from long ago, that the king's astrologers said would help channel the power.

"Hougen had no real idea what kind of power he was toying with. He'd heard tales of mages in the Cross-Sea Kingdoms who could harness magic to make it do their bidding. There were stories that the magic had been bound here on the Continent, and then lost. If that was true, there had been no magic for at least a hundred years. Hougen wanted that for himself, for the kingdom he intended to create."

"What happened that night, Audun? What did Sverre tell you?" Penhallow pressed, leaning forward.

Audun's gaze took on a faraway look. "He and his brood

were on guard to assure that the king was not disturbed. They feared that one of the king's rivals might bring a force against them. But the threat did not come from men."

Audun turned to meet Penhallow's gaze. "Fire came down, as if by the hand of the gods that night," he said quietly. "It struck all around, too quickly even for *talishte* to avoid. The wild magic held them motionless, in agony, and then it disappeared as quickly as it came."

He fell silent for a moment, and Connor feared Audun would not continue. Finally, Audun resumed his tale. "My maker had never seen power like that. He feared that, in the hands of mortals, it might be turned against our kind. And it was. Hougen did not betray him, but others did."

"What else did your maker say about that night? What of Hougen and the lords?" Penhallow prompted.

"Hougen and the lords came out of the ritual chamber changed," Audun replied. "Each of the Lords of the Blood found that a talent had been enhanced. For some, it was foresight. For others, battle prowess or healing skills, or the ability to navigate without the stars. For each lord, there was a special ability, even for Hougen, who after that could sense the truth in a man's words. Many of the others, including my maker, also gained abilities."

"Was it just those who were present that night who gained the ability to control magic?" Again, Lowrey broke in, too engrossed in Audun's tale to heed Penhallow's warning. "Did the magic come to others?"

Audun nodded. "Gradually, certain abilities became enhanced. Within a few generations, small magics were widespread, like being able to slow milk from spoiling or keep pests out of the grain. Powerful magic remained rare, and coveted. After that night at Mirdalur, the wild magic storms that often laid waste to the countryside grew scarce. The monsters were eventually destroyed. And the madness that the wild magic caused no longer gripped our people. Until the Great Fire, when the magic slipped from our grasp."

"What of the disks?" Penhallow asked intently. "Did your maker say more of them?"

Audun grew quiet as he searched his thoughts. "Sverre told me that he heard the king speak to the Lords of the Blood and charge them to guard their disks well. He told them that their disks helped to bind the magic."

"Did Sverre believe the disks themselves held power?"

Audun nodded again. "Yes, he did." His expression grew sullen. "I've told you all I know."

"You've been very gracious," Penhallow said smoothly. "I have one more question, and then we'll trouble you no more." He held out the map once again. "Take another look at this. Many of the places of power are familiar: Quillarth Castle, Mirdalur, the original fortresses of the Lords of the Blood." He looked at Audun intently. "One of those places of power is also the tower of the Knights of Esthrane. The Knights had both mortal and *talishte* members, but all were mages. Do they still exist?"

Audun handed back the map with a snap of his wrist. His dark eyes had grown cold, and his expression was grim. "You overstep, Lanyon, and meddle in things that are none of your business." He cast a dark glance toward Connor and Lowrey. "Certainly not for mortals to know."

Audun's voice sounded a warning that chilled Connor, but Penhallow appeared unfazed by their host's sudden change of mood. He took back the map and rolled it up, slipping it back into its wooden box, then handed both the box and disk back to Connor. "You've been most helpful, Audun," Penhallow said, as if nothing had happened. "I'm grateful."

"What do you have planned for Reese?" Audun asked. His eyes held a predatory glint, and his expression took on a sudden hunger.

"As always, I plan to be a thorn in his side," Penhallow replied, standing. Connor and Lowrey got to their feet as well, a mite too quickly to look unhurried. "*Talishte* like you and me function quite well amidst magic. Helps to maintain a balance of power. Without magic, there's a void, and Reese would like to fill it." Penhallow gave a casual shrug, as if the two vampires were not discussing anything more momentous than the weather. "I prefer to see Reese reined in."

"Leave the Knights to the legends, Lanyon. Let the dead stay buried." There was no mistaking the warning in Audun's tone.

Penhallow's smile made his sharp teeth plain. "Except that the dead don't stay buried, do they, Audun? We don't even stay dead." With that, Penhallow ushered Connor and Lowrey from the house and into the night.

CHAPTER THREE

"ONCE AGAIN, MCFADDEN ELUDED YOU. HOW DIF-
ficult can it be to catch one criminal—with a private
army at your disposal?" Pentreath Reese did not raise his voice.
Volume would not have magnified the anger, the barely harnessed power, the implied threat.

Vedran Pollard kept what he hoped was a suitably neutral
expression. Now that he was in his early fifties his dark hair
had thinned, and what remained as a short-cropped fringe was
sprinkled with gray. Pollard had been a military man in his
youth, and it showed in his bearing. Tall, hawk-faced, with
sharp gray eyes and angular, uncompromising features, he was
accustomed to intimidating others to get what he wanted. He
had set aside his cloak and wore a black coat and pants with the
cut of a military uniform, though the jacket bore no insignia
of any kingdom's troops. These were the uniforms of Reese's
private army, the army Pollard commanded. And while at the
moment the 'army' numbered no more than a few hundred,
Pollard knew that Reese intended to build it into a mighty military machine.

A glint of satisfaction in Reese's eyes told him that the *talishte* had seen the flinch Pollard had tried not to display and been satisfied that the threat was delivered and understood.

"The man is annoyingly lucky," Pollard replied. "But all luck runs out eventually."

Reese stood near the fireplace, holding a goblet casually in one hand. He was dressed as if he had just come in from the hunt, with high leather boots and a well-fitted waistcoat. Reese looked to be in his late fourth decade, though Pollard knew that he was hundreds of years old. Reese was not of unusual height, nor uncommonly handsome. But he had a sense of presence that commanded the room. He was an imposing figure, even before one factored in his *talishte* speed, strength, and fighting skills.

"I expected better from you, Vedran," Reese said. "Your man failed me in Edgeland. McFadden lived to return. Once again, your traps failed at Mirdalur. You've failed to take Glenreith either by force or by diplomacy. You had better become useful to me soon, Vedran. Very soon."

Reese paused. "McFadden is an unwelcome distraction. I'd like to be done with him and move on." He gave Pollard an evaluating look. "I want your full report of just how you intend to bring him to me."

Pollard fought down mortal fear and cursed himself for his weakness. He knew Reese could spot the smallest nuances of his stance, the most minor changes in his facial expression. That level of observation had long ago earned *talishte* the reputation for being able to read minds.

Pollard removed the jacket of his uniform, moving deliberately to mask the way his hands shook. Slowly he turned up the cuff of his left sleeve, until his arm was exposed above the elbow. With more bravado than he felt, he thrust his bare arm forward. "See for yourself. The plan is solid."

Reese set aside his goblet and moved toward him at a leisurely pace Pollard knew was calculated to increase his own uneasiness. Pollard resisted the urge to brace himself, to close his eyes and stiffen, knowing it would make what was to come even worse, and that it would increase Reese's satisfaction immensely.

Reese lifted Pollard's arm, and in one brutal blur of motion, he buried his fangs in the vein that throbbed in the hollow of his elbow. Pollard set his jaw, willing himself not to cry out. Reese increased the pressure of the bite, forcing the fangs deeper into Pollard's arm.

With every mouthful of blood that Reese drew, he also took in Pollard's memories, his thoughts, his fears. Pollard knew that the process could be relatively painless. When Reese did not intend to make a point or inflict punishment, Pollard had experienced the bloodletting with minor injury and minimal pain. Today, Reese was angry, allowing his fangs to tear rather than puncture, taking more blood than Pollard guessed was necessary, until his head swam.

Show me everything, Reese voice said in Pollard's mind. He knew better than to resist. He had tried that once, early in his partnership with the vampire lord. Reese had broken through his mental barriers with sheer psychic force, then ransacked his thoughts like a thief rummaging through a chest of drawers. Reese had made certain that Pollard knew he had gained access to every hidden secret, every unpunished transgression, every mortifying memory. They all belonged to Reese now, to be wielded like weapons.

Reese clamped down harder, and Pollard could not stifle a groan. Through the blood bond, he felt Reese's satisfaction at the acknowledgement. Pollard tried to remain completely still, tried to keep his mind totally blank, tried to vacate his body until the 'reporting' was complete.

Pollard's breathing was fast and shallow, and his heart was thudding. He had seen what happened to the people Reese deemed no longer useful. More than once, Pollard had seen men drained beyond the ability to be revived, left as empty husks. Worse, he knew something of just how Reese could bend the blood bond, the *kruvgaldur*, to his will.

In the cells below Reese's fortress at Westbain were other wretches who had displeased the *talishte* lord. They were fed upon regularly by Reese's vampire guards, but their real punishment was within their own skulls: the tampered, heightened memories Reese had left them of their greatest fear, their most crippling pain, compulsive thoughts that drove them mad.

Reese tore his mouth free, leaving a deep gash in Pollard's arm. His mouth was bloody, something else Pollard knew was for show. He had seen Reese take blood for reporting or for feeding with not a drop spilled. Reese spat into his palm and pressed a bit of the spittle against Pollard's savaged skin. The skin began to close over rapidly, but Pollard was a veteran of such things and he knew that while Reese had provided enough of his spit to close the wound, it was not sufficient to quicken the deep healing. He'd intended Pollard to be left with a painful injury that would take time to heal and produce a wicked bruise as a memento. All the better to make his point.

"Your report is complete," Reese said, licking his lips as his fangs retracted. "Understand this: I want McFadden stopped before he can make another attempt at bringing back the magic. Bring him to me. I want to know what he knows."

"We've got spies all over Donderath with instructions to kill him on sight," Pollard replied. "It's going to be hard to get the message out to them that there's been a change of plans." It took all of Pollard's strength not to let the vertigo claim him. The loss of blood, the imposition of Reese's will, and then the sudden removal of his presence swirled Pollard's thoughts and blurred his vision.

Reese shrugged. "That's your problem. Make it happen."

"I understand," Pollard replied, his voice as steady as he could make it.

"I'll have your horse ready at daybreak. Go back to your men and this time, get it right."

"I understand," Pollard repeated. He knew Reese could feel how weak he was right now, how close to losing consciousness, and wondered if Reese intended to humiliate him by keeping him standing in the warm parlor until his knees buckled and he dropped to the ground.

"Leave me," Reese commanded.

Pollard forced down the impulse to run, made himself cross the short distance to the door slowly to preserve the shred of dignity he retained. He made his way up the stairs, trying to cling to the balustrade without looking as it were the only thing holding him upright. He reached his room, shut the door behind him, and fell to his knees as his vision went gray.

Damn, damn, damn, damn! Pollard thought. The vertigo was winning, so he eased himself down onto his back, nursing his injured arm. He lay staring at the ceiling. Before the Great Fire, the ceiling had been a work of art, plastered with an elaborate design of cornices and embellishments.

Now, the fine old ceiling was cracked the width of the room, with bare spots where a number of the geometric three-dimensional plaster shapes had fallen. Reese's home sustained less damage than many of the other manor houses. But the telltale signs were all around: a fire-damaged wing and burned dependencies. Scorch marks on the stone, new repairs, or places where repairs had not been done at all. Cracks that ran through the thick stone walls, a testimony to the sheer power of the magical strike. Pollard's own manor had fared much worse.

Precious good your own title is doing you, Lord Pollard, his own voice mocked in his mind. *Who holds the reins—and who wears the bit?*

Pollard's right hand dug his fingers into the thick pile of the carpet in frustration, and he murmured a litany of curses. After a few moments, the worst of the vertigo passed. Pride more than prudence forced him to his feet. He staggered and dropped heavily into a chair near the fireplace. It did not surprise him to find a bottle of fine brandy and a crystal glass waiting for him, as well as a selection of cheeses and a platter of roasted venison, still warm from the kitchen. Such was the nature of fealty to Pentreath Reese, a dizzying swing between generosity and fear.

Pollard stripped off his shirt and threw it to the ground. It was spattered with blood, and he had no intention of wearing it when he went to meet with his men. Thus far, the humiliations Reese chose to deliver had been private, and Pollard intended to keep it that way as long as possible. Knowing Reese, there would be a fresh shirt hanging in the wardrobe, perhaps with an entirely new cloak and pants as well. *Generous. And terrifying at the same time*, Pollard thought.

Pollard distracted himself by focusing on his dinner. Though Reese had no need to eat, he maintained a kitchen staff that was the equal of that of any of the great houses. It was whispered that Reese's title had been purchased, not earned, and that his wealth had been extorted over the centuries. *Perhaps.* If so, Reese had learned how to handle himself with as true an aristocratic mien as any of the lords of Donderath. Now, with the kingdom in ruins, the provenance of a man's title mattered little. Except, perhaps, in the case of Blaine McFadden.

Pollard finished the venison and washed it down with half of the brandy before his nerves felt steady enough for him to sleep and the ache in his arm had dulled. He wondered, as he climbed into the high four-poster bed, whether Reese had tampered with his dreams, but his sleep, when it came, was untroubled.

The next morning, Pollard's mood was sour as he rode back to his encampment. He dismounted and thrust the reins into the hands of a waiting groom, then strode toward his tent. Inside, he allowed himself a deep breath, trying to put the horrors of the previous night behind him. The canvas tent was a mark of both rank and privilege. It was twice as large as the officers' tents, big enough for a table and chairs for strategy meetings and a few portable luxuries: throw rugs, a small silver set for serving *fet*, pewter drinking goblets, and a brassbound trunk with a selection of what brandy and spirits could still be found.

A pot of water boiled on a small brazier in the center of the room. The brazier took the chill off the tent, although with the days growing shorter and solstice not far off, the harshest days of winter were yet to come, and the most comfortable tent would not afford the warmth of a real house.

"Welcome back, Lord Pollard," Kerr said, bustling through the tent flap. He bent immediately to take the steaming kettle from the brazier, pouring it over the dark syrup in the silver pot to make the strong, bitter drink that would clear Pollard's head and revive him.

"What did I miss?"

"Nothing but the usual drills and the incessant archery practice," Kerr replied, unflappable despite Pollard's moods. "I've set out a bit of sausage and dried fruit in case your lordship did not have a chance to eat before you left Lord Reese's fortress."

Without a word, Kerr helped Pollard out of his cloak, not needing to be told to be gentle with Pollard's wounded left arm.

Under any circumstances, Kerr would have been frighteningly efficient. But without ever acknowledging what he knew or letting on to how he came by the knowledge, Kerr understood that visits to Reese took a toll on Pollard. Kerr made it a point to have food ready, a hot pot of *fet* waiting, and a box of bandages and ointment discreetly set out on Pollard's cot. Pollard suspected that his valet had discerned the nature of Pollard's fealty to Reese one of the times Kerr had bandaged him after a battle and could not help but have seen the scars of old puncture marks on Pollard's skin.

"Thank you, Kerr."

Kerr handed Pollard a cup of the steaming, strong mixture, and Pollard let the vapors rouse him for a moment before he lifted the cup to his lips. "Per your instructions, m'lord, I've notified your commanders to meet with you at tenth bells. Is there anything else you require?"

"That will be all," Pollard said, his voice flat, a mixture of distraction and exhaustion. Meeting with Reese always had that effect on him, just another reminder of who really held the power. Pollard downed the rest of his cup of *fet* as Kerr left the tent, then poured a second cup to steady his nerves before sitting down on his cot beside the box of bandages.

He set his cup aside, eased himself gingerly out of his uniform jacket, and rolled up his sleeve. Although the skin was already healed, the middle of his arm, from a handsbreadth above his elbow to the same distance below the joint, was swollen and purpled. He winced as his fingers brushed the wound, and the arm hurt when bent. Pollard dug in the box for some of the powders the healer had supplied to dull the pain without dulling his wits, and he added an ample dosage to his already-bitter *fet*.

Pollard had just finished the food Kerr had set out for him and drained the last of the pot of *fet* when the others arrived. Each man paused in the door of the tent to make a shallow bow before entering, then took his place at the small portable table.

"Reconnaissance report," Pollard snapped.

Captain Anton, a dark-haired man in his early thirties, looked up as if he had been expecting the command. "We've increased the watch on all roads leading from Glenreith toward Castle Reach and the eastern cities," Anton reported.

"Why not on all roads, Captain?"

Anton grimaced. "There's nothing to the west of Glenreith except farmland, least not for quite a ways out. We've only got so many men, m'lord. They're stretched thin as it is."

"How did McFadden get past your men to reach Mirdalur?" Pollard demanded.

Chagrin flashed across Anton, and then resignation. "They disguised themselves as tinkers, m'lord. We'd not blockaded the roads, merely kept a watch for McFadden. Now that we know he's willing to move in disguise, we'll watch more closely."

He paused. "Your orders had been to patrol but not raise suspicions," he added, a touch of defensiveness coloring his tone. "Stopping and searching all travelers is bound to raise questions, as well as protest."

Pollard swore under his breath. "Lord Reese doesn't want to tip his hand as to the strength of his forces—at least, not yet," he replied. "Some discretion is necessary, I agree." His tone hardened. "Yet I am quite certain Lord Reese would prefer to smooth over the ruffled feathers of a few villagers or motley caravans in order to apprehend McFadden and his companions."

"Noted, sir."

"Berit," Pollard said, turning his attention to the next officer at the table.

"Sir."

"I'd like to know exactly how McFadden and a handful of men managed to outfight your soldiers and get free."

Berit was a blond man with the manner and look of a dockhand. His hair was cut short for a helm, making his neck appear even thicker than it was. A scar ran across the left side of his face, from the bridge of his nose across one cheek. His right temple was still bruised from the altercation with McFadden's group, and his eye was blackened.

"It wasn't just McFadden and his guards, sir," he replied. "We got attacked by another force of armed men who joined in the middle of the fight." He paused. "Gods' truth, m'lord, I think the second group happened upon the battle. We couldn't make out their uniforms. They were a mangy lot, but they fought like real soldiers, and they were better armed than I'd have expected from their appearance."

Pollard began to pace. "So you're telling me, Captain, that you were fighting with McFadden and his guards and a second set of soldiers appeared, out of nowhere, and took up McFadden's part?"

Berit nodded. "Aye, that's exactly what I'm saying."

"What makes you think they weren't with McFadden all along?"

"They didn't hail him or join ranks with his men, sir," Berit replied after taking a moment to replay the scene in his mind. "They fired on us from a distance and ordered us back. I believe they thought we were brigands attacking a group of peddlers."

Pollard shook his head. "Amazing. McFadden and his con-

vict friends get rescued by a group of wandering soldiers looking to rid the kingdom of highwaymen?"

Berit looked abashed, but he nodded once more. "I don't say
that it makes sense, m'lord, but then again, few things do these
days."

"So where is McFadden now?"

Berit shifted in his chair. "Our survivors retreated, then we
sent back a scout. Once we were gone, the other soldiers moved
in and captured McFadden's men, then marched them all back
to their camp."

"How in the name of the gods did your scouts miss the camp
of rogue soldiers?" Pollard thundered.

Berit stiffened his spine. "Like McFadden, they weren't keeping to the main roads. Their camp was set back, out of sight,
and more of a beggars' village than a proper army encampment. There were more of them than there were of our men, so
we fell back to await new orders."

Pollard ran a hand through his thinning hair. The terror of
his encounter with Reese was still fresh in his memory. "Unless
you'd like to explain, in person, to Lord Reese how McFadden
keeps escaping your men, I suggest you adjust your patrols," he
replied.

Fear and defiance sparked in Berit's eyes, but the man merely
nodded. "Yes, sir."

Pollard looked to the third man, Nilo Jansen, his second-
in-command. Nilo was small and wiry, with dark eyes that
missed nothing and hair close-shorn in a soldier's cut. Inven-
tive, ruthless, and fiercely loyal, Nilo was one of the few people
Pollard trusted to have his back.

"What have we heard about Penhallow?" Pollard asked.

Nilo smiled, reminding Pollard of one of the fish he had

seen down on the wharves, a monstrous thing with a maw of needle-sharp teeth. "He hasn't been back to Rodestead House since the Great Fire. It's empty, badly damaged, and even his mortal servants appear to have left for good. Our *talishte* soldiers burned out one of his crypts and nearly caught McFadden in the process, but we know we injured several of Penhallow's people and killed more than a few of his brood."

"Good," Pollard grunted, "but not quite good enough."

Nilo nodded in agreement. "We put watchers on places he had been known to go and people he was known to contact. We managed to bottle him up inside Traher Voss's fortress, along with the mortal who's been traveling with him, Lord Garnoc's former assistant."

Pollard looked up. "So you have him pinned down with Voss?"

Nilo sighed. "No. Voss is a clever bastard. I've had reports that Penhallow and his servant and a man my source couldn't identify have been seen since then. I don't know how, but they got out."

The sheer audacity made Pollard smile. "That's why he was one of the most successful mercenaries Donderath ever fielded." The smile faded. "What of the siege?"

Nilo shrugged. "Still under way, for all the good it does us."

Pollard let loose a lengthy stream of curses. Nilo and the others sat motionless, their faces showing no expression until Pollard had vented his frustration. "Lord Reese tires of excuses and failures," he growled. "Surely one *talishte* cannot outrun this entire army?"

When they said nothing, he felt his temper rise. "I want Penhallow! Do whatever you have to do to bring him down. Kill the servant, but stake Penhallow in the heart and bring him to me. Lord Reese wants to question him."

Despite the cold outside, the tent had grown warm, or at least, Pollard thought, his anger had raised his own temperature until sweat beaded his brow. "And to the man who brings me Blaine McFadden, a dozen gold pieces. Maybe that will put some incentive into the soldiers if orders and the wrath of Lord Reese aren't enough."

"Aye, sir."

Pollard turned away. "Berit. Anton. Return to your men. Nilo, a word in private."

They remained silent until the two other men were gone. Pollard sank down into a campaign chair near the brazier and took out a bottle of brandy and two pewter cups. His temper had stirred his heartbeat so that his wounded arm ached afresh. Pollard poured a measure of whiskey into both glasses and held one out to Nilo.

"Have a drink." It was more an order than an offer, and Nilo walked around the table, pulling up a chair to join Pollard. He accepted the whiskey and eyed Pollard with concern.

"I take it the meeting with Reese went badly."

Pollard knocked back the whiskey in his glass and poured another. "What do you think?"

"How badly?"

Pollard let his head fall back and studied the ceiling of his tent for a moment before speaking. "Lord Reese does not tolerate continued failure."

Nilo cursed. "He took blood?"

Pollard drew up his sleeve, and Nilo gave a soft whistle. Nilo leaned forward, swirling the whiskey in his cup. "Mirdalur wasn't the first place magic was raised. According to my sources, it's not the only place it can be raised again. Reese didn't invent this whole story about McFadden being a Lord of the Blood." He drained his own cup. "It's true. And if the gods so will it and the stars align, it's possible he could bring the magic back."

"If that happens, Reese loses his bid to become the dominant warlord on the Continent," Pollard replied, eyeing the bottle and deciding there wasn't enough whiskey in Donderath to make him feel better. "And I lose my chance at the crown."

Nilo nodded. "All our preparations are for naught if McFadden survives long enough to bring back the magic."

Pollard let out a long breath. "Reese wants McFadden brought to him alive, so he can drain his knowledge with his blood, know what he knows."

"It would be better for our plans if McFadden died sooner," Nilo said quietly. They both knew they were skirting a dangerous topic, and that Reese was not forgiving of disobedience.

"I have no way to give my spies revised orders," Pollard replied. "If McFadden dies before I can update them—well, such things are unfortunate." He turned his cup in his hand as he thought. "Without McFadden, Glenreith will have no choice but to accept my offers. And I will finally have my revenge on Ian McFadden."

"Unless Reese loses," Nilo said.

Pollard frowned. "If he loses, and we're really, really lucky, we'll be dead."

CHAPTER FOUR

G IVE US OUR WEAPONS BACK!" BLAINE DEMANDED.
"If we're being attacked by *talishte*, then Reese won't stop
until he's taken us. That's what he's after. I don't know if we
can win, but we can damn well give him a good fight."

Niklas Theilsson nodded and bent to retrieve the weapons
his men had confiscated from Blaine and his friends. Blaine
paused when he had belted on his sword. "I'm sorry we brought
this on you."

Niklas shot back a roguish smile. "Why apologize? It's like
old times: you, me, and trouble."

"But do there have to be vampires?" Piran grumbled. "I hate
fighting vampires."

Kestel caught Blaine by the arm as he moved for the doorway. "You're not going out there, are you? If you die, the magic
might be gone for good."

Blaine met her gaze. "I'm not going to let Niklas or his men
get killed on my account. What's my option? If it's Reese out
there, he'll find me no matter where I hide. I can't outrun *talishte*. At least in a fight, I've got a chance."

Piran clapped him on the shoulder. "My thoughts exactly. Let's go whack off some vampire heads, shall we?"

Niklas had already sprinted from the tent, shouting orders as he rallied his men. Blaine and the others followed, weapons at the ready. Outside, the camp was in chaos. Blaine saw one of Niklas's soldiers thrown a dozen feet as casually as a child might toss a rag doll. The soldier lay crumpled where he fell. Across the camp, soldiers shouted and cursed as they tried to fight an enemy that moved too quickly for them to see.

Tents appeared to explode, ripped from their moorings and thrown up in the air. Torches were doused with dirt or water, giving the advantage to the *talishte* who did not need light to see.

A few feet away, a soldier screamed as he was lifted a dozen feet into the air, vainly attempting to strike at his attacker with his sword. With a rush of air, the man fell, landing with a thud. A few tent rows to the right, another man rose screaming into the sky, his attacker seeming to be no more than shadow. He, too, fell back to the ground, shouting and flailing.

Blaine and Piran headed one direction, Kestel and Dawe in the other. Verran ran low, keeping to the shadows, scouting for trouble, his knife clutched in his hand.

Blaine caught movement out of the corner of his eye and slashed with his sword, anticipating his attacker's movement. The blade caught and held for a moment, though Blaine saw only a blur before the sword came free, its edge bloodied.

"You got one!" Piran shouted.

"No good if you don't take the head or heart," Blaine grated, glancing around warily.

Something moved, close on the left. "Run!" Blaine shouted, as he and Piran began sprinting toward the center of the camp, where the fighting was heaviest. Around them were the bodies of injured soldiers who lay where they had been thrown from the sky. Tents littered the ground, flung aside as the attackers ripped them from their tethers, or kicked to the side as desperate soldiers fought to free themselves when the canvases dropped like nets from above.

Piran stopped to bend over an injured soldier. "Where are you hurt?"

"Leg's broken. It twisted when I fell."

"Were you bitten?"

"Gods, no! I'd know, wouldn't I? By Esthrane, I'm not going to be turned, am I?" For an instant, fear surpassed his pain.

"You'd know," Piran said grimly. "I'll send someone back for you when I can," he promised, then rose and sprinted to rejoin Blaine.

"If it's Reese attacking, he's changed his tactics," Piran observed. "Compared to the way his people fought the last time, they're playing nicely. No head-ripping, no throat-gouging."

Blaine and Piran were fighting back-to-back, barely keeping the swiftly moving attackers at bay. Blaine's mouth set in a hard line as he swung his sword, and more than once, he managed to strike an attacker on the shoulder or arm despite the *talishte*'s greater speed.

"They don't have to stop until dawn. But we can't keep up the fight that long," Blaine replied through gritted teeth.

Just then, a hoarse scream cut through the night air. Blaine turned to see Dawe in the grip of one of the *talishte* attackers, struggling to get free as his assailant lifted him into the air above the melee. Kestel grabbed Dawe's fallen crossbow, but there was no way for her to get off a clean shot without striking Dawe, and by the potent curses she screamed, it was clear she realized the standoff. Blaine steeled himself, expecting the *talishte* to drop Dawe as the attackers had let all their victims fall, but this time, the vampire kept rising, disappearing into the night sky with Dawe in his grip.

"They're looking for us," Piran said as a trio of *talishte* came at them. "That's why they took Dawe instead of dropping him."

From across the commons, Verran gave a sharp cry as he was lifted into the night. "Get out of here!" he shouted, twisting in vain to get loose before he and the *talishte* ascended too high for a safe fall.

Around them, men scrambled to evade the fast-moving *talishte* only to be seized and dropped. Across the vista of flattened tents and ruined wagons, Blaine saw men struggling to rise from where they had fallen or limping away from the thick of battle. Some charged back into the fray despite their injuries. Yet as Blaine surveyed the damage, nowhere did he see heads severed from bodies or throats torn open. In fact, he realized, he saw no corpses at all, just soldiers injured enough to take them out of the fight.

"It's not Reese," Blaine said. "These aren't Reese's men."

"How in Raka can you be sure?" Piran shouted above the noise.

Blaine stepped away from Piran and let his sword fall.

"What are you doing? Have you lost your mind?" Piran shouted, rushing to interpose himself between Blaine and a *talishte* who was heading their way.

"Nobody needs to get hurt," Blaine said. "It's a misunderstanding."

"Reese is messing with your mind, Mick. Get your godsdamned sword!"

The *talishte* stopped just out of reach of Piran's sword. "We're here to get your people out safely," the vampire said. "Geir's waiting."

"Geir?" Piran said, lowering his sword just a bit.

"That's why the soldiers aren't getting killed," Blaine replied. "Why they aren't fighting like Reese's men. They're just trying to get us out of here.

"Call off the attack," he said, turning to the *talishte*. "The soldiers are on our side. We're not captives."

"Geir won't believe it unless you tell him yourself," Piran said, lowering his sword the rest of the way. "Go. Get Geir to call off his troops, and I'll find Niklas and get him to have his men stand down."

"Ready?" the *talishte* asked. But before Blaine could reply, strong hands seized him in a vice grip. They lifted up from the ground so quickly that Blaine felt his stomach lurch, and then the movement made everything around him a dark blur until finally the *talishte* set him down lightly at the edge of a copse of trees not far from the camp. Geir was waiting for him, looking worried. Verran and Dawe were behind him, and from the sound of it, they were already arguing for a cease-fire.

Geir stepped toward Blaine. The *talishte* was tall and slender, dressed in black, with dark hair that fell shoulder-length. He took in Blaine's appearance with a worried look. "What's going on? I found shelter for the day when you were hidden in the barn, and when I woke, you were captives. I feared the soldiers belonged to Pollard, so I returned as soon as I could gather enough of Penhallow's brood in the hope I could free you."

"Great idea. Much appreciated. Only the soldiers turned out to be good guys. Captain's an old friend. We need to stop the attack. They're on our side—or they were, before this," Blaine replied.

Geir's eyes took on a distant look, and for a moment, Blaine wondered if the other had heard him. Then the *talishte* roused and returned his gaze to Blaine. He looked skyward as several dark shapes grew closer, then set down near the forest's edge. "All my men have been recalled."

Blaine let out a long breath. "Now somehow we've got to explain to Niklas that you were trying to save us from him, after his soldiers saved us from Pollard."

Geir winced. "My apologies, although that is insufficient."

Blaine shrugged. "You came to a logical conclusion. Under different circumstances, I'd be grateful for the rescue. But we've got to patch things up because if Reese and Pollard do attack, it would be helpful if your people and Niklas's soldiers all know they're on the same side." He met Geir's gaze. "But we'd better get back, or, if I know Niklas, he'll send a war party after us."

Within half a candlemark, Blaine and Geir stood within sight of Niklas's encampment, far enough away to be out of range of archers. They stood side by side, with Verran and Dawe behind them. A line of soldiers stood on guard, and after a moment, Niklas Theilsson stepped out in front. Just behind the line, Blaine spotted Piran and Kestel.

"What's going on, Blaine? We were trying to protect you." Niklas looked as angry as Blaine had ever seen him.

Blaine moved forward. "And these particular *talishte* were trying to protect us from you. They knew we'd been taken away from the barn. The last soldiers they'd encountered were Pollard's."

Niklas glared at Geir. "I've got men who were dropped out of the sky or thrown across the compound, a camp that's been torn apart, and you're telling me it was all just a mistake?"

"No one got killed, Niklas. Geir's *talishte* were being careful. They could have made it a bloodbath," Blaine said. "If they'd have walked up to the camp and asked nicely, what would your guards have done?"

"Put a quarrel through their chests," Niklas growled. He

eyed Geir and the other *talishte* as if unconvinced of their intentions.

"While we stand out here yelling back and forth, we're vulnerable to a real attack," Blaine replied. "Will your men accept a truce? It's still a long way home, and we'll be stronger together."

It was plain from Niklas's expression that he wasn't happy with the idea, but after a moment, he turned and shouted orders to his men. It might have been years since Blaine had last seen his friend, but he had not forgotten just how stubborn Niklas could be.

"You have your truce," Niklas snapped. "But it's probably best if the *talishte* keep their distance until tempers cool and we get the camp functioning again."

"Understood."

Blaine turned back to Geir as Niklas walked away. "Since we're the cause of the attack, the least my people can do is help them put the camp back together. Tomorrow, perhaps things will have cooled down. I hope to convince Niklas to ally with us."

"Raising an army?"

"Why not? Pollard and Reese have their own soldiers. And they'll be back to attack us. Niklas needs a lord to serve now that the king is dead. We could use the help. Better to have them with us than go it alone."

Geir nodded. "I can't fault your logic, but I'd feel more sure of our next steps if Penhallow were here."

"Does your bond give you any idea of where he is?" Blaine watched Geir for a clue to the *talishte*'s thoughts, and as usual, saw nothing.

"Whatever situation had put him in danger, I have the distinct feeling that Penhallow and Connor escaped," Geir replied. "And an impression that they would rejoin us, after they accomplish...something."

"No idea what?"

Geir shook his head. "As I've mentioned, the *kruvgaldur* is imperfect, especially at a distance. Flashes of strong emotion, brief pictures send much better than actual words."

Blaine grimaced. "So they'll show up when they show up," he said, making no effort to hide his impatience. A sudden thought struck him. "Geir, did your party encounter any scouts?"

Geir frowned. "Two. I used the glamour to put them to sleep. I thought you might want to question them. They're unconscious and bound just beyond the tree line." He seemed to see something in Blaine's expression that made him wary. "Why?"

"One of them may be my brother." Blaine turned to Verran and Dawe. "Go give Niklas a hand on the cleanup and tell Kestel and Piran what's going on. I'll be there as soon as I see whether Carr is among the guards."

Dawe and Verran strode off toward Niklas's camp while Blaine accompanied Geir back to the forest. Two men in tattered, dirty uniforms lay bound and gagged on the ground. As Blaine approached, he found that he was holding his breath.

Carr was just a child when I was exiled. Will I even recognize him? Blaine wondered, feeling his stomach tighten.

He looked at the two unconscious men. One man was pale as moonlight, his face framed by lank hair the color of dried blood. No recognition stirred in Blaine's mind, and his worry rose. He turned his attention to the other man. The second was tall and lean, and while he was still shy of twenty seasons by several years, his body had been toned and hardened by war. Muddy brown hair fell across one cheek, but even so, Blaine felt his throat tighten at the surge of recognition. "That's Carr," he said, his voice tight.

Geir lifted the first man in his arms as if the soldier were a child. "I'll take this one out where the others are, and I'll lift the compulsion on your brother. Give him a moment or two to rouse. And be careful if you cut his bonds: he may wake fighting."

"One more thing we have in common," Blaine murmured, thinking of how many times Piran and Dawe had complained back in Edgeland that Blaine often woke from dark dreams thrashing and struggling.

Geir disappeared among the trees and Blaine was glad for the privacy, though now that the reunion awaited, he found himself at a total loss for words. With a sigh, Blaine knelt next to Carr, who was beginning to stir. Drawing his knife, he cut the bonds on Carr's wrists and ankles, took Carr's sword and the long knife that hung from his belt, then stood back. He sheathed his knife but stood ready for an attack should Carr suddenly launch himself at his 'captor.'

Carr struggled awake as the *talishte*'s compulsion cleared from his head. His eyes blinked and he stood up quickly, defensive and reaching for his missing weapons.

"You're safe," Blaine said quietly.

Carr's eyes were wild with fear and rage. But as he fixed on Blaine's features, Carr sat back down with a thud and the blood drained from his face. "Oh gods above, I'm dead, aren't I?"

"You're not dead."

"Blaine? You can't be Blaine. My brother's dead, gone to Velant. People don't come back from Velant."

"I did."

Carr reached again for his weapons, and this time he met Blaine's gaze with suspicion. "Why take my blades, brother?" There was no mistaking the skepticism and mistrust in the last word, and Blaine winced.

"I've awakened a time or two fighting my way out of

nightmares. My mates objected to getting slugged for no fault of their own," Blaine said with a shrug. "Your weapons are here for you."

"Why did you come back?" Now that he was fully awake, Carr studied his brother with a dark glare.

"Long story better told when we're somewhere else," Blaine replied. He toed the weapons closer to Carr and stepped back. "Niklas will want to know you're safe."

"Does he know about you?" Carr moved for his weapons without taking his eyes off Blaine, still alert for deception.

"He knows. And before you ask, the *talishte* who captured you are on our side. They meant no harm. They thought Niklas had captured my friends and me."

Carr snatched his weapons and moved backward, out of reach. " 'Our side'? I don't know whose side you're on yet."

"There isn't time—"

Carr's expression twisted with anger. "I was on patrol and got attacked by a pack of bloodsuckers. Now I wake up and my dead brother is back, talking to me like I'm still a child. For all I know, those damned biters got inside my head and you're not even real."

Blaine extended his right hand. "I'm real enough, Carr. But we need to get out of here."

Carr sprang from where he crouched, landing a fist to the side of Blaine's jaw hard enough that Blaine staggered back a step. Blood started from his lip. Unwilling to harm Carr, Blaine fell into a defensive stance but did not draw his sword. Carr stepped back, flexing and clenching the fingers of his right hand at the pain of the blow.

"You're solid. Doesn't mean you're real."

"By Torven's horns! What was that for? I'm your brother for the gods' sake."

"The brother who left us to starve? Dammit, Blaine, I know why you killed Father. I know he dishonored Mari. Gods above, I was sick enough of his beatings. But without Father, and without you, Aunt Judith and Mari and I had nothing left. The scandal meant that almost no one would trade with us, sell to us, buy our surplus crops. We were outcasts, unwelcome at court, and even the village peasants spit when we crossed their paths!" Carr was shouting now, and while his face was red with anger, tears glistened at the corners of his eyes. "We lost everything!"

"So did I." Despite himself, Blaine's temper rose. "The king took my title, my claim to the land, and the sentence took Carensa from me," he returned. "My betrothed married another man, bore his child. I spent three years in Velant, starving and freezing, under the commander's boot. Three more years starving and freezing as a colonist, in the mines or on the boats. I would have preferred that Merrill execute me. But I went to Velant knowing that at least I had stopped Father from beating you and raping Mari, and that was enough."

"And after six years you show up out of nowhere and want it all back?" Carr challenged.

"Keep the godsdamned title, if that's what matters to you," Blaine snapped. "But Glenreith is still my home. Aunt Judith welcomed us. That's where we're going, if I can ever get your stubborn ass out of this forest before we're attacked again."

"'Us'? You brought a bunch of convicts back with you? How wonderful. Did Judith tell you we sold the silver to pay for food, so there's naught left to steal?"

Blaine's fists clenched at his sides, and it took all his will to keep himself from landing a punch. "There are bigger things at stake than your hurt feelings," Blaine grated. "By Charrot! Grow up."

Carr fixed him with a baleful look. "Oh, I grew up, Blaine. I grew up working like a man in the fields when I was naught but a slip of a boy. I grew up hearing Judith sob herself to sleep because we had no food and no money to buy any. I grew up seeing my sister marry beneath her station because no one wanted the taint of the McFadden name. And I grew up with every kill I made in the name of king and country on the front lines."

"Carr—"

"Damn you! I mourned you at first, and then I learned to hate you for what you cost us. So now you're back. To Raka with you! We learned to get by without your help. Go back to Edgeland. We don't need you. I can't imagine why in the name of the gods you came here."

"Because I may be the only one who can restore the magic." Blaine met Carr's angry gaze as the other took in the words. Disbelief gave way to an angry smirk.

"Have you figured the cost, dear brother? I've been saved once by you, and the price was too damn high." With that, Carr strode for the edge of the forest, shoving his way past Blaine and disappearing into the darkness.

CHAPTER FIVE

I T'S HARD TO BELIEVE THAT ONLY HALF A YEAR HAS gone past since..." Connor's voice drifted off to nothing, but the others did not need him to finish the sentence to know where his thoughts strayed.

Castle Reach, once the bustling palace city of the kingdom of Donderath, was now a ruin. Much of the city had burned in the Great Fire on the night that Donderath fell, when a ribbon of fire, called down by the battle mages of Meroven, laid waste both to Quillarth Castle and to the city around it.

Trapped at the top of the castle's bell tower, Connor had watched the city fall. In the rubble of the castle and the Fire that consumed the city, Connor had lost all he had: his master, his king, and his home. All that had remained was duty, and his dying master's charge to safeguard the disk and the map that Connor had found hidden in the royal library. A map Penhallow had hoped might change the course of the war, found too late to stop the carnage.

"For once I did not see such things happen with my own eyes," Penhallow replied. "I have seen so many things come to ruin in my time." There was an edge of sorrow in his voice.

Connor felt for the wooden map box that he kept in a pouch beneath his cloak, and the obsidian disk on a leather strap under his shirt. He did not want to think about how many times the vampire had seen kings and kingdoms come to ruin.

"I don't know how you manage it," Connor said quietly. "Once was more than enough for me."

Penhallow did not reply, and Connor wondered if such things were beyond words, even for one of the immortals.

Before the Great Fire, the king's census had numbered more than eighty thousand people in the environs of Castle Reach. Thriving, noisy, bustling with life, the palace city had teemed with merchants, sailors, criminals, soldiers, wanderers, scholars, and all manner of travelers. The air had smelled of cooking meat and the press of unwashed bodies, of cart horses and torch smoke, and on occasion, of the flowers, incense, and perfumes offered by merchants in the crowded market. A forest of ships' masts once filled the wharf front, and the shouts of stevedores and the clatter of the cargo they moved mingled with the salt air. The din of wagon wheels and the shouts of street vendors had echoed from the walls along the narrow, winding streets, and raucous music spilled out of the dark doorways of the innumerable taverns, public houses, and brothels that met the every need of Castle Reach's residents and visitors. Now...

When the magic failed, so did the protective spells that held back the sea. The wharves and the street nearest the seawall were now buried beneath the tide. Many of the buildings that had not burned, collapsed when the small magics used to patch and support them disappeared. The war with Meroven had never brought an invading army to Castle Reach, yet the city looked as if it had been besieged, overrun, and cruelly conquered.

The streets were quiet, but not empty. Though the night was

cold, ragged forms huddled in the shadows of the burned and ruined buildings or shuffled along the scorched cobblestones. The air still smelled of salt spray, but the ships that once filled the wharves were long gone, fleeing the city's devastation or burned to the waterline where they sat at anchor. Connor had managed to get a place on one of the last ships to leave the city in the aftermath of the fall, and he had watched the skyline burn as the ship set sail, course unknown.

That ship had taken him eventually to the northernmost site in the world, Edgeland, a place so harsh and unforgiving that it was colonized by force with exiles and criminals. There he had met Blaine McFadden and discovered that the map and disk he carried might yet play a role in bringing back the shattered magic.

"I wouldn't have believed it if I hadn't seen it myself," Treven Lowrey said. Connor stole a glance at Lowrey, whose expression of shock and dismay so clearly mirrored Connor's own feelings.

"I watched from the castle tower as the Fire fell," Connor replied in a voice just above a whisper. "And I still can't believe it."

"Stay sharp," Penhallow murmured. "We're being followed."

Connor rested his hand on his sword. Lowrey gripped the walking stick he had cut in the forest, a stout stave at least six feet in length and almost as thick as a man's wrist. Penhallow did not reach for his weapon, and Connor knew why. Unless they faced other *talishte* in battle, Penhallow's speed, strength, and fangs presented a formidable array of weapons.

Moving through the alleyways, Connor could feel unseen eyes watching them. Here and there, groups of men huddled around small fires, talking in low tones. The lower floors of the least-damaged buildings had been reclaimed, and lamplight spilled from the glassless windows, along with the unmistakable smell of rough-brewed whiskey and cooked fish.

"Lookin' for company, are you?" a woman's voice called from a doorway. Clad in tattered, tawdry finery, the woman swaggered toward them. She looked as raw as the whiskey on her breath, and her thin face was gaunt and wan.

"We have no need of your services," Penhallow said quietly, but Connor felt the tingle of the *talishte*'s compulsion.

The woman returned to her place with a dazed look, and Connor had no doubt that within a moment, she would not recall their passing.

"If you can send her away, why not get rid of whoever's following us?" Connor whispered.

"It doesn't work that way," Penhallow said, and despite the situation, he managed a terse chuckle. "I wish it did. I can only compel one person at a time. Keep your eyes open. Our 'friends' are getting closer." Walking single file, Penhallow led the way as they moved through the small crowd outside the reclaimed tavern, doing their best to pass unnoticed.

They turned a corner and found four men with drawn swords standing shoulder to shoulder, blocking their path. Connor heard footsteps behind them, and three more armed men appeared from the shadows, cutting off their exit.

"We'll be having your coins, and anything else we take a liking to, like that fine coat of yours," the tallest of the men said, and with his sword point he indicated Lowrey's cloak.

"Not tonight." Penhallow had barely spoken before he moved as a blur, going for the two men on his right. Connor drew his sword and went after the men on the left. He hoped that the surprise of Penhallow's attack might make up for his own lack of sword skills.

That left Lowrey to face the rear. Robbed of his magic by the Great Fire, Lowrey glowered at the men and lifted his long staff. He bellowed a cry as he ran at the man in the center of the line, swinging his staff so wildly that the other two were forced to jump aside or be bludgeoned. "Take my cloak will you, blackguards?" he challenged.

Connor found himself facing two well-armed opponents. He struck first at the man on the left, managing to bloody his shoulder before the second man attacked and scored a gash on Connor's forearm. Connor parried, acutely aware that his time as Lord Garnoc's assistant had never included any serious training at arms. His opponents, eyeing an easy kill, closed in on him, one from the left and one from the right.

The man on his right feinted, but Connor caught the flicker of movement on his left in time to parry the second man's strike, a blow that reverberated down Connor's arm from wrist to shoulder. Knowing that the man on his right would strike in earnest, Connor pivoted more by instinct than by sight, rounding on his attacker, his sword leveled at the man's chest. The brigand's momentum drove him into Connor's sword, even as his own sword slashed deep into Connor's shoulder.

Penhallow easily evaded the swords of his quarry. He lifted the man on the far right in one hand and hurled him down the alleyway as if he were a child's ball. Striking before the second man could run, Penhallow's arm lashed out and his hand caught the man by the throat, crushing his windpipe and snapping his neck before the startled thief could raise his sword.

As the second crumpled body fell to the bloodstained cobblestones, the remaining thieves fled for their lives. Penhallow went to Connor's aid as Connor freed his sword from the dead brigand. Connor turned to see Lowrey standing over the fallen form of one of the thieves who had been downed and bloodied by Lowrey's frenzied attack. What the mage lacked in skill he made up for in bluster, and this time luck was on his side.

"And don't come back!" Lowrey shouted after the fleeing bandits, shaking his staff in the air after them.

"You're wounded," Penhallow said as Connor swayed on his feet, as much from the nervous energy of the fight as from the blood that soaked his shirt at the shoulder and forearm.

"I'll be all right," Connor assured him, but he stumbled and would have fallen if Penhallow had not gotten under his good shoulder and slipped an arm around his waist.

"You'll need attention, but we've got to get away from here," Penhallow said, his undead strength effortlessly supporting Connor's weight. Without turning, he addressed Lowrey. "Treven! For the gods' sake, stop looting the dead and get moving!"

"We've got more need of his copper and silver than he does," Lowrey muttered, but he got to his feet and followed, staff raised should further trouble come their way.

"Did you see that, Lanyon? I took the blackguard down with my stave in two strokes. Never had a chance to lay a hand on me," Lowrey said.

"Good for you," Connor muttered, ashamed that he needed Penhallow's support yet feeling the world around him begin to spin.

They walked for a few blocks, then turned again, and the road in front of them broadened as the boulevard neared the castle. Once, the homes along this wide avenue had been those of prosperous merchants and sea captains. Farther up the hill, when the road broadened yet again, were the city homes of the nobility. Unlike the crowded tenements of the twisting, narrow streets at the heart of the city, these homes had been sprawling and grand, walled to keep out inquisitive looks from passersby, secured with ornate wrought-iron gates, and defended by household guards.

Though the tenements that remained standing were still occupied, despite their squalor, it appeared that the nobles and merchants had fled their homes when the Fire rained down. Gates hung askew, leaving what remained within open to looters and squatters.

"This will do," Penhallow said, veering into one of the gateways.

"What if there's someone hiding in there?" Connor asked, though in truth, he was so light-headed he feared he would soon collapse.

Penhallow strode toward the ruined home as if he were its owner. "If someone were here, I'd know it, mortal or *talishte*. We're safe—for now."

The courtyard had once been beautiful, Connor guessed. A broken fountain sat in the center of the garden, filled now with leaves and debris. Where the magic tendrils of power had struck during the Great Fire, part of the outer wall was blackened and reduced to rubble. The house itself appeared to be intact, though a tree from the walled yard had fallen over, crashing into the roof. The shutters on the downstairs windows had been pulled aside, and all of the windows were shattered.

They entered through the main door, which sagged on its hinges. The darkness smelled of mold, decay, and urine.

"Close the shutters, Treven," Penhallow commanded. "Then light a lantern."

Penhallow's voice left no room for argument. While it was too dark to see Lowrey's expression, Connor could only imagine the scholar opening his mouth to retort and then shutting it again to do as he was bid. Penhallow found a tattered mattress and eased Connor onto it. Outside, Connor heard the clatter of the shutters and Lowrey swearing as he struggled to find the latches, followed by the click of flint on steel as he tried to light his lantern in the moonlit courtyard. Finally, Lowrey strode back into the house, carrying a small, shuttered lantern. He opened the shutters, and light flooded the room.

Intricate mosaics covered one wall, while frescoes decorated two more. A tapestry hung against the fourth wall, though it had seen better days, dirtied and soot-streaked from the Fire, stained by whatever goings-on had occurred after the home's owners had fled. Connor tried to focus on the details to keep himself from passing out. A broken ale cask, filthy blankets, and an old, torn shoe gave him to guess that squatters had laid claim to the house in the aftermath of the city's fall.

"Let's see those gashes," Penhallow said in a voice that would have brooked no denial, had Connor felt well enough to protest. He pulled open the remnants of Connor's torn shirt to reveal the deep, bloody cuts.

"Not as bad as the last time," Penhallow muttered.

"I almost died the last time," Connor argued, his voice weak.

"As I said." Penhallow spat into his palm and laid his hand over the worst of Connor's injuries. Connor cried out and writhed as the energy began to heal his wound.

"I still don't know why your magic works and mine doesn't," Lowrey murmured, coming to stand behind Penhallow but facing away, watching the door with his staff at the ready.

"Your magic—the *hasithara*—is external, and its binding to be usable by humans was artificial. The *kruvgaldur* is part of what I am," Penhallow replied without taking his eyes off Connor. "The power that sustains the immortals is as much a force of nature as the storms and floods—or the wild, untamed magic that you mages call *visithara*."

"Yet when the magic, the *hasithara*, moved beyond our grasp, even your *talishte* mages lost their power," Lowrey responded.

"But they did not lose the *kruvgaldur*," Penhallow replied, his attention still on Connor. "It is our essence."

Connor dropped back against the mattress, which smelled of rats and mold. He was sweating, and his breathing was shallow and rapid from the pain and blood loss. When Penhallow removed his hand, the shoulder wound had healed. Once more, Penhallow spat into his palm and pressed it against the deep cut in Connor's forearm. His touch felt like fire, and Connor bit back a curse. After a moment the pain eased and the gash closed, healing without a scar. Connor sank into the old mattress, too spent to care about its smell.

Penhallow rose and wiped his bloody hand on a rag. "It's near dawn," he said. "I must feed, then find shelter." He looked down at Connor. "We need to reach the castle before the night is spent."

Connor nodded, pushing himself up. His wounds were healed and no longer hurt, but his body still reacted to the trauma, arguing for whiskey and a good night's sleep. Connor shook his head when Penhallow offered him a hand, managing to get to his feet on his own. "I can walk," he said. "Let's just hope I don't have to fight."

Penhallow chuckled. "If I'm to be your new master, perhaps some salle training is in order. As soon as people stop trying to kill us, I'll make arrangements."

"Thanks," Connor muttered. He was hungry and so tired that he would have gladly slept the night on the cast-off mattress, but he knew Penhallow was right: They had to reach the castle before dawn.

Penhallow scouted the courtyard and signaled for the others to follow him. Connor gritted his teeth and resolved to keep up, knowing that Penhallow was holding himself back to mortal speed for his and Lowrey's sake.

The road sloped steeply above the houses of the nobility, leading up the hills to where the ruins of the castle sat at the crest. Just months before, Quillarth Castle had been an imposing structure, a walled fortification hundreds of years old, reigning supreme from its lofty perch. Connor looked up at the dark summit and shuddered. The castle had always been lit like a beacon, its bailey awash in torchlight, its windows glowing brightly. The tall, round bell tower was the castle's highest point, with bells that could be heard all the way to the seaside and beyond. It was said that the bells of Quillarth Castle had guided many a sailor safely to port.

"You're quiet, lad," Lowrey said, falling in step with him.

Connor shrugged, uncomfortable with the emotions his memories roiled. "Whenever I'd go into town to run an errand for Lord Garnoc or to bring back buckets of bitterbeer, I would always keep my eye on the bell tower. You could see it from anywhere in Castle Reach." He paused.

"Quillarth Castle was seven hundred years old. It looked so mighty on the hilltop, like it sprang from the bones of the world. It had been there long before I was born, and I figured it would stand long after my death. To have outlived it..." Connor's voice trailed off, his gaze on Penhallow's back. Though the *talishte* had not spoken and appeared to be ignoring the conversation between Connor and Lowrey, Connor was well aware that vampire hearing was sharp enough to pick up every word. The grief he had felt all day at the sight of the ruined city, and now, the damaged castle, crushed down on Connor, giving him a new respect for Penhallow.

As they neared the castle ruins, the horizon had begun to lighten from black to deep indigo. Penhallow quickened his step, forcing Connor and Lowrey to move faster as well. When they reached what remained of the castle walls, Connor was surprised to find guards stationed at the gate and at the places where the walls had collapsed.

"Looks like someone's home after all," Lowrey murmured.

The guard at the gate stepped out to stop their progress. "State your business." Though it was difficult to see much by the torchlight, it appeared the main gate had been repaired, and as Connor glanced to his left and right, it looked as though an effort was being made to restore the castle wall.

"Lord Penhallow, to see Seneschal Lynge," Penhallow announced himself, as casually as if the Great Fire had never happened and they were arriving at the king's invitation for a ball or a fine dinner.

The guard eyed Connor and Lowrey, then returned his gaze to Penhallow. Connor fully expected them to be turned away or detained while the guard checked with his superiors, but to Connor's surprise, the guard made an awkward bow.

"Lord Penhallow. You are expected." His gaze flickered back to Connor and Lowrey. "I was not told there would be others in your party."

"My assistant, Bevin Connor, former assistant to the late Lord Garnoc," Penhallow said smoothly. "And mage-scholar Treven Lowrey, from the university."

"If you vouch for them, m'lord, they may pass, seeing as you're expected by the seneschal."

Penhallow nodded. "Thank you, soldier."

At that, the guard stepped aside, and Connor followed Penhallow into the castle's walled bailey. The once-formidable walls had crumbled in many places, and the stones were blackened from the heat of the Great Fire. The bell tower had withstood the Cataclysm, but subsequent storms had badly damaged it, and the top levels had crumbled, making it significantly shorter than it had been. The dependencies, mostly wooden, had been consumed in the Fire, as their blackened outlines against the stone confirmed.

Connor turned to survey the castle itself. Quillarth Castle had been one of the thirteen original fortified keeps in the kingdom of Donderath, built when most of the Continent was wild and lawless. It was a fortification first, and the residence of a monarch second. Though King Merrill and his predecessors had built onto the original castle over the centuries, Quillarth had never lost the sense of being a defensible outpost. Its façade was unadorned granite, its windows narrow enough to shield from siege, as strong and stoically silent as the soldiers who had guarded it through the centuries.

Of the castle itself, only half of the massive original structure survived. Connor's gaze wandered to where his window had been, in the suite of rooms he had shared with Lord Garnoc. That portion of the castle still stood, but like the rest, it had been badly damaged. The Great Fire on the night of Donderath's fall had taken its toll, but so had the magic storms and the anarchy that followed, dangerous aftereffects that survivors called the Cataclysm. It took all of Connor's will not to sink to his knees and weep for what had been lost and might never be again.

Penhallow laid a hand on his shoulder. "We need to be about our business, Bevin," he said quietly. "If I believed Blaine's efforts to be a lost cause, we would not be here." He glanced at the sky, growing lighter with the impending dawn. "But we must hurry."

Connor nodded. He took a deep breath and squared his shoulders, then followed Penhallow and Lowrey up the cracked, broken front steps and into the grand entranceway.

"Bevin Connor. I did not think to see you again this side of the Sea of Souls," a voice proclaimed. Lars Lynge, seneschal to the late King Merrill, stepped out of the shadows and embraced Connor. "Welcome back."

Lynge had been Merrill's seneschal for nearly twenty years, the cool, efficient force that held the complex court together. Tall, slender, and in the old days, always immaculately groomed, Lynge had struck Connor as an intelligent man for whom any show of humor or emotion was uncomfortable. At a complete loss for words, Connor awkwardly returned Lynge's embrace before stepping backward to free himself. Lynge motioned to a passing servant and spoke in low tones to the man, who scurried off.

Var Geddy stood just a pace behind Lynge. As Lynge's assistant, Geddy was usually seen but not heard. He was close to Connor's age, sharp-featured, with dark, lank hair that hung in his face. Geddy had always reminded Connor of a blackbird, nervous and fidgety. Connor and Geddy had been together the night of the Great Fire, searching for the map and pendant in the royal library, and from the bell tower, the two men had watched in horror as their kingdom burned.

Connor met Geddy's gaze, and in the man's green eyes, he saw acknowledgement of a shared grief. "Thought you'd hopped a ship to somewhere—anywhere but here."

"Long story," Connor said, his attention straying to where Penhallow and Lynge were deep in hushed conversation. Lowrey, seemingly forgotten for the moment, was wandering around the stately entranceway examining the walls, and Connor was surprised to see that tears were streaking down Lowrey's face.

Bereft, Lowrey turned to the group. "What of the paintings and the tapestries that hung here?" he cried. "Surely they didn't all perish in the Great Fire?"

Conversation ceased as the others looked at Lowrey. Connor

eyed the walls and realized that he had never seen them bare. Massive oil paintings of Charrot, the High God, and his consorts, Esthrane and Torven, had graced the bare granite walls. Tapestries told the stories of the gods and their lovers, their battles and dalliances, their celebrations and mourning. Gone, too, Connor noted, were the gilt-framed mirrors that had filled the entranceway with reflected light. Swags and buntings of elaborate draperies had once softened the austere lines of the grand staircase. Unadorned, Quillarth Castle looked even more like a fortress.

"They're down below, m'lord," Geddy replied. "What with the fires and such, and the magic storms, we didn't want to lose anything else. They're safe, m'lord. Or as safe as anything remains these days."

Lowrey breathed a sigh of relief, letting his head fall back as though he were saying a prayer of thanks to the gods. Treven Lowrey could be overly dramatic, but in this, Connor suspected, the man's lifelong passion as a scholar gave him to speak from the heart. "Thank Esthrane," he murmured. "Is there hope, then, that perhaps some of the library was spared?"

"We saved what we could," Lynge answered. "Not everything, I'm sorry to say. But most of the books, and all of the Special Collections." He gave a knowing look at Penhallow. "When we received your message, we cleared a room in the tunnels beneath the castle. It's very secure. You can take your rest there and study the collections without interruption."

Lynge frowned. "Given your message, we had expected you to arrive considerably sooner. Did you meet with problems on the journey?"

Penhallow chuckled. "Nothing major," he assured Lynge. "The roads are not as easy to navigate as they once were."

"Let's get the three of you belowground, and we can talk

when you've rested," Lynge replied. "There's a flagon of fresh deer blood waiting for you, Lord Penhallow, and refreshment for Connor and Scholar Lowrey as well."

They followed Lynge down a winding stone staircase into the depths of the castle's many cellars. Despite his years of service in the castle, Connor had never seen this area before. The stairway had been carved out of the rock itself, and this part of the castle was obviously the oldest. Torches burned at intervals in iron sconces affixed to the rock walls, but they did not completely dispel the shadows. Lynge led them down a maze of passageways, until the corridor narrowed to be barely wider than a man's shoulders, and the ceiling was low enough that Lynge and Penhallow had to duck their heads.

Finally, Lynge stopped at an oak door bound with iron. He swung the door open and lifted a torch to light the interior. It was a good-sized room, wide enough for a wooden table and chairs with space enough for two straw mattresses. On the table sat a flagon and a goblet for Penhallow, and nearby, two pitchers of ale, tankards, and a wooden tray heaped with cheese, honey, bread, dried meat, and fruits.

"Hardly a feast," Lynge said, "but there should be enough to fill your stomachs." He glanced toward Penhallow. "There's a separate room for you, Lord Penhallow, where you won't be disturbed. As for the rest of what you requested, let me show you, and then I'll leave you to your meal."

A servant stayed behind to light the torches in the room with the table and mattresses, while Lynge led them back into the narrow corridor. "How did you send him a message to expect us?" Connor whispered to Penhallow. "We were under siege in Voss's fortress."

Penhallow nodded. "I'd sent the message before that, expecting our stay with Voss to be shorter. So I can imagine that our friends here were worried when we were delayed a good bit beyond the time I'd indicated they should look for us to arrive."

Lynge gestured toward a door on his left. "That's your room, Lord Penhallow. It locks from within, so you'll be quite secure." He fell silent as they walked on until they came to a room at the end of the corridor. Its door was of the same heavy oak as the others they had passed, but this door was reinforced with iron, and a complex locking mechanism secured it.

They hung back as Lynge worked the complicated lock. The bolts and levers that slid clear echoed in the confines of the stone walls. Finally, Lynge opened the door and stepped inside. The room smelled musty, with the scent of old leather and the dusty aroma of ancient parchment.

Lynge's torch illuminated the room, which was much larger than Connor had imagined. The seneschal walked around the perimeter, lighting several of the torches.

"It's a library," Lowrey breathed, with a passion usually reserved for the sight of a beautiful woman.

"Not just a library," Penhallow said, and a faint smile touched his lips.

"No, indeed," Lynge agreed. "This is all that remains of the archives of the banished Knights of Esthrane."

CHAPTER SIX

"IT ALWAYS COMES BACK TO BLOOD." PENTREATH REESE moved slowly around the perimeter of the dimly lit parlor. His hand trailed across the surface of a table, then stopped to linger on the ancient obsidian knife that lay in front of them. "Always blood," he murmured, as if he had forgotten that Pollard was in the room.

Pollard knew better than to interrupt. Since the Great Fire, Reese's moods, always mercurial, had grown more extreme. Reese continued to pace the edge of the room, lifting items, examining them as if he had never seen them before, or caressing them with his fingertips before moving on.

"Wild magic is a beautiful thing," Reese said, his deep voice smooth as brandy. "Lovely and terrible." He seemed to remember Pollard's presence. "Did you possess magic before the Great Fire?"

"You know I didn't."

Reese nodded. "Yes, I did know that. I have no magic either, save for the dark gift that flows in my blood." He looked up and met Pollard's gaze. "You see, once again, it comes back to blood."

"What of the wild magic, m'lord?" Pollard asked. He had learned from experience that it was better to humor Reese when he was in a pensive mood. Reese's melancholy could shift into deadly rage with frightening speed. Once, he had seen Reese casually eviscerate a servant who accidently disturbed him when he was feeling introspective. Pollard had no desire to push the limits of Reese's self-control, nor did he harbor any assumptions about being irreplaceable to his lord. Patience was not Pollard's strong point, but where it stood to yield tactical advantage, he could make an exception.

"Have you ever watched a forest burn, Vedran? Or seen the sea rise up into a wave that reaches the sky and then surges forward onto the shore?"

"No, m'lord."

Reese's voice held a note of wonder that sent a chill down Pollard's spine. "I have. The wild magic is just untamed. Without agenda or conscience or remorse. Beautiful, unharnessed power."

He paused his pacing in front of a set of shelves that held a variety of unusual objects. Small, intricately carved stone boxes. Focusing balls of crystal and gemstone. Athames made of polished, exotic wood or smooth, rare, semiprecious stone. Silver amulets and rings, rough stone bowls, and delicately wrought goblets: All of these treasures Pollard recognized as ones his men had systematically looted from the hidden stores of mages and scholars. "What a crime to bind such power to the will of insignificant men," Reese mused, "men whose ability to harness magic is nothing but an inherited fluke, no more their doing than the color of their eyes."

He turned to Pollard, moving so quickly that Pollard stepped back, wary of an attack. But Reese did not advance. "*Talishte* are not created by accident of birth," he said quietly.

"We are chosen by our makers, tested to determine whether we are suitable to receive the dark blood-gift of the *kruvgaldur*. That is something for which mages can never forgive my kind," he said, staring past Pollard into the dimly lit room as if seeing a memory.

Pollard gently cleared his throat. "My lord," he said with great care. "My men have returned from searching the ruins of the university at Aldomar. I came to make a report."

Reese nodded, but it was clear his attention was not yet fully engaged. "In good time, Vedran. In good time." He gave an absent wave in the direction of one of the upholstered chairs near the fireplace. "Have a seat."

Pollard sat down, and his gaze was drawn upward above the blaze that burned in the fireplace to a large oil painting that hung above the mantel. Most of the manor houses and grand homes boasted fine portraits in such a spot, of the current owner of the manse or one of his or her illustrious ancestors. Still others favored scenes from the hunt, or perhaps an artist's fantasy taken from the stories of the gods.

A dark vision loomed on the wall above the mantel. The landscape was the stuff of nightmares, with leafless trees stripped of their bark and a sky filled with storm clouds. The foreground showed twisted images of animals and men that seemed to have been painted by someone who had never seen such things. Deformed figures limped and scrabbled their way across the canvas with hunched backs and foreshortened or elongated limbs.

Reese chuckled as he noted the direction of Pollard's gaze. "Does it frighten you, Vedran?"

"It is disquieting, m'lord." Pollard kept his face as neutral as possible.

Reese leaned against the massive study table in the center of the room and looked up at the painting. "A very long time ago, when I was a mortal child, a man came through our village with a traveling carnival. He promised us that, in exchange for a few coppers, he would show us monsters that would haunt our dreams forever. Monsters from the depths of Raka itself."

Reese's voice had taken on a quiet tone, and his gaze was distant. "I stole the coppers I needed to see such wonders," he said. "I was not disappointed. I saw a parade of things that had the flesh and faces of men, but whose bodies had been twisted into unnatural shapes, with malformed limbs and faces too hideous to look upon and too fascinating to look away from." He shook his head in wonderment. "There were men, women, and children—or at least, things that were at once human and totally alien. Animals, too, that looked as if they had been sewn together from the pieces of several different species, or like a rag doll twisted by a vengeful child and allowed to remain so. And some creatures the like of which do not often walk upon this world."

He returned his attention to Pollard in time to see him shudder. "I learned later that these oddities, these freaks, had not been born thus. It was not the hand of the gods that made them magnificently horrible. Most were made by the carnival owner, who spirited them away as babies, using all manner of iron bonds and intricate straps to bend and shape their bodies to his will. Others were made by magic, brought from some other realm by the *visithara* magic and left here to prove that monsters are real.

"I learned then that what is bound becomes warped," Reese said, and his voice grew stronger, more passionate. "And I realized that true power means the absence of restraints."

In the blink of an eye, Reese straightened, sloughing off his reflective mood and growing businesslike. "Tell me what you found at Aldomar."

Pollard had grown accustomed to such whiplash-quick changes in topic. "The university was badly damaged in the Great Fire. Of course, none of the mages who survived retain any ability to wield magic. We interrogated them at length, and my men were their most persuasive," he said with a dangerous smile. "Yet we learned nothing new about either Treven Lowrey or Vigus Quintrel. Both mages seem to have vanished into thin air."

Reese brought down his fist so hard on the end of the reading table that it smashed through the polished mahogany surface. "Unacceptable! I do not entrust these errands to you, Vedran, for you to come back to me empty-handed."

Pollard remained very still, a survival skill he had perfected long ago. He refused to give Reese the satisfaction of seeing him react, though he was well aware that the *talishte* could hear the rapid beating of his heart and the shallow rhythm of his breath. "I did not say that we returned with nothing, m'lord."

"Tell me."

"Our sources report that Lowrey was taken by Traher Voss—"

"Voss again?" Reese interrupted and muttered a curse.

"We're certain it was Voss's men who bested our own kidnappers," Pollard continued, undeterred. "And we have reason to think that Voss sent them on orders from Lanyon Penhallow."

"Son of a bitch," Reese said.

"My men have caught sight of Penhallow once since he and his servant escaped from the siege at Voss's fortress." Pollard resisted the urge to wet his lips, refusing to show his nervousness. "There was a third man with them who matches Lowrey's description. We believe they are heading toward Castle Reach, and very possibly, Quillarth Castle. I've activated the spies in the city and set men on every highway and footpath."

"Rescind the order," Reese directed.

Pollard frowned. "My lord?"

Reese pushed away from the damaged table and began to pace, a dark, powerful shadow in the dim room. "If Penhallow has Lowrey with him, then odds are he's on to something that has to do with McFadden. Don't move on him until we know what it is. He may lead us right to McFadden himself, or to whatever McFadden and Lowrey believe is required to restore the magic."

Pollard resisted the urge to scream. "M'lord, I don't possess your blood bond with my men. As I have previously cautioned, once the spies receive a mission, I have no reliable way to update their orders."

Reese made a dismissive gesture. "How you do your job is none of my concern. Just do it."

Pollard's gaze took in the hundreds of old volumes on the library's shelves. Most of them, he knew, fed Reese's long obsession with the histories of Donderath's oldest families, the genealogies of the thirteen Lords of the Blood. His own family was among those of the thirteen lords chosen by King Hougen four hundred years ago, one of the Lords of the Blood that raised the magic at Mirdalur. Yet Pollard's blood was not of interest to Reese. It had been an open secret among Donderath's nobility that Vedran Pollard was illegitimate, the product of an impotent father and a faithless mother. He inherited the title and the lands as the sole surviving heir, but that inheritance did not include magic.

"What of the items I desire, Vedran? The ones held by the Lords of the Blood?"

Pollard motioned to the box he had laid on the table when he arrived. "What we've found so far is in the box," he reported. "Some odd old drawings and a few trinkets, but nothing that matches the sketch you gave me."

Months before, Reese had happened upon a sketch of a strange pendant in one of the books Pollard had looted from the scholars' libraries. A very old drawing showed a wide, dark disk with cryptic markings and a strange arrangement of slits carved into its surface. On the same page, the drawing showed thirteen men costumed as of old, each wearing a similar pendant, standing in what was clearly meant to depict a ritual chamber.

Since then, Reese had become obsessed with finding anything related to the old Lords of the Blood, anything that might deny McFadden his ability to restore the magic.

Reese tore open the box and lifted each item from inside as if it were a hallowed relic. Pollard recognized them as they were removed. A yellowed scrap of a star map, showing constellations in the sky. A faded drawing of a strange pattern that might have been a magical symbol or ancient, forgotten heraldry. A few torn, water-stained, and partially burned pages ripped from a journal that might once have belonged to Archus Quintrel, ancestor of the elusive Vigus.

"You've done well, Vedran, very well," Reese said with a tone of satisfaction usually reserved for praise of a fine racehorse or a prize stag.

"Thank you, m'lord. My men continue to comb through the ruins of the old manors," Pollard replied, silently exhaling in relief.

"Treven Lowrey uncovered information about how these elements raised the magic at Mirdalur, and Quintrel thought he knew something about even older attempts. I want what they know, Vedran," Reese said, the insatiable hunger of an obsessed collector clear in his voice. "I want to find them and destroy them before McFadden can gain their knowledge."

"I rather liked the idea of just eliminating McFadden,"

Pollard said drolly. "By the way, we've identified the soldiers who intervened near Mirdalur," he added. He shook his head in amazement. "They're actually King Merrill's soldiers, or what's left of them, returned at last from the war. Their captain is a man named Niklas Theilsson."

Pollard gave a snort of derision. "I knew of his father, Lars Theilsson. He had a large farm near the McFadden holdings. Called it Arengarte, as if it were a manor. Managed to put up with Ian McFadden enough to trade with him, although rumor had it that it was because his son was a friend of Blaine McFadden."

"So McFadden's aligned with the army," Reese murmured. "How interesting."

"I'd hardly call such a ragged band of vagabonds an 'army.'"

"They'll complicate your plans to lay siege now, won't they?"

Pollard shrugged. "Sieges take too long and tie up too many men. There will be better ways to get our hands on Glenreith."

"What of the items our man said he saw on the ship from Edgeland?" Reese inquired, still examining the artifacts Pollard had brought for him.

Pollard grimaced. "It would help if he'd gotten a good look at whatever it was they had," he observed dryly. "He thinks he saw some kind of map case in the courtesan's possession, and a similar case and perhaps a disk being closely guarded by Lord Garnoc's servant, Bevin Connor."

"Penhallow's spy," Reese replied absently.

"The problem is, we don't really know what they had. They might have nothing to do with magic, or with McFadden."

"Oh, they're important, I'm sure of it," Reese said, bending to examine the scrap of parchment even more closely. Pollard wondered what the *talishte*, with his heightened senses, could make out that had evaded Pollard's mortal vision. "McFadden came back for a reason. Your spy said he had a comfortable life in exile, one he seemed happy to keep. He cared little enough for his lands and title that he was willing to sacrifice them to rid the kingdom of his miserable father. He didn't return because he was homesick."

Reese put down the map fragment and stared at Pollard intently with a gaze that made Pollard acutely aware of the *talishte*'s power. "I'm counting on you to stop him."

"If you hate him so much, why not kill him yourself?" Pollard asked.

Reese paused as if debating whether to consider the question curious or insolent. "His alignment with Penhallow complicates the matter. Much as I dislike Penhallow, I have no desire to attract the attention—and meddling—of other *talishte*. Your actions are much less likely to be noticed. I don't want the Elders involved—at least, not yet."

Reese fixed Pollard with a glance that chilled him to the bone. "Bring me Blaine McFadden, and when I'm through with him, you may be the one to kill him."

Pollard found Nilo already waiting in his tent when he returned. A supper of stew, hard biscuits, and baked apples with a tankard of ale sat ready for Pollard, and he picked at his food, distracted by his thoughts.

"What did you find out?" Pollard asked when he pushed his plate aside.

"One of our men who returned on the ship from Velant confirmed that the barkeeper in Edgeland had once been an assistant to Lord Arrington's mage," Nilo replied. "We also know that another man, Silas Lum, was a scholar who was banished to Velant some years ago. Both men, while not mages themselves, would be quite knowledgeable about magic and possibly about the rituals used at Mirdalur."

Pollard nodded. "Good. What else?"

"There's a rumor that a *talishte*-mage by the name of Arin Grimur was sent into hiding in Edgeland by Lanyon Penhallow."

"The king drove the *talishte* from court," Pollard mused, drawing out old memories. "It was a dangerous time for the *talishte*, and Grimur wasn't the only one to disappear. But he is the only mage-*talishte* to take up residence on Edgeland, and it's more than a little suspicious that his maker was Penhallow."

"My spy confirmed that McFadden and Grimur were acquainted. Grimur kept a very low profile, but he was seen with McFadden in Skalgerston Bay after the magic failed, and it was likely Grimur who killed your assassin," Nilo said.

"So it's quite possible that McFadden knew about the Lords of the Blood before he left Edgeland," Pollard mused. "How interesting." He set his jaw firmly. "Reese grows increasingly unstable."

"Agreed."

"The longer he remains fixed on Blaine McFadden, the more distracted he is from the more important goal: gathering an army that can dominate this broken land." He paused. "We need to consolidate Reese's hold on the kingdom."

"And move you one step closer to the crown?" Nilo mused. "What do you propose?"

"We need to step up the program to capture McFadden," Pollard said, his voice cold. "Put one of our men in every place legend links with magic. McFadden's a step ahead of us, and it's time to bring him to heel." He paused. "And I still intend to have Glenreith for my own, no matter what it takes." Pollard smiled. "A final humiliation for the McFadden family."

"Blaine McFadden didn't succeed in raising the magic at Mirdalur," Nilo said. "Why do you think he's a threat?"

Pollard settled back in his chair. "My mother told me a tale on her deathbed. She said that when my father was dying, mages came to the manor. I was off on campaign with the army. The mages demanded to see my father, and to her surprise, he permitted them a private audience. Something about their visit was so urgent that my father rose from his deathbed to take them to the family vault. He would not permit any servants to accompany him, nor would he allow my mother to assist him. They were gone briefly, and the mages helped my father back to his room. They left with a small velvet bag, and my father would permit no one to question them. He died soon afterward."

Nilo met his gaze. "The mages took something away, but what?"

Pollard leaned forward intently. "My father was a Lord of the Blood. By that time, he had no heirs but me, and he knew my mother had been unfaithful. Despite that, he left me the lands and title. What if he knew there was another inheritance, an inheritance of blood, that could never be mine?"

"Meaning?"

"I think the mages carried off magical items they knew could only be used by a true Lord of the Blood. Since my father's line, by blood, ended with him, there would be no more Pollard males who inherited whatever magic was linked to that old heritage.

"I am betting that whatever they took from my father was something each Lord of the Blood had. McFadden knows—or guesses—what that is. But he didn't have enough of what it takes to raise the magic when he went to Mirdalur." He tented his fingers. "So he's going after what he needs. And when he does, I want your men to be there.

"When the time comes, we'll capture McFadden and break him," Pollard continued, "and he'll tell us what he knows. Let him collect whatever he thinks he needs to work the magic, and we'll present a rich package to Lord Reese with no loose ends—and there'll be no remaining Lords of the Blood to challenge my claim to the crown."

"What if Penhallow is protecting him?"

Pollard shrugged. "Reese doesn't fear Penhallow, and neither do I."

"Velant didn't break him. Prokief couldn't kill him. What makes you think we can?" Nilo asked.

"McFadden's weakness is what sent him to Velant," Pollard replied. "He's willing to sacrifice himself for those he loves. Strike at them, hurt them, endanger them, and his honor will demand that he risk himself to protect them. He'll give us the opportunity."

Nilo poured ale for both of them and lifted a tankard.

"Here's to the future," he said.

Pollard grinned. "Here's to the future—as we decide to make it."

CHAPTER
SEVEN

———

Y OU'VE BEEN BACK TO GLENREITH THEN, SINCE YOU
returned to Donderath?" Niklas asked as he rode next to
Blaine. Behind them followed Dawe and Kestel, who were deep
in their own conversation, and then Piran and Verran, with the
rest of Niklas's soldiers riding in ranks of four. Geir had gone to
ground for the day, promising to meet them when they stopped
for the night. Carr, Blaine noted, had disappeared among the
soldiers, though Blaine had invited him to ride with the group
at the front.

"We made for Glenreith as soon as we could," Blaine replied,
pulling his attention back to the conversation. "I wanted to see
if there was anything left."

Niklas nodded. Temperatures had fallen during the night, a
reminder that winter was at hand. A chill blast of wind ruffled
his horse's mane and swept his hood back, exposing his face.
Blaine got a better look at his friend in daylight, surprised to
see the difference six years had wrought.

Before Blaine's exile and before the war, it had been Niklas's
boyish charm that had won him the attentions of many a pretty
girl. Years of war and hardship had given Niklas a weathered,

rougher look. But it was his eyes that had changed the most. Before, there had been a careless good cheer that made Niklas a favorite at the local pub or village festival. Now, the look in Niklas's blue eyes was harder, shuttered, weary. And after six years of his own hardship in the mines of Velant and the wastes of Edgeland, Blaine wondered if his friend saw the same changes in him.

"I've been gone for a long time," Niklas said. "Three years on the war front, and most of another year trying to get home." His smile was sad. "Can't believe you made it back first." There was a pause.

"How did Glenreith fare?" he asked, and Blaine realized he had fallen silent for several minutes. "And what of Arengarte?" Niklas's father, Lars Theilsson, had been a wealthy farmer and landowner who managed the rise to prominence without a title or family connections. Arengarte, the Theilsson family home, was less grand than Blaine's manor at Glenreith, but still large and comfortable.

Blaine sighed. "The original manor house at Glenreith was destroyed in the Great Fire. The new house suffered some damage, but it was spared." He drew a deep breath. "We have reason to think the strike that leveled the old manor was deliberate, a plan by the Meroven mages to wipe out the Donderath nobility. What they didn't realize, at least what we don't think they knew, was that the manors and the eldest heirs to the titles of the thirteen oldest noble families were also the anchors for usable magic."

"So when they destroyed the manors, and then if the eldest heirs died—"

Blaine nodded. "The magic also died."

"Except for you," Niklas said quietly. "The last Lord of the Blood."

"So the theory goes," Blaine replied.

"Glenreith was livable?" Niklas asked.

"Habitable, yes. But far from its better days." Blaine looked away. "I played a part in that, I'm afraid. My exile, and the scandal over killing Father, fell hard on the others. Aunt Judith downplayed it, but Carr was brutally straightforward," he said. "I may have saved Mari and Carr from Father's beatings, but at the cost of the family fortunes."

Niklas was watching him closely, perhaps making the same assessment of how the years had treated Blaine that Blaine had just made of him. "I remember some of that," Niklas said quietly. "Father never liked Ian McFadden, thought you did the world a favor by killing him. But there were some who had a different opinion." His voice was angry. "Those people made it hard for Judith."

"I never meant to make it more difficult," Blaine said, looking into the distance. "But someone had to stop Father. The beatings...and worse...it had to end."

"Would you do it again, knowing the cost?"

Blaine was silent for a long while. "To stop him from hurting Mari and Carr, yes. I thought that I'd be executed, that it would be over quickly. I didn't count on Merrill being merciful and sending me into exile. And for several years, I didn't see the mercy in his sentence. Velant deserves its reputation."

"What of Carensa?" Niklas asked, his voice quiet. "She mourned you long after you were sent away. For years, she defied every attempt her father made to marry her off. But I've been gone for a long time, with no real news from home. Did Rhystorp survive?"

Blaine looked down and swallowed. "Rhystorp burned to the ground in the Great Fire," he said slowly. "Aunt Judith told me that Carensa's father finally arranged a marriage for her with an older man who needed the Rhystorp fortune badly enough to overlook the taint of her association with me," he added bitterly. "When the manor burned, they found the bodies of Carensa's husband and son. She's presumed dead, but no one ever found the body."

"I'm sorry, Blaine."

Blaine shrugged, uncomfortable. "My sentence ended our betrothal. I begged her to renounce me, to go on with her life. I fully expected to die in Velant."

"But you didn't."

Blaine shook his head slowly. "Not for lack of wishing, sometimes. But I guess I was too stubborn to give in. I survived three years in the prison stockade, and in the ruby mines, before I earned my Ticket of Leave to become a colonist. I met Verran on the boat to Edgeland, and Piran and Dawe and I were chained together in the mines. Kestel, I met in the prison. When we got our Tickets, we pooled the pittance sum and the land grant each freed prisoner received, and we built a homestead together. We've had each others' backs for a long time now."

"And you and Kestel?" Niklas said, with a glance over his shoulder where Kestel was talking with Dawe.

"Very good friends," Blaine said, the hint of a smile touching his lips. "When we all moved into the homestead together, Kestel made it clear that none of us would be getting any special favors." He chuckled. "So there we were, four men living with one of the most notorious courtesans from the royal palace, completely out of luck."

Niklas laughed. "Although everyone assumed—"

"Uh-huh. Which only made it worse," Blaine replied. He paused. "The year I got out of Velant, I married a girl named Selane. Sweet girl, sent to Velant on false charges. She died of fever."

Niklas regarded him in silence for a moment. "Offhand, I'd say you've paid your price several times over. But you and your mates came all the way back to Donderath on the rumor that you might be able to save the magic. After all Donderath cost you, why would you, of anyone, care?"

Blaine's gaze found the horizon, and he did not answer for a moment. "It wasn't just Donderath," he said finally. "The magic died in Edgeland, too. It's a brutal place, but we'd managed to find a way to make it livable, and in the best moments, it was home. Without magic, I don't know if the colony can survive, especially with the storms growing worse. There are two thousand people up there who have no place left to go, no part back here in Donderath, who paid for their homesteads with blood and tears. If I can save that, well, it's worth the cost."

Niklas studied him carefully, as if weighing all his friend had said. "So everything you told me, about Pollard and Reese, and the vampire who was helping you—"

"Penhallow."

"All this about bringing back the magic, you mean to try again." It was not a question. Niklas looked at him intently.

"If I can," Blaine replied. "Penhallow's long overdue. We got separated from him and Connor, the fellow with the map and pendant, when we were attacked by Reese's men. Geir believes they escaped, but they've been delayed, maybe even detained."

"You went to Mirdalur. It didn't work. What next?"

"I don't know. We've got some old books, and one of the maps. Maybe there'll be a clue."

"You're going on hunches?" Niklas asked, skepticism clear in his voice.

Blaine shook his head. "More than that. There's information in the books and maps—we just have to decode it. Penhallow knows more, I'm sure of it. It's like putting a puzzle together with some pieces missing. We'll gather as much information as we can and plan our strategy from there."

"Not so different from war," Niklas agreed. "You never have all the information you need, so you do the best with what you've got."

"Either way, we need to go back to Glenreith, recoup. And let your men recover."

Niklas grimaced. "Don't remind me. Your *talishte* friend mounted an effective assault. I'm glad he's on our side." It was Niklas's turn to be quiet for a few moments. "You never answered me about Arengarte."

Blaine sighed. "We rode past on our way to Mirdalur. I didn't have the chance to stop and explore. From what I saw, the main house was still standing. It was damaged, but it didn't look like a direct hit by the Great Fire."

"If your theory's right, the Meroven mages wouldn't have bothered with us. We certainly weren't descended from the old, noble families," Niklas replied.

Blaine nodded. "It looks abandoned. When Aunt Judith said you'd gone to war and not returned, I feared the worst."

Niklas swallowed hard. "It hasn't been the best few years for any of us. My father died a year or so after you were exiled. Bad heart. I tried to keep the lands going, but when the war came, and so many of the lads who worked the land were conscripted to the army, I couldn't handle the farm alone. So I agreed to soldier up myself."

"And you took Carr with you," Blaine added, an edge to his voice.

The look on Niklas's face gave Blaine to realize that his friend had some inkling of how Blaine's reunion had gone. "Don't be too hard on Carr. If I have to guess, he's more of a mind that he failed you than the other way around."

"How so?" Blaine asked, frowning.

"He was just a boy when they sent you away. He tried to be the man of the house, take care of your sister and aunt. But he was too young. Then Mari found a young man and got married, and Carr figured they didn't need him anymore. He badgered me into letting him sign on, and I finally said yes. But Mari's husband wasn't a noble, and he was conscripted into my unit. He died on the first day we saw battle, just a few feet away from where Carr was standing."

Niklas shook his head. "Gods help us, but the fighting was vicious. Even the seasoned soldiers said it was bloodier than they had ever seen. Donderath was losing badly, hemorrhaging men. Carr was in the thick of it and somehow he survived. But he blames himself for the death of Mari's husband, and I've always suspected he felt responsible for you killing your father."

"That was on no one's head but mine," Blaine said sharply.

Niklas gave him a knowing look. "Ah, but part of the reason you did it was to keep your father from thrashing Carr and taking liberties with Mari."

"No one was supposed to know about what happened to Mari," Blaine said, meeting Niklas's eyes.

"Carr took a bad sword wound in one of the battles, and it poisoned his blood. He was fevered, dying. The healers almost didn't think they could save him. I sat with him, because he was calling for you and you couldn't be there," Niklas said with a forced smile. "You and me, growing up, we were thick as brothers, so I let him think I was you. That's how I found out what really happened. Carr wasn't talking out of turn. He believed he was talking with you."

Blaine looked away, struggling with his feelings. "Yeah, well. He hates me now. Pretty clear about that."

"Give him time," Niklas said. "He's still young, and he's been through a lot. After all, for us, it's a bit like having you back from the grave."

Blaine sighed. "Let's talk of something else, shall we? What are your plans, when we reach Arengarte?"

Niklas sighed. "I stopped making plans when we lost the war. We've spent the last six months foraging our way across a scorched landscape, fighting off highwaymen, dodging magic storms." He gave Blaine a sideways glance. "It's not just the storms. So many strange things have happened since the magic went bad. Nightmare creatures, men gone mad." He sighed. "It's taken all we had in us just to survive. I never really got farther than leading them home, because to tell you the truth, I didn't think we'd make it."

"Then you won't mind if Kestel made a few plans on your behalf?" Blaine said and smiled at Niklas's astonishment.

"Kestel?"

At the mention of her name, Kestel left Dawe with a nod and urged her horse to catch up, flanking Niklas. "Is it arranged?" she asked, her eyes alight. Her tunic and trews were cut for a man, but they could not completely hide the contours of her figure. Kestel had bound her red hair back in a braid, and she wore neither cosmetics nor jewelry, but her green eyes sparkled like emeralds, and the winter wind brought a glow to her cheeks.

"Why don't you tell him, since you're the one who had the idea?" Blaine urged.

Kestel smiled broadly, and despite the dust from the road that smudged her features, it was impossible to overlook the fact that she was a beautiful woman. Intelligence and cunning glinted in her eyes, the traits that had made her equally skilled as a spy and assassin at court. Blaine knew that any man who overlooked her abilities for her beauty did so at his own peril.

"You need a base. Glenreith needs protection, and come spring, men to work the land. I suggest that you and Mick strike an alliance. Billet what troops you can at Arengarte, and send the ones who need healers to Glenreith." She winced. "It's the least we can do since Geir attacked them on our behalf.

"It's more mouths to feed, but also more hands to harvest the root crops left in the fields and to hunt for game over the winter," Kestel went on enthusiastically, leaning forward in her saddle to make eye contact with Niklas. "And if I'm not mistaken, Captain, a respectable military man such as yourself leads his men in service to a lord. King Merrill is dead, so your duty there is finished. Only two mortal lords remain, to our knowledge: Lord Pollard, and the Lord of Glenreith," she said, with a meaningful glance toward Blaine. "In whose service would you find honor best served?"

Niklas chuckled. "She really is a marvel, Blaine," he said with a grin, then turned his attention back to Kestel. "M'lady makes a fine case, and, truth be told, similar thoughts had occurred to me."

He looked to Blaine. "Well, Blaine, what do you have to say? Are you agreeable?"

"Completely. And I can't imagine Aunt Judith having any qualms about it. If we do make another attempt to bring back the magic, having your men along will make it somewhat less risky than going out on our own. And if we can't bring the magic back," he said and paused, hesitant to put that scenario into words, "then we really are on our own, without a king or king's guardsmen to keep the peace. I hope it doesn't come to that. But either way, support from you and your men would be much appreciated."

"Consider it done," Niklas said. "Although we'll arrange a bit more of a show for the men once we're settled. I've spoken with them, and most left nothing behind, so they have nothing to return to. They can't sell their swords, since even the mercenaries have no work without kingdoms or lords."

"It won't last," Kestel said soberly, and both men looked at her. "Haven't you read the histories? Before there was a king, there were warlords, fighting over land and water. A continual state of war, until the victors divided the spoils among themselves. Even if the magic comes back, that's what's to come. The pattern repeats."

"Then we'd best stand united," Niklas said. "You can count on us."

CHAPTER EIGHT

IT LOOKS LIKE A WASTELAND," NIKLAS SAID AS THEY rode through the countryside. Before the war, this section of Donderath had been known for iron mines that supplied the kingdom with the raw material for weapons, armor, tools, and cookware. Now, the towns were deserted, and many of the miners' small shacks had burned in the Great Fire. In the daytime Niklas knew that it was easy to spot the dark tunnels that led into the Broadhill mines, but now they were as silent as the towns that had once prospered around them.

Niklas scanned the hills, though at night it was impossible to see the mine openings from this distance. On this road, the hills were never out of sight. Niklas wondered whether the mines were actually deserted, or whether, in the months since Donderath's fall, desperate men had made them their homes.

"It's like this, or worse, all the way from the Meroven border," Niklas said, his tone grim. "The fighting spilled over to both sides of the actual border, so it's a muddy mess filled with bloated corpses and all the wreckage an army leaves behind." He grimaced. "We scavenged what we could, but there wasn't much left."

Blaine nodded. "We sailed into Castle Reach," he said quietly. "Most of the city burned. What's left is a ruin. Even the brick and stone buildings took quite a bit of damage."

Niklas shook his head. "Funny, isn't it?" he said drily. "We go to war to prevent Meroven from wreaking this kind of damage on Donderath, only to have it all destroyed without the enemy's ever invading."

Blaine didn't reply for a few moments. "Up in Edgeland, when we heard about what happened, I don't think most people really believed what Connor said about everything being gone." He sighed. "It wasn't until the ship sailed into the harbor and we could see for ourselves that people really understood the truth. It's still hard to believe it's like this across the whole kingdom."

Niklas shrugged. "Since I haven't been all the way across Donderath, I can't say for sure, but from what we've seen on our return from the front line, odds are good that conditions aren't any better anywhere else."

In the distance, Niklas could see a small village. After the scarred landscape and ruined towns they had passed, it was a pleasant relief to see smoke wafting from the chimneys. On the outskirts of town, near a wide stream, was a gristmill, its wheel turning with the water.

"We can hardly march an army into town," Niklas said, "but we're short on flour, and biscuits keep my men on the march. I'm going to see if I can find someone who'll sell to me, maybe see who else has been this way lately."

"I'll come with you," Blaine offered. "I'd like to hear what passes for news in these parts."

After a short discussion with the others, Blaine and Niklas rode toward the mill. As the daylight faded, lantern light shone through the building's lower windows, indicating that the miller was likely still at his task. Outside, on the road into the village, they saw no one.

Niklas cast a glance toward the village. Lights glowed in many of the windows, and in the distance, they could hear faint strains of music and voices carried on the wind from the village alehouse.

"Wonder where everybody is?" Niklas said quietly.

"By the sound of it, lifting a pint or two in the village," Blaine replied. "Not buying their grain, that's certain."

The two men kept a wary eye but saw nothing to give alarm as they rode up to the mill. They looped their reins over the hitching rail outside and approached the door. Niklas took the lead, and Blaine hung back with his hand close enough to his sword to draw the weapon if need be, but mindful of not making the miller fear an attack by brigands.

After three loud knocks, the door opened. A portly man in his middle years appeared in the entranceway. He had a bald pate with a fringe of white, closely cropped hair, and the burly shoulders of a man used to hard work. "Ho there!" he greeted them. "A bit late to be comin' round, don't you think?"

Niklas gave a shallow bow and managed the grin Blaine had seen him use many a time to get out of trouble. "My pardon, sir. We meant no harm. I had hoped to buy a sack or two of flour."

The miller regarded them for a moment, and his gaze lingered on the swords they wore. "You have coin to pay for it?"

Niklas nodded. "Aye."

With a harrumph that seemed to indicate the miller would believe when he saw the coins himself, he moved out of the doorway. "You're in luck. I don't always have flour for sale," he said, ushering them into a small room that was obviously where he handled his accounts. There was a writing desk with a lantern and a ledger, a solid wooden chair, and a worktable to one side. A narrow stairway led up from the corner, and Niklas wondered if the miller had his home on the upper floor. In the background, Niklas could hear the squeal of the gears in the waterwheel and the crunch of the millstones.

The miller had gone to retrieve a sack of flour, and he came back to flop it onto the table. "You're not from here."

"No, sir," Niklas replied. "Had to ride a while to find a mill with flour to sell."

The man went back to retrieve a second sack, and he thudded it onto the table next to the first. "True enough, and with the way the harvest was, you're lucky to find it. It's been slim enough for the folks who brought their own grain to mill," the man said. He gave Niklas a measured look. "That'll be two silvers for the flour."

Niklas withdrew two silver coins from his pouch and put them on the table. "Not much traffic on the road in these parts," he said with feigned casualness.

The miller scooped up the coins and gave a snort. "It's on account of the madness," he said. "Started a few months ago, when Old Man Turney's boy went wild. Killed a cow and nearly beat one of the hired men senseless before they got him tied up."

"You say it 'started' then," Blaine said. "There have been more?"

The miller gave him an incredulous look. "You're really not from these parts, are you?"

Blaine shrugged. "Just passing through."

"Gods have pity on us," the miller replied. "Turney's boy was just the first. One of the scullery maids over at the tavern lost her wits a month or so later, and then the butcher's wife." He shook his head. "It's an awful thing, not knowing where it'll strike next."

"There was no warning? No change before they went mad?" Niklas asked.

The miller shrugged. "I wasn't with them, so I can't say for certain, but none that gave much warning, that's for certain." He shook his head. "That girl over at the tavern started talking crazy, like she was looking for a child that ran off, only there weren't no such thing. The cook there told me the girl looked at her like she'd never seen her before, although that girl had worked in the kitchen for two years. Came after her with an iron pan, she did, shrieking about how the cook had stolen her baby. Almost brained her with that skillet, too, I heard," he said with a chuckle.

"And the butcher's wife?" Niklas said.

"Same sort of thing," the miller replied. "Went after one of the customers with a big knife and nearly killed the man. Them that saw it said her eyes were wild, like she'd never seen him before, although he bought his meat there all the time." He shook his head. "Then Davey, the blacksmith's son, ran off a few days ago. No one knows whether the madness took him or whether he just lit out looking for something better." He sighed. "No making sense of it. World's comin' to an end, I guess, what with the Fire and the war and all."

Niklas hefted one of the bags of flour, careful to put the load on his left shoulder so he could still draw his sword if need be. He fought a smile as he realized Blaine had done the same. "See any unusual traffic on the road?" Blaine asked casually.

The miller's eyes narrowed as if he realized his two visitors were getting a lot of information with their flour. "No highwaymen, if that's what you're a-fearin'," he said. "Saw a group of men in black cloaks riding off west a few days ago," he said with a jerk of his head in the direction they had come. "They didn't bother anyone, but I wouldn't have wanted to get in their way. Well armed, they were."

More of the men we fought by the barn? Niklas wondered. "We'll keep an eye out," he said. He and Blaine moved toward the door.

"If you're not staying at the alehouse, I hope you're not far from home," the miller said as Niklas opened the door.

"Why's that?" Niklas asked, turning.

"On account of the ghost knights, that's why."

Niklas froze in the doorway. " 'Ghost knights'?"

"Renegade knights that King Merrill's grandfather banished long ago," the miller said. "Some biters, some mortals, all the fiercest fighters ever seen. Got too dangerous, so the old king tried to wipe them out. Killed some, but the others just disappeared." His voice fell.

"But there were always stories that they'd just gone into hiding," the miller added. "That when the king needed them most, they would return." He shook his head. "Well, if they've come back, they're late. Won't be doing Merrill any good, I wager."

"Have you seen them?" Blaine asked.

The miller shook his head. "Not me. But Jeb the peddler swears that he saw gray-cloaked men riding on warhorses along the ridge road near midnight one night. Claims he wasn't drunk, although I'm not so sure."

"Why did he think they were the ghost knights?" Niklas asked.

"He said he got a look at the crest on the shields they carried, and a glimpse of the uniforms they wore when the wind blew one man's cloak. They had a blue diagonal bar, like the tales tell." He shrugged. "But where they were going, or why they came back, no one knows."

The sacks of flour were getting heavy, and Niklas was anxious to return to their group. "Thank you for the flour, and for the news."

"Don't get much chance to tell tales nowadays. Ride carefully."

They did not speak until they had secured the flour sacks behind their saddles and ridden clear of the mill. "Madness and ghost knights," Blaine said. "And a sighting of Pollard's men. What's next?"

Niklas shook his head. Night had fallen, and the air had turned colder. A headache was starting in his temples, and he cast an eye at the sky, hoping it did not mean that snow was likely. "Well, we know where Pollard's men were headed," he said. "As for the 'ghost knights,' they're almost certainly the Knights of Esthrane. The question is, are they real?"

A dark figure hurtled from the woods with a shrill cry, and Niklas's horse reared. A wild-eyed young man stood in the road brandishing a broken tree limb as if it were a broadsword. His hair was long and matted, and his face and skin were as dirty as if he had rolled down a hillside. The homespun clothing he wore was stained and torn.

"You may not pass!" he shouted, swinging the branch in such a wide circle that the horses shied back.

Blaine and Niklas had already drawn their swords. "We want no trouble," Niklas said. "We have no quarrel with you."

"Can't let you pass," the man replied emphatically. "The ghosts wouldn't like it."

"Ghosts?" Niklas asked, eyeing the trees around them to see if their attacker had any friends waiting to strike. He could see no motion in the shadows. *I wonder if this is the black-smith's boy who went missing*, Niklas thought. *Another case of the madness.*

"Can't you see them?" the young man challenged as if they were daft. "They're all around us, and they don't like people disturbing them."

"We won't disturb them," Niklas said in a soothing tone. "We're just trying to get home."

"Liars!" The man advanced and thrust the branch at Niklas, nearly striking him. "That's not what they tell me. Not what the ghosts say."

Blaine and Niklas exchanged a glance. "What do they say?" Blaine asked, watching the young man closely.

"They don't like you." The wild man ran at them with a cry. Niklas pulled back on the reins and the horse reared, its front hooves kicking at the air around their attacker's head.

"Leave now, and we won't hurt you," Blaine shouted.

The young man did not seem to hear. His eyes were wide, gripped by mania. He feared neither the horse's hooves nor the swords and ran again at Niklas brandishing the tree branch in one hand and a large knife that he had snatched from his belt in the other.

Niklas kicked at the man with his boot, trying to push him away so he could ride past, hoping to escape the situation without needing to harm the addled young man.

The man gave a deep-throated bellow and charged once more, snagging Niklas with one of the knots on the branch. Alarmed that he might actually be able to throw Niklas from the horse, Blaine rode in from the other side, sword raised.

Too bad I can't get close enough to thump him on the head, Niklas thought, but their attacker's single-mindedness and the frenzy of his attack made that impossible.

Blaine brought his blade down on the man's shoulder, slicing to the bone. The man howled, but madness won out over pain, and he gave a vicious jerk that nearly unseated Niklas.

Blocked from a clean strike by the branch, Niklas kicked again and swung. His blow was not quite enough to cut through the wood, and the attacker shoved hard, throwing Niklas off balance. The branch came free, and the attacker swung high, landing a bone-crunching strike on Niklas's shoulder.

This time Niklas did lose his seat as his horse reared. Blaine dismounted as Niklas hit the ground. Niklas managed to keep his feet, but barely—as he tried to get his footing, the attacker came at Niklas with a two-handed foray, scything his wide-bladed knife and jabbing with the branch, which was just long enough to keep out of range of Niklas's sword.

Blaine came up behind their attacker, but just as he brought his sword down, the attacker turned, whipping the branch in Blaine's direction and catching him on the side of the head. Blaine staggered, and the man came at him fast, angling the knife for Blaine's chest.

Blaine brought his sword up in time to parry the blow, and the blade skittered down the steel and bit into his arm. The wild man raked the branch at knee level, catching Blaine's right leg so hard that it nearly folded under him. The man's eyes were alight with madness, cheered on by ghostly voices only he could hear.

Before the man could make another strike at Blaine, Niklas came at him from behind with a blow that severed his sword arm. Numbed by his frenzy, the man made a wild swing at Niklas with his makeshift club as blood flowed freely from the stump of his shoulder onto the rutted road.

The branch slammed against Niklas's side, but as Niklas staggered he saw a blur of movement as Blaine rushed the mad-man from behind. Blaine's sword tore into the man's back, sliding between his ribs, propelled by Blaine's momentum until it sank hilt deep and the blade protruded from his chest.

Only then, taken through the heart, did the man slow his attack. He staggered, eyes uncomprehending, and the branch fell from his hand. One more step and he sank to his knees, still in the grip of the madness that drove him past normal endurance.

"They said I could not lose," he whispered. Blood dribbled from the corner of his mouth. "They promised me." His breath came in one last, rattling wheeze, and he fell forward onto the road.

Winded and battered, Blaine and Niklas watched the man's still form as they recovered from the attack.

"So we just leave him here?" Niklas said as Blaine pulled his sword free of the body and wiped it clean on the dry grass along the road.

Blaine looked up at him. "Do you fancy taking him back to the village and explaining to the blacksmith how two larger, older, heavily armed strangers were forced to defend themselves against his son?"

Niklas grimaced. He knew Blaine was right, but it galled his sense of honor. "Not really," he said. "Damn."

Blaine headed down the road to reclaim his horse. He was limping from the force of the blow he had taken to the knee. When they reached the horses, they saw that, despite the attack, the precious sacks of flour had managed to remain unscathed. "At least your men will have biscuits," Blaine observed.

"Saves us a fight or two over scarce rations," Niklas replied. He swung up to his saddle, favoring his right arm.

"Look at the bright side," Blaine said. "Once we make camp, Kestel will insist on fussing over our injuries."

Niklas chuckled. "I know you say she's only a good friend, but you might want to stake your claim. She's pretty, smart, and knows how to fight. Hard to find that in a woman." He grinned. "If you're not going to make a move, I just might."

"Just remember that 'assassin' is one of her many talents,"

Blaine replied. "I wouldn't start something if you don't mean to finish it."

Niklas grinned. "I always finish what I start," he said, laughing.

Blaine chuckled, but as they rode toward camp, something in his eyes gave Niklas to gather that Blaine did not find the comment funny at all.

CHAPTER NINE

B Y THE TIME THEY SET OUT FROM CAMP THE NEXT day, Blaine found himself edgy and anxious to get back to Glenreith.

"Another day, and we should be home," Blaine said. The camp healer had done an admirable job binding up the gash on his forearm and applying a poultice to his bruised leg, but today, both were sore and made riding miserable. From the way Niklas sat his horse, it was clear he was also feeling the after-effects of their fight with the madman.

"We've been gone for a long time," Niklas said. "I know your exile was much longer, but it's been far too much time away from home for me."

Blaine looked out over the horizon. They had ridden for much of the day, and twilight had fallen before they found a suitable place to camp for the night. With the solstice not far off, the days were getting shorter. They were still riding through hill country, past the ramshackle mining villages and the deserted mines sunk like abandoned tombs into the sides of the mountains. There was no sign of life in the tumbledown villages, as if their former residents had abandoned them to the ravages of the Great Fire and the magic storms.

"Just remember, you're not the same man who left," Blaine said quietly.

Niklas gave him a glance that seemed to see too much. "Spoken from experience?"

Blaine shrugged. "People move on. Things change. Even without the Great Fire, things would be different."

Just then, a strange whistling sound caught their attention. Blaine's horse began to sidestep nervously, and Blaine felt sudden, blinding pain in his temples. He pulled on the reins, struggling to control his horse, and caught the pommel of his saddle to steady himself.

"Magic storm coming," he said in a hoarse voice.

"We've got to get shelter," Niklas said.

Blaine glanced at his friend. Niklas's face was ashen, his eyes wide with fear.

"You never had any magic," Blaine observed. "But you feel the storm?"

Niklas shook his head. "I don't feel it, but I've survived enough of them to know how dangerous they are. And even without magic, they always give me a nasty headache."

"Ride for the mines!" Blaine shouted. He turned in his saddle. Looking out over the contingent of men who rode with them, Blaine could see that some looked as if it took effort to remain on their horses. *I'm betting they're the ones who had a touch of magic.*

He did not have to urge twice. In the darkness, it was difficult to see the coming storm. But the high-pitched whistling was louder now, and it seemed to come from everywhere at once. Blaine turned his horse toward the hills, hoping they could reach the shelter of the mines before the storm tore them apart.

Ahead he saw a man standing in the wide, empty mine road. As his horse pounded closer, he recognized Geir.

"Storm's coming in from the south!" Geir shouted. "Moving fast. I've found an entrance that should shelter us. Follow me."

Blaine cast a glance toward Niklas, knowing that only the night before, Geir had led an assault on Niklas's men. To Blaine's relief, Niklas's strong practical streak won out over any other feelings he might have had.

"Follow him!" Niklas shouted to his soldiers. "We've got to get to the mines."

Blaine could feel a shift in the air. The storm was moving closer. Breathing was difficult, as if the air had become heavier. His headache threatened to make him black out, but Blaine held on to his horse as they closed on the hills. It was still impossible for him to separate the shadows from the entrances to the mines, but he could make out Geir's form ahead of them, waving his arms to guide them.

The wind had picked up, bitter cold as the temperature fell. The high-pitched whistle had grown to a dull roar that was disturbingly close.

Blaine heard a crash as one of the sheds along the mine road blew apart, sending boards and stone fragments flying through the air. The next building sent a shower of stones and wood raining down on them and churned the dirt road into a blinding dust storm.

Horses whinnied in fear, and men railed at the storm with curses or shouted prayers to the gods. Blaine and Piran were riding on either side of Kestel. She looked ghostly pale, but she held on to her saddle with a white-knuckled grip. Verran and Dawe were right behind, urging their horses on.

They were close enough now that in the moonlight, Blaine could make out the entrance to which Geir was directing them.

Two more storage buildings smashed to pieces as the magic storm howled louder behind them. A phosphorescent glow filled the air. Ahead, Blaine could see Geir waving them toward the entrance where torchlight streamed from the opening. Blaine rode toward him at full speed, reaching the mine entrance at the same time as Niklas.

"Quickly now. Dismount and lead your horses inside," Geir said. "There's a broad ramp and a big antechamber. It'll be tight with the horses, but I think we can all fit."

Piran helped Kestel safely inside, followed by Dawe and Verran. "Go toward the back," Blaine said to Piran. "Make sure we've got an orderly process."

Piran gave a curt nod and led his and Kestel's horses deeper into the cave. Geir also moved toward the back, and Blaine was completely confident that between the two of them, no one would get out of hand.

Verran and Dawe began to light more torches, and within a few moments they could glimpse the scale of the mine's antechamber. They were in a vast rock room that appeared to Blaine to be part natural cave and part dug-out rock. It was easily as large as the entire first floor of Glenreith, with a high ceiling that sloped lower toward the back of the room. From the rear of the cavern, tunnels led off into darkness. The air smelled of brackish water, soot, and pitch.

"Keep it moving!" Niklas shouted to the constant stream of men who entered the mine, leading their skittish horses. Outside, Blaine glimpsed the whirlwind he knew to be the magic storm. The air in the whirlwind sparkled like snow in the sunlight, casting an eerie glow across the deserted ruins of the village.

Two of the last men in line were struggling with their horses, trying to get them into the mine's entrance. "Leave the horses!" Blaine shouted. "If they won't come in, forget them and save yourselves!"

One of the men cursed at his stubborn horse and ran for the mine. The spooked horse bolted. The other soldier continued to struggle with his stallion.

"To Raka with that idea! I'm not losing a good horse!" he shouted, trying unsuccessfully to drag the frightened animal toward the mine entrance.

"Get into the mine!" Blaine shouted. The magic storm was dangerously close, and Blaine winced as the pain in his temples grew blinding. His knees buckled, and then strong arms tightened around his chest like iron bands and whisked him into the depths of the mine.

"Godsforsaken fool," he heard Geir mutter, but whether the *talishte* was referring to the obstinate man with the horse, or to Blaine's attempt to coax the man to safety, Blaine was not sure.

A man's bloodcurdling scream and the death cry of a horse echoed at the mine entrance. The magic storm howled outside, and its mass of swirling, coruscating particles lit the entranceway of the mining chamber with a supernatural glow. The wild *visithara* magic pounded the hills with the physical force of a tornado, while the unharnessed power seemed to ripple through the entire mountainside in waves as powerful as the sea.

The horses gathered toward the back of the mine stood trembling as if finding themselves in the gaze of a predator. Whether the storm caused them pain, Blaine had no way of knowing, but the horses didn't bolt, as if they understood how dire the danger.

Blaine struggled to hold on to consciousness as he collapsed to the ground. He could hear Niklas shouting, but he could not make out the words. Kestel screamed. Others cried out, and Blaine could not say whether or not he had been among them. Pain ebbed and flowed with the storm's power. Visions danced on the edge of consciousness, in the gray area between waking and nightmares. The shimmering light seemed to be inside his mind, behind his eyelids, and in that deadly glow, Blaine saw the faces of the dead. Prokief. Ian McFadden. His mother. Selane, and so many of those he had known and buried back in Edgeland.

But the images the storm showed him were not of the dead at rest. In the visions of the *visithara* magic, the dead faces stared back at him as corpses, ashen, lifeless, their glassy eyes staring accusingly. Trapped in the grip of the storm, reason offered no escape. Like ghouls newly risen from old graves, their images stalked him, surrounded him, incoherent in their anger, relentless in their need.

The rock walls amplified the roar of the storm so that it felt as if the mountain itself shook to its roots. Blaine feared that at any moment the mine would crash down upon them, but the storm kept him pinned against the floor, unable to move.

Just when Blaine had become certain that the pressure on his chest and the pounding pain in his temples would kill him, the storm began to abate. Blaine felt the awful weight lift from his chest and gasped in lungfuls of sweet, cold air. The blinding headache faded next, receding from his forehead, his eyes, his temples, and finally from the nexus of pain at the base of his skull.

By now, Blaine was familiar with the aftereffects: the full-body ache from convulsions and spasms he did not remember, the dry mouth, the raw throat from screams over which he had no control. He groaned and closed his eyes, surrendering for a moment to complete exhaustion.

"Mick, can you hear me?" Piran bent over him, looking worried.

Blaine groaned again and accepted Piran's hand to help him sit up. "What about the others?" Blaine managed.

Piran cursed. "Kestel, Dawe, and Verran are on their feet, although they were taken down like everyone else. Niklas says his men have lived through storms before, so they know what to expect."

Piran was looking at him strangely, and Blaine had the feeling his friend had not said everything he was thinking. "What?"

Piran shrugged. "Just wonderin' why you're the last to get your wits about you. You've been out a good few minutes longer than everyone else, and there was no rousing you, even when I shouted in your ear."

"No idea," Blaine said, mustering all his energy to stand. "Just lucky, I guess."

"Glad to see you on your feet." Niklas strode up. He looked worried and tired. "Was starting to wonder if we were going to have to throw you in the back of the wagon with the supplies." His words were joking, but his tone made clear his concern.

"I'll be all right," Blaine assured him with more confidence than he felt. "How about your men?"

"They're fine, except for the idiot who didn't leave his horse," Niklas replied.

Geir joined them, and Blaine thought even the *talishte* looked haggard from the storm's violence. "Judging from the blood, the storm took them both." He grimaced.

"Let's get out of here," Niklas said, his expression hard. "I'm ready to go home."

CHAPTER
TEN

————

A DAY LATER, GLENREITH LOOMED AGAINST THE twilight sky. Blaine and Piran rode on ahead to warn the guards that the large force approaching the walls was not an invasion. A brief stop at Arengarte had made it plain that while Niklas's family home could be repaired enough to billet his men, it was going to take some work. In the meantime, a winter storm was brewing, and rations were running thin. Pressing on to Glenreith had been the only real option, and Blaine wanted to prepare his aunt and Edward, the seneschal, for the new arrivals.

"So that young bloke, the one with a chip on his shoulder, he's your brother?" Piran asked as the Glenreith gates neared.

"Yeah," Blaine said with a sigh. "That's Carr."

"Doesn't seem real pleased to see you," Piran observed.

Blaine grimaced. "I brought trouble down on their heads. It wasn't what I intended, but intentions don't change results."

Piran shrugged. "The way I see it, you gave him freedom, and freedom can be a real bitch. Ever wonder why some men will put up with a master who beats the shit out of them rather than run away? Because they're more afraid of making their own decisions than they are of being beaten. When you're indentured, you can blame your lot on the sorry son of a bitch who's your master. But a free man, well, he's only got himself to blame, don't he?"

"I hurt people badly enough when I got sent away," Blaine replied. "I didn't mean to hurt them more by coming back."

"Your brother will get over it, or he'll move on. Either way, he'll have made a decision, and he'll have to live with it."

"You may be right," Blaine conceded.

"You know I'm right." Piran gave a glance over his shoulder. "Your friend the captain seems to have taken a shine to our Kestel."

"If I know Kestel, she's pumping him for information about what he saw on the warfront," Blaine replied, resisting the urge to follow Piran's glance.

Piran shrugged. "Maybe. Maybe not. I wager the ladies think he's a fair-looking bloke. Kestel's been cooped up with the likes of us, and a bunch of convicts, for several years now. Wouldn't be surprised if she has a look around now that we're back in civilization."

"I wasn't sure we *were* back in civilization," Blaine countered, unsure why Piran's comment made him uneasy. But by then they had reached the gates of Glenreith, and Blaine swung down from his horse.

"I'm back, and we've got reinforcements!" Blaine shouted up to the guard at the gate. "Call for Edward and Lady Judith, and let's get the gates open before someone makes a target of us."

They waited for what seemed like forever, and the evening wind whipped around them, carrying with it the first flurries of snow. The dying glow of the sunset was replaced by the light of torches, both on the manor's outer wall and among the soldiers behind Blaine and Piran. Darkness fell, and finally, the heavy doors creaked open to reveal several of Glenreith's guards. Geir and Edward stood behind the guards in the entranceway.

"We're relieved to see you home once more, m'lord," Edward said. "Sir Geir reached us last night, just after full dark. Tell Captain Theilsson that his men are welcome here, though as you know, our provisions are not bountiful."

"Niklas sent out a hunting party early in the day," Blaine said, turning to motion for the others to advance, then walking toward the gates with Piran, both of them leading their horses. "They brought down several deer, so those are dressed and ready to be roasted."

"I take it that your efforts at Mirdalur did not go quite as you had hoped," Edward said as they walked into the manor's large courtyard. "That's unfortunate, but at least you've come back safe."

Blaine glanced at Geir. "Did you tell him the other news?"

Edward chuckled. "Sir Geir did let it slip that Master Carr was among the soldiers returning with Captain Theilsson. Lady Judith is making a few preparations to welcome both of you home, and she's asked me to bring you and Carr, and of course your friends and Captain Theilsson, along to the dining room as soon as the captain has seen to his men." He smiled. "She said to be quick about washing up."

Blaine exchanged a look with Piran. "We've been on the road, ridden through sleet, and had a few skirmishes. It's going to take a bit more than soaping up hands and face. I'm quite sure you wouldn't want to be in a warm room with us."

Edward chuckled. "M'lady was merely asking that you move with all haste."

Blaine smiled. "I do my best not to keep Aunt Judith waiting, but I need to help Niklas get his soldiers situated before I can make myself presentable."

Nearly a candlemark later, Blaine headed into the manor house. It had taken some maneuvering, but Blaine, Edward, and Niklas had managed to find quarters for all of Niklas's soldiers and a few casks of ale to go with the venison roasting in the courtyard.

Carr followed a few paces behind Blaine, refusing to speak except in clipped replies even to Niklas. Kestel and the others had already returned to their rooms to clean up.

Lady Judith McFadden Ainsworth stood framed in the doorway. Although she was in her middle years, she was still a handsome woman with a trim build. The hardship of the last years showed in her face, but when she laughed, it was still possible to imagine just how pretty she had been in her youth. With a joyful cry, she embraced Blaine. "Thank the gods you've returned safely. Sir Geir gave us only the barest information—I want to hear all that happened."

By this time, Mari had joined Judith in the hallway. Mari's dark hair was caught back in a braided bun, making her look older than her twenty-two years, but fitting for a widowed mother of a young son. Although Mari was smiling, there was a sadness that never left her dark eyes. Blaine hugged his sister and bent to receive a kiss on the cheek. Blaine stepped to the side, guiding Judith to move with him. "We brought someone home with us," he said and caught Carr with a warning glance. *Be as angry as you want with me, but don't you dare deny Judith her reunion.*

"Carr!" Judith and Mari exclaimed at once and rushed to enfold Carr in their embrace. A variety of emotions flickered across Carr's features. Alarm, uncertainty, and embarrassment warred with each other as he surrendered to Mari's kisses and Judith's hugs. Whether Carr had read the intent in Blaine's glare or reserved his ill will solely for his brother, he did not, to Blaine's relief, give vent to the anger he had shown before.

Judith was the first to step away, and she turned from Carr to find Niklas, who hung back, allowing the family to reunite. "Niklas," she said, moving to take his hand and draw him forward. "We're in your debt for returning Carr to us safely."

Blaine's gaze wandered to where Mari stood. She had moved away from Carr, and now she eyed Niklas with a painful look that tore at Blaine's heart. *She wants to know what really happened to Evaret, but she's afraid to hear the details,* he thought. Blaine moved closer and put an arm around Mari's shoulders. She looked up at him appreciatively and leaned into him, as if the finality of Niklas's return without her husband put an end to all hope.

"As Blaine may have told you, we're stretched a bit thin these days," Judith said apologetically. Despite her worn dress and frayed bodice, she was, as ever, the elegant hostess. "But such a wonderful occasion deserves a celebration. My nephews have both returned home safely. For that we thank Charrot, Esthrane, and all the many gods, above and below."

A candlemark later, the small group gathered around the table in the manor's large dining hall, where a spread of cheese and dried meats, small cakes and dried fruits, brined vegetables, and a cask of homemade wine awaited them. One of three large fireplaces at the far end of the room blazed, and a large cauldron simmering with stew warmed in the embers.

Blaine had found a change of clothing among the items he had left behind when he went to Velant, although years of hard work in the prison's mines meant the waistcoat was snug through the shoulders and chest. Still, the dark brown velvet flattered his coloring, as did the burgundy shirt. Judith had somehow procured fresh clothing for the others, and as Blaine looked across the room, he saw that Verran was resplendent in a silk shirt of midnight purple and black trews.

Dawe's height had obviously posed a challenge for Judith, for while his satin shirt fit across the chest, both his sleeves and the hem of his brocade trews were a bit too short. Piran, stockier in the chest and thicker through the neck than any of the others, wore a black linen shirt and brocade vest Blaine recognized as having belonged to Ian McFadden. From a distance, the wardrobe Judith had assembled looked quite festive, but up close, Blaine saw the telltale signs of heavy wear, mending, and patches that bore witness to Glenreith's fall from prosperity.

Everyone turned as Kestel entered the dining room. She wore an emerald silk gown with an intricately embroidered bodice, a dress she had borrowed from either Mari or Judith. Though the fabric showed wear around the edges, the gown flattered her. Her full skirt rustled as she moved gracefully across the room. Kestel's red hair was swept up into a twist, exposing her slim neck and setting off her features. She had added a touch of rouge to her cheeks and kohl to her eyes. Blaine's gaze signaled his appreciation and Kestel smiled, inclining her head just a bit, as she joined the group near the table.

Verran pulled a pennywhistle out from a pouch beneath his coat and struck up a merry tune. Dawe grabbed and drained a goblet of wine, shoved a handful of dried fruits into his mouth, and sat next to Verran. He began to tap a rhythm to accompany the melody, something he had done many a time back in Edgeland to while away the endless nights.

Judith took Carr's arm and steered him around the table, loading a plate for him until he protested, and pressed a goblet into his hand. Blaine could not hear their conversation, but it appeared that Carr was resigned to Judith's gentle questioning. Mari and Niklas had withdrawn to a far corner of the room, where they spoke together in low tones. From Mari's stance, Blaine guessed that she pressed Niklas for details about Evaret's death. As her shoulders began to shake and Niklas drew her to him, allowing her to sob against his chest, Blaine knew Mari had the answers she needed but did not want to hear.

Piran, left on his own, filled a trencher and refilled his goblet, finding a spot by the fire to enjoy both the warmth and the music. Kestel caught up with Blaine as he poured himself a glass of wine and took a selection of the cheese and dried meat. "Glad to be home?" she asked as she held out a glass for Blaine to fill.

"Still getting used to the idea," Blaine replied.

Kestel's gaze strayed to where Carr and Judith were talking. "Piran told me that Carr wasn't completely happy to see you."

Blaine grimaced. "You could say that." He sighed. "Maybe he'll come around. He saw a lot of action in the war. That changes a man, and Carr was barely old enough to enlist when he went off with the army."

"I'm pleased to see that you made the rest of the journey back safely," Geir said, and Blaine startled at the *talishte*'s silent approach.

"Just be glad none of Niklas's men got worse than some broken bones and bruised egos," Blaine replied. "Although he seemed willing to accept a truce."

Geir shrugged. "The captain appears to be a reasonable man." He fingered his goblet, which was filled with fresh deer blood. "Between his men and the *talishte* I've gathered, we should be better prepared for the next attempt to restore the magic." He met Blaine's gaze. "I'm assuming you intend to try again."

Blaine sipped his wine. "We've got the journal we found when we got out of the Mirdalur ruins. Now that we're safe, I intend to have a good look at it. But I'd welcome Penhallow's opinion."

Geir nodded. "What I sense of him and Connor is that the two of them are safe, for now. I also get a strong image of Quillarth Castle, so I'm guessing that, for some reason, Penhallow felt the need to go there before rejoining us."

"It's not going to take Pollard too long to figure out where we've gone. I've no desire to see him try to lay siege again," Blaine remarked. "Once the winter storms begin, we could just as easily be bottled up by the weather as by Pollard." He shook his head. "If that journal did belong to Vigus Quintrel, then I'm hoping it gives us something to work on if there really is a chance to restore the magic."

Geir drained his cup. "I came by to welcome you and your brother home, but I need to see to the *talishte*. Tomorrow night, let's have a look at that journal and see whether there are any clues to be gleaned." With a bow, he slipped out of the room.

Blaine looked up to see Judith approaching. Carr drifted to stand alone along one wall, eyeing the gathering as if unsure where he fit. Mari was gone, and Niklas was now talking with Piran.

"Does Mari need someone to look in on her?" Blaine asked, concerned.

Judith sighed. "I will, in a little bit. She needs some time to be alone with her grief. She had resigned herself to Evaret's death, but having it confirmed reopens the wound."

"How did your conversation go with Carr?" Blaine asked. Kestel drifted over to join Piran and Niklas, giving Blaine and his aunt privacy.

Judith frowned. "Carr turned in on himself after you were exiled, and I fear the horrors he saw in the war made him more pensive. It may help him to have Niklas and the regiment nearby. As you know, homecomings are not simple, no matter how long desired."

"It might be best for all of us if my friends and I leave soon to hunt for another way to restore the magic," Blaine observed. "I think Carr would prefer we weren't at Glenreith."

Judith's expression hardened. "Glenreith is your home, and no matter what King Merrill decreed, you are Glenreith's lord. The gods have answered my prayers by returning the two of you safely. There is room enough for both you and Carr here."

Just then, Verran struck up a dance tune, shifting from the quieter ballads he had been playing. Kestel tugged at Niklas's arm, pulling him to an open area of the floor and making a curtsey. She motioned to Blaine. "Enough talking! This is a celebration. It calls for a dance or two."

Blaine smiled and offered his arm to Judith. "How about it? I seem to recall that you used to adore the winter ball at court."

Judith chuckled, taking his arm. "That was many years ago, when I was much younger. I haven't danced in years."

"Then perhaps you're long overdue," Blaine replied, making a formal bow.

The tune Verran played was for a country dance, where two or more couples faced each other and then proceeded through a series of steps, changing and exchanging partners. It was a sprightly song, one Blaine vaguely remembered from long ago, and although he and Niklas both missed a number of the steps, Judith and Kestel both laughed aloud with delight as the steps grew faster and more complicated.

Kestel's cheeks flushed with the energy of the dance, and her expression was vibrant. Niklas swung her through the pattern, one arm around her waist, spinning her out from him and then gathering her back into a light embrace before she was whisked away by Blaine and Judith took her place. Judith, too, was alight with enjoyment, and Blaine decided that the embarrassment he felt at making a mess of the steps was well worth it to see both Kestel and Judith so happy.

After three dances, Blaine and Niklas finally begged off. Kestel and Judith, both still laughing from the dance, leaned against the table and fanned themselves. Niklas collapsed into a chair and loosened the collar of his shirt. Blaine wandered toward the double doors that led out to a loggia that stretched along the side of the manor house. He stepped into the cool night air, closing his eyes as the wind rushed against his face. He could still hear the strains of Verran's music through the doors, and the light from the dining room's candelabra cast the loggia in a soft glow.

By the gods! I haven't actually laughed like that in...I don't even remember how long, Blaine thought. Though Kestel had made certain to drag all of her housemates out to the dances at the bonfires and holidays in Edgeland, it was one thing to lumber through the steps outside around a fire in the freezing cold, and another to dance indoors, in civilized attire.

Kestel's laughter carried on the night air, and Blaine thought about how it had felt for the moments when he had held her in his arms as they danced, as her hand clasped his when they moved through the dance steps. In Edgeland, it had seemed easy to think of Kestel as no more than a friend. But since their return to Donderath, he had caught himself noticing her as a woman, and he felt a stirring of something more than friendship. Resolutely, he pushed the thoughts from his mind.

All those years in Edgeland, she hid her beauty, her liveliness, he thought. *What did it cost her?* He stood still, listening to the sound of the muffled voices. *When we've brought back the magic—or failed—what will Kestel do then? There's no court, no grand society. Glenreith hardly seems enough for her.* He turned back to the railing, looking out past the wall, down the rolling slopes.

He heard the click of the doors opening and turned to see

Carr heading toward him. From his brother's gait, Blaine guessed Carr was well into his cups. Carr withdrew a flask from his pocket and poured a draught into his mouth, snapping the lid shut and replacing the container.

"Why not get some rest, Carr?" Blaine said. "It's been a long day."

"It wasn't enough that you had to disgrace the family once," Carr growled as he closed the distance between them. "Now you bring a pack of thieves and whores and biters into the house."

Blaine tensed, feeling his anger flash. "You're drunk. I'm going to pretend I didn't hear you."

Carr's mouth twisted in a nasty smile. "I meant for you to hear me. I've a mind to throw you and your whore and your thieving friends out of this house," he said, growing louder.

"You're out of line," Blaine grated.

Carr's eyes glinted. "Defending a whore's honor? That's precious."

"Shut your mouth and get out of my sight."

"You've brought enough trouble to us," Carr pressed, taking another step forward. "You deserted us, left us defenseless. Why don't you go back to where you came from and leave us alone?"

Carr might have been drunk, but his aim was true. His fist swung for Blaine's chin and Blaine blocked it, but the force sent him back a step. Enraged, Carr came at him again, both fists flying, and Blaine ducked, catching a strike on the shoulder that was meant for the side of his head. Carr was Blaine's height, and the demands of soldiering had made him solid. Angry and bent on fighting, Carr meant to do damage.

Blaine came up swinging. One fist caught Carr in the ribs, while the other clipped him in the jaw. Carr lashed out with one foot, a high kick that caught Blaine hard in the thigh. Carr launched at him with fists pummeling. Blaine's lip was split, and one eye was beginning to swell where Carr had clipped him on the side of the head.

"I've had enough of this," Blaine muttered as his own anger rose, canceling out any concern to avoid injuring Carr. He landed one solid blow and then another, forcing Carr to loosen his hold. He drew back his arm and punched hard, catching Carr on the side of the head and sending him sprawling.

Footsteps sounded on the loggia's stone floor as the others came running. Niklas grabbed Carr by the arms and hauled him to his feet, and Piran circled to stand behind Blaine, laying a cautioning hand on his shoulder.

"Get him out of here," Blaine said, his heart still pounding from the fight. "And keep a watch on him until he sobers up."

"Oh, you're certainly the Lord of Glenreith, all right," Carr snarled, spitting blood. "Just like Father. Well, I've got this to tell you, Lord McFadden. I took Father's thrashings, but I'll be damned if I'll take yours. You don't belong here. Get out."

Niklas tightened his grip on Carr's arms. "That's enough, soldier," he said. "Shut your mouth before I shut it for you." Carr said nothing else, but the baleful look in his eyes gave Blaine to know the matter was far from settled. Niklas half-shoved and half-dragged Carr back out of the dining room.

Judith sank into one of the chairs near the fire and covered her face with her hands. Blaine dropped to one knee in front of her. "I'm so sorry, Aunt Judith," he said, his words slightly slurred by his swollen lip. "I tried to pull my punches, but Carr meant to do damage."

Judith raised her head and reached out a hand to gently touch the growing bruise on Blaine's temple and his swelling eye. "I'm the one who's sorry, Blaine. I knew Carr was angry before he left for the war. At first I thought it was just his way of dealing with everything that had happened. It was...very difficult for us after you were exiled. Mari was older, she understood, and she bore up under the hardship. But Carr...I fear he got Ian's temper."

"Niklas will make sure he cools down," Blaine said. As the heat of the fight drained away, his head throbbed and he could feel every strike Carr had landed. "Before long, we'll be gone from Glenreith, and maybe then Carr can get settled."

Judith's eyes were troubled, and she rested her hand on his shoulder. "I've only just had the two of you returned to me. I'm not keen to lose either of you again."

I made a mistake coming back to Glenreith, Blaine thought, looking away. *I've caused my family nothing but pain.*

Judith seemed to guess his thoughts, because she gently turned his chin until he was looking at her. "At every turn, you've done what you had to do to protect us. There's no shame in that, Blaine. Carr will come to his senses. I'm sure of it."

Pollard and Reese aren't through looking for me. And without finding a way to tame the magic, we can't stop the storms. Carr doesn't realize it, but he's the least dangerous thing I have to worry about right now, and if he wants a piece of me, he's going to have to stand in line to get it.

CHAPTER
ELEVEN

HOW IS IT THAT YOU HAVE NOT YET BREACHED THE walls?" Vedran Pollard sat on his horse, staring at Traher Voss's fortress. The fortress that, despite his soldiers' efforts, *still* belonged to Voss.

Major Stanwik was a man approaching his middle years, a man who had served a decorated career in the king's army back when there was a king, and an army. Stanwik was of medium height, with a muscular build and a full head of short-cropped, wavy, dark hair. His gray eyes showed intelligence, the only thing remarkable about his otherwise ordinary face. Stanwik was extraordinary in one important way: He had the tenacity of a mastiff, and Pollard had never seen the man give up on a fight.

They had a good view of Voss's fortress without being within range of the smuggler's weapons. Voss had apparently chosen to spend his money on structural soundness rather than aesthetics, because there was nothing remotely good-looking about the fortress. Thick walls, strong gates, heavy iron, and towers high enough to give an observation advantage made the building an excellent fortification despite its lack of architectural embellishment. *Even more like Voss*, Pollard thought. *The man makes it easy to take him for a fool, right before he picks your pocket, steals your horse, and plunders your supply wagon.*

"The walls are very well reinforced, sir," Stanwik replied. "I'm not entirely sure what Voss used, but they're more resilient than anything I've ever come up against. Nothing the catapults have sent against the walls seems to have much of an effect. The outbuildings and all the roofs are made of stone, so there's nothing to burn. As for the gates, we're not sure how many sets there are, because every time the battering ram knocks down one, there's another behind it."

Pollard cursed under his breath. "Can you cut off his water supply? Starve him out?"

Stanwik shook his head. "Not so far, although we've tried. We've compromised the escape tunnels under the fortress, but it didn't stop Penhallow from getting out."

"And how did Penhallow escape, with two mortals in tow, without your men noticing?"

Stanwik flinched. "There's an underground river beneath the fortress. It's the source of their water, we presume. It comes out in a cave some distance away. We found three dead patrols nearby the night Penhallow escaped."

Pollard gave a predatory smile. "If Penhallow can bring out two mortals, can you send men in?"

Stanwik's expression gave Pollard to believe the military man would have preferred to be anywhere but where he was at the moment. "We tried that, sir. Sent in two of our best swimmers, mortals. They drowned. Stiff current, narrow passageways. No idea how Penhallow got his mortal servants out alive." He paused. "So, we sent in *talishte*, since they didn't need to breathe."

"And?"

"They died," Stanwik replied. "The bodies floated back to us badly cut up, with quarrels studding their chests."

"You've got *talishte* fighters," Pollard replied. "Have you brought them in from the air?"

Stanwik nodded. "Aye. Voss has archers with flaming arrows. We've lost several good men that way."

Pollard's next curse was creatively obscene. "What of their food supply? He can't have an unlimited amount."

Stanwik sighed. "True. But depending on how prepared he was, it could take months for him to run out."

"I have no intention of keeping an army in the field for months to drive down a smuggler!" Pollard roared.

Stanwik's expression was unchanged. Pollard noted that Stanwik's expression never changed. It looked the same in victory or defeat, on a good day and after a rout. "That is certainly not my intent, sir. We're working on new plans."

"Which are?"

"We're bringing in heavier war machines," Stanwik said. "No walls should be able to withstand them."

"Lord Reese will not be patient much longer," Pollard warned. "Voss is an asset to the opposition. It's not enough to keep him bottled up. We need to destroy him."

"Understood, sir."

They rode back to the camp in silence, Pollard stewing over Voss's continued ability to evade capture, and Stanwik quiet and unreadable as ever. It was dark when they arrived, though the camp was awash in torchlight. When Pollard reached his tent, he was pleased to find a bottle of brandy and a warm meal awaiting him. He shouldered out of his cloak and found that even with a fire in the brazier, the tent was still quite cold.

He sat down to his dinner, a large bowl of stew and a hearty hunk of bread. Pollard was hungry and cold enough to eat just about any camp ration. He reached for the bottle of brandy and poured the amber liquid into the tankard that had been set out for him. Just as he finished his dinner, a thundering crash sounded from the center of the camp. Pollard stood up so quickly he knocked over his chair. He grabbed his cloak and ran for the tent door, sword already in hand.

Another blast rocked the ground, and then another. By the time Pollard reached the outside, he could see flames shooting up from multiple points within the camp. There was another resounding boom, and a fire flared high into the sky from the strike point.

Throughout the camp, Pollard could hear running footsteps along with the shouts of commanders attempting to restore order. At least half a dozen tents were afire, and a charred circle of ground stood where other tents had been just moments before. Another explosion rocked the camp, and then more. A burning man staggered from one of the tents, his clothes and hair aflame, screaming and flailing. He lurched into Pollard's path, twisting in agony. Pollard swung his sword, slicing the man's head from his shoulders. The body took one more step and collapsed, while the head, hair still afire, rolled to the side.

Pollard grabbed a passing soldier by the shoulder. "Report!" he growled.

"We're under attack from the gods!" the man cried, more terrified of the fire that was raining down on the camp than of Pollard.

Pollard tightened his grip and wrenched the man toward him. "Soldier, report!"

The young fighter looked at him with wild, dilated eyes, his face ashen with fear. "It's the gods, I tell you. Look! It burns without being consumed."

Pollard frowned, and his gaze followed the direction in which the panicked soldier pointed.

Flames soared into the night sky from the roofs of the buildings within Voss's fortress. As Pollard watched, unbelieving, it did indeed appear that the massive fortress burned without looking worse for the conflagration.

"He's dancing on the parapets, like a madman," the soldier murmured, awestruck.

"Who is?" Pollard demanded.

"Voss. He's surrounded by fire, but it doesn't touch him. How can we fight a man who doesn't burn?" The soldier's words choked off as he stared at the horizon and suddenly looked as if he might faint. "Gods have mercy! Vessa herself is rising!"

At that, the terrified soldier dropped to his knees in supplication, babbling the words to a prayer. Pollard stood staring, openmouthed, at the spectacle he saw but could not comprehend.

A fiery figure of a woman rose into the night sky, hovering above the camp, garbed in burning robes. Men cried out in terror or prostrated themselves, begging the apparition for mercy. Pollard had long ago dismissed belief in the gods as mere myth, but even he had to admit that what appeared in the sky fit the legends' description of Vessa, the notoriously ill-tempered goddess of fire.

Another blast rocked the camp. With a curse, Pollard took off at a run to find Stanwik. He was running toward the front of the camp, toward Voss's fortress, and as he closed the distance, he could make out what appeared to be the figure of a man dancing against a backdrop of fire.

"No man could survive that," he muttered to himself, but he was as much at a loss to explain the sight as the soldiers who were pointing toward the walls in panic. From the height of the fire, he doubted any mortal could remain nearby for more than a few minutes. Yet the dancing figure seemed completely untouched.

As he crossed the camp, Pollard saw a dark shape fall from the sky, but before he could make out what it was, it crashed to the ground and exploded, sending up a sheet of flame that scorched the soil and lit the surrounding tents on fire. Much of the camp was on fire, and in several places, the explosions had blown small craters into the dirt.

He caught sight of Stanwik and ran toward him. Pollard heard a whistling sound behind him and then an explosion. Flames licked his heels and caught at the hems of his pants. He found Stanwik shouting at his men, regaining order in the front lines. The whole plain was awash in firelight, from the burning tents and from the firestorm that lit the roof of Voss's fortress. Fire shot toward the heavens, but the buildings and walls in Voss's stronghold seemed impervious to the fire.

In the next breath, a mighty roar shook the camp. The ground beneath the camp collapsed, opening a maw into darkness. Men, horses, tents, and siege machines tumbled into a vast and rapidly spreading chasm that descended into darkness.

"Run!" he heard Stanwik shout amid the screams of men and the squeals of the terrified horses. The lip of the chasm was expanding, and the ground was collapsing at an alarming rate. Stanwik and his soldiers fled. Overhead, the figure of Vessa outshone the moon, and if the goddess was ever inclined to pity mortals, she seemed to feel none for the panicked men. Pollard stole a backward glance toward Voss's fortress, only to see the dancing smuggler against the flames.

The collapsing ground forced the fleeing soldiers to run toward the fortress. But once the men reached solid ground, cascades of arrows rained down on them. Pollard felt an arrow slice through his upper arm, and the man next to him fell with a gasp and a gurgle, a shaft through his heart.

"We've got to run along the chasm's edge!" Pollard shouted, his voice barely audible in the rout. Running along the lip of the massive sinkhole would mean dodging burning tents, but it was preferable, in Pollard's opinion, to being cut down by a hail of arrows.

Two men behind Pollard dropped in their tracks, arrows in their backs. Another arrow barely missed Pollard, flying close enough to his head that it nicked his ear. Stanwik was a few steps ahead of him, running a gauntlet among arrows and blazing tents. The soldier nearest to Stanwik stumbled and careened toward the sinkhole. Stanwik grabbed for him, catching his arm, as the ground crumbled under the man's feet.

In one move, Stanwik twisted, hurling the soldier toward Pollard, who had no choice except to catch the flailing man. Stanwik leaped toward solid ground and landed on his feet just outside the lip of the hole. He grinned in triumph, then cried out as two fiery arrows hit him with enough force that their tips cut through the chest of his uniform shirt, drenching him in blood.

For just an instant, Stanwik teetered on the cusp, his clothing and hair afire, his expression agonized, and then he fell backward into the darkness.

Pollard disentangled himself from the panicked soldier and gave a momentary glance toward the pit, but Stanwik was gone from view. Cursing under his breath, Pollard strode away from the flames and the maw of the sinkhole.

"Rally here, men!" he shouted, holding his sword aloft. It would be hours before he had a full report, but it was clear that the attack had killed many of the soldiers and destroyed much of their materiel.

Has Voss somehow discovered a way to use magic? Pollard wondered. *Surely not. Has he managed to invoke the gods against us? Impossible. And yet...*

The camp was a complete ruin, its siege machines swallowed in the maw of the pit or set aflame, its soldiers dead, missing, or running for their lives. The sky was still dominated by the fiery image of Vessa and the fiery fortress with its mad brigand owner.

Terrified, soot-streaked, and injured by fire and arrows, the sorry band of survivors regrouped along the camp's rear perimeter with the horses and a few wagons they managed to rescue. The entire center of the camp had collapsed deep into the ground. What remained aboveground was afire or reduced to the cindered skeletons of tents, wagons, and catapults.

"Report!" Pollard snapped.

"Three-quarters of the soldiers are dead or missing," one of the lieutenants replied. "The tents, supplies, and war machines are a total loss. We were able to save about half the horses and a dozen wagons. Other than the sidearms the men were wearing when they ran from their tents, the majority of weapons were destroyed or disappeared into the chasm, sir." He looked around, lost. "Where is the commander, sir?"

"Major Stanwik is dead," Pollard replied. It stuck in Pollard's craw to slink off in the night, routed by a mercenary like Voss, but even he saw no alternative. He cut loose a string of invective. "We can't hold the position," he growled. "Move the men out." He turned back for one last look at Voss's fortress. "But I swear by Torven and all the gods, I will make sure Traher Voss pays for this and pays dearly."

CHAPTER
TWELVE

I T'S JUST A LIBRARY, M'BOY," TREVEN LOWREY SAID
encouragingly. "There's no need to hang back like that."

Deep below the ruins of Quillarth Castle, Lowrey stood in
the doorway of the hidden library of the Knights of Esthrane.
Penhallow had already stepped into the room as Var Geddy
rushed to light lanterns. Curiosity pulled Connor forward.
Common sense made him hesitate.

"You two are hoping there will be more documents by Vigus
Quintrel hidden away in there," Connor said, still unwilling to
cross the threshold. "And you're hoping Quintrel left us a clue
to jog another of my hidden memories."

Lowrey smiled. "Quintrel tampered with your memory so
you could read the code he used in documents. He's left us a
puzzle, so to speak, and you're the key."

"He waylaid me, planted ideas in my head, then made me
forget hours of my life," Connor replied testily. "For months,
I feared I had betrayed either Lord Garnoc or Penhallow. I
haven't forgiven Quintrel for that."

Lowrey tut-tutted. "Inconvenient, I'm sure, but important in
the grand scheme."

"I felt wretched after the last time," Connor responded. "It's an awful feeling, as if someone has taken over your mind. I'm not keen to have it happen again."

"Penhallow said you were perfectly safe," Lowrey coaxed.

"It wasn't happening inside his head, now was it?" Connor tried to look past Lowrey to get a better glimpse of the library. Part of him itched to see what had been hidden in the archive, kept locked away for generations.

"Admit it, lad. You want to see what's in there," Lowrey said, grinning.

"I've heard the legends about the Knights of Esthrane all my life," Connor murmured, venturing a step closer. "Mage-warriors, both mortal and *talishte*, the king's left hand, moving in the shadows, dealing with traitors and threats to the crown, and ultimately, betrayed by the king they served."

"It might be that Quintrel never got into this library," Lowrey said with a crafty gleam in his eye. "After all, before the kingdom fell, this was heavily guarded. You might have nothing to worry about."

With a sigh, Connor stepped into the room. "All right," he said. "You win." He looked at his surroundings. Though relatively small, the room was well appointed, fit for nobility. The library was elaborately paneled in wood, and a large rectangular table sat in the center of the room, covered with stacks of books. Tall shelves were recessed into the walls, all of them stacked with old leather folios, rolled-up parchments, and a selection of arcane instruments and talismans.

"Be careful," Penhallow warned. "Tamed magic might not work, but wild magic is as dangerous as ever. I don't want to take any chances with any of the objects accidentally bringing a magic storm down on our heads."

Connor slowly walked the perimeter of the room. "This

reminds me of the king's library upstairs," he said quietly. "It's laid out much the same, only this is a bit smaller."

Penhallow nodded. "Legend has it that the Knights had a private, secret place where they met with the king." He gestured toward the hall. "A number of the Knights were billeted there to protect the king, castle, and palace city. They came and went by hidden passageways so that no one in the castle above them could track their comings and goings."

"Powerful mages, skilled warriors, and *talishte* on top of that," Connor murmured. "No wonder the king grew to fear them." One side of the room was hung with tapestries that, while faded with age, were still beautiful for their workmanship and detail.

The first tapestry depicted the High God Charrot: the diune God, a being at once both male and female. Above the figure's head, the tapestry showed the constellation in the night sky that bore Charrot's name. Charrot was the Source, ruler of gods and men. The male side of his body was masculinity perfected: facial features that were decisive and compelling, strong, broad shoulders, corded muscles in his arms and legs, and generously endowed manhood. The female side of Charrot was intelligent and surpassingly beautiful, with indigo skin and long, midnight-black hair. Everything about her body promised fertility, from the full breasts to the curved hips.

Charrot was rarely depicted without his two consorts: Torven, the god of illusion, and Esthrane, the goddess of life. Torven was the ruler of air and sea, water and ice, metals and gems, darkness and twilight, as well as the Sea of Souls. Esthrane ruled fertility of the ground, crops, and herds and kept watch over the Unseen Realm, where incomplete souls wandered after death.

Charrot's female side held out a hand to the god Torven, while the god's male side extended a hand to caress Esthrane's cheek. At the gods' feet were smaller representations of the hundreds of lesser gods whom devout Donderans revered. Place gods and household deities, family patron spirits and the sentient essence that dwelled in ancient trees, quiet grottos, mountains, lakes, and other natural places were depicted with an artist's fancy. Such tapestries had been common in Donderath before the fall; those who could not afford elaborate pieces showed their devotion to the gods with paintings or murals.

Connor stared at the images of the second tapestry. They told another story he knew well, that of Vessa, the goddess of fire. Vessa was a slim, willowy figure with red hair that flowed around her, covering her nakedness and reaching below her knees. She had been a minor deity who had risen, by the craft of her fire and her own wit, to sit as a counselor to the higher gods, gaining the trust of Charrot himself. But Torven had grown jealous and schemed to make it look as if Charrot had taken Vessa as a lover, knowing that would anger Esthrane and hoping it would cause Charrot to cast Vessa aside. Esthrane, recognizing Torven's perfidy, took Vessa as her own confidante, putting Vessa beyond Torven's reach while securing fire under the control of mortals and denying Torven and his realms of light and heat.

"They were the Knights of Esthrane," Connor murmured. "Which would have meant that, like Esthrane, they trusted in fire."

"Not fire," Lowrey replied. "Magic. Vessa is the patron of mages. Think about it, m'boy. Esthrane is the goddess of life, and Vessa is the goddess of magic. The Knights were mage-warriors, with both mortal and *talishte* members, and the *talishte*—"

"Belong to Esthrane, as ruler of the Unseen Realm," Penhallow finished for him. He looked from Lowrey to Connor. "And if we're to figure out the secrets the Knights left behind, we'd best get started."

He looked at Connor. "We'll sort through the books and objects and divide things up," Penhallow said. "Connor, you'll take historic documents."

Connor eyed the shelves piled high with manuscripts and sighed. "What, exactly, am I looking for?"

"The Knights were privy to the origin of *hasithara*, tamed magic," Penhallow replied. "They were the protectors of Mirdalur until their exile. Look for anything that has to do with maps like the one of Valtyr's you have, or the disks that the Lords of the Blood wore to summon the magic, or Mirdalur itself."

Penhallow turned to Lowrey, who was eyeing the documents with undisguised curiosity. "Treven, start on the books of magic. If you see anything that looks newer than the other items, that might be a 'gift' from Quintrel. Let's let Connor have a look at it. Anything you think might be useful, set it aside." He leveled a meaningful glare at Lowrey. "Focus on *useful*, Treven, not merely 'interesting.' We have to carry anything we remove.

"I'll take the tools and amulets," Penhallow continued. "Being *talishte*, I'm a tad safer, perhaps, than the two of you when it comes to handling them, or at least more resilient should I manage to trip anything nasty."

"Going to need more light in here," Treven grumbled and looked to Var Geddy, who sat against one wall, doing his best to remain unnoticed. "See if your master can spare some oil lamps, and bring them down as quickly as you can," he said, shooing Geddy on his way. Lowrey began moving items off of the table, clearing a space by stacking manuscripts on the floor, then filling the space with new books as he began to ransack the shelves.

Connor moved around the large bookshelves, straining to see the gold lettering on some of the older bindings and brushing away dust as he searched for historical tomes. Finally, he selected a few old leather-bound folios and settled into his chair at the table, coughing at the dust that filled the air as he opened the cover of the first collection of papers.

Connor and Lowrey took turns grabbing a few candlemarks of sleep, then returning to help with the search. They paused briefly to eat when Geddy brought food for Connor and Lowrey and fresh deer blood for Penhallow, then returned to their tasks. Penhallow slept during the height of the day but returned as soon as he could to help. Though no one spoke of it, they all understood the urgency. Pollard and Reese were after Blaine— and apparently, after them as well. Thus far, Connor and the others had only barely eluded capture. At some point, it was very likely either Reese or Pollard would try to attack the castle to deprive them of any information that might help Blaine restore the magic. It would be best, Connor thought, if they were long gone when that happened.

Connor rubbed his eyes. He hunched in a chair over a yellowed parchment, hedged in on both sides by crumbling leather portfolios and bound illuminated manuscripts. Already he had lost track of the candlemarks they had spent examining the library's content. Connor yawned and stretched, glancing around to see how his companions were doing.

Lowrey had cleared one end of the large table, so that his place was ringed with oil lamps that gave him bright light to read by and dispelled the gloom of the small, windowless library. Connor had already scooted down to create a place for himself near enough to Lowrey so that he could take advantage of the lamps' light. Even so, he found himself squinting to make out the cramped, faded handwriting.

At the other end of the table, Penhallow handled the artifacts. Dim lighting posed no problem for his heightened sight, and Connor watched Penhallow examine an odd-looking object, a cross between an astrolabe and a sextant.

Connor returned his attention to the document in front of him and blinked, then widened his eyes trying to focus. He turned the page, and a small length of blue ribbon fluttered to the floor. Puzzled, Connor reached down and picked it up. It was unfaded and looked much newer than anything in the room. Curious, he skimmed down through the careful lines of script. "Hold on," he said, looking up. "I think this may be important."

Both Lowrey and Penhallow turned their attention to him. "I found this ribbon marking a page," Connor said. He held up the bit of satin for the others to see. "It doesn't look like it's been in here for hundreds of years." Connor looked back at the book. "It's marking what appears to be a genealogy of the thirteen Lords of the Blood."

Lowrey leaned back in his chair and gave a loud harrumph. "Why would that be important? We know who the lords were."

Connor frowned as he read further. He began to chuckle, even as he felt his cheeks flush. "I think I see why the Knights became unpopular," he said. "This isn't just a regular genealogy. It notes every bastard child and has a detailed list of the partners of the lords and ladies who were unfaithful. It's also rather clear on which lords, or their wives, were unable to bear children."

He shook his head. "According to this, two of the original

Lords of the Blood were unable to father children, so their wives secretly took lovers to produce offspring that the lords claimed as their own."

"The magic that kept the *hasithara* anchored only cared about true bloodlines," Lowrey remarked, looking over the tops of his lenses at Connor. "So that would invalidate the links to those two houses." He gave Connor a knowing look. "Does it give the names of the luckless lords?"

Connor nodded. "Doranset, which would be Lord Edenfarr's holdings," he began. "Gilholt," he continued.

"That's Lord Correnders manor," Penhallow supplied. "Interesting. If that book dates from before the Knights were exiled, then there is a third illegitimate, Vedran Pollard."

Connor nodded. "There are two more houses where the eldest sons died without direct heirs, breaking the line of succession. Solsiden, the holding of Lord Arvo, and Mirdalur, the lands of King Hougen." He let out a low whistle. "Well, that explains why King Merrill's ancestors decided to challenge Hougen's throne—and won."

"There's another note here, about a fifth house," Connor said. "Lundmyhre, the holding of Lord Arnbech Vandholt. The last eldest son was Kierken Vandholt, who was born a thousand years ago." He frowned as he reread the notation. "It says that he was turned *talishte* in the thirty-fifth year of his life, and almost four hundred years ago, he was cursed to pass beyond death into the Unseen Realm, denied rest in the Sea of Souls." He paused. "It also says his heirs were murdered, so his line would have ended with him."

Connor frowned. "Those dates can't be right."

Penhallow looked up. "Magic is a funny thing," he said quietly. "So precise. Blaine McFadden is the last *living* Lord of the Blood. But not the last such lord in existence."

Lowrey leveled a skeptical look at Penhallow. "Surely, Lanyon, you don't believe those rumors about Vandholt, do you?"

"What rumors?" Connor asked.

"The story of the Wraith Lord," Penhallow answered. "And I don't think it's mere rumor."

"Wraith Lord?" Connor's eyes widened.

Penhallow looked at Lowrey for a moment, as if debating how to answer. "Kierken Vandholt was a six-hundred year-old *talishte*-mage when he used his magic to save the life of King Hougen, at the cost of his own soul. It happened not long after the magic was raised at Mirdalur. He exchanged his soul for that of the king at the instant of Reaping, cheating Etelscurion, the Taker of Souls, who is master of the Sea of Souls. Etelscurion was so enraged that she refused to allow Vandholt's soul rest in the Sea of Souls. Esthrane took pity and permitted him sanctuary in the Unseen Realm. Hougen was grateful. But much later, King Merrill's grandfather was afraid when he saw that Vandholt's magic had the power to cheat death," Penhallow continued. "It was one of the things, ironically, that turned him against the *talishte* and the Knights of Esthrane. When Merrill's grandfather betrayed the Knights, he also had Vandholt's descendents murdered for good measure."

"How did he become a wraith?" Connor asked.

"It's said that Esthrane could not fully negate Etelscurion's curse," Penhallow replied, "so Vandholt is not truly living, dead, or undead, as we *talishte* are. He remains a shadow, sentient, wandering, forever separate."

"Could he be a Lord of the Blood if he was a wraith?" Connor asked.

Lowrey shook his head. "Doubtful. Wraiths don't have blood—they don't even have bodies."

Penhallow nodded. "Vandholt was one of the Lords of the Blood who raised the magic long ago, and then again at Mirdalur, before he became a wraith. Remember, magic has risen and fallen many times. Before magic was reclaimed at Mirdalur, the Continent had been without it for a hundred years."

Lowrey rubbed his hands together, warming to the tale. "When King Merrill's grandfather betrayed the Knights of Esthrane and the surviving Knights fled for their lives, they embraced the story of the Wraith Lord for obvious reasons. Like Vandholt, they had been betrayed by their monarch and forced into a half-life existence."

"Vandholt had been a patron and supporter of the Knights before he became a wraith," Penhallow said. "His sacrifice on behalf of the king would have gained him further esteem among the Order, especially when he—like they—was betrayed by the monarch for whom he had suffered so much."

Lowrey grinned. "There's a legend that the Knights who survived the purge escaped to a hidden place in the mountains." He paused. "The lost city of Valshoa. Find it, and you'll probably find the surviving Knights of Esthrane."

"If it were easy to find the Knights, don't you think the king's grandfather would have done it?" Connor challenged.

Lowrey shrugged. "King Merrill's grandfather got what he wanted. He broke the power of the knights and destroyed many of them. He may not have thought it necessary to pursue them." He smiled. "It does raise intriguing possibilities, doesn't it?"

Lowrey went on. "Legend has it that Valshoa was once protected by spells that kept unwanted visitors away, along with physical traps that assured only the most hardy—or foolish—seekers would reach their goal. The Knights were both mages and *talishte*. I'm sure they fortified the approach to keep out intruders, but all the magical protections would have failed the night of the Great Fire."

"Which leaves the Knights themselves to protect the city, and whatever physical traps they've maintained over the years to keep out intruders," Penhallow mused.

"Makes you wonder how Quintrel got in," Connor muttered.

"Vigus Quintrel loved a challenge," Lowrey replied. "The scholars in his family were obsessed with the legend of Valshoa. It would be like Quintrel to find a back way in or figure out how to best the traps." He chuckled. "He's a rather singular fellow."

Penhallow tented his fingers as he thought. He cleared his throat to bring the conversation back on track. "Can you follow Merrill's line? Is it unbroken and legitimate?"

Lowrey chuckled. "A little late to be digging up scandal, isn't it, Lanyon?"

Penhallow shook his head. "It's not scandal I'm after. If Merrill came from an unbroken, legitimate line, then he must have possessed a disk. The next logical question is, if the Lords of the Blood and their original fortresses were anchors for the *hasithara*, then are the disks themselves important, and could they . . . I don't know . . . stand in for the other lords if Blaine has another chance to restore the magic?"

"I can answer part of that question." Connor and Lowrey startled at the voice and turned to see Lynge in the doorway. "Please don't think that I meant to eavesdrop. Geddy's readying your supper, and I came down to see if you required anything more than food." Lynge paused. "I heard your question about whether or not the king possessed a disk. Is this what you're looking for?"

Lynge slipped his hand into his waistcoat and produced a small linen bag closed with a drawstring. He opened the bag and pulled out an obsidian disk on a leather cord. At Penhallow's nod, Connor withdrew the pendant he carried on a lanyard around his neck. "The disks are identical, save for their markings," Connor murmured, looking closely at the disk in Lynge's hand.

"How did you come to have the king's disk?" Penhallow asked.

Lynge sighed. "As you've probably guessed, the role of seneschal is as much that of a secret-keeper as it is of an administrator. One of the secrets King Merrill entrusted to me was about the disk. He may not have fully understood its use, but he knew it was significant to the kingdom. He kept it locked up with the ceremonial crown, and I was under strict instructions that, should anything ever befall His Majesty, I should safeguard it and deliver it to his heir. He feared that should something happen to the disk, a calamity would befall the kingdom."

Lynge looked down. "Unfortunately, the king's heir died in the Great Fire. I can't imagine a greater calamity than what has already happened, but I dared not take a chance. I removed the disk from the safe room the night the king died, and I have carried it with me ever since."

"May I see it?" Penhallow asked. When Lynge nodded, Penhallow stood and walked to where the others crowded in the lamplight. Penhallow took the disk and turned it in the light. The obsidian disk had been polished to a high gloss, save for the strange, unreadable markings and thin slits carved into its surface.

The markings they knew to be a very old magic code, and the slits, Connor had discovered, enabled the bearer to read some of the coded markings on Valtyr's maps that showed the places where magic had been at its strongest and weakest. Two of the maps were still known to exist; one of them was carried in a box beneath Connor's cloak. Blaine and his friends had a second map. Two more maps were rumored to have been created by Valtyr, but they had been stolen long ago, and whether or not they still existed was a matter of legend.

"We'll need to see what this disk reveals on your map, and Blaine's," Penhallow said. "But for the moment, let's focus on the task at hand." He reached down and picked up the snippet of blue ribbon that had marked Connor's book.

"It's something of a leap to believe that Quintrel left the ribbon," Penhallow admitted. "Let's indulge it. If so, then he thought the bloodlines to be important. Four lines died out long before the war—Arvo, Hougen, Corrender, and Edenfarr. One more line ended with the Wraith Lord. Merrill's line also ended when his heir was killed. And we know that Blaine McFadden is the last living Lord of the Blood. Pollard was illegitimate, so that line also died out as far as the magic is concerned. That's eight of the Lords of the Blood. But what of the other six?"

Connor flipped ahead a few pages. "There's a list of names here," he said. "And the word 'Mirdalur.'" He paused to count. "Thirteen names exactly." He held it up. "I'd say this accounts for your 'missing' names."

Penhallow looked to Lynge. "Do you know the fates of the old Donderan nobility?"

Lynge sighed. "I know what befell quite a few. Many died in battle, and others were killed when the Great Fire struck. Read me the names, and I'll tell you what I know."

Connor read down through the cramped, handwritten lines. "Lord Radenou."

Lynge met his eyes. Together, they had found Lord Radenou's body the night Meroven's mages sent their deadly onslaught. "Dead. His heirs died in the Great Fire as well."

"Lord Alarian."

"Died of the pox," Treven Lowrey said quietly. "He only had daughters, so his line also had died out. Vedran Pollard murdered Alarian's widow. That's the disk Connor has."

"Lord Rhystorp."

"Died after the Cataclysm. He had no sons."

"Lord Taneral."

"Beheaded in the Battle of Asera-shan. His eldest son died of blood poisoning from a wound gone bad."

"Lord Lorens."

"The last Lord Lorens was *talishte*," Penhallow said, his expression thoughtful. "He went mad and made a habit of slaughtering mortals." He paused. "King Merrill's grandfather used Lorens as another reason to step up his oppression of the *talishte*. Lorens had a very public trial, and the king condemned him to starve to death."

"Then it's certainly possible that Blaine McFadden is indeed the last living Lord of the Blood," Lynge mused.

"What of the disks that belonged to the dead lords?" Connor asked. "The Great Fire was sent by the Meroven mages against the palace and the holdings of the nobles, to wipe out the kingdom's leadership. Knowing the fates of the lords is only half the issue. What became of their disks?"

"If the disks weren't buried or burned when the manors were destroyed, then they've most likely been looted by now," Lynge replied. "Things are bad enough in Castle Reach without the King's Law and the guards to keep order. I've heard that it is even worse in the countryside, where the Great Fire and the magic storms have left people to survive by their wits."

Connor looked to Penhallow. "Do you think Reese or Pollard have the disks?"

Penhallow thought for a moment. "Impossible to know for certain."

"Pollard and Reese became very interested in the research I had done on the old lords," Lowrey said, chagrin clear in his face. "I'm afraid I'm to blame for bringing it to their attention, although I never thought my research was of the slightest importance to anyone outside the university." He sighed. "They followed me to Kaskinnen, Lady Alarian's manor. But she had already entrusted the disk to me, and the servant who escaped swore she died without telling Pollard anything." Lowrey's voice hardened. "I still owe that Son of the Damned One for what he did to her."

"Pollard was descended from the old lords, so might he have heard the legend of the disks from his father," Lynge said.

Penhallow nodded. "Certainly possible, although the real question is, when did it occur to Reese and Pollard that the disks might be part of the way to restore the magic? After all, Reese didn't know that magic would be destroyed."

"Pollard sent an assassin to Edgeland to kill Blaine," Connor said. "But the assassin didn't come after him until it was clear that the Donderath was going to lose the war. Blaine said that King Merrill had made a note on his record forbidding the Velant commander from killing him." He paused, thinking about the timing. "And even so, the assassin didn't seek out Blaine until after I was shipwrecked there, and the colonists found the ghost ship to take them home to Donderath."

"So it might not have been about the magic," Penhallow replied. "Pollard could have sent the assassin because he wanted the McFadden land holdings, or because he truly hated Blaine's family. There had been no ships from Donderath to Velant in several months before the Great Fire. That makes it unlikely that Reese somehow foresaw the collapse of magic."

Lowrey drummed his fingers as he thought. "Thirteen lords, and only one bloodline remains unbroken." He looked toward the shelves and stacks of manuscripts. "If the Knights knew about the importance of the Lords of the Blood, and four of the bloodlines had died out by their time," he mused, looking from Connor to Penhallow, "then might they have secured the disks from those four noble houses for safekeeping?"

Penhallow nodded. "If so, then the disk might have already been removed from Pollard's family's keeping before he learned of it. That idea favors us, because if it was your research, Treven, that brought the old lords to Pollard's and Reese's attention, we might still be a step or two ahead of them."

Lowrey smiled. "I think Connor had a good idea. Let's see if we can find any more bits of blue ribbon. If Quintrel's left us a trail, then we'll make the best use of time trying to pick up his scent."

This time, even Lynge and Geddy joined in the search. Each man took a section of shelves or a stack of crates and carefully checked each item for the telltale blue ribbon.

"I've got one," Lowrey crowed. "There's a ribbon in this old journal."

"Set it aside," Penhallow instructed. "We'll go through everything once we've finished the search."

"I've found another one," Connor said, gingerly handling a rolled parchment tied with a blue ribbon.

They searched in silence for a few candlemarks. Geddy had taken on the crates, and suddenly he let out a whoop of exultation. "Look what I found!" He held up an ornate old key with a blue ribbon tied in one of its looping bows.

Lynge frowned. "If I'm not mistaken, that is a key no one has seen in many years."

"What does it unlock?" Connor asked.

"Someplace no living man has entered in many years," Lynge replied. "The crypt of the Knights of Esthrane."

CHAPTER THIRTEEN

BLAINE MCFADDEN STOOD ON THE ROOF OF Glenreith with a spyglass, peering at the stars. The winter wind whipped his cloak around him and stung his face. By Donderath standards, the night was bitter cold. But six years in Edgeland had given Blaine an entirely new appreciation for truly frigid weather. Despite the light snow that fell and the brisk wind, the night's temperature likely rivaled that of one of the warmest days on Edgeland.

Blaine looked up at the stars, then sank to his knees, studying the map he had secured with four rocks. The shuttered lantern flickered in the wind, only partially protected by the crenellations that rimmed the catwalk around the sloping peaks of the roof.

"What in the name of the gods are you doing up here?" Kestel's voice barely carried above the wind. A cloak blanketed her against the wind, but she, too, had grown accustomed to Edgeland's arctic winters.

"Stargazing," Blaine replied, with a nod toward the map.

Kestel frowned and knelt to have a better look. "What's the connection between the stars and the map?" she asked.

Blaine had turned away to get another sighting with the spyglass. "This would be so much easier with a real telescope," he muttered before turning back toward her. "Remember when we realized that Connor's map of the Continent not only showed the places of strong magic and no magic, but that the old noble houses were aligned in a way that traced the major constellations?"

Kestel nodded. "I remember. Is there a reason you chose to stargaze from up here, when you could be looking out the window in your nice, warm study?"

Blaine chuckled. "For one thing, I can see the full sky. And since I'm not entirely sure what I'm doing, I had hoped to avoid questions until I came up with something convincing."

"If you don't want questions, don't disappear after dinner. The map was gone, you were gone, and so was your cloak. I took it as a challenge and came looking for you."

"Just as well, I could use a fresh perspective," Blaine said, and his breath clouded in the cold air. "Take a look at what I've marked on the map."

Kestel knelt next to the map, brushing away a few flakes of snow, and settling herself into the folds of her voluminous cloak. "I see you've made do with a standard map of the kingdom," she noted.

Blaine grimaced. "It should serve the purpose. I've marked the approximate position of the oldest manor houses, the ones that would have belonged to the original Lords of the Blood, and the other key points I could remember from Connor's map."

"Including Mirdalur," Kestel noted.

"And I've done my best to mark the groupings that corresponded to the constellations," Blaine said, still turning his spyglass on the night sky.

Kestel shifted, looking up to follow Blaine's focus on the stars above. "So far, it's all information we already knew. Why bother?"

Blaine turned from the sky and knelt down, marking the map with a piece of graphite. "Because there are other points that correspond with the constellations that don't match up with the original manors."

He turned to Kestel. "What if...there were null places and places of power in addition to the manors, places that the mages used for themselves, or even hidden places that they didn't want other people to know about?" He sighed. "They're likely marked on Connor's map, but you wouldn't have had a reason to mark them on the copy you made, since you were looking for the major houses."

She looked at the map in the flickering glow of the lantern. "You're gambling that the relationship works in reverse, that you can predict where those spots would be by the constellations, instead of just drawing lines between sites that already existed and creating a connection to the stars."

Blaine nodded. "We know the stars are sacred to the gods, and that the constellations have power. That's how astrologers read the will of the gods and predict the future. And all the stories of the gods begin with 'As above, so below.' What if that wasn't just a poetic flourish?" he asked, excitement bringing a flush to his cheeks despite the chill.

Kestel traced the patterns with her finger gliding just above the surface of the map. "If you're right...And you're making some big guesses here—"

"I know."

"Then if this is us, here at Glenreith, and this is Mirdalur, there should be another place of power here," she said, letting her finger hover above the mark Blaine had just made.

He nodded. "That would be the closest spot, and the easiest to verify. There could be other places of power here, and here," he said, pointing to two other marks. "Maybe more." He paused.

"Up till now, we've been so focused on bringing back the magic that we've only looked at the places of power," he said, sitting back on his haunches. "But Connor said that when the Great Fire struck, he thought Penhallow had gone to a null place, somewhere he thought the magic might not be able to strike as hard." He looked up, meeting her gaze excitedly.

"Connor and Penhallow thought that Vigus Quintrel was important." A smile crept over Blaine's face as he saw Kestel catching on. "Now Quintrel's gone missing. What if he's gone to one of the null places?"

Kestel shivered as the wind rippled her cloak. "The problem is, there could be dozens of places of power and null places spread across entire kingdoms, maybe the whole Continent. We could spend a lifetime trying to find them all."

Blaine nodded. "And like the spot we found on Edgeland, most of them are probably just shrines if they focus power, or areas people go out of their way to avoid if they're the null places. But what if the places aren't all equal? What if some are stronger than others? I figure there was a reason the old lords chose Mirdalur for the working that raised the magic. Maybe it was one of the especially strong places."

Kestel studied the map carefully. "Mirdalur also was struck particularly hard when the Meroven mages sent the Great Fire. If there are places where the power is stronger, they may also have been damaged worse by the Cataclysm."

Blaine sighed. He retracted the spyglass and tucked it into a pouch on his belt, then reached past Kestel to roll up the map and put it safely beneath his cloak. Blaine helped Kestel to her feet and then bent down to retrieve the lantern. "We came back for a purpose, and sitting here at Glenreith won't bring back the magic. You're right—we could go out to these spots and find nothing. But without knowing where to find Vigus Quintrel, and without Penhallow or Connor to give us direction, it's the best guess I can make, given what we've got to go on."

Kestel's eyes sparkled. "You'll need a search party, one that is small enough to slip through Pollard's net, but able to defend itself. Count me in."

Blaine chuckled. "I had a feeling you'd want to come. I was thinking Piran and Verran should also go with us."

"What about the others?"

Blaine held the door to the access stairs that wound from the roof down the servants' staircase to the lower floors of the manor house. He let Kestel step inside first. His lantern illuminated the narrow, twisting stairs. "Dawe's been busy in the forge. He wants to create some new weapons for us. I have the feeling we're going to need them, so I'd like to give him the chance to make progress."

"Won't Niklas think we should have a regiment of soldiers with us?" Kestel teased, but Blaine could hear the concern beneath her tone.

"He'd probably prefer we take extra guards, but I'm not sure having more people with us made us any safer when we went to Mirdalur," Blaine replied. "If anything, it slowed us down, made us more noticeable. I'm hoping Geir can scout for us and join us after dark. If we're lucky, we might even find an inn or a tavern where we can get shelter. A couple of these spots will require more travel than we can finish in one day."

They reached the landing for the main floor, and Kestel opened the door to let them into the parlor at the end of the corridor. Blaine thought how quiet Glenreith had become.

When he was growing up, it seemed the house was bustling with servants night and day. Now, the house seemed strangely empty.

"Niklas is going to have his hands full getting his men back on their feet and trying to provision them," Blaine said, pulling himself out of his memories. "If this does turn out to be for naught, I'll feel a little better if we haven't wasted his time as well as ours."

"What about your brother?" Kestel asked. She had thrown back the hood of her cloak, and her red hair spilled over her shoulders. As she shrugged out of the heavy coat, Blaine saw that her gown was another of Mari's everyday dresses, a tan, woolen dress without ornamentation, not meant for social occasions. Still, it flattered her.

"Niklas can handle Carr," Blaine replied, a touch of bitterness coloring his voice.

Kestel studied his face. "I'm sorry your reunion with Carr didn't go well."

Blaine sighed. "At least Mari and Judith are happy to see me." He looked away. "I'm sorry Carr was rude to you. His comments were unforgivable."

Kestel set aside her cloak. "It was sweet of you to defend me. But I'm accustomed to the fact that Carr's opinion is that of the nobility, including my former patrons."

"Yeah, well, it's not my opinion," Blaine replied. Kestel's face was flushed from being outside, and her eyes were alight. As simple as the borrowed dress was, it looked good on her. Despite having just returned from the cold, Blaine felt uncomfortably warm, acutely aware that Kestel was standing close enough to touch.

How did leaving Edgeland change everything? he wondered. *Kestel's one of my best friends. If she were interested in being more, she certainly would know how to indicate it. I don't want to spoil what we've already got. And besides,* Blaine thought, *I'm bad luck. The last two women I loved ended up dead. I'm a penniless, outcast lord with powerful enemies. Kestel could do much better than me.*

Blaine turned away and crossed the room to pour them both glasses of brandy. He brought one to Kestel. "Have some. It'll warm you up." She accepted the glass, and he took a sip from his drink. "I swore that nothing would ever seem cold again after Edgeland. I guess it doesn't work like that."

Kestel chuckled and sank into one of the armchairs. "So, when do we leave to test your theory?"

"Tomorrow," Blaine replied, leaning against the mantel of the fireplace. "We'll be heading away from Castle Reach and away from where Geir spotted Pollard's troops. After all, they've got no reason to think we'd head for a village at the foothills of the mountains. We'll ride out, have a look around, and come home."

Kestel toyed with the rim of her glass. "Without magic, how will we be able to sense whether the place is null or strong?"

Blaine grimaced. "That's where it's an imperfect theory. I'm hoping we'll turn up some kind of evidence one way or the other. The question is, if Vigus Quintrel expected something like the Great Fire to happen, would he go to a place of power and hope the magic was strong enough to protect him, or hide in a null place?" He shrugged. "Let's try going to a null place and put the theory to the test. Maybe someone there will know something about Quintrel or about the magic."

"On the other hand," Kestel replied, with a pause as she sipped the brandy, "Mirdalur was a place of power. If there's another way to bring back the magic, then odds are it will be at another place of power. Quintrel might have thought the same.

Or he might have taken refuge at a null place until after the Great Fire and moved his exiles to a place of power later."

Blaine nodded. "And it's a good bet that all places of power were hit during the Meroven attack. So I wonder, if there was another ritual space we can still access, has it been completely destroyed?"

Kestel withdrew a small book from a pouch beneath her cloak. "I've been reading that book Arin Grimur gave us, back in Edgeland."

"Did you find anything useful?" Blaine asked.

Kestel rifled through the pages. "I swear, mages seem incapable of saying anything straight out. Everything is in rhymes and riddles, and some pages can't be read at all without knowing their secret code. But from what I can make out, the mages spent a good bit of their time and energy on rituals to thank the gods for the magic." She looked up at Blaine. "Suppose those rituals weren't really for the gods. Could they have been shoring up the magic, even before the war with Meroven?"

"It's possible," Blaine conceded. "And if they had been doing those rituals for long enough, they might not understand the real reason."

Kestel fluffed her skirt as she shifted in her chair. "What if the magic really is gone for good, Mick?" She met his gaze, and her green eyes were worried. "I mean, what if it can't be restored?"

Blaine sighed. "Penhallow and Grimur have lived for centuries, and they both believe it can be restored. And if Pentreath Reese didn't think we had a shot at bringing the magic back, why would he send Pollard after me?"

Kestel looked away, watching the flames dance in the fireplace. "What if you can't do it? Can we survive?"

Blaine walked away from the fireplace to sit in a wing chair across from Kestel. For a moment, he watched the flames in silence. "Without the small magics, I imagine we could learn to get along. It would be harder." He frowned as he thought.

"Then again, farmers used their magic to keep crops from rotting after a rain, or to heal a sick cow," he said. "Healers depended on their magic. Maybe we'd find or remember a way to do those things without magic, but it would take a while. And in the meantime, there would be a price to pay."

"We're already paying a price," Kestel said. "You've heard Niklas tell about strange beasts that came from the storms, and we've seen the madness for ourselves."

"Without magic of our own, there's no way to limit the storms," Blaine agreed. "They're dangerous, and they seem to be getting stronger." He sighed. "And without magic, mortals can't hold their own against men like Pentreath Reese."

"Then we'd better hope that we can track down Quintrel," Kestel replied. She rose from her seat and stretched. "I'd best go back to my room and pack for our outing. Just let me know when you and Piran and Verran want to get going in the morning, and I'll be ready."

"Something's wrong." Piran reined in his horse and stood in his stirrups, scanning the horizon.

"See anything?" Blaine asked, turning in his saddle to look.

Several candlemarks had passed since they left Glenreith. It was mid-morning, and they had left the main road behind them more than a candlemark ago, journeying forward on a narrow road that seemed more farm trail than byway. Their roads had led them steadily uphill, into the foothills of the Belhovan Mountains, though the sharp, rocky peaks were still many leagues away.

"The air feels...thick," Kestel remarked, looking around worriedly. "Let's get going. I don't like this place."

"Doesn't look as if anyone else has been through here in a while, at least not since the snow fell," Verran observed, looking ahead of them at the road with its unbroken covering. "The only things we've seen all day are some wild dogs and goats." He looked out across the open field.

"Kestel's right, let's get out of here," Blaine muttered. But before he could shift in his saddle, a dark line on the horizon caught his eye.

"Look there," he said, pointing. Already the dark line had grown closer, and it undulated as it moved.

"If that's a magic storm, we've got nowhere to hide," Piran replied. "We'll have to outride it. Move!"

They spurred their horses forward, slowed by the heavy snow. The darkness on the horizon appeared to be moving on an intersect course with the road. The goats in the field raised their heads, and one of them bleated an alarm that was taken up by the rest of the herd. Terrified, the goats ran in the opposite direction of the storm, nearly getting themselves trampled as they ran across the road dodging the horses and sliding on the slippery snow.

Blaine eyed the growing darkness, which still seemed to head directly for the road. "The goats have the right idea!" he shouted. "Leave the road. If we ride at an angle, we might outrun the storm."

Blaine urged his horse on, galloping across the fields. It was reckless to ride at full speed across unknown ground— his horse could easily step into a hole and break a leg. But the ground held solid, frozen by the bitter cold, and Blaine took comfort in the fact that with the Great Fire, the fields were unlikely to have been turned this season. Still, he held on to his reins tightly and gripped his horse with his legs to keep his seat.

On the horizon, Blaine could see the rooftops of a village. He hoped it was Riker's Ferry, the small hamlet that should be a null zone if his theory was correct. "Ride for the village!" Blaine shouted. "If I'm right, if it really is a null place, the storm won't follow us."

They easily outrode the goats, thundering across the open fields. Blaine could feel the nearness of the magic storm as his head began to throb.

"It's gaining on us," Verran called, fear in his voice.

Blaine spared a glance over his shoulder. The storm moved like a billowing curtain, sweeping across the land, close enough that its power pulled the snow up into it. As the storm grew closer, they could see the air sparkle and glow as the wild *visithara* magic pulsed. A growing hum filled the air, rising in pitch as the magic storm grew closer, and Blaine knew from the storms he had survived that the hum would grow to an earsplitting screech. Blaine fought to retain control as his horse began to panic.

Kestel and Verran had leaned over far enough that they were gripping their horses' manes. Both of them rode as if they were just trying to hang on, almost completely at the mercy of their horses. Piran's expression was grim.

"Look out!" Piran yelled. "There's another one!"

Blaine looked up. A shining ribbon of light hung in midair, dangerous and terrible in its beauty. Where the storm to their right had already touched down and carried with it snow and debris, the new storm had yet to descend. Worse, it was heading straight for them and moving fast.

"Veer!" Blaine shouted, angling his horse toward the open space between the two approaching storms. The pounding in his head was amplified by the thud of his horse's hooves, and his vision blurred with the pain.

Behind him, Blaine heard frantic squeals from the herd of goats, which were running, wide-eyed in terror, stumbling and staggering across the snowy ground. The first storm was closing in on the goats, and as the wild magic reached the slowest animal in the herd, the goat was lifted off its feet to hang suspended in air for an instant, its hooves still pawing frantically for traction. There was a wet *pop* and the goat exploded, sending a gruesome spray of blood, flesh, and entrails over the rest of the herd, which scattered. The storm moved forward relentlessly, and one by one, the hapless goats were pulled into the maelstrom, screaming their fear. Blood seemed to feed the wild magic, and the color of the storm shifted, growing red with the gore of the slaughtered goats. Even the smell of the storm changed. It had first smelled like the tang in the air after a nearby lightning strike—now it was the metallic scent of blood.

Blaine shot a worried glance toward Verran and Kestel. Kestel had grown pale, and Blaine could see that she grasped the mane with balled fists. Verran looked as if he was fighting for consciousness, hanging on for his life. Piran, out in front, was sitting tall, shoulders back, defying the storm. Blaine came up behind Verran and Kestel, unwilling to allow them to take up the rear, and smacked the rumps of their horses to urge them forward, even as the storms thundered closer.

The ground behind Blaine began to shimmer, and he shivered as he recalled stories that amid such storms men had fallen into mere mud puddles, never to be seen again. He dug his heels into his horse's ribs, but the frightened beast needed no urging to run for its life.

The air around them glowed, full of luminous, tiny particles. Blaine's lungs strained for breath, and the gasps he took felt thin, depleted. His vision tinged with red as he struggled for breath. His chest burned, lungs ached, and his heart thumped. Blaine felt as if he could sense the movement of the blood through his veins, as if the blood itself were on fire, and as if everything—blood, breath, and will—was gradually being pulled into the dark, roaring maw behind them.

The village was in sight and growing closer with every hoof-beat. Whether the villagers knew of the storm or were just going about their business, no one was in sight, with the doors shut and the windows shuttered. A low stone wall separated the village from the fields beyond.

The two storms closed in on each other. The hum had become a shriek, loud enough that Blaine could feel it reverberating in his bones, piercing enough that it forced a groan. With one final, desperate burst of speed, Blaine's horse shot forward just as the two storms collided.

Sure they were all about to die, Blaine sent his horse leaping over the stone wall, and it felt to him as if they were pushed by a wave of sound and light.

Blaine reeled, barely clinging to consciousness. His vision was clouding, and his head hurt as if it might explode. Dimly he realized that it had grown easier to breathe. Their horses came to a halt, and both Kestel and Verran tumbled from their saddles. Blaine kept enough presence of mind to control his descent, but his knees gave out when he reached the ground and he fell to the snow. As if from far away, Blaine could hear Piran shouting his name, but then the darkness closed in and he heard nothing more.

CHAPTER FOURTEEN

I HATE CRYPTS." CONNOR TRUDGED BEHIND LYNGE and Penhallow while Geddy and Lowrey brought up the rear of the small procession. Geddy and Connor carried packs on their backs filled with supplies. Geddy, who was holding a lantern, fell a step behind and let Lowrey walk beside Connor.

"You're missing the point, lad," Lowrey said in a voice tinged with wonder. "I'm sure that, before the magic died, these crypts were fairly quivering with power. Preservation spells. Memory spells to assure that descendents didn't forget an ancestor's legacy. Even binding spells, I'd wager, on a corpse or two someone wanted to make damn sure stayed buried." He sounded as if he had just been invited on a treasure hunt, and for once, academic enthusiasm triumphed over his usual curmudgeonly outlook.

"It's still full of dead people," Connor argued, unwilling to be distracted and perversely committed to sulking. "Not even living dead people, like when we were in Penhallow's hiding place. That was a nice crypt, more like a parlor. This is just a tomb."

"Would it cheer you up to know that for several hundred

years, the only ones permitted to step foot in these crypts were the priests and priestesses of the gods, the seneschal, and the direct descendants of the crown?" Lynge said, but his placating tone barely hid a chuckle.

Connor knew he was being unreasonable, but he wasn't ready to give in. He had nearly been killed in Penhallow's underground hiding place when Reese and his *talishte* had attacked and the roof had caved in. Twice he had run for his life from monsters in the dark through narrow, twisting tunnels belowground. The harrowing escape from Voss's fortress via the underground river was still fresh in his mind. "Not really," he grumbled.

Despite himself, Connor was impressed by the grandeur of the royal necropolis. In the bedrock beneath Quillarth Castle, artisans had gone to considerable work to sculpt an entire city for the dead. Façades of the oldest buildings in Castle Reach had been meticulously duplicated, as had Quillarth Castle itself. The detailed stone models looked to be scale models of the originals.

"It's said that inside the models, everything is just as it was in their full-size counterparts," Lynge continued, taking Connor's mood in stride.

Connor could not help but be intrigued as he looked around. Dozens of buildings were represented, and at the far edge, he could hear running water and he glimpsed a quayside much like the Castle Reach harbor.

"I don't understand," he protested. "If the kings believed that the dead are taken to the Sea of Souls, why bother?"

Penhallow chuckled. "The crown forces a king to sacrifice his conscience many times over," he replied. "Even the best king may fear such sacrifices doom him to wander the Unseen Realms. This city of the dead, and others like it, provided a bit of insurance, just in case the king did not merit the gods' favor in the afterlife."

The chamber with the scale model of Quillarth Castle and Castle Reach opened into another equally large chamber. The room was easily as large as the castle's huge dining hall, but instead of a table that could seat one hundred guests, row upon row of catafalques stretched from one end of the room to the other.

"Behold: the final resting place of the kings of Donderath," Penhallow said in a quiet voice.

Carved, life-sized figures lay atop granite biers with heavy, engraved pediments. In the row closest to the doorway was a catafalque that did not appear to be shrouded by the cobwebs and dust of the centuries. Connor caught his breath as he recognized the figure atop the bier. King Merrill lay as if asleep, his hands on his chest intertwined above a carved sword, his eyes closed in rest.

"Merrill commissioned his bier several years ago," Lynge said sadly. "We implored him to have the sculptor carve an image of him as an old man, but Merrill insisted it look as he did at the time." He sighed. "Who knows? Perhaps the king or his seer had a premonition. Geddy and I prepared the king for burial and brought him down here the day after the Great Fire."

"No funeral?" Connor asked, trying to hide his shock.

Lynge shook his head, and from the expression on his face, Connor guessed that the seneschal was reliving the memory. "Our world had burned. Parts of the castle and much of the city were still afire. Most people had fled the castle. Those who didn't were far too busy digging out the survivors and finding corpses amid the rubble to bother with a funeral or having the king lie in state. At least the king had a proper burial. We did our best by those who perished, but many were buried in a common grave."

Connor caught back a gasp thinking of Lord Garnoc. Lynge seemed to guess his thoughts. "Your master was one of the few we were able to bury with honor. His family had served Donderath's kings for generations, and for that, Lord Garnoc could be buried in one of the sections of the crypt reserved for favored nobility," Lynge said.

"When Meroven's mages struck the great houses, it meant there was little chance anyone would reclaim the bodies of the dead lords who were at court. The survivors had other priorities and no means to bring home the bodies, even if they wanted to," Lynge added sadly. He drew a deep breath and squared his shoulders, lifting his head. "It's time to move on."

Three new tunnels opened off the catafalque chamber, requiring them to thread their way among the biers. Connor glanced at the figures as he passed them, awed by the presence of the kings and queens of long ago. Many of the faces he recognized from statues, paintings, or tapestries that had graced the castle's walls. So many of these men and women had loomed larger than life, commemorated long after their deaths for their valor in battle, their wise rule, or their cunning defeat of adversaries. Just as many were remembered more for their dark deeds and oppression.

He glanced toward Penhallow, whose expression was pensive. *How many of these kings has Penhallow served in his long lifetime?* Connor wondered. *How many of the men in these chambers did Penhallow know, either as a mortal or as* talishte? *Does immortality remove the sting of loss?* Given the look on Penhallow's face, Connor doubted it.

"What's down those other tunnels?" Connor asked.

Lynge answered without turning. "One of the corridors holds the bodies of the royal consorts and their families. The second corridor has crypts for the nobility. Warriors of great valor are buried in vaults down the third corridor."

Lynge led them on, holding his lantern aloft to light the way down the center corridor. More tunnels opened off of their corridor, and Connor hoped with all his might that Lynge would be able to remember the way out.

Out of the corner of his eye, Connor caught a glimpse of movement. Quillarth Castle's age meant that many ghosts haunted its corridors. Connor had encountered several of the spirits that frequented the castle. Disembodied voices, sudden cold spots, doors or cabinets that opened or closed on their own, even moving shadows were not unusual. Once, Connor had glimpsed someone standing behind him in a mirror, only to find the room empty when he turned.

"It's just the ghosts, lad," Lowrey said. "Nothing to fear."

Connor looked at him askance. "I'm not so sure of that."

"When a building's this old, it's not surprising a number of souls don't want to leave when it's their time," Lowrey replied. "And a place like this, a king's castle, with all the important doings that have gone on here: the war councils, the executions, the betrayals and love affairs," he said with a shrug. "Well, you can see why some spirits might not be in a hurry to go elsewhere."

Another movement caught Connor's attention. It was as if he glimpsed the edge of someone's long robe, or the last bit of a passing shadow. He shivered. "Have you ever had one try to get inside your skin?"

Lowrey frowned. "What's that? How do you mean?"

Connor drew a long breath before speaking. He had never told anyone about his experience, not even his former master,

Lord Garnoc. *Will the others think me mad?* He wondered. *No madder, perhaps, than the tales I've told thus far, of ribbons of light descending from the sky to burn the world, or of vampires at war over whether to restore magic. I can hardly see where one more tale can hurt.*

"I was coming back late one night from doing an errand for Lord Garnoc," Connor began, casting caution aside. "I was alone in one of the lower corridors. I saw a man farther down the corridor, holding up a hand and signaling for me to stop." Connor paused and stole a glance at Lowrey, to see if the mage-scholar was laughing at him. To his surprise, Lowrey was listening intently.

"Go on," Lowrey urged.

Connor cleared his throat, surprised to have his story taken seriously. "I called out to the man. He started to move toward me, and all of a sudden, I felt him overtake me, as if he were trying to get beneath my skin." He shuddered. "Memories that weren't my own flooded over me. I felt as if, for a moment, I had become someone different." He paused. "I was terrified, and— odd as it sounds—I flung the ghost away from me, and I ran."

Connor took a deep breath. Even now, the memory was unsettling. "He just…vanished. There was nowhere for him to have gone that I couldn't have seen him. But I swear, he looked as solid as you or me when he was coming toward me."

Lowrey peered over his spectacles at Connor. "You're a medium."

Connor's eyes widened. "A what?"

"There's something about you that attracts ghosts and allows them to take you over."

"You mean, possess me?" Connor asked, horrified.

Lowrey nodded. "Aye, in a manner of speaking. It's not common, for all that the tavern charlatans seem to be able to talk to anyone's dead husband or brother or son for the price of an ale." He paused. "Interesting."

"Interesting?" Connor yelped. "Damn terrifying if you ask me. Do you mean to tell me that ghost might not have let go of me?"

Lowrey shrugged. "No. You may not know how you did it, but you obviously had some natural protection that let you break free. Interesting thing about mediums: Unlike necromancers, you didn't lose your abilities when the magic died."

"What's the difference? I don't have magic," Connor asked, interested despite himself.

"Mediums aren't thought to have true magic, not in the way a necromancer does," Penhallow mused. "I've heard it said that a medium's ability to interact with the dead is similar to the power of our *kruvgaldur*—something intrinsic to our being, not external magic. Mediums usually don't initiate the contact with a ghost."

Penhallow eyed Connor as if seeing him for the first time. "Necromancers can actually raise the dead, bind spirits to their will. Lowrey here can probably explain it better, but I suspect they're two very different abilities."

Lowrey sighed. "Unfortunately, mediums often bear the risk without the power. It's rare for a necromancer to be possessed against his will, but mediums are always at risk. You'll have to be on your guard, m'boy. There are more ghosts than usual since the Great Fire."

Connor drew a deep breath. "I thought I was just nervous, but I keep seeing things down here just out of the corner of my eye."

Lowrey's expression became serious. "You're nervous, all right," he replied. "But that's not why you're seeing things. Kings and queens, as well as powerful warriors and ambitious members of the court, are buried here. Most had secrets they took to the grave with them—and beyond. Secrets, lies, treachery, and forbidden love produce strong emotions. They don't fade with death. I have no doubt you've glimpsed some spirits. Stay sharp."

The corridor widened and opened into a large circular room. Like spokes from a wheel, five corridors led away from the central chamber. In the center of the chamber floor was a large mosaic made of inlaid stone, gems, and bits of gold and silver. It glittered even by the lantern's glow, and Connor imagined that the mosaic would have been breathtaking if the torches on the walls had been lit.

The mosaic was a depiction of Esthrane and her eldest child, the minor god Veo the Trickster. Esthrane stood with arms upraised and stretched far apart, her feet planted wide and solid on the ground. Veo sat at Esthrane's feet, represented as a toddler with a preternaturally wise and knowing expression. A nimbus glowed around Esthrane's hands and feet, and a light encircled Veo's head, suggesting the constellation that bore the goddess's name. It was no accident, Connor was sure, that each of the corridors aligned with one of the points in the mosaic.

The chamber's walls also had floor-to-ceiling mosaics between the corridor openings. Each mosaic showed a scene from stories about the goddess. As with the floor mosaic, the panels were crafted from precious and semiprecious stones and joined with seams of gold and silver. One scene showed the handfasting between Esthrane and Charrot, with a cord of lightning bolts encircling their joined hands to form a permanent union. In the background, Torven watched the marriage with a jealous expression. A second panel showed Torven enticing Charrot from Esthrane's bower with gifts of gems and gold, as an angry Esthrane looked on.

The third and fourth panels depicted two of the many wars between the gods. In the third panel, those lesser gods loyal to Torven led an assault on Esthrane's palace amid the clouds of the gods. Many died, both among the demigods and on the world below, as the devoted followers of Torven and Esthrane battled in the names of their patrons. Torven's expression was triumphant as Esthrane's forces fled in retreat.

In the fourth panel, the situation was reversed. Esthrane, leading a large army of lesser gods and mortal warriors, laid siege to Torven's fortified castle on the shore of the Sea of Souls. Rivers of blood flowed from the castle to the sea. Esthrane's army slew its opponents, and the goddess was shown sending the souls of her enemies into the obsidian depths of the Unseen Realm.

In the fifth panel, Charrot—the High God himself—descended from the sun to broker a truce between his warring consorts. Yet even as Charrot stood hand in hand with Torven and Esthrane, it took only one look at the faces of his consorts to know that this battle would not be their last. Around the feet of the gods and goddesses, the lesser gods and mortals continued to struggle, and standing behind Esthrane, just barely visible in the shadows, stood a cluster of figures with alabaster faces, the *talishte*, and with them, clad in blue and gold, the Knights of Esthrane, with both mortal and *talishte* mage-warriors.

The entrance to each corridor was carved with figures and symbols, so that their archways were both works of art and icons depicting the legends of the gods. "This was hallowed ground for the Knights of Esthrane," Penhallow said quietly. "Strangers did not venture here, on penalty of death."

"It seems odd they had to come through the crypts," Connor replied.

"Remember what was said about secret entrances?" Lowrey said, turning away from the mosaic he had been eyeing. "That applied to more than just their library. The Knights always had secret escape routes, and it was rumored that they had multiple secret passages, some of which even the king did not know about. When King Merrill's grandfather betrayed the Knights, those few from the castle who survived were the ones who could reach their hidden passageways in time."

Lynge made a circuit of the room, illuminating the mosaics. Finally, Lynge led them down one of the corridors. Along the walls were several doors made of heavy, dark wood with ornate carvings, bound with iron, secured with huge iron locks.

Lynge stopped in front of Penhallow and withdrew the key. "Your key should fit one of the locks in this corridor," Lynge said.

Penhallow took the key from Lynge and held it up in the lantern's light. Its top had been molded with a scene of figures and images. Penhallow studied the iron key, then slowly walked along the corridor, trying to determine where the scene on the key best matched the door and its adjacent murals.

Finally, he stopped in front of one of the doors and inserted the key into the lock. The old lock stuck for a moment, and its heavy mechanism groaned as Penhallow turned the key. Finally, the tumblers thudded open. Penhallow took hold of the door's ring and pulled. Connor could see that, even with Penhallow's *talishte* strength, the door was difficult to budge. It yielded, creaking open on iron hinges, revealing darkness. Cold air heavy with a dank, musty scent filled the chamber.

"I'm guessing we have to go in there," Connor muttered.

"That door hasn't opened in a very long time," Lowrey replied. "I don't think anything is waiting to jump out at you."

"Nothing living, anyhow," Connor murmured.

Lynge held up the lantern and was the first to step into the room. "It's a crypt," he called over his shoulder. "There's a catafalque in here."

They followed Lynge into the room. The catafalque sat in the center of the room. Against one side was a large stone table that looked as if it might have functioned as an altar. The room was round, and on its walls was a mural. Unlike the elaborate mosaic in the prior chamber, this mural had been done as a fresco, and in places, time and decay had blurred some of the images or cracked through the stucco base. Still, as Lynge and Geddy held their lanterns aloft, enough of the mural survived to make out the story.

"It's the history of the Knights of Esthrane," Lowrey said, excitement coloring his words. "It picks up from where the mosaic ended, with Esthrane choosing the Knights to keep Torven's forces in line."

The images unfolded from the left of the doorway through which they had entered. In the first scene, Esthrane conveyed her charge to a broad-shouldered warrior with long, brown hair and a dark beard. Beside Esthrane stood a burly man wearing a crown who bestowed both a charter and a sword on the warrior. Various battles made up the bulk of the other images, depicting triumphs over Torven's forces or slaughters at the hands of the Knights' foes.

Connor paused as he stared at the last panel to the right of the door where they had entered. Though space remained for another mural, the stucco was blank.

"They never finished the mural," Connor murmured.

"Or the king's loyalists had the images plastered over," Penhallow replied, a note of bitterness in his voice.

There was a clatter behind them, and they looked up to see Geddy emptying his pack onto the stone table. From it, he withdrew several lanterns, which he lit. After the long trek through darkened tunnels, Connor had to squint as his eyes adjusted to the light. He noticed a movement outside the door, but when he looked again, there was nothing.

Connor grabbed a lantern and leaned out of the doorway.

"What's wrong?" Lynge asked.

Connor's lantern illuminated the corridor. It was empty. With a sigh, he moved back into the room. "Nothing. Thought I saw something. I was wrong."

Lowrey gave him a suspicious glance, but Connor refused to meet the mage's gaze. Connor moved back toward the middle of the room, where everyone's attention was focused on the bier.

The catafalque in the center of the chamber was less ornate than those they had seen in the Crypt of the Ancient Kings. The pediments and bier were simple, with a few inscriptions but no decorative carving. Atop the bier lay a figure of a warrior, forever clad in his battle armor, helmetless but surrounded, even in death, by depictions of the weapons he favored in life.

"This is the tomb of Torsten Almstedt," Lynge said quietly. "He was the founder of the Knights of Esthrane. The Knights who fell in battle are also buried here."

"Did Almstedt live to see the Knights betrayed?" Connor asked.

Penhallow shook his head. "Almstedt was killed in battle before the Knights were disbanded. As the founder of the Order, his tomb was a shrine for the Knights. When the Order was disbanded and the surviving Knights fled for their lives, I have heard it said that one of their keenest losses was that they could no longer tend the crypts of their brothers-at-arms entombed below the castle."

Connor moved closer, studying the warrior's statue. He had expected to see the image of a man killed in his prime. Instead, this warrior was in his middle years, with a face that showed dignity and intelligence. A shield was carved next to the man's legs, and as Connor blew away the dust, he realized that the surface of the shield was covered with both recognizable heraldic images and with more subtle symbols that were startlingly familiar.

"Bring the light over here!" he said, bending closer for a better look.

"What did you find?" Lowrey asked, crowding closer.

Connor withdrew the obsidian pendant from beneath his shirt. "Look," he said, holding the pendant close to the shield. It was clear that several of the symbols carved into the surface of the pendant matched those on the Knight's shield.

Lowrey came around to peer down at the shield and its markings. "Those are definitely mage symbols," he said. "Not surprising, given the Knights' abilities as mage-warriors."

"So why did Quintrel want us to find this chamber?" Penhallow asked.

Connor went to the table where Geddy had laid out his lanterns and set down his own pack. "I guess I'm going to have to see if anything triggers one of Quintrel's messages here," he said, distaste clear in his voice. "Gods, I hate this part of it."

Connor took a deep breath to still his apprehension, then reached into his pack and withdrew the parchments and journals they had found marked with blue ribbons in the Knights' library. He let his hand hover over each of the items, a journal, a rolled parchment, and an old bound manuscript. The worn leather cover of the journal drew his attention, and bracing himself, he picked up the journal and held it in both hands, turning the yellowed pages to where the blue ribbon marked a spot. The ribbon had not triggered memories when he had read the journal before, but Connor wondered if this new location would have a different effect.

As soon as he touched the ribbon, Connor swayed on his feet as a new memory flooded him. "The bravest Knight guards more than bones. The markers of blood ties forever severed are shielded from prying eyes. Show one marker to the eternal guard to remove the shield."

With a jolt, Connor came back to himself. This time he remembered what he had said, and he wondered if the triggering of Quintrel's hidden memories would get easier with each clue uncovered. "What does it mean, 'the eternal guard'?" he asked, still feeling a little shaky.

The temperature in the crypt plummeted, and Connor could see his breath misting. A blue-green glow began to swirl next to the catafalque, forcing Penhallow and the others to back away from the bier. As they watched, the glow took shape until Almstedt's image became clearly recognizable. The ghost wore the same armor as the carved figure atop the catafalque, but his sword was drawn and he carried no shield. His stance conveyed a challenge, and his gaze was stern.

The spectral figure held up one arm, displaying an outstretched palm to signal that they keep their distance. As they watched, Almstedt's ghostly gaze swept over them, and he turned his hand palm up.

"By the gods!" Geddy croaked from where he had backed up against the wall of the crypt. "What does he want from us?"

"Show him your disk, Connor," Penhallow said. His voice was steady, though Connor could see from Penhallow's posture that he was ready should danger arise. "I believe that's the 'marker' Quintrel mentioned. If I'm not mistaken, Almstedt's ghost is guarding the four disks we're looking for."

"We're not going to have to open the coffin, are we?" Geddy's voice rose an octave. "I didn't sign on for looting coffins!"

"Hush," Lynge admonished, though Connor could see that the seneschal had blanched at the sight of the ghost.

Mustering his courage, Connor withdrew the obsidian disk from beneath his tunic and slipped the leather strap over his head. He stepped forward, offering the disk on his outstretched hand, forcing himself to move closer.

Connor's hand shook as he felt the ice-cold touch of Almstedt's ghost. Almstedt passed his hand over the disk, then turned and laid his hand on the carved shield atop the catafalque and pointed to a raised decoration. He looked to Connor as if awaiting a response. Connor stepped forward hesitantly and pushed on the embellishment.

The stone shield began to move, slowly grinding open to reveal a small compartment beneath it. Almstedt pointed to the compartment, meeting Connor's gaze with an expression that communicated his imperative.

Swallowing hard, Connor moved around the catafalque, avoiding the ghost, and grimaced as he reached into the dark compartment. He relaxed as his hand gripped four smooth obsidian disks and he withdrew them from their hiding place. Almstedt's expression softened to express his approval, and the stone shield slowly moved back into place. But to Connor's surprise, the ghost did not vanish once Connor found the disks. Instead, Almstedt pointed to the rolled parchment on the desk.

"I think he wants you to have a look at that piece of parchment," Lynge said quietly.

Heart thudding, Connor brought the disks back to the table and laid them to one side, returning his own disk to its place around his neck. Swallowing his uneasiness, he loosened the blue ribbon that bound the old parchment and spread it flat.

"It's a map of the stars," Lynge murmured.

Penhallow shook his head. "More than that. It's part of a set of coordinates to find a particular place. Look," he said, pointing. "There's a longitude, but no latitude, and a month and day. I'm betting that on that date, if the sky overhead matches that map, you're where you're supposed to be."

"Yeah, but where is that, and why would we want to be there?" Connor muttered.

Connor felt a lurch as Quintrel's hidden memory surged to the front of his consciousness.

"Hidden allies will arise. Turn to the exiles, for you will find them among the dead men's bones."

At that, Almstedt's revenant began to fade, his form blurring until it was nothing but a shimmering light, and then vanished altogether.

"Exiles again," Connor said. "First, I'm told to seek the 'exiled man.' Now, more exiles. Do you think he means the convicts in Velant?"

Penhallow had moved closer to the map and was studying it carefully, even as Lowrey jostled for a spot to do the same. "I don't think Quintrel meant Edgeland," Lowrey said. "For one thing, these stars," he said, pointing to two marks on the map, "can't be seen above the horizon that far north at that time of the year."

"Does that mean we need to be at a certain place on that date?" Connor asked, puzzled.

Penhallow shook his head. "I don't think so, but we don't have enough information to be certain." He raised his head to look at Lowrey. "You told me that the equinox would be a time when the power would be strong."

Lowrey nodded, still studying the map. "So is the solstice, which is just a month away. They're times when the natural world creates 'channels' for power. So it might be easier to bring back the magic then, but that doesn't mean it would be impossible at other times."

Connor stared at the date on the torn parchment. "Would an astronomer be able to fix the location given this map?"

Lowrey straightened. "My interests at the university included astronomy and cartography," he replied. "So I'm qualified to comment. Without the latitude, you might narrow it down to an area, but not a precise point. If by 'the exiles' Quintrel means himself and the mages he took into hiding, I don't think he's going to make it too easy to find him, just in case the knowledge were to fall into the wrong hands."

"There's another possibility," Penhallow said. "From the Knights' point of view, they, too, were exiled. It's been widely rumored that some of the Knights who escaped and went into hiding were never found. Quintrel may be steering us toward the Knights, for whatever reason."

He paused. "If so, we must proceed with caution. The Knights have not wished to be found for a long time."

Connor looked at the manuscript. "What about that?" he asked. "I handled it, and it didn't open any memories."

Lowrey smiled. "All in due time, lad. As we suspected, Quintrel left memories that trigger to time and place. Take the book with you. When the time is right, you'll be able to tell us what it means." Connor gathered up the journal, map, and manuscript, along with the four disks, and placed them in his pack as the others readied to return to the castle.

Outside Almstedt's crypt, they moved through the corridor toward the central chamber but halted abruptly at the sound of rushing wind, and the hue and cry of men rushing to battle.

"We've been discovered!" Geddy cried, terror clear in his features.

The temperature in the main chamber was now icy. The sound of running feet echoed from every direction, yet what they saw hurtling down each of the five corridors were blue-green orbs of light, bouncing and bobbing, moving with fearsome speed.

"What's happening?" Connor asked, feeling his throat constrict with fear as they began to back toward Almstedt's crypt.

As they watched, the orbs began to cluster, expanding and shifting until the forms of men appeared. Within a heartbeat, they stared out into the chamber to see two opposing spectral armies facing off against each other. One side wore the livery of the king's guard of Donderath, while the others were outfitted in the armor of the Knights of Esthrane.

Battle cries echoed from the stone walls as the two sides rushed toward each other. Though neither side had physical form, Connor and the others could clearly hear the clang of swords, the pounding of footsteps, and the curses and cries of men as the two sides battled fiercely.

"By Torven's horns, what's happening?" Geddy stared wide-eyed at the spectral battle. "If they turn on us, we're trapped like rats."

"They don't want us," Penhallow said quietly. "They don't even know we're here. This isn't a show for our benefit." He looked to Lynge. "There's more than one reason the necropolis is off-limits to all but a few, isn't there, Lars?"

Lynge nodded. He watched the spirits battle with an expression that was unnerved, but far from Geddy's unabashed terror or the fright that paralyzed Connor. "The spirits of those buried beneath the castle do not rest," he said quietly. "Over the years, there have been many reports of spirits reenacting the circumstances of their death. Lovers' fatal quarrels, duels to the death, assassinations: Down here, they never end." He paused.

"Some of the early kings who fell in battle were buried near the mass grave that held their soldiers' remains."

"So what we're seeing is a battle between the king's troops and the Knights, relived by the spirits of the dead?" Lowrey murmured. "Fascinating."

" 'Fascinating' isn't the word I would have picked," Connor retorted. "We're trapped."

"If they're just ghosts, then they can't hurt us, right?" Geddy asked in a quivering voice.

Connor was relieved, because the same question burned in his mind, though he was loath to be the one to ask.

"That depends," Penhallow replied, his body tensing as he watched the flow of battle.

"On what?" Geddy squeaked.

"On which side won this particular battle," Lowrey finished the sentence. "And by my estimate, the Knights are losing."

Lynge paled. "Which means, from the point of view of the king's forces, we stand on the side of the traitors."

Connor's heart thudded in his throat as he watched the ghostly battle. With every moment, more of the Knights fell to the swords of the king's forces. The Knights were badly outnumbered though they fought valiantly. "What happens if the king's men win, and they find us?" Connor asked, dry-mouthed.

"Treason is punishable by death, lad," Lowrey replied.

"Can ghosts kill?" Geddy asked in a small voice.

"If they're strong enough," Lowrey answered. "And here in the place of the dead, they're at their greatest strength."

"It would be best not to test your theory," Penhallow said, never taking his gaze off the battle as it surged and ebbed. "We need to leave, and we can't return the way we came." He looked to Lynge. "You said the Knights had multiple escape routes. Can you lead us out?"

Lynge shook his head. "For obvious reasons, exploration of the older areas has been limited," he said, nervously wetting his lips.

They backed away from the sound of battle, toward Almstedt's crypt. "Let's see if we can find an entrance to a passageway from the crypt," Lynge said. Geddy stood watch at the door as the others began to work their way around the room searching for a hidden opening.

It was only then that Connor realized that the temperature within the crypt had fallen to reach the icy cold of the corridor beyond. He felt the hair on the back of his neck rise and turned to see Almstedt's ghost standing behind them. "Lynge might not know how to get us out, but I bet he does," Connor whispered.

Penhallow turned to face the ghost. "Will you help us escape?"

Almstedt nodded and wordlessly raised his right arm, pointing toward one of the walls of his crypt. Lowrey poked Connor in the shoulder to nudge him closer to where the ghost stood. "Maybe he'll show you how to open a secret door," Lowrey whispered.

"We can't wait long. Our side isn't doing too well," Geddy muttered, watching the battle in the corridors.

Almstedt's spirit glided over to the wall and laid a hand over one of the images of Esthrane on the mural. In the painting, the goddess was conveying a pennant with the heraldic emblem of a diagonal blue bar to the kneeling Knights. Connor edged closer, his heart thudding, and let his fingers feel their way over the image of the pennant. He found a depression and pressed, hearing a satisfying click. One segment of the mural swung inward, exposing a hidden passageway.

"Thank you," Connor murmured to the ghost, who stepped aside to let the others pass.

Penhallow led the way. Lynge followed, with Lowrey right behind him. Connor held the panel open, waiting for Geddy to catch up. Geddy remained frozen in place, watching the battle in the corridor, too afraid to move.

"Come on!" Connor hissed, as the battle began to work its way toward them, rushing down the corridor and spilling into Almstedt's crypt.

A bright light flared, and Almstedt's ghost appeared, standing between the escape corridor and the thick of battle. Geddy found the nerve to begin his run toward freedom across the crypt with Almstedt in the center, blocking the advance of the enemy soldiers. But as Almstedt turned to engage one of the combatants, two ghostly soldiers nearest Geddy stumbled with the momentum of their sword blows, staggering backward into Geddy's path. The soldier's blade slashed downward, and the Knight's spirit swung his own sword to parry, but the blow went wild, catching Geddy through the chest.

Blood spurted from a gash in Geddy's chest. Connor shouted Geddy's name, but Geddy clutched at his bloody shirt, the look on his face a mixture of shock and horror. Connor started forward, but an ice-cold hand grabbed Connor's wrist and dragged him into the darkness of the corridor, pulling the panel shut behind him.

"We can't just leave him!" Connor protested, fighting to break Penhallow's grip on his wrist.

"We have no choice. It was a mortal wound," Penhallow replied grimly. "He's beyond our help. Almstedt will hold the entrance. With luck, the battle will play itself out and no one will come after us."

Numb with shock, Connor stumbled along, barely keeping his footing on the rock floor of the corridor as they ran down the passageway. Lynge's lantern bobbed ahead of them. Connor depended on Penhallow's ability to see in the dark to guide them, as little of the lantern's glow reached them. Twice Connor slammed into rocky outcroppings, bruising his shoulder and leaving a gash on his temple.

Gradually, the corridor warmed from the icy chill of the ghostly battle. The passageway twisted and turned and eventually led them to a carved stone wall.

"We're trapped," Lynge said, feeling his way across the rock face with his free hand as he held the lantern aloft, looking for a hidden opening.

Behind them, the sounds of battle carried up the corridor. "Almstedt may not be able to hold them much longer," Connor warned.

Penhallow slipped toward the front and began to press his fingers into the stone carvings, stopping after a few moments to tap the wall. He stood back, and a smile crept over his features. "Aha," he murmured.

"Anytime would be good now, Lanyon," Lowrey prodded.

Penhallow arranged his hands over a section in the center of the carvings so that his fingers formed the shape of Esthrane's constellation. He gave a push on the five points simultaneously, and they heard a *click* as a hidden latch gave way. The heavy door pivoted on a central fulcrum, opening a narrow access through which they slid one man at a time, latching the door behind them.

A dozen more steps brought them to an opening in the foothills above the city. Connor drank in the cool, fresh air and the sight of stars in the night sky overhead.

"We should be safe now," Penhallow said. "The spirits are bound to their crypt. They can't follow us here."

"That doesn't help Geddy," Connor said.

Penhallow laid a hand on Connor's shoulder. "Your grief

is admirable, but it would not serve his sacrifice to allow the enemy to gain the advantage. Now that we know which disks are missing, we need to find them."

"Four pendants, plus the one Connor wears and King Merrill's disk," Lowrey observed. "Perhaps McFadden has found his family's pendant. That's seven disks accounted for out of thirteen. And we know Reese has interest in the old families." He met Penhallow's gaze. "I'd say the race is on."

CHAPTER FIFTEEN

"COME ON, MICK, WAKE UP!" PIRAN ROWSE'S VOICE seemed painfully loud, but Blaine guessed that might have more to do with the pounding in his temples than Piran's actual volume.

With a groan, Blaine felt consciousness return. Every bone in his body ached. He lay in the snow, gradually becoming aware of just how cold he was and realizing that his feet and hands were numb. He tried to move his arms and legs. Everything hurt, but at least his body still worked.

Piran extended his hand and Blaine pulled himself up to a seated position, then swayed as his head threatened to explode and his vision blurred. "The others—" he began, then winced at the throbbing in his head.

"We all made it over the fence," Piran replied. "Skin of our teeth, it was, with those storms behind us. But we made it." He gave a nod to the right, where Blaine saw Kestel and Verran moving gingerly. Kestel carefully shook the snow free from the folds of her cloak, and Verran brushed snow from his tunic and trews. Piran appeared to be the most recovered of any of them.

Their horses, looking no worse for the long, frantic chase, were milling about well inside the stone wall.

Piran was crouched in front of Blaine, and now he cast a worried glance behind him, toward the hamlet of Riker's Ferry. "Can you stand?" he asked quietly. "Because we've attracted the attention of the town folk."

Blaine gritted his teeth and forced himself to stand, doing his best to ignore every aching joint and a blinding headache. Piran also got to his feet, carefully keeping his hands away from the sword that hung at his belt.

Blaine looked at the small crowd that had started to gather. Fortunately, they were not brandishing swords, but he could see that most of the men were carrying staves and small tools that could quickly become weapons should introductions go poorly.

Blaine took a step forward, making sure both hands were in plain view and far from his sword. "My friends and I barely outrode two storms. We mean no harm."

An older man at the forefront of the crowd nodded. The others looked to him, and Blaine guessed he was the village elder. "It's fortunate none of your companions were hurt," he said. "Welcome to Riker's Ferry."

"I'm Mick," Blaine said, deliberately not using his given name, "and my friends are Piran, Verran, and Kestel."

"I am Helgen," the older man replied. "I head the village council. What brings you and your friends so far into the back-country?"

Blaine had been expecting the question. Given how far Riker's Ferry was from more heavily traveled roads and major towns, it was inevitable. He had not, however, expected to have to pass the scrutiny of the entire town at once. "We came from

Castle Reach," Blaine said. "We're looking for a friend of ours who went missing after the Great Fire."

Helgen's eyes narrowed, and he looked up at the lingering crowd to wave them off. "Go on, get about your business. I'll see to our visitors." Gradually the small group dispersed, looking disappointed there hadn't been more to the incident.

"Bring your horses, and let's go get a pint at the pub. The tavern master can see to your horses, we'll get you warmed up, and you can tell me what you're really doing out here on the backside of nowhere," he said with a glance at Blaine.

Piran shot a look at Blaine, who shrugged. They gathered their horses, and Blaine fell in step with Helgen. Piran and Kestel followed, with Verran bringing up the rear.

Blaine looked around as they walked down the main street of Riker's Ferry. From the map, he knew that the Pelaran River bordered the far side of town, where the ferry was located. Before the Great Fire, most traffic bound for Castle Reach and the harbor would most likely have taken the bridge, a day's ride to the south. Riker's Ferry was off the main route for the majority of the merchants, caravans, and traveling fairs that had moved freely about the kingdom before the war. The town's less-than-ideal location no doubt accounted in part for the fact that it had the look of a small farming village rather than a bustling hub of commerce.

"Looks like your town weathered the Great Fire pretty well," Piran observed.

Helgen nodded. "Out here, we're not much of a target," he replied.

He's conveniently not mentioning the fact that they're null magic, Blaine thought. *Yet that has to be the main reason nothing here looks as if it was even touched.* He looked from side to side as they traveled up the village's broad main street, noting that the taverns, shops, brothel, and stable looked weathered by the years. *In other words*, Blaine thought, *they look completely normal, not as if they'd been blown to bits and cobbled back together.*

"It's rather nice to see buildings that aren't smashed to pieces or burned to a crisp," Verran observed. "Most places near Castle Reach took a pounding in the war."

Helgen gave a wan smile that did not reach his eyes. "For once, our inconvenient location was a blessing."

Blaine glanced around the Ram and Boar as they entered. It was modest but not shabby. Near the bar, he saw several men with the look of farmers or herders standing with mugs of ale, while a handful of other men played cards or dice at tables near the fire. Everyone looked up as they entered.

Helgen spoke a few words to the barkeeper and motioned them to sit with him at a table near the back. Blaine noticed two young men seated at a nearby table. Both of the men looked like peddlers or tinkers, dressed in worn jackets with ragged sleeves and scuffed boots. They were deep in their own conversation and did not look up as Blaine's group settled in at a table.

"Bring some food with that ale!" Helgen shouted back to the barkeeper. "It's cold outside." From the kitchen, they heard a muffled assent.

A stout woman, probably the barkeeper's wife, bustled to bring them their drinks. "He's got stew tonight. Mostly potatoes and onion and some deer meat. A bit of that and some bread should warm you up," she said. "If you're needing a room, we've got beds upstairs. If you're early to bed, you'll get a spot. If not, there's room on the floor and plenty of blankets."

She paused, her gaze lingering on Kestel, as if trying to make out what a woman was doing traveling among men and attired in tunic and trews. "If you'd like, dearie, you can sleep down here or in the kitchen, keep you away from the gods-awful snoring."

Kestel smiled warmly at the woman. "That's kind of you."

If she had any concerns over the nature of Kestel's business in town, the woman seemed mollified by Kestel's answer and relaxed a bit. "All right then, it's settled. He'll be out with that stew in a moment. Holler if you'll be needing more ale." At that, she turned away and bustled back toward the bar, where several of the other customers were holding aloft empty tankards to be filled.

Helgen looked at Blaine, and his blue eyes held a wary intelligence. "Now please, if you will, I'd like the real reason you happened upon our little village."

Blaine took a sip of his ale, watching Helgen carefully. "As I said, we are looking for a friend of ours who went missing just before the Great Fire. He was a mage named Vigus Quintrel."

Helgen's mouth turned up slightly at the corners, bemused. "Why would a mage come to a farming town like this?"

"Because magic doesn't work here," Kestel replied, smiling at Helgen. Her smile, coupled with her blunt observation, seemed to surprise the man.

"Magic doesn't work anywhere, not since the Great Fire," Helgen said, eyeing Kestel warily.

"But it didn't work in Riker's Ferry even before that, did it?" Kestel pressed, leaning closer. "That's why we thought our friend might have come here. We think he was afraid something like the Great Fire might happen, and he thought this was safe."

Helgen was silent for a moment. "We may not be one of the main trading stops on the river," he said finally, "but before the Great Fire, we had our share of strangers coming and going.

When the fires came, people stopped traveling. There wasn't anywhere for them to go, once the castle and its city burned." He gave a sharp, short bark of a laugh.

"At first, everyone was afraid to go anywhere. Then when it got closer to winter, people got up the nerve to leave. Since then, there's been a steady trickle of people finding their way here. Some just travel until they run out of provisions, and so they stay. Others, well, I imagine there are as many stories as there are vagabonds. So long as they don't cause trouble, and they'll work for their food, we don't usually care if they stay."

"What about before the fires?" Kestel asked, leaning forward and turning the full glow of her attention on Helgen. Piran sighed and leaned back in his chair, and Blaine knew his friend was resigned to watching the master interrogator go to work. Verran looked amused, but his attention was elsewhere and his gaze darted around the room. Blaine guessed Verran was scouting the room for easy marks or taking in the details with the practiced eye of an experienced thief.

Before Helgen could say more, the barkeeper announced that he had just tapped a fresh keg, precipitating a rush of patrons to the bar. When the ruckus died down, Blaine returned his attention to Helgen.

"Before the fires, we were an unlikely destination for a mage of any sort," Helgen replied. "As you've obviously guessed, our location is…unusual. Our boundaries roughly match the area where magic didn't function. That spared us from the Great Fire, and it's protected us from magic storms like the ones you fled."

"A null spot," Blaine said. Helgen startled just a bit at the term, and Blaine had his confirmation that the council head had heard the term before. "Hard to believe that some in the village didn't realize the opportunity that presented. Riker's

Ferry would have been the perfect sanctuary for people who'd gotten on the wrong side of a mage, or were under a curse, or had some unfortunate run-in with magic."

A flicker in Helgen's eyes preceded a curt nod of his head. "In some circles, it's been quietly known for a long time that our little village could be a good place to disappear. We didn't get a lot of folks like that, but so long as they kept their heads down and didn't attract anything dangerous, we let them stay. There are other folks who settled here because magic was a burden for them," Helgen said quietly. He fixed Blaine with a challenging look. "Out here, people mind their own business."

A kitchen wench approached with a tray laden with bowls of steaming stew and loaves of freshly baked bread. They fell silent as she set the meal on the table and bustled to refill their tankards. When she had gone, Blaine cleared his throat as the others began to eat.

"We didn't come to make trouble, or to bring any trouble with us. We're just looking for Quintrel or for information about him. We know Quintrel traveled around, and that right before the fires, he had some powerful enemies. He might have wanted to disappear," Blaine added. "A place like Riker's Ferry would have been the perfect place for him to do that. If you can steer us to the right people to talk with, we'll be on our way tomorrow."

Helgen said nothing for a few moments as he ate his stew, and Blaine wondered if the man intended to answer. When Helgen had finished his meal, he wiped his mouth, took a long draught of his drink, and sat back in his chair. "Vin at the bar sees most of the strangers who pass this way. Ellie, over at the Rogue and Damsel, meets most of the men sooner or later." He leveled a glance at them. "She runs our whorehouse.

"They're your best bets, I'd imagine, for finding what you

want to know—assuming your friend even passed this way," Helgen continued. He pushed his chair back from the table.

"I'm glad you and your friends weren't hurt by the storm," he said, looking at Blaine. "I've already made arrangements with Vin for this meal and your lodging tonight. But tomorrow, perhaps it's best if you and your friends head back toward the city. No telling when another storm might come our way." With that, Helgen bid them farewell and made his way to the door.

When Helgen was gone, Piran leaned forward, frustration clear on his face. "What a load of shit! I'd bet a gold piece he knows more than he's telling."

"You don't have a gold piece, so it's a safe bet," Verran replied. "But I agree that he's either lying or hiding something—or both."

"And if he wants us to talk with the barkeeper and the madam, it's also a good bet that they either don't know anything or wouldn't tell us if they did," Kestel added.

Blaine nodded. "Agreed. So we're going to look like we're taking his advice, then do a little sniffing around on our own." Blaine looked toward Verran. "Verran, stay here at the tavern and see what you can find out, from Vin or from the patrons. Pull out your pennywhistle, play them some tunes: You know how to work the crowd. I doubt Quintrel broadcast that he was a mage or used his real name, so just ask around about strangers from the city. Maybe we'll get lucky."

"What about me?" Piran asked.

Blaine grinned. "I've got the perfect job for you. Go over to the Rogue and Damsel, and see what the ladies have heard." He palmed a few silver coins and passed them to Piran. "Mind, I'm not paying for your entertainment," he warned. "Just be on your best behavior and see what you can learn from the ladies."

Piran grinned. "Not to boast, mates, but I'm more likely to do the teachin' in a place like that than the learnin'— Ow!" He glared at Kestel. "Why'd you kick me in the shin? What was that for?"

"Did I?" Kestel replied, her face the picture of innocence. "Maybe I was warning you that the gods hate boasters." She leaned forward conspiratorially. "Or maybe I'm just reminding you that until we know whether these folks are friends or foe, you might want to keep your pants fastened and your jewels guarded."

"Very funny," Piran grumbled. He brightened. "Still, I've never had any problem getting the ladies to talk to me."

"As I recall, most of them say, 'Get your hands off me, you lout,'" Verran said.

"Enough, all of you," Blaine said, struggling to keep a straight face. He quickly sobered. "Just remember Helgen obviously doesn't want us hanging around, and I'm betting he's got a stake in making sure this town's secrets stay secret. Watch your back."

Verran cocked his head and looked at Blaine. "What about you and our Sour Rose? Where will you be?"

"Kestel and I are going to take a little stroll around town," Blaine said. "See if we can figure out who Helgen didn't want us to talk to."

"Let's gather back here by eleventh bells," Kestel suggested. "Riker's Ferry isn't that large, and it's cold enough people aren't likely to be about in the streets late."

Verran looked over his shoulder, then back to Kestel and Blaine. "You think we're safe here?"

Blaine shrugged. "Compared to what? I don't fancy sleeping in the cold, and sure as Raka, I don't want to head outside the null area tonight. We'll take turns on watch. If we find out what we need, we can be on our way tomorrow and Helgen will be rid of us."

The tall tower at the far end of the street chimed sixth bells as Blaine and Kestel exited the tavern. Kestel's long cloak neatly hid the fact that she wore trews instead of a ladies' gown, and she had her hood up, covering her hair, in a show of modesty common among well-to-do women. Blaine offered her his arm, and together they walked along the snowy main road.

"We've been followed," Kestel said quietly.

"I saw. If he's this bad at being discreet, maybe he won't be difficult to lose," Blaine replied.

"I don't think he was trying to be discreet," Kestel murmured. "I think we were meant to see him."

"So, let him watch," Blaine said, "until we decide to do something worth watching. Then we'll lose him."

Kestel chuckled. "I like how you think." She gripped his arm, leaning against him as if they were a proper couple out for an evening stroll. *Too bad she's only playacting*, Blaine thought, then forced his attention elsewhere.

"Butcher, baker, seamstress—or maybe tailor." Kestel counted off the shops on the village's main street. "Chandler, cobbler, cooper. All the essentials, no more, no less. By comparison, it almost makes Bay-town back in Edgeland look like a huge city!"

Blaine smiled. "That's because before the supply and convict ships stopped coming from home, Bay-town played host to a bunch of hungry, thirsty, randy sailors with coppers in their pockets to spend." He sighed and looked down the quiet street. "With Castle Reach destroyed, there aren't traders headed toward the city anymore. Between the magic storms and the brigands on the roads, not as many travelers going anywhere, I wager."

"Do you think it will ever be like it used to be?" Kestel asked wistfully, and Blaine knew she was thinking about the once-glittering court at Quillarth Castle and the prosperous chaos of Castle Reach's busy streets.

"I don't know," Blaine replied. "Even if we can get the magic to work again, it's going to take a lot to rebuild. I don't imagine it will ever be quite like it was. Maybe different, even better. But not the same."

They were quiet for a while after that. The village shops were closed. Other than the tavern and the brothel at the other end of the streets, windows were dark down on the street level, while lanterns in the windows of the upper floors signaled that the shopkeepers and tradesmen had gone home for dinner. Yet there were more than a few people about on the street. Some were headed in the direction Blaine and Kestel had come, no doubt planning to avail themselves of a good meal or some companionship. Despite the closed shops, a steady stream of people was heading toward the far end of town. Intrigued, Blaine and Kestel followed the crowd.

"There's something going on in the village green," Kestel said quietly.

She and Blaine edged closer, until they could see what had attracted the crowd. The village square was lit with torches on posts that stood in a semicircle to create a makeshift stage. The painted side of an enclosed peddler's wagon read: KOMOROK TROUBADOURS.

Despite the cold winter night, a small crowd had gathered. Two men played a jaunty tune on drum and lute while two young women danced in as few clothes as the frigid temperature would permit. A tall, lanky man dressed from head to toe in black with a high black hat stood a few paces in front of the performers, exhorting the crowd to show their appreciation for the music and barking out an invitation to any and all passersby to come to the show.

Kestel watched the troubadours with a measured glance. "I wonder where they come from?" she said under her breath, so softly only Blaine could hear. "I doubt Riker's Ferry is big enough to support them."

"From the look of them and their wagon, they've traveled the hard way," Blaine observed.

"They look like they rummaged through the castoffs of some down-at-the-heels noble's wardrobe," Kestel murmured.

"Which we know something about, having done it ourselves recently," Blaine chuckled.

Kestel jabbed him playfully in the ribs. "That wasn't what I meant."

Kestel's assessment was accurate, Blaine thought. If the performers had heavy coats, they were stashed in the wagon. The two young men playing the drone and the drum wore a strange mix of shabby brocade waistcoats and frock coats over silk shirts that might once have been vibrantly colored, but were now stained and torn. Worn velvet breeches and scuffed boots completed their outfits.

"Those are the men who were at the table behind us at the tavern," Kestel whispered. "They left just before we did, and they were wearing long coats so I didn't notice their outfits, but I'm sure of their faces."

The dancers wore dresses that reminded Blaine of the loose, unconstructed shifts favored by women in Edgeland, women who needed freedom of movement for real work, unconstrained by corsets, heavy skirts, and bodices. Such outfits would have raised scandal in Castle Reach, but Blaine had heard they were quite common in the rural areas. These simple shifts were a riot of piebald colors, bits of silk, velvet, and brocade stitched together in magnificent motley, with a magpie's treasury of shiny bits of metal, beads, and common gemstones that glistened in the firelight.

Both dancers looked to be in their early twenties. One wore her long, black hair in elaborate braids that hung down her back and swayed seductively with every movement. The other woman's dark blonde hair was pinned atop her head in a tousled pile. Both women had high cheekbones and dark eyes, with skin the color of light caramel, giving them an exotic beauty.

The dark-haired woman smiled and flirted with the crowd, but there was a wariness beneath her joviality. The blonde woman did not seem to notice the crowd at all, reacting to her companion's comments, focused on her tasks with a dreamy, faraway expression. The men in the audience shouted their appreciation and made suggestive comments. The dark-haired woman deflected the come-ons with banter, and the blonde went about her dancing as if she did not hear the catcalls. Blaine's attention flickered back to the two young men, who watched the crowd with caution. He was quite sure that they heard, and resented, the lewd suggestions.

Blaine followed Kestel's glance to see that the man who followed them had stayed near the back of the crowd and now was bobbing up and down looking for them. Kestel took Blaine's hand and led him deeper into the crowd, intentionally choosing a place to stand in front of a man who was a head taller than Blaine.

The troubadours' leader, the tall man in black, wore a threadbare velvet frock coat over a stained burgundy vest and dark woolen pants that were a bit too short for his height. The deep-green silk jabot of a popinjay's shirt flounced down the front of the man's vest, matching the hatband on his tall hat, giving him a measure of disheveled dignity.

By now, a good-sized crowd had gathered, and the audience began to hoot and clap for a show. The man in black bowed low, sweeping his hat in an exaggerated arc. "Good gentles all!" he boomed. "Thank you for your esteemed presence. I am Illarion, the master of the stage, and we are the Komorok Troubadours. Tonight, beneath the torches, on this very stage, we will present feats of valor and acts of daring the like of which you will not see anywhere else! Be prepared to be astounded! Ready yourself to be amazed! Your mind will not believe what your eyes will see!"

As Illarion spoke, the drummer and the lute player set aside their instruments and stripped off their topmost garments. The two young men shared a strong resemblance, making Blaine wonder if they were twins. Both had long, dark hair and thin faces with sharp features that made Blaine think of them as a pair of ravens. Yet when they moved, their motions were as fluid as dancers', and Blaine rethought his comparison. *Not ravens*, Blaine thought. *More like the mountain cats that feed on the villagers' sheep and are bold enough to steal a colt or calf.* The pair separated, moving so that one stood on either side of Illarion at the far wings of the 'stage.'

"Ladies and gentlemen, I give you Borya and Desya, the Shadow Twins, our master musicians and acclaimed acrobats!" With a flourish, Illarion walked backward off the stage area as Borya and Desya spun across the open space in a blur of motion, executing a series of breathtaking back-bends and aerial somersaults. Without the frock coats, the acrobats' silks and brocades became a wild panoply of color and motion, and from the way their clothing glistened and sparkled in the torchlight, Blaine suspected that glass beads had been sewn onto the garments to further enhance the effect. Illarion had taken up the drumming, and the hypnotic beat echoed from the walls of the village buildings.

Having reached the opposite ends of the stage, Borya and Desya launched themselves into motion once more, hurtling toward each other as if they meant to do battle. At the last moment, Borya leaped high into the air, landing with impossible grace on Desya's shoulders. The dancers, who had moved to where several large knapsacks lay in the shadows just behind the torches, began to throw objects to the acrobats. Brightly colored plates, gleaming chalices, and silver candlesticks flew through the air, caught by the two acrobats and juggled into a colorful blur. Each man juggled items of his own and then began to pass items up and down to the other in patterns that were nearly impossible for the eye to follow.

Kestel elbowed Blaine. "Look at their eyes," she murmured.

Blaine caught a glimpse of Desya's eyes and startled. At least from where he stood, they appeared to have the narrow, vertical pupils and the yellow irises of a cat's eyes.

"Borya's are the same," Kestel whispered.

Borya began throwing objects back to the dancers, who caught them with uncanny grace. He dismounted with a twist and somersault, and without a pause he caught the other man's forearms, bracing their bent knees against each other and leaning back as counterweights. The two dancers came tumbling toward them in perfect handsprings, landing so one was atop each of the men's shoulders. The crowd cheered, but the pose was not yet complete. The dancers leaned forward, inverting themselves so that they braced their hands on the men's thighs, daringly straightening their legs and in doing so, revealing that their 'skirts' had been full, flounced pantaloons made with layers of brightly colored silks.

The crowd cheered as the performers moved into ever more complex contortions that defied gravity. Sometimes the four performers danced into solo poses, bending and twisting with such flexibility that their bones almost seemed malleable. Blaine marveled at the skill and grace of the troupe and saw that, despite the cold, the effort was raising a sheen of sweat on their faces. Their final form was a circle, with the dancers atop the two men's shoulders, with the two couples engaged in a delicate counterbalance. As if from nowhere, the top two performers unfurled a black sheet of silk. The sheet bore embroidery in shining threads with the symbols of the gods' constellations and with arcane runes that gave Blaine an uncomfortable jolt.

Blaine exchanged a silent, surprised glance with Kestel. *The markings from the disks*, he thought. *This can't be a coincidence.*

A moment later, the silk fluttered to the ground and the performers exploded from their positions in twirls, somersaults, and handsprings. All of the troupe left the stage except for the blonde woman, who stood at the center. She wore a dreamy expression as if despite the cheering audience, she was in a world of her own. It gave her a vulnerable, childlike air, although Blaine guessed that she was close to the age of the dark-haired dancer.

"Kata, beautiful and dangerous as a dancing flame," Illarion intoned. The dark-haired woman began playing a drone as Illarion remained drumming, and Borya took up the lute. Kata remained still, and then two arcs of flame soared across the air and she snatched them with effortless accuracy, revealing them to be fiery batons.

As if hypnotized, the crowd watched Kata toss the flaming batons into the air, spinning like falling stars, only to snatch them again and again and hurl them even higher. She danced as she sent the batons arcing overhead, combining graceful steps that matched the music with bends, twists, and acrobatic movements. Her face was a mask of concentration, as if she did not see the crowd and focused only on the blazing batons. Desya tossed her a ring the size of a wagon wheel with an interior, metal ring. Kata tossed the ring into the air, dropped one of the flaming batons into the snow, and used the last baton to light the outer ring.

Kata stood completely still as the ring dropped down over her and she caught it by its inner circle, then raised it overhead as she gracefully spun the fiery ring by one hand and then the other, tossing it aloft and catching it again. She bent double and lifted one long leg into the air, catching and spinning the blazing wheel, then straightened, holding her leg out in front of her and launching the ring once more. This time she caught it again with her hand, and from the sidelines flew a long, thin skewer with a thickened end. Kata lit the end of the skewer and straightened, allowing the flaming ring to fall to the ground, wreathing her in fire. She let her head fall back as she opened her mouth. The crowd gasped as Kata seemed to swallow flame, and as the skewer in her mouth extinguished, the ring at her feet flared one final time and went dark.

Illarion bounded to the center of the stage as Kata bowed and the crowd roared its astonished approval. She gave a vague smile. Illarion whispered a comment, and Kata's smile broadened. She gave a shy wave, made a bow, then ran off the stage.

Borya moved the charred ring and burned batons to the side of the performance area as Desya brought a trunk from the sidelines and opened it so that it faced Illarion.

"Behold!" Desya intoned. "Illarion, master of knives."

Kata began to drum as the other dancer began to play the lyre. Desya withdrew a lethal-looking, large, curved knife and blithely tossed it toward Illarion, who snatched it from the air as if it were nothing of consequence. Four more times Desya threw the knives and Illarion caught them all, keeping the other knives deftly wheeling through the air.

At first, Illarion juggled slowly, but the pace grew faster and faster until the knives blurred into a single silver ring in the firelight. The crowd clapped in rhythm to the drum, but Illarion's concentration remained absolute.

Desya moved to stand just behind Illarion, then lay down on the ground, arms and legs splayed. Without turning, Illarion suddenly shouted, "One!" and threw one of his daggers into the air so that it arced behind him, but he made no move to catch it. The blade wheeled and embedded itself just outside Desya's right thigh. Desya remained motionless, and Illarion appeared oblivious, but one of the women in the audience screamed and fainted.

"Two!" Illarion shouted, sending another blade up and behind him. This fell to earth, point down, to the outside of Desya's left thigh.

"Three, four, five!" Knives flew, each in a different direction. One landed between Desya's thighs, close enough to his groin to make Blaine wince. The last two landed just outside Desya's shoulders, one on each side, so close they nearly pinned the fabric of his shirt to the snow.

The crowd howled in approval. Illarion gave a deep bow. "Good gentlemen and gentle ladies," he boomed, as Kata tossed him his tall hat. "If you have enjoyed the marvels of this performance, please be so kind as to toss us a copper or two." He spun his hat through the air and it landed at his feet, brim up.

"For those who would like a glimpse into the beyond, our charming Zaryae is also a true seer," Illarion said, inclining his head toward the dark-haired dancer. "For a single silver coin, Zaryae will tell you the future."

Many in the crowd surged forward to toss coins into Illarion's hat. Zaryae came to the edge of the performance area and a few people called out to her, but no one moved to offer her the silver Illarion requested. After dropping a few copper coins into the hat, Blaine and Kestel turned to go.

Over and over again, circles and fire, Blaine thought. *And symbols that match the disk. Were they mages?* Blaine wondered, stealing a glance toward the performers as they eased through the waning crowd. *What do they know? Or am I so obsessed with a failed quest that I see symbols and augers in the shadows?*

"M'lady, if you please!" A slender hand reached out to pluck at the sleeve of Kestel's coat, and they realized Zaryae had moved to stand beside them. "I have a reading for you, a warning from the gods." Zaryae's dark eyes were intelligent and canny. Up close, Blaine saw that her features were a bit too angular to be pretty in a conventional sense, though under any circumstances, she was quite striking.

Kestel exchanged a glance with Blaine, and it was clear that each wondered if the girl's offer was a trap. "What kind of reading?" Kestel asked warily, and Blaine caught a slight motion as Kestel's hand fell to her side, where a dagger was hidden among the folds of her clothing.

Zaryae glanced around them and pulled Kestel and Blaine closer to the performance area and away from the thinning crowd, so that the wagon blocked them from view. "You and your friends are in danger," she murmured. "Borya and Desya were not the only ones to notice your arrival at the tavern. A black circle haunts your dreams, and you wish to restore what the Fire took away. Please, m'lady, come to our camp with me and I will tell you there what I dare not say aloud among so many curious ears."

"Where is your camp?" Blaine asked, moving closer to Kestel to signal that the invitation had better include him.

Zaryae gave a nod of her head toward the left, toward an open space between buildings. "By the outer wall, beyond the stables. I have to go beyond the wall to receive the messages."

That makes sense, Blaine thought, *since the village is in a null zone and whatever magic remains lies beyond.*

"I assure you, m'lady, you are as safe among my friends and me as you will ever be in this village," Zaryae said, reading the expressions of mistrust that were clear on their faces. "The dreams foretold that you would come. Please, you must hear me."

CHAPTER SIXTEEN

B Y NOW, THE CROWD HAD GONE, AS HAD THE MAN who followed them from the pub. Borya and Desya gathered up the last of the batons and other props that lay scattered across the snow, while Illarion snuffed out the torches and carried them back to their wagon. Kata led a horse from a copse of nearby trees and hitched him to the wagon. Illarion strode over to join them.

"M'lady," he said with a deep bow to Kestel. He met Blaine's eyes for a moment. "And m'lord," he said. "Borya and Desya heard part of your conversation earlier this evening and told Zaryae that the watched-for ones had arrived. Helgen cannot help you in your quest, and his first loyalty is to caution. Zaryae's gift has told her something of your burden and she can help, if you will honor us with your presence at our camp."

"All right," Kestel answered, with a glance to alert Blaine that she knew the risk of accepting the invitation. Blaine let out a deep breath. He had already come to the same conclusion, yet he wished there were a way to let Piran and Verran know where they were going.

Out of habit, his hand fell to the pommel of his sword.

Illarion caught the movement and a smile ghosted across his face. "You are wise to be cautious, but our camp is safe."

Alert for danger, Blaine and Kestel watched as the performers loaded the last of the gear into their wagon. Zaryae and Kata climbed up onto the driver's bench and signaled for Kestel to join them. With a shrug and a glance toward Blaine, Kestel swung up to the high bench, leaving Blaine with the other men who walked behind the wagon as it made its way slowly through the slush.

"Your performance was very good," Blaine said, falling into step with Illarion. Borya and Desya walked behind them, but whether they were merely following or acting as bodyguards, Blaine could not be certain.

Illarion gave a shallow bow. "We're thrilled to have pleased you. Our audiences are not as varied as they once were."

Blaine raised an eyebrow. "How long have you been in Riker's Ferry?"

Illarion gave an enigmatic smile. "Patience. Questions are best answered when we will not be overheard."

Blaine glanced around them. A few people lingered in the streets, talking with one another after the performance, but by now the village green was deserted, and the rest of the pedestrians were hunched against the cold, hurrying to their destinations. He chafed at waiting to ask about the symbols and the recurring circles and flame but held his tongue. Laughter wafted back to them from where the three women rode at the front of the wagon, and Blaine smiled, guessing that Kestel was giving a performance of her own to win over the dancers and gain their trust.

The performers' camp was not far. Blaine was grateful since

the wind had picked up, swirling snow into the air and cutting through his cloak. Illarion offered Kestel a hand down from the wagon, which she accepted with a smile.

Blaine looked around the camp. A second wagon lay unhitched near the rock wall that marked the edge of Riker's Ferry and the magic-null zone. The wagon was a little larger than the one the troupe had used for the performance, and Blaine wondered if it was where they slept when the weather was at its worst. To one side, a large plow horse was tethered along with two small goats. A ring of stones had been set to mark the camp, and within it was a well-used fire pit with a rudimentary spit to roast meat. In a makeshift wooden enclosure, a half-dozen chickens clucked and waddled across a cleared patch of ground. Cords of wood were stacked neatly near the fence.

"Share a meal with us," Illarion invited with a grin and an exaggerated bow, tipping his tall hat. "Our food is plain, but our conversation is witty and you may find that which you seek."

Kestel laughed and gave a curtsey. "We would be honored."

Despite his wariness, Blaine could not resist the good spirits of the troupe. Zaryae and Kata began to sing as they set about readying the meal, while Borya and Desya chimed in on the chorus as they brought wood to make a fire and trudged to the well to draw water. Soon, a merry fire blazed within the fire pit, and Kata set a kettle near the flames for tea. There were five wide log segments set on end around the fire to serve as chairs. Desya went to the woodpile to bring two more for their guests.

"Come. Sit," Illarion said. As Kata and Zaryae assembled the meal from the provisions in the wagon, the others took their places around the fire. Borya withdrew a large flask from inside his coat and passed it around the circle. Blaine took a small mouthful. The home-brewed whiskey was as strong as any distilled on Edgeland, and for a few seconds it took his breath away.

"We saw you in the pub earlier," Kestel said, leaning forward with a look toward Borya and Desya.

Just then, Kata and Zaryae approached, each bearing two wooden bowls. One bowl held a pile of hearth cakes, small loaves of bread made of rough-ground flour and cooked on the hot rocks of a fire. There was another bowl of dried sausages, a third with hunks of cheese. With a sigh of resignation, Blaine saw that the fourth bowl was filled with pickled herring, something he had hoped never to eat again after he left Edgeland. The bread was passed around the circle first, followed by the other items, which each person took using the bread as a plate. Borya's flask was offered more than once, but both Blaine and Kestel declined, mindful not only of the cold but also of the danger of their situation.

Finally, Illarion spoke. "You asked how long we have been in Riker's Ferry," he said, taking another drink from the flask. "We've been here for almost two months. Long enough to take the measure of this place."

"Which is?" Blaine asked.

Illarion's eyes lost their merriment. "As you already know, something about this land repelled magic. Before the Great Fire, the town drew those with a reason to elude magic—their own or someone else's. Some came because they couldn't control their powers and thought exile better than being consumed. Others came because they'd angered a mage and figured their chances to be better if the enemy had to use a physical, rather than magical, attack."

"So why did you come?" Kestel asked. "This is a small town, and by the look of it, not prosperous. They seem unlikely patrons."

"We barely gather enough coppers to feed ourselves and our animals in this godsforsaken backwater," Desya said, his voice thick with contempt. He spoke with the heavy accent of the lands along the border with the Lesser Kingdoms, and Blaine had to listen closely to catch his words.

Illarion stared at the fire as he spoke. "The night of the Great Fire, the night flames fell from the skies and magic died, we were camped outside Castle Reach. One of our patrons, Lord Radenou, had been so pleased by our performance at his manor house that he had secured us a performance for the king." His voice glowed with bitter pride. "Such an honor nearly killed us."

Kestel frowned. "How so?"

"Because we were too close to the bloody castle when the fire-ribbon fell," Borya said. He had the same heavy accent as his brother. In the firelight, there was no mistaking his strange cat eyes. Desya saw Kestel look at him and defiantly met her gaze, as if daring her to look away first.

Illarion resumed his story. "We were delayed by broken axles and muddy roads. As much as we cursed the mud it saved our lives. Had we arrived earlier, we might have camped even closer to the city, and we would have surely burned."

"As it was, we still prayed for death," Zaryae said bitterly. Kata, still humming the song she and Zaryae had been singing, wandered back toward the wagons.

Illarion's expression grew somber. "We did not burn. But we were not entirely spared. A powerful blast of magic swept across Donderath that night, like the hand of the gods."

"You were caught in a magic storm?" Kestel asked, drawn to look at Desya's eyes once more.

"It came on us without warning," Borya said roughly. "Three of our players and several of our horses died."

Illarion continued quietly, "I can't tell you how long the storm was upon us. It felt like hours."

"Those of us who survived were changed," Zaryae said. "Our magic was gone. But it was more than that."

"The wild magic changed our eyes," Borya said. "Before the Fire, our magic was unusual agility. What agility remains is merely mortal. We could do so much more with magic."

Zaryae gave a quick glance over her shoulder, as if to assure herself that Kata was out of earshot. "Kata was badly hurt," Zaryae said. "The storm was cruel to her. It took her magic, which had given her unusual speed—quite an asset for a juggler and a dancer. She was amazing," Zaryae said quietly. "But it also affected her mind. She's like a child now, simple, happy for the most part, but not herself. She still loves to dance, but the Kata we knew is gone."

"Before the storm," Illarion said, "I was quite the minstrel. The storm took my music along with my singing voice. Of those of us who survived, I caught the worst of the storm's fury, and it left me badly injured. Beneath my costumes, I am covered with scars," he said sadly. "I broke enough bones that things never healed right. I used to be the third acrobat with the twins." He shrugged. "Now, I'm lucky to walk and do a little drumming."

"Yet you still dream prophecies?" Kestel asked, looking to Zaryae.

The dark-haired dancer drew a long breath before answering, and her brown eyes held sorrow. "Before the Great Fire, I saw visions. I could touch a person's cloak and see his past. If

I held an object in my hand, I knew the secrets of the person who had owned it. People paid well for my visions—and some paid well for my silence." She paused.

"Illarion's body was most damaged by the storm. Kata lost herself, and the twins were changed. But when the storm stripped away my magic, its power roared in my mind."

Her voice faltered. "I have never felt such pain. I went mad for a time," she said, shooting an uncertain glance toward Illarion, who nodded and gave an encouraging smile.

"All I know is that for a while, I heard the voices of the gods, and the past, present, and future swirled around me like dust in a storm," Zaryae said. "When I finally came to myself, my dreams were no longer my own. Every night, I descend back into the madness, and every morning, I wake from it. It's as if the wild magic rages in my mind. Within the walls of the village, I can't hear the voices. But if I venture outside, they return. I have learned that it goes easier on me if I don't try to hide from the dreams. So every night, for a little while, I step outside the wall and let the dreams speak."

"And now?" Kestel asked. "You said you had a warning for me."

Zaryae smiled. "Knowing Riker's Ferry, one doesn't need a seer to get a warning. This town is filled with people who are desperate to remain hidden or to keep their secrets. But this warning came to me last week, during a storm."

"What did you see?" Blaine's voice was quiet.

Zaryae's eyes fluttered shut. "I saw a dark disk ringed with fire. It floated into the air and covered the sun. Then I saw symbols, but I didn't know what they meant. The disk fell and landed beneath a gallows, at the feet of a hanged man. The man slipped the noose and took the disk." She opened her eyes and looked at Blaine. "The man in my dream looked like you."

"Were those the symbols from your dance?" Kestel asked.

Zaryae nodded. "We often create our performances based on my dreams. When I dream things I don't understand, performing helps me find an answer." She paused. "We believed it would draw the hanged man to us. Then we heard from Desya and Borya that strangers had come looking for a mage. At the performance, when I saw you." She looked at Blaine. "I knew the message was for you."

"You said you wanted to warn us," Kestel said quietly. "Warn us about what?"

Zaryae met her gaze. "When the hanged man lifted up the disk, bolts of fire struck the disk, and he burned."

Which sounds a little too close to what happened at Mirdalur, Blaine thought, remembering their failed attempt to bring back the magic. *Is the dream warning me away from trying again? Or just showing something that has already happened?*

"We're grateful for your warning," Kestel replied. "And we'll heed it. But do you know anything else about the symbols?"

Illarion and Zaryae exchanged a glance, and Zaryae nodded. Illarion reached inside his shirt and withdrew an obsidian disk. "After the Great Fire, we took refuge in one of the manor houses that had nearly been destroyed. It was deserted, but we found shelter in the ruins. As Zaryae and I healed from our injuries, the others picked through the rubble for anything that might help us survive. Borya found this in a metal box that was hidden inside one of the manor's walls. When the wall collapsed, the hiding place broke open. Zaryae insisted we bring it with us."

Kestel nudged Blaine with her elbow. He drew a deep breath and drew out his own disk. "Once upon a time, there were thirteen of these," Blaine said quietly. "They were used to harness magic on this Continent." He looked up to meet Illarion's gaze. "If we're lucky, they might help us bring the magic back."

Illarion took the disk from beneath his shirt, lifting its leather strap over his head. He handed the disk to Blaine. "Then take it." He looked at Blaine intently. "Can the magic be restored?"

Blaine grimaced. "We think so, but we don't have all the pieces. That's why we came to Riker's Ferry. Before the Great Fire, there was a mage-scholar named Vigus Quintrel. He and his students went into hiding. But he left a trail of clues. We're trying to find him. The disks are part of that, we think."

"You're not the first person to come to Riker's Ferry looking for Quintrel," Zaryae said quietly. "Several weeks ago, another man came. He also asked Helgen about a mage named Quintrel. I had a dream where a cloud covered the black disk, and I took it to mean we should hide from this man."

"Did he give a name?" Blaine asked, leaning forward.

Zaryae shook her head. "He said he represented a wealthy man who would reward anyone who helped him. And," she added, "he was dead."

"*Talishte*?" Kestel asked.

Zaryae nodded. "Few *talishte* pass through this town. I have been told that it unsettles them."

Blaine looked at Kestel. It was clear from her expression that she, too, was thinking that the stranger was likely employed by Reese.

"We'd appreciate it if you wouldn't tell anyone about the disk," Blaine said.

Illarion chuckled. "We've spoken of it to no one, except yourselves."

"Now that you've found us, I'd suggest you drop the symbols from your performance," Kestel warned. "There are powerful men who gain from keeping magic out of reach. They've already shown that they're not afraid to kill. If they link us to you, you may be in danger."

"Helgen made it clear that he wanted us to leave Riker's Ferry tomorrow," Blaine said.

"Helgen's motives are often framed by what is best for Helgen," Illarion replied. "But in this, I believe his counsel is true." He paused. "Yet I'm curious. You couldn't have known about us and our disk. Why did you come to Riker's Ferry?"

Blaine paused, unwilling to admit to the existence of the maps. "We gambled that a mage or two might have sought refuge in the null places, and that perhaps those mages could lead us a step closer to Vigus Quintrel."

Illarion nodded. "I know of no true mages in Riker's Ferry, but then again, now that the magic is gone and mages are vulnerable, such people may not want their presence known. I can't help you."

"What will you do with the disk?" Zaryae asked.

Blaine shrugged. "That's why I was hoping to find Quintrel. We made one attempt to bring back the magic. It ended badly."

"We will also be moving on," Illarion replied. "Where we go, I'm sure the gods will show us." He paused. "There is something else that might be important for you to know." He took a deep breath. "I've heard it whispered that long ago, a small group of mages fled for their lives when the king withdrew his favor and betrayed them. They fled to a forsaken place where the magic was strong, a place of the gods." He paused. "They were not the first," Illarion said. "There were ruins of a much older city, and the legend says that the ancient city will rise again birthed in flame."

"Where is this place?" Kestel asked.

Illarion smiled and shrugged. "No one knows. The mages, so the story goes, were never seen again. But I wonder whether such a place is real, and whether your missing mage knew the legend and followed in their footsteps."

Without Valtyr's map, even a place of power might remain unnoticed if it were remote enough, Blaine thought. *Illarion's story sounds awfully close to what Geir said about the Knights of Esthrane.*

Their meal was long finished, and the fire was burning low. Blaine and Kestel stood. "You've been generous with your provisions, and with your information," Blaine said. "Thank you. Now, it's time for us to rejoin our friends."

Illarion stood as well. "Keep a watch," he advised. "I fear that you're not safe here. Had we room, I would offer you lodging, but as you can see," he said, spreading his hands to indicate the camp, "we barely have shelter for ourselves." He met Blaine's gaze. "Tell no one your business, and leave with first light. May Esthrane's hand be upon you."

Blaine and Kestel turned to leave. To their surprise, Borya and Desya stood and followed them. "We'll make sure you get back to the inn," Borya said. "A little extra muscle never hurts." His strange yellow eyes flashed, and Kestel shivered.

They reached the pub without incident and bade Borya and Desya good night. As they entered the Ram and Boar, the common room grew uncomfortably quiet when they made their way to the stairs. Feeling the gaze of the pub's patrons upon them, Blaine and Kestel moved quickly out of view and were glad when they reached the door to their room.

Piran and Verran both rose from their seats near the fire. "Where in Raka were you?" Piran demanded as they entered. "Geir got here some time ago. He's gone out searching."

In response, Blaine held up the new disk. "We went to watch the traveling performers and came back with more information than we expected." He gave Piran and Verran a quick recap.

"Not bad," Piran said, settling back into his chair. "But Verran and I turned up some information, too."

Verran moved away from the fire and propped one foot up on a bench. "I passed the evening in the common room. After I bought a round of drinks, people were happy to talk to me, and I fell in with the musicians who were playing tonight," he said, tapping the pennywhistle in his pocket. "We're not the first people to come this way looking for mages."

Blaine grimaced. "So we heard."

Verran's expression sobered. "Yeah. Either we were followed, or someone had watchers in place, looking for you, Blaine. A man I'd never seen before came to the bar asking about 'the strangers' who had come in with the storm. I stayed out of sight, but I could hear what was being said. Whoever was looking for you gave the impression that we were trouble. After that, the room wasn't quite so friendly."

"Was he *talishte*?" Blaine asked.

"No," Verran replied.

"Probably not Reese's man then," Blaine said. "I wonder if he was connected to the fellow who followed us."

"Did you learn anything from the musicians?" Kestel asked.

Verran shrugged. "They had a few opinions about the acrobat troupe and freak show that came into town a while ago. Been some accusations—never proven—that they're petty thieves. There's a rumor going around that the performers are under some kind of curse." He ran a hand back through his straw-colored hair. "Gods above! I wish we could leave tonight."

Kestel sauntered toward the fireplace and sank into the chair Verran had vacated. She looked at Piran and grinned. "How did your research go, Piran? Did you use your wiles to get the ladies to bare their secrets?"

"You've got no faith in me at all, do you, Kestel?" Piran returned with mock exasperation.

"If you mean, do I think you'll keep your wits about you in a whorehouse, the answer is no."

Piran sighed. "Well, then, you'd be surprised. I spent a pleasant candlemark in the parlor having a drink or two with the ladies. One of the girls, Calia, allowed as how she had seen a newcomer to town more than a week ago, a man who seemed to be looking for someone." He grinned. "As you can imagine, she's the one I paid for some companionship."

"We don't want a report of your escapades," Kestel replied with good-natured impatience. "You were supposed to be spying."

Piran drew himself up as if offended, although the mirth in his eyes said otherwise. "I'll have you know I denied myself the pleasure of Calia's significant charms and asked if we could use the time my coin bought to talk. She said it was all the same to her, so that's what we did."

Blaine and Verran smirked while Kestel rolled her eyes. "Yeah, we'd heard that you were all talk. Tell us something we don't know," Kestel jibed.

"How about this?" Piran said, growing serious. "Pollard's got at least one spy here."

The joking mood vanished. "How do you know?" Blaine asked.

"Turns out the spy took a fancy to Calia. He got drunk and started bragging. Said he worked for a very wealthy man and that he was sent to keep an eye on a group of escaped criminals. Gave her the impression he was the leader of a military team."

"Shit," Blaine murmured. "What else? Are you sure he

meant Pollard? I hate to say it, but he might not be the only wealthy man with a reason to keep an eye on us."

"He told her that his boss had powerful friends among the *talishte*," Piran replied. "It's got to be Pollard."

"How do you know she wasn't trying to pump you for information?" Kestel said, fixing Piran with a gaze that had suddenly lost all humor. "Maybe she's in league with him."

Piran shook his head. "Doubtful. She was angry. Turns out when she wasn't properly impressed by the man's story, he roughed her up. Madam Ellie had him thrown out, and he's not welcome back."

Before anyone could reply, the glass in both of the room's windows shattered and two streaks of fire arched through the air. Blaine barely caught a glimpse of what appeared to be a pitcher stuffed with burning rags before the vessel shattered on the bare-wood floor, sending shards of pottery and tongues of flames in every direction.

"Get away from the windows!" Blaine shouted. The flames caught quickly amid the tinder of the bedding and the dry wood. Already the room was filling with smoke and the noxious smell of pitch and burning oil.

Kestel's quick reflexes served her well. She ducked the worst of the flying shards and was on her feet in a heartbeat, grabbing her cloak and what she could of their gear on her way toward the door. Verran and Piran snatched what they could easily carry and Blaine followed, barreling out of the door and down the stairs into the chaos of the common room.

"The house is on fire!" someone in the crowded room shouted as Blaine and the others cleared the last of the stairs. Smoke was beginning to billow down the steps behind them. Screams, cries, and shouts filled the air as the drunken patrons shouldered each other to get out the door.

"This way!" Kestel said, grabbing Blaine's arm. He signaled to Verran and Piran and followed Kestel as she ran in the opposite direction of the crowd, into the pub's back hallway and through the kitchen.

"Head for the stables," Blaine instructed. "Grab the horses. We need to get out of here."

They plunged out of the doorway and into the cold night. A crowd had gathered behind the pub as well as in front. As they cleared the doorway, there was a roar and the flames burst from every window on the second story, showering the yard with glass.

"Those are the ones!" a voice shouted from the crowd. "They brought this on us."

The crowd closed ranks, forcing Blaine and the others to stop in their tracks. "We had nothing to do with this," Blaine countered, holding up his hands as if to ward off the crowd.

"We heard you were trouble!" another voice shouted. "We were warned."

"Someone threw pitchers with burning rags through our window," Kestel answered, taking a step toward the crowd. "We had nothing to do with it."

"Happened because you were here, din't it?" a man replied. "I'd say that's on account of you."

"Drive 'em out!" a woman yelled from deep within the crowd. "Get rid of them!"

"I say hang 'em all," another man dissented.

"Run them out!"

"If you want to blame someone, here's your man." Blaine and the others turned sharply at the sound of Geir's voice. He was standing at the back of the crowd, and he held a man by the shoulder so that his feet barely touched the ground.

The crowd hushed, staring at Geir. "I saw him throw the

pitchers, but I was too far away to stop him." Geir shouted. "I caught him as he tried to run."

The man twisted in Geir's iron grip. "Help me! He's a biter and he's got me!"

Behind them, the roof of the pub caught fire. Flames shot from every window and door, and Blaine could hear the shouts of the bucket brigade in the front of the pub as they relayed buckets from the well to wet down adjacent buildings and keep the fire from spreading. It had grown warm enough where they stood to raise a sheen of sweat on Blaine's forehead, and the firelight cast a flickering red light across everything.

"The biter's in league with them! Run them all out!" Voices took up the cry, and the crowd surged forward.

The clatter of a wagon and the thunder of horses running at full speed stopped the movement of the crowd. To Blaine's astonishment, the troubadours' wagon drove toward them at breakneck speed, with Zaryae in the driver's seat, her dark hair flying around her on the wind. She reined in the horses so hard that they nearly reared, stopping so the wagon stood between Blaine's group and the crowd. Borya and Desya, who had been hanging on to the outside of the wagon, standing on the running board and clinging to the top rail, jumped down, each now armed with long swords in both hands.

"Get in!" Zaryae shouted to Blaine and the others. "The boys will see to your horses."

Caught between the crowd and the heat of the flames, Blaine and his friends climbed into the wagon. As he ducked his head to enter the wagon, Blaine caught a glimpse of Geir rising straight up, still holding the arsonist.

No sooner had Piran closed the door of the wagon when Zaryae gave an earsplitting whistle to the horses, who took off at a gallop. Blaine had to grab for the sides of the wagon to keep from being thrown from his feet. Kestel lost her footing as they rounded a curve at full speed but was prevented from tumbling to the other side of the wagon when Verran grabbed her by the arm.

"We're heading away from the crowd and the fire," Piran observed. "Question is, what are we headed toward?"

"And can we trust the people who saved us, or did we just land in worse trouble?" Kestel asked as she pulled herself to her feet.

The wagon slowed after a few minutes so they did not have to cling to the sides to avoid being injured, but they were still riding fast enough that every rut and stone in the road jarred their bones and knocked their jaws together. Finally, the wagon's speed decreased and they gradually came to a stop.

Blaine poked his head out of the wagon's doorway, holding his sword. "Where are we?" he asked.

"Safe. For now," Zaryae replied.

Blaine jumped down from the wagon and looked around. They were outside of the wall, close enough to Riker's Ferry that he could see the lights of town and the flare of the pub fire, but far enough that the unruly crowd was unlikely to follow. The cold wind was a relief. Steam rose from the horses, and their frames heaved as they breathed.

A moment later, Geir touched down next to them. The arsonist was limp in Geir's grip, and when Geir let go of the man, he crumpled to the ground.

"If he's dead, we'll never know who sent him," Piran complained.

"He's not dead. He fainted when I went up in the air," Geir replied. "He'll come around. We'll find out who sent him."

"Pretty good drivin', don't you think?" Zaryae's voice made them jump. The seer was still in the clothing she had worn at the show, with a worn coat and a stained scarf pulled over her outfit. "You're lucky the warning came to me in time."

"Warning?" Verran asked.

"Zaryae's a seer," Kestel explained. "She's with the troubadours we saw in town, the ones who gave us the disk."

"I went to the wall when you left us," Zaryae answered. "I sought a sign. I lost consciousness, and a dream came to me. I saw flames, and danger, and a journey. It was so clear, I couldn't wait. I shouted to the others to pack up the camp, and I took the wagon after you. Borya and Desya had just seen you to the pub, and when the explosion came, they jumped on and we rode as hard as we could."

"We're in your debt," Blaine said. "Thank you."

"What about the others?" Kestel asked.

"Illarion and Kata will leave by the back gate. We're to meet them there. I don't like being outside the walls at night," Zaryae said, casting a nervous glance at the starlit sky, "but staying where you were wasn't really an option."

"Without our horses, we're stranded," Verran said.

As he spoke, they heard the sound of hoofbeats. Fearing that the mob had indeed come after them, Blaine gripped his sword and the others unsheathed their weapons.

"Look, they're coming!" Zaryae shouted, but her tone held a note of glee.

Four horses were galloping toward them. Borya and Desya rode the rearmost horses and stood in their saddles, driving the other two horses forward with drovers' calls and keeping them on course with the movement of their own horses. After a few minutes, they slowed, and as they neared the wagon, Borya and Desya dismounted and gathered the reins, leading the horses to where the group was standing.

"That was some good riding," Piran said appreciatively. "You've herded before?"

Borya laughed and brushed his dark hair from his yellow eyes. "Desya and I grew up traveling in the Flatlands. If it's got four legs and hooves, we've driven it from one side of the grasslands to the other. Your horses were much easier than a herd of goats!"

A moan drew their attention. The man lying at Geir's feet stirred. "Let's see what our guest has to say," Geir said, leaning down to grab the man by his shoulder. He jostled him awake and pulled him into a sitting position. The man eyed Geir with terror and seemed only barely aware that the others were nearby.

Geir squatted down so he was on eye level with the man. "Look at me," Geir said softly, his voice quiet, thick with compulsion. The arsonist resisted for a second, and then despite his terror, he raised his head until he was looking Geir in the eyes. No one spoke, but the arsonist's face relaxed, his eyes heavy-lidded though open, and his body lost its tension.

"Very good," Geir said in a voice that was firm, yet reassuring. "Now. Who sent you?"

"My commander."

Blaine could see the irritation in Geir's face, but the *talishte*'s voice remained smooth. "You're a soldier?"

"Yes."

"Did you swear your oaths to the king, or to a lord?"

"To a lord."

Geir nodded. "Very good. To which lord are you oathbound?"

"Lord Pollard."

Blaine and his friends exchanged a glance. Geir moved a little closer to the arsonist, and Blaine knew that the *talishte* was strengthening the depth of his compulsion. "What was your task?" Geir asked.

"I was to track a man, note his movements, discover his contacts, and report back," the arsonist answered, in a voice that sounded on the edge of sleep.

"Were you sent to kill him?"

"If the opportunity presented itself."

"That's why you started the fire tonight," Geir responded.

"Seemed as good a chance as any," the arsonist replied.

"What was he doing in Riker's Ferry?" Blaine asked. "He got here before we did."

"Answer the question," Geir prompted.

"My commander said you didn't seem interested in going back to Castle Reach, so Lord Pollard sent us out to the towns that remained, watching for you and asking questions."

Blaine looked up sharply. "There are more spies?"

"Yes."

"How many more?" Geir asked, his voice soothing.

"Don't know. Just more."

Behind them, Piran began to curse. "That's just great. Now we're being hunted."

"Pipe down. We already knew that. This just means the hunt's fresh," Kestel replied with a sidelong glare at Piran.

"Why did Pollard care where we went?" Verran asked. "What's he think we're doing?"

"Answer him," Geir directed.

"He doesn't know. Commander says Lord Pollard don't like mysteries."

"Did your commander send spies to all locations, or just to some?" Geir pressed.

"Lots of places aren't there no more," the arsonist replied. "Lots more got no people livin' there since the storms got bad.

That cut down on the number some. Commander said towns known for magic might draw you, or spots with no magic. Said you might be looking for a hocus, guy with a funny name. If you found him, we were supposed to kill you for sure. If not, like I said, report in, unless the opportunity was too good to pass up."

"You've done very well," Geir said quietly. "Now, rest." At his words, the arsonist slumped forward, motionless.

"What are we going to do with him?" Blaine asked. "Everyone in Riker's Ferry saw you leave with him, and they know you're with us."

Geir nodded. "Unfortunately for him, that restricts our options. The last time Piran caught a spy, I could make him forget everything and send him on his way. There are too many witnesses to do that this time."

Kestel nodded, and the look in her eyes was steely. "He can't return to report."

Zaryae looked from Geir to the arsonist. Blaine had expected her to react with horror, but her voice was matter-of-fact. "Have you fed recently?" she asked Geir. Her dark eyes betrayed no emotion.

He gave a cold smile. "No." He grimaced. "I don't care for the circumstances, but it's our most expedient option."

Blaine looked at the unconscious man. "He didn't mind the idea of burning us to death, along with everyone else in the tavern. We can't let him go." He met Geir's gaze. "He's yours."

Geir hefted the arsonist into his arms and walked away from the group, behind a copse of trees. When he had gone, Blaine looked to Zaryae and the twins. "*Talishte* don't bother you." It was a statement, not a question.

Zaryae shook her head. "We're from the southern plains, near the border of the Lesser Kingdoms. Our people have herded on those lands from times before memory. When a wolf threatens the flock, there is no shame to the dog who kills it."

She reached up to twist her long hair and secured it with a long brass pin at the nape of her neck. "An unfortunate analogy, but true. *Talishte* are predators. They and my people have long been able to live in accord. We understand each other. If your friend were not what he is, we would have had to handle the matter ourselves. A wolf cannot be allowed to harry the herd."

There were stories in her dark eyes, Blaine thought, but few of them had happy endings.

"Where now?" Verran asked.

"Illarion and Kata are waiting for us," Zaryae replied. "We join them, make camp as near the city wall as we dare, and set a watch for storms. Tomorrow, you can be on your way."

"I agree," Blaine said. "There's safety in numbers. We'll camp together tonight."

"And tomorrow?" Kestel asked.

Blaine smiled and patted the part of his coat that held the map. "We found some pretty exciting things in a place where there isn't any magic. Next we'll see what we find where magic used to be strong."

"I had a feeling you weren't ready to head back yet," Verran said, in a voice that indicated he clearly wished they were.

"How far?" Kestel met Blaine's gaze.

He shrugged. "About a day due west."

"Even before the Great Fire, towns were scarce in the foothills," Zaryae said, her gaze following the shadows toward the dark outline of the mountains that loomed against the night sky. "You mean to go to Durantha."

Blaine nodded. "You know the place?"

"I've heard of it."

"Does your gift give you any hint about whether going there is a good idea?" Verran asked nervously.

Zaryae smiled. "I'll see what the dreams say tonight. We're outside the walls." She turned her attention back to Blaine.

"Before the Great Fire, there was a mages' collegium in Durantha, the Lyceum of Tobar," Zaryae said. "Whether or not it still stands, I don't know. But if anything survives, you may find it worth the ride."

"All I want right now is a good night's sleep," Blaine replied, feeling weariness in every bone and bruise. "I'll worry about everything else tomorrow."

"If the storms don't come tonight," Verran added darkly.

CHAPTER SEVENTEEN

—

"PUT YOUR BACKS INTO IT, LADS, OR THERE'LL BE NO shelter the next time one of those magic storms comes around!" Niklas Theilsson shouted the order to his men and pulled the rope tight across his shoulder, one of a team of eight men pulling on stout lines to drag away the heavy stones that blocked entrance to Arengarte's cellars.

Niklas was sweating despite the winter cold, and he had laid his coat aside a candlemark ago, trusting to exertion and his heavy wool shirt to shelter him from the elements. "Pull!" he shouted.

Grunting and sweating, they pulled the heavy rock on skids far enough away from the cellar opening to clear a space. It had taken two days to reach the bottom of the pile of tumbled rocks that were all that remained of the grand home's main barn. With the final stone dislodged, Niklas dropped the lines and walked over to observe the opening they had uncovered.

A few years earlier, Niklas might not have been so quick to take a place alongside his soldiers for such dirty work. His superiors would have reprimanded him for acting beneath the dignity of his rank, and the farmer's son who had won his prized commission with luck, sweat, and blood would have taken their chiding to heart and stood to the side, directing.

That Captain Theilsson belonged in a different world, a different life, Niklas thought. He could barely remember those days, when Donderath's army swaggered off to war certain of its supremacy, and its officers were assured of their own extraordinary abilities. One by one, those generals had fallen, while the troops that had been Donderath's pride fell by the tens of thousands.

There had been a time, Niklas thought, when he would have been quite upset to find a smudge on his uniform or a button missing from his jacket. That was before he learned what it was like to go hungry for days, to crawl on his belly through mud and blood and entrails, pushing aside the severed limbs of dead men. It was before he had learned to be grateful for water wherever he could find it, even from brackish pools and old horse troughs, when he had thought so highly of himself that he would have thrown aside a moldy biscuit or a bit of maggoty meat instead of understanding that hunger can make the unthinkable palatable. It was before he had seen his army humbled, his men slaughtered, and his kingdom brought to ruin. Before he and the survivors, many of them maimed in mind or body, had begun their long, painful march across half a continent to find the wreckage of what they had once called home.

"Captain!" A man's voice roused Niklas from his thoughts. To these men, for the rest of his life, his name would be "Captain," and he knew that nothing would ever change that.

"What is it, Ayers?"

Ayers, a stout man with thinning red hair and a stubborn jaw, barely restrained himself from saluting. "The hunting parties have returned, sir. They've made good work of it, too. Each party brought down a deer." He paused and looked around nervously. "Beggin' your pardon, sir, but are you absolutely certain it's legal, poaching deer?"

Niklas laughed. "If there's no king, there's no king's forest, and hence, no poaching."

Ayers looked relieved. "Not that I doubt your word, m'lord, but my mate and I got in a bit of trouble over such things, before I went to war. We went out to do a bit of hunting and got caught by one of the king's wardens. I outran him, but my friend wasn't so lucky." He looked chagrined. "That had a lot to do with me joining up, if you know what I mean."

Niklas had no doubt that Ayers's story was common among those who had volunteered for the war. Some had joined for adventure, and others for honor, but most were running toward the war because they were running away from something else. His gaze strayed to where Carr McFadden was helping another work team lever the salvaged rocks into place to repair the holes in the stone fence. *Running away is usually easier than coming back*, he thought. *Blaine knows that. But does Carr?*

"Give the teams my hearty thanks," Niklas said, clapping Ayers on the shoulder. "Make sure the deer are dressed and save the blood, in case we have more visits from our *talishte* friends."

Ayers grimaced. "You don't think that's likely, do you, Captain?"

Ayers had been one of the men dropped from the sky by the *talishte*, and he'd been one of the lucky ones to emerge with bruises but no broken bones. Niklas could not fault his caution.

"Lord Penhallow's *talishte* are allies of Lord McFadden," Niklas replied. "That makes them our allies as well."

Ayers looked even more ill at ease. "There's a rumor, Captain, and I hope it ain't true. Some of the men are saying that you've sworn your fealty to Lord Penhallow. They're not keen to be bound to a biter."

Niklas grew sober. "I've pledged my fealty, but not to Lord Penhallow. Blaine McFadden is our lord now, and I am his liege man." He had always been at Blaine's side, from the time they were boys together, and more than once, he had bound up the wounds inflicted by the elder McFadden or talked Blaine out of running away, or worse. Old guilt stabbed at him. *Perhaps if I'd been around, I might have kept Blaine from killing Old Man McFadden. I let him down once. I won't do it again.*

Ayers looked relieved. "I'll let the men know, sir. They were afraid to ask."

Niklas forced his attention back to the present. "If that's what's being said, I'd appreciate your help in setting it right," he said. "I'd like to put the men's minds at ease." He paused. "Lord Penhallow is, by all accounts, an honorable *talishte*, and a patron of Lord McFadden's. Please let the men know they need to be mindful of how they talk."

Ayers saluted. "Consider it done, sir."

Niklas turned back to the work crew, who had regrouped to clean out the cellar beneath the collapsed barn. Durron, one of his lieutenants, organized the men so that whatever rubble was found in the cellar could be handed up along a human chain, passed from man to man until it could be discarded. Satisfied that the procedure no longer needed his help, Niklas retrieved his coat and was headed toward the ragged cluster of tents and lean-tos that was the camp.

"Captain Theilsson!"

Niklas looked up to see Ordel, the healer, striding toward him. The look on Ordel's face gave Niklas to know that it was not a social call. "What's wrong?" Niklas asked as soon as the man was close enough for conversation.

"We've got two men down," Ordel said. "I don't like the look of it. I think it's fire frenzy."

Niklas sighed. 'Fire frenzy' was one of the names given to the strange madness that had begun to appear around the time of the Great Fire. Some called it "Meroven madness," as if Donderath's opponent had seeded an outbreak. Still others just called it "the madness," making no attempt to explain its origin. "Tell me," Niklas said, falling into step beside Ordel.

"Both of the men complained of feeling poorly for the last few days," Ordel said. "One of the men, Eidar, became confused and then collapsed while he was mending fences. The men who brought him to me said he started convulsing and grunting before he lost consciousness."

"And the other?"

Ordel shrugged. "It came on him a little differently, but we've seen the like of it before. He had mentioned not feeling well, and his tent-mate said he hadn't slept well for several nights, thrashing and calling out in his sleep."

"If that's the mark of madness, then we're all madmen," Niklas said, his tone dark. "These men have seen real nightmares and lived to tell it. Everybody's dreams are haunted." *Mine certainly are.*

Ordel nodded. "Aye, sir. That's true. But this morning Roderon, the second man, didn't seem to know where he was or who he was. His friends thought he might have had too much to drink, and so they got him up and out for the work detail, but it's as if he's in a fog that doesn't lift," Ordel said. "He's forgotten the most basic things, like how to use a saw or a hatchet or tie off knots."

"Do you think it was an act, to get a few days in the infirmary?" Niklas asked.

Ordel barked a harsh laugh. "You mean lounge in luxury in the sick tent, where the canvas leaks and the brazier can't keep out the chill?"

Niklas grimaced. "Some men will do just about anything to shirk a task they don't like."

"True enough, but in this case, I don't think so. I gave Roderon a purgative, just in case he'd eaten something that caused the symptoms." He chuckled. "Usually that separates the real sick men from the pretenders very quickly."

"How is he now?"

Ordel sighed. "He collapsed, and then he started to shake and cry out. We had to restrain both men by tying them to their cots."

"Are you certain it's the madness?" Niklas asked. "You've ruled out bad whiskey, eating or smoking or brewing the wrong kind of plants, being bitten by a snake—anything?"

Ordel favored him with a forbearing smile. "Yes, Captain. No one saw them eat or drink anything that wasn't shared by the rest of the camp. There are no bite marks of any kind."

"Were they using witch potions?" Niklas asked, still hoping to find any explanation other than the madness.

Ordel shook his head. "We found none in their tents, nor any of it on their skin." Niklas knew that Ordel was well acquainted with the potent mixture the men called 'witch potions.' Some of the men whose battle scars were more mental than physical had taken to creating dangerous mixtures of nightshade, hensbane, and other wild plants that could be made into an ointment to produce visions. Despite Niklas's condemnation of the dangerous potions and the healers' efforts to confiscate the substances, the plants were so plentiful and the recipes so basic that it had been impossible to completely eliminate them.

Niklas cursed. "What now?"

"We've given them both sedatives, and they're quiet for now." He turned to look at Niklas. "You've seen this happen as often as I have. We both know how it goes from here."

Niklas let out a long breath. "Yes, we do." Once seized by the madness, few men recovered. They thrashed and wailed, tormented by visions and monsters they alone could see, as if the wild magic of the storms had found a home inside their minds. Some lingered for several days or weeks, until they refused all sustenance and died of starvation. A lucky few had survived, but thus far, none of Ordel's healers could determine what enabled these men to recover. Eight of the men who had left the Meroven battlefront with Niklas had fallen to the madness, and only two had survived. What little they knew about the madness came from the rumors and gossip they had picked up as they traveled, since it seemed to have struck in every town and village where they had journeyed.

"Have your healers learned anything more about the madness?" Niklas asked. They had reached the infirmary tent, and Ordel held open the tent flap for Niklas to enter.

"We've seen no link to anything they've consumed, and it doesn't appear to spread from man to man like flux or fever," Ordel said.

"Thank the gods for small favors," Niklas replied. A plague of madness was more than he wished to contemplate.

"There they are," Ordel said, indicating the two men with a nod of his head.

The healers' tent was one of the largest in the camp, and while it was in no better repair than the others, it offered room for six cots as well as space enough for two healers to eat, sleep, and work among their charges. Right now, the cots were empty except for the two sick soldiers. Niklas walked between the two cots and regarded the men in silence.

Under the influence of the healers' sedative, the men appeared to be sleeping soundly. The ropes that bound their wrists and ankles to the cots betrayed the truth, as did the fresh burns on their skin where the men had rubbed raw against their bonds. Their breathing was shallow, and their skin was ashen.

"We've done our best to make them comfortable," Ordel said quietly, his voice sad.

"Naught to do now but wait," Niklas said. "What are the men in the camp saying?"

Ordel shrugged. "You know an army camp moves on its belly and lives for gossip. I'm sure by now the rumors say that these two poor blokes turned into wolves and bayed at the moon. Let them imagine all the reasons they like. I suspect that it would terrify them more to know that we have no idea what causes or cures it."

Niklas nodded. "I agree. Keep me posted. If anything changes with their conditions, or any others succumb, I want to hear about it."

"Aye, sir." Ordel sighed. "And may Esthrane favor us. Gods know, we've seen more than our share of bad fortune."

"I stopped asking the gods for their favor the night Donderath fell," Niklas said. "They didn't deliver us then. I wonder if they were ever listening at all."

Ordel gave a sad smile. "You've led a regiment of injured and heartsick men through the wreckage of their kingdom and brought them home again. I believe the gods favor you more than you know."

"I hope so, Ordel. I hope so."

Niklas left the healers' tent and stepped into the cold wind.

He headed up the path to what remained of Arengarte, his family home. His father had made his own way in the world, turning what began as a small bit of land into a thriving farm. Lars Theilsson had been a clever man, and he had developed arrangements with the nearby miller to gain a preferred price for his own wheat and barley. He had employed spinners, weavers, and dyers to turn the wool from his herds of sheep into sought-after yarn and cloth. The farm's kitchen had produced jams, pies, and breads that were quite popular with the nearby town folk. Over time, the Theilsson family had prospered despite their lack of a noble title.

Now, Niklas thought sadly, most of what his father had built was gone. Arengarte's roof had been damaged by winds and weather, but thankfully, it had been spared from the Great Fire. The large farmhouse, built of fieldstone, had withstood the elements fairly well. A tree had fallen on one corner of the house, the chimney had collapsed, and the wind had torn off the shutters. The smaller dependency buildings had been made of wood, and most had been severely damaged. Those were all problems Niklas intended to rectify, now that he had returned with a ready-made workforce that badly needed a self-sufficient home.

"Copper for your thoughts," Ordel said, following him outside.

Niklas shrugged. "In spite of everything, it's good to be back."

Ordel nodded. "I overheard some of the men talking. The soldiers who bartered for ale at the last tavern we passed mentioned something you need to warn your friend about. There was talk at the pub about strangers who'd been through, asking questions. They were looking for Blaine McFadden."

Niklas sobered quickly. "What cause did they have to be looking for Blaine?"

Ordel shook his head. "They never said, but the barkeeper told me they were flashing coins around, willing to pay for information."

"Pollard's men?"

Ordel shrugged. "These men were *talishte.*"

"Pentreath Reese," Niklas muttered. "That means trouble."

CHAPTER EIGHTEEN

F OR WHAT IT'S WORTH, I REALLY DON'T LIKE THIS."
Bevin Connor followed Lanyon Penhallow through the
debris-strewn streets of Castle Reach.

"Liking has nothing to do with it," Penhallow murmured.
"Necessity does."

Connor kept his hand close to the pommel of his sword,
though he knew his skill as a fighter was no match against a
serious opponent. He and Penhallow had left the relative safety
of Quillarth Castle nearly a candlemark ago, on an errand
Penhallow had deemed 'urgent.' It was not so urgent that it
required Treven Lowrey to accompany them, Connor thought
sourly. The former mage-scholar had insisted he was better left
behind to study the books they had found in the hidden vaults
of the Knights of Esthrane.

Before the Great Fire, Connor had always enjoyed the
errands that took him into the palace city. Now he watched
uneasily as they made their way through the darkened streets.

"We're almost there," Penhallow said.

"How can you be sure the shop is still standing?" Connor

argued, nervousness getting the best of him. "Everything's changed."

"I'd had some dealings with them just before that unfortunate incident in the crypt," Penhallow replied. Connor shuddered, remembering. Pentreath Reese's men had stormed Penhallow's hiding place. Blaine and the others had narrowly escaped, and Connor had nearly died. "Granted, it's been a few weeks, but the odds are good—"

Penhallow stopped in his tracks and looked at the row of storefronts. "And here we are," he said.

Connor eyed the building warily. Most of the shops were deserted, their windows broken, their signs charred and askew. Several of the adjacent buildings' roofs had burned in the Great Fire, and the walls of the remaining buildings were dark with soot.

TRINKETS, the sign read, and three balls, the symbol of a pawnbroker, hung beneath the sign. The window was cracked and smudged, but the dim light of a lantern shone from within. A variety of old keepsakes were haphazardly displayed in the window: A carved ivory statue, a large, ornate snuffbox, and an old, red battle flag were the items that caught Connor's eye. "Not much to look at, is it?" he muttered.

Penhallow smiled. "Looks can be deceiving."

Connor followed Penhallow into the shop. It smelled of dust and smoke and was cluttered with everything imaginable. Jewelry, weapons, books, and decorative objects of all sorts crowded into every corner and shelf. "How does this shop get left alone?" Connor wondered. "Everything else has been looted clean."

"Most shops don't have a *talishte* as a proprietor."

Connor startled at the voice. He was half-hidden by shadows

so that in the lantern light, Connor saw only part of his face. The man appeared to be in his fourth decade. He had black hair shot through with gray, which he wore back in a queue. His waistcoat was of good brocade, now shabby with wear.

"Ambrose, it's good to see you," Penhallow said warmly and clapped the man on the shoulder. "This is my associate, Bevin Connor, until recently in the service of the late Lord Garnoc."

"Come here, boy. Let me get a look at you," Ambrose said, his voice gravelly. Connor shot a concerned glance toward Penhallow, who nodded. Ambrose caught the movement and chuckled. "That's all right. I won't bite…this time."

"Ambrose has agreed to keep an eye out for things that might pertain to our problem," Penhallow said.

"Meaning that I watch out for magical items that have been looted from their rightful owners, things taken from the old manors when they were destroyed, things that shouldn't be in circulation," Ambrose said, sparing Connor a glance.

"And what have you heard?" Penhallow asked. "People who come to pawn stolen goods often carry tales."

Ambrose nodded and motioned for them to follow him into the rear of the crowded shop. A large black mastiff growled menacingly as Penhallow approached, only to be silenced by a slight movement of Ambrose's hand. "I let Farod bare his teeth so I don't have to bare mine," Ambrose said.

Ambrose had fashioned a small, shabby parlor in the store's back room. A fire burned in the fireplace, taking the chill from the space. Above the mantel hung four swords against a battered family crest. On the mantel, a variety of blackened silver objects lay on haphazard display: candlesticks, goblets, and teapots. On either end of the mantel, old battle flags hung from staves flush against the walls. Two tapestries, stained and ragged along the edges, hung against the walls, one beside the door, and the other to the right of the fireplace. The worn furniture looked as if the pieces might have been among Ambrose's inventory of distressed items. A velvet couch, its pile rubbed thin in places and faded along the back from long-ago sun, sat facing the fireplace. Two armchairs covered in a dowdy brocade were nearest the fire. Ambrose sat in an armchair and motioned for them to take their seats. Connor sat, but Penhallow walked closer to the fireplace and leaned against the mantel.

"You asked what I've heard," Ambrose said. "The usual half-truths, gossip, and lies. The kind of people who come to trade with me don't frequent the better parts of town."

"There aren't any better parts left," Connor muttered under his breath.

Ambrose chuckled. "Quite true, m'lad. But beneath the prattle, I hear dark rumors. It's said that the Knights of Esthrane are stirring."

Penhallow frowned. "The Knights? Why now?"

Ambrose leaned back in his chair. "The king is dead. The king's soldiers are dead. There's no law for them to fear in Donderath. Perhaps their return would not be a bad thing. It's often the fear that a guardsman is about that gives the thief pause."

"The Knights never bothered themselves with petty issues like keeping the peace," Penhallow replied. "They were as likely to hunt *talishte* as humans. They did as the king bid."

"Until the king himself grew to fear them," Ambrose replied. "I remember those days as well as you do. Yet I tell you, I have heard rumors that the Knights are taking an interest in affairs. Tread carefully."

"What else do you hear?" Penhallow pressed.

Ambrose's face grew somber. "The outbreaks of madness are growing worse."

Penhallow frowned. "How so?"

Ambrose watched the fire as he answered. "The last time we talked, it was just a few cases." He shook his head sadly. "But there have been more incidents. As I hear about it, I track it," he said. "Best I can tally, there've been about a thousand cases in the city proper." He met Penhallow's gaze. "It's starting again."

"What's starting? And what do you mean, 'again'?" Connor asked.

Ambrose turned his gaze on Connor. "Magic isn't just convenient, m'boy. It's necessary. Without it, bad things happen."

"Like crop failures and floods and plague," Connor supplied.

Ambrose replied, "The magic has 'broken' before over the millennia. We know that, from what our oldest *talishte* have seen themselves. Each time, when the magic failed, it was a period of great hardship." His eyes transfixed Connor. "Without tamed magic, men go mad."

"What do you mean?"

Ambrose's gaze had a faraway look. "No one really knows why it happens, but each time, the records show an outbreak of madness. A few at first, then more. If it's not put right quickly, thousands of people go raving mad." He drew his eyes back to meet Connor's. "Can you imagine? I hear about more cases of madness each day." Ambrose shook his head. "I don't know how bad it is outside the city, but it will get worse."

Connor stole a glance toward Penhallow, who nodded in confirmation. He looked back to Ambrose and leaned forward. "As I said, magic has failed before."

Ambrose nodded.

"And each time, society fell apart, chaos and madness ensued. Then someone put the magic right once more. It must be possible."

Ambrose's expression grew cold, and he leaned back in his chair. "Such things are best not discussed."

Before Connor could reply, Penhallow shifted his position, taking a step nearer the fireplace. Something had changed in his posture, and Connor sensed a new tension in the room.

"What of Reese?" Penhallow asked.

Ambrose leaned back, drumming his fingers on the arm of his chair. "Pentreath Reese is a slippery fellow," he said. "I understand he has a new obsession: finding a man named Blaine McFadden."

Connor looked sharply toward Penhallow, but Penhallow's expression gave him no clue as to his thoughts, and Connor remained silent. "Why is Reese interested in McFadden?"

"His real reason? Who knows? I remember the name. Killed his father in cold blood. Should have hanged for murder, but King Merrill went soft and sent him to Velant instead."

"Some might say hanging is preferable to exile to the arctic," Penhallow noted.

"Perhaps," Ambrose allowed. "Still, it would be like Reese to want the services of a murderer. He has enough of them in his employ."

"If so, what does he want with McFadden?" Penhallow asked, his face giving nothing away.

"Well, that's where it gets interesting," Ambrose said. "Reese's men say one thing, and the word on the street says something else. Rumor has it there's a bounty on McFadden's head, a dozen gold pieces to the man who brings McFadden in alive. That's enough money to make quite a few men sell their souls. Word on the street is that Reese says McFadden double-crossed him, and he wants to make an example of him."

"Interesting theory," Penhallow said. "Is that all Reese's men are saying?"

Ambrose straightened. "No. It's not. A couple of them came by here. Would have turned the place upside down looking for something."

"For what?" Penhallow asked, and Ambrose smiled like a fisherman with a taut line.

"I imagine they were looking for this." Ambrose held up a slim obsidian disk by a silken cord. "Same as you."

Penhallow smiled. "How did you keep it from them?"

Ambrose's expression grew melancholy. "I didn't."

"Nobody move." A fighter dressed all in black stood in the doorway, and behind him, Connor could see more men. Connor had not heard the fighters approach, which likely meant they were *talishte*. Farod, seated beside Ambrose's chair, stood, his hackles raised, and gave a low growl.

"They got here two days ago," Ambrose said. "Bloody poor houseguests, the lot of them."

Connor looked around the small parlor. There were no windows, and no other door. *Trapped.*

The lead fighter stepped into the room and drew his sword. "You are the prisoners of Lord Reese. You will come with us." He turned to Ambrose. "And now that we have Penhallow, you will surrender the disk."

Penhallow's motion was a blur. In the blink of an eye, the swords above the mantel were in his hands. There was a glint of silver, and then one of the swords was in Ambrose's grip. Connor caught the second sword an instant before the fighter moved toward him. Penhallow stood with a sword in each hand.

Connor ducked the fighter's swing, and the man's sword sank into the back of the couch behind where Connor had been standing. Two more fighters swarmed into the small room, blocking their exit. Connor shoved the couch toward his attacker, stumbling out of the way of another killing stroke. He parried the next swing, holding his sword with both hands, but the *talishte*'s greater strength sent a shock down his arms strong enough that he feared his bones would snap.

Penhallow and his attacker were moving so quickly that Connor could scarcely trace their motions. Ambrose, too, was holding his opponent at bay. The *talishte* who advanced on Connor smiled, and Connor knew the man realized he had the weakest prey.

The *talishte* swung again, and Connor dove and rolled. His attacker's blade came down hard on a small table, cracking it down the middle, momentarily jamming the blade. Connor reached the fireplace and snatched one of the short, heavy candlesticks from the mantel. He lobbed it at the *talishte*'s head with all his strength as the fighter's attention was on freeing his blade. The candlestick hit the *talishte*'s temple with a satisfying thunk, but though the man staggered, he did not fall.

"I'm going to kill you very slowly for that," the *talishte* snarled as his blade came clear.

Connor tore one of the flags from its mooring above the mantel and let it drag through the fire. The old fabric caught immediately, and with a battle cry that was more an exclamation of terror than of bravado, Connor lunged toward the *talishte*, swinging the burning flag.

The flag caught the *talishte* as he moved, setting his clothes and hair ablaze. Connor pivoted, coming at Ambrose's opponent, who was the closest of the enemy *talishte*. Caught between Ambrose's sword and the blazing pennant, the *talishte* fighter gave a roar of anger. Ambrose dove forward, sinking his blade into the fighter's chest as Connor dipped the fiery flag to pull it across the fighter, who burst into flame.

"Mind where you wave that thing!" Ambrose cried, jumping back.

Penhallow had backed his opponent to the wall, and in one stroke he ripped the sword from the fighter's hands. The fighter sank to his knees. Penhallow brought his blades down and across each other, scissoring the *talishte*'s head from his body.

More fighters poured through the doorway, but the narrow entrance and the small room limited their numbers. Penhallow seized the nearest armchair and grabbed the other flag from the wall. He thrust the flag into the fire, then stabbed the flag-pole into the back of the armchair. In the instant before the entire chair went up in flames, he kicked it toward the fighters in the doorway. They shrieked as the flames caught them, and Connor watched in horror as the fire spread rapidly through the tawdry collection of papers and maps piled on the floor and the threadbare tapestry that hung against one wall.

"We'll burn with them!" Connor shouted.

"Not yet we won't," Ambrose said. Smoke was rapidly filling the room, tinged with the acrid smell of burnt flesh and the tang of blood. Connor could barely make out the shadow of Ambrose's form as the shop's proprietor moved along the fire-place wall.

Choking and gasping for breath, his eyes tearing too hard to see, Connor fell to his knees. He felt a viselike grip on his arm, and Penhallow hauled him to his feet. "Come on."

Stumbling as Penhallow dragged him forward, Connor could see Ambrose feeling his way down the wall. There was the *snick* of a catch releasing, and then a narrow, dark opening appeared as a panel slid back. Ambrose stepped into the dark-ness with Farod bounding behind him.

"After you," Penhallow said, giving Connor a shove.

The air in the tunnel was cold and clear, and as Connor

stumbled and ran, he gasped for breath, his eyes and lungs stinging from the smoke. Penhallow came last. They had barely started down the passageway when flames billowed through the doorway, and they heard a mighty crash.

"I'm afraid we've cost you the shop," Penhallow said as they ran through the narrow tunnel.

"I've got your disk. It's a shame about the rest, though. Ah well. Nothing lasts forever," Ambrose replied.

Connor felt as if he were hurtling through the darkness. He scraped painfully against the rough rock walls and banged against outcroppings so that he was certain he would be bruised and bleeding when they emerged. Finally Ambrose slowed, and in another minute, Connor saw the flash of flint on steel and then the welcome glow of a lantern. In the light, he could see that they had reached a way station of sorts, with lanterns and candles, a few small bundles of wood, and leather knapsacks.

"How can you trust him?" Connor demanded. "He was going to betray us!" He gasped and bent over, bracing his hands on his knees as he tried to catch his breath.

Penhallow smiled. "He warned us before we ever entered that we were compromised."

"How?"

"Did you see a red battle flag in the window, lad?" Ambrose asked, chuckling. "Lanyon and I have been using flags to send messages for a long, long time."

"I didn't dare tell you because I didn't want to endanger Ambrose," Penhallow added.

"What about endangering me?" Connor said, still unwilling to back down.

Ambrose grinned. "He's got fight, I'll say that for him." The *talishte* shopkeeper leaned against the stone wall. "I knew the shop was being watched before I knew what the watchers wanted. None of them cared about my window display, but I knew Lanyon would get the message immediately."

"Ambrose always has a variety of weapons close at hand," Penhallow said. "Old army habit. I didn't want to risk Reese's men destroying him if we didn't show up at all, but I was fairly certain we could fight our way out."

"Just in case I ever actually had to use this passageway, I thought it best to be prepared," Ambrose said. "I set this up before Reese's men came. Figured that sooner or later, someone would try to kill me." He gave Penhallow a sidelong glance. "Seemed logical if you were involved. Oh, and there's even some food for your pet mortal."

"I'm not a pet," Connor grumbled.

Ambrose looked from Connor to Farod and back again. "Whatever you say. I also put some dried meat away for the dog, just in case." He smiled. "I took your advice that I'd better be prepared for the worst, Lanyon. Then again, you've always had a genius for getting me into trouble."

"Just like old times," Penhallow replied, and in the dim light, Connor could see a faint smile on the *talishte's* face.

"Old times? You two have done this sort of thing before?"

"Aye. That we have," Ambrose said. "Served in His Majesty's army together long ago."

Connor looked from Ambrose to Penhallow. "Exactly which 'Majesty' are we discussing?"

"King Drostan," Ambrose replied, "most recently."

Connor's eyes widened. "King Drostan lived over three hundred years ago," he said quietly.

"And a fine king he was," Ambrose said wistfully. "He was the grandson of King Hougen, who brought back the magic at Mirdalur."

"Let's get moving and tell the tale when we're a bit safer," Penhallow cautioned.

They picked up the knapsacks and continued on their way, but a score of questions formed in Connor's mind as they walked. He put them aside in favor of more practical concerns but vowed to press both Penhallow and Ambrose for answers as soon as he could.

"Where does this tunnel lead?" Connor asked after they had walked for a long time in near darkness.

"We go under the city for a ways," Ambrose replied. "There's a warren of tunnels below Castle Reach, and before the Great Fire, they all connected. Tunnels run all the way down to the wharves and come up under the Rooster and Pig, among other places."

"Do you think Reese's men will be waiting for us?"

In the lantern light, Connor saw Ambrose shrug. "The tunnels don't run in a straight line. Some of them have been blocked, and the rest come up in enough different places that Reese would be hard-pressed to watch them all. And there would have to be survivors to know we didn't die in the blaze. I'd say our odds are good."

"Reese already knows we've destroyed his men," Penhallow observed.

"He'll have expected casualties," Ambrose replied. "It may take longer to figure out that we've escaped."

"We can't make it back to the castle before daylight," Connor added.

"We'll have to spend the day here in the tunnels. Tomorrow night, we'll move on," Penhallow replied. "It's too dangerous for us to stay in the city. We've gotten what we came for."

They reached a wide, dry spot in the rocky passageway, and Penhallow signaled a stop. Connor sank to the ground, exhausted, and realized how hungry he was. He rummaged through his knapsack to find hard sausage and a filled wineskin. Ambrose fished out dried meat for Farod, who finished it with a snap and a gulp, then looked longingly at Ambrose for more. When Connor finished eating, he returned his attention to Ambrose and Penhallow.

"What about you? Have you fed?" Although Penhallow had earned his trust, Connor was not yet completely sure of Ambrose's loyalty, and it had occurred to him that he might be stranded in a dark tunnel with two hungry *talishte*.

"You've naught to fear from me, boy," Ambrose said. "And even if I were a mind to taste you, I'm quite sure Lanyon wouldn't permit it. No matter. I fed before you came." He patted Farod. "So did Farod, although the greedy thing is always begging a treat." The large dog wagged his tail, then settled down beside his master.

"I'll hunt tomorrow night, when I scout our exit," Penhallow replied. "So you can put your fears to rest," he said with amused forbearance.

"You said you'd seen the madness come before," Connor said, returning to his questions.

"Sometimes, when the magic dies, it's just a single continent," Ambrose said. "There are legends of times when it failed throughout the known world, and those were dark times indeed." He leaned forward, his eyes glowing in the lantern light. "Can you even conceive of what it would mean to have much of the world gone mad?"

Connor shivered, but it had nothing to do with the chill in the tunnel. "I don't think I want to."

"It isn't just the madness," Ambrose continued. "The magic storms grow more frequent, larger. Cities wither because people prefer to move about to avoid the storms. All the things that make a civilization great die with the grand cities." He paused. "And as the storms grow, the monsters come."

Connor looked up. "Monsters?"

Penhallow nodded. "No one's quite sure where they come from, whether the magic spawns them or it rips a hole in the fabric of the universe that allows them to come through from somewhere else. But the longer the *hasithara* is gone, the stronger the *visithara* becomes. And the more monsters begin appearing."

"What kind of monsters?"

Ambrose had settled down on the rocky floor of the tunnel, angled so that he would be alerted should anyone approach from the passageway ahead of them. He stared into the darkness. "Things with teeth much bigger than mine," he replied. "Flying creatures, with talons strong enough to snatch a man from the ground the way a hawk catches mice, and with beaks sharp enough to peck out his heart in a single strike. Shadows that can kill a man just by passing over him and taking his breath. Scaled things with bulbous heads and fish eyes and teeth like a shark, that walk on land and run faster than a horse—and other things just as bad."

Connor watched Ambrose and felt a chill down his back. *If such things frighten a* talishte, *what hope do mortals have?* he wondered.

Penhallow's expression had grown sad. "The legends say ancient civilizations possessed great magic and then were destroyed when the magic died. I've walked among the ruins, just dust and memories."

"Do we know how they raised the magic?"

"Each time, the magic rises differently," Ambrose replied. "It may be that the nodes of power require different things to bind the magic. Or it may vary depending on who does the binding.

But on one thing the legends agree: It's bound to the blood of those who harness it."

"The Lords of the Blood," Connor replied.

Penhallow nodded. "And it means that, among the thirteen lords who bound the magic four hundred years ago at Mirdalur, at least one of them was a direct descendant of someone who had bound the magic before."

"And the disks?" Connor asked.

"Insurance," Penhallow answered. "Since we don't know exactly how the magic was raised before Mirdalur, it makes sense to gather the objects that were important to the men who raised it. That's why we need to find Vigus Quintrel. If my hunch is correct, he had it figured out, and he went into hiding to preserve that knowledge, knowing that there would be men like Reese who wanted to keep it from rising again."

Connor leaned back against the rock wall and closed his eyes. "But why would Reese want a world filled with madmen and monsters?"

"Pentreath Reese thrives on chaos," Ambrose replied. "Just as vultures feast on a battlefield, Reese is strongest when the world is in tatters and there is no one to constrain him."

"A kingdom of madmen," Connor murmured. "What honor lies in such a thing?"

"It's not honor Reese seeks," Penhallow replied. "It's power. When everything falls apart, Reese fills the void."

Connor drew his cloak around him. He had enough food in his belly to let him sleep, and the wine warmed him. Farod lay between Connor and Ambrose and appeared to have accepted Connor, so the big dog did not stir when he stretched out next to him. Penhallow settled himself in a position so he could see anyone who might approach from the way they had just come.

"Where next?" Connor asked.

"I've contacted Geir through the *kruvgaldur*," Penhallow replied. "Once we get out of the tunnels, you and I have business elsewhere."

"Do I want to know?"

A faint smile touched the corners of Penhallow's lips. "I intend to request an audience with the Wraith Lord."

CHAPTER
NINETEEN

I'VE NEVER REALLY BEEN THIS FAR WEST," VERRAN said, staring out across the rolling land. "I didn't know it was this beautiful."

"Or dangerous," Blaine agreed. They had woken with the dawn. Now, spread before them was a landscape they had not seen by daylight. On the way to Riker's Ferry, they had ridden across flatlands that, before the Great Fire, had been cattle pastures. They rode into the foothills of the Belhoven Mountains, just beyond the Pelaran River.

"The only mountains I've ever seen were in Edgeland," Kestel said, coming up to stand beside Blaine. "These are just as beautiful."

The sharp stone peaks of the Belhoven Mountains slashed across Donderath like a bony spine. The tallest crags stretched into the clouds, capped year-round with snow. While Blaine and the others were still a distance from the mountains themselves, the rocky spires dominated the westward horizon.

"Durantha lies at the base of Mount Elom, over there," Blaine said, pointing toward one of the smaller distant peaks. "But first we've got to get across the river."

"And crossing by ferry is definitely not an option," Kestel remarked, with a backward glance in the direction of the town from which they had fled.

"According to the maps, there's a bridge to the south," Blaine replied. "It means backtracking, but it can't be helped."

"This place we're going to, it was a spot where the magic was especially strong?" Kestel asked.

Blaine nodded. "I found it in the book Grimur gave you. The Lyceum of Tobar at Durantha was a place for mage-scholars and archivists. There was a grand library, a collection of magical objects, relics, even the bones of powerful magic users."

"Bones?" Kestel asked, with a sharp look at Blaine. "Why bones?"

Blaine shrugged. "Grimur's book doesn't come right out and say it, maybe because it was written for people who already understood, but I get the feeling the keepers of the lyceum thought that preserving the bones would help protect them."

"So it's haunted?" Verran said. "That's just great."

"Just because there are bones doesn't mean there are ghosts," Kestel said, landing a good-natured punch to Verran's shoulder.

"How else do dead people protect a place?" Verran challenged.

"It depends on how 'dead' they actually are," Blaine replied. "Geir does a pretty good job of protecting us."

"Geir's undead, not just dead. There's a difference," Verran sniffed.

A gust of wind came across the plain, and despite her heavy cloak, Kestel shivered. Blaine put his arm around her and she did not pull away. From the camp behind them came the smell of a fire, and the tangy scent of a pot of *fet* brewing over the coals. Blaine turned to look. Piran was deep in conversation with Borya and Desya. Illarion was tending the troupe's goats and chickens. Kata bent over the fire, poking at the coals with a stick and singing quietly to herself. Zaryae sat at the edge of their camp, facing outward, utterly still.

"What about the troupe?" Kestel asked quietly. "Last night it sounded as if they intended to come with us."

"They didn't have to save us, but they did," Blaine replied. He nodded toward Zaryae. "I think she's the reason why."

Kestel looked up at him. "What do you think she's seen in her dreams? About us, I mean?"

Blaine shook his head. "I don't know. But the rest of them defer to her, even Illarion."

"I'm worried more about Pollard than the performers," Verran said. "I don't like the idea that there are spies on the lookout for us. Do you think Pollard's got someone at the lyceum?"

Blaine shrugged. "There's no way to tell if the lyceum even survived the Great Fire until we get there. I don't underestimate Pollard. Then again, if the mages are still alive, it may not be that easy for us to get in, let alone one of Pollard's assassins."

"Unless he sends a former mage," Kestel replied.

There was no answer to that, so they walked slowly back toward the fire, where the others were giving Kata their tankards for some of the thick, bitter *fet* that would jolt them toward wakefulness. There was a battered pot on the coals, and Blaine smelled porridge and wild berries. With Piran and Desya on watch, the others sat down around the fire to eat.

Even Zaryae had rejoined the group. She said nothing, but from beneath the dark hair that fell into her eyes, she watched Blaine with disconcerting intensity.

"The gods are with us," Illarion said in a hearty voice. "No magic storms last night." Although the others had changed out of their elaborate performance costumes, Illarion was still dressed all in black, with his tall hat perched atop his head.

"And no monsters," Borya added. He grinned and his catlike eyes flashed. "Perhaps our new companions are favored."

"Not yet favored, except with the gods' curiosity," Zaryae said, and her voice, though quiet, drew the others' attention. Although Zaryae was a young woman in her twenties, the look in her dark eyes suggested wisdom and suffering far beyond her years.

Verran sat up and wiped his mouth with the back of his hand. "I traveled with a few caravans and faires before I went to Velant. Some of them had... *unusual* people," he said with a nod toward the twins and their catlike eyes, "people with odd skills," he added, glancing toward Illarion, "and jugglers, musicians, and acrobats. But they were motley groups." He leveled another look at Illarion. "The five of you are more like a family."

Illarion paused for a moment, then nodded. "Kata and Zaryae are nieces. Borya and Desya are grandsons. We were once a group of twenty, with my brothers and sisters and our families." His eyes took on a haunted look. "The changes that the wild magic worked on our group were cruel. Three of our group died in the Great Fire. Twelve of the others fell to sickness, or injuries, or madness in the months since then. Now we're all that's left."

"You're Wanderers," Verran said. "I've heard about your people, but I never expected to meet any."

"The Wanderers are the last of an old race from a homeland lost to legend," Illarion replied, with a trace of the heavy accent that was thick in the twin's voices. He reached up to adjust his tall black hat. "Our oldest stories tell of a great civilization that fell in a firestorm more than a thousand years ago. Since that time, our people have roamed at will with their herds and wagons, moving with the seasons and going where they found good water and plentiful food.

"My people have never sworn allegiance to any king, so the kings and their soldiers have never trusted us." Illarion shrugged. "We follow our own ways. We're traders, tinkers, peddlers, and entertainers." His eyes flashed. "Regardless of what some say, we are not thieves."

"You said that Zaryae's dreams brought you to Riker's Ferry," Verran said. "How is it that her gift still functions when magic failed?"

"My gift is much less powerful than it once was," Zaryae said quietly. "I received visions when I was awake, while now the power of the wild storms burns through me when I sleep. I have no magic that I can control, as I once did." She sighed. "When I touch an object, I no longer see its past. Yet I'm attuned to the storms, and it's as if I can see glimpses in the whirlwind."

"Your people aren't known for welcoming strangers," Verran said. "Can we thank your dreams for that as well?"

"My dreams have been troubled for many weeks." Zaryae's voice was quiet. "Since the Great Fire, the images are disjointed, difficult to read. But when we found the disk, the dreams grew clearer."

"What have your dreams told you?" Blaine asked.

Zaryae smiled, but the look in her dark eyes was distant. "Our paths wind together, for now."

"We've got company!" Borya called down from where he sat atop one of the wagons on watch. "Eight riders, coming this way."

Piran scrambled atop the other wagon so that he and Borya had an advantage as archers. Blaine, Desya, Kestel, and Illarion mounted their horses, while Zaryae and Kata went to secure the livestock. Verran gathered rocks and took shelter behind one of the wagons. When the riders drew closer, Blaine could see the armed men.

Blaine and the others rode out a bit from the camp to present themselves as a line to be crossed. Their weapons were drawn and ready.

The riders stopped a few paces in front of them. Their swords flashed, ready for action. Cloaks covered any uniforms that might have identified them. A broad-shouldered man with dark hair in a military cut gave a cold smile in greeting.

"We're willing to make this easy," the rider said. "Give us Blaine McFadden and we'll leave you in peace."

"Go to Raka," Desya snapped.

"We're not looking for a fight," Blaine said. "But that's what you'll get if you don't turn around right now."

The dark-haired man chuckled. "You hire street rabble to fight for you? Be a man. Give yourself up and we won't kill your friends."

There was a silver flash, and one of the cloaked riders stiffened in his saddle with the pommel of one of Kestel's throwing knives protruding from his chest. For a breath, he kept his seat and then he slowly toppled to the ground as his horse reared and fled. An instant later, the twang of bow strings sounded and arrows downed two more of the riders from their mounts.

With a howl of rage, the dark-haired man spurred his horse forward, sword raised, riding straight for Blaine. One of his companions rode for Kestel, making the mistake of thinking her an easy mark. Two of the others took on Illarion and

Desya, while the fifth man teamed up with the first attacker against Blaine.

Piran cursed as one of his shots ripped through the shoulder of an attacker's cloak without damaging more than fabric. Borya's shot opened a slice along the temple of one of the other attackers but missed its mark. A well-aimed rock struck the nearest attacker's mount on the flank, giving Illarion an instant's advantage. Blaine caught just a glimpse of Verran as he dodged back between the wagons.

Two opponents left Blaine no time to worry about how his companions fared. He had both his blades in hand. Up close, he could see the bloodlust in his attackers' eyes. Shouts and curses filled the air along with the sound of hoofbeats and the rough breathing of their mounts.

The two opponents circled and Blaine moved as well, doing his best to keep either from getting behind him. The attackers intended to work in tandem, and Blaine wondered how long he could keep both at bay. He scored a gash on the first attacker's thigh, but the second man managed to nick Blaine's forearm.

Another arrow sang through the air, and this time it caught one of Blaine's opponents in the right bicep. Before the man could recover, Blaine thrust with his sword, driving it deep between the man's ribs as the attacker slipped from his horse. Blood gushed from the wound, and the man fell to the ground as his mount bolted.

Blaine's victory came at the cost of a deep cut to his own left shoulder as the second man seized the advantage of his momentary distraction. Blaine cursed under his breath as he turned to face his remaining attacker. Out of the corner of his eye, he glimpsed Kestel holding her own with her surprised opponent, while Illarion and his attacker seemed well matched enough to be at a stalemate. Desya was giving his foe more of a battle than the man seemed prepared to fight, driving him back with pounding blows. Verran lobbed rocks whenever the fight came within range of his hiding place, sparing neither horses nor riders.

Borya and Piran continued to fire at the attackers when they could get a clear shot, but the quick movements of the fighters made it difficult to shoot the enemy without endangering their own side. The man fighting Illarion yelped in pain and twisted in his saddle as an arrow sank deep into his thigh. Illarion seized the advantage, tossing his perfectly balanced sword into the air as if it were part of his juggling act but angling the blade to slash his opponent across the throat.

What Kestel lacked in power she made up for in speed and style. She had the sword-fighting skill of a trained duelist and the dirty tricks of an assassin. Blaine saw that she was gradually drawing her opponent to reach beyond his balance, and when the man realized his mistake, Kestel took the offensive, bringing her sword down hard enough on his wrist to nearly sever the hand. The fight had taken them into range of Verran's rocks, and a rock the size of a man's fist flew through the air, striking Kestel's opponent squarely in the temple.

Blaine tried to maneuver his attacker closer to the archers, but the man would not be drawn into the trap. Illarion had gone to Borya's aid, and out of the corner of Blaine's eye he could see that together they were making short work of their opponent.

"You're the last man left," Blaine said, dodging a hard strike. Despite the odds, the man continued his single-minded assault. "Who sent you?"

"Do you have to ask?" the man replied through gritted teeth, swinging his sword in a two-handed grip. Blaine blocked the blow but had to brace himself to keep from being swept off his horse.

"Surrender and I'll spare your life," Blaine said, delivering a pounding blow of his own that the man nearly did not block. "I've got a message I'd like to send Lord Pollard."

"I have my orders," the soldier grated, readying for another swing. "Succeed or die."

Blaine got under the man's guard, twisting out of the way of his sword and driving his own point deep into the man's belly just as his opponent gasped and stiffened with Kestel's knife between his shoulder blades. His mouth worked soundlessly like a hooked fish, his eyes wide with pain, and then he fell sideways from his horse, leaving his mount covered with his blood. With their riders dead, the horses bolted. Borya and Desya rode after them, returning with four prime geldings.

"Good horses are hard to find," Desya said with a grin.

Breathing hard, Blaine looked around. Illarion and Desya each bore several gashes, but they looked no worse than he imagined he appeared. Kestel was flushed with the fight and sweat beaded on her forehead despite the cold wind. While blood spattered her clothing, none of it was her own. Piran had jumped down from his perch and was walking among the downed enemy fighters, his crossbow cocked to dispatch them if they were not already dead. Borya remained atop the wagon, watching the horizon for threats.

They regrouped near the wagons. Zaryae was singing a song in praise of Esthrane for their deliverance, and Kestel joined in with quiet fervor. Kata looked confused and alarmed, but Zaryae patted her arm and murmured something the others could not hear. Kata brightened and went back to sit in the wagon, humming to herself.

"Do you think they were working with the assassin in Riker's Ferry?" Kestel asked, dropping to a seat next to the fire.

"Probably," Blaine replied. "Maybe they were the insurance

in case the first attack failed. Pollard may just be casting his net wide and hoping he gets lucky."

"He may know about the lyceum," Kestel said quietly, "especially if he figured out why we were at Mirdalur." She met Blaine's gaze. "If he didn't suspect before that you were trying to restore the magic, that must have tipped our hand."

Before Blaine could reply, Zaryae took hold of him by his uninjured arm. "Sit down. I've put on hot water to make poultices. You're hurt." She leveled her gaze at Piran, Illarion, and Desya. "All of you. Sit."

Kestel chuckled as the men did as Zaryae bid them. Zaryae's mouth twitched a bit at the edges, satisfied. Then she turned to Kestel. "If you're as undamaged as you appear, come help me." She bustled back toward the fire. "Once we patch you up, I've got raisin cakes for breakfast. Figured you'd want to eat while we rode."

To Blaine's relief, none of the injuries were serious, and once their wounds were treated with Zaryae's poultices and bound up, they broke camp quickly, eager to be on their way. Zaryae and Illarion drove one of the wagons; Kata and Desya drove the other. Borya took up a position in the back of one of the wagons where he could keep an eye out behind them. Blaine and his group rode their horses alongside the wagons. Kata was singing one of the songs from the performance, and her clear, pleasant voice carried back to where they rode.

Kestel brought her horse up to ride next to Blaine's, while Piran and Verran took their turn as the rear guard. "Did you expect them to travel with us to the lyceum?"

Blaine shook his head. "Then again, I didn't expect them to come to our rescue."

"Do you believe Zaryae? That her dreams foretold our coming?"

Blaine shrugged. "You're talking to someone who sailed from the edge of the world to try to bring back magic. Apparently, I'll believe anything."

Kestel grinned. "You're no one's fool, Mick."

Blaine sighed. "I felt a little more certain of that before Mirdalur. Now..." His voice drifted off.

"We still don't have any word from Penhallow," Kestel replied.

"I wish we had Connor's map," Blaine replied. "The tracing you did is some help, but now that we've gotten another disk, I'd like to see if we could make anything more from the markings on the map—or from that book Grimur gave you. I have the awful feeling that we're running out of time."

"What do you expect to find at the lyceum?" Kestel asked.

Blaine shook his head. "I don't know. A book, a map, maybe another disk. Maybe someone who could translate the marks on the map, or on the disks. I believe Quintrel is out there. I think he's left clues for the right people to find him. We just have to put the pieces together."

After a few candlemarks' ride, the bridge over the Pelaran River was visible in the distance. Blaine let his gaze stray past it into the foothills, where the old map indicated there was a spot where magic once was exceptionally strong. Ancient mages believed that invisible lines, *meridians*, were where the wild *visithara* magic was naturally strongest and built their important buildings along those lines to tap into that power.

"Look there!" Piran pointed to the sky. In the distance, off to the right of the Pelaran bridge, Blaine could see dark shapes circling.

"Vultures," Blaine guessed. "So?"

Piran shook his head. "Too far away. Vultures wouldn't look

so big from this distance. Problem is, I can't think of anything that could be so big and that far away."

"They're gryps," Borya said, and Blaine could hear an undercurrent of worry in the acrobat's voice. Borya stood and turned toward the front of the wagon. "Gryps!" he shouted.

Abruptly the two wagons halted. Desya leaped down from his perch, and Borya opened one of the wagons. From it they withdrew two crossbows, two large quivers of quarrels tipped with razor-sharp blades and wrapped, just above the tips, with blackened rags. Verran hesitated for a moment, then jumped down from his horse and began collecting an arsenal of rocks for throwing and slipping them into a bag. Blaine caught a strong whiff of what smelled like pitch.

"What in Raka is going on?" Piran demanded. "What are gryps?"

"Bad news," Borya answered, keeping his eye on the circling forms. "We think they came out of the magic storms. From where, I don't know. They've got bodies the size of a man, with leathery wings that stretch, tip to tip, a good eight feet, and very sharp teeth. They're fast, and they hunt in packs."

Piran let out a particularly potent string of curses. "Oh, that's just great. And let me guess: They eat people."

Borya shrugged. "They eat anything that moves, and some things that don't."

"How do we keep them at bay?" Kestel asked.

Desya held up his crossbow and bucket. "Fire. Flaming arrows." He angled his head toward the tree line on the opposite side of the river. "If we can get to cover, we may be safe. They only hunt in the open, and only during the day."

"Give me some of your arrows." Piran had dismounted and walked over to where the brothers stood. He cradled the modified crossbow Dawe had made for him. "I can ride and shoot."

Desya dug in the wagon for more arrows. He also brought a lit oil lantern, so that Piran could set the pitch-soaked tips ablaze. "Borya and I can shoot from atop the wagons. We might get lucky, and the gryps will be busy with whatever they're circling. But if they notice us, we can only hold them off so long. We've got to make it to the forest."

Blaine nodded. "Understood."

Borya eyed the horses Blaine and his friends rode. "Put your group between our wagons. You'll be safest that way." Once more, he cast a wary glance toward the circling gryps. "Let's get moving."

They rearranged their riding order and set off at a brisk pace. Borya and Desya had fastened themselves to the tops of the wagons. They strapped themselves so that they lay flat on their backs in harnesses, with their oil lanterns clipped firmly beside them. With hats drawn low to shield against the sun, they were in position to ward off an aerial attack. Piran had lashed his lantern to the pommel of his saddle with a few straps of leather. He rode with his crossbow cocked and ready, the horse's reins clenched between his teeth. They set off at a gallop, desperate to cross the bridge before the gryps noticed them.

Within a few minutes, they were close enough to the bridge to see that it was an old, arched span made with massive stones. Beneath it, the Pelaran River flowed, deep, swift, and dangerous. Beyond the bridge, the forest nearly came down to the shoreline, and Blaine could just make out a road that might take them farther up the mountains to the lyceum in Durantha.

A shriek like the sound of steel on stone split the air.

"Here they come!" Borya shouted.

Blaine chanced a look toward the sky. The dark shapes had left off circling and were heading toward them like a jagged black line against the gray winter sky. Another shriek, closer now, spooked the horses so that they were running, wild-eyed.

They were nearly to the Pelaran Bridge. Its stone sides came as high as the horses' haunches and were blackened with age. Beneath it, the waters of the Pelaran rumbled by, gray and cold, with white hunks of ice swept along by its current.

One of the creatures was nearly upon them. It gave an ear-splitting screech and dove for the horses. Desya launched an arrow. The flaming quarrel blazed through the air, tearing through the gryp's right wing. The gryp screamed in pain and frustration, its wing dripping a dark ichor.

Piran sent another burning quarrel into the air, and this one took the gryp at the base of its throat. The flying predator was close enough that Blaine could see the gryp's long, bony neck and narrow, scaled head. As it shrieked, he could see the rows of needle-sharp teeth and its black, cold eyes.

Twisting and writhing to free itself of the quarrels, the first gryp gyred off to the side and landed, bleeding, on the ground. Three of its companions, smelling blood, veered to attack. Four more gryps followed the humans, easily keeping pace even with the horses running at full gallop.

The first wagon clattered onto the bridge's stone bed, and the horses' hooves quickly pounded behind it. Yet now, on the bridge's length, Blaine and the others were exposed to the gryps, and the huge beasts circled over the river, diving and weaving above and under the bridge, their wings barely skimming the roiling waves below, then propelling them high into the sky so they could dive once more.

Blaine, Kestel, and Verran hunched over their horses,

making themselves the smallest targets possible. Piran rode standing upright in his stirrups, squinting against the sun, careful to make his shots count.

They were halfway across the bridge now, and Blaine kept his eye on the tree line, refusing to look over his shoulder at the gryps. The archers kept up a steady barrage, and the horses' hooves thundered across the old stone bridge as the wagons creaked in protest at the strain. He looked over to Kestel. Her face was taut with focus, and she gripped a dagger in her right hand. Verran's eyes were white with fear, and he was muttering a string of curses beneath his breath, but he watched the gryps carefully, lobbing rocks at them whenever they came within range.

The other end of the bridge was growing nearer with every thud of the horses' hooves. Blaine caught himself holding his breath, willing his horse to move faster. They were nearly across, and then just a short expanse of rocky shore separated them from the thick forest.

Three gryps came at them at once. The archers took aim and fired, hitting their targets, and two of the gryps beat their wings, backing away. The third flew straight at the riders between the wagons. Blaine was riding on the group's flank, and his horse reared when the gryp dove for them, bucking Blaine from his saddle. He drew his sword and settled into a defensive stance.

"Get Verran out of here!" he yelled to Kestel. "I'll meet you on the other side."

The gryp came at Blaine fast, and he dodged as its leathery wings struck at him. His sword sliced upward, and its tip skimmed the creature's tough hide but did not penetrate. The gryp screeched in rage and lunged toward him with its long, snakelike neck. Blaine swung again, and this time his sword sliced into the gryp's wing, sending a spray of dark blood into the cold air.

The stone bed of the bridge was slippery with the icy spray of the river that crashed below. Blaine had no desire to fight alone on the bridge, and when he dodged the next strike, he ran to catch up as Borya and Desya gave him cover.

The wounded gryp dove for Blaine, and he threw himself to one side to avoid its talons. A rock struck the gryp in the head, giving Blaine the chance to regain his feet and strike at the gryp's uninjured wing. Just then, the fourth creature seemed to appear from nowhere, coming up from beneath the bridge in front of the lead wagon, and the group came to a sudden halt.

The gryp Blaine battled struck again, going for his legs with its sharp beak. Blaine jumped aside just as the gryp lunged, although one of its talons raked his thigh, and he brought his sword down, hard, on the juncture between the gryp's body and its right wing. A dagger sang through the air, flashing past Blaine's face, and sinking deep into the gryp's side. For good measure, another rock crashed into the gryp's injured wing. Blaine could not spare a glance behind him, but he knew Kestel and Verran were doing their best to back him up.

From the shouts of the others and the thud of the crossbows, Blaine knew the gryps were coming at them from all sides. He could not afford to take his gaze off the gryp he battled, and it watched him with clever, cold eyes, waiting for the chance to kill.

Blaine and the gryp lunged at the same time. The gryp's beak sliced across Blaine's left arm, and he choked back a cry of pain as blood flowed down his forearm. The attack did not slow his strike, and this time his sword got a clean hit, slicing through hide and sinew, so that the gryp's wing, partially cut off at the shoulder, dangled uselessly.

The gryp reared and bellowed, and Blaine threw himself forward, his blade leveled for a killing blow. His sword struck the gryp in its ribs, sinking deep into its chest. The dying gryp flailed its ruined wings, falling backward toward the river, sweeping Blaine along with it.

Blaine scrabbled for a foothold as he yanked his sword free. Caught in the gryp's death throes, Blaine battled to keep from plunging over the side of the bridge along with his kill. The gryp began to fall over the stone wall, and Blaine splayed his legs, trying to slow his own movement, twisting to free himself from the leathery wings and the talon that grabbed his cloak in the dying creature's panic. The shrieking gryp tipped over the side, pulling Blaine with it as he tried desperately to stop himself from falling.

He could see the swift, icy river beneath the bridge, watched the gryp lose its grasp on the rocks as its talon held on to his cloak. Just as he was about to tumble in, he felt rough hands yank his legs back onto the bridge. He fell backward onto solid ground, landing in a heap beside Kestel and Verran.

"You almost went swimming," Verran said, out of breath.

The shrieks of the three remaining gryps cut off anything else they might have said, and they scrambled to their feet, weapons at the ready.

The gryp that harried the front wagon had gotten closer, while another flew at the group from behind. Borya, harnessed atop the wagon, twisted for a shot. Piran loosed a flaming bolt, but the gryp veered at the last moment, and the arrow merely grazed its wing.

They heard a woman's scream and a man's shouted curse. Then the gryp spiraled upward, holding Kata in its talons.

"Don't hit her with your arrows!" Illarion shouted, his anguish clear in his voice. But even as Illarion cried out, Blaine could see that one of the gryp's talons had pierced Kata's body. She convulsed, then hung limply in the predator's clutch.

Desya cursed wildly in a language Blaine did not understand. Freeing himself of his harness, Desya climbed to his feet atop the wagon, lobbing shots at the gryps as fast as he could reload his crossbow. In another instant, Borya had done the same, screaming curses, his aim made more true by grief and anger. Their arrows pierced the gryps' leathery wings, too fast and accurate for the beasts to evade. Badly wounded, the beasts twisted away and left off the chase.

Piran's expression was hard, battle-focused, and Blaine guessed it was what his enemies had seen when they faced Piran in war. While Blaine had always thought of Dawe as the archer in their group, it was clear that Piran was well acquainted with the bow. He drew and fired with practiced speed, and his arrows flew straight.

The gryp that carried Kata's body angled away from them, satisfied with its prize, and Blaine tried not to think about the young dancer becoming the gryp's meal. But carrying the corpse made the gryp slow. As Piran drew aim on the last gryp that harried the group, Borya and Desya targeted the killer.

One flaming bolt hit the gryp that had killed Kata in its back at the juncture of its wings. Desya drew his bow and muttered a prayer. His arrow struck Kata's motionless body, setting her cloak and clothing ablaze. The gryp shrieked and loosened its hold, dropping the fiery bundle into the swift current of the Pelaran. Borya sent another arrow, and this one ripped through the gryp's wing. Robbed of its prize, its wings in burned tatters, the gryp gave one more cry and plunged into the icy river.

By the time Borya and Desya could turn their attention to the gryp Piran battled, it was already over. Piran's aim had sent the badly wounded gryp blundering away on bleeding wings.

Blaine searched the sky. No other gryps circled. Now, only the dangers of the forest awaited them.

"You're injured," Kestel noted as they moved to calm their frightened horses.

Blaine looked down at himself. The gryp's talons had sliced through his pants, and blood stuck the fabric to his leg. His left arm had a deep gash. As the adrenaline of the fight faded, the pain made him catch his breath.

"We've got to get to shelter, get off the bridge," he said, gritting his teeth as he swung up into the saddle. Kestel gave him a look that said the discussion was not over, but she and Verran saddled up as well, and the wagons began to move toward the forest road. They did not stop again until they were well hidden by the forest canopy. Just a few feet from the old road, a stream poured down the slope toward where it would join the river.

At a wide spot in the road, they halted the wagons and let the horses rest. The sun was high overhead, but in the shadow of the huge, old trees, the air was cold. The tree canopy was thick and the undergrowth was sparse, so Blaine felt reasonably assured that some new predator could not approach without being seen.

Illarion helped Zaryae down from the wagon. She was pale and trembling, sobbing as she leaned against him. Borya and Desya, still flushed from the battle, wore their grief clearly in their faces, and their altered eyes gave them the look of angry wildcats. Piran's whole form was taut with rage.

"I'm so sorry about Kata," Kestel said, and the others murmured their agreement.

Illarion's expression was disconsolate. "The thing that killed her is dead," he said in a hollow voice. "It was better to lose her body to the flames than to have that creature savage her." Blaine could see the depth of the man's loss in his eyes.

Kestel pressed Blaine to sit down on a large rock, and she

drew a tankard of water from the stream to cleanse his wounds as the men led the horses to the stream to drink. Zaryae sat alone, her arms wrapped around herself, face hidden by her long, dark hair. Her shoulders shook as she sobbed.

"I'll go to her, after she's had some time to herself," Kestel murmured so only Blaine could hear. "First, let's have a look where that thing got you. We can't have the wound going sour." Gently, she pulled back the tatters of his pant leg to wash the three deep cuts where the gryp had sliced at him. It stung, and Blaine bit back a curse.

Kestel sighed. "The best I can do is wash it for now. Once we get to real shelter, I have some medicinal herbs in my bag. They should help."

She turned her attention to the gash on his forearm. Blaine reached out to touch her cheek and gently turned her face so she met his gaze. "Thank you," he said. "I would have gone into the river if you two hadn't grabbed me."

Something flickered in her eyes and she smiled. "Can't have that," she murmured. "Without you, the magic is gone for good." Her voice was light, but her expression gave him to know that she understood just how close a call it had been.

He folded his hand around hers. "I'm glad you have my back."

"You know I do," she replied, and for a heartbeat she did not pull her hand away. The moment passed and she broke the gaze, returning to the task of cleaning his arm. The gashes were deep, and she took strips from his torn pant leg to bind up the wounds until they could reach the lyceum.

"Was anyone else hurt?" Blaine asked.

Kestel shook her head. "No one else got as close as you did. Maybe you should swap your sword for a bow."

Blaine grimaced as he tried to stand. "I'd take you up on that, but I've always had lousy aim."

He looked up to see Illarion standing in front of him. "How far to the lyceum?" the troupe's leader asked.

Blaine took a deep breath and shrugged. "I don't know for sure. After all this time, and the Great Fire, I'm not even certain it's still standing. I'm hoping we'll find shelter, and something that makes the trip worth the cost."

Illarion nodded. "If there's something here that could return magic to the world, our loss is small by comparison." Blaine could see what Illarion's admission cost, and he nodded. There was nothing he could say.

CHAPTER TWENTY

NIKLAS THEILSSON ADJUSTED THE COLLAR OF HIS best shirt and took a deep breath as he stood in front of Glenreith's massive front door. In all the years his friendship with Blaine had made him a regular visitor at the manor house, he never remembered feeling awkward. *I've put a lot of miles on my boots since then*, he thought. *I barely recognize the boy I used to be.*

Edward, Glenreith's seneschal, opened the door. "Welcome, Master Niklas," he said. Niklas nodded his head.

"Good morning, Edward." To Niklas's eye, Edward had always been old. He seemed unchanged from Niklas's memories of childhood visits, although more than twenty years must have lined his features, whitened his hair, or made his rail-thin body more stooped.

"Lady Judith is expecting you in the parlor," Edward said. "Thank you for giving Master Carr leave from the camp to visit. He came by earlier this morning."

Niklas smiled. "I've offered to give him leave to stay here, but he says that, for now, he prefers the camp."

Edward's face betrayed no emotion. "Ah. Very well. If he

changes his mind, his room is as he left it." He stopped in front of the parlor door. "Here we are." He opened the door and stood aside for Niklas to enter.

Lady Judith McFadden Ainsworth was seated on a brocade couch near the center of the room. A fire burned in the fireplace, but Niklas remembered that Glenreith never seemed warm enough in the winter.

Judith welcomed him with a smile and open arms. Her dark hair had a noticeable amount of gray, while worry and hardship had added lines around her eyes and mouth, but she was still quite a good-looking woman. "Niklas! So good to see you. Please, come in and sit down." She favored him with a kiss on the cheek and hugged him as if reclaiming a lost child. Niklas grinned. He had been a favorite visitor at Glenreith for as long as he could remember. If the downturn in her circumstances worried Judith, she did not show it. She insisted on pouring his tea and pressed a plate filled with small sandwiches and tarts on him as if he had not eaten in days.

As he ate, Judith settled back in her chair. "I'm in your debt for bringing the boys back to us safely," she said. "It was quite a shock, you can imagine, when Blaine and his friends showed up unannounced. Like seeing a ghost—but a welcome one!" She sighed. "We'd almost given up on seeing you and Carr again when the war ended and there'd been no word for so long." It seemed to Niklas that the mention of Carr seemed to take some of the sparkle out of Judith's eyes.

"It's been a long road for everyone," Niklas replied. He savored the warm tea. It was not the same quality that Judith had favored before the war, but such luxuries were a casualty of hard times. Whatever the mixture, it was better than what he had in the camp, and Niklas was determined to enjoy it.

Judith was watching him with a gaze that seemed to take in

the changes of the last years, and Niklas guessed that she was comparing the reckless boy he had been to the somber soldier he had become. "Thank you for giving Mari the confirmation she needed about Everet's death," she said quietly.

And withholding what she could be spared knowing, Niklas added silently. Mari did not need to have her dreams haunted with the image of Everet's staring corpse, of the quarrel that had taken him through the chest, and the mutilations inflicted by the vengeful Merovenian troops. Mari did not need to know those things, but Niklas wished by all the gods that he could stop knowing them. Everet's death was just one of hundreds that would haunt Niklas's sleep forever.

Niklas ducked his head, afraid Judith might read his thoughts in his eyes. "There are things about the army I enjoyed. Notifying their next of kin isn't one of them."

Judith nodded. "I understand." She paused. "Congratulations on your promotion to captain."

"Thank you," Niklas said. "Rank doesn't mean much these days, but I imagine my men will call me 'Captain' until we're all old and gray." It was his turn to be silent for a moment, and then he set down his cup and leaned forward.

"I know Blaine's gone off looking for something he thinks will help bring back the magic," he said and pushed a lock of dark blond hair out of his eyes. "He was never one for damn-fool quests, so if he thinks it's possible, it probably is."

He drew a breath. "The way I see it, I've got two priorities now: to keep Glenreith safe, and to keep Blaine alive." He met Judith's gaze. "He told you that I swore fealty to him?"

Judith smiled. "He told me. And he was rather chagrined by it, I'll add. I think he had well and truly put the notion of being lord of anything behind him when he was exiled, and he hasn't quite made peace with reclaiming the title."

Niklas shrugged. "My men needed a purpose. We swore our vows to the king, but the king is dead. These last few months, just getting home alive was cause enough. But most of my men have no family or fortune to return to, and many of them lost what lands, wives, or children they had to the Great Fire. I was going to make it my business to keep Blaine safe anyhow," he said with a conspiratorial grin. "This just makes it official."

"How do you think you're going to keep Blaine safe?"

Niklas grimaced. "First, I've got to get him to stop riding off without telling anyone."

Judith shook her head. "This is Blaine we're talking about."

"I'm proposing that I split my men into two forces. One will stay as a garrison to protect Glenreith. This quest of his has stirred up some powerful enemies. We want to keep them from posing a threat to the manor."

Niklas took a deep breath. "The other force will back up Blaine. Provide the protection that he didn't have at Mirdalur." *That almost got him killed*, he thought but didn't say aloud.

Judith nodded, and all levity had vanished from her manner. Niklas saw the glint of intelligence and will in her eyes that had enabled her to carry the beleaguered manor through hardship. "I agree, but can you persuade Blaine?"

"It's what I aim to do as soon as he returns," Niklas said.

"Good. I'm glad you already made plans. It saves me trying to talk you into it," she said with a smile.

Niklas leaned back in his chair, relieved that Judith was in agreement. "Edward said that Carr came up to the manor this morning." He let his voice trail off, looking to Judith's reaction for information.

Judith drew a deep breath. "War changes people, doesn't it?" she said quietly. "Carr was so young when he went off, but there was no talking him out of it, and I knew you'd watch out for him as best you could. It's a hard way to grow up."

Niklas looked away. "Carr saw far more action than I wanted for him, but keeping him out of the fray wasn't really an option."

It was a charnel house, Niklas thought, passing a hand over his face and pushing his hair out of his eyes. *Toward the end, it was almost impossible to tell which forces belonged to which side, we were so covered with muck and blood and soot. As if the horror of gut wounds and severed arms and legs wasn't bad enough, the mages had to bring their own particular brand of misery down on us. Gods above and below! It's a wonder we didn't all go barking mad.*

He realized that he'd fallen silent, and from the look in Judith's gaze, he guessed that his expression exposed more of his thoughts than he intended.

"Carr said he wasn't feeling well, and he went up to his room. I sent Edward up with tea and a bit of lunch for him. I imagine Mari will look in on him when she comes in."

Niklas looked puzzled. "Where's Mari?"

Judith chuckled. "Doing her best to ferret out her brother's secrets from his friend, the silversmith. Dawe, I believe, was his name. He's been doing something down at the forge, and Mari's taken it upon herself to wander down there each day. She says she's lending a hand, but given how few visitors we've gotten in the last years, I suspect she's starved for news of any kind."

"I may just have a few questions for Dawe myself, especially if Blaine isn't around," Niklas said. "They're a tight little group, and I'm trying to sort out the connections."

Judith gave him a knowing look. "You mean, you want to know if Mistress Kestel has a prior claim on her."

Niklas chuckled. "Don't get me in trouble! But I will allow that she's a fine-looking woman."

Judith sighed. "Blaine's had his share of heartache when it comes to women. First Carensa. Then the woman he made a handfasting with up in Edgeland died of fever." She looked at the fire and seemed to be staring into the past. "It would have been so different if Blaine hadn't killed Ian."

Niklas drew a deep breath. "I'd best check in on the supplies we've stored up here and then see what information I can pry loose from Dawe before I head back to the camp. Just wanted to let you know that we'll do our very best to make sure Glenreith is safe."

"As safe as anywhere can be these days," Judith added. "Thank you."

Niklas left Judith and headed down the stairs. Glenreith had always been like a second home to him, and it was easy to take momentary comfort in the familiar surroundings. For just an instant, he could imagine that all was as it had been, with Blaine awaiting him to take off on an adventure, dodging Ian McFadden's temper. Before Velant and the war, before everything changed.

He headed for the forge and was surprised to hear raised voices coming from that direction. Concerned, Niklas picked up his pace and rounded the corner in time to see Carr swing a punch at Dawe.

Before he could close the distance, Mari jumped down from the fence where she was sitting and launched herself at Carr, fighting like a wildcat to pull him off Dawe. Dawe was defending himself, but Niklas could see that Blaine's friend was trying not to injure Carr, although Carr showed no such compunctions and looked livid with rage.

"Stay away from her!" Carr shouted, pummeling Dawe. "Keep your filthy convict hands off my sister!"

"He didn't touch me!" Mari protested. "I just came down to bring him some lunch. We were talking, Carr. Go away!"

Carr wrested free of Mari's hold, giving her a shove so hard that she stumbled and fell. Dawe, who had been willing to hold his punches, glowered and bucked Carr free. Before Niklas could wade into the fray, Dawe had sent his fist to connect hard with Carr's jaw and managed to put himself between Carr and Mari.

Niklas adjusted his course to come in behind Carr, but he caught a look at the young man's face. Carr's eyes were dilated, his hair was wild, and his features were twisted with unreasoning fury. *Sweet Charrot, Carr's got the madness!* Niklas thought.

Carr reached for a weapon and grabbed one of the pokers from the forge. Dawe barely managed to snatch up a pair of tongs in time to deflect the blow. Dawe pushed Mari behind him, shielding her with his body, and ducked another swing from the iron poker Carr wielded. Mari was shrieking at Carr to stop, Carr was screaming curses at Dawe. Out of the corner of his eye, Niklas saw several of the groomsmen and servants heading toward the disturbance.

Before Carr could get in another swing, Niklas tackled Carr. "Drop it!" Niklas commanded, but Carr kept thrashing, the poker still in his hand. "I order you to drop it, soldier!"

Carr fought even harder, nearly breaking free of Niklas's grip. They were surrounded now by several men who had come at the sound of the scuffle. The flailing poker kept Dawe and the others from getting close enough to intervene. Niklas managed to wrestle Carr backward until they were near one of the large wooden pillars that held up the roof of the forge. Carr hurled himself to the side, trying to break free, and Niklas used his momentum against him, slamming Carr's right wrist against the wooden post hard enough that Carr howled with pain and dropped the poker.

"Get off me!" Carr shouted. His words were slurred as if he were drunk, but Niklas could smell no alcohol on him.

"You're a fool, Carr, and a brute," Mari snapped. "Go back to the camp and stay there."

Two of the other men came forward to help Niklas wrestle Carr to the ground. Carr bucked and kicked, fighting with all his might, until one of the men returned from the stable with a length of rope. It took four men to pin Carr while Niklas tied him up, and even bound, Carr rocked back and forth, straining against his bonds, shouting threats until Mari took a kerchief from her belt and stuffed it in his mouth.

"Get him into the house and up to his room," Niklas said grimly. "I'll explain what happened to Lady Judith. He's been taken by the madness, so we don't dare untie him."

Mari stared at her brother with a mixture of pity and fear. Carr was fighting and attempting to bite his captors; none of the men looked as if untying him had crossed their minds.

Niklas glanced over his shoulder at Dawe and Mari. "Are the two of you all right?" he asked.

Dawe looked shaken, while Mari's fists were clenched as if she would like to have taken a swing at her brother. "We're fine," Dawe said, although Niklas could see that one side of his face was already beginning to bruise from where Carr had struck him.

"I'll get a cold cloth for Dawe's eye," Mari said. "Take care of Carr." She paused, and the anger drained from her face. She looked to Niklas. "Will he be all right?"

Niklas sighed. "No way to tell, Mari. We'll have to wait and see."

Two men hefted Carr between them, one holding Carr's shoulders and the other his feet. Carr had finally stopped fighting, although the look in his eyes was murderous. With a sigh, Niklas followed behind them, wondering how he was going to explain this to Judith.

"Head for the servants' door," Niklas instructed. "We'll make less of a spectacle that way."

Word had already reached the house, because the cook and scullery maid were on the back stoop craning for a look. They moved out of the way for Niklas and the two men carrying Carr, watching wide-eyed.

"Send for Lady Judith," Niklas instructed the maid. "Carr's been taken ill. We're taking him to his room."

It took all three of them to wrestle Carr up the back stairs and into his room. When Carr was safely deposited on the bed, Niklas turned to the groomsman. "Ordel, my battle healer, has experience with the madness. I need you to bring him here as quickly as you can."

The young man looked as if he wanted to be anywhere but in the room. He ducked his head in acceptance. "Yes, m'lord. I'll be back shortly."

He had barely left when Judith rushed into the room, followed by Edward. She took one look at Carr, bound securely and looking worse for the wear from the fight, and then looked to Niklas.

"The servants were abuzz about a fight in the yard. Sweet Esthrane, what did Carr do?"

Niklas sighed. "He was raving about Dawe being a convict and not wanting him to have anything to do with Mari, and then he attacked him," he replied wearily. "He could have killed Dawe."

"Was anyone hurt?" Judith asked, her eyes widening.

Niklas shook his head. "Mari's shaken up. Carr clipped Dawe pretty hard." He paused. "I suspect Carr's got a broken wrist. I didn't have a choice: No one could get close to him while he was swinging that damn poker around. I'll have my healer tend him."

Carr began to strain against his bonds, managing to hurl himself back and forth on the bed. The gag in his mouth only muffled the string of curses he was shrieking. Judith blanched. "Oh dear," she murmured as Carr's language grew increasingly obscene.

"It's the madness." Niklas took Judith by the elbow and steered her out of the room. "We've seen several cases in the camp. He didn't recognize me when I intervened, and even a direct order made no impact."

Judith turned to him and met his gaze. "Is Carr going to die?"

Niklas sighed and looked down. "Hard to say. Most of the time, the madness kills. We haven't been able to figure out why, or how it falls on some but not on others. On occasion, someone pulls through. My battle healer has powders and potions that will put Carr to sleep and keep him sedated so he can't hurt himself or anyone else. I'll post a guard around the clock. Then we'll have to trust the gods."

Judith nodded. "What of the others? Are we all at risk?"

Niklas shrugged. "My healer doesn't believe it's catching. All we can do is let it run its course."

"And pray to the gods for mercy," Judith murmured.

"If you still believe in that sort of thing, yes," Niklas replied.

Over the next two candlemarks, Niklas stood silently in the back of the room as Ordel, the army healer, worked on Carr. Between the two of them, they had forced a sleeping potion down Carr's throat, and Carr now lay quietly, still bound. Niklas had watched as Ordel applied a poultice and splint to Carr's broken wrist, then treated the bruises and cuts from the fight.

"I've mixed some fragrant plant leaves in with the candle wax to soothe his sleep," Ordel said as he stood and stretched. "And I've mixed powders with the wine in the carafe," he said with a nod toward the table, "to help keep him drugged while the madness runs its course."

"What are his chances?"

Ordel looked back at Carr and shrugged. "No way to tell. It's often not the madness that kills them—it's that they won't take food or drink and they starve. If we can keep him fed and get water into him, and keep him from damaging himself further, there's a chance." He grimaced. "Some take fever, others don't. If he doesn't, his odds are better. We won't know for a while."

Niklas nodded. "Thank you for coming up to the house."

"Sure thing, Captain." He managed a grin. "Never thought I'd get to be personal healer to a noble house."

"With luck, Carr will be the only one who requires your attention," Niklas replied. The soldier arrived who would stand on guard through the night, and Niklas slipped out, leaving the healer to his patient. Judith was nowhere to be seen, so Niklas slipped down the back steps.

Dawe was back at the forge, although his eye was purpled and swollen. Niklas stood by the forge door for a few moments, watching as the lanky man moved with confidence born of long practice. He was heating a length of iron in the fire but had not resumed pounding with his mallet. Mari had taken a seat on the fence that ran along the open side of the forge. Despite the cold, the heat from the blacksmith's fire made it far too warm for a cloak, and Mari had only a light shawl wrapped around her shoulders over her work dress.

"How is he?" Niklas asked Mari with a nod toward Dawe.

" 'He' can hear just fine, and he's all right," Dawe responded without looking up.

"I'm sorry," Niklas said, grimacing.

Mari snorted. "You're sorry? For what? Carr's my brother. If he's an idiot, it's to our shame, not yours."

Niklas shrugged. "He's my soldier. Hard to stop feeling responsible just because we're back home."

Mari smiled sadly, and for a moment, Niklas could see her as the half-grown girl she had been when she would tag along, unbidden, whenever he and Blaine would head off on their boyhood adventures. "Carr was going to war with or without you, Niklas." She shook her head. "Gods above, Blaine was right. Without him to lighten you up, you're positively grim with responsibility."

Niklas managed to chuckle. It was an old joke among the three of them, from what felt like a lifetime ago. Back then, when he and Blaine were in their teens, Mari was just a slip of a girl, and she was out to prove that she could keep up with both her brothers. Carr, much younger, had not been included on the forays.

"Did he hurt you?" Niklas asked.

"He knows better," Mari said. "I swore I'd never let anyone lay a hand on me like that, after Father—" She broke off abruptly. "After what happened," she finished quietly and looked away.

Dawe finished the iron bar he was working on, set it in water to cool, and dusted off his hands on his leather apron. "Thanks for lending a hand," he said. "I didn't want to thrash Mick's little brother, but I also didn't fancy being pounded on." He wiped the sweat from his forehead with his arm. "Took enough of that in Velant." Dawe's sleeves were pushed up, and Niklas could clearly see the brand on his forearm.

"I can send my camp healer over if you need him," Niklas offered.

Dawe shook his head. "Got over worse than this in Velant on my own. Mari got a cloth with cold water to put on it, and I'll find some ice in the yard tonight. Good thing it's winter." He grinned. "In Edgeland, finding ice was never a problem."

Niklas leaned back against a post. "How well did you know Blaine—Mick—up there?"

Dawe chuckled. "Shared a cell in Velant, worked chained together in the mines for a few years, spent time in the fishing fleet. And when we earned our Tickets of Leave, I shared a house with him and the others that we built ourselves." He shrugged. "Pretty well, except that Mick never once mentioned he was a lord."

"The five of you must have been pretty tight," Niklas said.

Dawe poured a cup of water from the pitcher that sat on a table to one side of the forge. "If you don't have people watching your back in Velant, you don't survive," he said. "Mick, Verran, Piran, Kestel, and me, we made the oddest bunch you could imagine, but we lived through it."

Niklas nodded. "Sounds like the army."

Dawe cast a look at the fire and pumped the bellows until the flames roared hotter. "Don't know much about the army myself. I used to be a silversmith."

"What's that you're making?" Niklas asked.

Dawe grinned, his teeth bright against the soot that streaked his face. "I like to tinker. I've been fiddling with the crossbows, trying to make them fire faster, since we keep having to fight off Pollard's men and the biters move too damn fast." He held up one of the versions he had made in Edgeland.

"I've made a few improvements to the mechanism," Dawe said, pride coloring his voice. "Experimented with the range.

It's always a trade-off between range and force. For my money, I'll take range, especially if we're fighting biters. Rather not have them get close to me, if you know what I mean."

"I thought Lord Penhallow was your ally," Niklas replied.

"Penhallow's all right, I guess, though he and Connor disappeared and haven't shown back up again. Not sure I completely trust anyone who's dead, if you know what I mean." Dawe chuckled. "Whenever I say things like that around Kestel, she reminds me that I'd have never been able to navigate the politics at court being so blunt. Good thing I didn't have to."

"How does Kestel figure into this?" Niklas asked. "She seems like an odd match for you four."

Dawe moved a new iron bar to the fire. "Mick fought off a guard in Velant who was beating Kestel—she was chained at the time, or she might not have needed the assist, being an assassin and all. Spent a day and a night in the Hole for it, too."

"The Hole?" Niklas asked, although he could formulate a guess.

Dawe shot a glance at Mari as if unsure how much to say. "Prokief's oubliette. A pit in the ice where the guards would throw you after they worked you over. If you didn't bleed out or freeze to death, they'd haul you back out later—assuming they remembered to come back for you." Mari shuddered but said nothing and looked away.

"By the time I met Mick, he and Piran and Kestel were pretty thick. Mick met Verran on the ship to Edgeland, so that's their history. Mick and I spent a couple of years sharing a cell, then chained together on a work crew. You get to know someone pretty well when you've only got a few feet of chain between you and them," Dawe said. He withdrew the iron bar, gave it a practiced glance to determine whether or not it was ready to be worked, and put it back in the fire.

Niklas debated how best to ask the question on his mind. "So Kestel and Blaine are friends? Lovers?"

Dawe didn't answer, and Niklas wondered if he had intruded too far on the group's secrets. Dawe eyed Niklas for a moment, then chewed his lip, as if trying to figure out what to say. "Kestel kept all of us at arm's length at the homestead, but I always figured that if she'd have made an exception for anyone, it would have been Blaine."

"He wasn't interested?" Niklas asked.

"Why do you want to know?"

Niklas looked away. "She's a very pretty woman."

Dawe sighed. "If you and Mick weren't old friends, I wouldn't say anything and just let you figure it out the hard way. Seein' how you go back so far with him, I'll give you my opinion. I think there's a powerful attraction between Mick and Kestel, always has been. At the homestead, it kept the peace to keep it friendly."

Dawe stared out over the courtyard for a moment, then went on. "Mick was all torn up over losing the girl he was betrothed to when he was sent away."

"Carensa," Niklas supplied.

Dawe nodded. "After Selane died of fever, Mick didn't let anyone get too close."

"And Kestel?"

Dawe looked away. "Kestel fancies Mick. I don't think she realized how much until he married Selane. Kestel spent their wedding night out in the barn, crying, although she'd probably slit my throat if she knew I told anyone that."

"She was the most sought-after courtesan at the castle," Niklas said. "Surely she knows how to let a man know when she's interested in him."

Dawe glanced at Mari and his cheeks colored, as if the

conversation had edged into topics improper for a lady's ears. Mari picked up on it immediately. "I'm a widow," she snapped. "I've got a son. I know what goes on between men and women."

"Kestel told me once that she could seduce any man she set her eye on," Dawe said. "And I think that was the problem. She wanted more than that from Mick. I think she didn't trust anything that would come from her advances. She wanted him to make the first move."

"And knowing my brother, he was being all honor-bound because he'd agreed to just be friends," Mari chimed in.

"Yeah," Dawe said with a grin. "That's Mick. The most honorable convict I know. He didn't want to mess up what we had at the homestead or lose her friendship."

Niklas sighed. "I was afraid the story would be something like that." He frowned. "Now that you're all here in Donderath, do you think things will change?"

Dawe shrugged. "I guess that's up to Mick and Kestel."

CHAPTER TWENTY-ONE

───────

SILENCE FELL OVER THE GROUP AS THEY RESUMED their journey. The wind was cold, sweeping down the mountains toward the river. Blaine pulled his cloak closer around him, trying to ignore the pain of his injuries. The road was rocky, and their horses picked their way carefully on the steep ascent as the wagons clattered and jostled along the rutted surface.

"We're making enough noise that we're not going to surprise anyone," Piran grumbled.

"If it's a mages' lyceum, maybe that's a good thing," Kestel replied.

Piran grimaced. "I'd worry about that if magic still worked. What are they going to do? Throw rocks?"

Verran sat up straighter in his saddle. "I'll thank you not to impugn my rocks. A few of them distracted that gryp you were fighting."

Piran rolled his eyes and turned away. From the set of his jaw, Blaine guessed that the failure to prevent Kata's death still bothered Piran more than he chose to let on.

The trail wound through the forest. While they rode on

alert, watching for the approach of either men or wild animals, nothing stirred. Borya hiked ahead of the group, scouting the road. Not long after they reached the cover of the forest, Blaine looked up to see Borya striding their way, looking very unhappy.

"Someone beat us here," he said grimly. "The road was too washed out before to see the hoofprints. Their bodies are in the clearing up ahead."

"Bodies?" Kestel echoed.

Blaine and Piran immediately turned to scan the tree line, expecting an attack. "How many?" Blaine asked.

The distaste on Borya's face was clear. "Hard to say. The gryps didn't leave much of them or their horses."

"How old were the corpses?" Piran asked.

"A day or two at most. What the gryps didn't eat, the wolves and scavengers picked clean. But what's left hasn't been out in the weather too long, and there's still enough of the soft bits left to rot and stink," Borya replied.

"Does it look like they were attacked on their way to the lyceum, or on their way back?" Kestel asked, eyeing the road ahead.

Borya put his hands on his hips and surveyed the forest around them. "My guess is that they were on their way to the lyceum when they were attacked. I went up the road a piece looking for tracks, and even under the trees where the road's been protected from the rain and snow, I didn't see any."

"Someone could have escaped on foot, gone through the forest," Kestel said, turning in a slow arc to look at the dense woods around them.

Borya shrugged. "Maybe. But I'd have guessed from the bones that there were ten of them, and the number of bones for horses and men were equal."

"Anything left—saddlebags, weapons, packs—to indicate who they were?" Blaine asked, although he could guess.

"From what's left, I'd say they were friends of those dark riders who chased us a while back," Borya replied. "They beat us here, maybe intended to wait for you," he said with a pointed glance toward Blaine.

"Or the timing's a coincidence, and they came to loot the lyceum or search for clues about Quintrel," Kestel said.

Borya stole a glance back to where Zaryae, Desya, and Illarion waited with the horses. "After what happened to Kata, I want to get the others past that place as quickly as possible." He paled. "Bad enough that I saw it and thought of what might have happened to her—"

Kestel laid a hand on his arm. "She was spared that, at least," she said quietly.

Borya nodded, tight-lipped. "Let's get moving."

It was impossible to ignore the smell of the dead soldiers, but Blaine and his friends made sure they rode on the side of the road that had a view of the corpses, shielding the others from having to see the carnage. Even so, it was all too easy for their imaginations to fill in the details, and Zaryae sobbed quietly as she rode, letting her long dark hair fall over her shoulders, guarding her mourning like a veil.

"I led us here because that's where the clues seemed to point," Blaine said to Kestel as they rode up the rocky trail. "Between the maps, the disks, Grimur's book, and the other things we've pieced together, it made sense." He sighed. "But maybe I'm wrong. Maybe we don't have all the pieces yet. I don't know how I can live with it if I've cost Kata her life for nothing."

"Vigus Quintrel hasn't made it easy to figure out how to bring the magic back," Kestel replied. "The gryps exist because magic was broken. If the magic stays broken, how many more monsters will appear? And how many more people will die?"

The same questions had badgered Blaine's thoughts since they left the bridge. He shrugged in reply, at a loss for a better answer. "I guess we'll have to see what we find when we get there."

The sun had passed its highest point by the time the road reached the lyceum. It was a three-story stone building set among the trees. Most of its roof was burned away, and scorch marks marred the walls. The group came to a halt a distance from the building's front entrance. The road in front of the lyceum did not look as if anyone had passed this way all season. Many of the building's windows had been shattered and the rest stared at them like eyeless sockets.

The lyceum was built in the shelter of a high cliff, with rocky outcroppings on the north and east, the forest sprawling down toward the river on the west and south. The grounds included several outbuildings. Cut into the rock behind the lyceum was a set of steps leading up to a squat stone building perched on the edge of the cliff.

"Borya and I will scout the buildings and grounds before we go farther," Piran said.

Blaine nudged his horse out of the riding order to draw up alongside the lead wagon where Illarion sat and peered up at the lyceum while Piran and Borya completed the search. Nothing stirred beyond the darkened windows. "Doesn't look like there's anybody home," Blaine said.

"There's no sign that anyone's been here recently," Borya called as he and Piran returned.

"Not entirely true." They startled as Zaryae spoke. She was staring at the lyceum with an expression of concentration. "There is no one here. And yet, they have not gone." Her gaze seemed fixed on something no one else could see. "The bones of the dead still protect this place."

"That doesn't make any sense," Piran muttered.

Kestel led her horse up to stand beside Blaine and Illarion. "Hush, Piran." She looked up at Zaryae, who still sat in the wagon driver's seat. Zaryae's dark hair fell across her shoulders, accentuating her high cheekbones and angular features. Her eyes were red-rimmed from crying, and the grief made her look older, tired. "Do you mean that the people who lived here are buried on the grounds? Did they become *talishte*?" Kestel asked.

Zaryae had a faraway look in her eyes, but she shook her head. "Not *talishte*. And not buried. There was no one left to bury the bodies." Her gaze remained fixed on the windowless ruin. "But their spirits remain. The bones still stand guard."

Kestel looked at Blaine. "Didn't you say that the lyceum's keepers thought the relics they kept would protect them?" She shivered. "Maybe those are the 'bones' Zaryae means."

"Let's go see what we came to see," Blaine said. He dismounted from his horse and led it over to a small copse of trees, where he lashed the reins to one of the tree trunks. The others did the same while Illarion and Desya drove the wagons up.

"Desya will stay with the horses," Illarion said.

"I'll stay with him," Verran volunteered. "If you need me to steal something or pick a lock, you'll know where to find me. I'm in no hurry to meet dead mages."

Illarion looked to Zaryae. "Do you feel up to—"

Zaryae waved away his concern. "Of course I'm going in. I'm the one who can sense the spirits. The magic may be dead, but spirits walk, regardless of magic." Despite her protest, Blaine thought that Zaryae looked worn.

They approached the door to the lyceum carefully, weapons at the ready. No sounds broke the forest stillness save for the wind in the branches. The forest was a mixture of tall pines with some leafless hardwoods. Wind skittered the dry leaves across patches of hardened snow in the shadowed places. Blaine felt a chill run down his spine that had nothing to do with the temperature.

The double main doors opened when Blaine pushed them. "Not locked," he mused. "Whoever left was either in a big hurry or expected to come back very quickly."

"Or no longer cared," Kestel murmured.

They stepped into a large entranceway worthy of any manor house. The mosaic floor was elaborately tiled in a variety of hues, testimony that whoever had established this lyceum had spared no expense. Enough light streamed in through the windows that they could see well despite the gloom of the unlit interior. A damp chill permeated the space, and Blaine wondered whether the coldness ever really went away, even when the lyceum was populated and its fireplaces were lit.

"So a lyceum is a school?" Piran asked, looking around himself warily. The entranceway walls were covered in murals that looked very old. Some of the murals showed the gods. A few panels venerated Torven, god of illusion, patron of the dark places, the god scholars beseeched to find out hidden truths. Other panels honored Esthrane, goddess of life, and patron of the souls that wandered in the Unseen Realms, the favorite of inventors and explorers. Yet another panel showed Vessa, goddess of fire, patron of knowledge. The murals were beautifully done, and it was obvious that, whatever neglect they had suffered recently, they had been tended faithfully for a long time.

"A lyceum is a school and a library," Kestel replied. "And often an alchemist's laboratory as well. It's a place dedicated to knowledge. The university near Castle Reach was a lyceum founded by King Merrill's grandfather." She cast a meaningful look at Blaine. "I believe Vigus Quintrel was on its faculty, until he disappeared."

Blaine moved around the entranceway, engrossed in the mural. After the tribute to the gods, a panel showed Esthrane handing a set of keys to a robed man. The lyceum building was depicted, along with elaborate grounds with gardens, mazes, and statuary. In the background stood several men in chain-mail armor, holding a furled flag. "Look there," Blaine murmured, pointing to the armored men who were nearly hidden in the shadows of the forest.

Kestel nodded. "The Knights of Esthrane?"

Blaine shrugged. "That would be my guess. It might also explain why someone built this lyceum so far away from the palace and the major cities."

Kestel frowned. "Then where are the Knights? Why did they leave?"

Blaine followed the murals to the next panel. It showed a bloody battle, one with hopelessly unbalanced forces. The armored figures from the previous panel were hunted down by men on horseback, impaled with pikes, chained in the sun, or forced to kneel before the executioner's ax. In the background, the lyceum sat upon a hill, and the robed figures around it appeared to be weeping. Off to one side, a handful of the armored men trudged off toward the horizon, into exile.

"Maybe that's your answer," he said quietly, pointing. "The Knights were killed by the king's men or forced into exile— somewhere even more remote than this. I imagine that once your patrons have been executed, it makes a place like this much less popular."

The next panel showed men and women in scholars' robes about their daily business, milling flour, baking bread, harvesting the vineyard, and pressing grapes. Other figures sat at the feet of teachers, studied from manuscripts, or handled the instruments of astronomers and alchemists.

"Look there," Kestel said. In the final mural, a much-reduced number of scholars tended the lyceum, and the artist showed them grayed and bowed with age. Both the drawing of the building and of the dependencies made it clear that the entire complex had fallen on hard times. The last drawing lacked the skill and finish of the other murals. It showed several scholars bedridden, being cared for by their comrades, and then finally, a funeral procession.

Kestel lifted a hand to touch the rough drawing. "I can almost imagine the last survivor, deciding to leave a record of what happened," she said quietly. "You can tell whoever did the last panel wasn't an artist, but you can almost feel the desperation." She was quiet for a moment. "It's almost as if, once the Knights were destroyed, everyone forgot about the lyceum. So nobody persecuted them—"

"But new members didn't come, either," Blaine finished her sentence. "Even if the scholars weren't celibate, their numbers were bound to dwindle." His gaze lingered on the drawing of the sickbeds and the funeral. "Perhaps an outbreak of something hurried them on their way."

Blaine's head throbbed. Though Kestel had done an excellent job binding up his injuries, Blaine knew he was warmer than he should be on such a cold autumn day. His wounds ached, and he feared the gryps' talons had carried infection. He gritted his teeth and wondered whether Illarion and his group had any remedies, or whether the mage-scholars had left anything behind. *The cuts weren't that deep. I survived three years in Velant. I'll get through this.* He looked up to see that Kestel was watching him closely.

"I need to put a poultice on those wounds," Kestel said

archly. "Piran dear, please fetch me some water," she added. Piran grumbled but went back outside toward where they had seen a well.

"Sit down," she instructed and steered Blaine toward the steps. Piran returned in a moment with a bucket full of water, and the others wandered around the entranceway, studying the murals, as Kestel and Zaryae made a paste of medicinal herbs and healing oils from their packs, along with the ice-cold water from the well. Kestel tore strips from Blaine's ruined shirt for bandages.

"We'll see if we can find you another shirt," she said, standing back to admire her handiwork with the bandages.

"I should have a spare in my pack with the horses," Blaine said. He knew the poultices would take time to work. His headache pounded, making conversation difficult. Once more, Kestel dispatched Piran on an errand to bring back the shirt, and with good-natured grumbling, Piran did as she directed. Blaine shouldered gingerly into the fresh shirt, ruefully accepting that his slashed pants would have to last until they found replacements or returned to Glenreith.

"That poultice should help," Kestel said, a look of concern on her face. "But tell me if the wounds don't seem to get any better."

A sudden gust of cold air slammed the rickety doors shut. Piran jumped and pivoted, crossbow drawn, then swore under his breath.

"The spirits are watching us," Zaryae said quietly. "Wondering why we've come."

Blaine looked at the seer. "Should we tell them?"

Zaryae smiled. "You can, but they will believe what they observe, not what we say."

"Zaryae," Kestel said, her gaze still focused on the mural

and its depiction of the Knights of Esthrane, "can you sense whether or not there are *talishte* here?"

"Just the spirits."

"Let's have a look around," Blaine said, turning away from the mural. "Let's start at the top and work our way downward." He cast a glance toward Zaryae. "Assuming you're right, and there won't be any surprises from the cellars once night falls, this should be as good a place as any to make camp."

"No *talishte*," Zaryae repeated. "I would know."

Something in Zaryae's reassurance seemed incomplete, but Blaine did not press the issue. *She's just seen her kinswoman murdered by the gryp*, he thought. *Anyone would seem a bit off, considering.*

Piran and Borya led the way up the wide, curved stairway. As they climbed, Blaine and Kestel looked around, keeping their weapons at the ready. Illarion accompanied Zaryae.

When nothing burst forth as they reached the second floor, Blaine felt himself relax, just a little. He resolutely ignored the headache. Despite Kestel's poultice, he could feel a fever that threatened to have him sweating despite the cold. "Piran, Borya. Check out the stairs to the next floor—just in case," he said.

They waited until the two returned. "Stairs to nowhere," Piran reported. "Floor's there, and some of the walls. Anything above this level burned." He reached out to pat the stone wall nearest him. "Good thing this place is built like a fortress, from the look of how hot it got."

"A fortress," Kestel echoed. "Do you think the Knights originally built this as a place they could fall back to and defend?"

Blaine shrugged. "If so, they changed their minds. Or something kept them from reaching sanctuary here."

Satisfied nothing was hiding above them, the group split into armed teams of two, moving down the long corridor.

Piran and Borya went to the far end of the hallway and began working toward the stairs, opening doors and searching the rooms. Blaine and Kestel worked their way forward, down the left side, while Zaryae and Illarion took the right side.

Blaine pushed open a door and stood ready, sword raised. The old wooden door creaked back on its iron hinges. A dusty room met their gaze, filled with two neat rows of cots. "Dormitory," Blaine said.

Kestel nodded. "But look. The bedding's pulled up neatly on each of them. It doesn't look as if something roused them from their sleep or sent them off on a moment's notice."

A quick search found personal items around each bed. A pair of spectacles lay atop the covers, next to a book on one cot. A dressing gown was folded neatly at the foot of another bed. Blaine bent down and found that beneath each bed was a small wooden box.

He pulled out the box from beneath the nearest bed and looked down at the contents. "A clean shirt, pants, and undergarments," he reported, disliking the need to rifle through the personal effects of strangers. "A small devotional carving of Esthrane. A set of prayer beads. From the look of it, the mages were ascetics."

Kestel was moving methodically from bed to bed, making a quick examination of the storage boxes. Finally she straightened, holding a pair of trews and grinning victoriously. "These should fit you," she said, and tossed the pair of pants toward Blaine.

"You're looting the dead?"

Kestel rolled her eyes. "Not like they can use the things anymore, is it? Blame Verran. I learned thieving from a master."

Blaine motioned for Kestel to turn her back and quickly changed pants.

"We lived together in a small house for three years, and you don't think I've already seen you without pants?" Kestel jibed.

"We're back in civilization now," Blaine replied.

Kestel snorted. "What's left of it." She turned around without awaiting an invitation as Blaine tied the drawstring on his trews.

She frowned as she looked around the room. "You know, from the mural, I thought the mages had died off within memory of when the Knights were exiled. But the lyceum hasn't been abandoned that long, maybe only since the Great Fire," she said.

Blaine nodded. "You're right. Which means that, while the mage-scholars might have been dwindling in numbers, they survived a lot longer than the Knights without going into hiding."

Kestel looked around the room. "Then again, as we've mentioned, this place is pretty far off the main roads. Maybe they made it so they just wouldn't be noticed, and let people forget about them."

"Could be. They could have recruited new members quietly," Blaine agreed. "Just a few each year to keep the order going. It wouldn't have been in their interest to have too many people here. Too difficult to stay hidden."

He was about to turn toward the door when movement at the edge of his peripheral vision caught his attention. He turned his head sharply only to see an empty room.

"What's the matter?" Kestel asked.

Blaine shook his head to clear his thoughts. "Nothing. Just thought I saw something move."

"I didn't see anything," she said, but he could hear worry in her voice. "Do you think Zaryae was right, about the mages' spirits remaining here?"

The possibility had already occurred to Blaine, and he didn't like it. "If she's got half the ability Illarion and the others think she has, that's exactly what I was thinking."

"If it's true, they aren't trying to stop us," Kestel remarked.

Or maybe, Blaine thought, *they're just biding their time.*

They left the dormitory room and opened the next door. Two more identical rooms followed. By this time, they had reached the center of the corridor. Piran and Borya emerged from the last rooms on their half. "There's another dormitory room down at the end," Piran said. "And a large room with a big table and a number of chairs—kind of far away from the kitchen for a dining hall, isn't it?"

"Probably a study room," Illarion replied. He motioned toward the rooms he and Zaryae had just searched. "We found a sleeping room, with a few personal items beneath each bed."

"I wonder what was on the top floor," Kestel mused.

"No way to know," Blaine replied. "Let's go down and see what we find."

As they headed downstairs, Blaine felt the weight of the morning's wild ride and Kata's death settle heavily on him.

The floor plan on the main floor was quite different from that of the simple single corridor above. Three different wings opened off the main entranceway. Kestel and Blaine took the hallway on the right, while Illarion and Zaryae headed into the central hallway, and Piran and Borya went to the left.

As Blaine and Kestel started down the hallway, they found several small, austere rooms that sat forlorn and empty, save one heavy wooden chair in each. "Classroom," Blaine said. "Reminds me of the ones at the collegium my father sent me off to, near Glenreith. The master sat in that chair," he said, pointing, "and the students gathered at his feet, asking questions, soaking in knowledge."

Blaine shifted to turn toward the door and grimaced. The ache in his head had grown worse, so that it was difficult to think. Despite the poultice, his wounds throbbed, and he was sweating. He caught another glimpse of something, as if a shadow moved just at the edge of his vision.

"Did you see that?" he asked, turning to stare in the direction of the movement, though nothing was there.

Kestel shook her head. "I didn't see anything."

"Damn. I keep catching a glimpse of something moving, but when I look at it, nothing's there," Blaine replied.

Kestel regarded him skeptically. "You don't look well. Is the poultice helping?"

Blaine made a dismissive gesture. "I'm sure it is. I saw worse in Velant."

"Uh-huh. Let's find an infirmary and see if the scholars had anything stronger than the herbs and oils Zaryae and I have. We've got a long ride back to Glenreith."

"It can wait," Blaine said. "We need to see what we're dealing with. I'll be fine."

They found several more classrooms and another larger study room before reaching the end of the corridor. "I hope the others have found something more interesting," Blaine remarked. "We'll have come a long way—and paid too high a cost."

Kestel touched his arm. "It's not your fault, what happened on the bridge."

Just then, a shout echoed down the corridor. "I think we've found something!" Illarion's voice carried through the empty building.

Blaine and Kestel headed back, walking as quickly as Blaine's injured leg would permit. Blaine did not mention it to Kestel, but the shadow shapes he glimpsed now seemed to be all around them, moving closer than the periphery of his vision. He still felt feverish, and despite the poultices, his battle wounds ached. *Can't be good if I'm hallucinating*, Blaine thought. *Maybe the talons were poisoned. Then again, it wouldn't be good if what I'm seeing is really there. Which is worse?*

They reached the entranceway just after Piran and Borya. "Nothing down the corridor we searched except the kitchens and the dining room," Piran said, anticipating the question. "And before you ask, yes, we checked. Some of the food spoiled, but what was dried or preserved is still in good shape. We've definitely got provisions for the trip back, and some to share." He grinned. "I vote to grab those casks of wine and brandy and the grain we found in the dependencies as well. Things like that are harder to come by than they used to be."

"We've found a library," Zaryae said excitedly. "And a shrine. Come and see."

They followed Zaryae and Illarion back down the central corridor. It was now mid-afternoon, and the winter light was fading.

Shadows lengthened in the hallway, and it seemed to Blaine that whatever moved on the edge of his vision was growing more agitated, moving more frequently, and losing any fear that might have persuaded it to keep its distance. *If what I see is real, how can we fight shadows?* he wondered. He looked at Zaryae, who was talking animatedly with Illarion, but she did not appear to be paying particular heed to the darker edges of the room.

"Zaryae," Blaine said, getting the seer's attention. "You said the mages hadn't left, that their spirits remained. Can you sense them?"

Zaryae looked at him, her eyes alight. "Oh yes. They're here. They're watching."

"What do they want?" Kestel asked.

Zaryae met her gaze. "They want to know our measure. Then they'll decide."

"Decide what?" Blaine asked.

"What to do about us."

"That doesn't sound good," Blaine said.

Zaryae shrugged. "We chose to come here. This place belongs to them. It's theirs to protect."

"And what are they protecting?" Kestel asked.

"If we're meant to know, we'll find it," Zaryae answered.

They reached a set of wooden double doors. The doors were made of cherry, stained dark, and rubbed to a fine, smooth finish. Into the satiny finish was carved a series of symbols. An arc of six circles, each a phase of the moon, rose above a horizon line, with a similar and opposite arc beneath adorned one door. A sheaf of wheat, and an ear of corn, along with a vine heavy with grapes were carved into the other door. Spanning the two doors was a star map showing the constellation they had seen so often.

"They're all symbols of Esthrane," Kestel murmured.

"More proof that they were associated with the Knights?" Blaine mused. He gave the doors a push and they opened at his touch, swinging wide to reveal the large room inside.

"Now this is a real library!" Kestel exclaimed with appreciation as Illarion led them into the scholars' sanctuary. Despite the austerity of the rest of the building, the library was comfortably provisioned, perhaps because it was the focus of the inhabitants' existence. One wall was covered with a tapestry panel that showed scholars and soldiers working side by side, and above them, the night sky aglow with Esthrane's constellation.

The other three walls were lined with bookshelves made from the same cherry wood as the doors, equally well crafted.

The shelves were filled with manuscripts and scrolls, and on the study tables there lay a large astrolabe and sextant, quill pens and inkwells, and parchment paper left as if the users had just gotten up to stretch their legs. A large brass armillary sphere sat on one of the tables. The stone floor was covered with beautifully woven carpets with elaborate motifs in shades of ochre and green, colors of the harvest, sacred to Esthrane.

"This could take a while," Blaine said quietly, looking around.

"You're looking for another disk?" Zaryae asked.

Blaine shrugged. "Perhaps. If each Lord of the Blood received a disk, then there are—or were—thirteen of them. Whether they all still exist, and whether or not they're important, we don't know."

"What else should we look for?" Illarion asked. "It'll be dark soon. We can easily pass the night in here." He inclined his head toward the fireplace. "We saw enough wood to make a fire, take the chill off the room. Piran and Borya say there are food and wine as well." He grinned. "We've spent the night in far worse places."

Kestel slowly made her way around the room, looking at the manuscripts. She reached up to select a leather-covered volume from a shelf at shoulder-height.

"Oh!" she cried out as a book fell from above her, and she jumped to the side, barely avoiding being hit by the wood-bound tome. It clattered loudly on the stone floor at the edge of the carpet. Blaine turned sharply at the noise, just in time to see the shadows shift, and felt a sudden chill.

Kestel turned to the others and stepped back from the shelves. Her face was ashen. "I wasn't anywhere near the shelf that fell from," she said. "And the shelves are set into the wall, so I don't think I wobbled the case when I pulled out a book."

Illarion moved to where the fallen manuscript lay. It had a carved wooden cover bound together with leather straps, and the stack of parchment held between the covers was nearly as broad as a man's hand. With a wary glance upward, Illarion retrieved the volume. "It's good you're quick. You could have been hurt if this had hit you. It's heavy." He carried the tome to one of the study tables and laid it aside.

"It wasn't an accident," Blaine said. "I saw the shadows move."

"You're saying ghosts threw that at Kestel?" Piran said incredulously.

Blaine shrugged. "That's my guess. Now the question is, were they warning her away from something or trying to get her attention?"

"Do you think Geir will find us, once the sun sets?" Piran asked. "Odd as it sounds, if we've got to spend a night or two in here with dead mage ghosts, I'd feel better with a biter on our side."

"He knew where we were headed. He'll be here," Blaine replied. He looked toward the large fireplace, where a painting of Charrot, Torven, and Esthrane hung above the mantel. Images of the High God and his consorts were common, but something caught Blaine's attention.

"Take a look at the painting. Does it strike you as odd?" he asked.

The others studied the image for a moment. "In other paintings, Charrot is always the dominant figure," Kestel said after a pause. "But in this one, Esthrane is larger than either Charrot or Torven. She's been painted to look luminous, while the others almost look mortal next to her. And both Torven and Charrot are looking at her with complete adoration." She frowned. "In every other paining I've seen, Esthrane and Torven are always looking at Charrot."

"Esthrane is definitely the main figure," Illarion said. "Some might say such a painting is blasphemous."

"But if we're right, and the scholars here were supported by the Knights of Esthrane, then it would make sense that they held her in high regard," Blaine mused. "I get the feeling we're in the right place."

Zaryae had crossed to stand in the large window. The wooden shutters had wide enough slats so Zaryae could still see out. "There's a storm coming," she murmured.

Blaine looked up sharply. "A magic storm?"

Zaryae shook her head. "No. But the clouds are dark. Snow."

Kestel shivered. "We're pretty high up. A heavy snow could make it difficult to get back down the mountain."

Blaine shrugged. "Not much to be done about it. Let's see what we can learn—about what happened to the scholars, and about where the Knights may have gone."

"What about Vigus Quintrel?" Kestel asked.

"The longer we're at this, the more I think Quintrel and the Knights may be bound together somehow. That doesn't mean Quintrel is with the Knights, but if they had old *talishte* among them, and they created hidden fortresses for themselves, who better for Quintrel to learn from if he wanted to create a place for his followers to disappear?" Blaine reasoned.

Illarion had joined Zaryae at the window. "The clouds are moving in," he said. "I suggest we get the animals settled and bring Verran and Desya inside. Perhaps some food and wine would do us all good."

Piran and Borya went to help Verran and Desya shelter the horses and wagons, with the promise they would bring back both wine and firewood. Zaryae and Kestel went to see what in the kitchen's stocks might supply them with dinner. Illarion and Blaine headed back upstairs to borrow bedding from the dormitory rooms to make their night's stay more comfortable.

They had gathered up armloads of blankets and pillows and turned to leave when Blaine heard the sound of voices and footsteps in the corridor. He and Illarion set down their burdens and drew their weapons. Slowly, they moved toward the doorway. But when they reached the corridor, it was empty.

"If someone was up here, he didn't have time to go far," Illarion said, a hard set to his jaw.

Together they searched the rooms on either side of the hallway but found nothing. "You heard it, too?" Blaine asked.

Illarion nodded. "It sounded like several people were moving down the hallway, talking, although I couldn't make out what they said." He frowned. "They were too loud to be trying to take us by surprise."

"As if they were just students, going about their business?"

Illarion met Blaine's gaze, then nodded again. "Yes. Exactly like that."

Blaine went back and gathered up the bedding, and Illarion followed him. "Perhaps our 'hosts' are starting to make themselves known. The question is—are we welcome or not?"

CHAPTER TWENTY-TWO

I DON'T LIKE THIS PLACE," PIRAN SAID, BRUSHING snow off his cloak. Desya knelt next to the hearth, building a fire, as Verran handed him bits of kindling and pieces of wood. Borya began to light the lanterns atop the library tables, adjusting the mirrors behind them to dispel the gloom.

"We kept hearing things that weren't there," Desya agreed. "I know the woods. Been a tracker all my life. I know what the wind sounds like in the trees, and the sound of a fox or a rabbit. What we heard wasn't anything natural. Or alive."

"Kept seeing shadows moving, and there wasn't a wind," Verran added, moving closer to the fireplace although the small blaze was hardly yet enough to warm him. "And I know that, after Edgeland, I should be the last to complain about the cold, but whenever the shadows would move, I swear it felt like a wind off the glacier. It chilled me to the bone."

"Did anything try to harm you?" Illarion asked, concern clear in his face. His tall hat was perched atop his head, adding to his height, and the long, wavy hair that fell to his shoulders framed his narrow face.

"Not when we were standing watch," Desya said, standing

and brushing off his hands on his pants. His odd cat's eyes looked even more golden in the firelight. "But when we went into the buildings for supplies, things kept falling on us. A piece of wood nearly clipped me on the head when we went to get the wine, and I still don't know where it came from."

"The shed with the firewood had farming and gardening tools in it," Verran said, his angular features drawn with cold and peaked with uneasiness. "One minute they were leaning against the wall, and the next, they fell over on me. I got hit in the head with a rake, and a scythe nearly took off my ear."

"I saw the tools fall," Desya said. "Nothing had been near them." He frowned. "There was something interesting about the stables. They were built of large blocks of stone and partially carved into the side of the cliff. There are bands of iron running around all four walls, as well as a couple of bands across the ceiling. I don't think they have anything to do with holding the place together." He shook his head. "I've never seen a stable built like that. It seemed like a keep."

"The horses were restless," Borya added. "We put them all the way in the back, in the part that was carved into the cliff, just in case we get any magic storms." He shook his head. "After I heard about what happened to Desya and Verran, I took down everything from the walls that I could move, just in case. There was enough hay to feed them, and we drew water from the well." He frowned. "It's clear the scholars had some animals of their own. But they're gone and no bones to be found."

"Just like the mages," Piran said. He looked toward Blaine. "If I get a vote, I vote we get out of here."

"Unfortunately, that's not going to happen soon." Geir's voice came from the doorway. His sudden appearance startled everyone. Snow still clung to his hair and his cloak. "The roads across the river are already deep with snow. It looked to me like the storm was heading this way."

He walked into the room and set his cloak aside, then looked askance at Blaine. "You're injured. I can smell the blood. What happened?"

Blaine gave a terse recap of the attack of the gryps and the battle on the bridge. Geir listened in silence, but his expression was worried.

"I'm sorry I wasn't with you to fight those things," Geir said. "Best we travel by night when we leave here, until we're well out of the plains. There are other hazards to be reckoned with in the dark, but the gryps only fly by day."

He moved closer to where Blaine stood. "You're running a fever."

Blaine made a dismissive gesture. "I've been worse. Let me get some food and wine, and a good night's sleep, and I should be fine."

Geir gave him a look that told Blaine the *talishte* disagreed, but he said nothing else about the matter. "What have you found?"

Blaine quickly recapped their explorations. "We left the library and shrine for last," he finished, "as well as the cellars."

Geir gave a cold smile. "Leave the cellars to me. I'll need to make use of them come dawn. And if there are any surprises down there, I'm best equipped to deal with them."

"I don't think the spirits are fond of us eating their food," Kestel said when she and Zaryae returned from the lyceum's kitchen. They each carried wooden platters heaped with dried fruit, smoked meat, hard biscuits, and cheese.

"To them, we're invaders, thieves," Zaryae said. "They didn't invite us here."

"And the bones of the relics? Do those spirits have an opinion about us?" Kestel asked.

Zaryae shrugged. "I won't know until I dream."

"What happened?" Blaine asked.

"Small things," Kestel replied. "Doors opening after they'd been shut and latched. Pans falling off the wall when no one was nearby." She paused. "Then Zaryae told the spirits to stop. She said we were friends of the Knights, and that we had come to bring back the magic."

"And?" Blaine asked.

Kestel shrugged. "Everything got quiet. We gathered up the food and left."

Blaine looked to Zaryae. "You spoke to them. Do you think they understood you?"

Zaryae's expression took on a distant look. "I'm quite certain that they heard me. What they decide to do about what they heard is up to them."

"Are you a medium?" Blaine asked.

"No," she replied. "I can see and hear the spirits, but I can't control them like a necromancer could, and they can't possess me, as they could with a medium."

Everyone except Geir sat down around the library's study table to eat. Piran had brought back a cask of wine, and with the food Kestel and Zaryae found in the kitchen, everyone had more than enough. The fire took the chill off the large room, but despite the welcoming glow of the dancing flames, Blaine did not feel that the library's inhabitants had fully accepted their presence.

"Since I've already had my dinner," Geir said, "I have a few things to report." He stood near the hearth. The combination of a recent feeding and the glow of the fire softened his usual pallor.

"I scouted the area before I came inside," Geir said. "The forest harbors no threats beyond a pack of wolves and a family of bears." He leaned against the wall. "It appears that magic storms have struck near this area several times since the Great Fire. There are places where the trees have been flattened or uprooted. Some look fairly recent."

Blaine nodded. "It would make sense, since magic was stronger than usual, for the wild magic to be drawn here."

Geir folded his arms across his chest. "Agreed. I also spotted an observatory atop the cliff. I thought it would bear investigating."

Blaine nodded. "The sooner the better, between the chance of snow and the risk of getting caught in a magic storm."

"Shouldn't you wait for daylight?" Kestel asked, worried. She gave Blaine a wary look. "And are you sure you're up to it?"

"If we get a storm—snow or magic—we might not get another opportunity," Blaine replied. "And once the storm hits, I'll have plenty of time to recuperate." Geir's glance told him that the *talishte* suspected Blaine might be more injured than he let on, but he said nothing more.

"I'll come with you," Borya volunteered. "I'm not bothered by either the cliff or the snow."

While the others continued to search the library, Blaine, Borya, and Geir gathered the supplies they needed for their climb to the observatory. Geir needed no extra light, but Borya and Blaine both lit lanterns, and Borya grabbed a coil of rope.

The three men hiked the short trek to where the steps began at the edge of a steep cliff. "I'll go first," Geir said. "Rope yourselves to me, the way the goatherders do. Put Blaine in the middle. I've got enough strength to keep you both anchored, and Borya's got the advantage of being an acrobat."

They tied off the rope and began the climb. The winds

buffeted them and made the flame in Blaine's lantern flicker wildly. He shuttered all but a sliver of the globe, hoping to avoid attracting attention. Borya did the same, leaving only enough light to guide their path.

The stone steps were old and snow covered, sloping in places and too narrow for Blaine to place his whole foot on the risers. Geir kept a steady pace that accommodated his mortal companions. Blaine kept one hand on the rock of the cliff wall, resolutely refusing to think about the sheer drop to the left. The ache in his injured leg was growing worse, but Blaine did his best not to limp.

"I'm not looking forward to the return trip," Blaine muttered.

Despite his heavy cloak and hat, the cold wind chilled Blaine to the bone. He eyed the sky warily. A light snow had begun to fall, but from the look of the clouds, there was more to come. By the time they reached the top of the cliff, Blaine's heart was pounding and he was breathing hard, his breath clouding in the cold air. Geir was unaffected by the effort, and while Borya seemed as winded as Blaine felt, the acrobat was actually grinning.

"That was fun," Borya said.

"We would be unwise to linger," Geir cautioned. "The weather in these mountains can change without warning. You'd mind the cold being stuck here for the night, and I would regret the trip come dawn."

They made their way warily toward the old observatory, on guard for attack. To Blaine's relief, they reached the building without incident. If the others noticed that Blaine was moving more slowly than usual and favoring his injured leg, they said nothing.

Compared to the size of the lyceum, the observatory was small and unimposing. Built like a lighthouse, the observatory was a tall cylinder of stone. Blaine could not see all the way to the top of the tower, and he wondered how badly the upper floors had been damaged in the Fire that destroyed part of the lyceum.

Geir entered first, alert for danger, but if any predators lurked in the darkness, they chose not to attack a *talishte*.

"More stairs," Blaine muttered as they lifted their lanterns in the gloom of the tower's entranceway. The first level of the observatory was strictly functional, without ornamentation on its walls or floors. The walls were whitewashed, and the floor was rough-hewn planking, weathered by use and age. The stairs wound around the inside of the tower, cantilevered from the walls. A wooden railing bordered the open side of the steps, but given its age, Blaine was leery of trusting it. Borya untied them from their climbing rope and coiled it over his shoulder.

"Let's see what remains above," Geir said, heading toward the stairs.

The first landing held three rough cots with straw mattresses, a few chairs, and a table.

"No fireplace," Blaine noted.

Geir chuckled. "Occupational hazard. Hard to see the stars if smoke is rising from the chimney. But I doubt anyone lived here for long. I suspect the mages stayed for short periods when they were studying the stars and were probably as glad to return to the lyceum as we'll be when this is over."

From the look of the room, it had been a while since it was last occupied. They returned to the stairs and climbed to the next level. "This is promising," Geir mused as they entered a rudimentary library. A broad table sat in the center of the room. Shelves around the walls held astrolabes and sextants, as well as a number of scrolls and manuscripts. The windows on this level were still intact, mullioned glass in a leaded honeycomb pattern.

Borya wandered over to a side table where several oil lamps with mirrored reflectors sat awaiting the vanished scholars. He lifted one of the lamps and smiled. "Still has oil in it," he remarked. He hunted around until he found some straw in a basket next to a small brazier the scholars probably used to heat the drafty room and lit several of the lanterns.

"Now we have light for a proper search," he said.

"And we've just announced our presence to the world," Geir replied drily, with a nod toward the windows. "But it can't be helped. Let's be quick. We still have another level to search, and we don't want any company."

Geir, Borya, and Blaine spread out, each examining a third of the room. They gathered up armfuls of the parchment scrolls and carried them to the table, carefully unrolling them to discover their contents.

"Star maps," Borya said with annoyance. "I guess that shouldn't be a surprise."

"Nothing out of the ordinary," Geir said. "From what I can see, it appears the scholars were tracking the movement of the constellations at the seasons, the equinox, and the solstice." He lifted one of the manuscripts and paged through it.

"This book, at least, is filled with theories about the 'traveling bodies,' the stars that fall through the sky or streak across the heavens and are not seen again, or that reappear only after many years," Geir added. "It's what I'd expect to find in an observatory, but not of consequence to your task."

Between the pain and fever, Blaine was growing lightheaded. He tried to keep his focus and concentrate on the task at hand, refusing to give in to his injuries until they completed their search. Blaine had finished going through the manuscripts and scrolls in his section, finding them to be as Geir described. Then a small chest under the side table caught his eye, and he knelt to examine it. "That's interesting," he mused. "This looks to have a Tollerby mechanism lock. I wonder what the scholars thought was important enough to put in a box like this?"

"Bring it with you," Geir said. "I don't want to stay here any longer than necessary."

Borya laid a canvas pack on the table. "It should fit in here," he said. "There's room for some of the scrolls, too, if you think they're important." Blaine slipped the Tollerby box into the pack, along with the more unusual scrolls, and tied it shut.

"Let's take a look at the top floor, then get back to the lyceum before the weather shifts," Geir said.

It grew colder as they climbed, so Blaine was not surprised to find that the windows on the topmost floor of the observatory were broken, leaving it exposed to the elements. A telescope remained, but it had been left to the weather long enough that Blaine was sure it was ruined. If the scholars had left scrolls or other papers on the rain-roughened desk, they had long ago blown away or been destroyed by the birds that had claimed the observatory for their own.

"Let's hope there was nothing of value here," Geir said. "We'll make a quick search and then it's time to go."

They made their way carefully down the winding stairs, then paused in the entranceway to secure themselves to the rope once more. Blaine shivered as Geir opened the door and reached out a hand to steady himself. His head spun for a moment as the fever raged inside him. The wind had picked up, and snow had begun to fall heavily. Clouds drifted across the moon, deepening the shadows. A layer of fresh snow covered the paving stones outside the observatory's doorway, making the footing slippery.

Once again, they filed down the steep rocky steps. While

Blaine had been able to force his attention away from the sheer drop on the way up, it was impossible to descend without being constantly aware that the right side of the steps fell away into nothingness. Snow made the footing tricky, and by the time they were a third of the way down, Blaine's left hand was bruised and cut from grasping the stone cliff side to steady him. His injured leg threatened to buckle under him, and the gash in his arm made his grip too weak to trust. Even Borya moved cautiously, though Geir seemed unaffected by either the weather or the steep descent.

Borya may have grown up on the flatlands, but he has the dexterity of a mountain goat, Blaine thought. *Geir could have probably levitated up here on his own. The mines in Velant were as steep, but too dark for us to see the drop-offs, and belowground we didn't have snow, thank the gods.*

Blaine's boot slipped on an icy stair, and he grabbed for the rock wall an instant too late. "Watch out!" he shouted, but he was already falling over the side, into the shadows. Blaine flailed, trying to reach a handhold, and the sharp rock sliced into his skin. For an awful moment, he feared he would pull the others with him, but then he jerked to a halt as the rope caught around his waist, nearly causing him to heave up his dinner. He swung back to slam against the rocky side of the steps with a bone-jarring thud.

"Still with us, Blaine?" Borya called.

"Yeah, I'm here," Blaine responded, catching his breath as his heart thudded.

"I'm going to pull you up," Geir said. "I can't levitate down with both of you. Grip the rope—it will make it easier on you," he added. Blaine kicked against the rock to right himself and hung on to the rope as Geir lifted hand over hand. Finally, Blaine scrabbled back onto the narrow staircase.

"Thank the gods for the rope. Though I was afraid you'd be pulled with me," he said, still feeling his heart pounding in his throat.

"Even if both of you fell, you wouldn't budge me," Geir assured him, "though it would be uncomfortable for everyone."

"I managed to grab a handhold, but you gave me a nasty jolt," Borya said. "Glad we had the rope."

The rest of the descent went without incident, though Blaine was glad for the darkness, because he was certain he was still shaking even after they reached the ground. His fever was making it difficult to think clearly, and while he was likely to have bruises and rope burns from the mishap on the stairs, the injuries from the fight with the gryps were painful enough that he barely noticed.

Blaine had not thought that after Edgeland he would ever feel cold again, but the wind was bitter, and small ice crystals in the air stung his face. He was grateful when they reached the lyceum and stepped into the entranceway. Kestel and Piran rushed out to meet them.

"Well?" Kestel asked, eyes bright with curiosity. "Did you find anything?"

Blaine untied Borya's pack and carefully withdrew the Tollerby box. "I've got a puzzle for Verran," he said. "Everything else was out in the open. Makes me wonder what they thought was important enough to lock up."

Kestel led them up the stairs into the library, where a fire danced in the fireplace and the room smelled of dinner and old parchment. Blaine was glad that Kestel was in the front, otherwise she might have noticed the limp he could no longer hide. He wondered if he looked as pale as he felt.

When they reached the library, Blaine, Geir, and Borya recounted their search of the observatory, and Blaine was grateful they did not dwell on his mishap. Kestel gave him a worried glance but said nothing.

"Oh, that's a beauty," Verran said when he finally had the chance to examine the box. "Inlaid mahogany, hidden hinges, and the scrollwork on the lock itself is magnificent."

"Just open the bloody thing," Piran grumbled.

Verran sighed. "Barbarian."

Piran leaned toward him. "You know I am. So get going before I find a big rock and smash it open."

"No appreciation for fine art," Verran muttered, but he bent to his task. He worked in silence for several moments, and they could hear the quiet clicking of the mechanism. "You've got to give me space when I open the lock," he warned. "These Tollerby mechanisms shoot out a dart, just in case you're the wrong person."

They moved away from the table, and Verran gently angled the box as he depressed the lock. A small dart shot out with deadly speed and thudded into the wood of the bookshelf. Verran straightened, laced his fingers, and cracked his knuckles, then stood over the box grinning. "Let's see what was so important," he said as he opened the lid.

Inside was a curled scrap of old parchment. Kestel reached in and carefully unrolled the parchment, then sharply drew in her breath. "I think it's part of one of Valtyr's maps," she said, holding the paper to Blaine. "It's the right age, and it has symbols that match the ones on the obsidian disks. But I'm not sure why they thought it needed to be locked away."

Blaine cleared away the remnants of dinner and pushed aside the heavy, wood-bound book that had nearly fallen on Kestel, then he spread out the torn map. He was growing unsteady on his feet and wished for nothing more than the chance to lie down, but instead he pulled up a chair and turned his attention to the maps.

Kestel, Zaryae, and Illarion crowded behind him. "Long ago, there were four maps made by a mage named Valtyr," Blaine said for the benefit of Illarion's troupe. "Three of them were stolen. We've found two of them: one of Edgeland, and one of the Continent."

"Where are those maps now?" Illarion asked.

"We have the Edgeland map with us," Blaine replied. "Connor has his map of the Continent, and another disk. We were separated from him and from Lord Penhallow when we were attacked by Lord Reese's *talishte*."

"I have a tracing of that map," Kestel said and produced the thin silk scarf onto which she had marked the main nodes and null places from Connor's map. "This map from the observatory would be the third of Valtyr's missing maps."

Blaine studied the yellowed parchment. "This is a star map—or part of one," he said. "Similar to what I was trying to re-create at Glenreith. Look, there's Torven's constellation, and Esthrane's stars, Woman in Childbirth." The map clearly showed and named the stars and also gave the faint tracing for the fanciful pictures that had been ascribed to the constellations long ago.

Illarion bent closer for a better look. "If I'm not mistaken, some of the stars are noted differently from the others. Look," he said, pointing to the top star in Torven's K-shaped grouping, the tip of the conjuror's outstretched wand. "This star is noted with two concentric circles. While this one," he said, noting the star at the bottom of the left foot, "has only a hollow circle. Most of the rest of the stars are marked with a solid circle."

"We know that the pattern of null and powerful places on the Continent correlated to the patterns of the constellations for Torven, Charrot, and Esthrane," Kestel mused. "Do you think the stars themselves may have figured in the magic?"

"Of course they do," Zaryae answered. "This star, Arktoriphe," she said, pointing to the tip in Torven's wand, "has very strong magic. When it's overhead, both magic and divination are easier to work, with better results."

She pointed to the star in the heel of Torven's foot. "But this star, Letikonon, is bad magic. When it's brightest, magic dims. Seers can't read the signs. Working magic becomes dangerous."

"But we've only got part of the map," Kestel said, straightening. "We don't even know whether we've got the most important part or not. And for all we know, the other piece could have been destroyed centuries ago."

"Or maybe the most important piece was salvaged," Blaine countered. "There's no way of knowing. It would help to find the fourth map."

"The night's still young, and we've got nowhere else to go," Kestel said, stretching. "Why don't we see what we can find here in the library?"

"I agree," Geir said. "While the lyceum is a comfortable shelter from the storm, it would be unwise to stay long. Best to find what we can and be on our way as soon as possible."

"All right, I'm game," Piran replied. "What are we looking for?"

Blaine drew a deep breath and looked around the library. Its walls were covered with bookshelves from floor to ceiling, and each of the shelves was full. "Maps, for starters. If you find anything that looks like a disk, give a shout. Beyond that," he said, and gave a shrug, "if a book seems to call to you, perhaps it's our spirits at work."

The others set about their tasks, but Kestel hung back. She laid a hand on his arm. "You don't look so good," she said worriedly. She raised the back of her hand to touch his forehead, and her eyes widened in concern. "You're hot with fever."

Blaine shrugged. "Just tired. I'll be all right." Kestel's expression let him know that she did not believe him.

The next few candlemarks passed in near-silence as they worked. From time to time, someone would select a book and lay it to the side for closer inspection. Blaine remained alert to the movement of the shadows, but for now, they were still.

Kestel carefully laid out Ifrem's map of Edgeland and the drawing she had made on a silk shawl that allowed her to overlay that map with Connor's map of the Continent. She took out the two disks and began to compare them to the markings on the maps. The heavy wood-bound book was useful for anchoring the top of Ifrem's map to keep it from curling, and she used some coins from her pouch to secure the bottom corners. After a few moments, she left the study table and began to rummage in the drawers of a nearby desk until she found blank parchment, a quill, and ink so she could note her findings.

Geir's ability to climb and levitate meant he was the choice to examine the topmost volumes. Borya took his turn at watch, taking up a position in the darkened entranceway. That left the others to divide up the bookcases.

"Here's hoping that the information we need is in a language we can read," Verran muttered, paging through a volume in a language Blaine did not recognize. "It could take forever to look through all the books that aren't written in the Common Tongue or in Donderan."

"A map is a map," Piran said. "If you find something that looks like that damn map of Ifrem's, it doesn't bloody matter what language it's in." He gestured toward where Kestel was comparing the maps. "It's not as if we can read all the squiggles and marks anyway."

"The null spots and places of power on the star map definitely match up to my drawing of Connor's map," Kestel announced, glowing with pride. She put her hands at the small of her back and bent backward, stretching. "And from what I can tell, there are several places, both null and powerful, that are like the lyceum—not main cities or manor houses. A few of them are completely in the wilderness, either in the mountains or out on the far plains."

"Good hiding places, perhaps, if you were being hunted by the king," Geir remarked. "The Knights were warriors, and many of them were *talishte*. Being in the wilderness would be a small price to pay for safety."

Outside, the wind whipped through the ruined upper floor, howling past the opening where the stairs had been. Geir and Borya maneuvered a few large wooden panels into place to keep the cold gusts from sweeping through the entranceway, but the storm still whistled across the broken timbers.

"Blaine, Kestel, come here," Geir called suddenly. "Bring a lantern." Blaine and the others moved into the large foyer.

"Look at the ceiling," Geir said.

Blaine lifted the lantern. He could make out a random pattern of dots. "All right…" he said skeptically.

"Now come up onto the stairway, and look down at the mosaic on the floor," Geir replied.

"I'll go," Kestel said quietly, guessing that Blaine had no desire to climb more steps. She took the lantern and moved to where Geir stood.

For the first time in several candlemarks, Blaine noticed that the shadows seemed to move on their own again, shifting even when his lantern did not reach their depths. *Our ghost friends are interested in what we find*, he thought.

From the top of the stairs, Kestel looked at the floor below. "Down there, it just looks like a rather pretty bunch of colors," she said. "But from up here—"

"It's a map of the Continent," Geir finished. "And I'm betting that the dots overhead match the star map."

Piran had followed them out to the entranceway. "I don't get it," he said. "If the maps are a big secret, why make them into something everyone sees?"

Kestel chuckled. "It's called 'hiding in plain sight,'" she replied. "So what if the lyceum had a map of the Continent on the floor? No one would think anything of it, unless they knew about Valtyr's maps. Even if someone figured out that the dots were stars, who would care? They'd expect to see sky over land."

"This building is old," Geir said. "Whoever created the ceiling and floor art would have done it before the maps were stolen."

"I've got the tracing of Connor's map of the Continent, showing the places of power," Kestel said excitedly. "In daylight, we can find a way to transfer the tracing to the map on the floor." She looked upward. "Then, if we take the tracing up to the ceiling, we should be able to match the places of power and no-power to the stars. That should give us the missing portion of the star map," she said with a grin.

"But what does that tell us?" Piran grumbled. "That we don't already know?"

"It shows the position of the stars over the land at a specific time of the year," Illarion answered. "From that, an astronomer could calculate the date—and the location."

"The time of year is important for a mage," Zaryae said. "The solstice and the equinox are dates of great power, and many mages plan their workings for those dates because the magic is strongest then."

Blaine looked to Illarion. "We're not far out from the solstice. If the Cataclysm disrupted the magic, would the solstice be our best shot to bind the magic again?"

"It's something to consider," Illarion replied. "But if you believe the solstice would help you restore the magic, it doesn't leave much time to figure out exactly how you're supposed to do that."

They filed back into the library, and Blaine sank into a chair by the fire, while Geir began to pace. Blaine stretched out his injured leg, trying to find a comfortable position. He rested his hand on his thigh, then quickly moved it when even the light pressure was too painful to bear.

"Magic waxes and wanes for many reasons," Zaryae said. She had taken a seat next to the fireplace, and the flickering flames cast her face in light and shadow. "The time of day, the weather, the skill, and the power of the one wielding the power—and the time of the year."

The wind tore at the shutters, whistling across the slats, while outside the storm raged, and the wind made the fire billow. Somewhere in an adjacent room, a loose shutter banged against the stone walls.

"So magic is stronger some days than others?" Blaine mused. He looked to Geir and Illarion. "And an astrologer could tell the date by the position of the stars?"

Both men nodded. "Certainly, if the stars and their positions were detailed enough."

"Which means that the entranceway marks a particular date," Verran said, his previous reluctance gone now that he was warm. "But we have no way to know what was special about that date. It might not have anything to do with bringing back magic. Maybe it's the date the lyceum was built, or the head mage's birthday."

"Perhaps," Illarion said. "But I doubt mages would go to that much expense for vanity. No, the map in the entrance serves a purpose, but we don't yet know whether it aligns with your concerns."

Just then, a loud thump made them turn. "That damn book!" Piran said. The wood-bound book lay on the floor.

"Wait," Kestel said. She walked over and picked up the heavy tome. Then she looked toward the corners of the room, where even the lanterns and firelight did not fully dispel the shadows. "I'm a little dim, but you keep moving this book around," Kestel said to the shadows. "All right. You've got my attention." She looked at the others. "Maybe the ghosts weren't trying to kill me when they pushed this off the shelves. Maybe they were trying to get us to look at this particular book."

She lifted it to the table and began to page through the book as the others gathered around her. "The cover is heavy," Kestel murmured. The two pieces of burnished wood were tied together rather than bound with a spine. In between were hundreds of parchment pages, yellowed with age, all cut to fit between the covers.

"What's the subject?" Blaine asked.

Kestel frowned and shook her head. "This can't be right. It's a storybook—or a history—about Valshoa." She looked up, mystified. "But Valshoa is only a legend."

"May I take a look?" Geir exchanged places with Kestel and began to leaf through the parchment. "Valshoa is a legend, but most legends have root in fact," he said. "Valshoa disappeared centuries ago."

"Maybe a big storm wiped it out," Piran countered. "Or a volcano. When I soldiered, we passed through a lot of places where there were just ruins of old buildings or towns."

"Valshoa was a city of mages," Illarion said. "The legends say that the mages didn't want to be distracted from their magic, so they built a city for themselves and used their magic to discourage visitors. Over the years, they became more and more reclusive. Their magic made people avoid their city and helped outsiders forget about them." He shrugged. "So the stories say."

"So they made people forget they were there, and people thought the city disappeared?" Piran asked, pouring himself another tankard of wine.

"There are many stories, but who knows how much is true?" Illarion said. "If they are true, then at least a few people managed to visit the city and return—or escape."

Blaine stared at the wood-bound book. "And at least a few who may have wanted their privacy as much as the mages," he said quietly.

"What are you thinking?" Geir asked.

Blaine frowned. "We've got a city that vanished—a city that must have been in a place of power to be known for its mages—and a group of immortals who needed a secure place to hide. And we've got Vigus Quintrel, who suspected that something terrible was going to happen and needed sanctuary for the mages and scholars he gathered."

"You think the Knights of Esthrane found the ruins of Valshoa and made it their sanctuary?" Kestel asked as Geir continued to page through the parchments held between the wooden covers.

"Who knows? But it's possible there could be *talishte* who actually remembered Valshoa, isn't it?" Blaine asked.

Geir nodded. "Yes, although most don't survive that long." He paused. "A small number of Elders remain. It's certainly possible that they could have had firsthand knowledge of Valshoa."

Piran gave Blaine a horrified look. "I don't care what you say, I'm not hunting up some thousand-year-old *talishte* and asking for directions," he said and drained the tankard.

"I would counsel caution as well," Geir said. "The Elders are not known to welcome strangers, especially mortals. They live in seclusion and rarely even see others of our kind. If we must seek the counsel of the Elders, it's a task best left to Penhallow."

"Listen to the vampire," Piran said. "He's talking sense."

Kestel's gaze had not left the book in Geir's hands. "What else did you find in the manuscript?" she asked.

Geir continued to turn the pages. "It's a fairly complete history of Valshoa, from what I can make out. Oddly enough, it was marked with a blue ribbon. But no map." He paused. "And a note from our mysterious friend." He held up a loose sheet of parchment that was much newer than the rest of the manuscript.

"What's that?" Blaine asked.

Geir gave a thin smile. "Another coded set of jottings signed with a 'VQ,'" he reported.

"Vigus Quintrel," Kestel said. "How is it that he's always a few steps ahead of us?"

"More like we're a few steps behind him," Blaine replied, taking a look at the paper. "After all, Quintrel knew what he was planning. We're scrambling to figure out the puzzle before time runs out."

Blaine looked at the notations on the loose sheet. Some of the markings resembled those on the obsidian disks. Names and initials were jotted on the sheet, along with words in a language Blaine did not recognize, and a series of numbers.

"The numbers appear to be longitude and latitude," Geir said. "But what they direct us to, I don't know."

"Could it be Valshoa?" Kestel asked, excitement coloring her voice. "Let me see." Geir obligingly placed the heavy book back on the table. Kestel carefully turned the manuscript over and let her fingers move slowly over the back cover.

"Kestel?" Verran said tentatively. "What are you doing?"

"I noticed when I picked the book up that the back cover seemed different from the front," she said, still examining the wood. "Then when Geir picked it up, I could see that the back cover is thicker."

"You think there's a hidden compartment?" Verran's interest grew livelier with the prospect of secreted valuables.

Kestel grinned. "I think the back cover is hollow. Do you want to do the honors?"

Verran's eyes were alight as he traded places with Kestel and let his fingers play over the old wood. "It's inlaid, but someone went to a lot of trouble to make it look ordinary," he mused. "Usually it's the other way around. Someone who can only afford a simple thing wants it to look like more than it is."

Verran bent to have a closer look. "Wait, I can see the lines where the pieces fit together. Between the grain and the finish, whoever made this did a good job."

"Can you open it?" Kestel asked excitedly.

It seemed to Blaine as if even the shadows gathered closer to where Verran hunched over the book. "Don't be doubting me, Kestel dear," Verran quipped. "Of course I can open it."

"If it was worth going to that much trouble to hide something, would the book's owner have spelled the compartment shut?" Piran asked.

Verran gave him a sour look. "Might have. But the magic died, remember? So did binding spells and the like. Ah!" he said suddenly, and he smiled. "I think I found a catch."

There was a quiet *click*, and a thin panel of wood came loose in Verran's hands. "Oh yes," he enthused. "Oh yes."

"Don't make love to the bloody thing," Piran grumbled. "Just tell us what's inside."

Verran was enthralled enough with his find that he did not spare a look for Piran. His slender fingers worked at the small compartment until he had teased out a folded piece of brown parchment. "Yes!" he shouted, then suddenly realized how loud his voice was.

"What have you got?" Kestel asked, moving closer. This time, Blaine was certain he saw the shadows shift in corners of the room quite apart from where the fire cast their silhouettes.

"A rather old piece of parchment," Verran said, handing the folded square to Geir. Geir carefully opened it. "Now this is interesting," he said quietly.

"What?" Verran asked, stretching onto his toes to see over Geir's shoulder.

"By the looks of it, we've found Valtyr's last map," Geir replied. "And it's of Valshoa."

"Valshoa?" Kestel said, frowning. "I mean, it makes sense, given where we found it, but why would Valtyr bother with creating a map like that—"

"Because Valshoa did exist," Zaryae said triumphantly, her eyes shining.

Geir studied the faded writing on the map. "More so than the other three, it seems to be a detailed map of a fairly small area. Two maps were of entire continents, and the third was of the heavens. This is a map of the city itself and its immediate environs. And perhaps," he added, looking more closely, "of places where the power waxes or wanes inside the city."

"Are there any clues that might help us find the city itself?" Illarion asked, peering over Zaryae and Kestel for a glimpse.

"Nothing that I can see," Geir said and placed the map with the others on the table.

Blaine's head pounded, and his fever left him sweating and flushed. As the others clustered around the maps, he poured himself another glass of wine.

Kestel studied the maps. "I wonder whether Connor and Penhallow found any more disks."

Geir shook his head. "I have no news, other than the sense that Penhallow and Connor are reasonably safe. We'll have to wait for them to rejoin us to find out more."

Zaryae bent close to the wood-bound manuscript. She turned the manuscript over, focusing on the carving on the front cover. "Look at this," she said, holding one of the disks next to the carved wood.

"Do you see?" She pointed to a downward-facing curve with a slash through it. "This is the same on both the disk and the cover." Zaryae frowned. "I've seen this symbol somewhere else. Somewhere recently." She looked up and grinned broadly. "I remember! It was carved into the door of the shrine."

"Then let's have a look," Kestel said excitedly.

"I'm not much for shrines," Piran said. "And it's nearly my turn to take over the watch from Desya. I'll stay here and make sure nothing happens to the maps." He glanced around himself. "I don't trust this place. The sooner we're gone, the better." Borya nodded his agreement.

"I agree," Geir said, "but likely for different reasons."

"I'm staying near the fire," Verran said. "If there's a lock to pick, come and get me."

They could hear the storm tugging at the wood that blocked off the stairs in the entranceway. Blaine, Illarion, Kestel, and Zaryae made their way down the darkened corridor, lanterns held aloft. Once they left the glow of the firelight that radiated from the library's doorway, the hallway seemed oppressively dark, and each step took them deeper into the shadows.

"You're limping," Kestel said quietly. She moved to walk on the same side as his injured leg and slipped an arm around

Blaine's waist. "Lean on me. We'll have a look at that leg when we get back to the library."

"I'd be happy for a stiff shot of whiskey to dull the pain, and the chance to sleep it off," Blaine murmured. "I feel terrible."

"I sure hope this place was a little more comfortable when the mage-scholars lived here," Zaryae said with a shiver. "Even ascetics can freeze to death."

As they passed the kitchen there was a loud, metallic clatter. It echoed against the stone walls of the corridor, making them jump. Kestel and Zaryae exchanged wary glances. "Sounds like the spirits in the kitchen are still at work," Zaryae remarked.

Illarion was in the lead with a lantern. He stopped in front of a wooden door. Like the library entrance, the door was made from cherry wood, and it was carved with an equally impressive motif. But even in the lantern light, Blaine could see the symbols for Torven, Charrot, and Esthrane.

"Did you go in when you found the room?" Kestel asked, her voice just above a whisper although the four were alone in the corridor.

Zaryae shook her head. "We peered in the door, enough to get a sense of its purpose. We thought it best to explore it with a larger group. I had a strong sense that it and the library would be where we would find what we sought."

Illarion gave the heavy door a push. Inside was completely dark, and Blaine guessed that the shrine lacked even the shuttered windows of the library. Illarion stepped into the room, holding the lantern aloft.

The corridor had been much colder than the library, but the shrine was colder still. The lantern's light did not reach to the four corners of the room. It was enough to see a darkened altar, the melted remnants of candles, and a shadowy sculpture that loomed against the far wall.

Blaine's head throbbed harder, and he reeled. Kestel reached out to steady him, and he could see concern in her features. "Are you all right?"

Blaine grimaced. "I've been better. Let's be done with this so I can go back to the library and sleep off this headache."

Another step into the shrine revealed a room that might be able to accommodate about twenty-five people. Ornate boxes of metal and wood had windowed panels displaying yellowed bones.

"Looks as if we found those relics you were talking about," Kestel murmured with a nod toward the boxes.

Against the far wall was a full-sized figure of a robed skeleton holding a scythe in one hand and an astrolabe in the other. The wall behind the figure was painted in brightly colored symbols.

"Look at what the skeleton is wearing," Kestel whispered to Blaine. He moved a step closer for a better look in the dim light. Nearly hidden by the figure's robes, an obsidian disk on a leather strap hung on the bony rib cage.

"Do you see?" Blaine whispered to Zaryae.

She nodded but touched his arm in warning as he reached toward the skeleton. "We must ask the goddess's permission. She takes a dim view of those who desecrate her holy places."

Whispered voices seemed just beyond the threshold of Blaine's hearing, and he inclined his head to listen better, but the voices were too distant to make out.

"This is all wrong," Kestel murmured. "Torven is the harvester of souls. But the color of the robe is green, Esthrane's color."

"Esthrane rules the Unseen Realm, where the wandering souls reside," Zaryae replied in a hushed voice. "Look at the

symbols in the background. Sheaves of wheat. Herd animals."
She pointed toward the wall behind the skeletal figure. "And
Esthrane's constellation. This is Mother Esthrane," Zaryae
said. "But I've never seen her shown this way before."

All around them in the darkened shrine, Blaine could hear
voices whispering. They were louder now, but still indistinct.
He felt the skin prickle at the back of his neck.

"Here's a taper," Kestel said. "Let's light some candles and
get a better look at the mural behind the figure." She lit several
candles and turned to Zaryae. "What do you make of it?"

The mural behind the skeletal statue began on the right with
figures of the mage-scholars at work in the fields and going
about their daily business, milling wheat, baking bread, tending herds. Over them all, in the sky, were symbols of Esthrane's
protection: hawks, crows, and falcons.

In the next panel, directly behind the death-mother figure,
the mage-scholars were at their books, studying and teaching
or venerating Esthrane with prayer and offerings.

"Look there," Zaryae said quietly, pointing to the third
panel. A gray-green sky replaced the bright blue of the first
panel. The birds of protection had been replaced by ravens,
owls, and vultures. A faint green ribbon of light could be seen
in the gray sky, and a skeletal hand protruding from a burgundy robe hovered, as if to hold the image fixed. Below that,
translucent images of men milled about on the banks of a black
river. Unlike the first two panels, there was nothing to suggest
their purpose or how they passed their time, no daily chores,
no study or worship.

"The Unseen Realm," Zaryae murmured. "The place of
restless souls."

"And for some reason, the mages believed that was their
fate," Kestel said, drawing closer to the mural and leaning

forward for a better look. "See—the faces of the ghosts are the same faces of the mages in the first two murals."

"Why would they believe that they would linger in the Unseen Realm instead of passing to the Sea of Souls?" Kestel murmured. "Or worse, to Raka if they had done something to anger the gods?"

Blaine's fever flared, and he felt the blood leave his head in a rush. He fell, vaguely aware of Kestel's cry and Zaryae's shout. Illarion was speaking, but his voice seemed far away. In its place were the voices of the dead. The shadows surrounded Blaine, cooling his fevered skin with their touch, and their words grew clear as the living voices receded.

Lord of the Blood, you have come, a voice said.

Our seer foretold that one remained. We awaited you, but we did not live to greet you, added another voice.

Blaine's body thrashed in the throes of fever, and he groaned, feeling as if he were burning from the inside out. He struggled to ask the questions he wanted to ask, fighting his failing body.

Where did you go? he managed. *Why did you wait for me?*

The voices murmured, drawing away as if in conference with each other. Blaine's head swam. *Tell me*, he urged.

We will show you. The world around Blaine went black, and the panicked voices of his friends receded. In their place, he saw the lyceum standing whole and undamaged, with twenty mage-scholars rising before dawn to be about their daily chores. The ground under his feet shook, and the sky seemed to split as a wide, bright-green ribbon snaked across the heavens.

He heard the scholars' cries of fear and dismay, then saw them rally as the eldest mages called them all to shelter within the lyceum. It was as if he huddled with them in the shrine. He listened as some prayed to Esthrane for deliverance, while others tried in vain to harness the magic.

Wild magic was all around them, and as the *hasithara* slipped beyond the mages' grasp, the rogue *visithara* seemed all the stronger. The ground beneath the lyceum trembled, and cracks appeared in the walls. The air itself crackled with unharnessed power as the ribbon passed overhead.

A mighty roar sounded above the frightened scholars, the sound of snapping beams and crumbling stone. The air was filled with the acrid tang of lightning close at hand, and billows of smoke followed quickly after as the ribbon of light burned and smashed its way through the top floor of the lyceum, overcoming the mage's wards and protection.

Among the scholars' ghosts, Blaine felt the loss as the mages had felt it and understood how vast a difference it had made for those who had possessed far more than just a hint of power. It felt as if his soul, his essence was being flayed from him, inch by inch, pulled out through his skin, white-hot, ripping at the sinews of his being. He screamed, raw-throated, bucking and writhing with the pain, his back arching and his hands scrabbling for purchase on the stone floor.

He saw the mages downed by the sudden disappearance of their power, helpless as their lyceum burned, frightened and in agony as their magic was stripped from them. Wild power coursed in its place, searing them from the inside, torturing them with visions and horrors.

Then, all was still. The wild power left as quickly as it came, and the harnessed magic, the *hasithara*, did not come in its place, leaving the mages empty and broken. Blaine, who possesed a minor power, had felt the loss of it keenly, but for true mages, the absence was as if someone had stripped them of sight, sound, and hearing. Blaine heard the whispers of the mages' ghosts, and he knew that many of them had not survived the loss of the magic.

The scene shifted, and Blaine saw the mages struggling to recover, beating out the last of the flames to save the lower floors of the lyceum and daring to go outside to recover their farm animals.

A raptor's cry split the air, and instinctively, Blaine flinched. He knew that cry. He had heard it on the bridge as the gryps attacked. It sounded all around him, around the scholars, as their sky filled with the beating of leathery wings and gryps attacked the mages who were tending their crops and herds.

Just nine of the original twenty mages survived the first attack, and Blaine felt the ghosts' sorrow as keenly as if it were his own. Other images filled his mind, of magic storms and the monsters conjured by rifts in the fabric of the world torn by the wild *visithara* magic. Blaine saw the survivors try to go about their lives, tending the animals, working on the mural that told the story of the lyceum. One by one, they fell to the gryps. Finally, only one old man remained, and his heart failed him as he fled from the winged predators.

The loss of the mages was keen, overwhelming Blaine. A familiar image filled his mind, and he recognized it as the ceiling mural and floor design from the lyceum's entranceway. Blaine felt as if he hung suspended between the two, belonging to neither land nor sky. Ghostly figures moved at the edge of his vision, then one of the shadows stepped forward. *Lord of the Blood, you have come*, the voice repeated. *Yet you are almost one of the dead.*

Tell me how to save the magic, Blaine begged.

When we saw that you had come, and we knew it to be you, we brought a manuscript to your attention, the ghost replied. *The mage you seek took refuge among us. He spoke little of his plans, but he was consumed with tales of Valshoa. Take the manuscript and the disk. Continue his search.*

Why Valshoa? Does it really exist?

For a few seconds, the voices were silent. *Valshoa is a place of great power, a crossroads of the meridians*, the voice answered finally. *Find it, and you may find him.*

Blaine's life force was fading with the poison of the gryp's talons, and as it did, he felt his bond with the ghosts grow stronger, even as his connection with the living frayed.

Then Blaine saw a faint glow in the darkness, and as he watched it, the glow grew brighter until it became the figure of a young woman with long, dark hair. Zaryae, Blaine thought, and he realized he could hear the seer's voice.

If you believe he can save the magic, help me save him, Zaryae beseeched the ghosts, but Blaine could not tell whether she spoke the words aloud or whether he heard them in the same way he could hear the ghosts. *He must live for the magic to be restored in our time. I can't raise him up without your help.*

We had potions and powders that will be of use to counter the gryps' poison. We will show you where they are hidden and how to use them, one of the ghosts said.

Fever raged through Blaine's body, alternating with chills so intense that his muscles seized painfully and it was hard, so hard, to breathe. Far away, Blaine could hear a woman crying. There were other voices, men's voices, some shouting, others arguing. And farther away, at the edge of his senses, Blaine could hear Geir's urgent warnings that they needed to go below to take cover from the magic storm.

Illarion forced Blaine's jaws open, and Zaryae poured a bitter elixir into his mouth, stroking his throat to make him swallow. "He's burning up," Zaryae murmured. "The wounds have gone bad. It's poisoned his blood. He's dying."

"Do something!" Kestel begged. "Please don't let him die."

"The spirits are thick around us," Zaryae said. "I've asked them for their help. I've done all I know to do."

Voices chanted. Time stood still. Power raged. In the maelstrom, Blaine felt as if the bonds that tied his soul to his flesh loosened so that he was hovering, caught between the frantic efforts of the living and the prayers of the dead. Torn between worlds, Blaine saw his friends kneeling around his still form at the feet of the skeletal goddess, hands linked, eyes closed.

In the gray vale of the Unseen Realm, Blaine heard the chant of scholars as the ghosts drew near, their shadows gathering around the mortals in the shrine, surrounding him. Once more, Illarion pried Blaine's mouth open and forced a vile mixture down his throat. Kestel and Zaryae gentled Blaine out of his clothing so that Zaryae could dress the wounds with a new poultice. Distantly, Blaine heard Zaryae muttering, perhaps to herself, perhaps to the spirits that gathered around them.

Zaryae rose from where she knelt next to Blaine. In the candlelight, he saw her move from one relic box to the next, stopping in front of each to make a shallow bow. "Please," she begged. "Show me how to hold on to him. I'm losing him. The elixirs need time to work. I need to delay his spirit's passage until his body can heal."

Zaryae returned and laid her hands on Blaine's wounds, one on his thigh and one on his shoulder. She began to chant. Blaine felt the press of spirits grow thick around him. One by one, the relic boxes took on a faint glow, and the air in the shrine grew even colder. Power stirred around Blaine, and he knew he was in the presence of the dead. Illarion and Kestel must have felt the ghosts' presence as well, because Blaine heard them cry out.

Blaine watched his body convulse, and he felt the bonds that tied his soul to his body grow slack. He looked around and saw dozens of ghosts filling the shrine. They formed an unbroken ring around him, and he knew he could not break through their cordon.

"The spirits have come," Zaryae said. "They will keep his soul from passing over."

Abruptly Blaine plunged back into his body. The elixir was burning through him, as if red-hot pokers had been laid on his flesh. His whole body stiffened in pain as the elixir warred with the poison in his veins. Blaine felt as if he were tumbling in the airless depths of the ocean, held in the grip of the cold sea. Finally, darkness took him and he was too exhausted to wonder whether it would ever release him.

CHAPTER TWENTY-THREE

CONSCIOUSNESS RETURNED SLOWLY. AS BLAINE came around, he realized first that the terrible pounding in his head had stopped. His body ached as if he had recently done hard labor in the mines of Velant, but the fever had broken. Instead of waves of chills, he felt the cold stone beneath him, and shivered.

The voices of the shadows were silent. In their place, Blaine could hear worried whispers, and the catch of a woman's breath as she cried. His eyes struggled open. He still lay where he had fallen, in the small shrine to Esthrane. Torches now lit the enclosure as well as the candles that circled the feet of the skeleton statue. The crackle of power that had filled the air was gone.

"How do you feel?" The voice was Kestel's, and it sounded as if her throat was raw. Blaine looked up and saw that her face was tearstained, and her eyes were red from crying. She managed a self-conscious half smile and wiped her face with the back of her hand.

"Pretty awful," Blaine admitted.

Kestel leaned down and kissed him on the cheek. "I'm glad you're back," she murmured. "You gave us all a scare."

"What happened after I blacked out?" Blaine's mouth was dry, and his tongue felt thick. He was exhausted and sore and hungry, but his forearm and thigh where the gryp had gashed him no longer burned, and he realized that he did not feel the slow poison of the wounds in his blood.

Kestel was kneeling next to him, and she smoothed back his sweat-soaked hair. "We got hit with a magic storm, on top of the snowstorm we already had," she said. "And I'm not completely sure, but I think Zaryae received a vision from the ghosts that helped her use the mages' potions to heal you."

"A magic storm," Blaine repeated. "But we're not belowground."

"It came up fast," Kestel said. "Geir got Piran, Verran, Borya, and Desya into the cellars. But we didn't dare try to move you. So we rode it out here." She shrugged. "The lyceum's survived magic storms before—what's one more?"

"You could have all been killed," Blaine murmured.

"Zaryae was in the middle of a vision," Kestel replied, touching his cheek gently. "We couldn't get the potions we needed if we went below. And you were busy dying."

Blaine met her eyes. "I felt...as if the fever took over completely."

Kestel nodded, and Blaine could see her eyes well up once more. "You collapsed. It was so cold, but you were burning up. You started raving about the shadows, and then you went into convulsions. While Zaryae was trying to heal you, you stopped breathing." Her voice caught, and she touched his face lightly with her fingertips, as if to reassure herself that the worst had passed.

"You saw and heard things in those moments," Zaryae said.

She leaned against the wall near the skeleton statue, and even in the torchlight, Blaine thought Zaryae looked haggard. She had bound back her long, dark hair, and her eyes were shadowed as if from lack of sleep.

"Thank you," Blaine said quietly. Zaryae inclined her head in acknowledgement. Blaine tried to shift positions but realized he still felt too weak to sit up.

"You don't need to move. The danger has passed," Illarion said. He paused. "I'd very much like to know what it is you saw right before—"

"Right before I died?" Blaine finished for him. "Ghosts. I saw ghosts."

Zaryae nodded. "It's not uncommon for the dying to see the dead. You were the one all along to see the shadows moving, when the rest did not."

"You knew they were there," Blaine said.

Once more, Zaryae nodded. "Yes. Before the magic failed, seeing the spirits was part of my gift. Now, I can only sense them when the wild magic is very strong. I could feel the storm coming, and I hoped it would help me communicate with the mage spirits and the ghosts who were bound to the relics. I gambled that it might be enough to save your life, and that the thick rock walls might protect the rest of us."

"Too dangerous," Blaine murmured. "You should have gotten to the cellars."

"And let you die? I don't think so," Kestel said. She reached for his hand and squeezed it hard. "After all, you're the last Lord of the Blood. We've got to take care of you." Her tone was joking, but the look in her eyes was not.

"What did the ghosts show you?" Illarion asked.

"The scholars knew Quintrel," Blaine said. "He came here.

That's why the ghosts made sure we found that book. He left the map, and that disk," he said, with a nod toward the statue. "We have their blessing to take both items, plus the book. The ghosts told me that if we find Valshoa, I'm likely to find Quintrel."

"I think we'd better study that book carefully," Kestel said, "as well as the murals in the entranceway."

They looked up at the sound of footsteps in the corridor, then Geir and the others appeared in the doorway.

"The storm has passed," Geir said. "It's nearly dawn. I'll need to head into the cellars, but I wanted to make sure that you had all survived."

"Glad to see you made it," Verran said, the note of cheer in his voice masking his worry. "We've got the fire going again in the library and brought in food enough for breakfast." He looked to Geir. "What about you? You're not feeling peckish, are you?"

Geir smiled. "There are rats enough in the cellars to sustain me." Distaste colored his voice. "It's not my preferred meal, but I've made do many a time on worse."

Kestel looked at Geir. "The ghosts of the scholars came to Blaine. They confirmed that Quintrel was here—and that he was interested in Valshoa. That's where they think he's gone."

Geir grimaced. "That would be great news—assuming the coordinates we've found for Valshoa are accurate." He paused. "Now that the storm has passed, I'll copy the drawings of the sky and land in the entranceway. Best we get that done before anything else happens."

"Never tempt a thief with a hidden treasure," Verran said with a grin. "It's going to take us a bit to dig our way out with the snow. And when I'm not digging, I fully intend to be studying those maps. We'll find it."

"Don't forget Pollard and Reese," Blaine said quietly, still exhausted from his ordeal. "They're likely to be hot on the trail as well. And if any of the men who attacked us were bonded to Reese, he may already know their attempt failed."

Verran shrugged. "All in a day's work. After all, any treasure worth stealing means someone else wants to steal it from you." He grinned. "Stick with me, and I'll make proper thieves of the lot of you."

Zaryae had hung back, leaning quietly against the wall near the statue. Blaine looked to her. "Thank you," he said quietly.

Zaryae gave a tired smile and nodded. "Thank the goddess. I was just the vessel."

Blaine made it back to the library, supported between Verran and Illarion. Geir, who could have easily carried him, refrained for the sake of Blaine's dignity and instead hung back in case Blaine collapsed. Zaryae leaned heavily on Kestel, exhausted but otherwise undamaged. The few feet of corridor seemed endless, but they arrived at the library, and Blaine gratefully accepted the bed that had been fixed for him from the scavenged materials of the scholars' dormitory rooms.

Geir took shelter from the day, but the others remained awake long enough to eat something to replenish them after the events of the night before. Tonight, Blaine would join the others to force the manuscript to give up its secrets. Today, he wanted nothing more than sleep.

The torches in the library had been extinguished, as had the lanterns. The gray light of dawn filled the room, muting its colors. Someone had banked the fire. Everyone except Desya, who had the first watch, had found a place on the floor to make a bed for the day. Even the shadows did not move, and Blaine wondered if, after what happened in the shrine, the shadows would speak to them again. For now, they were silent.

Kestel had moved her bedroll next to his. Blaine managed a weak grin. "So now you're my nurse?" he bantered shakily.

She smiled, but it did not reach her eyes. "Bodyguard, if you prefer." Her expression grew serious. "You almost died, Mick. It was too close. Dammit! Why didn't you tell us something was wrong?"

"Didn't seem to be much purpose in worrying anyone, when the poison was going to have to run its course," Blaine said.

"You wouldn't have made it if the ghosts hadn't told Zaryae where to find the herbs for the potions, and if she hadn't asked the relics' spirits to keep your soul from crossing to the gods before the elixir could work." She shivered. "I thought we were going to lose both of you."

Blaine reached out to take her hand. "Thank you for staying with me."

Kestel managed a half smile. "Don't push your luck like that again." She leaned down and kissed him lightly on the lips. "Now that you're back from the dead," she said quietly, "don't be afraid to go after what you really want."

Blaine met her eyes, then brought a hand up to cup her head, tangling his fingers in her red hair, drawing her back down for another, longer kiss. Kestel did not pull away, and she returned the kiss with gentle interest.

When they finally separated, Blaine looked at her in slightly dazed wonder. "If I'd known I needed to die to get your attention," he joked weakly, "I would have done it before this." He was still holding her hand, and he lifted their twined fingers to his lips. "I love you, Kestel."

She squeezed his hand. "I love you too, Mick," she said in a voice low enough that only he could hear. "I think we've both been figuring out how to say it for a while now."

Exhaustion threatened to overwhelm Blaine. "Don't go," he murmured. He let go of her hand and slipped his arm around her, guiding her to settle down against him. "Stay close, please."

Kestel nestled closer. "Don't worry. I'm not going anywhere without you."

CHAPTER
TWENTY-FOUR

NIKLAS LEANED BACK IN HIS CHAIR, LET HIS HEAD fall backward, and closed his eyes. The need to sign documents and fill out forms had died with the king, but a captain was never truly off duty.

"Maybe I should promote myself to general," he muttered aloud, though the tent was empty. "Field promotion. Gods know I've earned it, even if there's no raise in pay." *There's no pay at all*, he thought. *What's left of His Majesty's army has become a group of squatters, looters, and thieves.* They weren't the first army to be reduced to those conditions, he thought with a sigh. And they wouldn't be the last.

It hadn't been his best day. Two more cases of madness in the camp, with damage and injuries to be cleaned up. *I wonder how Carr is doing?* he thought. Losing any of his men distressed him, regardless of the cause. Over the long march home, he had come to know all of his soldiers by name, and he knew their stories. *To have survived the war, the Great Fire, the march, and then to die of madness, it's just wrong.* Seeing Carr succumb was even harder. Not only for what Niklas knew it would mean to Blaine and his family, but because Carr had been a link to the time before the war, before Blaine's exile, before the kingdom's fall.

The scouting parties had returned, with fewer provisions than he had hoped, even though several *talishte* had been among the hunters. *Good thing we brought back that flour,* he thought. *Not much meat to go around tonight.*

He sat up, and his gaze wandered to the half-empty bottle of whiskey. They had looted it, and several others, from the ruins of what had once been a grand home, destroyed and abandoned in the Great Fire. It was too easy to pour a drink and dull the pain. *We lost the war, saw our kingdom destroyed, our king dead, our cities burned. We're vagabonds and drifters in a land where even magic didn't survive. There's not enough whiskey in the world to make me forget that.*

In addition to the madness, there'd been the usual: fighting between the men, disciplinary procedures, a briefing by the morning scouts, and several candlemarks spent poring over maps, trying to figure out where Vedran Pollard had troops stationed and how best they could navigate around them.

Blaine's been gone for nearly a week, Niklas thought and pushed a hand back through his hair, fighting a headache as he stared at the maps. *No one's even entirely sure where he went.* He shook his head. *When he gets back, we're going to have a talk about riding off without backup.* He resolutely refused to consider the alternative, that perhaps Pollard or Reese had intercepted Blaine, and that he and his friends had been captured or killed. *I won't believe they're not coming back. Not until I've seen proof,* he vowed silently. *And maybe not even then.*

Like most of the soldiers he knew, Niklas had no magic of his own. He'd always joked that the army was for people who had no choice about doing things the hard way. Before the Great Fire, even the small magics were enough to make a person valuable to the community, prosperous, perhaps even wealthy. Great magic usually led to an appointment at court or at least a position in a lord's house.

Magic determined whose farms prospered, whose trades were most valued, whose healing or insight commanded respect. *Without magic, all you had was the strength in your hands and back, a more trainable sort of ox*, Niklas thought. And though his father had balked at that comparison, they both knew it in their hearts to be true. Lars Theilsson, blessed with magic that gave him a talent for turning raw materials into wealth, built his family's farmland into a profitable estate that rivaled those of the nobility. Niklas, with none of his father's magic, went to war.

Now, the advantage is reversed, Niklas mused. *The people who needed magic to do everything can't do anything at all, and those of us who had to do things the hard way have the skills it takes to survive.*

He found himself staring at the glowing coals of the brazier. The small fire wasn't enough to warm his tent, but it took away the worst of the chill. His thoughts were far away. *If Blaine returns, we'll have to fight Pollard and Reese to help him bring back the magic. And if he doesn't*, he thought, *we'll still end up fighting Pollard and Reese or let them claim most of Donderath for themselves*. He sighed. *Gods, I'm tired of war.*

Niklas looked up when someone rapped on the tent post outside his door. "Come in," he said.

The soldier was one of Geir's men, a *talishte* Geir had left behind with Niklas's troops for support. Niklas had promptly assigned the half dozen *talishte* to night guard duty and night hunting, and their success had decreased the skepticism the other soldiers felt toward their new comrades.

"We've intercepted a spy, sir. On the far edge of the camp. Think he might be one of Pollard's men. We've brought him to you for questioning."

Niklas took a deep breath and let it out. *This evening has just managed to go from bad to worse.* "Bring him in."

Two other guards entered, dragging a bound man between them. The prisoner looked to be in his late twenties, with close-cropped dark hair and dark eyes, clad in black from head to toe. A few days' stubble darkened his face.

"Did he infiltrate the camp?" Niklas asked the guard. *Not that there's much intelligence to be gained from it. No military plans to steal, no secret communications from the king to see. The worst he'd learn would be our numbers, and just how badly provisioned we are. And that might be enough to make a difference.*

"We don't believe so, sir. We caught him just beyond the camp perimeter. We think he was going to wait until the camp was quiet," the soldier reported.

Niklas stood and brought a chair away from the side of his desk. He set it in the middle of the tent and motioned for the prisoner to be put there. The soldiers dumped the bound man into the seat, and the man glared at Niklas but did not say anything.

"Why were you spying on our camp?"

"I wasn't spying," the man said, trying to shift his position to keep from falling out of the chair. "I was traveling. Something spooked my horse, and it threw me, then ran off. That's not a crime, is it?" he challenged.

Niklas looked at the two guards. "We didn't find a horse or recent hoofprints, sir," one of the guards replied. "And we confiscated his weapons when we caught him. If he's a traveler now, he used to be a soldier, because his weapons are military issue."

Niklas returned his attention to the prisoner. "Why did Pollard send you?"

"I don't know anyone named Pollard."

"What were you sent to find out?"

"I told you, I wasn't sent," the man snapped. "My horse ran off."

Niklas regarded him and looked toward his guards. "Did you read his blood?"

The guard, a young man who looked to have been in his late teens when he was turned, shook his head. *For all I know, he could be old enough to be my great-great-grandfather*, Niklas thought. "No, sir. We figured you should decide that."

Niklas began to pace in front of the prisoner's chair. He drew out his knife and let the flat of the wicked blade slap against his palm. "What to do, what to do," he mused aloud.

"I could give you to my men for their amusement," Niklas said. "After what they've been through, they might enjoy a way to take out their frustration." He sighed, as if considering his options. "As a general rule, I don't hold with torturing prisoners, but I haven't had a good day, and my men deserve a little recreation, don't you think?"

Niklas continued pacing. "Since you don't have any information, we lose nothing by killing you. We don't need another mouth to feed." He toyed with his knife. "I might even enjoy it, given how much aggravation your master put us through at Mirdalur."

He turned away from the prisoner, but he'd glimpsed nervousness in the man's face. "Not that your master cares what happens to you," he went on. "I've known Vedran Pollard for years. He's a son of a bitch. So it would be like him to let you die." He chuckled. "And here you are, being oh-so-loyal. Pathetic."

"I don't have a master," the prisoner argued, but Niklas could hear the fear in his voice.

"But I think, given the circumstances, that reading your blood is a better option," Niklas continued as if he had not heard the man. He turned back and stared straight into the prisoner's eyes. "Do you know what it means to have your blood read?"

The prisoner paled. Niklas was willing to bet that Pollard was regularly read by his own master, Pentreath Reese, and that rumors of what that entailed had been whispered among his men. The prisoner, who had been so sure of himself before, was sweating although the night was cold, and his breathing was shallow.

"I think you do know," Niklas said with a cold smile. "So here's what's going to happen. My *talishte* friend here is going to rip into your arm with his fangs and drink your blood. He gets a meal, and we get everything you know. I'll make sure he stops before you're quite dead."

He paused, then said, "After that, we'll take you out to that big tree on the edge of camp and hang you. Haven't had much cause to hang many men, but my soldiers are getting better at it. They haven't figured out how to tie a noose so that the neck snaps right away, but the last man we hanged didn't choke all that long before he died." He watched the prisoner's pupils dilate. "I imagine you'll dance right pretty for us."

"Wait!" the prisoner finally said. "I can be valuable."

Niklas had turned away. "Oh?" he asked, his tone bored.

"You're right," the man confessed, speaking quickly. "Pollard sent me. He's lost track of McFadden, and he wanted us to find out what your orders were."

Niklas repressed the urge to chuckle. *Orders? I haven't had orders from anyone in nearly a year. But if Pollard can't find Blaine, that's a point in our favor.* "Go on."

"I was supposed to report on your troop strength, how many *talishte*, your weapons," the prisoner confessed. "If possible, I was to torch your supply tent. Pollard intends to bring siege against Glenreith, and your camp is in the way."

"Glad to know we've inconvenienced him," Niklas said. He poured himself a glass of whiskey and swirled the liquid, hoping he looked nonchalant. *Gods above, I hate this part of the job.*

"And? That's all?" Niklas asked in a bored tone.

"That's all I was supposed to do. By Torven, I swear, that's everything."

Niklas took a sip of the whiskey. He shrugged. "Nothing we didn't already know."

"There's one more thing," the captive said, looking as if he might swallow his tongue. "I overheard it when I was waiting for Pollard's orders. That biter master of his, Reese, he's powerful upset about McFadden. He's sent men out to canvass the countryside looking for some old magic things that don't even work anymore."

"Like what?" Niklas asked, making an effort not to sound interested.

"Maps. Strange round pendants. Old carvings. They don't work, because the magic is gone, but Reese, he's fixed on getting them. Thinks McFadden's going to beat him to some kind of treasure."

"Very interesting."

The prisoner looked up hopefully. "Let me go, and I'll run away. Pollard, he'll know that I betrayed him. Just let me go, and I'll disappear. I won't work for Pollard anymore."

Niklas let out a long breath. "I'm afraid we can't do that." He nodded to the *talishte* guard, who stepped forward as the other guard pinned the prisoner to the chair.

The captive began to struggle. "Wait! You said if I told you what I knew, he wouldn't bite me!"

Niklas met the prisoner's gaze. "No, I didn't. I told you what was going to happen. You tried to bargain." He shook his head. "Always negotiate the terms up-front. Sorry, but we can't trust you not to return to Pollard or be captured and tell him what you've observed. We don't have the food to take prisoners, or a dungeon to keep you in."

The prisoner eyed the *talishte* in terror. "Just hang me then. I don't want to be eaten." He struggled, but the second *talishte* guard kept him firmly in his chair.

Niklas turned away. "We can't overlook the fact that you might know something else, something you don't realize is valuable. I've learned not to be wasteful."

The *talishte* took the prisoner by the chin and forced him to meet his gaze. "Don't fight me, and you'll feel no pain," he promised. The captive slumped, and his eyes fluttered closed. The *talishte* guard lifted the man's arm and sank his fangs into the soft flesh of the wrist. Niklas forced himself not to look away. *Enemy or not, the captive is a mortal. He's someone's son. If I can order his death, I can have the balls to bear witness.*

After a few moments, the *talishte* guard let the wrist fall and stood. No blood marked his mouth or lips. Niklas cast a glance toward the prisoner, who was still breathing. "Report."

"The story he told you was mostly true," the *talishte* said. "Pollard's got spies throughout the countryside, not only to keep an eye on us, but to dog McFadden. He's got them at least as far away as Castle Reach and Riker's Ferry, I guess on the off chance McFadden shows up." He nodded toward the prisoner.

"One of his friends got sent to Riker's Ferry and never came back."

Niklas smiled. "That's one point for Blaine." He paused. "What else?"

The *talishte* frowned. "This man wasn't alone. He came with a team of six other spies."

Niklas held up a hand. "Hold on." He leaned out of the tent and spoke to the guards at the entrance. In a moment, he returned. "I've sent scouts looking for the other spies, if they stuck around."

"He told the truth about Reese wanting old, magic objects," the *talishte* said. "This man was part of a group that looted one of the mage libraries near here shortly after the Great Fire." He grimaced. "They tortured the mages for their knowledge, then stole whatever relics they could find and burned the place to the ground with the mages inside."

"Anything about Penhallow?" Niklas asked.

The *talishte* guard was silent for a moment, and Niklas wondered how, exactly, he processed the thoughts that he read from the blood. *I probably don't want to know.*

"Rumor again, gossip in the barracks. Patrols said Penhallow was pinned down under siege, but escaped. Some of the soldiers said they saw him in Castle Reach, and he escaped again. Pollard was very angry and Reese made examples of those who failed."

"I wonder what game Penhallow's playing, and how it relates to Blaine," Niklas mused. "Who was being besieged?"

The *talishte* thought for a moment. "He wasn't sure of the name. Ross?"

Niklas raised an eyebrow. "Traher Voss? Now that's interesting." *Voss didn't get to be the most storied mercenary in Donderath without cause. And come to think of it, his troops were strangely absent at the front. What does Penhallow intend to do with Voss? One thing's for certain: I sure wouldn't mind some backup.* "Nothing else?" he asked.

The guard shook his head. "Nothing of strategic value."

Niklas knocked back the rest of his whiskey. "Drain him."

The guard nodded. "What should we do with the body?"

Niklas turned away. "Once he's dead, hang the body from the tree. Maybe Pollard will get the message."

"Yes, sir." The *talishte* paused. "You showed him mercy. Why?"

Niklas met the *talishte*'s gaze, unafraid of being glamoured. "Something has to separate us from the other side," he said quietly. "Maybe it's proof that war hasn't made us all beasts."

The *talishte* nodded, and Niklas was reminded that his undead guards followed him on Geir's orders, not their oath to him or to what remained of his army. "As time passes, that line gets harder to draw," he replied. Something in his eyes gave Niklas the impression that the *talishte* knew a thing or two about that struggle.

Niklas forced himself to watch as the *talishte* drank deeply. Gradually the prisoner's breathing slowed, and his skin grew ashen. When the *talishte* finished, Niklas moved to the side to allow the guards to remove the body. "Hang him high," Niklas said, hearing the utter tiredness in his own voice. "Make sure he feeds the vultures and not the wolves."

When they were gone, Niklas poured himself another glass of whiskey and stepped outside the tent. He needed some fresh air. The camp had quieted, and Niklas heard the bell ring midnight. The soldiers were in their tents, except for the *talishte* patrols. It would be another four candlemarks until the bakers awoke to start making bread and readying breakfast. This was as quiet as the camp would get.

Niklas leaned against a barrel and took a sip of his whiskey.

The night was cold, and the wind hit his face like a bracing slap. *It's come to a sorry place when draining a man of blood before hanging his corpse passes for mercy*, Niklas thought. The whiskey burned down his throat, but it did nothing to ease his mood, or his worry.

And after all that, I still don't know for certain that Blaine is alive, or where Pollard will strike next, or whether Penhallow—and now Voss—is really on our side. He let out a long breath and watched the mist rise in the frigid air. *I'm not even completely sure where the battle lines are drawn.*

A faint motion caught his eye. Niklas looked up, and his attention was drawn to the hanging tree, and the shadow of its new burden, the prisoner's body dangling high in the air with its head snapped to one side. A few paces away stood a man. *Or maybe the ghost of a man*, Niklas thought.

For what Niklas could make out, the visitor was dressed in gray, with a dark slash of color across his chest. His cloak and uniform looked military, but his silhouette when he turned showed a style of cloak not worn for a long time. The man made no move to come closer and seemed to pay the corpse no mind. In the moonlight, Niklas wasn't entirely sure the newcomer was solid, but he felt the man's gaze on him.

How did he get past the talishte *guards?* Niklas wondered. But the weight of the man's gaze gave him the answer. *Whoever he is, he's talishte, too.* He let his hand fall to his sword, ready to sound the alarm. *Is he one of Reese's men?*

Something familiar about the uniform made him pause. *I've seen that before*, Niklas thought. He searched his memories, of the regiments he had fought with—or against—in the war, the mercenaries, the rogues. Then he remembered the tapestries. Recognition dawned, and he slowly lowered his drink, returning the shadowy visitor's gaze. *I could swear it looks like the uniform of the Knights of Esthrane*, he thought, feeling a mixture of curiosity and concern. *But that's not possible—is it?*

Niklas remained staring toward the hanging tree for a few moments as the import of what he had seen sank in. *A talishte warlord wants to stop Blaine from bringing back the magic. Another* talishte *lord is playing a dangerous game of cat and mouse, and what's left of Donderath is the prize. Traher Voss is a wild card. Now, a knight from an exiled band of mage-warriors shows up—but whose side is he on? Is he alone, or are there others like him? And is his appearance a show of support, or a warning?*

Niklas drained the last of his whiskey and turned back toward his tent. *Whatever we've just gotten ourselves mixed up in, it's as big as the war we left behind.*

CHAPTER
TWENTY-FIVE

"HOW CAN THE WRAITH LORD BE DEADER THAN a *talishte*?" Connor asked as he followed Penhallow up the winding trail.

"Mortals think that dead is dead," Penhallow replied. "In my experience, it's more of a range. *Talishte* remain the closest to what we were as mortals. There are other, less pleasant ways to remain active after death. Wraiths retain their memories, but they wander for eternity without bodies."

"But before he became the Wraith Lord, he was *talishte*?" Connor asked, torn between horror and fascination. He had grown increasingly used to that feeling and found himself daring to ask questions that would have been unthinkable a few months earlier.

Penhallow nodded. "The Wraith Lord was one of us, which is why he is among the Elders."

"He's not going to mistake me for a food offering, is he?" The thought had bothered Connor the entire trek up the barren hillside. "He'll recognize and respect your bond, right?"

Penhallow chuckled, but Connor thought he heard a hint of uneasiness. "You are under my protection. You are as safe as I am."

Connor slid a sideways glance toward Penhallow. "You've left some room for interpretation, I notice."

"You are a singularly persistent mortal," Penhallow replied. "With a penchant for asking uncomfortable questions."

"I just like an idea of what I'm walking into," Connor retorted. He was quiet for a few moments as they made their way up the rocky trail. "With everything that's happened, the Great Fire and all, how can you be certain the Wraith Lord will still be here? He could go anywhere, couldn't he?" Connor had been trying to wrap his thoughts around the idea of being a spirit without a body, yet something more substantial than a ghost.

"Without a body, the Wraith Lord hasn't wandered far from the ruins of his home in quite some time," Penhallow said. "It's said that he is nearly one thousand years old. Great age commands respect, and a certain amount of fear."

"So he's old enough to remember before when the magic was raised at Mirdalur?" Connor said, excitement edging out fear.

"I'm quite certain that he remembers," Penhallow said. "Whether or not he'll speak of what he knows remains to be seen."

"Do you think he might know something that would help Blaine bring back the magic?" Connor asked, doing his best to keep up with Penhallow. "More to the point—whose side is he on? Ours or Reese's?"

Penhallow paused. "I'm not sure that the Wraith Lord thinks of such things in the same way as mortals do... Or even as *talishte* do. I'm hundreds of years old, yet I am not one of the Elders. The Wraith Lord is among the eldest of our kind, but he is as different from other *talishte* as *talishte* are from mortals. What he chooses to share with us will be for his own purposes, likely to have little to do with our interests or even our benefit. He's not our enemy, but neither is he our friend. He merely is."

"I feel so much better about this now," Connor muttered under his breath. Penhallow chuckled.

"How do you know he'll even see us?" Connor asked.

"I petitioned him for an audience as soon as I heard about Blaine's quest," Penhallow replied as they climbed to the top of the hill. "My petition has been accepted. We have been granted an audience."

As they reached the crest of the hill, Connor could see the ruins of an ancient fortress. Thick stone walls still stood, but the building's roof was long gone, and the grounds were heavily overgrown. Connor could see the sky through the empty window openings, and several tall trees grew up through the center of the ruins in what would have once been the middle of the main keep.

Even if he had not known that the ruins were the domain of an immortal wraith, something about the area warned him to run as far away as possible. His skin prickled, and he felt as jumpy as a stray dog before a storm. Connor looked to Penhallow and saw for the first time a hint of hesitation in the other's features. *Even Penhallow is wary of the Wraith Lord,* Connor thought. *If the Wraith Lord can frighten someone like Penhallow, then I'm not such a coward for feeling a bit terrified.*

"Have you forgotten that I can sense your emotions through the bond?" Penhallow said quietly. "As if I couldn't read them in your face."

"Sorry."

"I would be more worried if we were approaching the Wraith Lord and you did not feel fear," Penhallow replied. "Yet you were often in the presence of the king with your last master, were you not? Were you constantly in fear of Merrill, when he could have spoken a word and sent you to your death?"

Connor let out a long breath and shook his head. "No,

although I knew my place and stayed well out of the king's way. King Merrill never spoke an unkind word to me or noticed me much at all."

"The comparison isn't perfect, but it will do," Penhallow said. "The Wraith Lord will see you as my human servant, much as Merrill understood you were Lord Garnoc's man. Your part in this is to be a second set of eyes and ears for me. I'll ask you for your observations and impressions later. The Wraith Lord may well want to hear what you know of Blaine McFadden and the effort to bring back the magic."

"And what do I tell him?" Connor asked nervously. "Do you trust him? Should I tell him the truth?"

A cold smile hinted at Penhallow's lips. "You must tell him the truth. He will sense a lie. But you do not need to reveal everything you know. Tell him what happened the night of the Great Fire, and in Edgeland, up to when we were attacked by Reese in Traher Voss's keep. But say nothing about where Blaine might be or what he might be doing." He paused. "I trust the Wraith Lord to act in a way consistent with his interests. So long as our interests coincide with his, we are allied."

"You never really said whether or not I'm in danger," Connor said, narrowing his eyes a bit.

"You are as safe as I am in the presence of the Wraith Lord," Penhallow repeated. "It's all I can say. That will have to suffice."

They walked the rest of the way in silence. The closer they got to the ruins of the keep, the more the land itself seemed to dissuade them from approaching. Rocks and brambles made the going difficult, causing Connor to stumble frequently. Dread haunted him from the time they reached the summit of the hill, but he was also aware of Penhallow's light compulsion, tempering the fear. Connor felt certain that they were being watched. Penhallow moved forward undaunted, and Connor mustered all his bluff to do the same.

"You are trespassing. State your business." The man came out of nowhere, and his voice made Connor jump. A guard dressed all in black stepped out of the shadows with *talishte* speed, blocking their path.

"We're here at the invitation of the Wraith Lord. He's expecting us." Penhallow's tone managed to convey both privilege and mild annoyance.

It was clear that the guard had been told to expect them. The man gave a curt nod and stepped aside, then raised one hand high and made a gesture that Connor assumed was a signal to the other unseen watchers to allow them through. "Go to the old keep. The Master will find you there."

Connor surveyed the approach to the keep, but the night was still and quiet, and he could not see any other guards. Connor squared his shoulders and held his head high, hoping that his projected confidence would mask the mortal fear that twisted his stomach.

They came to a stop at the battered front wall. Up close, Connor could see that the old keep's stone walls were twice as thick as the distance from his fingertips to his shoulder, massive blocks of granite laid atop each other. The ruins' age was unmistakable, and Connor could feel the spirits of the dead around them.

Another black-clad figure stepped from the shadows of the doorway. "You will come with me," the man said. Penhallow followed. Moonlight cast harsh shadows as they moved through the overgrowth. Now that he was closer, Connor could see that some of the interior walls were still standing. Beneath his feet, dirt, debris, and crumbled rock hid an old stone-mosaic floor. Connor could imagine what the building had once looked like, both keep and rough castle, the stronghold of a warlord.

Their guide led them to the best-preserved portion of the ruins. They ascended a few steps and found the floor here intact. Three of the room's four walls were standing, as well as a portion of its ceiling. From the large size of the area, Connor imagined it had been a gathering space, the place where a powerful noble would host his friends and hold court.

"You have come a long way to see me." The voice spoke from the shadowed corner. Connor glimpsed movement and saw a flash of something gray.

Penhallow gave a low bow, and Connor did the same. "My lord," Penhallow said, his voice grave and respectful, "thank you for granting us an audience."

"Your message was cryptic, but intriguing," the Wraith Lord replied, and as Connor squinted to get a better look at the shadows, he saw a figure shrouded in mist. It had the height and proportions of a tall man, but the mist blurred the man's features and swirled around him like a cloak.

Once more, Penhallow dipped his head in respect. "It was too dangerous to speak plainly in my message, my lord. I came to ask what you would share with us about Mirdalur, and times before that."

"Mirdalur." The Wraith Lord seemed to mull over the word. "I was at Mirdalur when the lords raised the magic. I stood among them as one of the Lords of the Blood, no longer mortal, but not yet as you see me now." The gray figure seemed to study Penhallow for a moment before speaking again. "What do you wish to know about Mirdalur, and why?"

"We know that magic has fallen and been raised again many times," Penhallow said carefully. "I believe it is to the benefit of the *talishte* for magic to rise once more." He paused. "If you were a Lord of the Blood, could you help to raise the magic again?"

The Wraith Lord laughed, an unpleasant sound like the

rattling of dry bones. "No. I am just a shadow of my former self, without physical form, and most certainly without blood. I dwell in the space between the living, the dead, and the undead. I cannot help you with the ritual."

"One living Lord of the Blood remains," Penhallow said. "He has vowed to restore the magic."

"Why have you involved yourself?"

"Because another of our kind opposes him," Penhallow replied. "This *talishte* would set himself up to rule."

"Are we not meant to rule?" the Wraith Lord asked. "Mortals are weak, slow. We are superior in every way: strength, speed, endurance. Does not that superiority convey a mandate from the gods that we should rule?"

Penhallow once again inclined his head in deference, then straightened to look directly at the Wraith Lord. "My lord, I would disagree," he said in a careful voice. "We possess those strengths—that is true. Yet we are vulnerable. We must hide by day, and we can be easily destroyed when we are weakened by the sun. Mortals breed faster than we can turn our followers. You know, my lord, that when our kind has tried to rule, it has nearly destroyed us."

"I remember." The Wraith Lord's voice was low, rumbling like distant thunder. There was silence for a moment. "Who is this man, the one who would restore the magic?"

"Blaine McFadden, lord of Glenreith," Penhallow replied. "He is the last mortal Lord of the Blood."

"McFadden. Yes, there was a McFadden at Mirdalur," the Wraith Lord mused. "So long ago."

"My lord, what can you tell us that might help McFadden bring back the magic?" Penhallow asked.

Connor felt the shift in the Wraith Lord's manner and knew that somehow, Penhallow had attracted their host's interest.

"Why have you brought a mortal with you—and one who is a medium?" The Wraith Lord's voice was a challenge that chilled Connor to the bone. Connor mustered his courage, lifted his head, and took a step forward.

"I serve Lord Penhallow," Connor said. His voice shook despite his best efforts.

"Penhallow, did you know that he was a medium?" the Wraith Lord asked.

"Yes," Penhallow said.

"You trust too much, Penhallow," the Wraith Lord said. "His ability calls to me even more than his warm blood." He turned to Connor.

"You see and hear ghosts that others do not," the Wraith Lord said. "And sometimes the ghosts try to speak through you. Do you deny it?"

Connor flushed. "No. Sometimes I feared they would succeed."

"They did not have the power to possess you," the Wraith Lord said. "But I do." Connor shivered and took a step closer to Penhallow.

"He is under my protection," Penhallow warned.

The Wraith Lord chuckled. "If I wished to take him, I would have already done so." There was silence for a moment, and then he turned to Connor. "Tell me about McFadden," the Wraith Lord replied. "And I will determine whether I will help you."

Penhallow gave Connor a nod of encouragement. Connor told his tale, beginning with the night Penhallow had sent him to find Valtyr's map in the castle library. He recounted the night of the Great Fire, his flight on the doomed ship, the shipwreck on Edgeland, and all that had happened since then, culminating with Blaine McFadden's return to Donderath and Pentreath Reese's attempts to stop the magic from coming back. Connor's heart thudded in his chest, and his palms were sweating despite the cold of the evening, but he carried on in a clear voice that grew stronger as he recounted his story. When he ended, the Wraith Lord was silent for a few moments.

"Lord Reese is known to me," the Wraith Lord said. "I admire his ruthlessness, but he is reckless and brings danger to all of our kind. I prefer a world in which magic functions. Even in my state, magic makes many things much easier, and it keeps the livestock healthier."

Livestock. The word took Connor's breath away. He was quite certain that humans were included in the Wraith Lord's definition of the word.

"Why did you come here, Penhallow?" the Wraith Lord asked. "Surely it was not for my blessing, or to hear old tales."

"On the contrary, old tales are exactly what I would hear from you, my lord. I want to learn what you know about how magic can be restored."

The Wraith Lord paused. "I saw the magic raised before Mirdalur," he said at last. "When I was a mortal, magic eluded the grasp of men, as it does now. The *hasithara* magic had been broken for more than a generation. Those who survived lived out a wretched existence in a savage, lawless land. I have no desire to see those times return," the Wraith Lord said, with more emotion than Connor would have expected.

"The strongest lords of the time followed a holy man to a place in the wilderness where the wild storms came most ferociously. There, they made a working to raise and bind the magic to bring it under men's control once more."

"Were you there?" Penhallow pressed, his face taut with excitement.

"Yes."

"And in time, something destroyed the magic again, so that

it was necessary to raise it once again at Mirdalur?" Penhallow asked.

"Yes. A conspiracy of mages destroyed the kingdom and brought our people to their knees," the Wraith Lord replied, anger coloring his tone.

"Was the older ritual the same as the one that raised the magic at Mirdalur?" Penhallow could not hide the excitement in his voice.

"No. Not exactly. Magic is not an alchemist's formula. I was told that every time the power is raised, the ritual must fit the needs of those who seek to bind the magic," the Wraith Lord replied.

"And it has been done many times?"

"Yes." It seemed to Connor that the Wraith Lord had grown more solid as they spoke, and as the moon rose in the sky. Where at first his shape had been a blurred form hidden in the mist, now Connor could glimpse a man veiled in fog, broad-shouldered with a warrior's build, clad in a style of clothing not seen for several hundred years.

"Do you know anything we might use to bring the magic back?" Penhallow asked.

There was a long pause, so long that Connor wondered whether or not the Wraith Lord would speak again. Finally, the gray form shifted, and the Wraith Lord roused from his thoughts. "There was a mage named Archus Quintrel who was obsessed with the history of magic. He disappeared, along with his notes, never to be seen again." He paused. "He left a descendant. I have heard it said that the descendant followed in his footsteps."

"Was Archus Quintrel killed? Did he truly vanish by choice?" Penhallow asked.

The Wraith Lord shrugged. "It was said that the Knights

of Esthrane spirited him away to protect the forbidden knowledge he had uncovered." Another pause. "There were rumors that before he disappeared, Archus Quintrel rambled on about finding the long-lost city Valshoa. Most people dismissed it as empty bragging, but I do not. I have heard recounts of its fall from those who saw it firsthand."

"Do you believe the Knights hid him?" Penhallow pressed. "Or did they destroy him?"

The Wraith Lord inclined his head. "Either is likely." There was another long pause, this one more uncomfortable. "Is this the sole reason that you requested an audience, Lord Penhallow? I do not like to be disturbed."

Penhallow bowed low, making a gesture of deference. "A thousand pardons, my lord," Penhallow said smoothly. "But there is another pressing matter. I petition you to convene the Elders. I claim the right to neutrality."

I've got no idea what that means, but it doesn't sound good, Connor thought. *And if Penhallow isn't among the Elders, I'm damned if I want to be anywhere near a bunch of even older* talishte. His heart was thudding, and he was acutely aware that its rapid beat made him more noticeable, and attractive, to the Wraith Lord.

Penhallow's playing a dangerous game, Connor thought. *I don't think the Elders convene on a whim.*

"You understand that if the Elders find your petition to be unworthy, they can destroy you and your servants without penalty," the Wraith Lord cautioned.

"I understand," Penhallow said gravely. "Reese is putting his considerable resources against McFadden to stop the magic from coming back. All I want is a guarantee of neutrality from the Elders, that they will not aid or hinder either Reese or McFadden. Just their word that the Elders will not become involved."

For the first time, Connor thought he saw a flash of emotion on the Wraith Lord's features. "Nothing is simple when it comes to the Elders." He was silent for a moment. "I will convey your petition."

Through the bond, Connor felt a tinge of Penhallow's emotions: worry about McFadden, and a sense of solidarity that Connor found reassuring. Connor nodded to show that he understood. Then he drew a deep breath, said a prayer to Esthrane, and prepared to die.

The Wraith Lord gathered himself from the mists once more. "The petition has been made. I will summon you when a time has been chosen—if they agree to hear your plea." He paused. "We have an intruder," he remarked.

Penhallow exchanged a glance with Connor. "On your land?"

"Pentreath Reese has presented himself and demands an audience," the Wraith Lord said. "I've sensed his presence at the edge of my territory. It was as if he were waiting for something—or someone. Perhaps he suspected that you would come?" His tone conveyed amusement, but underneath was anger. "I've given him permission to join us. I would hear what he has to say."

Pentreath Reese strode toward them, his long cloak billowing about him as he moved. The moonlight glinted from his hair, washing out its color and accentuating his pallor.

"You were not called to this meeting," the Wraith Lord replied. Connor could feel anger radiating from the Wraith Lord, although he could not see his mist-shrouded features.

"An oversight, don't you agree? Since your decision involves me." Reese's confidence appeared unshakable. He stood with his head high, shoulders squared, his demeanor just shy of throwing down a challenge.

"It is forbidden to appear before an Elder uninvited," the Wraith Lord said.

"No more forbidden than it is to summon the Elders without due cause," Reese answered. "Penhallow runs from shadows of his own imagining. The plot he fears does not exist."

"Reese lies." Penhallow's voice revealed all of the anger that flashed in his eyes. "His loyalists burned my sanctuary, cut down my fledglings. He brought an army against Traher Voss and demanded my surrender."

"Ruffians abound," Reese replied smoothly. "The fact that they used my name doesn't prove that I had anything to do with their actions. As for Voss, the man cannot be trusted."

"No one said Voss could be trusted," Penhallow responded. "The man plays by his own rules. In that, he is more like *talishte*. I saw the soldiers myself. I was there when they demanded my surrender."

"Yet here you are, apparently unscathed," Reese said. "Perhaps I should be doubly offended, first, that you think I brought siege against Voss, and second, that you claim my soldiers were such incompetents as to let you escape." His tone was light, but the anger that glinted in his eyes was fierce.

"Is it your intent to stop magic from being restored?" the Wraith Lord asked in a neutral tone.

"It is my intent to stop a convicted murderer from bringing down a worse cataclysm on our heads than has already befallen us," Reese answered. His deep voice echoed from the standing stones, his manner totally confident. "Blaine McFadden is a danger to our kind, and Lanyon Penhallow is abetting him."

"I have heard Penhallow," the Wraith Lord said. "I will hear you."

"The McFaddens have had no love for *talishte*. Ian McFadden supported King Merrill's decree banishing us from court. He has never tolerated *talishte* presence on his lands. There were ugly whispers that Ian McFadden was to blame for the disappearance, and presumed destruction, of several *talishte* within the borders of his holdings."

"No one defends Ian McFadden, especially not his son," Penhallow countered. "Ian McFadden is dead. This is not about him."

"The son is no better than the father," Reese replied. "I placed a spy in Edgeland to watch Blaine McFadden, because I did not believe that any prison short of death could hold him. I was correct. He led the assault on the Velant camp, murdered its commander, and used a ship he hijacked to return to Donderath. He seeks a renegade mage and his goal is to harness the power of magic for himself, to set himself up as king."

Connor started forward, so angry at Reese's words that he forgot himself. Just as he was about to speak, he felt the icy grip of the Wraith Lord on his shoulder. His throat constricted, making it impossible for words to form, and he could not break free of the cold fingers that held him. The Wraith Lord shifted slightly, putting his form between Connor and Reese.

"Blaine McFadden does indeed seek the counsel of mages," Penhallow said. "But his purpose is to restore the magic, not to take it for himself. He had little magical power before the Great Fire. He killed the Velant commander because Prokief was well known as a tyrant, a man so savage that Merrill exiled him along with his prisoners. The ship was abandoned, not hijacked. He left Edgeland out of obligation, as the last living Lord of the Blood."

Penhallow's eyes narrowed. "Lord Reese has also conveniently forgotten to mention that he sent an assassin, not an observer, to Edgeland. An assassin charged with eliminating McFadden so that he could not return to raise the magic."

"My man had the discretion to decide when the threat was sufficient to require elimination," Reese replied coolly.

"The threat to your plans," Penhallow charged. "The threat to your intent to rise as the new warlord-king of Donderath."

Reese laughed. "Really, Lanyon, is that your fear? Do you suppose me so great a threat that you seek to gather the Elders?"

"I don't fear you, Pentreath. But I have no desire to be ruled by you, or to see what you would make of a kingdom with Donderath under your boot," Penhallow replied. "I wish to see Blaine McFadden succeed in his quest to restore the magic. To do that, I must stop you from killing him."

"The *talishte* have become weak!" Reese thundered. "Listen to yourself! We are predators, and we need magic no more than do the wolves and the great forest cats."

"I don't consider myself a wild beast," Penhallow countered. "Just because I'm immortal doesn't mean that I disdain the comforts civilization offers me. And without magic, we are not truly civilized." He paused. "It's also no secret among this group that we have often used magic to keep the peace among ourselves, so that the less powerful are not ground beneath the heel of those who would rule over us."

Reese laughed. "Is that how you see me, Lanyon? As the would-be conqueror of *talishte*? I would not have expected such fears from one of your age and power."

"My age and power are sufficient to have shown me much about the nature of our hearts," Penhallow replied. "Without forces to counterbalance our considerable powers, we do a remarkably thorough job of fighting among ourselves. Our greatest threat is not mortals—it comes from unbridled ambition among our own." He paused. "And it is against the law of the Elders for you and your brood to attack me, or those under my protection."

"Then put the matter to a vote." Reese's voice had become steel. "I trust the Elders' wisdom."

"Is that why you have a company of men and *talishte* gathered just beyond our gathering?" the Wraith Lord asked in a dangerously flat tone. "Did you plan to force the matter? Or did you think I could not tell that you were lying?"

"I came here to apprehend Penhallow and his servant, assuming you let them live after discovering Penhallow's deception," Reese replied.

"Penhallow is not on trial, nor has he used deception." The Wraith Lord's voice was cold, and Connor felt the immortal's mood shift like a gathering storm. While Connor doubted that the Wraith Lord cared for Penhallow or about their safety, he was quite certain that their host was growing angrier by the moment at Reese's provocation.

"Leave this place," the Wraith Lord said to Reese. "Do not come again unbidden."

"Don't be too certain of the Elders' support," Reese replied with a smirk. "We aren't finished." He disappeared in a burst of *talishte* speed.

No sooner had Reese left them than a dozen armed men swarmed toward them, swords flashing. In the distance, they could hear the guards fighting a battle of their own.

Penhallow drew his sword and squared off against one of Reese's fighters, another *talishte*, judging from the speed with which the attacker moved.

I'm a dead man, Connor thought as fighting erupted around him. *If an arrow doesn't get me, a* talishte *certainly will.* He drew his sword, fighting down panic, and braced himself for an attack.

"Are you truly Penhallow's man?" The Wraith Lord's voice sounded in Connor's ears, although he was not entirely sure the words had been spoken aloud.

"Yes," Connor replied. "I am."

"I have need of your body." With that, cold mist enveloped Connor. He felt as if he had just stepped into the thickest fog that cut off both sight and hearing. Pain flared as fangs punctured his shoulder, and Connor gasped. An instant later, he felt a dizzying shift. Vertigo dazed him, and he stumbled.

Such a strong, young form. The Wraith Lord's voice sounded inside Connor's mind. One of Reese's men came at Connor, and Connor watched in amazement as his body seemed to move of its own accord. With the practiced grace of a skilled swordsman, he parried the attack, then went on the offensive, executing a series of quick parries and thrusts that Connor was quite certain he had never learned.

Penhallow was holding his own, but Connor despaired at the odds against them. Two opponents rushed Connor, and he felt a combination of fear and exhilaration as his body, under the Wraith Lord's control, snatched a sword from one of the downed fighters to hold off the attack with a weapon in each hand. With strength and agility Connor did not know he possessed, the Wraith Lord held off the pounding onslaught, moving at *talishte* speed so that the swords' motion blurred in the moonlight.

The Wraith Lord and Penhallow were fighting back-to-back. Bodies littered the ground within the circle of the standing stones. Connor was certain that as a mortal, he would have wearied under the relentless attack, but the Wraith Lord never slowed. One of the attackers came at him for a killing blow, point angled for the heart. The Wraith Lord blocked the blow, sword clashing against sword as he deflected the force of the attack.

The second opponent was fighting two-handed, landing a series of numbing strikes that reverberated through Connor's bones until he feared his arm might break. The attacker moved within Connor's guard, and the point of his sword gashed Connor's shoulder. Warm, red blood soaked through Connor's cloak.

"You are not immortal in this body, Vandholt," the fighter taunted. "You bleed."

Heedless of the pain, the Wraith Lord managed to fend off the next strike, sending the attacker reeling. In that instant, the Wraith Lord pivoted and drove his sword home through the chest of the first attacker, who fell to the ground. Momentarily freed of distraction, the Wraith Lord went for the kill, wielding his own sword with a two-handed grip, setting to with such ferocity that Connor feared for the Wraith Lord's sanity.

Did they think they could best me? What arrogant fools! The longer the Wraith Lord possessed Connor, the clearer his thoughts became. Anger, vengeance, and confidence washed over Connor, intoxicating in the strength of the emotions, threatening to carry him away with the tide so that he feared he might never be able to sort himself out again.

Despite the fight Penhallow and the Wraith Lord put up, it was clear to Connor that Reese stood to triumph from the sheer number of his forces. *I'll die here, not even in possession of myself,* Connor despaired. *I'll be a corpse and the Wraith Lord will shed my body like an outgrown skin.*

Sudden movement from beyond the standing stones made Connor blink, and when he looked once more, dozens of warriors were pouring between the standing stones, driving back Reese's fighters. These new soldiers were clad in gray uniforms, and across their chests was a diagonal blue slash.

The Knights of Esthrane, said the Wraith Lord. *I called to them, and they have come.*

Penhallow gave a cry of triumph as he landed a killing blow, dispatching one of the two fighters he battled. The Wraith

Lord, having killed his own opponents, pivoted to attack the second man fighting Penhallow.

"Have a care with that body!" Penhallow commented. "I want him back when this is over."

So do I, Connor thought. Yet as the Wraith Lord animated his form with the dexterity of a consummate fighter, part of Connor yearned for the same level of strength and grace. He wondered how much of the Wraith Lord's power was shielding him from pain and fatigue. His body was bleeding from several gashes, and under normal circumstances, Connor was quite certain he would have faltered from sheer exhaustion.

Is this what it is to be a god? Connor wondered.

Not a god, came the answer in his mind, in the voice of the Wraith Lord. *But much more than mortal.*

The Wraith Lord's attention was fixed on striking down as many of Reese's soldiers as he could, working together with Penhallow to harry and kill as a team. Connor watched in awe as the Knights battled their way through the chaos like an efficient killing machine. Dispassionate, swift, and deadly, the Knights easily turned the tide of the conflict.

Connor's heart thudded with the adrenaline of the fight. The Wraith Lord's exhilaration was as heady as the strongest whiskey, deadening the pain of Connor's injuries and the weariness that only now began to make itself known at the edges of his consciousness. Everything seemed to be moving very quickly, and he was flushed with the exertion of battle, so that his hair hung wet with sweat around his face and his shirt beneath the cloak clung to his body.

The leader of the Knights stared at Penhallow, then looked around, searching the faces of those still standing. "I was summoned by the Wraith Lord," he said.

"And I am here," the Wraith Lord answered in Connor's voice.

"M'lord?"

Connor smiled stiffly. "I borrowed this form out of necessity."

"And it is time for you to give it back," Penhallow said quietly. "Before you burn it up."

The Wraith Lord sighed. "You cannot understand what it is like to feel once more, to grip a sword, to touch something and have it be solid to my hand."

"Kierken, it is time."

The Wraith Lord nodded. "I know." He paused. "Take him back to my home tonight. The Knights will protect you. Your man will need medical attention, and you will need a place to go to ground, because dawn is not far off."

He paused again, longer this time. "When you came, my intent was to remain neutral. Now that I see Reese's treachery, I will give you what aid I can—and something more." He was silent for a moment. "I believe you will need my disk—and all the other disks—to raise the magic. I will show you its hiding place."

"Thank you," Penhallow replied.

Connor realized that it was growing difficult for him to breathe. What he had first taken as the flush of battle now felt like a raging fever, and his heart beat so rapidly that he felt as if he would lose consciousness. Throughout the battle, the Wraith Lord's consciousness had calmed him, but now sheer primal panic threatened to overwhelm him.

"Let him go, Kierken. He'll die if you stay longer," Penhallow said, his voice sharp.

"As you wish. Thank him for me, if he survives."

As abruptly as the Wraith Lord had seized possession, he was gone. Pain, confusion, and exhaustion overwhelmed Connor and he sank to the ground, barely clinging to consciousness.

Penhallow caught him and lifted him as easily as if he were a child. Connor's head lolled, and he stared at the night sky as darkness threatened to blot out the stars in his field of vision.

There was a rush of air, and the stars were gone. A shaft of moonlight barely illuminated the small room through the open door, but all Connor could see was a stone ceiling. The room smelled of mold, of decaying leaves, and of long disuse. Penhallow laid Connor on a stone slab. Distantly, Connor could hear Penhallow giving orders to the Knights who had accompanied them, then he felt Penhallow beside him once more.

"Hang on, Connor," Penhallow murmured. Connor could feel Penhallow's presence and will strengthening him and keeping him from losing consciousness. Somehow, Connor knew that if the darkness took him now, he would not awaken.

He felt Penhallow rip away his tattered and stained cloak, then remove the torn, blood-soaked shirt. "Look at me, Connor," Penhallow said, his voice sounding with the strongest compulsion Connor had ever felt.

Connor managed to open his eyes, but he lacked the strength to turn his head. Penhallow moved into his field of view and met his gaze. "Feel no fear. Feel no pain. Trust me completely, and you will live."

Connor let himself be carried by the dark tide of the compulsion, with no will or strength left to resist. He felt Penhallow's hands press against his wounds, and then the heat and now-familiar burn of Penhallow's healing saliva. Connor could hear Penhallow cursing under his breath, and yet he felt more curious than alarmed.

"Bevin, listen to me. Even with my saliva and blood, your body is healing too slowly to save your life. I need you to take my blood, or you'll die."

It took all of Connor's will to force the words from his lips, and even so, he had barely enough breath to voice them. "Don't turn me."

"I'm not going to turn you, Bevin. You've lost a lot of blood and you're badly wounded, but I will not turn you. I swear it. The *kruvgaldur* can still heal you, but it needs more blood to do so," Penhallow said. There was a moment's pause, and then Connor felt cold flesh pressing against his lips.

"Take the blood, Bevin. You'll still be mortal, I swear to you. If you don't take the blood, you'll die."

Cool ichor slipped between Connor's lips, trickling into his mouth. Penhallow cursed once more and removed his wrist, and when it returned the flow of blood was stronger, flowing in a steady stream. The ichor that passed for Penhallow's blood had none of the coppery tang of human blood. It had a sharp, bitter taste, devoid of life yet filled with the power of the *talishte* bond.

Connor's heart had slowed from its rapid pace during the battle. Now, his heartbeat was sluggish. Every muscle and bone seemed too heavy to move. He was colder than he had ever been, even in his brief time on Edgeland. This time, the cold seemed to be in his very bones. Connor felt the darkness begin to enfold him when a silver point of light forced itself into his consciousness.

I forbid you to die, Bevin. Fight the darkness. The voice was the Wraith Lord's, and a dim memory surfaced: Kierken Vandholt had been banished to the Unseen Realms, the place between the living and the dead. Connor could feel the Wraith Lord's presence, but unlike on the battlefield, the voice sounded near him, not inside his own skull.

The pinpoint of light burned brilliantly, driving back the shadows. Connor clung to the silver glow like a lifeline. He was excruciatingly aware of every intake and exhale of breath, of his struggling heartbeat, of the blood coursing in his veins. Every sensation was heightened, as if Penhallow had overridden his dying brain to assure that Connor's body did not fail him.

Slowly, very slowly, the darkness began to dissipate. Connor's heartbeat, which had labored to keep a stuttering rhythm, gradually grew more regular. Breath came easier, so that the rising and falling of his chest did not seem to be a strain beyond endurance. The bitter cold receded. The silver light never faltered, nor did the sense that Penhallow and the Wraith Lord were constant presences, both in the physical realm and in the gray place between life and death.

Connor drew a shuddering breath. He grew more aware of the solid body that encased his consciousness. His fingers twitched, a feeble attempt to prove to himself that his body had returned to his volition. The honeyed warmth of Penhallow's compulsion receded, and for the first time since the battle, Connor felt the throb of overtaxed muscles and the pain of bruised and broken bones. The pain made him flinch, reassuring him that he was still among the living.

Connor's sense of the Wraith Lord's presence, and the silver light, faded. For the first time since Penhallow had placed his broken body on the stone slab, Connor felt the cold granite beneath him. A cool hand rested gently on his shoulder.

"You'll live," Penhallow said in a ragged voice. "Now, I must feed. Rest. When you awaken, your healing will be complete."

Connor tried to murmur thanks, but his body would not obey his command. He listened to the sound of his breath and heartbeat, comforted in their assurance that he would wake from the darkness that claimed him.

CHAPTER
TWENTY-SIX

O H, I HAVE SO MANY QUESTIONS FOR YOU!"
Treven Lowrey rubbed his hands together gleefully, staring at the man in the uniform of the Knights of Esthrane.

"Focus, Treven," Penhallow said. "The important information first, then you can research to your heart's desire."

"Piffle," Lowrey groused. "All well and good for you—you
live for hundreds of years, so you see history unfold on a scale
the rest of us can't imagine. You don't understand how fascinating it is to actually have the actual Knights here, close enough
to touch—"

"It would be better if you didn't do that," the Knight said,
and Lowrey hastily withdrew his hand from the Knight's arm.

"Please excuse my associate," Penhallow chuckled. "He's a
scholar, and his love of history sometimes cancels out his common sense."

Lowrey grimaced. "Oh really? Who had the common sense
to stay safely inside a fortress instead of traipsing around, making a target of myself?"

Penhallow, Lowrey, Connor, and the leader of the Knights

of Esthrane, a *talishte* named Nidhud, stood in the hidden library room beneath Quillarth Castle. Nidhud was a stocky man who stood no taller than Connor but was twice as broad. His black hair was cut in a fashion Connor had seen only in old tapestries, and his armor, though of the highest quality, was likewise of a style several generations old. Nidhud's dark eyes had the cold, flinty gaze of a seasoned warrior, and his hands were covered with battle scars, telling Connor that even before Nidhud had been turned, he had been a man of war.

"While you and Connor have been out brawling, I've uncovered important information, and I'm betting Nidhud can fill in the parts I couldn't piece together from the record," Lowrey said with a smug smile.

Connor and Penhallow had returned the previous night, accompanied by a half dozen of the Knights for protection, thanks to the Wraith Lord. Lars Lynge and Lowrey had listened with rapt attention as they told the story of the adventures that had befallen them since they left the castle. Lowrey had promised them an equally adventurous tale for the next evening, and they gathered after supper with Lowrey adoring his place at the center of attention.

"We suspected Vigus Quintrel had been dropping bread crumbs for us to follow," Lowrey said. "He's left us a trail in the form of hidden clues, as well as buried memories locked in Connor's mind. But after days and sleepless nights of scholarly research, pushing myself nearly to the breaking point, I believe I have finally unlocked the code," he said triumphantly.

"Enough self-congratulation, Treven," Penhallow said. "We all know you're a very, very clever fellow. Now—what did you find?"

Lowrey was excited enough about his breakthrough to

completely ignore Penhallow's comment. "Look, look—it's all here. I made a copy of Connor's map, and I've been studying it against the maps in the Knights' library."

In their absence, the small hidden library had been completely transformed. Lowrey had constructed moveable wooden frames to which he had tacked up his notes, map, and drawings, using different colored thread to point out relationships among the various pieces. Tables and chairs had been moved to allow for a wider working area, and on the largest table, Lowrey had laid out more maps and notes along with piles of manuscripts, an astrolabe, and a sextant. The library now reminded Connor of a war room, and Lowrey strode back and forth in front of his diagrams with the enthusiasm of a confident general.

"I'm certain that Vigus Quintrel believed there was a correlation between the location of the wells and deserts of natural magical power, the nodes, and the constellations," Lowrey said excitedly. "The map Connor stole for you the night of the Great Fire shows the nodes of power and no-power here on the Continent. Good enough—so far," he said and moved animatedly to display another drawing.

"Look here. I've overlaid my copy of Connor's map of the nodes with a star chart of the constellations," Lowrey said. "And I've marked the location of the great manor houses of the first thirteen Lords of the Blood, the ones who raised the magic at Mirdalur. They correspond to the nodes, and to the constellations."

"Yes, yes, Treven! But what does it all mean?" Penhallow said. "It's all terribly interesting, but unless we can find Quintrel or figure out the best location for Blaine to attempt to raise the magic, it's all rather useless."

"Useless!" Lowrey sputtered. "No research is ever useless. Some pieces are just more timely than others." He straightened to his full height. "And I've discovered some important information."

"Remember, Treven, if you draw this out too long, I might be tempted to just nip you and get the answers out of your blood," Penhallow warned, although the corner of his mouth quirked as he fought back a smile.

"You wouldn't dare!"

"I might." Nidhud stood near the doorway with his arms crossed across his chest. "Get on with it."

Lowrey gave an uncertain glance in Nidhud's direction, then regained his confidence. "As I was saying, I've discovered some items of importance. First, I've worked out a connection between the outbreaks of madness and the wild magic."

Connor perked up at that. "And?"

"Lynge was able to help me talk with nearly three dozen people near the castle who had a friend or family member succumb to the madness," Lowrey said. "Here's the thing: None of the people who have gone mad—as far as we can tell—were mages or *talishte*. They either had a very small bit of magic, or none at all."

Penhallow leaned forward and tented his fingers as he thought. "Interesting. I might have thought that those with the most magic would feel the absence the keenest."

"That's what I thought, going into it," Lowrey said, his head bobbing up and down. "And since a different sort of power animates the *talishte* and your *kruvgaldur* bond has remained in place when the other magic failed, I thought that there might be madness cropping up among the vampires due to the strain. But that's not what happened."

Lowrey's eyes glinted with excitement. "Do you realize what that means?"

"The longer we go without finding a way to bring back the

magic, the more we are at risk of being overrun by mobs of crazed villagers," Nidhud replied. "We already knew that."

"The rate of new incidents seems to be accelerating," Lowrey added. "When the magic first failed, there were no reports of madness. Within a few weeks, several cases appeared. To the best of my ability to connect the dots, the more time passes, the more people are affected."

"Another reason why we must resolve this as quickly as possible," Penhallow agreed.

"Here's my second discovery," Lowrey said, with a look toward Nidhud. "I also interviewed as many of the guards as I could. From their experience, the monsters are spawning most often in the places that are between the nodes and deserts. From what I could piece together from Quintrel's journal and the manuscripts in the library, the tension between the null places and the out-of-control wells of power actually rip apart the veil between our world and the places of the gods, allowing creatures to come through that have no business among mortals."

Lowrey leaned forward. "But here's the most important thing. I was wrong."

"You, Treven? Mistaken?" Penhallow clucked his tongue, and Connor stifled a laugh.

Lowrey grimaced. "It has been known to happen," he said in a dry tone. "I was wrong about the best time to try to restore the magic. It isn't the spring equinox. The most powerful times are the solstices—and we're only a few weeks away from the winter solstice."

Penhallow and Nidhud exchanged glances. "How much of a difference do you think the timing makes?" Penhallow asked.

Lowrey shrugged. "Enough for Quintrel to make note of

it. The men at Mirdalur raised the magic at the summer solstice. I found a chart where Quintrel used what he found in
old inscriptions, manuscript fragments, and mage journals to
estimate when the magic has risen and fallen before, at least
the times that he could document. Five hundred years ago, the
magic fell. It was a hundred years before it was restored—at
Mirdalur—on the summer solstice," he added.

"Before that, it gets murkier, but Quintrel thought he had
found inscriptions on ruins to suggest that at least once every
thousand years, the magic rose and fell. The locations varied,
but to the best of my ability to map them, they were all wells of
power," Lowrey said.

Penhallow nodded. "That makes sense. But there are many
places where the magic was exceptionally strong. Does it matter where Blaine makes the attempt?"

Lowrey turned his gaze toward Connor. "I think Quintrel
had an opinion on that," Lowrey said. "I can't read his code,
but I'm betting if it's important, you can."

Connor took a step backward. "I've had enough of other
people rummaging around in my brain," he said, holding up
his hands in protest. "It's getting so I hardly recognize my own
thoughts."

"Ah, but you're still alive to be annoyed," replied Penhallow.
"You handled the journal several times before we left to see the
Wraith Lord, and nothing happened. So I believe Quintrel's
trance also attuned to time and place." He paused.

"This is important, Bevin, just as it was urgent for me to
intrude, and for the Wraith Lord before that. Quintrel left his
clues with you. You're the only one who can do this."

Connor sighed and moved forward to where Lowrey had
Quintrel's handwritten journal laid open on the table. He

stared down at the yellowed journal page, and at an obviously newer note written in code. Quintrel's tight scrawl ran from one side of the page to the other in neat lines of faded ink, yet the symbols were meaningless, to Connor and even to Lowrey, a former mage.

Connor steeled himself and reached out to touch the lettering. A strange feeling washed over him and his head spun. Memories flooded to the fore, and when he looked down at the page, he could read the coded notes.

"Long ago, long before the kingdoms of Donderath and Meroven ruled the Continent, other great powers controlled these lands," Connor read. "For a time, the gods favored them, to see how high they might rise. They bound magic to their will. They built a vast city filled with riches and comforts. Their mages increased the yield of their fields. Their chirurgeons learned the secrets of healing. Then the gods became angry, and fire rained down on the city. So great was the destruction that the city itself disappeared."

Connor paused and turned his attention to the newer piece of loose parchment that had been used to mark the page. "The rogue mage awaits those who would restore the magic. One of the thirteen must find the valley where the last of the disks rests secure."

Abruptly, Connor stopped reading as the memory that Quintrel had embedded suddenly ended. He felt light-headed as he returned to himself, and the vertigo made him reach out to steady himself on the edge of the table. Lowrey grabbed his shoulder, but Connor shook himself free, angry over Quintrel's invasion of his memories.

"Well?" Connor asked, looking from Lowrey to Penhallow. He knew he was in a foul mood and that his tone was insolent, but at the moment, he didn't care. "Was that worth it? All I remember is a children's tale. How in Raka is that going to help when it never even mentions the place by name?"

"It doesn't have to." Nidhud had not moved from his place near the doorway. "You spoke of Valshoa."

"Dolan, the *talishte* who became the leader of the Knights just before we were exiled, believed that Valshoa was real," Nidhud said. "If he was correct, and we are fortunate enough to find Valshoa, we may also find a contingent of Knights awaiting us."

Connor frowned. "You're saying that the exiled Knights of Esthrane went looking for a place that might not even exist?"

Nidhud shook his head. "Not all of the Knights. When we were driven out, many of our company were destroyed. To increase the odds that some among us would endure, the survivors split up to escape detection." His eyes took on the faraway look of old grief that Connor had seen in Penhallow's gaze.

"Some fled to the Lyceum of Tobar in Durantha," Nidhud said quietly. "They hoped to hide among the scholars and mages. Others fled to the null places, to take up a trade and lose themselves in obscurity. But Dolan was not a scholar or farmer or tradesman. He was a warrior, and though he was *talishte*, he had never forgotten the thrill of adventure. He and a small group of Knights swore to find Valshoa."

"And did they?" Lowrey asked, his expression showing just how excited he was about the possibility.

Nidhud shrugged. "I don't know. I never saw him again."

"What about the *kruvgaldur*? Couldn't you sense whether or not they made it?" Connor asked.

Nidhud shook his head. "Dolan was quite particular about which Knights he chose to accompany him. He chose only those whose makers were gone, and who had made no fledglings—or those whom he had turned himself. They took their human servants with them. He made sure there would be no connection to the outside world."

Connor threw his hands into the air. "That's what we've got to go on?"

"No." Lowrey's voice made Connor turn. "Quintrel seemed sure he had discovered clues to the place he named in his code—the place you've all confirmed is Valshoa. If that's true, then that's where he's waiting for us to find him, the place he believes Blaine would have the best odds to bring back the magic."

"Why Valshoa?" Connor asked. "If anything is even left of it—assuming it ever existed. Aren't there other places of power that would be just as good?"

Lowrey shrugged. "Possibly. If McFadden tried to restore the magic at Mirdalur, it obviously failed. Maybe there's something special about Valshoa's location, or perhaps Quintrel has a few more secrets that he'll only share with the people dedicated enough to follow his clues."

"Not 'dedicated,' obsessed," Connor muttered. "Isn't he taking a huge chance with all this business of hidden clues? It was risky enough for Blaine to return to Donderath from Edgeland."

"Perhaps by the time of the Great Fire, Quintrel realized that there were some, like Reese, who would want to stop the magic from returning," Penhallow said. "He might have guessed it wouldn't be wise to speak plainly."

"We're only weeks away from the solstice, and now we've got to find—and travel to—a lost, ancient city that might not even exist?" Connor questioned, running a hand back through his hair in frustration.

"Quintrel seemed to believe that was the most likely way to succeed," Lowrey replied. "And there's another reason to find him. Did you hear what he said? He has the thirteenth disk."

"But we don't have all twelve of the other disks," Connor protested. "We're still missing some."

"We can hope that by now Blaine has come into possession of his father's disk," Penhallow said. "Until we rejoin Blaine, we don't know what else he's found."

"And if the disks are essential, then Quintrel has assured that whoever is serious about reviving the magic must come to him," Lynge summarized. "Brilliant—or incredibly reckless."

"Oh, Vigus Quintrel was both, I assure you," Lowrey said.

Penhallow looked to Nidhud. "You know, the Wraith Lord didn't have the chance to explain how a small company of long-exiled Knights just happened to be in place to rescue us from Reese's men."

A look passed between the two *talishte*, and then Nidhud nodded. "Very well. The Wraith Lord was punished by banishment to the Unseen Realm. He lost his physical body, while his consciousness remained within the mist, as you have seen. Yet Esthrane did not desert him. She could not undo Etelscurion's curse, but the Mother Goddess is clever, and she found a way to ease the Wraith Lord's suffering," Nidhud explained. "She gave him the ability to allow his consciousness to wander the Paths of the Dead and strengthened his power in the *kruvgaldur*. In that way, he was able to summon the Knights who did not go into exile in Valshoa to his aid."

"Can he communicate with the Valshoa Knights?" Connor asked.

Nidhud shrugged. "I don't know. He has never mentioned such a bond, but then again, the Wraith Lord keeps much to himself. No one except the Wraith Lord knows what limits—if any—hinder his spirit's travels. And I would not advise asking him.

"The Wraith Lord has existed for a thousand years," Nidhud said. "And in that time, he bound many people to him through the *kruvgaldur*. When Esthrane strengthened that bond, it gave the Wraith Lord a network of spies and informants that would have been the envy of any king. Through that network, he heard about your interest in the disks, and about the threat Pentreath Reese posed to restoring the magic. He knew that eventually you would come to him, either for the disk or to ask his counsel. He was a patron of the Knights before we were banished, and when the king betrayed us, the Wraith Lord did everything in his power to protect us. We are oath-bound to him. He called the Knights to him so that, if he deemed you worthy, we would assist you in your quest."

"Yet with that network, you don't think the Wraith Lord has connections to the Knights in Valshoa—assuming they still exist?" Penhallow asked.

Nidhud frowned. "Even among *talishte* there is politics. You, of all people, should know that. Dolan was something of a rogue, even among the Knights. He respected—and feared—the Wraith Lord. But he was careful never to make a blood bond with him, and he made every effort to keep his loyalists from bonding with the Wraith Lord. In a way, I think Dolan welcomed exile. It gave him the opportunity to follow no orders but his own."

"How many Knights are in your company?" Lowrey asked.

"I've gathered twenty-five from those who were exiled and still survive," Nidhud replied. "At our strongest, there were just two hundred Knights. King Merrill's grandfather slew half of the Knights when he betrayed us. Twenty knights went with Dolan to search for Valshoa. Exile has taken a toll on those who remained. Some were killed when assassins discovered their hiding places. Others gave up in despair and let themselves be killed in battle. Some just disappeared. Maybe they allowed the dawn to take them."

"What are your orders?" Penhallow's voice was cautious.

"We are to give our assistance and protection to Blaine McFadden's attempt to restore the magic," Nidhud said.

"How can we stand against Reese's army?" Connor asked.

Penhallow frowned, thinking. "Perhaps the odds are not so lopsided as they seem," he mused. "Traher Voss and his men are yet to be accounted for. I hardly believe Reese and Pollard were able to bottle him up forever." He clapped Connor on the shoulder. "Cheer up, Bevin. Although I sincerely hope we won't have to do battle with Reese, if a fight comes, we won't stand alone."

"Without the twelve disks, it may be in vain," Lowrey reminded them. "Don't forget about that."

Nidhud grinned. "I might be able to help, a little, with that. I know where we can find a disk that I'm almost positive Reese can't get his hands on."

"Where?" Connor asked skeptically.

Nidhud's smile was wolfish. "The oubliette beneath the castle." He met Connor's gaze. "But to get it, we'll need the Wraith Lord's help—and he'll need your help."

A candlemark later, Connor, Nidhud, and Penhallow made their way through a cramped tunnel beneath the ruins of Quillarth Castle. Stagnant water ran in a trickle along the floor, and heavy cobwebs festooned the corners of the upper walls. Connor carried a lantern. In the darkness, the lantern's dim glow bolstered Connor's courage, as long as he did not think about where they were headed.

Once again, I'm stuck in a dark tunnel with a couple of vampires, Connor thought. *When this is all over, assuming I survive, I'm never going belowground again.*

"You're telling me there's a *talishte* in an oubliette who's been down here so long that even Lynge didn't know about it?" Connor asked in a whisper.

"I'm not even certain Merrill knew, to tell you the truth," Nidhud replied.

"And you thought it was too dangerous for Lynge to come with us, but it's perfectly fine to bring me?" There was no hiding the challenge in Connor's voice.

"We've been over this before," Nidhud said. "Hemming Lorens has been locked away for almost one hundred years. King Merrill's grandfather grew to hate our kind," he said. "Lorens certainly didn't help our cause. He was a powerful *talishte* who enjoyed preying on mortals. In fact, he did so boldly, mocking the king's authority."

Penhallow's expression showed his distaste. "I remember. There was such an outcry, it's amazing we weren't all hunted and burned."

Nidhud nodded. "There were certainly those who tried."

"So Lorens has been locked in an oubliette for one hundred years? How has he fed?" Connor asked, a new horror gradually dawning in his imagination.

"He hasn't," Nidhud replied.

"And he still . . . exists?" Connor said, aghast.

"Merrill's grandfather was a ruthless man. He betrayed the Knights when they no longer served his purpose. Lorens's slaughter of mortals helped the king turn public opinion against the Knights," Nidhud said.

"Merrill's grandfather could have destroyed Lorens," Penhallow added. "He certainly exterminated enough of the

Knights of Esthrane. It's clear he knew how to do it. He publicly slandered the Knights, destroying any support they might have received from mortals, and made a spectacle out of their execution."

"Once Lorens's usefulness was over, the king decided to bolster his reputation as a fearless hunter of *talishte* even further by inflicting a punishment so severe, it drove the remaining *talishte* into hiding," Nidhud said. "He locked him in the deepest oubliette and left him to starve." Nidhud turned to meet Connor's gaze, and his expression was grim. "Do you have any idea how long it takes a *talishte* of Lorens's power to starve?"

Connor shook his head.

"Neither did the king."

No one said anything for a few moments, and Connor wrestled with his thoughts. *We're just going to drop by and then leave Lorens there to finish starving? On the other hand, he slaughtered mortals. Would it be a greater kindness for Penhallow or Nidhud to destroy Lorens altogether? Or is any existence better than none at all?*

Connor had heard of oubliettes, but he had prayed fervently to the gods that he would never see one. His lantern was the only light as they made their way through a dank corridor. Connor was certain that, by now, the corridor had led them far beyond Quillarth Castle, but where they were, he had no idea. Rats scurried by his feet, and a faint green glow from luminescent fungi on the corridor walls gave the passageway an eerie feel.

The oubliette was a deep hole in the rock covered with a heavy iron grate. The lantern's light did not extend far enough to see the bottom of the pit, but there was a sense of presence that made the hair stand up on the back of Connor's neck.

"I don't understand," he said in a hushed voice to Penhallow.

"Can't *talishte* fly—or at least levitate? Couldn't Lorens just come up to the top and rip off the grating?"

"The king thought of everything," Nidhud said, a bitter note coloring his voice. "He drove a stake through Lorens's heart. For those *talishte* who are old and strong, a stake alone is not enough to kill—beheading is necessary." He turned to meet Connor's gaze.

"Lorens is conscious but immobile. He can hear us, speak to us, but he cannot move. He has been that way for nearly three generations. Unless he is beheaded, he will be that way for a very long time."

Connor felt bile rise in his stomach. "Is there no way to end his suffering?"

Nidhud's eyes narrowed as he peered at Connor in the dim light. "Lorens slaughtered dozens of mortals. Yet you would end his suffering if you could?"

"Yes."

Nidhud looked away. "We have a job to do. Let's do it." He strode up to the iron grate and rattled it with his boot. "Lorens," he called out. "A word with you."

"Leave me." The voice was as brittle as dry leaves, a painful wheeze.

"Your maker requires a word with you," Nidhud said, his tone hard.

"His maker?" Connor asked under his breath.

"The Wraith Lord," Penhallow replied.

Connor shot a worried glance toward Penhallow. "Now wait a minute! I'm tired of being taken over by *talishte*. Am I the only one who thinks this is a bad idea?"

I cannot travel to the oubliette except through another, the Wraith Lord's voice spoke in Connor's mind. *He has a key to the puzzle. There is no other way.*

All right then, Connor thought, angry but resigned. *But be quick about it.*

Connor thought he heard the Wraith Lord chuckle. The now-familiar vertigo of possession made him stumble, and both Penhallow and Nidhud put out a hand to steady him. When Connor straightened, he felt the Wraith Lord come to the fore.

"Lorens. You survive." The voice that came from Connor's mouth was not his own, and Connor wondered how much it sounded like the disembodied *talishte* who spoke from inside his mind.

"Master? How can it be?"

"Do you have the disk?"

There was silence for a moment. "Yes. I wear it still around my neck. The king left me with it to taunt me, I suppose. Its voice keeps me company."

Disk? Voice? Connor questioned silently.

Lorens is a descendent of one of the original thirteen Lords of the Blood, the Wraith Lord explained. *As madness took him, he believed that the disk itself had occult power and that it spoke to him in his mother's voice. The voice he heard drove him to kill.*

"Lorens. Do you regret your deeds?"

A chilling laugh echoed in the stone corridor. "I regret only that I did not make the rivers run with sweet, warm blood."

"See," Nidhud murmured. "All this time, and he repents of nothing."

"We must take the disk. The time is come," the Wraith Lord said with Connor's voice.

"No, please. Master, I beg of you. In the darkness, the disk sings to me. We speak to each other, she and I. Please don't leave me here without it."

"There is no choice, Lorens. We need the disk." The voice

belonged to Connor, but everything about it was foreign, his tone, his phrasing, and the strange hint of an accent.

How, exactly, are we going to get the disk? Connor asked the Wraith Lord. *We're up here. He's down there.*

We're going down to take it.

Damn. I knew you were going to say that.

Penhallow took hold of Connor's arm and steered him away from the oubliette, back to the corridor from which they had come. "I don't like this, Kierken," Penhallow said. "We've already seen how hard it is on Connor for him to host you."

Go down there? No, definitely no! Connor argued silently.

Kierken, speaking through Connor, sighed. "There is no choice. When the king sent Lorens to the oubliette, he feared other *talishte* might try to free him. He set traps. Even without magic, those traps are potent. The chains that bind Lorens are overlaid with rope made from rowan-wood fibers to prevent unquiet dead from rising. Masterwort was burned and the ashes sprinkled on his skin and all around him. A tincture made with moonflower, prized for its ability to banish monsters, was allowed to seep into his clothing and bonds. Who knows what other spells of binding and protection were also used?" He paused. "While we no longer need fear the magic, the other traps remain dangerous."

Penhallow's expression was grave. "So all these years, he's been tormented as well as left alone?"

The Wraith Lord nodded. "I don't dispute that his crimes were grievous. But the king's penalty was merciless. One of us cannot touch him without harm. But none of the elements used were dangerous to mortals."

Do I get a vote? You're not listening. I am not going down there, Connor protested.

"I gave Connor my word that he would not be harmed,"

Penhallow said. His voice was terse, and his eyes glinted in challenge.

"Then perhaps you'd best rethink your promises, Lanyon. These are dangerous times, for *talishte* and for mortals. I don't know that it's possible to assure anyone's safety." He met Penhallow's gaze. "But if you value the life of your remaining Lord of the Blood, and you hope for the ritual to succeed, you'll need the disk."

"Connor's the one who needs to give permission. It's his life," Penhallow said.

Relegated to a corner of his own consciousness, Connor felt a wave of panic. *I am not going down there. Do you hear me?*

Do you wish to see the magic restored? The voice that answered Connor was that of the Wraith Lord.

Yes. You know I do.

The disks have been present for the last two rituals to raise the magic, and perhaps for longer. This is your one chance to take Lorens's disk: Only I can control him, and I need your body to do it.

Connor was quiet for a moment as the logic of the Wraith Lord's argument warred with his own instinct for self-preservation. *I'll go*, he said finally. *But then, you knew that already.*

The Wraith Lord chuckled. *You are a most interesting servant, Bevin Connor. Penhallow chose you well.*

"We are agreed," the Wraith Lord reported aloud.

Penhallow muttered a curse under his breath. "What's your plan? I don't trust Lorens, no matter how much the king thought he was incapacitated."

"Lorens is my get. Although I don't expect him to be able to fight us, I should be able to compel him, since I have the use of a physical body."

" 'Should' be able to compel him," Penhallow repeated, distaste clear in his voice. "But there's no real way of knowing until you—and Connor—are committed to the action, is there?"

"No. There isn't."

Penhallow was quiet for a moment. "All right. Let's get going. I've only just healed Connor, and I don't want you burning him up again."

Neither do I, Connor seconded silently.

They returned to where Nidhud waited near the metal grate that capped Lorens's prison. "While you two were gone, I took a look at the grating," he said. "The king may have trusted a bit too much in his magical precautions. The lock is heavy, but not particularly difficult to pick. I believe I can get it open."

"Can you fasten it again when we're through?" Penhallow asked. "I don't wish to be responsible for loosing that monster. The kingdom has sorrows enough as it is."

Nidhud nodded. "I should be able to lock it again." He met Penhallow's gaze. "You mean to leave him as he is?"

"That's entirely up to Lorens," Penhallow replied. From a scabbard on his belt, he withdrew a short sword, one he kept for fighting with blades in both hands. He gave the sword to Connor.

"Take this down with you, Kierken," Penhallow said to the Wraith Lord. "You'll have to leave Connor's sword with me—the oubliette is too narrow for you to draw it anyway. Lorens should be completely incapacitated. But if not—" The razor-sharp edge of the blade made Penhallow's meaning clear.

"How, exactly, do you mean to descend?" Penhallow asked, and it took Connor a moment to realize that the question was directed to his body, but not to him.

"The oubliette isn't designed to have visitors," the Wraith

Lord replied. "Or for anyone to ever exit. For all we know, the king might have thrown Lorens into the pit. There's no way down—or back up, for that matter. Since I can't levitate in this body, we shall have to descend the mortal way: with a rope."

Connor fidgeted as Nidhud constructed a harness for him with part of the rope he carried on his belt. "Stand still," Nidhud commanded.

"Make sure those knots hold," Penhallow said. "I want him brought back up safe and sound."

That makes two of us, Connor thought fervently.

"Are you sure you're going to have enough rope left to lower him all the way down?" Penhallow asked.

"Should be enough," Nidhud said, his attention still on the harness. "We tested the drop with a stone, so we know where the bottom is."

"We can lower the lantern with the chain over there," Penhallow said, giving a nod to a length of chain he had found pushed to the side of the room. "You and I may not need light, but if Kierken is using Connor's body, he won't be able to see in the dark."

"After all that time down there, Lorens won't be pretty to look at," Nidhud replied. "I hope your man has a strong stomach."

As Nidhud worked, Connor's eye was drawn to a deep crack in the room's far wall. He looked at the floor and saw that the crack extended down through the paving stones and had split the rocks at the upper lip of the oubliette so they gaped nearly the width of his hand. *It must have taken something pretty powerful to make that crack*, Connor thought.

The night of the Great Fire, earthquakes were felt all across Donderath, the Wraith Lord's voice answered him silently.

Since then, quakes have often accompanied the magic storms. In the years that Lorens has been captive, a powerful quake or two would not be surprising.

Finally, the harness was ready. Nidhud bent beside the lock on the oubliette's grate, working at the massive lock. After a while, the old tumblers clicked open. Even with their *talishte* strength, it took both Nidhud and Penhallow to lift the heavy iron grating.

"I'm coming down, Lorens," the Wraith Lord said. "Prepare yourself."

Possessed by the Wraith Lord, Connor stepped to the edge of the oubliette. The Wraith Lord's spirit was confident, yet wary. Locked away in a corner of his consciousness, Connor choked down fear. He sat down with his legs dangling into the darkness. The pit was just slightly farther across than he was tall, meaning that he would have to crouch a bit to avoid scraping the stone sides of the shaft. From the top, the pit appeared bottomless, and even when Penhallow readied the lantern, Connor could see nothing but blackness. The Wraith Lord gripped his sword like a seasoned fighter.

"Let yourself over the side," Nidhud said. "I'll keep the rope taut so you can walk down the wall if it makes you feel better. There isn't room for you to lie flat and swing, at least not without hitting your head. Move slowly, and you'll be all right."

Mortal terror welled up so strongly that for a moment, Connor could not breathe. The Wraith Lord pushed off from the edge. For a few seconds, Connor fell forward, and then the rope caught. It jerked him, and his breath exhaled in a rush.

So long since I felt fear as a mortal, the Wraith Lord said in his mind. *I had forgotten how it feels to be so . . . fragile.*

Since you're using my body, best you start remembering, Connor reprimanded, made bold by his utter terror. *I've got no intention of being eaten, dropped, crushed, or otherwise killed. Let's be clear about that.*

Utterly, the Wraith Lord said with the hint of a chuckle.

Penhallow had dropped the lantern over first so that it descended a few feet sooner than Connor, lighting his way. The walls of the oubliette were dark, stained with water that had seeped in over the years. Here and there, patches of fungus glowed. Connor's boot slid on a patch of slime.

He had expected the oubliette to smell like a tomb. After his association with Penhallow, Connor had grown more accustomed than he had ever imagined possible with tombs, crypts, and underground hiding places. Cellars often smelled of mold and damp ground. Crypts had a musty smell, of dust and decaying clothing and the scent of old death. Yet the oubliette's odor did not evoke any of those places.

Perhaps it would have been different, Connor thought, if Lorens had been mortal, consigned to a lingering death at the bottom of the pit. Maybe then the darkness would have smelled of stale urine, desiccated flesh, and old blood. Instead, the oubliette had the loamy scent of mushrooms and lichen, with a sharp tang Connor could not identify. He did not know the origin of the scent, but in his mind, he named it all the same: fear.

He doesn't merit your pity, the Wraith Lord reprimanded Connor silently. *He more than earned his punishment.*

The lantern bobbed for a few moments, twisting on the chain until it steadied. Its light did not go all the way to the bottom of the pit, but what it illuminated made the part of him that was still Connor recoil. Festooned down the pit, angled from the side to side, was a tangle of filmy spiderwebs.

I really don't want to go down there, he thought. *Those webs didn't spin themselves.*

He strained to see in the dim light, but he could not make out any spiders on the webs. *Maybe they're old webs. Maybe the spiders are long gone*, he thought.

No, he corrected himself before the Wraith Lord could speak. *Old webs would be in tatters. Those are new enough to be in good shape. And, Sweet Mother Esthrane, there are so many of them!*

No helping it, lad, the Wraith Lord said. *We've got to go down.*

Stop calling me 'lad.'

The Wraith Lord chuckled. *I am over one thousand years old. To me, even Penhallow is a youth.*

For a moment or two, Connor let himself think about the Wraith Lord's words, and what it would be like to be so great an age. It was a pleasant, but brief, respite from dwelling on the task at hand. The Wraith Lord slashed through the webs, kicking at them to clear a path through the filmy strands. Even so, tendrils of the sticky fibers brushed his neck and arms, clinging to his hair, like the breath of a ghostly lover.

With the Wraith Lord controlling his movements, Connor worked his way toward the bottom of the pit, rappelling down the wall. The oubliette was a narrow stone tube. To remain upright during the descent meant that Connor faced the wall. He would have preferred to keep his focus on the vampire below, even if there was nothing to see in the darkness.

His boot slipped, and the abrupt movement jostled the lantern, sending it twirling, so that for a moment, as Connor dangled in midair, the lantern spun: light, dark, light, dark. Spiderwebs festooned around him, clinging to his face and his clothing. He fought panic.

Don't lose your nerve, boy, the Wraith Lord said in his mind.

It's not your body in the harness, Connor snapped.

For now it is, the Wraith Lord replied. *Not too much farther. What do we do when we get down there?*

Lorens wore the disk on a strap around his neck, under his shirt. We reach beneath what remains of his clothing and take the disk. Mind not to dislodge the stake.

That would be bad, Connor said.

That would be very bad.

His boot found purchase on the rough stone once more, and he steadied himself to resume the descent. But as he worked his way down the wet stones, he noticed that the crack in the wall continued from the lip of the oubliette. It narrowed somewhat from the gaping, hand-width fissure at the top, but the crack was still several fingers wide.

That's a pretty deep crack, he noted. *Do you think the walls are still sturdy?*

If the prison hadn't been built to withstand the worst that men and nature could hurl at it, the entire room would have caved in by now, the Wraith Lord replied.

The top of the shaft seemed small and dim, so that Connor could barely make out the shadows of Penhallow and Nidhud, who were anxiously peering over the edge. The lantern cast flickering shadows, and more than once, Connor caught the movement of his own silhouette out of the corner of his eye, startling him and sending his pulse racing.

Steady, Connor. Nearly there, the Wraith Lord's voice coached.

What's that? In the silence of the pit, even the slightest noise attracted attention. Connor glanced up to see a large black spider scrabbling from inside the crack in the wall. He shuddered reflexively.

Up above, he heard a sudden shift and saw Nidhud and Penhallow disappear from their vigil. There were footsteps, and the swish of a sword through the air, then a loud screech. "What's happening up there?" the Wraith Lord called.

"Rats!" Penhallow shouted. "Nothing to be concerned about. We've got it taken care of."

Scratching noises sounded, close at hand. More spiders emerged from the crack in the wall. They were shiny and black, and counting the reach of their legs, as big around as a gold coin. The body of each spider was easily as thick as his finger.

The Wraith Lord's movements were swift and sure, though Connor kept a wary eye on the crack in the wall. Several more spiders had made their way out of it, and in the half-light there was no way he could see where they had gone on the black walls of the oubliette. Between the seeping dampness and the patches of slime, Connor could not make out the difference between dark spots on the walls and the spiders, and he was grateful that the Wraith Lord controlled his movements.

Connor could hear the clink of a sword up at the top of the shaft, scraping against rock, hurried footsteps, and more desperate squeaking. A large, flailing object hurtled over the lip of the oubliette and straight toward Connor.

The Wraith Lord shifted to get out of the way, heedless of the wall of spiderwebs Connor's body brushed against. The walls above them were now crawling with spiders, with more being disgorged from the crevice between the stones. The rope brushed against the wall, sending a dozen or more of the spiders falling toward him, but the Wraith Lord brushed them off as if they were gnats.

The rope gave a sudden jerk and Connor plummeted several feet, ripping his way through the gauzy webs. The rope caught, and he jolted to a stop. The lantern was overhead, too far away to illuminate his new position, and for a breath, it was as if he had been plunged into darkness.

The Wraith Lord regained a foothold against the wall. He moved with a focused battle-calm that Connor guessed had been honed over centuries. In the dim light of the glowing fungus, shadows seemed to creep across the stones. The lantern's chain clanked and rattled, dropping the light down to where Connor hung.

For just a moment, the lantern illuminated the dirt floor of the oubliette. In that instant, Connor had time to see just one thing: A wooden stake lay broken on the earthen floor.

There was a rush of air and something hard hit him in the chest, slamming him against the wall of the pit. Connor felt spiders fall into his hair and onto his neck. A bony hand pinned him against the stone and a leering, leathery face appeared before him. For an instant, Connor took it for a death mask before he realized that it was Lorens.

Hunger glinted in Lorens's eyes, and he moved swiftly for Connor's throat.

Fever heat surged through all of Connor's form at once, and the Wraith Lord broke Lorens's hold. Lorens hurtled backward, slamming against the wall of the oubliette in a shower of falling spiders.

Connor was free of Lorens's grip but he fell, jerking to a sudden stop several feet above the floor of the oubliette, hanging facedown by the rope. In an instant, Lorens landed on his back, wrapping his arms so tightly around Connor's chest that Connor gasped for breath.

The movement sent Connor swinging like a pendulum, and he kicked off the far wall with the Wraith Lord's might, turning as he did so that he drove Lorens into the other wall. The impact made Connor's head pound, but it loosened Lorens's grip, giving the Wraith Lord the space to drive his elbow back hard into his attacker's chest.

"How did you get free?" the Wraith Lord roared.

Lorens released Connor and disappeared into the shadows. An instant later, the lantern slammed against the wall, sending a shower of glass down into the oubliette and extinguishing the light.

"Down here in the ground, the quakes were quite severe," Lorens replied. Connor could not have located him, but the Wraith Lord's heightened senses narrowed in on Lorens's hiding place. "They jostled me, and the stake loosened. The rats finished it."

The Wraith Lord was in complete control, leaving Connor a terrified spectator. "You learned to compel the rats?" the Wraith Lord asked, and Connor knew that the ancient *talishte* was trying to get a fix on Lorens's position.

The only light was the faint glow that came from the distant lip of the oubliette. From the sounds that reached him, Connor guessed that Penhallow and Nidhud were locked in a battle of some sort. His rope neither pulled him up nor let him descend, giving Connor to surmise that it had been tied off to allow Nidhud to deal with whatever threat had presented itself.

Connor could feel movement where several of the spiders had gotten into his shirt, crawling beneath his collar. The Wraith Lord's movement triggered bites on Connor's forearms and through the cloth of his pants, but the *talishte*'s spirit seemed heedless of the pain.

A shadow moved, and strong hands clutched his shoulders. Lorens's wizened face loomed just inches from his own, and the *talishte* had a death grip on his shoulders with bony hands. Lorens leered and began to spin them, hoping to foul Connor in his own line. The Wraith Lord brought the pommel of the short sword down hard on Lorens's back, snapping ribs.

Lorens let him drop, and Connor's head swam, but the Wraith Lord was unaffected, slashing at the shadows.

Feathery bits of spiderweb drifted down on him, and Connor heard the soft crunch of hard carapaces skittering against his coat. The sword hit bone, and Lorens cursed, jerking free.

In the darkness, Connor could smell sweat and ichor. Above, he heard sounds of battle. His rope remained taut, but he was certain now that Nidhud's attention was elsewhere, as he did not move up or down.

A rush of air, a muttered curse, and Connor was body-slammed so hard that it drove the breath from his lungs. His rope snapped, cutting painfully into his skin and nearly dislocating his shoulder as his harness gave way and the knots dug into his flesh. The force of the blow sent him cartwheeling into the darkness. Connor landed hard on the floor, banging his head so hard that his vision swam. His sword flew out of his grip, and a powerful hand closed around his throat.

"I have waited a very long time for human blood," Lorens whispered, his lips against Connor's ear.

The Wraith Lord's power surged, and Connor's body bucked, breaking Lorens's grip.

Connor swept his arm along the packed dirt floor, seeking a weapon. His hand closed on the broken stake, and he could sense the Wraith Lord's satisfaction. He brought the stake up in front of his chest just as a gust of air signaled another attack. Its jagged wood tore into leathery flesh, and Lorens screamed in pain and anger, vanishing as quickly as he had come.

"You existed on the rats," the Wraith Lord guessed.

"We called to them, the disk and I." Lorens's voice was a whisper, seeming to come from everywhere at once. "And to the spiders. I held court, here in the darkness. Blood and companionship. It was . . . barely enough."

He's summoned the rats to attack Penhallow and Nidhud, distract them, Connor thought. *By the time they fight their way free, it's going to be too late for me.*

The Wraith Lord easily regained his feet. Connor was certain that the fall had broken a couple of ribs, and a sharp pain told him that his left collarbone was probably also broken. The Wraith Lord scanned the darkness, and then Connor gave a mighty leap, one that he knew exceeded his own abilities. One hand caught at the darkness and tangled in long, matted hair. Connor grabbed a fistful of the hair, yanking Lorens back toward him with enough force that it would have snapped a mortal's neck.

"Stop this. I command you," the Wraith Lord rasped.

"Can't see me, can't compel me," Lorens returned.

They were falling once more, but this time, the Wraith Lord twisted so Lorens's body absorbed the worst of the impact. The force still jarred Connor to the bone, making his teeth hit together and sending a jolt down his spine. His sword fell from his hand and clattered to the floor.

Now that Connor was on the floor of the oubliette, the faint shaft of light from the torches above was enough to enable him to make out some of his surroundings. The bones of countless rats littered the floor.

Lorens bucked against the Wraith Lord's grip, shifting just enough to sink his fangs into Connor's shoulder. Connor cried out, and the Wraith Lord shoved Lorens away as his fang tore through Connor's flesh.

The Wraith Lord and Lorens both dove toward the fallen sword at the same instant, but the Wraith Lord closed Connor's hand around the pommel first and pivoted just as Lorens sprang for the kill. The Wraith Lord thrust with the sword as Lorens's momentum carried him forward and the sword plunged into the vampire's rib cage.

Connor felt the full brunt of the Wraith Lord's fury coursing through him as he came almost nose to nose with Lorens. Connor's sword protruded from Lorens's back, and the hilt rested against Lorens's chest. Ichor, thick and cold, oozed from the wound, coursing over Connor's fingers.

Lorens's face was taut with pain, but he managed a grimacing half smile. "Rest," he wheezed. "Finally."

Moving with *talishte* speed, Connor's left hand tore down through the rags that covered Lorens's body. The obsidian disk swung away from Lorens's chest, and Connor, moving with the Wraith Lord's strength, effortlessly snapped the leather. A swing of his sword severed Lorens's head from his body, and both crumbled into dust.

Connor stood. The fever of the Wraith Lord's presence sent rivulets of sweat down his back despite the chill of the deep pit. In one hand, he clutched the obsidian disk, and in the other, he gripped the sword so tightly Connor did not think he would be able to let go. Movement sent stabbing pain down his left side from the gash Lorens's fangs had torn in his flesh, the dislocated shoulder, and the broken collarbone. Just breathing made his cracked ribs ache.

I'm alive! Connor thought, though he lacked the energy to move in celebration.

And I'm stranded at the bottom of an oubliette and possessed by the spirit of an ancient vampire, who's burning up my life force with every breath. The second thought made the prior elation evaporate.

If I leave now, you'll die, the Wraith Lord said. *You need my strength to get out of here. I'll try not to kill you in the process.*

"Connor! Connor, can you hear me?" Penhallow's voice echoed from the sides of the shaft.

"We're here," the Wraith Lord called back. "We've got the

disk. Lorens is dead. But you'd best get down here if you want your servant back alive. None of the traps remain."

A moment later, Connor could see Penhallow descending through the gloom, heedless of the torn remnants of spiderweb that had not been destroyed in the battle. The spiders themselves had vanished, although Connor felt the pain of several swollen bites along his back and down his arms and legs.

Penhallow touched down beside them. The three of them took up nearly all of the space in the oubliette's small circle. He took in Connor's bloodied and battered appearance, the ichor-stained sword, the pile of ash that had been Lorens, and muttered a curse under his breath.

"We've got to get you out of here," he said to Connor. "I'll carry you, since I don't imagine you'd like us to loop a rope under your arms and hoist you up."

Just envisioning the alternative sent a jolt of pain through Connor's body. "I'll swallow my pride," the Wraith Lord relayed on Connor's behalf. Penhallow lifted him as gently as possible for the ascent. As the darkness fell away behind them and they ascended, Connor thought he had never seen anything as beautiful as the torchlight that awaited them.

At the top of the oubliette, Penhallow stepped onto the stone rim. Nidhud looked Connor over with a concerned expression. "What happened?"

"The quakes dislodged the stake," the Wraith Lord explained in a weary voice. "Lorens had been calling to the rats and spiders to do his bidding, trying to regain the strength to break loose. Imprisonment weakened him, but it didn't destroy him."

Connor's eyes were half-closed, but he could see that the room at the top of the oubliette was littered from wall to wall with the butchered bodies of rats. Blood splattered on the walls, and rivulets of blood ran between the stones in the floor. The whole room stank of offal and blood.

"You can leave him now," Penhallow commanded the Wraith Lord. "He's too injured to handle your presence any longer."

Connor convulsed as the Wraith Lord left him. Without the Wraith Lord's power, Connor no longer had the strength to stand.

With me you burn, but without me, you are merely mortal, said a voice in his mind.

"We've got to get him back to the castle," Penhallow said.

"What about the grate?" Nidhud protested.

Penhallow shook his head. "Lorens is gone."

Nidhud toed one of the rat corpses. "Go on ahead. I'll clean up and meet you there."

Penhallow nodded and turned his attention back to Connor. "Rest. When all is well, I will awaken you." The words enveloped Connor like a warm tide, and he drifted into the darkness.

"I hear you were quite the hero." Lynge's voice penetrated the fog inside Connor's head and drew him to consciousness.

Connor opened his eyes and squinted against the light from the window. He was in an unfamiliar room, lying on a comfortable bed. Two facts stood out: First, he was alive, and in relatively little pain, with his shoulder put back into place and his broken ribs wrapped. Second, he lay on crisp, smooth sheets of fine fabric, a luxury he had not experienced since he fled the castle months ago. "Just trying to stay alive," he murmured.

Lynge pressed the thin lip of a porcelain cup against Connor's mouth and supported him to rise far enough to sip some of the tea. "Lord Garnoc would have been impressed," he said as Connor sank back against the pillow.

"Where's Penhallow?"

Lynge bit his lip nervously. "Lord Penhallow healed you, at considerable effort, I must say. He appeared quite spent by the end of it. He has gone to ground for the day, with instructions for me to care for you, and assurance to you that he will return once he is rested."

"Nidhud?"

"He came back from the tunnels looking as if he'd been to war—you all did," Lynge replied. "He made sure you and Penhallow had what you needed, asked for a change of clothing and water to wash with, and has presumably also found shelter from the day."

"We got it," Connor said wearily. "We got the pendant."

Lynge nodded. "So I was informed by Lord Penhallow." He frowned. "Surely there must have been a better way to go about it. You were on the threshold of the Sea of Souls when Lord Penhallow brought you here."

"I'm getting used to it," Connor murmured. If he moved, he could feel the ache in his ribs and collarbone, telling him that even Penhallow's spit and blood could not knit bone immediately.

"I brought you food," Lynge said, inclining his head toward a small stand at the side of Connor's bed that held a tankard of ale and a plate of cheese, bread, dried herring, and sausages. "It's not quite the fare you were accustomed to finding in the castle, but these days, we're lucky to have enough to fill our bellies."

"It looks like a feast," Connor said groggily. Another thought jarred him awake. "What of the Knights of Esthrane?"

Lynge leaned back in his chair, and Connor could see how

much the last months had aged the seneschal. Lynge had not been a young man before the Cataclysm. All that had transpired since then had turned the seneschal's hair completely white and lined his face so he looked as if a score of years and not months had passed since Connor fled the Great Fire. The death of the king, and the loss of Lynge's assistant, Geddy, had gone hard on him.

"Where will you go, once you're well enough to travel?" Lynge asked. "Lord Penhallow asked me to do what I could to put some fresh clothes and a few necessities together for you."

Connor eyed the food, decided that eating was too much trouble, and sank back into his pillow. "I don't think I can quite handle the thought of going farther than the garderobe," he said. "Perhaps somewhere completely nonexciting?"

Lynge gave him a skeptical look. "I was instructed to have your sword cleaned and sharpened and to find you a set of daggers and a short sword."

"Damn," Connor murmured.

Lynge nodded. "You've become quite the adventurer since you left Lord Garnoc's service, Bevin."

Connor closed his eyes and his expression tightened with a twinge of old grief. "I'd take my boring, comfortable life in an instant to have him back again."

"Aye," Lynge replied. He was silent for a moment. "You know, we buried Lord Garnoc with the picture of Millicent that he carried around with him," he said quietly. "Her crypt was on the grounds of his manor, and with the turmoil, we didn't dare leave the castle to bury him next to her. It was the best we could do."

A faint smile tugged at the corners of Connor's lips. "He was utterly devoted to her," he said, remembering all the times he had brought the small oil painting of Garnoc's beloved wife to keep the old lord company while he ate his dinner. "Perhaps it's for the best that he didn't live to see what's become of Donderath."

"Ah, but he had an inkling what you were made of, m'boy," Lynge said. "He'd be quite proud of you."

"I hope so," Connor said quietly. He opened his eyes, just a slit, to look at the seneschal. "You know something about shouldering what comes your way, don't you? After all, these last months haven't been within your normal duties."

Lynge looked away and made a dismissive gesture. "Nonsense. A good seneschal does whatever is required to keep the castle functioning."

It occurred to Connor how odd it was to be having this conversation with Lynge. Before the Great Fire, Lynge had always been polite but distant, as befitted the vast gap in status between the king's seneschal and an assistant to one of the nobility. Now, as survivors of the Cataclysm, they shared an understanding that far transcended the old hierarchies.

"If the world were as it should be, I would be getting the castle ready for the Solstice Festival," Lynge said quietly. "Balls to plan. Feasts to prepare. Minstrels practicing their music night and day. Lords and ladies all a-chatter about the holiday gossip. Seamstresses and tailors fitting the king for new robes." There was no mistaking the wistfulness in his voice. His gaze was on the fireplace, but Connor was quite certain that Lynge was looking past the fire to another place and time that were gone forever.

"I always liked the bonfires best," Connor said, managing a smile at the memory. "And the lanterns. Oh, and the roasted duck with currants and dates, washed down with a bucket of bitterbeer from the Rooster and Pig."

Lynge gave a soft chuckle. "A finer beer I've never tasted," he said with a sigh. "I wonder what became of its tavern master?"

"That I can tell you," Connor replied. "Engraham got me passage on a ship to Edgeland. When it foundered off the coast, he and I were among the survivors." He grinned. "Have no fear. His bitterbeer isn't lost to the world. He's just brewing it up in the frozen north, for a very appreciative audience."

Lynge sighed. "That's a fine story. And one with a happy ending. Few of those these days." He roused himself and stood. "I shouldn't be keeping you from your food, or from your rest. You've more than earned both," he said, stretching. "I need to see to the billeting of our soldier guests," he said, his tone coloring to indicate that he was somewhat ambivalent about the castle's visitors.

Connor looked toward the window. "So it's morning already?"

Lynge gave him a glance that Connor could not read. "It's morning, m'boy, but it's been two full days since Penhallow brought you to me. You've only just awakened. I feared, for a while, you might not."

Well, then, Connor thought, *that explains why I still feel like shit.*

"Come sundown, I'll let Lord Penhallow know that you're awake," Lynge said. "He's been by each night to sit with you and do what he could to help you heal. I don't know that I would have believed, before this, that a *talishte* would be so concerned for a mortal servant."

"He's a decent fellow, if you don't count all the times he's nearly gotten me killed," Connor said. He looked at the window once more, saw daylight, and felt a surge of relief.

However badly I was injured, whatever Penhallow's done to save me, he didn't turn me, or I couldn't see daylight, Connor thought.

Lynge chuckled, as if guessing his thoughts. "You're still quite mortal," he said. "Lord Penhallow said you might need to be reassured of that. Although, after all that's happened, I'm not sure I'd mind having a *talishte*'s knack for survival."

"Penhallow's seen kingdoms fall like this before," Connor said quietly. "The Wraith Lord has existed for a thousand years, and he's seen the magic destroyed several times." He met Lynge's gaze. "Would you wish that? Or is once enough?"

Lynge shuddered. "Point taken. Once is quite enough." He squared his shoulders and was again the unflappable seneschal. "Now I'd best be about my duties, and best you return to healing." He had the barest trace of a smile. "I shouldn't care to inform your new master that I've kept you from your rest."

"No," Connor said, stifling a yawn. "We can't have that." He gave one last look at the food, decided that it would still be there when he awoke, and was almost asleep when Lynge pulled the door shut behind him.

CHAPTER TWENTY-SEVEN

———

I'LL BE GLAD TO GET BACK TO GLENREITH," BLAINE said, riding between Kestel and Verran. The lyceum was two days' ride behind them, and they had most of a day's ride left before reaching home. Two of the horses they had reclaimed from Pollard's routed soldiers were tethered behind one of the wagons, while Borya and Desya rode the other two. Illarion drove one of the troubadours' wagons while Zaryae drove the other. Piran, Borya, and Desya took turns riding in front and behind the group, keeping watch.

"I'll be glad to get back to civilization—or what's left of it," Kestel said. She had bound up her red hair in a tight braid against the dust from the road, but all of their cloaks were streaked with mud and dirt. A cold wind swept across what had, not long ago, been farm fields and grazing pastures. Kestel had drawn her scarf over her face, and it muffled her voice.

"I'll be happy for a warm supper and a pint or two of ale," Verran sighed. He shrugged. "What can I say? Give me good food, good beer, and a lock to pick, and I'm a happy man."

"Now that we have the last two of Valtyr's maps, do you

think we're any closer to being able to bring back the magic?" Kestel asked.

"I've been asking myself that over and over," Blaine said. "Maybe." He let out a long breath. "I wish Penhallow and Connor would show up. Maybe they'll know what we're missing."

"Riders, coming from the east!" Borya shouted.

Blaine reined in his horse as the group slowed. "How many?"

"Can't say for certain from this distance, but I'd say at least ten, maybe more," Piran replied. "And they've picked up speed."

"More of Pollard's men?" Kestel asked, frowning.

"No way to tell," Borya called back. "But we'd better get going if we want to stay ahead of them."

"Damn," Blaine said. His gaze swept the countryside around them. It was wide-open land, so there were no forests or hills to shelter them. Blaine had no intention of being pinned down in any of the barns. "Assume they're Pollard's men. Let's ride!"

Illarion and Zaryae called to their horses, and their pace immediately picked up. They were heading away from the riders and passed a large crossroads, so Blaine hoped against the odds that the riders might turn off, but a glance over his shoulder told him that the riders remained behind them and had increased their speed.

"They're gaining on us!" Piran shouted. "Faster!"

Blaine spurred his horse to a gallop as the others did the same. Illarion and Zaryae snapped the reins, and their wagon's horses moved more quickly than they would have thought possible. Still, a rearward glance told him that the riders had also begun to gallop, and all hope that the others were merely fellow travelers faded.

"We can't keep up this pace forever," Verran said, holding tight to his reins and leaning forward on his horse. "What happens when they catch up?"

"Let's keep that from happening," Blaine said, setting his jaw and spurring on his horse.

The rough road flew beneath their hooves. The cold air stung their faces, and steam rose from the horses' breath. Yet with every length of road they covered, the riders drew closer. They were too far from Glenreith to hope that Niklas's soldiers might ride to the rescue. A fight wasn't likely to end well, and yet the chances of avoiding a battle were decreasing rapidly.

"Gryps to the right!" Desya shouted and pointed to the sky.

Eight of the dark-winged monsters circled in the pale-gray winter sky to the right of the road. Piran cursed fluently, and Kestel muttered several choice imprecations under her breath. With no apparent livestock nearby to sate the gryps' appetite, it would not be long before they turned their attention to the travelers.

Another crossroads was fast approaching. They could veer left, away from the gryps, but the riders behind them could easily ride cross-country and cut over to confront them. Ride straight and they might avoid the gryps, although that was far from guaranteed. Turning right would take them directly under the gryps.

"Turn to the right!" Blaine shouted.

"Are you mad?" Piran demanded.

"Borya, Desya, Piran, grab the lanterns and get your arrows ready!" Blaine said.

"You *want* to fight the gryps?" Verran asked, astonished.

Kestel laughed, and it was clear from the look on her face that she had guessed Blaine's intent. "The enemy of my enemy is my friend," she quoted. "It's mad—but it just might work."

They veered off so sharply that the wagon's wheels lifted from the road on one side. The gryps saw their movement and winged their way toward the horses. Blaine tightened his hold on the reins as his horse protested riding straight toward the flying monsters.

Zaryae handed down two lanterns to Borya and Desya, who each readied an arrow. Piran rode up to join them and lit an arrow from theirs. The three men galloped to the front of the group as the gryps swooped toward them.

Three fiery arrows flew through the air. One arrow caught a gryp through the wing and it shrieked, careening away. Another arrow dug into the body of a second gryp, spattering the group with the creature's dark blood and attracting the attention of one of its fellows, which began to chase the wounded gryp for an easy kill. A third arrow pierced the wing of another gryp, which gave a maddened screech and dove for the archers. Borya had loosed the arrow but Desya was first to reload, and his second shot nearly took the gryp through its neck. Wary, the injured gryp winged away.

"Keep firing!" Blaine shouted. "Make them go after easier prey!"

Verran had a white-knuckled grip on his reins, but he had opened the bag of rocks he kept tied to the pommel of his saddle and lobbed missile after missile with enough accuracy to clip the nearest of the beasts in the body or wing, making them pull back. Kestel and Blaine had each drawn swords, although Blaine recalled his nearly fatal fight on the bridge to the lyceum and hoped it would not come down to combat. Illarion and Zaryae each had managed to light torches, which they brandished upraised, remembering the fate that had befallen Kata.

"It's working!" Kestel cried. "Keep it up!"

The gryps had drawn away to a higher altitude, and while they were circling, they did not dive. The riders were not far behind, but they were so intent on catching up with Blaine's group that they did not recognize the danger until the gryps shrieked and wheeled out of their formation, winging their way toward the riders. Too late, the riders realized their peril, but without ready access to fire and armed only with swords, they were soon beset by the gryps.

Blaine and the others did not wait to watch the aftermath. Fearing the gryps might still be hungry after finishing off the riders, Blaine's group rode hard until they could not hear the screams of the dying men or the hunting calls of the gryps. Finally, they slowed their horses.

"I really, really don't want to do that again," Piran said, patting his horse, which was breathing hard.

Blaine gave him a sidelong look. "I'd rather outrun them than fight them again, any day."

"I hope there's some whiskey at Glenreith, Mick," Verran said, "because after all we've been through, I'm going to need fortification."

"Hear, hear," Kestel seconded.

"Let's get back to Glenreith in one piece, and I'll be happy to serve up a whole cask of whiskey—or whatever we've got in the storeroom."

"I'd even drink some of Adger's rotgut," Piran grumbled. "Take the chill off and calm my nerves."

"After the turns we've taken, are we even on the right road for Glenreith?" Kestel asked.

Blaine stood in his stirrups and had a look around. The Great Fire had leveled some of the barns and mills that had once been landmarks, but the lay of the land was familiar. "We didn't go out of our way. Most of the roads in these parts led toward the mill and the town farther down the river." He pointed toward the east. "That way."

Cold, hungry, and more unnerved by the attack from the gryps and the riders than he wanted to let on, Blaine would be grateful to get home without further incident. He had no doubt his companions felt the same. They were wary as they rode the next few candlemarks, but to Blaine's great relief, neither riders nor gryps harried them.

Just before sundown, they reached a point in the road from which Blaine could spot the lights of Glenreith. "Almost there," he said. "And I'm certain Edward can find us some stew or soup to warm our bones."

"That's an awful lot of lights for just the manor, Mick," Piran observed. "Your aunt having a party?"

Blaine frowned and tried to make sense of what he saw. Finally, he began to chuckle. "Don't blame Judith. I think Niklas expanded his camp to put a perimeter around the manor wall."

"You've got good taste in friends, Mick, if I do say so myself," Verran said and grinned. "And when we get back to your place, I'll be the first to pour Niklas a drink."

Kestel kicked him in the shin. "It's Mick's whiskey you're pouring, you lout."

Verran grinned more broadly. "All the better!"

"Is that all?" Niklas asked sarcastically as Blaine finished recounting what had happened since they had ridden for Riker's Ferry and then to the lyceum.

They had gathered in the main parlor at Glenreith. Dawe and Mari sat near the fire. Judith was in one of the high-backed chairs, and Edward, as always, stood behind her. Niklas had sprinted up from the camp when word came that Blaine had returned, and now he leaned against a side table.

Blaine stood near the fireplace, and Kestel was curled in a nearby chair. Piran sat cross-legged near the hearth polishing his knives. Verran worked a rope finger puzzle over and over again. Illarion and the rest of the troupe were busy getting themselves and their wagons settled into a small camp within the outer wall.

Blaine grinned. "No. We also found these." Kestel produced the new disks they had found as well as the map and fragment, and the wood-bound manuscript.

Niklas looked askance at him. "You're looting libraries now?"

Blaine had maneuvered a small table into the center of the parlor, and Kestel laid out the new items as Blaine gave the others a quick recap of their importance.

"So because of the map, you think this Valshoa is a real place?" Judith asked.

"Vigus Quintrel thought so," Blaine replied. "And it's possible that the Knights of Esthrane did, too."

Edward frowned. "The Knights were destroyed a long time ago."

"Not all of them." They turned to look at Niklas. He recounted the ghostly visitor he had glimpsed a few nights before.

"I wish Penhallow would show up," Blaine said. "I have the feeling he has pieces that would fill in the gap."

Geir had been listening from near the door to the parlor, casually on guard. "He and Connor are on their way to meet us here."

Kestel looked up at Blaine. "Connor has the other disk and the second map," she said, her eyes alight with excitement. "We don't know what else they've collected. With those pieces, we could have everything we need."

"It's also possible that at least some of the Knights of Esthrane also sought refuge in Valshoa," Geir added.

"Yeah, but whose side are the Knights on?" Niklas asked.

"The man I saw—if he wasn't a ghost—could have been protecting us or threatening us."

"Maybe Penhallow will know," Geir said.

"Speaking of Penhallow," Niklas said, "the spy we interrogated seemed to believe Penhallow had some connection with Traher Voss, the mercenary." He grinned. "Voss is the second craziest soldier I've ever heard about."

Blaine shot him a questioning look. "Who's the craziest?"

Niklas looked over to where Piran was sitting. "He is."

Kestel stood and sashayed over to Piran and made a show of lazily running her fingers across his bald head. "Piran, dear. If we're really heading into battle, perhaps now is a good time to tell us what actually landed you in Velant."

Piran leveled a glare at Niklas. "It's not a story for proper company."

"We're not proper company," Judith informed him. "Please continue."

Blaine grinned. Even he had never heard Piran's story, and from the look on Niklas's face, it was going to be interesting.

Piran set his sword aside. "I was fighting with a regiment near the border of the Lesser Kingdoms. We were supposed to put down a local rebellion, but the conditions were terrible. The mountains were damn near impassable, the locals were hostile, and we ended up foraging for food because our supply line got cut."

Piran sighed. "Our captain was a soft little fop who didn't want to leave his tent. The only time he ever saw battle, he peed himself. He refused to give the order to fall back because he didn't want to lose face, and meanwhile, we were hungry and the lines were closing around us."

He grimaced. "We ended up having to fetch water from a stream, and the water gave us all dysentery."

Kestel snickered, and Piran glared at her. "You don't understand. Our regiment got the runs, down to the last man, worse than your worst nightmare. We couldn't stop shitting." He gave a contrite glance in Judith's direction, but Judith merely nodded.

"So there we were, surrounded by hostile mountain people, cut off from reinforcements, and no one could keep their pants up because of the runs. And the bloody locals attacked," Piran recounted.

"I don't see how that got you court-martialed," Kestel said.

Niklas was laughing so hard he was almost doubled over. "Tell her the rest of it, Piran." He looked at the others. "This is why he's a legend in the king's army."

Piran sighed. "Our bloody fop of a captain wouldn't give the order to attack. I didn't want to die. So I clobbered him with the pommel of my sword, stole his cloak, hat, and horse, and led the troops out." He cleared his throat. "The men followed, but they were all still sick as dogs. We fought the battle pantless."

"You what?" Kestel whooped.

"We were in no mood to be attacked," Piran retorted. "We were a bunch of miserable sons of bitches looking for someone to take it out on."

"When the locals saw themselves being attacked by a regiment of pantless men covered in shit, they were so startled they ran away and surrendered," Niklas said, holding his stomach as he laughed.

"'Startled' doesn't quite do it justice," Piran said with a defensive tone in his voice. "We won the battle. Our cowardly commander lived through the fight. And what thanks did we get? The regiment got disciplined, and I got court-martialed for assaulting and impersonating an officer and stealing his horse and was sent to Velant."

Kestel was laughing so hard she sat down on the floor, and the others echoed her laughter. Even Judith and Edward chuckled heartily.

Verran wiped his eyes and struggled for breath. "I can't believe you held out on us! Blimey, that's one of the best stories I've ever heard."

Piran looked simultaneously disgruntled by the revelation and gratified by the story's reception. "It's not exactly the crowning achievement I want to be remembered for," he grumbled. "Now do you see why I wasn't keen on telling them?"

Blaine caught his breath, still chuckling. *I can't remember the last time I laughed that hard*, he thought. *I'd forgotten how good it feels.*

With a sigh, Blaine turned his attention back to the maps on the table. "Now that we know Piran's deep dark secret," he said, "and I think we can safely dismiss the idea of using that particular tactic," he said with a glance in Piran's direction. "Perhaps we'd better plan our strategy."

Niklas, too, had sobered. "There's a problem. The spy we interrogated confirmed that Reese and Pollard know it's a race. Pollard's been looting universities and libraries and torturing mages. Reese has him stealing old, magical objects."

"Damn." Blaine let out a long breath. "I was afraid of that. It was the only reason for Pollard having an assassin in Riker's Ferry: He had to know about the null places and that means he knows about the places of power, too."

"But we're the ones with the maps," Kestel said.

Blaine grimaced. "For all we know, he's found copies. Or found a mage who remembered old stories. We've got to assume that we'll encounter them on the way to Valshoa. Reese might even have possession of some of the disks."

"That could be a problem if you actually need the disks for the ritual," Kestel said.

Blaine shrugged. "We've got no way of knowing what will work at Valshoa until we get there."

"We tried that approach at Mirdalur, Mick," Verran said. "It didn't work so well."

"The thing is, if the solstice is a time when the magic is easier to bind, we don't have much choice," Blaine said. "The solstice is just over a week away. It's going to take several days to get to the place indicated on the map—assuming we can find it." He paused. "And assuming we don't have to fight Pollard every step of the way."

"You've got support from my men," Niklas pledged. "Although we should leave some of them here to protect Glenreith, in case Pollard decides to strike again."

"I'd feel better if we knew where we stood with those ghost knights," Dawe said. "But I've been busy in the forge. Mari's been a big help. I've gotten a number of modified crossbows ready."

"What do you know about Voss?" Blaine asked, directing his question to Geir.

Geir thought for a moment. "He's Penhallow's man, as much as Traher Voss belongs to anyone. Before the Great Fire, he was one of Lanyon's best sources of information."

"Any idea why he and his mercs weren't at the war front?" Niklas asked with an edge in his voice.

Geir shrugged. "Nothing for certain. I do know that, in the final months, Lanyon feared a mage strike. He may have gotten word to Voss and told him to pull back."

"Would have been nice if he'd warned the rest of us," Niklas said darkly.

Geir turned his gaze on Niklas. "Penhallow did his best to warn the king. Ask Connor when he arrives—he'll tell you firsthand. Merrill wasn't getting accurate information from his generals, and in the end, he underestimated Edgar of Meroven until it was too late."

Niklas looked away. "A lot of good men died in the war," he said quietly. "A lot of my men."

"We can't change what happened during the war," Kestel said, "but it would be nice to have all the help we can get now." She looked to Geir. "Do you think Voss will throw in with us?"

Geir grimaced. "No idea. Let's wait for Penhallow to arrive. If he's seen Voss recently, he may know his plans."

For the next several candlemarks, they pored over the maps, debating possible routes to reach the location Blaine had grown certain was Valshoa. Finally, Niklas rose.

"I'm glad you're back safe, Blaine," he said. "I need to get back to the camp. Keep me posted about the plans to head for Valshoa." He fixed Blaine with a stare. "This time, a contingent of my men will go with you. No more running off on your own."

Blaine chuckled, but after the danger they had faced on their last journey, he was more than willing to agree. "We won't leave without you," he promised. "And with luck, perhaps Penhallow will bring reinforcements."

Niklas bade them all good night, and Kestel gathered up the charts and amulets. Judith rose and went over to where Blaine stood.

"There's one more thing that happened while you were gone," she said, her expression grave.

Blaine sobered, and Kestel moved to stand next to him. "What is it?" Blaine asked. *It's got to be something to do with Carr*, he thought. *He's not here, and nobody's mentioned him all night.*

"Carr's been struck with the madness," Judith said.

Blaine let out a long breath. *I thought maybe he had run off in anger, gotten in another fight, torn up the camp or the manor. But madness?*

Kestel laid a hand on Blaine's arm. "What happened?" Blaine asked. He listened quietly as Judith and Dawe took turns recounting Carr's attack.

"I didn't want to hurt him," Dawe ended his story apologetically. "I know he's your brother, Mick. But he was swinging like he meant to bash in my head. I managed to get him down before he hurt Mari or did any real damage to me."

Blaine saw the bruise that was fading on the side of Dawe's face and felt a flush of shame, although he knew in his heart he could not have prevented the attack. He met Mari's gaze, and the mixture of sadness and challenge in her eyes made him look away. *She's got a right to be disappointed*, he thought. *Since I've come back, I seem to have brought hardship with me. They deserve better.*

"The madness isn't anyone's fault, Mick," Kestel said quietly. "It strikes wherever it chooses."

"It would have been worse if he'd been taken by the madness somewhere else, while they were on the road," Judith said, and her voice sounded weary. "At least he's in his own home, where we can care for him until it runs its course."

That realization shook Blaine to the bone. *She means, until he dies*, he thought. *Unless Carr is very, very lucky. And that kind of luck hasn't been with our family lately.*

A few candlemarks later, Glenreith was quiet. Piran had announced an impromptu game of cards in the kitchen, complete with a bottle of whiskey he had liberated from the lyceum. Niklas was already back in the camp and Judith had begged off, but Dawe, Kestel, and Verran insisted that Blaine join them, and to Blaine's surprise, Edward and Mari showed up as well.

As it turned out, Edward was quite good at games of chance, with skill that on occasion trumped Piran's sleight of hand. Kestel and the others, knowing Piran's penchant for cheating, had long ago perfected compensatory strategies. Mari watched from a seat nearby, and as the game progressed, she edged closer to where Dawe sat.

"I think you've met your match, Piran," Kestel chuckled as Edward gathered his winnings.

"Personally, I'm impressed," Blaine said. "I've seen a side of Edward I'd never glimpsed before," he said.

Edward colored. "In the years since your departure, it's required a variety of methods to keep the manor supplied," he said, gathering his dignity with the coppers.

Mari chuckled. "What Edward means is that we've begged, borrowed, wagered, and stolen to make ends meet. It's the new fashion."

Edward blushed deeper. "It sounds quite unsavory when you put it that way."

Piran clapped Edward on the shoulder. "Personally, I applaud a man who can adjust with the times. And I especially applaud any man who can get the better of me at cards." He peered enticingly at Edward and grinned. "Best two out of three?"

Edward smiled self-consciously. "The real secret to success at cards, Captain Rowse, is to quit when one is ahead."

Piran knocked back the rest of his whiskey. "You know, that's the part I never mastered."

The group dispersed, but Blaine managed to fall into step with Mari. "I'm sorry I wasn't here to keep Carr from causing trouble."

Mari sighed. "Carr's caused trouble for a long time, Blaine. I think he'd rather be angry than sad, and maybe he got stuck that way. The madness just pushed him a little further. He might have gone there anyway on his own."

"I want to look in on him," Blaine said.

Mari looked at him worriedly. "It can't help."

"I know. But I need to see." They paused as they reached Carr's room, and the guard at the door nodded assent, then unlocked the door and stood to the side.

Carr lay on his bed, head turned to one side, wrists and ankles secured with ropes to the bedposts. Other than the rise and fall of his chest, he did not move. Even from the doorway, in the moonlight that fell through the window, Blaine could see bruises and scratches on Carr's face from the fight. Wordlessly, he and Mari left the room, and the guard secured the door and took up his place on watch.

Neither Blaine nor Mari spoke until they had moved down the hallway. "It's not your fault," Mari said.

Blaine glanced at her. "I didn't say anything."

Mari managed a sad smile. "You don't have to. You were thinking it."

Blaine looked away. "Yeah, maybe I was." He changed the subject. "How's Robbe doing?"

Mari perked up at the mention of her son. "He's nearly four years old, and the picture of his father," she said, her smile growing sad again.

"Do you miss Evaret?" Blaine asked.

Mari looked down at the floor as they walked. At the end of the hallway, double doors opened onto a balcony. They paused in the moonlight, and Mari looked out through the glass, wiping it free of frost. "Yes, although it gets a bit easier with time. Hearing confirmation from Niklas was hard, although by now, in my heart, I had accepted that he wasn't going to come home."

She paused. "I grew quite fond of him, and it was awful to hear nothing for so long." Mari looked away. "The truth is, he was a very good friend but not the love of my life. The marriage was a matter of practicality for both of us," she said. The cold, blue light cast her face in angles and shadows, and Blaine saw once more just how much the last years had affected her.

"It wasn't really love, if such a thing exists," she said quietly. "He was willing to have me, after all that happened. I was willing to accept, since he wasn't a rotter. He tried to do right by me and Robbe. If the war hadn't taken him, I think things would have turned out passably well."

She paused. "Do you miss Carensa?"

Blaine looked away. "I was heartsick when I went to Velant. As the years passed, everything here seemed like a dim memory. I was fond of Selane, and if the fever hadn't taken her, I think we would have been happy. But it wasn't love."

Mari was still looking out over the moonlit landscape. From here, Blaine could see the hills all the way to the river. "Do you fancy Dawe?" he asked.

Mari blushed and looked down. "Are you going to warn me off him?"

Blaine chuckled. "If you're serious, I was going to encourage you. He's a good man. Unlike the rest of us, he didn't commit any crimes. Got framed by a jealous rival because he was too good at his craft. His wife left him—for the rival. He'd take good care of you and Robbe."

Mari gave a faint smile. "We've talked a couple of times. He's…nice." She was quiet for a while, then looked up. "What about you and Kestel?"

It was Blaine's turn to look away. "It all sort of depends on how things go with the magic, doesn't it?" *And whether or not I'm still alive.*

Mari stretched up to kiss him on the cheek. "I'd worry less about you, maybe, if you were married to an assassin. Someone to watch your back."

Blaine kissed the top of her head, as he had done since she was a small child. "Should I consider that your blessing?"

Mari chuckled. "Mine, and Judith's, and Edward's, too. We all think it's about time you settled down. And before you ask, no one's concerned about anything in her past. That would be a little silly, coming from this family, wouldn't it?"

Blaine saw Mari to her room and said good night. He thought about returning to his own room, but there was too much bouncing around in his mind to make it likely he would fall asleep. Instead, he took the back stairs down through the kitchen, a route he was certain would afford few interruptions.

At this time of night, the kitchen was dark, save for the banked fire in the massive hearth. Blaine paused for a moment and breathed in the comforting smells of baked bread and wood smoke, of roasted meat and onions. It smelled like the best of his memories of home, and for a few seconds, he let that warmth enfold him.

Reluctantly, he moved on, slipping through the kitchen into the darkened parlor. Everyone had gone to bed. Blaine lit one of the lanterns, stirred the embers into a fire, and poured himself a glass of whiskey. He settled into one of the chairs by the hearth, feeling the effects of the dangerous ride back from the lyceum.

The whiskey burned down his throat, but it did not warm him. He knew that there was no real question that he would go to look for Valshoa and try to find Vigus Quintrel. *If it were just risking myself, the matter would be settled. It's everyone else who'll go with me, who'll put themselves in danger. Gods above, I've seen enough death. I don't want their blood on my head.*

"I thought I might find you here." Kestel's voice startled him, and Blaine stirred from his thoughts to set his glass aside and rise from his chair.

"You're up late."

Kestel shrugged. "Couldn't sleep."

Blaine managed a wan smile. "Neither could I." Kestel was still dressed in the gown she had worn at dinner, a dark emerald dress that played up the deep red of her hair. Though frayed and worn in places, the satin in her dress still shimmered in the firelight. For several moments, neither of them said anything, and Blaine knew that the incident at the lyceum hung between them, although there had been no private moment since then for discussion.

We can't go on like this. It's worse than having said nothing, Blaine thought. He drew a deep breath, discovering that it was much harder to find the courage to broach the subject than to ready himself for battle.

"What you said…at the lyceum. Did you mean it?" His voice was quiet, and he wondered if she could hear the uncertainty he felt. *Perhaps she'll say it was the tension of the moment, that she was afraid I was going to die. Maybe I read more into it than she meant, and she's trying to figure out how to set me right.*

Kestel walked closer to the fireplace, but she did not meet his gaze. "I meant it," she said softly. "Did you?"

It was strange, Blaine thought, to see Kestel look uncertain. Even in Velant, despite the worst that happened to them, she had always seemed utterly sure of herself, completely in command. "Yes," he said, moving a step closer. "I'd been thinking about it for a long time, but I couldn't figure out how to say anything in case you didn't feel the same."

Kestel finally met his gaze. "You were dead, Mick. For a moment or two, you were gone. I'd been afraid to tell you, for fear I'd lose your friendship, and then I lost you anyway. Almost."

Blaine reached out to touch her cheek. "I didn't die. And I didn't run away."

Kestel lifted a hand to clasp his. "You don't have to go to Valshoa. You don't have to prove anything to anyone." She looked down. "I'm afraid for you, Mick. I'm afraid that the price to bring back the magic will be too high."

Blaine drew her into his arms, folding her against his chest, and to his pleased amazement, she did not draw back. Her arms slipped around his waist, and she leaned against him. "I'm a bad risk to fall in love with," he murmured, laying his cheek against her head.

"Too late." She paused. "This would be so much simpler if we were still in Edgeland."

Blaine tangled his fingers in her hair. "Because freezing our asses off with no sunlight for six months is so romantic?" He chuckled.

Kestel sighed. "No. Because I saw a way for it to work for us, without a war, without our pasts getting in the way."

Blaine tipped her chin so she met his gaze. "I can't avoid the battle that's coming. Reese and Pollard won't let the matter drop, even if I don't go to Valshoa. As for what happened in the past, yours or mine, I made peace with that in Velant."

Kestel slipped out of his arms and moved closer to the fire. "The problem is, I want more than I have a right to." She looked back at him defiantly. "If we begin this, I want more than to be your lover or your mistress. I'm only interested in playing for keeps, and while that could work in Edgeland, where we were on our own, I don't know how that can possibly work here."

"Why not?"

Kestel gave him a sidelong look, as if he had missed the obvious. "Because you're a lord, and I'm a courtesan. That defines what's possible, and I'm not willing to settle."

"Good. Because neither am I."

Kestel's gaze was wary. "Meaning?"

Blaine moved to stand behind her and gently turned her to look at him. "The way things appear to be shaping up, I'm not a lord—I'm a warlord. And I can't think of a more perfect partner for a warlord than an assassin." He leaned down to kiss her, savoring the moment.

"Your family—" she protested.

"Will learn to live with it," Blaine finished. "There is no court, no nobility: no rules. Donderath is like Edgeland, a barren land where we can make of it what we will. And I want you with me." *If I live through the battle*, he added silently.

CHAPTER TWENTY-EIGHT

"WHY DID PENHALLOW COME TO THE CASTLE?"
Pollard delivered a sharp kick, and the bound man on
the floor groaned in pain as Pollard's boot connected with his
ribs. Pollard's guards had already taken their turn at the man
who was bruised from head to toe, his clothing reduced to rags.

Lars Lynge, former seneschal of Quillarth Castle, lay in
a heap on the floor. His shock of white hair was filthy and
streaked with blood, and his eyes were purpled and swollen
almost shut.

"Answer me!" Pollard ordered, making sure that his boot
connected with the man's hip.

"He didn't tell me."

"I don't believe you," Pollard said, and this time he landed a
kick to the older man's knee that elicited a howl of pain. "Tell
me what you know."

"Penhallow stayed a few nights. He kept his own counsel."

Two of Pollard's soldiers dragged the battered man across the
room and dumped him into a chair. "Tell me about Penhallow
and Treven Lowrey," Pollard said in an icy voice.

"They came to the castle for refuge," Lynge replied. "Then they left. I don't know where they went."

"What did they do while they were in the castle?" Pollard tapped his toe against the stone floor, an indication that he would not wait forever to get the information he sought.

Lynge drew a labored breath. "They wanted to know the history of Donderath."

Pollard swore and kicked a wooden crate so hard that it skidded across the stone floor. He swung around and leaned down close to the seneschal's swollen face. "What were they researching?"

"History. Nothing but history," Lynge wheezed.

"What kind of history?" Pollard's voice was dangerously even.

"The old families of Donderath," Lynge replied. His skin was ashen where it wasn't bruised, and his lips had taken on a bluish hint. Pollard guessed that the beating had gone harder on the seneschal than his men intended. *No real loss. We were going to kill him anyhow. It's one more obstacle out of the way.*

Reese's *talishte* had arrived a week after Penhallow and the Knights of Esthrane left. Despite the castle's guards, it had been easy for Reese's men to break through the defenses. Pollard looked around the shambles of the castle's main dining room. The Great Fire had damaged the castle badly, but he would make a thorough search. He planned to be certain that nothing valuable to Lowrey—or to Blaine McFadden's cause—might still remain.

Pentreath Reese had slipped soundlessly into the room and stood in the shadows at the back.

"What did he want to know about the old families?" Pollard asked, gritting his teeth. *He was looking for the Lords of the Blood*, he thought. *The question is: What did he discover that Reese doesn't already know?*

"Lowrey was a thief. He was looking for valuable items," Lynge said. "To sell, I imagine."

From the look in Lynge's eyes, Pollard was sure that the man had no illusions of leaving alive. "What did Lowrey steal?"

"Anything he could," Lynge said. A fit of coughing took him, and blood flecked his spittle.

"Like what?" Pollard said, barely keeping his temper in check. He was certain Lynge was lying. Yet there was nothing to be gained by further injuring the man, and everything to be lost if it hastened his death before he could share what little he knew.

"When you stop having information for me, you stop having a reason to live," Pollard grated. "I'm going to look forward to gibbing you like a fish."

"No."

Reese's voice was sharp, and the command carried compulsion, freezing Pollard in place. Pollard swore under his breath, and when the compulsion eased, he leaned back, away from the old man. Lynge did not make a sound, but for the first time, there was real fear in his eyes.

In a few swift steps, Reese stood beside Pollard. He snatched up Lynge's thin arm so hard that the man came off the chair a few inches, dislocating his shoulder. Lynge gasped as Reese bowed his head and sank his fangs into the cleft of Lynge's elbow.

Pollard forced down a shudder. Reese was even more savage in the blood-taking than he had been with Pollard, making a gash like a hungry wolf. The old man's lips moved, but Reese paid no heed. Reese continued to feed long past the point that Pollard knew the *talishte* had enough blood to provide the needed information. The seneschal convulsed, then fell back, limp. Reese dropped the bony arm, and the body slid to the floor.

"Lowrey and Penhallow believe Vigus Quintrel knew the

secret of the origin of magic," Reese commented. He withdrew a kerchief from his vest and dabbed at the blood that stained his mouth, and even in the lantern light, Pollard could see a ruddy flush that colored Reese's cheeks from the feeding.

"Did they find anything that would locate Quintrel?" Pollard asked.

Reese stroked his chin as he thought, as if sorting through the memories he had gathered from Lynge's blood. "Penhallow certainly thought so," he said. "They were interested in the thirteen old families, the Lords of the Blood." His expression darkened. "And disks. Obsidian disks that Penhallow believed had something to do with raising the magic."

"What about McFadden?"

Reese's anger was clear in his face. "From what Lynge saw, it's clear Penhallow thinks McFadden can restore the magic." He fell silent as he parsed through the other memories he had stolen. "Interesting," he mused.

"What?"

Reese's voice was an angry growl. "Now I know why Penhallow took on Bevin Connor, Garnoc's servant. He's a medium." He let loose with a stream of invective. "That explains why things went so unexpectedly well for Penhallow with the Wraith Lord and why the Wraith Lord sided with him. He wants a body to possess."

"Perhaps Lynge was mistaken," Pollard said.

"Not in this. I could feel Lynge's fear: He didn't like the idea that the dead could possess the living. Damn," Reese said. "This complicates matters. The Wraith Lord should not have been involved."

"Did Penhallow learn anything else at the castle?" Pollard pressed.

Reese began to pace. "Yes. They went into the crypts

beneath the castle—into the forbidden tombs of the Knights of Esthrane. Penhallow found several of the disks, and he took them with him." Reese's temper was clearly at a breaking point, and Pollard made sure he was out of convenient reach.

"If the disks alone could restore the magic, they would have done so already," Pollard said.

Reese wheeled on him. "Not if they must be used by a Lord of the Blood."

"Blaine McFadden."

"Yes."

Pollard frowned. "Garnoc's servant—did he learn anything from the spirits?"

Reese frowned. "He was receiving information from someone, but Lynge was unclear about the source." He slammed his fist into a wooden table, and his *talishte* strength smashed the thick wood. "It means Penhallow has an advantage, and a dangerous one." Reese squared his shoulders. "He must be stopped."

"And McFadden?"

"McFadden is more dangerous than I thought. I want him brought to me before he gets any closer to a way to restore the magic." He began to pace. "If McFadden is chasing the old mages, it might explain why he turned up in Riker's Ferry and again at the lyceum, then eluded my agents there."

Reese turned to Pollard's guards. "Take the body, and leave us." He was silent until the men had dragged the corpse from the room.

"Why Riker's Ferry? It's in the middle of nowhere," Pollard said.

Reese began to pace once more. "The mages I interrogated said that Valtyr had a theory about how magic worked. He was quite interested in the null places and the places of strong magic. They say that's what his maps showed. McFadden's interest makes me quite sure that at least one of those maps has found its way into his hands. It would also account for his unhealthy fascination with

Mirdalur." Reese paused. "If Quintrel's obsessions are driving McFadden, and the Knights are now assisting Penhallow, then perhaps we should look more closely at Valshoa."

"Valshoa is a myth," Pollard challenged.

Reese shrugged. "'Myths' are what mortals call events they only half-remember. Valtyr was not the only one to believe Valshoa existed. It was rumored that at least some of the Knights of Esthrane sought out Valshoa when they were forced into exile."

Pollard began to laugh. "That's what McFadden is searching for? A place out of stories told around a campfire?"

Reese's gaze was cold. "Laugh if you like. But McFadden returned from Edgeland for a reason. It's possible he might have encountered Grimur there." He made an expression of distaste. "Probable, if Lanyon Penhallow was meddling. I find it particularly interesting that Garnoc's man also ended up in Edgeland and returned with McFadden and now seems to have become Penhallow's servant." He paused. "I do not believe in coincidence."

"And now, rumors that the Knights of Esthrane have returned, in the kingdom's direst hour," Pollard said, skepticism clear in his voice.

"Not rumor," Reese snapped. "They fought for the Wraith Lord and destroyed many of our men.

"What have you learned from your man in Riker's Ferry?" Reese asked. "Has he seen McFadden?"

Pollard stepped back without thinking and steeled himself before answering. "He's disappeared. But he was last seen being taken by a *talishte* who was with McFadden."

Reese turned on him with a glare, and in his eyes, Pollard saw barely restrained fury. "You continue to disappoint me. McFadden is free and is still a step ahead of you."

Pollard met Reese's gaze. "Not for much longer."

CHAPTER TWENTY-NINE

—

"WE'RE UNDER ATTACK!"

The shout woke Niklas from his sleep, and the sound of the camp rousing for battle snapped him instantly alert. He rolled from his cot, dressed in a rush, and belted on his sword. By the time he cleared the doorway of his tent, he could see his soldiers already mobilizing.

Thank the gods I decided to stay down here with the men instead of up at Glenreith, Niklas thought and gave a worried glance over his shoulder. Up on the hill, Glenreith loomed dark and silent.

"Report!" Niklas collared one of the soldiers who ran toward where the men were forming up into battle ranks.

"Don't know who or why, but we've got a godsdamned army closing in on us, sir," the man reported, his face flushed with excitement.

"Shit," Niklas muttered.

"Captain!" Niklas looked up as Ayers strode in his direction.

"Tell me what we're up against," Niklas replied, falling into step as he and Ayers made their way toward where the men were massing. He could hear his lieutenants rallying the soldiers, assigning posts, readying for battle.

"Best guess is that it's Pollard, and he's got more men than we do," Ayers replied tersely. "Wouldn't be surprised if he intends to take out our camp, then march on Glenreith."

"*Talishte*?" Niklas asked.

Ayers grinned. "That's one thing that went right, sir. They sent *talishte* against us as a sneak attack and didn't expect us to have biters of our own. We drove them back, and the scouts had a chance to report that there's a large force headed our way."

Niklas nodded grimly. "Now we get to see if all our preparation was worth a damn. I'm glad we've gotten some reinforcements."

Though they had not been camped long, Niklas's men had been busy in the time they had been at Arengarte. One contingent had dug out and secured the old cellars as a precaution against magic storms. The other three contingents had been tasked with fortifying both Arengarte and Glenreith. Both Blaine's manor house and Niklas's family home were included within the defensive line Niklas and his commanders had devised.

More important, word had spread that Niklas's straggler army had returned. Since they set up camp, two other bands of soldiers found their way to Arengarte and asked to swear allegiance to Niklas's lord and join his regiment. *Glad to have the extra help*, Niklas thought. *Something tells me we're going to need it.*

"Use the signal lantern to get word to Glenreith," Niklas ordered.

Niklas's troops had turned a large rectangular area connecting Arengarte and Glenreith into a no-man's-land, with a heavily defended perimeter. Four lines of defense were designed to make an advance as slow and costly as possible for attackers and to provide defenders with time to inflict a steep toll on their enemies. Only one clear path led to the camp and past it, to Glenreith, and it was well guarded and easily blocked.

The forest had yielded a wealth of trees from which abatises were formed: tangles of large trees felled or positioned so their sharp branches faced the enemy, impeding advance. Behind the abatises, Niklas's soldiers had dug deep trenches lined with sharpened pikes. Caltrops had been fashioned from old nails harvested from ruined buildings and bent into wicked, four-pronged shapes that always had one pointed end skyward, ready to impale a boot or a hoof. The caltrops were spread lavishly across the land on all sides of the defended area, where they became nearly invisible in the dry grass.

Behind the abatises and the trenches were line upon line of X-shaped wooden obstacles, logs studded with sharpened pikes designed to stop a mounted attack and slow men on foot. Behind the pike-logs the men had thrown up an embankment to hide archers who could pick off invaders as they wormed their way through the defenses. In the heart of the camp, small, mobile catapults were armed with a nearly inexhaustible supply of rocks to lob at an advancing force.

"Let them come," Niklas muttered. "We're as ready as we'll ever be."

"Captain Theilsson!"

Niklas turned, and in the blink of an eye, Gennedy, one of the *talishte* fighters Geir had assigned to the camp, seemed to appear out of nowhere to stand before him. *I'm never going to get used to that damn* talishte *speed*, Niklas thought, simultaneously grateful that, thanks to Geir, he could claim some of that advantage on his side.

"We struck camp, and the open area is secure. My archers are in place," Gennedy reported.

Niklas nodded. "Good, good. We've got to hold Pollard here, keep him from getting anywhere close to Glenreith." He gave a wolfish grin. "The more of Pollard's men we kill tonight, the fewer we'll have to deal with later."

Gennedy's smile mirrored his, even more predatory with his visible fangs. "I have no love for Reese's men. We'll clear the skies for you."

After the pounding Geir's *talishte* had given their camp over Blaine's capture, finding a way to avoid *talishte*-inflicted casualties had become a high priority. Once Geir's vampires and Niklas's men had patched up their misunderstanding, they had worked together to find a way to protect the camp—and Glenreith—from similar attack.

Niklas had a small number of *talishte* fighters, far too few to risk in hand-to-hand combat if it could be avoided. Instead, he had matched the *talishte* with his best mortal archers to make aerial attack expensive. Striking the tents and hiding them in the stone cellars meant the camp became far less vulnerable to fire.

Now it's time to see if it all works the way it's supposed to work, Niklas thought as he strode down the lines. His soldiers were the final defense, and they were ready.

"Pull!" Across the camp, the command echoed as one after the other, the catapult teams lobbed their missiles at the dark shapes just beyond the abatis line. Niklas heard the whirr and squeal of the mechanisms, the thunk as the central wooden rod slammed against the wooden mechanism, sending its deadly contents flying through the air.

High overhead, Niklas could make out more of the dark shapes. Arrows sang through the air as the *talishte* archers let fly and reloaded almost faster than mortal sight could follow. Both the archers and the catapult soldiers had a second round of defense, with oil-soaked rags and chunks of wood that could turn arrows and catapult rocks into fiery projectiles.

"They're attacking from the west, sir." The messenger was Taras, one of Niklas's men.

Niklas nodded, still watching the sky warily as volleys of arrows disappeared into the darkness. "How many?"

"Hard to say, Captain. Estimate about seventy-five on horseback, and at least as many on foot."

"Damn," Niklas muttered. "Are the battlements holding?"

Taras nodded. "For now."

"Has Glenreith seen the warning lantern?" Niklas asked, casting a worried glance toward the dark outline of the walled manor on the hill behind them.

"Aye. They've readied themselves." Niklas could see that, despite the hour, torchlight blazed along the archers' walks around the top of Glenreith's walls.

"Sir, you'd better see this!" Niklas and Taras both turned to follow the voice. Ayers pointed toward the western fortifications, where one line of the abatis had been set aflame.

"It was just a matter of time," Niklas muttered. "Did the men soak the wood first?"

Ayers nodded. "Most of the trees were still green when we felled them, so they won't take like tinder. But sooner or later, they'll take."

Niklas sighed. He'd never thought Pollard a fool, and any decent military man knew that fire and grappling hooks could dismantle even the best-laid abatis. All it took was time.

Ayers seemed to guess his thoughts. "We've moved the catapults, so we're making it difficult for them. They may be able to set the fires from a distance, but the grappling hooks will bring them out into the open where we can pound them." Satisfaction gleamed in his eyes, and a cold chill went down Niklas's back.

Does Pollard have any idea who he's taken on? Niklas wondered. *My men may not have been the king's crack troops, but they've been beaten and gotten back up again, marched across half a continent, and lived to tell the tale. They'd like nothing better than to give someone the whipping they couldn't deliver in person to Meroven.*

A man's scream echoed in the darkness. There was the sound of flapping cloth, and a sickening thud as a body fell from the sky with several arrows protruding from his back. A few yards farther, another body fell, and a cheer rose from Niklas's men. Two soldiers ran out with torches and lit the downed bodies of enemy *talishte*, which caught fire like dry leaves and burned with the smell of putrid meat, flashing into flame and then dissolving into cinders. Niklas watched the burning corpses with a mixture of satisfaction and dismay.

What do our talishte *allies think?* Niklas wondered. Yet he could not disavow his own feral pleasure at seeing such a nearly invincible opponent brought down. And it was not lost on him that the arrows were most likely fired by the undead fighters who had been assigned to protect his camp. *Reese and Penhallow have been enemies for a long time*, he thought. *Maybe they were itching for a reason to fight, and we just offered a convenient excuse.*

Two large sections of the abatis were on fire, with flames reaching high into the night sky. As Niklas watched, three other sections caught fire. Taras and Ayers returned to the line, but one after another, more runners came bearing news. Niklas squinted, trying to make out anything on the horizon, but Pollard's men were still too far away. *For now*, Niklas thought darkly. *Pollard's not the type to give up. But with luck, by the time he manages to break through, we'll have whittled his forces down to size.*

Niklas knew he was supposed to remain visible by pacing along the lines, cheering on his men. Yet he itched for hand-to-hand combat, the sheer physical release that came with launching himself into the fray and working out his anger with the blade of his sword.

The only warning Niklas had was the sound of rushing air, enough to cause his battle-heightened nerves to throw him sideways as a round object fell from the sky. The sphere exploded on impact, sending a rain of fire and shards in a wide burst. Another explosion sounded seconds later, then another and another, with a deadly hail of broken pottery and flame.

"What in Raka is that? Where are the archers?" Niklas shouted, beating out the places where his cloak had caught fire. One of the catapult crews had taken a direct hit; the men rolled on the ground, trying to douse the fires that burned their flesh while the catapult itself was a total loss.

"The archers are still firing, but Reese's *talishte* are dropping those godsdamned fire bombs from so high up, our arrows can't reach them!" Gennedy shouted.

Niklas stooped to examine the remains of the nearest bomb. Charred shards told him all he needed to know. *Some kind of pottery vessel, filled with oil, with a rag for a wick and lit just before it's dropped. When the flames hit the oil, it burns and spreads.*

Niklas helped drag the survivors free of the fires, then joined the men shoveling dirt and rocks onto the patches of still-flaming oil. Thanks to the precaution of striking the camp at the first sign of attack, the main area was free of nearly everything except catapults, archers' blinds, and a few shielded campfires. Their tents, provisions, and other materials awaited them in the underground storage chambers. *If we survive to retrieve them*, Niklas thought.

He stared up at the night sky, watching for the next round of firebombs. By now, his men knew to watch overhead, spot the falling objects, and scatter. Even so, fires flared across the inner camp, and men screamed in agony as the splattered oil set them aflame.

Niklas cast a worried glance toward Arengarte. *Thank Mother Esthrane that we thought to stable the horses in the granary threshing floor instead of out in the open. Arengarte, with its stone walls, is likely to survive. We'll have plenty of food and enough water from the mill to outlast the siege.*

"Look up!" one of the soldiers shouted. Niklas dodged for cover and looked skyward.

In the moonlight, he could just make out a dark shape streaking up, as a smaller shadow fell toward the ground. Before the pottery bomb could hit the ground, a man's silhouette snatched it from the air, doused its wick, then levitated gently down to land a few feet away from Niklas.

Gennedy was grinning broadly, his eyeteeth prominent. In his hands he carried one of the lethal oil bombs. "Can't promise we'll get all of them, but we'll catch as many as we can," he said. He handed off the sphere to Niklas. "You might want to keep these—could come in handy if we get to return the favor and besiege those sorry sons of bitches." With that he streaked upward, deftly evading the hail of arrows.

"Mind where you're shooting!" Niklas shouted to the archers. "Those are our men going up after the bombs!"

By now, a length of abatis along the right side of the camp was on fire. Inside the rows of brushy obstacles, wooden fence sections with pointed pikes would slow down the invasion, but if the force against them was sufficient, Niklas knew Pollard could afford to sacrifice troops to clear a path. If the fences were breeched, the trench and embankment hiding the archers was the camp's last defense.

Niklas lost all track of time as the night slipped past. He helped Ordel and the other healers triage the burn victims and gave his blessing for the healers to administer a toxic sleeping potion to those too severely injured to recover. Thanks to Gennedy and the other *talishte*, fewer of the firebombs struck the ground, but when they did, the damage was considerable.

"If we can make it to dawn, the sun will ground Pollard's *talishte* as well as ours," Niklas said as he carried an injured man to the triage area. "I prefer a fair fight with an enemy we can see."

Ordel wiped his brow with his sleeve. "That depends," he said, "on how many of the enemy there are to see."

"Perhaps it's time to get an idea of what we're facing," Niklas replied.

In the center of the camp, Niklas's men had built a wooden spy tower that rose two stories into the air. It was little more than an enclosed staircase with archer slits, but it afforded a better view than could be had from ground level. *Not to mention the fact that it also makes a nice target*, Niklas thought as he began to make his way up the narrow steps. Twice already the tower had been struck by oil bombs, but the quick reactions of nearby soldiers doused the flames with buckets of water.

At the top, he pulled his spyglass from his belt and waited for the clouds to clear. Moonlight shone across the plain, clearly illuminating the protected land that stretched from Arengarte to Glenreith. Niklas could make out a sea of shadows, some moving as if on horseback, most on foot. They appeared to outnumber his own regiment.

He swore under his breath, mentally combing through all the tactics he had witnessed on the battlefield for a way to repel the enemy. Nothing came to mind. Even from a distance, Niklas could see the smaller force at Glenreith on the archers' walk, catapults rolled into position on the manor's highest roofs.

Blaine's depending on us to keep Pollard at bay, Niklas thought. *It's all for naught if we can't drive them back.*

The next moments happened in a blur. Niklas heard a warning shout from outside the tower as he saw two dark shapes streaking toward where he stood. He heard a crash as pottery smashed against the wooden tower. Burning oil covered the top section, catching quickly in the rough-hewn wood and filling the observation post with smoke. Niklas covered his mouth and nose with his sleeve and hurtled down the steps, slamming against the sides of the narrow stairs in his haste to outrun the smoke. He heard the smash of a second bomb hitting near the bottom and more smoke rushed in, making it difficult to see or breathe. Niklas tumbled down the last length of stairs and ran for the door.

A sea of burning oil greeted him where the bomb had soaked the ground at the exit. Niklas could hear the flames eating at the top portion of the tower, and he knew it would not be long before the tower's roof fell in. Hot cinders were already falling in a fiery rain around him, burning his neck and shoulders.

Is this what it was like the night the Great Fire fell? he wondered. *I have a choice: Stay and burn, or see if I can outrun the flames.*

Just as he resolved to take his chances crossing the burning patch of oil, he spotted Ayers, who was holding a bucket of water.

"Captain! I'll make a path!" Ayers hurled the water across the burning oil, dousing a thin path to safety.

Niklas did not hesitate. He lurched from the tower door even as he could hear portions of the roof beginning to fall behind him. Flames licked at his trousers as he ran, and he hoped that his high leather boots and thick cloak would protect him. As he reached the safety of the other side, he heard the shouts of a bucket brigade rallying to contain the damage to the burning tower.

Niklas looked up at the flaming structure. It would be

impossible to save the tower, but with luck, the soldiers could keep the fire from spreading.

"You all right, Captain?" Ayers asked with a worried expression. "You're covered with soot, dark as a coal miner, you are!"

Niklas managed a relieved grin and dragged a sleeve across his face, noting that it came away black with grime. "Thanks for the path. I didn't fancy lighting up like a torch!"

Before long, the soldiers had the tower fire under control. Ayers and Niklas paused to drink a few dippers of water and wipe the soot and sweat from their faces. "We can't hold them off forever, sir. You know that."

Niklas nodded. "I know. But from what I saw in the tower, we can't take them head-on, either."

A runner came bounding up to where Niklas stood. Peters was one of the soldiers who had been under Niklas's direct command in the war, unlike the many stragglers who had joined up with them on the long march home. Despite the cold, the young man's dark hair was slicked back with sweat. His face was grimy, and the edges of his torn coat were singed.

"Something's going on out there, sir," Peters reported. "Can't rightly say what, but something's pulling the attack off our flank."

"Show me!" Niklas said and took off after the lieutenant.

Niklas scrambled to the makeshift observation post his men had constructed on the stone roof of a small storage building. "Look there, sir," Peters said, gesturing toward the shadows beyond the abatis wall.

Niklas peered into the darkness. Clouds streamed across the moon, so that the light waxed and waned. Between the distance and the darkness, it was difficult to see. Yet as Niklas adjusted his spyglass, it seemed as though the shadows were roiling. He could hear the shouts of men carried on the night wind, along with the clang of steel and the frightened cries of horses.

"Someone—or something—is attacking them," Peters said.

Niklas gave a cold smile. "Then let's take the offensive to them, shall we?"

Invigorated by the new advantage, Niklas was already shouting orders as he climbed down from the roof. "Catapults! Change your aim. Gennedy and the *talishte*—let's send those oil bombs back where they came from. Pound their rear flank, and let's drive them into the pikes and the trench where we can give them a proper battering!"

This was the part of soldiering that Niklas truly loved, the moment when a battle changed in a heartbeat and the odds shifted from impossible to probable.

"Who's out there, Captain? Are they for us or against us?" Peters asked, dogging Niklas.

"No idea, Lieutenant," Niklas replied as he moved down the lines, repeating his orders. He saw the dark shapes of *talishte* take flight and watched as they repositioned themselves and the catapult gunners dragged their war machines for a new vantage point. "All I care about is that they're fighting our enemy."

Peters moved to help one of the catapult crews with their heavy burden. "And if they come after us once they're done with Pollard? What then?"

Niklas's expression was grim. "Then we'll take them with us to Raka, soldier. By all that's holy to whatever gods exist, we're going to hold this ground."

All through the night, the catapults thumped and arrows sang through the air. Niklas continued working his way up and down through the ranks of the defenders, adjusting their aim, exhorting them to stay on their feet despite the long hours of assault. In the distance, Niklas could see flames light up the night where his *talishte* dropped the oil bombs. But as the night sky began to fade with the coming dawn, it became clear that his soldiers had not only held their position, but the new attackers had succeeded in severely damaging Pollard's strike force.

"They're retreating, sir!" Ayers shouted with jubilation, and a cheer echoed down the line.

"What of the strangers, the newcomers?" Niklas asked. He scrambled to the top of one of the catapult rigs for a better view.

"There's a man coming this direction under a white flag," Ayers reported.

Niklas glanced over his shoulder at the sky. "We've still got a bit before dawn breaks. Send Gennedy and another *talishte* to guide the soldier in. Let's find out if they're friends or whether we've got another fight coming."

Before long, two *talishte* returned with a third man. Niklas's eyes narrowed as he attempted to identify the man. From the way the *talishte* soldiers landed, it appeared that the emissary was also *talishte* because he touched down on his own accord, as if he had not been supported by his two escorts. The man was not remarkably tall but he was stocky, and he wore a cloak and uniform of military cut. *Whoever he is, he walks as if he owns the camp. I wonder if we've gotten rid of one threat just to greet another?*

"Captain Theilsson," the newcomer said before Niklas had a chance to speak. "I am Nidhud. I bring you congratulations from Lanyon Penhallow and offer you the support of my troops, the Knights of Esthrane."

CHAPTER
THIRTY

BLOODY HELL," PIRAN MURMURED UNDER HIS breath. "They're ghosts, I tell you. Nobody's seen the Knights of Esthrane for generations."

"They're not ghosts," Kestel said, motioning for Piran to pipe down. "We've been through this before, at the lyceum. They've just been in hiding for a while."

"And now things are so bad that they've come out of hiding?" Piran said, casting a skeptical glance at the man who waited for them in the cellar at Glenreith. "Is that supposed to make me feel better?"

"They're here with Penhallow and Connor," Blaine replied. "That means, at least in this matter, they're on our side."

"Uh-huh," Piran said, unwilling to give in, but he fell silent as they grew closer.

Penhallow and Connor stood with Niklas and a man Blaine did not recognize. All four men looked as if they had come from battle. Niklas was singed and sooty. Connor's cloak had been cut in places, and his shirt was spattered with blood. He looked rougher than Blaine remembered, unshaven, with the haggard look of a man who has seen the worst of battle and

returned with nightmares. Penhallow looked as coolly unruf-
fled as ever, but his clothing was muddy and torn, and the
ruddiness of his complexion told Blaine that the *talishte* had
recently fed well.

Blaine looked Nidhud over. He was solidly built, with strong
shoulders and a thick neck, his dark hair cut short for battle.
Blaine had seen the style of uniform that Nidhud wore in the
mosaics and murals at the lyceum, but it was still a shock to see
one of the legendary Knights in the flesh.

Nidhud met Blaine's gaze, and it was clear the Knight was
taking Blaine's measure as well. "Lord McFadden," Nidhud
said with a curt nod.

Maybe someday I'll get used to answering to that, Blaine
thought.

"Sir Knight," Blaine replied, meeting the *talishte*'s gaze.
"Welcome to Glenreith."

"Penhallow tells me you're the last living Lord of the Blood,"
Nidhud said, his voice matter-of-fact.

"Yes."

Nidhud seemed to consider that for a moment, then nodded.
"You seem to have made some powerful enemies."

Blaine managed a cold chuckle. "That's the story of my life,"
he replied. "We're grateful for your support in the battle. But
tell me: How does my being the last Lord of the Blood concern
the Knights of Esthrane?"

"I believe the real question is: What are you willing to risk to
find Vigus Quintrel?" Nidhud asked.

The cellar room had been outfitted for *talishte* occupation
shortly after Blaine's arrival, when they had expected Penhallow to show up any day. A worn table with several battered
chairs sat to one end of the room, while a few cots and more
comfortable chairs were arranged toward the other end.

"Sounds like we have a lot to talk about," Blaine said. "Please, have a seat." He paused. "Have you eaten?"

Penhallow smiled. "Nidhud and I have fed well, thank you. But I would imagine Connor is quite hungry after the battle."

Blaine could see the blood on Connor's shirt and surmised that not all of it came from Connor's foes, but he just nodded. He turned and spoke a word to one of the guards who had accompanied them down to the cellar, and the man went to retrieve food for Connor.

They sat down around the table, and Blaine listened in silence as Niklas described the battle from his perspective. "Just when we really thought we'd been outmanned, it was like someone had dropped a pack of wildcats into the middle of the enemy army," Niklas said with a grin. "We didn't know at first whether we'd found new friends or a different enemy, but either way, it spelled trouble for Pollard."

"I wish we could claim exceptional foresight," Penhallow said, taking up the story, "but as with most military victories, chance played a role. The truth is, Connor and Nidhud and I were on our way to Glenreith when we happened upon the battle. When it became clear that Vedran Pollard was involved, we made it our business."

"Glad for the help," Niklas said. He leaned back in his chair, and Blaine could see how weary his friend looked.

"We've had our own adventures aplenty since I left you, if you want to call nearly getting killed every other day an adventure," Connor said. "But I've brought back the map and disk I had in Edgeland, and all but a few of the other thirteen."

Connor withdrew a small locked box and set it on the table. When he opened the lock, Blaine could see a pile of the smooth obsidian disks inside. "We've also got a former mage-scholar with us, Treven Lowrey. He stayed behind with some guards when we realized there would be fighting. He'll join us here tomorrow." Connor looked at Blaine. "You'll want to hear him out, Mick. Between Nidhud and Treven, I think we've got a fix on how to find Vigus Quintrel."

"A matter in which Connor also plays a role," Penhallow added. Connor looked away, and Blaine wondered at his sudden look of discomfort. "It appears that Quintrel left some clues hidden in Bevin's memory without asking permission to do so, a liberty that has put Bevin in quite a bit of danger."

"Thanks to Quintrel, I can read his godsdamned coded writing and find the trail of bread crumbs he left to lead us to him—and the way to restore the magic," Connor said with an edge in his voice.

"There's more," Penhallow said quietly. "Connor is a medium."

Kestel frowned. "So you can hear spirits?"

Connor grimaced. "More than hear them. I see them more easily than other people, and they can communicate with me. If they're strong enough, they can take over my body."

Kestel met his gaze. "Do you get anything to say about that?"

"Not always." It was impossible to miss the touch of bitterness in his voice.

Penhallow cleared his throat. "We've also gained a new ally: Kierken Vandholt, the Wraith Lord. He has provided invaluable help."

"And nearly killed me twice," Connor muttered.

Zaryae had been quiet. She was dressed in muted colors, not at all like the flamboyant appearance she affected in her performances. She looked at Connor with understanding and placed a reassuring hand on his arm. "A medium's gift carries a heavy price," she said, reaching out to touch his hand. "Mediums don't control the possession, and they have few protections if a spirit decides to move in and stay. Hosting the spirit takes a toll on the body and mind." She gave a reproving glance toward Penhallow. "There's a reason most mediums die young." Zaryae paused. "I may be able to help you learn to control your gift, show you ways to protect yourself."

"Thank you." Connor looked down. "I'd give my life to bring back the magic," he said quietly. "I swore that I would do my part, and I will. I just prefer to be myself when I'm doing it, if you know what I mean." He paused. "Even if the Wraith Lord does fight a damn sight better than I do."

Penhallow nodded. "Understood."

Connor and Penhallow made a succinct report of all that they had seen and learned. When they finished, the others took a few moments to digest the new information.

"If it's true that we have a better chance if we work the ritual on the solstice, we don't have much time," Blaine said. "That's a little more than a week away. I've got maps that we think may show us where to go, but Valshoa is quite a distance from here. It will take most of that time just to get there—assuming we can find it when we arrive, and that we can figure out how to work the ritual once we're there."

"Lowrey seems to believe the solstice would be auspicious," Penhallow replied. "I defer to him on matters of magic."

"Some of the surviving Knights retreated to Valshoa when we were exiled," Nidhud said. He met Blaine's gaze. "It's quite possible they extended sanctuary to Vigus Quintrel and his refugee mages. If so, Quintrel left clues so Penhallow could find him. And a cipher," he added with a look at Connor.

"If the Knights retreated to Valshoa, does that mean you can lead us there?" Kestel asked Nihud, leaning forward expectantly.

"Unfortunately, no," Nidhud said. "When the Knights fled the king's persecution, we split into groups to avoid our persecutors." He paused. "My group fled to the lyceum, and when we feared discovery, we went farther into the hills to the west until the Wraith Lord called to us. But I believe that, with the maps and the other clues you have found, I may know enough that I can greatly increase your odds of success."

Nidhud's eyes gleamed with battle fire. "And I can think of another way in which we may be of help. My troops are quite prepared to battle Pollard's men. I propose that we draw them off, present a distraction, to buy Blaine and his party a chance to get a head start toward the mountains."

Niklas grinned. "While my men accompany him—leaving a force behind to guard Glenreith, of course," he said with a quick glance toward Judith.

"An excellent suggestion," Penhallow said as he stood. "Now, since it is quite late even by mortal standards, I suggest that we adjourn until Treven joins us."

Blaine turned to Connor. In the weeks since they had parted company in the battle at Penhallow's crypt, Connor seemed to have aged several years. When he had arrived as a shipwreck survivor in Edgeland a few months ago, Connor struck Blaine as young and untested. Blaine had admired Connor's grit for enduring the perilous sea journey and for throwing himself into the dangerous business of the maps, but he had wondered whether it was the first time Connor had ever faced grief and hardship.

Now there was a world-weariness in Connor's expression that had not been present before. He had seen it in Velant's youngest, least dangerous convicts as they lost the last of their innocence. Blaine was sure Niklas had seen such a change as well in young soldiers returning from their first real battle. Whatever had befallen Connor since their parting, it had changed him, hardened something deep inside. And right now, Connor looked tired enough to fall asleep where he sat.

"Why not leave the cellar to the *talishte*?" Blaine asked Connor. "We've got empty rooms upstairs. You look like you could use a good day's sleep."

Connor had finished the cheese, bread, and dried meat that Edward had brought, but he still looked as if he had skipped a few regular meals on the road to Glenreith. He gave Blaine a grateful, tired smile. "I'd appreciate that. Thanks."

Penhallow nodded approvingly. "Go. Spend some time in the sun," he said with a smile that might have held a touch of envy. "You've seen quite a bit of cellars and tunnels lately."

"That doesn't cover it by half," Connor muttered, but his voice held no rancor. "You know where to find me if you need me."

"I know," Penhallow said. "Now get some rest. I dare say such opportunities are likely to be limited."

Connor followed Blaine, Kestel, and Piran up the stairs to the main part of the manor. "I can't tell you how happy I am to have arrived here in one piece," he said.

Kestel threw her arms around him and planted a kiss on his cheek. Piran clapped him on the shoulder. "We weren't so sure you'd be coming," Piran said.

"I imagine you've got quite a story to tell," Blaine added. "We've been busy, too. But all that can wait until tomorrow, when your mage shows up."

Connor stifled a yawn, stretched, and looked around as the group emerged from below stairs into the main part of the manor and walked toward the large front hall. "So Engraham was right—you really are a lord," Connor said, taking in the entranceway.

"Fortunately the manor is in better shape than the Rooster and Pig," Blaine said. "Welcome to Glenreith, the place I spent twenty years trying to run away from and then crossed an ocean to come home to."

"I've seen enough of what's left of Castle Reach to know that you're lucky Glenreith is still standing," Connor said as they headed up the steps.

Blaine stopped in front of one of the empty bedrooms and opened the door. He was not surprised that Edward had anticipated his invitation, and they found the room freshly made up, the bed turned down, and a clean towel and nightshirt laid out next to a pitcher of water and basin.

"Once again, I'm in your debt for a roof over my head," Connor said, yawning broadly.

"Think of it as the new homestead," Kestel said. "Now go," she commanded, "before these two keep you up talking any longer. There will be time enough when you're rested. We'll make sure to save plenty of food for you, so get some sleep."

Connor gave a tired bow. "As you wish, m'lady Kestel," he said, and for the first time, the smile that touched his lips reached his eyes. "Tomorrow will be soon enough to tell tales."

Just after sunset, the dining room at Glenreith hosted the first large gathering it had seen in all the years since Blaine's exile. The heavy draperies were drawn to cover the windows, though it was full dark outside. Judith and Edward had conspired with the manor's remaining staff to muster a meal of venison, roasted parsnips, and baked apples washed down with plenty of wine. For the *talishte*, flagons of deer blood were sufficient to slake thirst. Although Blaine had apologized profusely to his aunt for the added strain on the household's slim resources, Judith had brushed off his protests with the wave of her hand,

and Blaine thought she actually seemed to be enjoying hosting the closest thing Glenreith had seen to a party in many a year.

Penhallow and Geir sat with Lowrey. Nidhud represented the contingent of the Knights who had arrived with Penhallow. Niklas and Ayers were present on behalf of the soldiers, and Illarion, Zaryae, Borya, and Desya came at Blaine's invitation. Blaine, Kestel, Piran, Verran, and Dawe sat with Connor, directly across the table from Penhallow. Judith, ever the gracious hostess, ate with the group and kept conversation on a lighter note, then tactfully withdrew, as did Mari.

When they had finished their meal, Blaine rose. "If we stand any chance of finding and reaching Valshoa before the solstice, we need to put together the information we've gathered and make a plan." He looked out over the assembled group.

Lowrey peered over his spectacles at Blaine. "Does he always worry this much?"

Kestel stifled a laugh. Piran sighed. "Actually, for Mick, this is pretty relaxed."

Penhallow looked as if he was holding back a smile. "Blaine is correct: We have an urgent task and a pressing deadline. Made more so by the fact that our destination is a matter of legend."

Nidhud looked to Blaine. "Let's get the maps and disks out onto the table. Then we'll know what we've got to work with."

Kestel laid out Ifrem's map as well as the map and map fragment they had found at the lyceum. Verran laid the disks they had gathered next to the maps, and Connor carefully withdrew his map and disks, laying them alongside.

Connor added to the trove with the other disks they had discovered, until twelve of the thirteen disks lay before them. From a worn backpack, Lowrey added the most important books they had found, the ones that contained Quintrel's clues.

Kestel added the manuscripts from the lyceum, and Connor eyed these last items warily.

Blaine and his friends recounted the stories behind their finds, with Zaryae and Illarion jumping in to add to the tale. When they finished, Connor told of their adventures.

Kestel studied the new disks intently, while Verran tried to decode the markings by comparing them to the maps. When everyone had had a chance to examine the items, Blaine looked to Lowrey and Nidhud.

"What do you make of it, now that you've heard everything?" Blaine asked.

"Not quite everything," Connor said. With a sigh, he looked to the items that had been retrieved from the lyceum. "Give them here. If they're going to wallop me, I might as well get it over with."

Connor sat down, and Piran slid the wood-bound collection of manuscripts toward him. Connor closed his eyes and took a few deep breaths to prepare himself, then spread his right hand and laid it palm down on the wooden cover.

The reaction was immediate. Connor's posture stiffened, but his expression took on a trancelike look. "You've done well to find this," Connor said in a distracted tone, as if an invisible someone were speaking in his ear and Connor was repeating what he heard. "If you have found the other pieces to the puzzle, you are close to having all you need."

"Can he answer questions when he's like this?" Kestel whispered to Lowrey.

Lowrey frowned, thinking, then shook his head. "No. It's more like Quintrel planted notes and clues in his mind. It's not a connection to Quintrel himself, just memories—more's the pity."

"Valtyr's maps of the Continent and the stars work together. If you desire to restore the magic, follow the stars to the hidden city. Bring the disks and one of the Blood. The Remnant awaits you." Connor went silent, and a moment later, he seemed to come back to himself with a shake.

"Was any of that useful?" he asked.

Kestel patted his arm. "You've confirmed what we suspected: The star map combined with the map of the power places on the Continent will lead us to Valshoa."

"I hate to say it, but there's another item that Connor should probably see as well," Blaine said. He slid the leather journal toward Connor.

Connor sighed. "Where did this come from?"

"We found it in a blocked-up tunnel at Mirdalur, right after we almost died," Blaine replied wryly.

Connor frowned and reached out to draw the journal toward him. Once again, his eyes lost focus and his face relaxed even as he sat upright, as if suddenly called to attention. "If you found this before attempting to use the ritual space at Mirdalur, reconsider. This space has been damaged, and it is dangerous."

"Now he tells us, after we got our balls fried," Piran muttered.

"I believe that the best chance will be to follow the map. Look to the missing soldiers, they can guide your way. Beware the Guardians. Come if you can at darkest night or brightest day. The Remnant awaits you."

Connor shook himself and looked from face-to-face. "What in Raka are the 'Guardians'? And who are the 'Remnant'? And what's all this about day and night?"

Lowrey had been chewing his lip in thought. "I'm almost positive that the Remnant are mages that Quintrel spirited away when he vanished. We know for a fact that quite a few mages went missing just before the Great Fire."

"As for the day and night comment," Lowrey continued, "I'd take that as a hint to come on either of the solstices, the longest and shortest days of the year." He smiled. "I'm betting the equinoxes work well in a pinch, too."

"And the Guardians?" Kestel asked.

"I believe I can be of assistance," Nidhud replied. "Although I have not been to Valshoa, the lore among the Knights has stories of such Guardians. It may be enough for us to pass safely past their precautions."

"What do you know?" Penhallow asked.

Nidhud was silent for a moment, searching his memories. "The original Valshoans valued their privacy. Their first line of defense would have been spells that made intruders forget their purpose or become distracted so that they did not see the path. They would have had sentries to determine whether visitors were welcome or not. When the magic still worked, the Guardians were a set of magical obstacles, plus physical traps designed to discourage casual intruders and assure that only the most determined—and most skilled—reached their goal."

"Then how did Quintrel manage it?" Piran challenged.

"Vigus Quintrel was an expert when it came to getting into places he shouldn't," Lowrey replied. "He was also a mage of great power, although he did his best to be underestimated. He might have figured out a way to cheat the obstacles. Or he might have found himself a guide. Perhaps he was able to get a message through and make his case for sheltering the survivors of the strike he knew would come." Lowrey shook his head. "Quintrel is a wily one, and not entirely to be trusted."

Nidhud smiled. "The good news for us is that the magical obstacles won't be of concern, since they failed with the loss of magic. That's something in our favor." He frowned. "The physical traps, however, still pose a danger. They were intended to be the backup plan, in case Valshoa was attacked by someone with sufficient power to defeat the magical precautions. They won't be easy to beat."

"Do you know anything that might help?" Blaine asked. "Anything you might have overheard?"

Nidhud's gaze was far away as he thought. "Each Guardian is more difficult than it first appears," he said. "There are traps within traps." He paused once more. "My fellow Knights sometimes are too fond of riddles. Here is what I remember: 'In the abyss, the last breath is taken. Beware the gardener, who prunes and harvests. Blood is the coin to pass among the shadows. Narrow is the path through the flames.'" He grimaced. "Not much to go on, is it?"

Connor looked to Nidhud. "What about the *kruvgaldur*? In all the years since the Knights went into exile, wouldn't some of those who went to Valshoa have contacted other *talishte* through the bond?"

Nidhud shook his head. "For *talishte* to communicate through the *kruvgaldur*, one must be the get of the other or have forged a blood bond. The Knights Dolan chose to go with him in search of Valshoa had outlived their makers and had made no fledges or blood bonds themselves. He did not wish to be found."

"I can also help," Zaryae said. "Valshoa was a place of power. That means the wild magic will be strong, and I will dream visions. They may be able to provide clues—or warnings."

Verran rubbed his hands together and looked gleeful. "If the Guardians are locks to be picked or traps to be sprung, I'm your man."

"It's not the Guardians that worry me, it's getting to the location," Niklas put in. "We've got to move a small armed force as well as this team over devastated ground, and for the most part, trust that we can live off the land." He shook his head. "I hope you weren't expecting stealth. If Pollard and Reese are looking for us, they're sure to find us. We can't hide that large an operation."

"There's no helping it," Penhallow said. "Much as I would prefer to do this quietly, we know that Reese has been stealing magical objects and capturing mages, so we have no way to know how much he's discovered about Quintrel or the clues to Valshoa."

"At least we know he doesn't have the disks," Kestel said. "Or more than one of them."

Penhallow nodded. "It looks like Pollard has been scavenging anything he finds, not looking for specific objects."

"You'll have armed protection day and night," Geir replied. "And after the drubbing Pollard received yesterday, he'll need time to regroup."

"We don't know how large a force he can muster," Blaine countered. "On the other hand, we aren't certain that Reese knows about the solstice. If we move quickly, we might be well on our way before Pollard recovers."

"I wish Voss were here," Connor said. "We could use the assistance."

Penhallow chuckled. "If I know Traher, he's taking his revenge on his way to joining us. He was quite fond of the fortress Pollard besieged, and Traher's not a forgiving person. I wouldn't put it past him to take a meandering route and destroy anything valuable to Pollard on the way."

"I'll have to leave a small garrison here to defend Glenreith, and my numbers aren't huge to begin with," Niklas said, "though we've gained some men since setting up at Arengarte."

"You have three more men at your command," Illarion said and nodded toward Borya and Desya. "We're prepared to fight."

Blaine looked to Niklas and Nidhud. "It's settled then. When can your men be ready?"

"We can leave tomorrow," Niklas said.

Nidhud nodded. "My men travel light. We're ready."

Blaine looked to the others. One by one, they nodded. "All right," Blaine said. "Tomorrow it is."

"And may the gods go with us," Kestel murmured.

Nidhud met her gaze. "It's not the gods we need to be worried about."

CHAPTER THIRTY-ONE

I DON'T LIKE THE LOOK OF THAT," BORYA SAID, reining in his horse. They were four days out from Glenreith, riding across what had once been some of the best farmland in Donderath.

"It's an empty field," Piran retorted. "What part don't you like?"

Borya squinted against the cold winter sun. "That part, over there," he said, pointing to places that looked to have less of a thatch of dead vegetation than most of the rest of the field.

Desya rode up beside them and scanned the ground ahead. Blaine was right behind them, close enough to hear the conversation, and he looked out over the field, straining to see whatever was worrying Borya.

"There's another spot, just like it, over there," Desya said.

"Just like what?" Piran asked, irritation clear in his voice.

"Look across the field," Borya replied. "Those spots are every fifty feet or so, all across the field, but not in a regular pattern."

"So you don't think they're just a trick of the wind," Blaine said.

"No, I don't," Borya replied.

Blaine surveyed the skyline. "There's no good way to go around—the flattened spots go on for as far as the eye can see."

Borya nodded. "Of course I may be too cautious. There's only one way to find out." Before anyone could reply, he gave a cry and put his heels to his horse, galloping into the field. An instant later, Desya was behind him, each of them riding straight for flattened spaces.

"I had the feeling they were going to do that," Piran said with a sigh.

The others had closed ranks behind Blaine and Piran. "What are they doing?" Kestel asked, raising a hand to shield her eyes against the sun.

"Stirring up trouble," Piran replied.

Borya was the first to near his destination. Before he could reach the flattened vegetation, his horse began to buck and fight, resisting Borya's urging to go closer, even when Borya dug in his heels. Desya also was fighting his balky horse as he reached the area just beyond where the grass was flattened.

"Looks like they found it," Blaine murmured.

A deep growl rumbled from the ground, then dark brown creatures sprang from the flattened grass, bounding toward the horses and riders with near-*talishte* speed. Desya and Borya wheeled their horses back toward the group. The creatures were the size of large hogs, with thick bodies and long, jointed legs.

"We can't outrun those things for long," Piran said, staring at the beetlelike creatures. Dome-shaped, with many legs and sharp, wide maws, the attackers moved unerringly to follow the two riders.

"And we can't get to the mountains without crossing this stretch of land," Blaine said, sword already in hand.

"What are those things?" Kestel's voice was muted by the wind.

"Mestids," Illarion said grimly. "We've seen them before—like the gryps, monsters born of wild magic."

"And they're coming our way!" Piran shouted. "Get ready!"

Borya pivoted his horse, smashing at the mestid with its hooves. The hard carapace sounded like stone against the hooves, and the mestid did not falter in its attack. From the other flattened places, more of the mestids began to swarm to the surface, one from each of the nests.

"If you've fought these before, what works to kill them?" Blaine called to Illarion.

"Fire!" Illarion yelled back. "They don't like fire any better than the gryps do!"

Wary of gryps, they had brought as many bottles of oil and batting for flaming arrows as they could carry, as well as long, straight pieces of wood suitable for torches. Illarion had already lit a torch and was riding toward Borya and Desya. Blaine, Piran, and Kestel rode to where Zaryae and Verran were grabbing bottles of oil and readying more of the baton-torches as the swarm of mestids closed in on them.

The mestids clicked as they moved, and as they neared, Blaine got a whiff of decaying leaves. The huge beetles' wide maws had jagged edges suitable for tearing meat. The front legs ended in vicious pincers that looked strong enough to do damage.

Borya was slashing at the pincers of one of the mestids. The mestid lunged at the legs of Borya's horse, snapping and nimbly evading Borya's strikes. More mestids swarmed toward the rest of the party, and Blaine could hear shouts passed down the line, warning those behind them of the danger.

Illarion jabbed at the mestid that harried Borya, while Piran handed off a burning torch to Desya and managed to get in several strikes on his attacker before drawing the attention of another beast.

At least thirty of the mestids had crawled from hiding and advanced on the party. Niklas and twenty of his men rode forward, swords at the ready, and waded into the fray, slashing with their broadswords and using their horses' hooves to kick at the hard carapaces.

Blaine slashed at the mestid that lunged toward him, barely evading its pincers. He dodged to the right and swung hard, connecting with his blade against one of the mestid's many leg joints. His sword drew blood but did little real damage except to further enrage the beast.

Connor's next strike went true, sinking hilt-deep into the space where its head was joined to its body, and he twisted out of the way of the pincers at the last instant. The mestid snapped at him, but the blade in Connor's other hand slashed across its neck, severing its head.

Blaine had little time to celebrate Connor's win. The mestid he fought rushed toward him with pincers and snapped its maw, but Blaine scored with the sword in his right hand, slicing through one of the mestid's legs. Blaine thrust with his left sword and felt the blade grind against bone as it slid deep into the mestid's thorax. He twisted the sword and the mestid screeched, but Blaine managed to stay clear of the thing's pincers.

A flaming arrow sailed past Connor's shoulder and struck the mestid Blaine battled but bounced away. A patch of dry grass caught fire, and the mestid let out a shriek, scrabbling backward.

Another arrow and then another streaked through the air, landing within inches of the mestids Niklas and his soldiers were fighting, driving the attackers back as the dry tangle of brush caught fire. Dawe let out a whoop of triumph. Blaine rose in his stirrups. "Niklas, pull back. I've got an idea."

"Are you crazy?" Niklas shouted. "If we pull back, those things will be on you in a heartbeat."

Blaine ignored the question and turned to Dawe and to the line of Niklas's soldiers behind him. "When Niklas pulls back, shoot burning arrows into the space between us and the mestids."

Piran had managed to bludgeon one of the mestids into submission with his horse's hooves and rode back. "Hand me a bottle of oil and some batting," he ordered breathlessly, grabbing the supplies from Zaryae's hands. He lit the batting from Zaryae's torch and stuffed it into the mouth of the bottle, then rode headlong toward the mestids, screaming a battle cry. He let the bottle fly and it crashed into the ground, sending up a wall of flames as the underbrush caught fire and the oil spread.

Dawe had already grabbed another bottle and batting, while Blaine did the same. "Box them in!" Blaine shouted. "Burn them!"

In moments, the broad, flat land in front of them was a roaring fire, and the air was heavy with the smell of smoke. Hemmed in on each side by flames, the mestids shrieked and scrambled toward the middle, piling atop each other in a frantic effort to avoid the fire. As the flames reached them, their carapaces burned and blackened, and the soft parts began to pop and sizzle, emitting an acrid stench.

Blaine and the others watched the pyre warily, swords still at the ready, alert should any of the mestids escape. Finally, when it appeared that the mestids were dead, Blaine sighed and turned to Connor.

"I thought Penhallow said reinforcements were on their way," Blaine said.

Connor grimaced. "Traher Voss is notorious for setting his own schedule."

"Can't Penhallow call him with his blood?"

"It's daytime—Penhallow is asleep," Connor replied. "And I don't know for certain that they share the *kruvgaldur* bond. Don't worry. Voss will catch up—eventually."

"Do you trust him?" Blaine asked, wiping his swords on the snow to clean off the mestids' fluid, then drying the blades on his cloak before resheathing them.

Connor gave a harsh laugh. "Voss? Hardly. He's a mercenary. But Penhallow seems to trust Voss. So that counts for something."

"You're a good bit better with that sword than you used to be," Blaine observed. When he had first met Connor after he was shipwrecked in Edgeland, the man had struck him as a courtier who had never been closer to battle than the verbal warfare at the palace. Blaine guessed that the improvement in his sword skills had come at a high price.

Connor looked away. "I've had a lot of practice."

They left the dead mestids where they lay amid a wide swath of blackened land. Niklas rode up to them, still eyeing the terrain ahead. He motioned to two of his soldiers.

"Burn us a corridor," Niklas commanded. "Save the oil—the underbrush is like tinder. Take us far enough that you can't see any more of the mestids' nests." The two soldiers gathered supplies and rode ahead, torching a path through the infested land.

"So much for stealth," Piran sighed, watching as black plumes of smoke rose in the sky.

"Pollard's going to have as much fun as we just did if he tries to ride across that field after us," Kestel noted. "And if those things have memories, they'll be plenty mad."

Niklas joined them. "Did either of you take any damage?"

Blaine and Connor shook their heads. "We're fine. How about the others?"

Niklas looked out across the fields. "Haven't had reports of any men down," he said. "Damn. I hate these things," he said, looking toward the blackened mestid corpses. "They came after us several times on the way home from the border. Lost more than a few soldiers to them."

Kestel, Dawe, Verran, and Piran were heading their way, as was Illarion's crew. "Everyone in one piece?" Blaine greeted them. They nodded.

"I'm guessing it's too much to hope that's the last we see of monsters," Kestel said. "Maybe they'll go after Pollard's soldiers for a change." She drew a deep breath. "If we've read the maps right, we don't have much farther," she added with a nervous glance toward the mountains.

"Which gives us precious little time to figure out how to work the ritual, assuming we find the right place," Blaine said, following Kestel's gaze. "Assuming Valshoa even exists."

"Let's get moving," Niklas said, signaling to his men. "We told Penhallow we'd make the outskirts of Hogstown by nightfall."

Traveling with a force of soldiers did not lend itself to stealth. The villagers and farmers they passed along the way eyed them suspiciously, and the few other travelers they encountered gave them a wide berth. The winter sky was gray, and wind howled down from the mountains, making the day seem even colder than the already freezing temperatures. Blaine glanced up at the sky often, trying to gauge how likely it was to snow. *Just the thing to make a miserable journey even more so*, he thought and pulled his cloak tighter around him.

The solstice was now only three days away. Days were short

and bleak with snow-laden skies, reminding Blaine of the long dark nights on Edgeland. The weather, along with the mestids' attack, had dampened the group's spirits, and they rode in silence. Even Verran, known for playing a tune on his pennywhistle as he rode, did not seem so inclined. Everyone's attention was on the mountains ahead of them, where Vigus Quintrel's clues indicated that whatever remained of Valshoa was located.

Midday, Blaine and Niklas stopped and consulted their maps. They had created a master map from the maps of the Continent, the stars, and the city of Valshoa. Connor and Lowrey had painstakingly added what else could be gleaned from Grimur's book and the notes Quintrel had left for them. The result, Blaine hoped, was a one-of-a-kind treasure map, with the hidden city at its heart.

"Anything from the mage?" Blaine asked Kestel, as he glanced back to where Lowrey rode with Connor. The older man had managed to stay out of danger during the fight with the mestids by hiding beneath one of the supply wagons.

Kestel shrugged. "Personally, I think he's scared to death whenever he's not in a library doing research."

"I don't think any of us signed on for this," Blaine said with a sigh. "It's gotten far out of hand from what I originally expected."

Kestel chuckled, though the scarf that warmed her face muffled her voice. "Hard to believe, considering we were expecting the end of the world."

Niklas lifted his face to the wind. "Think we'll have more trouble from Pollard's men?"

Blaine grimaced. "Count on it."

Niklas swore. "I'd almost welcome an all-out attack instead of this constant sniping."

"Hush!" Kestel admonished, making a warding sign. "Be careful what you wish for."

It had been clear that Pollard had them in his sights since they set out from Glenreith. Caltrops had been spread on the road not far from Glenreith, which might have lamed several horses or seriously damaged their wagons had the nighttime sabotage not been spotted and cleared by Penhallow's *talishte* fighters. Trees had been felled to block the roadway. Damage to a bridge could have sent them to the bottom of a steep ravine had it not been discovered and repaired. And at intervals, archers had shot at them from the cover of underbrush. So far, none of the attacks had inflicted major damage or injuries, but sooner or later, their luck would change.

"Maybe he's gotten ahead of us, if he found his own sources of information about Valshoa," Blaine said, scanning the horizon. He saw nothing but trees and the distant mountains.

Niklas shook his head. "Doubtful. The *talishte* scouts flew quite a distance out. They saw no indication that a large force—even a middling force—had passed this way." He paused. "On the other hand, Pollard no doubt knows we have *talishte* on our side. He may have found a way to move his men in small enough groups by day to evade our notice." He leveled a glance at Blaine. "If they suspect we're heading into the mountains, we may find that they rally to meet us."

"Maybe Nidhud succeeded in drawing them off," Blaine said. "Snipers might be the best Pollard can do until he can gather his forces, which means that he's likely to attack from the rear rather than get between us and Valshoa."

Kestel shrugged. "Let's hope Voss and Nidhud catch up by then. Maybe if we've got a big enough army, Pollard won't dare attack."

Niklas managed a smile. "I like the thought, but I don't see it working out that way." He gave a wary glance toward the sky. "Let's get moving. I want to make it to what's left of Lord Garnoc's manor before nightfall."

The road now led toward forest, a large swath of pines that spilled down the slopes of the mountains. Until now, the highway had been relatively open, threading its way past farms and villages, many of which had been abandoned.

"Still think we picked the right road?" Kestel asked as they rode.

Blaine eyed the shadows of the forest as they drew closer. "As Niklas pointed out, it's a toss-up. Ride in the open, and we can be spotted more easily, but we can also see if anyone's coming. Take the forest road, and while we're hidden, so is the enemy." He sighed. "And truth be told, no matter which way we ride, there are going to be stretches of forest. Can't get around it, this close to the mountains."

They fell silent as the road wound closer to the forest. It was late afternoon, and the angle of the winter sun sent long shadows across the road. Beneath the pines, it was nearly impossible to see if watchers waited in the darkness. By unspoken agreement, they rode as far to the side of the highway as possible, to keep a buffer between themselves and the forest.

The unbroken line of trees seemed to make them all edgy. Niklas insisted that Blaine and his friends, along with Lowrey and Connor, ride toward the middle of the group. The sense that something was waiting to happen grew stronger the farther they rode. Perhaps it was the unrelenting gray sky, Blaine thought, or the bitingly cold wind, or just the impenetrable depths of the old forest. But he doubted he was the only one holding his breath.

The twang of arrows and the thud of crossbow bolts broke the silence. On the edge of the formation nearest the forest, four men toppled from their mounts, arrows protruding from their bodies. Horses shrieked as riders pulled them up sharply. The archers might as well have been ghosts, as the shadows beneath the trees hid them completely from view.

"Ride!" Niklas shouted. "Get out of their range!"

Bent low over their horses to present more difficult targets, the riders broke into a gallop. A hail of arrows rained down on them, striking both soldiers and their horses, but the angle made it unlikely any of the hits would be fatal. Arrows sailed past them, making the horses skittish and difficult to control.

Blaine kept his head low and urged his horse forward. He dared a glance toward the forest, but the tree line was hidden from his view by the other riders. *Pollard can't possibly have archers the entire length of the forest,* he thought. *All his tactics have made good use of a limited force. He thought he'd catch us with our guard down, get in some lucky shots.*

More men cried out as arrows struck flesh. Even if they didn't lose many men or horses from the attack, Blaine knew that injuries were likely to slow them down, hinder their ability in a battle. *Pollard's smart. He knows we can't easily go after the archers in the forest, and any damage he does to us now is to his advantage if he's anticipating a real battle later.*

"We're outriding them!" Blaine heard a man shout as they galloped down the highway. Fewer arrows whistled overhead or swished past them, and Blaine fervently hoped that they were nearing the end of the archers' range.

Ahead of them, there was a rise in the road. They thundered up and over the summit, glad to be free from the arrows. A hedgerow lined the side of the road opposite of the forest, bushes as high as a man's waist, running as far as the eye could see. As the last of the soldiers cleared the crest of the hill, the sound of wood striking wood rang out, echoing in the winter stillness. Blaine glimpsed something glinting in the fading sunlight. The rider next to him jerked upright in his saddle and his mouth opened and closed wordlessly. Blaine saw a bit of metal protruding from the man's chest an instant before he toppled from his horse.

"They're launching blades from catapults!" Piran shouted behind him.

"We've been herded, nice as you please, into a slaughter," Verran muttered.

Just then, a new storm of arrows rained down on them, shot by archers at the tree line. All around Blaine shouts of panic rose, and the travelers reined in their horses or bolted ahead, into the deadly assault. Above the chaos, Blaine heard Niklas shouting to regain order, straining to be heard above the cries of wounded men and the panicked screams of horses.

"Damn!" A sharp fragment of metal flew past Blaine's shoulder and opened a bloody slice. Another metal splinter sank deep into the side of the horse next to Blaine's mount, and the horse reared and bucked.

"If we ride down the gauntlet, we're all dead!" Piran's voice carried above the pandemonium.

Blaine squinted toward the hedgerow. He could just make out the wooden mechanisms that were hidden behind the bushes. "They've got small catapults. Ride for the row!" Blaine shouted to his companions as he drew his sword. "Let's cut a way through their line!"

The move was pure suicide. Yet as more bits of deadly metal hurtled through the air, Niklas's soldiers were losing ground fast. Between the archers in the forest and the deadly hail of fragments from the hedgerow, the highway had become a killing field. Horses and men were down, some dead and others flailing.

They were likely to end up with their horses eviscerated and blades in their chests, Blaine knew as he struggled to bring his frightened horse under control. Yet his cry echoed down the line. Without sparing the time to think about the folly of his action, Blaine spurred his horse toward the point in the hedge that had most recently discharged its missiles, gambling that it would take a few moments to reload.

Blaine's horse sailed over the hedge and its hooves smashed into one of the gunnery men caught by surprise beside his small catapult. Swords in both hands, Blaine slashed at the two other gunners, even as silver flashed through the air and he felt something strike his belly.

Piran cleared the hedge a moment later, then Borya and Desya, who tumbled from their saddles to land on their feet, swords a blur of motion. Connor and Illarion were next, followed by Kestel and Zaryae, with Verran and Dawe after that. More of Niklas's soldiers followed the desperate gambit, and as they cut down the gunnery soldiers and disabled the catapults, the rest of the army stormed through behind them.

One of Blaine's opponents fell quickly, run through before he could even draw his sword. The other man got his wits about him in time to parry Blaine's attack.

"You're stuck," the gunner taunted. "You're bleeding."

From the pain in his side, Blaine guessed that one of the fragments had cut him badly, but he knew the gunner was waiting for an opening and he dared not look down. Instead, he roared in anger and dove forward, and his move caught the man by surprise. The gunner struggled to get his guard up, but Blaine struck with his full strength, landing a brutal blow with the sword in his right hand, followed by a thrust with the sword in his left. The gunner sank to his knees as Blaine pulled his sword back from between the man's ribs.

"See you in Raka," the man gasped. "You'll be joining me

soon, I think." Hands clasped to the wound in his chest, the man swayed and then fell face-forward into the snow.

All around Blaine, soldiers poured through the breach in the hedgerow and the catapults had fallen silent, their gunners chased down by Niklas's angry troops. Down the line, Blaine could see his friends, and over the fray, he could hear Niklas barking orders. *It worked*, he marveled.

Nearest to him, he saw Connor fighting off three of the gunners. Silhouetted against the sunset, Connor appeared to be struggling. His swordsmanship had improved, but it was not yet up to fending off three attackers at once. As the sun dipped lower, though, Connor straightened as if infused with new energy. His sword strokes grew surer and more powerful, and within a few moments he had bested his opponents in a display of skill that left Blaine completely puzzled.

As the adrenaline faded, Blaine felt the pain in his belly and it forced him to his knees. He pushed back his cloak to see a rapidly spreading stain. The world around him began to swim, even as he heard Piran shouting his name. He managed a response but felt himself topple to the ground as footsteps pounded in his direction. Overhead, the last light of day was fading with the sun.

By Vessa and Esthrane, don't let me come so close and die here, he thought. *I hadn't expected to survive the ritual, but don't let me die now, when I haven't even made the attempt.* He heard Piran's shout and Illarion's worried voice, but before he could respond, the darkness closed in around him.

CHAPTER
THIRTY-TWO

*B*LAINE. BLAINE, I KNOW YOU CAN HEAR ME. FIX *your attention on my voice. Follow my voice.*

The voice was familiar, but Blaine could not place it. Darkness engulfed him. He wondered if he still lay where he had fallen, in the snow near the hedgerow. He was so very cold.

Follow my voice, Blaine. The man's voice was firm, welcoming, irresistible in its compulsion. It was difficult to move, almost impossible to overcome inertia, but the voice gave him no choice. In the darkness, Blaine had no sense of up or down, of left or right, but the voice called, and he moved. Direction didn't seem to matter. He focused on the sound of the voice, and as it grew stronger, he knew he was getting closer.

Gradually the darkness dissipated, clearing like smoke. Blaine found himself in a darkened room, lying on a pallet, with Penhallow leaning over him, a worried expression on his face.

"He's with us once more," Penhallow murmured, but the concern was clear in his eyes.

"Where are we?" Blaine asked, finding it unusually hard to form the words.

"You're in Sondermoor, Lord Garnoc's manor," Penhallow replied. "Or, I should say, what's left of it."

Blaine swallowed hard. His mouth was dry, and his whole body felt sluggish. "I got hit," he murmured, closing his eyes and letting himself sink into the pallet.

"One of the blades caught you in the belly," Penhallow said quietly. "You lost a lot of blood."

Penhallow's voice felt like honey, warm and thick. Tired as he was, Blaine could not turn his attention away. "It was a bad wound," Penhallow continued. "By the time Niklas got you to Sondermoor, you were dying. You were beyond his healer's abilities."

"Am I turned?" Blaine managed. He thought he might feel horrified at the possibility, but caught in the magnetism of Penhallow's voice, he could feel nothing except warmth.

"No. But in order to heal you, I had to make a bargain, of sorts," Penhallow replied.

"What kind of bargain?" Blaine struggled to open his eyes. He met Penhallow's gaze and belatedly remembered that *talishte* could bind a mortal's will with their stare.

"To mend such a severe wound, I needed to create a bond between us. Not so strong a bond as turning you, but enough to make my power accessible to you."

"The *kruvgaldur*," Blaine replied, finding it difficult to think clearly. "Like Connor."

"There was no choice, if you were going to live," Penhallow said.

Distantly it occurred to Blaine that he should feel angry at having such a permanent decision made for him, but he lacked the energy to feel anything at all except relief. "What did you do?" Even to his own ears, his words sounded slurred.

"I drank your blood, then used the bond it created to reinforce my ability to heal you with saliva and my own blood," Penhallow replied.

"I'm bound to you?"

"In a manner of speaking," Penhallow said. The timbre of his voice was comforting, reassuring. "The bond creates an obligation for me as well. You are fully under my protection."

"Can you read my mind?"

Penhallow chuckled. "Not the way you may think. Your memories are clearest during the actual blood-taking. The bond grows stronger with repetition. Over time we can communicate, with limitations, even over distance. Geir or Connor have mentioned this, I believe?"

"Yes." Blaine was quiet for a moment. "How long—"

"Only a matter of a few candlemarks have passed since you were injured," Penhallow finished for him. "It was Connor who summoned me, although I was already on my way." He chuckled. "Lady Kestel was quite forceful about insisting I heal you. I will lend you my strength, and with rest, you should be ready to ride tomorrow."

Still alive, with a chance of actually reaching Valshoa in time, Blaine thought. *An acceptable trade.*

Penhallow laid a hand on his shoulder. "Your friends are safe and undamaged," Penhallow said, answering the unasked question. "Niklas's battle healer has his hands full with all the men who are injured, but most are in no danger. We're in the lower levels of the old manor, as safe a place as to be found. Now sleep. I'll make sure someone sits with you. And if you need my help, I will know."

Blaine started to protest, but exhaustion washed over him, and between it and the compulsion in Penhallow's voice, he sank into sleep before he could say another word.

*　　*　　*

"You're looking better," Connor said as Blaine opened his eyes sometime later. "Glad you're still with us."

Blaine drew a deep breath. He felt a dull pain in his side, but he had a vague memory of it being much sharper not long ago. For a moment, he felt completely disoriented. Then he remembered the conversation with Penhallow, the battle, and his near brush with death.

"Thank you," he said raggedly. "Penhallow said you called him to me."

Connor chuckled nervously. "At the time, I wasn't sure whether you'd thank me or not when you woke up, but I didn't think Kestel and Niklas intended to leave me any option, regardless." He sobered. "And if you hate me for it, I'll understand—although I still think it was the right thing to do. Your Edgeland mates took turns sitting with you. Kestel wouldn't leave your side until she knew you were going to live." He shuddered. "I didn't fancy facing her if you didn't."

"What...is it like?" Blaine asked.

Connor took his meaning immediately. "The *kruvgaldur*? Takes a little getting used to. Most of the time I don't think about it now. Being with Penhallow all the time makes it stronger."

Connor paused. "It still makes me nervous when he takes blood, but he's as kind as possible. I mean, someone can only be so gentle about it." Another pause. "I had to get used to the idea that I might not have any real privacy, any secrets. Not that I had much to be private about. It was the thought, really, of not being alone in my own mind that took a bit to adjust to."

He sighed. "Penhallow says he only wants certain information, that he doesn't go rooting around to see what he can find. I believe him—after all, I don't think about anything that's all that exciting." Connor met Blaine's gaze. "I don't think you have to worry. Whether you ever offer up your blood to him is up to you—unless you nearly get yourself killed again."

"Does he control you?" Blaine managed to meet Connor's gaze and found a mix of emotions swirling in the young man's eyes.

"Penhallow? I don't think so." He gave a nervous laugh. "If he could, I wouldn't have gotten banged up quite so badly in a few of the fights. He certainly doesn't control Traher Voss."

"I saw you fighting at the hedge," Blaine pressed. "You gained a lot of skill in a very short time."

Connor looked away. "Oh. That wasn't Penhallow. It was the Wraith Lord. He can take over my actions when he possesses me." He looked down, anywhere except at Blaine. "He's saved my life by taking me over, fighting through me."

"By possessing you?"

Connor nodded with an uncomfortable expression on his face. "Yes." He paused. "So far, he's been honorable and departed when it would harm me, or when the situation that required his presence was over." He paused. "There's something else you need to know. The Wraith Lord was one of the original Lords of the Blood. Before Mirdalur."

Blaine lay still for a moment, letting that bit of information sink in. "So I'm not the last Lord of the Blood," he said finally.

Connor shook his head. "Yes, and no. The Wraith Lord is the essence...maybe the soul...of one of the original Lords. But you are the last *living* Lord of the Blood, and from everything Treven's found in Quintrel's books, that's what really counts. The magic is in the blood—your blood."

"Will the *kruvgaldur* change anything?" Blaine asked.

Connor shrugged. "You and Penhallow are connected. Beyond that, I don't know how it will work for you. I thought about that when I asked for Penhallow's help, but if you were dead, there'd be no working the ritual at all."

"Has the Wraith Lord told you anything—about bringing back the magic, or Valshoa?"

Connor gave a grim smile. "When you're feeling better, he's requested a meeting with you and Nidhud."

Blaine looked at him skeptically. "He waits until I nearly die?"

"He needed to observe you. He wanted to come to his own conclusions about your motives, to assure himself that you were not aligned with Reese."

Blaine sighed. "Here's hoping he's got some ideas on what to do when we get there—assuming we find it. We may have come all this way for nothing."

"He believes in Valshoa. So does Nidhud."

"I wish I did," Blaine said tiredly. "Despite the maps, I'll believe it when I see it."

"Then you won't have long to wait," Connor replied. Blaine heard him push back his chair and stand. "One more thing," he said. "The *talishte* scouts have spotted magic storms. They're still a distance away, and their direction is always uncertain, but it's possible they could head this way."

"Just what we need. One more complication," Blaine murmured.

"Thought you'd want the warning. The only thing worse than being hit by one is not knowing it's coming."

"Thank you," Blaine murmured.

"Just save the magic, huh? That's all the thanks I need."

Blaine awoke sometime later to find that the pillar candle on the floor beside his pallet had burned down from its previous height, and he wondered how long he had been out.

"You slept for a couple of candlemarks," Kestel answered his unspoken question. "Verran came down to check on you, and he brought food for both of us."

She nodded toward a loaf of bread, a wineskin, a length of dried sausage, and a hunk of cheese that lay on a kerchief nearby. "Candlelight dinner. Romantic," she said, but the humor in her voice did not match the concern in her eyes.

"This almost-dying shit is getting old," Blaine muttered. "Bad enough in Velant, but I thought I'd gotten past those days."

"Not much fun for the rest of us, either."

Blaine sighed and reached out to take her hand. "Sorry."

"You're alive. That's all that matters." Kestel's voice was brisk, but her eyes told another story. She bent down to kiss him, and he drew her close. "I'm glad you accepted Penhallow's help." She paused. "Are you angry with us for asking him?"

Blaine grimaced. "I didn't have much choice."

"There's always a choice." Kestel paused. "If it makes you feel better, I knew Penhallow's reputation from court. Even people who didn't like *talishte* allowed that Penhallow was a man of honor. I took a risk and trusted him. It was better than losing you." Abruptly, she forced a smile and changed topics. "Eat your dinner. You'll feel better."

With a grunt, Blaine managed to sit up without her assistance. He winced at a sharp pain in his side, then realized it felt more like a pulled muscle than a nearly fatal injury. *Not too bad, considering.*

He leaned back against the stone wall and reached out to rip apart the bread. He offered some to Kestel, but she shook her head.

"No thanks. While you were sleeping, I ate. What's left is for you." She nodded toward a small cup Blaine had not noticed. "That's an elixir from Niklas's healer. Said it would help with the pain and promised that by morning, you'll feel good enough to ride."

Blaine ate his dinner and washed it down with wine. "Any word about Pollard's troops?"

Kestel shook her head. "After you went down and the sun set, Penhallow's men—and Nidhud's Knights—showed up, although by that time, our folks had taken quite a toll on Pollard's troops. Your crazy maneuver worked—except for the part where you almost died."

Blaine shrugged. "No plan is perfect." He paused. "How about Voss? We could use some reinforcements."

"Not yet, although Penhallow believes he'll be here before you work the ritual."

"Nothing like cutting it close."

Kestel sighed. "Speaking of which—I'm to tell you that Nidhud, Niklas, Lowrey, Penhallow, and Connor will be down to see you after eleventh bells. Piran and I would like to stay as well, and Zaryae asked to come along. It'll make for a tight fit in here." She smiled, and Blaine could see her concern. "After what you've been through, I figured we could be your ears and memory, in case you're not quite back to being yourself."

Blaine squeezed her hand. "I'd appreciate that." Food and wine fortified him, but the battle had taken its toll. Despite the elixir and Penhallow's healing, Blaine felt exhausted and laid back down on his pallet.

"Go ahead. Sleep," Kestel urged. "One of us will be here. We'll wake you before it's time for the meeting."

Blaine thought of several responses, but sleep took him before he could say anything more.

When Blaine next woke, he was surprised to find that the ache in his belly was almost gone, and he felt much improved. Enough so that he insisted on sitting up to greet his visitors,

"Vessa had to pass through fire to prove her ability to become the goddess of flame," Connor said.

"Darkness, ghosts, maze traps, and fire," Blaine said quietly. "So finding Valshoa's location is only the beginning. We still have to survive the journey."

"Who's to say Reese and Pollard won't be right behind us with an army?" Piran asked. "I'm more concerned about getting an arrow in my back than working out some ancient puzzle."

"We'll watch your back," Niklas assured him. "My men will hold the pass."

Penhallow nodded. "Mine as well. We won't be able to go with you, because we don't know what shelter is available from the daylight. But we will secure the entrance."

Nidhud grimaced. "Obviously if the Knights could navigate the Guardian path, there must be some provision for *talishte*, but since we aren't privy to all of the path's secrets, my men and I will remain where we can be of most assistance—to assure that you aren't attacked from the rear."

"The last impression I had from Voss tells me that he is quite close," Penhallow said. "He's been burning out Pollard's safe houses and hiding places, cutting his supply lines. That should mean that any force Pollard and Reese bring against us will be at less than their best."

"So it will be me, Piran, Dawe, Verran, Kestel, Illarion, Borya, Desya, and Zaryae, going in on foot," Blaine summarized.

"And me." They turned to look at Connor. "I've got to go. Quintrel planted his clues in my head for a reason. I'm the cipher. I'm also your link to the Wraith Lord, and anything he knows that could be of help. I'm coming."

"Count me in," Lowrey said. "I'll be more use to you if we

really do find Quintrel and his mages than I'll be out here with the soldiers."

"You won't be able to take your horses once we reach the foot of the mountains," Niklas said. "Our *talishte* scouts have checked the first part of the path and said it's too steep. I've got my men making packs for all of you with essentials: food, wineskins, rope, tools, and knives, as well as flint and steel and batting for torches, some candles, and lanterns. You'll be as prepared as possible."

Blaine looked around the group, meeting each person's gaze in turn. Every one of those gathered reflected clear resolve. *They're ready to walk into the shadowland for me*, he thought. The realization both humbled and frightened him. *We might not make it back. The ritual might not work. I could fail. They know—and they're ready to go anyway.*

"Valshoa has an interesting history," Lowrey said, puffing along behind them. Despite the cold day, he was already red in the face and a slight sheen of sweat dotted his forehead. "Since that's where we're headed, perhaps you'd care to hear…"

Lowrey regaled them for some time about the legendary exploits of the Valshoans and the extraordinary accomplishments of their city, which had, according to him, melded magic and technology in ways never seen before or since. Blaine was not sure that anyone was fully listening, but it kept Lowrey amused.

By midday they reached the first symbol on Kestel's map. The trail appeared to dead-end in a sheer rock face at the end of a canyon. Dawe, Boyra, and Desya had their bows out, keeping a wary eye on the ledges and sky overhead, alert for danger.

"Now what?" Illarion asked, scanning the rock walls around them.

Connor had been unusually silent all morning. Zaryae laid a hand on his arm. "Something's troubling you."

Connor nodded, and Blaine saw conflict in his eyes. A flush crept into his cheeks. "Quintrel left us a clue," he said, before a change came over his face and his eyes grew glassy.

"Over there." Connor pointed to the very back of the canyon, where a large rock jutted from the ground. "The path lies that way, then down. Light neither torch nor candle—they will destroy you. Take the guide stones to find the way."

Connor grew quiet, and his eyes regained their focus. He shook his head to clear it. Then his expression reflected chagrin. "I really hate when the memories take over," he said with a sigh. "If you didn't think I was completely mad before, this trip should prove it."

"What did he mean, go toward the rock then down?" Piran demanded. "It's a sheer rock cliff!"

"Let's go look," Verran said, enthusiastic for the first time since they had set out. "This has all the markings of a good treasure hunt." Verran led the way as the group filed through the narrow gap between the canyon walls.

Before long, he stood in front of a large chunk of stone that had fallen from one of the upper edges of the canyon. Sword at the ready in case a trap awaited, Verran licked his lips and the fingers of his right hand twitched expectantly.

"There's an opening here," he called to the others. "Definitely not something you'd see if you weren't looking for it."

Blaine and Kestel exchanged glances, then Blaine made his way toward where Verran stood. A dark hole barely wide enough for a man's shoulders loomed near the base of the stone.

"No torches, huh?" Blaine mused. "There's no telling whether it opens up into somewhere we can walk, or whether it's a hole straight down."

"I'll go," Desya said. "Borya can rig me a harness. We've both done rope work before. The two of us have the most experience climbing, and if there's a drop, we know how to fall."

"Quintrel was clear—no flame," Blaine repeated.

"The real question is, what are guide stones?" Kestel asked.

"No way to tell until I get in there," Desya replied, with a tone that said he relished the challenge.

Dawe, Piran, and Illarion remained on watch as Desya and Borya constructed a rough harness. Verran poked at the entrance to the opening with his sword and confirmed that the ground extended some distance inside. "It's not a sheer drop—at least, not right away," he said cheerily.

Borya said something to his brother in a language Blaine did not understand, but from his expression, he assumed the comment was a warning. Desya nodded, then walked to the opening as Borya and Blaine readied themselves to brace the rope that extended from the harness.

Zaryae made a sign of warding and murmured something that sounded like a prayer. Desya dropped to his hands and knees, then ducked his head and carefully began to inch his way into the hole.

"The ground slopes down, and the tunnel gets higher," Desya called back in a muffled voice.

"Any guide stones?" Borya called after him.

"No. Wait," Desya called an instant later. "I think I see something."

Blaine and Illarion carefully let out the rope as Desya shimmied farther down the passageway. The rope grew taut, then loosened as Desya moved back to be heard. "Glowing rocks. There are a lot of them not far inside the entrance."

He paused. "I'm going to take some of the rocks and go on. There's a path that winds through the cave chamber, and from what I can see, there are places where it drops off, so you couldn't come through here in the dark. But something's not right. There's nothing alive in here that I can see. That's strange. I think it might be the air."

"Should we pull you out?" Illarion asked, worried.

"No. I think the trap was to find a way through the bad air without flame. When I get to the other side, I'll get out of the harness and wrap it around some of the glowing stones. You can draw it back and use it for the next person." He coughed. "I'll leave a trail with the other guide rocks so you know the safest path to follow. Hurry. The air is very bad."

"Send Blaine through next," Illarion said. "That gives us another swordsman on the other side. Let Lowrey go through with him, in case the scholar needs assistance, then send

Connor. Kestel and Zaryae can go next, and Dawe, Borya, and I will come last."

When the harness and the guide rocks were pulled back to the entrance, Blaine shouldered into the ropes and hefted the rock with the brightest glow in one hand. Illarion and Borya fashioned a second harness for Lowrey from a smaller length of rope. "All right," he said. "Let's hope I have as good luck as Desya."

Blaine dropped to his hands and knees and found he needed to duck even lower, since he was several inches taller than Desya. Illarion had used a smaller length of rope to secure their packs and the other supplies, so they would not lose them. It made for a tight fit. Crawling on his belly and forearms, Blaine made it through the narrow opening. The guide rock glowed brightly. Lowrey scrabbled through the cave's mouth, muttering under his breath. Blaine moved forward carefully, mindful of the perils Desya had reported.

The floor of the cave was still solid as Blaine's feet cleared the entrance. Once inside, he held up the guide rock, trying to get a sense of how much room he had to maneuver. Tentatively he rose to a crouch and extended his arm over his head. When he did not touch the cave's ceiling, he breathed a sigh of relief.

Even with the guide rocks Desya left behind to light the path, Blaine could make out little about the cave. Careful not to move faster than the faint light of the phosphorescent stone in his hands, Blaine made small steps forward. From here he could see that a narrow causeway made a bridge between two steep drop-offs. The walkway was barely wide enough to cross.

"Move carefully," Blaine warned Lowrey.

Blaine took a breath and felt his head swim. Suddenly shaky, he dropped to his knees to steady himself. Whatever had affected him was also causing problems for Lowrey, because the scholar wove unpredictably, trying to control his fall. He landed badly and tumbled sideways onto the brink of the sheer drop, which crumbled beneath him.

Blaine scrambled to find a handhold to keep himself from plunging into darkness after Lowrey. "Stop the rope!" he shouted, but his voice echoed eerily in the empty cavern.

No guide stones glowed from the sides of the pit. There was no way to tell how far Lowrey had fallen. He could hear Lowrey gasping for air and feared that the air in the pit might be even worse than in the larger cavern above.

Just when Blaine was certain that Lowrey would fall to his death before the rope handlers realized something was wrong, the rope jerked to a sudden stop. Then slowly, the rope began to drag Lowrey back up toward the cusp of the pit. Lack of air was making his head spin, but Blaine had the presence of mind to lie flat and extend an arm over the pit's edge to help Lowrey haul himself over the brink.

"Got him!" Blaine shouted back to the others. "When you come, crawl across the narrow place."

This time, Blaine did not try to walk across the narrow causeway. Both he and Lowrey crawled on all fours, moving as quickly as they dared, and Blaine feared that one of them would pass out before they reached the other side. The faint glow of the guide stones gave Blaine a focal point, and he forced himself to think of nothing except reaching the next marker.

It seemed to take forever, but gradually, the rim of the pit came into view, and he could glimpse light from the cavern's exit. Lowrey was falling farther and farther behind so Blaine had to pull him forward with every movement. Blaine's lungs burned, and his eyes swam with tears, irritated by whatever noxious gases filled the cave. Heaving and gasping, he dragged himself into the cold, fresh air. He hauled Lowrey out of the cave and rolled over onto his back, utterly spent.

"Bad in there, didn't I tell you?" Desya said, helping Blaine sit up so he could unfasten the harness and loosen the rope that bound Blaine's supplies to his body. As Blaine struggled to catch his breath, Desya helped Lowrey out of his harness, then bundled up the guide stone and gave a jerk on the rope to signal Illarion to pull it back to the entrance. After a few moments, Blaine found that he could breathe more easily, although his lungs and throat still burned, and his eyes felt red and irritated. Lowrey took longer to recover. He rolled to the side and retched, then sat up, trembling.

"What in Raka is in there?" Blaine managed, his voice hoarse.

Desya stood watch, his bow drawn. "Not sure, but I've heard tell that men who go into the deep places often don't come out again."

As Blaine's head cleared, he took a sip from the wineskin Desya offered him. "When Piran and I were in the mines in Edgeland, there were shafts where the air would go so bad the men would die. Sometimes a candle or lantern would set off an explosion or cause a cave-in."

Desya nodded. "Mines can disturb the foul air of the deep places, but I've heard tell that sometimes it comes up naturally in caves, even wells." He nodded toward the cave mouth from which they had emerged. "Nasty Guardian, that one. If we hadn't had Connor's warning, we would have put a torch in there for a good look and probably blown ourselves to pieces."

The dangerous elegance of the Guardian and the multiple levels of threat it posed gave Blaine new respect for Valshoa's residents. "If the other three Guardians are like this one, we'd best be on our toes," he said.

Connor was the next to crawl from the cave, and Blaine was not surprised when he emerged wobbly and pale. Desya kept watch, his arrow nocked and ready, while Blaine helped Connor from the harness and offered him a sip of wine.

"By all the gods!" Connor exclaimed when he could talk again. "I feel as if I've breathed fire. Have I mentioned how tired I am of being buried alive, dragged through crypts, tunnels, and caves, suffocated, and drowned?"

"This sort of thing happens to you a lot?" Blaine asked, raising an eyebrow.

Connor glowered and took another drink of wine. "More than you can imagine."

Kestel shimmied through the opening, followed shortly by Zaryae. When they had recovered, they took over helping each of the others as they emerged, while Connor and Blaine took up watch with Desya. Blaine was fearful that the cave exit would be the perfect place for snipers to take advantage of the vulnerability of their group as one by one, they stumbled, gasping, from the cave. Though he could see no one, he felt a prickle at the back of his neck, warning him they were not alone.

Kestel shook the dirt and cobwebs out of her hair, patted her bandolier to make sure all her knives were where they should be, and looked around with a grin. "What's next?"

"I'm going to hate myself for suggesting this," Connor said, "but since I'm the one with Quintrel's helpful hints tucked away in my memory, I probably should go first."

"I think that's a good idea," Blaine agreed. "But we'll be right behind you."

Connor's expression spoke for him. They headed on, but the four bowmen kept their weapons out and ready. Blaine eyed the ridges of the canyon above them, but he did not spot any watchers.

The footing was rough and in many places, the passages were so tight that the group had to move in single file. *Perfect killing box*, Blaine thought grimly, and a look at Piran confirmed that the other had the same idea.

"How far in do we have to go to find this city?" Dawe asked.

Blaine grimaced. "From the map, assuming everything was to scale, it should take most of the day."

Dawe glanced at him. "Cutting it close, isn't it? The solstice is the day after tomorrow."

Blaine shrugged. "Then we'd better keep up the pace and hope for the best, huh?"

By the position of the sun overhead, Blaine knew they had walked for two candlemarks after emerging from the cave. Everyone was anxious to keep moving, so lunch was hurried, with only a brief break to rest.

Zaryae sat apart from the group, deep in concentration, seeking guidance from her cards and crystals. "Is she unwell?" Blaine asked Illarion when the group stopped to eat.

Illarion frowned. "She said her dreams have been dark. We're in an area where wild magic is strong. Until she can determine exactly what we're being warned about, she doesn't want to speak of it."

Blaine nodded. Piran ambled up to where they were sitting. "Does your bloody map give us any clues about what's ahead in the canyon?" he grumbled.

Kestel shook her head. "It wasn't that detailed, other than to indicate the route in. You wouldn't expect a hidden valley to be easy to find, would you?"

"Because then it wouldn't be hidden," Verran added, elbowing Piran. They began walking again.

They rounded a bend and came to a stop. "I think we've found the second Guardian," Connor said.

The narrow passage opened to a broad area enclosed by canyon walls. A wall of thornbushes nearly seven feet tall stretched from side to side in the canyon. There was an obvious opening, and close inside, another wall of thorns.

"Looks like a maze," Illarion said.

"Can we climb above it?" Piran asked, eyeing the rock walls of the canyon. "Get a bird's-eye view?"

Borya and Desya walked to either side of the canyon and ran their hands over the stone. Borya attempted to gain a handhold but slid down the wall. Desya also tried, with similar results. Borya climbed onto Desya's shoulders, looking for a hold farther up the wall. He found nothing suitable. The twins returned, shaking their heads.

"Someone's intentionally smoothed off the walls of the canyon," Desya reported.

"Can you drive pinions into the walls?" Kestel asked. "Use ropes to get above the maze?"

"It's worth a try," Borya said.

They unpacked the pinions and Desya took one of the lengths of rope, using the same harness that had gotten them through the cave. Borya helped him into the harness and once again climbed onto his shoulders to position the first pinion at the very top of his reach.

Borya jumped down, doing a somersault for good measure and landing on his feet. He helped Desya hoist himself up with the pinion and secured Desya's safety line as Desya carefully lodged several more pinions, each higher than the others. Finally Desya had managed to gain a vantage point halfway up the cliff wall.

For several moments, Desya surveyed the maze, using Blaine's spyglass. Kestel had given him a piece of charcoal and a bit of parchment on which to note the contours of the maze, and Desya balanced skillfully as he made swift, bold strokes, then tucked the map into his vest and let himself down, reclaiming the pinions as he descended.

"Anything?" Blaine asked when Desya and Borya rejoined him.

Desya shook his head. "Not as much as we hoped. Whoever set up the maze deliberately designed it so that anything I can see from this wall—and from the other wall as well, I wager—are just outer pathways. Whatever traps there are must be toward the center, and I couldn't see that section even with the spyglass."

"Don't forget the riddle Nidhud gave us," Piran said. "'In the abyss, the last breath is taken. Beware the gardener, who prunes and harvests. Blood is the coin to pass among the shadows. Narrow is the path through the flames,'" he quoted.

"We've been through the abyss, and now we know what they meant by 'last breath,'" Blaine said. "So in the maze, we need to watch out for a 'gardener'?"

"Or perhaps just keep an eye out for something that cuts down what doesn't belong," Piran pointed out.

"Were you at least able to map the maze pattern?" Kestel asked Desya. Excitement glinted in her eyes at the challenge.

Desya withdrew the parchment and charcoal and handed them to her. "What I could see, I drew. I couldn't make out the path we'd need to take through it. Whoever designed the thing didn't want to make it easy."

Kestel, Connor, and Blaine studied Desya's drawing. Lowrey crowded in and bent down to have a better look.

"From what he's drawn, the beginning of the maze is fairly straightforward," Lowrey said when he stood and pushed his spectacles back up on his nose. "Labyrinths and mazes are quite popular with mages because they are ways to focus the mind. This looks like a rather common configuration." He eyed them over his glasses. "Which means that the challenge may not be the maze itself. The challenge is more likely something inside it."

Blaine looked to Connor. "Does anything trigger your Quintrel memories?"

Connor looked uncomfortable, and Blaine guessed the drawing had indeed caused a reaction. "I've been getting a vision since I first saw the entrance to the maze." He shook his head. "The problem is, I'm only seeing the first turn, not the whole path through the maze, and nothing to indicate any traps. I'm hoping that more memories will come when I see landmarks within the maze."

"Let's hope so," Kestel murmured, making a sign of warding.

Connor headed toward the maze when Borya caught his arm. "You go first? Then you wear this." He thrust the harness at Connor. "Just in case."

Connor moved to protest then relented, and Blaine guessed he was thinking about the cave. In just a few moments, Borya and Desya had him in the harness, with the rope trailing behind where Blaine and Illarion kept a loose hold.

"I feel like a dog on a leash," Connor muttered.

"That 'leash' kept Lowrey and me from falling to our deaths," Blaine replied. "It's worth the damage to your dignity."

Connor led the way, followed by Blaine and Illarion. The others filed after them, with Piran, Borya, and Desya watching the rear and Dawe on alert in the center of the group. Guided by the prompting of Quintrel's embedded memories, Connor worked his way through the outer layers of the maze, stopping by each opening and branch to consult his inner sense.

"How about you?" Kestel asked Zaryae as they wound through the initial passageways. "Are you picking up anything?"

Zaryae nodded. "My dreams last night warned of danger. Things are not as they seem. We must watch for shadows."

Kestel frowned. "Shadows?"

Zaryae gave a weak smile. "The images are often not as clear as I would like them to be. I have a strong feeling of shadows and danger, but no specifics."

Kestel nodded. "Then we'll keep an eye out."

Around the next bend, Connor came to a halt and held up his hand. "Wait," he said. They had wound their way back and forth through the maze without obstacle, and the farther in they got without incident the more nervous Blaine became. *Someone wants us to stop being cautious*, he thought. *The maze-maker wants us to let our guard down. We're about due for a surprise.*

The next turn lay up a slight rise. The path beneath their feet was made of the same crushed rock as the floor of the canyon, and they were walled in on every side by the thick tangle of thornbushes. Connor stopped and stood very still, his eyes unfocused. After a moment, he shook himself and blinked.

"Another Quintrel memory," he said. "There's a drop-off up ahead, but as usual, he left a riddle: 'Beware the pit.' That's it—nothing more helpful," Connor said, spreading his hands palm up in a gesture of futility.

Connor moved carefully, step-by-step, pausing to rise on tiptoe and peer ahead.

"What do you see?" Blaine asked.

"Nothing. I really hate the son of a bitch who set up these Guardians," Connor replied. "I can't see anything—"

Connor's words vanished in a strangled cry as the ground gave way beneath his feet and he disappeared from view. Blaine and Illarion grabbed the rope. Kestel and Verran caught the rope as well. Digging in their heels, they managed to jerk the rope still.

"Connor! Are you all right?"

"Yeah!" Connor shouted, his voice muted. "The pit was

right at the rise and hidden by shadow so I didn't see it until it was too late."

"We'll pull you up," Illarion said.

"Wait a moment. This looks familiar. I need to look around," Connor said. He was silent for a few moments.

"It's like the cave. There's a way through it, but only if you know what to look for. Just falling brings you down on some nasty sharp stones. But in the corner the floor is smooth, and a ladder's been chipped into the far side of the pit. Drag me to the corner and then lower me down a little."

Blaine and Illarion did as Connor directed and felt the rope go slack as Connor reached the ground. "All right!" Connor shouted. "I'm going to cross the pit and climb out the other side, just to make sure. If it works, you can start coming down one at a time, but make sure you come down in the corner."

In a few moments, Connor emerged from the pit and stood much farther down the path. Lowering each person was a slow process, but finally Borya and Desya were the last ones left.

"Go on," Borya said. "I'll use the pinions." Desya nodded, and Borya lowered him down, then reclaimed the empty harness.

"I'll join you in a moment," he said, shrugging into the harness. Blaine and the others watched as Borya lay down on the path and leaned over the edge to secure a pinion in the wall, then wrapped the rope around the pinion and began to rappel down the side of the pit.

"I'm going to have to sacrifice a pinion," he shouted. "No way to get it back out, but if we have to come back this path, we'll have a way up the other side."

In a few moments, Borya had gathered his rope, crossed the pit, and climbed to the top. "Do you think that's the trap?" he asked, with a backward glance at the sharp rocks on the pit floor.

Connor shook his head. "No. Another one of Quintrel's memories came back while I was dangling: 'Beware the blades of the gods.'"

"What in Raka does that mean?" Piran demanded. "And why can't Quintrel say anything straight out?"

Connor shrugged. "I imagine he thought it was safer this way." He paused. "But there's another image along with it. I think I'll recognize the place when I see it. I hope."

They made their way through several more turns of the maze, with Connor stopping to concentrate and get his bearings at each juncture. After a dozen turns, they were near the center, and the high thorn hedge cast a shadow across the next stretch of the maze.

"Careful," Kestel warned with a glance toward Zaryae, who nodded. "Zaryae had a dream about dangerous shadows."

Connor was staring at the stretch ahead without moving, as if lost in thought. Finally, he bent down and picked up a handful of the fine rock dust that covered the path. He threw it into the air in front of him.

"What's that for?" Piran asked skeptically.

"Watch," Connor replied, nodding toward the path ahead.

Fine dust billowed, but instead of falling straight down to the ground, some of the particles appeared to hang in midair, as if suspended by the shadows themselves. "What is that?" Illarion asked.

Connor removed his cloak and let the hem of it flutter against the darkness. Four thin slices appeared in the heavy fabric, as if it were gossamer. "Hidden blades. Quintrel's 'blades of the gods.' They're made of something very thin and dark," Connor said, "placed on end in the shadows so they can't be seen. They look to be anchored in the ground."

Piran let out a low whistle. "Be a real bugger to run into

if you weren't looking," he said, eyeing the trap appreciatively. "How do we get past it?"

Connor threw another handful of dust into the shadows, and for good measure, tapped at the hidden blades with his sword. "There's a space on the right side," he said. "It's narrow, and you're likely to get torn up a bit by the thorns, but there's no room between the blades. There should be a second trap just past these blades, but I don't have a clear vision yet.

"I'll test the path to the right," he said warily. He threw his cloak over one shoulder and arm to protect him as much as possible from the thorns. Connor worked his way past the blades, which shaved a few threads off the edge of his cloak as he passed. "Damn, they're sharp," he muttered.

The shadows and the blades hid Connor from sight, but Blaine could hear Connor's footsteps crunching on the rock for several steps, then silence. "What's happening?" Blaine called out.

"There's a second set of blades," Connor said, "set vertically in the ground like the first ones. I imagine that's for any poor, overconfident blighter who makes it through the first set and starts to move ahead in a rush," he said with a grimace. "There's room for you to edge to the left and make your way down the far side along the hedge. Watch for the dust." He paused. "Then get as low as you can—there's a single wire set at neck height, sharp as a razor. Be careful," he added ruefully. "I lost some hair ducking under that one."

Blaine was the next to go. It was a tight fit between the last blade and the vicious thorns that tore at the fabric of his cloak and raised bloody scratches on his arms. Despite his best efforts, his shoulder rubbed some of the dust from the blade in passing. "Throw more dust once I'm through," he called back. "You'll have to do it after every person to see your way."

Blaine eyed the blades warily. He could not guess what they

were made of. They had the thin, razor-sharp edge of an obsidian blade but the strength of steel, like a finely honed sword. *They're a nasty piece of work*, he thought.

When they had gathered on the far side of the blades, Blaine looked to Connor. "Glad to have you along," he said with a tired grin. "I'd have hated to run into those without warning."

He paused and looked down the next corridor of the maze. The sun was past the midpoint, and the shadows were getting longer. "What next?"

Connor stared into the shadows, and Blaine wondered if he saw more than he let on. "Another remembered warning: We must cheat death."

CHAPTER THIRTY-FOUR

CONNOR MADE HIS WAY THROUGH THE MAZE, mindful of the lengthening afternoon shadows. The thought of spending a night in the maze was disquieting. *Then again, we have no idea what is waiting for us on the other side*, he thought. *Compared to that, the maze may seem friendly and safe.*

The others followed him through the maze, and Connor felt a crushing weight of responsibility for their safety. As he passed specific points, Quintrel's hidden memories surfaced randomly, popping unbidden into his head but denying him the security of being able to formulate a plan. Penhallow's presence was silent during the day. The Wraith Lord, no longer constrained by day and night as a passenger in his mind, was a more consistent voice than either Quintrel's or Penhallow's, though he spoke when it suited him and did not seem to feel obligated to answer Connor's questions.

How in Raka did I end up as the point man? he wondered. *They're all depending on me. Gods above! Before the Great Fire, I would have said that anyone who heard voices in his mind was insane, and now I've got two vampires and a mage rattling round in my brain, speaking up when they please and doling out bits and pieces at their leisure.*

The mountain air had been crisp by day; as night approached, the wind's bite grew sharper. Connor drew his cloak around him, but that did nothing to shield his face and hands. They had brought the bare minimum of supplies with them, leaving behind their tents and extra blankets with the horses. The prospect of a cold night was not appealing.

"We'll have to light lanterns before much longer," Blaine said. "Any idea how much more of the maze there is to navigate?"

Connor shrugged. His mood was grim. "I'm afraid Quintrel's memories don't trigger until there's a landmark, so I don't know about it until I see it."

Lowrey, who had stayed close to the front throughout the maze, nodded. "I've been marking down our path as we go, just in case we have to leave the way we came. If the maze holds to the familiar pattern, we should be nearly through. Not much farther until we're out." Zaryae slipped up beside Blaine so quietly he had not noticed until she spoke. "My dreams warn me that we will pay a price. I don't know exactly what that means, but I take the warning seriously." Grief was heavy in her voice, as if the loss had already occurred.

Blaine considered her warning for a moment before he spoke. "Is what you've seen certain? There isn't a possibility that circumstances could change the outcome?"

He could see the grief in Zaryae's dark eyes. "Perhaps. But I have found that the harder we try to avoid an outcome, the more certain it becomes."

More of the maze was shrouded in shadow as the sun moved west. The high thornbushes loomed large and menacing. Wicked-looking, inch-long thorns protruded from gnarled wooden stems that tangled around each other to form an impenetrable wall. Even Borya and Desya held no illusions about being able to climb the maze.

They turned right, and the maze passageway grew much narrower. The walkway was almost completely dark. Piran moved to go forward, but Connor thrust out an arm, blocking him.

"Wait," he said abruptly. He drew his sword and slashed at the darkness. There was a metallic ring as his blade struck something.

"What in Raka is that?" Piran demanded as Connor raised his lantern. A dull gleam reflected light, and Connor pressed at the area with his sword, exposing a thin, sharp wire fastened across the walkway at a height that would take the average man through the throat.

"More wire," Connor said with a grimace.

"Blimey," Verran said and swallowed hard, his hand going to his neck. "That'd take a bloke's head right off."

Connor nodded grimly. "Aye. And it may not be the only one. Keep your eyes open."

The narrow passageway allowed only one person at a time to pass without being snagged by the long thorns. Connor led the way, testing the air in front of him at every step with his sword. Three more wire traps blocked the passage before the walkway widened.

"We should be close to the end," Blaine observed. "We're far beyond what Desya was able to see from the start." They stopped for a moment, and Kestel studied the rough pattern Desya had sketched earlier in the day.

Connor paused as if listening to a voice only he could hear. "There's a new warning," he said, and his tone made the others look toward him.

"What's that?" Blaine asked.

Connor met his gaze. "'Beware the hunters in the maze. After dark, all become prey,'" he repeated from the clue Quintrel had planted in his memory. He sighed. "Apparently, there are things that live in the maze—more of Zaryae's 'shadows.' They come out after dark. We don't want to meet them."

Piran exploded with curses. "Well that's just bloody lovely, now, isn't it? And I'm betting these 'things' aren't friendly little puppy dogs, are they?"

"Probably not," Kestel observed dryly. "And I'd rather not find out what they are. So let's keep going."

Verran cast a nervous glance over one shoulder. "I could swear I heard something growling in the bushes."

Piran opened his mouth to make a sarcastic retort but just then, an unmistakable and unfriendly growl sounded from somewhere behind them in the tangled thorns. "Let's get out of here," Piran said, drawing his sword.

We've only conquered two Guardians, Connor thought. *If the Knights were right, we have two more to go.*

Blaine looked back at the maze and eyed the cliffs above them, searching.

"See something?" Kestel asked. The archers also looked skyward, although nothing was visible on the canyon rim.

Blaine shook his head. "No. But I can't shake the feeling that we're being watched."

Deep in the canyon, the shadows were long and much of the pathway was in shadow. They walked farther, weapons at the ready. When the canyon widened again, they found themselves facing rows of cairns.

"I don't like the look of that," Lowrey murmured. "Those are old graves. I didn't have any ability with death magic, but I knew mages who did, and they swore that old graves were powerful—and dangerous."

"What was Nidhud's riddle?" Kestel said. "'Blood is the coin to pass among the shadows. Narrow is the path through the flames.'" She frowned. "If that refers to the next two Guardians, it doesn't sound like fun."

Zaryae moved to the front of the group and pulled at Connor's sleeve. "Can you feel the spirits?"

Connor nodded. "They're waiting."

Piran gave a skeptical look toward the grave mounds. "There are ghosts, aren't there?"

"And they're angry," Zaryae replied. "They don't want us to pass." She paused. "This could be tricky, since Connor is a medium."

Blaine looked to Connor. "Now what?"

Connor let out a long breath. *The fate of the entire party rests with me, and because of Blaine, the fate of magic itself. No pressure at all.*

Before he could answer, a voice in his head spoke to him, and he recognized the presence of the Wraith Lord. *You'll need my help*, he said. *The spirits will be more likely to defer to me.*

With a sigh, Connor nodded his assent. *If you can help us get through here alive, then use me.*

I cannot promise that you all will live, but I will do everything in my power to protect you, the Wraith Lord replied.

Blaine frowned as if he noticed a change had taken place, and Connor felt the rush of power that coincided with possession by the vampire's ancient spirit.

"We will go first," Connor said. He noticed that everyone was looking at him as if trying to figure out what was different.

"Am I addressing the Wraith Lord?" Kestel asked, and Connor saw concern on her face as she searched his gaze.

"Yes."

"By 'we' you mean you—and Connor?"

"Yes."

"Be careful with him," Kestel admonished. "We'd like him back in good condition."

The Wraith Lord's laughter was a rich, rolling thunder in Connor's mind. "I have already given Lord Penhallow my word to that effect, but I will also give it to you, m'lady," the Wraith Lord replied.

Kestel looked askance at him but merely nodded. The others stepped back, giving way for Connor to move toward the cairns.

This area of the canyon was wide, filled with more cairns than Connor could quickly count. At least a hundred, he guessed, maybe more. Connor felt a smothering press of spirits, legions of grim-faced specters awaiting his entrance. Some stood near their tombs while others floated nearby. And all of them were staring straight at him.

A circle of stones on the ground indicated the boundaries of the cairns and signified where a warding had been cast. When Connor stepped across the stones, he felt a crushing weight of ominous power as if the air itself had become thick and heavy. The spirits left their places and swirled around him, and the air became far colder than the winter wind. Connor felt the heat leeching from his body, as if the spirits were drawing away his life and soul.

As the ghosts rushed toward Connor, he could sense their hunger. They descended on him like a cloud, and the strongest spirits forced themselves into his consciousness. *Sweet Esthrane*, Connor thought. *They're fighting over who can possess me!*

I'm with you now. I'll handle this, the Wraith Lord murmured to Connor.

Connor felt the Wraith Lord's presence fill him completely, forcing his consciousness to a small corner of his mind. The spirits of the cairns shrieked as they fled to a safe distance, where they withdrew to watch balefully as Connor walked into their midst.

"Enough!" the Wraith Lord roared. "You will allow me and my party to pass uninjured among your cairns."

The spirits had pulled back, enough so that Connor no longer felt as if they were drawing the breath from his body. But they circled hungrily, like wolves around prey, and Connor was painfully aware that the only thing holding them at bay was the Wraith Lord's presence, a presence that could not long be sustained.

What a choice. Allow the Wraith Lord's possession and burn alive. Lose his power and be sucked dry by vengeful spirits, Connor thought.

"You are no longer among the living," one of the spirits challenged in a voice like the rustle of wind through dry branches. He was dressed as a soldier, in an old style of uniform. His ghost was dark and menacing and looked at Connor with unconcealed malice.

"A sacrifice must be given," another spirit said. "We must have blood to allow any to pass. Those are the rules of the Guardians."

"The medium whose body carries your spirit can't sustain you forever," the soldier's spirit said, smiling unpleasantly. "If we detain you long enough, we're sure to have the blood we require."

Connor felt the ghosts gather once more, massing like a thunderhead. The spirits swelled toward him, smothering him. Their raw power rivaled that of the ocean. For an instant, Connor was overwhelmed by the memory of nearly drowning in the icy seawaters off the Edgeland coast. He gasped for air. The press of the spirits plunged him into a cloud of freezing mist,

cold enough to offset the warmth of the Wraith Lord's possession. *There are too many of them*, Connor thought. *I'm going
to die.*

Connor felt the Wraith Lord's spirit well up inside him. This
time, he did more than fling the ravenous ghosts away. Connor
felt the Wraith Lord's essence extend beyond the confines of his
body like a glowing aura. He might be bound by constraints
among the living, but here in the realm of the dead, his power
was unfettered.

Every spirit touched by the Wraith Lord's aura shrieked in
terror and screamed in pain. The Wraith Lord burned away
the cold, flashing across the cairns like lightning without ever
losing his hold on Connor. It happened in the blink of an eye,
but when it was over, the spirits had drawn back against their
cairns, cowed and trembling.

"I am changing your rules." Whether or not the others could
see it, Connor felt as if his whole form glowed with the indomi-
table will of the Wraith Lord.

"I am *talishte*. I was a patron and protector of the Knights of
Esthrane. You were put here by the Knights, and I can sweep
you into oblivion if you have outlasted your usefulness.

"Say now what you will do," the Wraith Lord continued.
"May my party pass unharmed, or will you go to Raka by my
hand?" The *talishte*'s voice seemed to echo from the cliff sides,
deafeningly loud. The power that filled his body made it difficult
to breathe, and Connor felt as if he would collapse with fever.

I might not be around for the fourth Guardian, Connor thought,
trying to hang on to the shred of consciousness that belonged to
him. The spirits shrank back at the ferocity of the Wraith Lord's
ultimatum. One by one, the ghosts sank to their knees.

"We will yield," the ghost soldier said. "Forgive us, my lord.
We did not recognize you."

"Allow us to pass," the Wraith Lord commanded. Around him a corridor cleared as the specters drew back.

"Come now. Be quick," the Wraith Lord said to the others who waited at the edge of the cairns.

As if he were physically holding back the storm, the Wraith Lord led the group past the rows of cairns as hundreds of angry ghosts stared at them, hungry for blood. Whether Blaine and the others could see the ghosts, Connor did not know, but they shrank from the edges of the path the Wraith Lord had cleared, as if on some primal level they understood the danger of what sight and sound could not communicate.

"If we must pass this way again, you will not threaten us," the Wraith Lord instructed the ghosts. "You will do nothing to cause us misfortune. This is your command."

"Yes, my lord," the ghost soldier replied with a deep bow.

"Then be at rest," the Wraith Lord said, holding up a hand in benediction. Connor could see the spectral soldiers melting into the shadows until the canyon appeared to be deserted except for his companions

They cleared the edge of the burying ground, and Connor felt the weight of the unseen power lift so he could breathe once more. Once the forbidding presence of the cairn ghosts was gone, Connor sank to his knees, burning up inside, gasping for air.

"You've got to let him go!" Kestel said, kneeling beside Connor and grasping his shoulders.

Zaryae knelt on Connor's other side, and Connor could hear her chanting in a strange language. Blood thundered, making it impossible to think, but somewhere in the chaos, Connor thought he sensed Penhallow's presence warning the Wraith Lord to withdraw.

I will leave you, for now, the Wraith Lord's voice spoke in

Connor's mind. *I regret if I have damaged you. The spirits of the cairns would not have been as gentle.* With that, the Wraith Lord's presence vanished, and Connor fell forward as the world swam around him.

When Connor came around, he found his companions watching him worriedly. Zaryae and Kestel helped him sit up. "We need to keep going," Connor said, his voice hoarse.

"We were waiting to make sure you were still alive," Piran remarked. "It was a little iffy."

Connor got to his feet, and although he was a bit unsteady he managed to stand without assistance. "I'll live. We've got to get through the last Guardian."

Zaryae eyed him as if she doubted his account but said nothing, although she stayed close behind him.

Blaine fell into step behind him. "Could we have gotten through the cairns without the Wraith Lord's help?"

Connor was exhausted enough that he took a while to answer. He could feel Penhallow lending him energy, but he could also feel tension through the *kruvgaldur* and guessed that Penhallow himself was facing some kind of challenge. *Is he under attack? Maybe Pollard and Reese made their final assault.*

"Not without cost," Connor replied. "They intended to demand a blood price, either my life or Zaryae's because our abilities called to them." He paused. "If Nidhud had come with us, he might have been able to appease the spirits, since he was one of the Knights." The memory of the spirit's lust for blood came back to Connor, and he shivered. "Then again, maybe not."

"We've got one more Guardian to pass," Lowrey reminded them. Connor was surprised that the old scholar was still chipper, but he seemed to be reveling in the adventure when he wasn't quailing with fright. "Did Quintrel leave you a clue?"

"Nothing yet," Connor said, wondering if the others could hear the exhaustion in his voice. "Let's hope I remember something useful once we get there."

They did not have far to go. They were quite far back in the canyon, and the next turn brought them to a strange sight. The air shimmered above a crack in the stone, presenting waves of heat despite the cold day.

"How do we get past that?" Borya asked and cursed.

"The fissures go from side to side," Blaine said. "And I don't relish the idea of trying to jump across."

"A narrow path through the flame," Kestel murmured, recalling the knight's riddle.

Connor had gone still, listening for the voice of Quintrel in his mind. He saw the stars burning overhead, then it seemed as if one constellation came into sharp contrast. Vessa, the Fire Bringer. The same constellation he had seen drawn on the star map in the king's library in Quillarth Castle the night of the Great Fire. He saw the points of light in the sky that were Vessa's constellation, and he knew.

"There's a path through the fire," Connor said. "It follows the outline of Vessa's constellation. The path isn't clear from the ground, but if you could see it from above, it would be the shape of the star figure."

"Where's the fire coming from? That's what I want to know," Piran said. "We never had volcanoes here in Donderath, not like we had in Edgeland."

Lowrey had ventured close enough that the hem of his cloak smoldered and as he ambled back to the group, his beard smelled of smoke. "Take a good whiff," he said, raising his nose and breathing in. "What do you smell?"

"Smells like a coal fire to me," Verran said.

Lowrey nodded. "Aye. And that's what's burning. One huge

coal fire." At their blank looks, he went on. "You've never heard of a coal seam catching on fire? Oh, it doesn't happen often, I grant you, but a burst of lightning can do it. Sometimes it just happens and no one knows why. Magic could start one, back when there was magic to be used. Once it began, it would go by itself, without the magic." He pushed his spectacles back up his nose. "I've heard tell of fires that have been burning for a hundred years without going out." He chuckled. "Very clever, using it as a trap."

"If I may intrude?" They looked up to see Illarion, flanked by Borya and Desya, who appeared to be quietly arguing. "Since the last Guardian was very taxing for Connor, I wanted to volunteer to take the lead this time. I was accustomed to juggling and tumbling with fire. I will scout the path."

"Let us go," Desya protested angrily. "Borya and I can do it." His yellow, catlike eyes flashed in the firelight.

Illarion drew himself up to his full height and straightened the tall hat he insisted on wearing. "You insult me."

"No, we don't want to see you get hurt," Borya shot back. "Before we were caught in the magic storm, you could make any jump, scale any wall. You've never gotten over what the storm did to you." His eyes, altered in that storm, glowed an eerie yellow.

Illarion turned away. "Then I am most expendable."

"You are never expendable!" Zaryae protested, pushing forward. "This is a foolish risk to take, especially when my dreams have been dark."

Illarion turned to her with a pained expression and reached out to touch his niece's cheek. "No, Zaryae. This is exactly the risk to take when your dreams are dark. Because I have the least to offer the group, while Borya and Desya are young and strong. Let me do this. Please, indulge my pride."

Zaryae looked as if she was holding back tears. She turned his palm and kissed it, then folded his fingers into a fist. "For luck," she said, although the look in her eyes was sad.

"For luck," Illarion replied. He gave a look of challenge to the twins, but Borya gave an audible sigh and shook his head.

"There's no stopping you when you're in a mood like this," he conceded. "But be careful. We've got many roads to follow together."

Desya's expression made his objection plain. "If you do this and die, I will refuse to mourn you," he threatened.

Illarion took the threat in stride. "Let's hope that's not necessary." He eyed the darkening sky. "Let's get moving. We're nearly out of daylight."

They had been cold all day, nearly frozen in the winter chill. But as they got closer to the split ground and the growing fire within, the canyon rapidly became uncomfortably hot. Connor insisted on walking near the front, in case another of Quintrel's memories awakened. He walked along the wall, keeping a careful distance from the fissures.

"There!" he said, pointing. "You hardly see it as an opening, because there's another seam offset from the first making it look as if the split goes all the way across. But there's a gap."

Illarion nodded, eyeing the space. "Aye. A bit tight, but there's an opening for sure." He looked back to the others. "Follow carefully. I'll call out what I find as I go. You'll excuse me if I've got no desire to make a return trip once I reach the other side."

"Let's get you into a harness," Borya said, catching Illarion by the shoulder.

Illarion looked at the cracked landscape and the fiery glow. "A rope won't hold in that. I'll find my way."

Zaryae tore a piece of fabric from her clothing and wet it in a pool of slush. She wrung it out and offered it to Illarion. "Put this across your nose and mouth. And be careful," she said, stretching up to give him a kiss on the cheek.

"I'll see you again," he said, bending to kiss her forehead. Then he took the wet cloth and made his way amid the fissures. The air shimmered with the heat, making it difficult to see far ahead. The others, taking a cue from Zaryae, soaked scarves or kerchiefs and also covered their faces against the fumes and heat.

"I don't think I can cross that." Lowrey's voice was barely audible. Blaine turned to the scholar, who was ashen with fear. "Leave me here. I'll never make it."

"Climb on my back," Borya said. "I'll carry you."

Connor was just a few steps behind Illarion, followed by Borya and Desya, and then Blaine. Illarion seemed to disappear into the shimmering air, but when Connor ventured after him, he realized that the path between the fissures was wider than it looked. *A good thing, or we'd be cooked before we made it out*, Connor thought.

Once inside the first set of fissures, a large patch of cracked stone stretched several wagon-lengths across the floor of the canyon. From between the cracks, plumes of smoke rose from the burning seam. Past the cracked stone area, the canyon floor appeared to return to its normal appearance.

It was dangerously hot among the fissures, and the fumes from the burning coal made the air difficult to breathe. Illarion traced the six-star figure of the Vessa constellation in the air to remind himself, then peered at the field of cracked stone and finally nodded.

"I think I see the path," he said. "It's narrow. There are places where it widens a bit. My bet is that the wide places form the same figure as the constellation's stars, and it's the way to safely navigate the trap."

"Are you certain?" Blaine asked, eyeing the burning cracks with concern. "If you're wrong—"

"If I'm wrong, I die, and Borya or Desya takes my place," Illarion said. "I respect the fire, but I'm not afraid." He chuckled. "I don't plan to die today. You watch. I will find the path."

Illarion eyed the pattern of the burning coal seams one more time, then carefully began to make his way, surrounded by smoking fissures.

Illarion tottered, and Connor feared he might lose his balance, but he straightened and surveyed the ground in front of him. Vessa's constellation was a zigzag of bright stars, which the ancient astronomers had fancied to be a woman with wild hair streaming behind her and flames flaring from a burning brand held in her right hand.

Illarion turned sharply to follow the narrow path to what would be the lowest point of the flames from Vessa's burning brand. The rock ridge that was the path through the glowing cracks was as narrow as an acrobat's balancing beam. Next, Illarion tacked in the other direction, to a point that made up the body of the astronomer's fanciful figure. Borya followed, carrying Lowrey on his back, and Desya found safe footing.

"Our turn," Blaine muttered. He motioned to Piran behind him, the signal for a few more of the group to cross over.

Illarion made another diagonal move to a point of the constellation that was Vessa's long, unbound hair. There was just one final stretch to the last point in the constellation, Vessa's head. From there, he had a short leap to unbroken stone. He turned to encourage Borya, who was close behind him.

The edge of the narrow ridge of stone began to crumble, and Borya lost his footing. Illarion caught him by the back of his cloak and hauled him upright. With Lowrey on his back, Borya lacked the agility that should have made the crossing simple.

They tottered for an instant, but the thin ridge of stone was too narrow for them both to secure a solid footing. Illarion twisted, giving Borya a shove toward the next wide place in the path. More rock crumbled from the narrow ridge and Illarion toppled backward, flailing, into the glowing fissure.

"Illarion!" Borya and Desya cried out.

"You've got to keep moving," Connor grated. He could see the grief in the twins' faces, and he was not immune to their sorrow, but intense heat, coupled with his heavy traveling clothes, was beginning to make him light-headed, and he was certain the same was true for the rest of the party. "We'll lose everyone if we don't keep moving."

Trying not to think about the burning coal in the fissures all around him, Connor inched his way toward the first widening in the path. Even though he had watched Illarion and the twins closely, it was difficult in the fiery glow to spot the islands of safety. "We'd better move people through one island at a time!" he shouted back to Blaine. "It's not easy to spot the path, and it can't bear much weight."

Blaine nodded. Connor had to heel-toe his feet to cross the narrow ridge.

"Keep your eyes on a focal point!" Desya shouted back to him. "Don't look at the path, look at something on the wide place."

Connor held his breath and fixed his gaze on a rock in the middle of the wide place. He moved with a combination of caution and panic, knowing that his delay was costing his companions endurance time. With a gasp of relief, he made it to the landing, and Blaine followed to the spot he had just vacated. Kestel was next in line, followed by Zaryae.

Connor moved to step onto the next ridge and realized too late that he had eyed the wrong spot. He twisted mid-step, and for a horrible instant, saw nothing but the gaping stone fissure and a burning maw of coal. Regaining his balance, Connor took a deep breath and stepped again, this time making sure not to take his eyes from the spot Desya left.

It seemed to take forever for the group to cross. On the far side of the coal seam it was marginally cooler, although the burning coal was close enough that they all opened their cloaks and mopped their foreheads. Connor's lungs ached from the smoke, and he longed to leave this area behind.

They moved a safe distance away from the flames and heat. Zaryae collapsed into Borya's arms, sobbing, and Desya stood next to them, his entire form rigid with anger and grief. The others stood apart, unwilling to intrude on their mourning, but mindful that they were still not out of danger. Lowrey was bent over, wheezing and gasping for breath, looking pale and terrified. Dawe had unsheathed his crossbow, and Piran had drawn his bow. Both men eyed the dark ridges of the canyon walls. Night had fallen, and after the brilliance of the fire seam, their lanterns gave a paltry glow that seemed to be mocked by the darkness of the canyon.

"I don't like this," Connor muttered. Nothing about the journey had been hospitable, but in the darkness, the canyon seemed ominous.

"We've got to make camp," Verran said. "For all we know, there could be a huge cliff in front of us, and we wouldn't know it until we fell off it, it's so dark."

"We can't stop here," Blaine said, "it's too exposed. We need to move farther back in the canyon, away from the fire."

"Give them a little more time," Kestel admonished. "Then we'll worry about making camp." She approached the huddled group and laid a hand on Zaryae's shoulder. "I'm so sorry," she said.

Zaryae drew a shuddering breath and nodded, unable to

speak. Borya was weeping, but Desya remained dry-eyed, his expression filled with suppressed rage.

Blaine moved up behind Kestel. "We're all sorry for your loss," he said quietly. "And when we get through this, you and the twins are welcome to make Glenreith your home if you wish. But now, we need to move on."

Zaryae nodded and linked arms with Borya, who seemed to be supporting her weight as they began to walk. The group drew closer together, watchful of the cliff sides as they started forward.

A crossbow thud echoed in the canyon, and a quarrel slammed into Desya's shoulder hard enough to spin him to the side before he collapsed. Zaryae screamed and would have run to him, but Borya held her back as three more shots laid down a line not to be crossed.

"Show yourselves!" Blaine shouted, moving to the fore.

An instant later, lanterns were unshuttered, and they saw a force of at least fifteen armed men, crossbows nocked and ready, blocking the path. A tall man with an unpleasant expression stepped forward.

"You are trespassing. You do not belong here. Now, you will die."

CHAPTER
THIRTY-FIVE

▬▬▬

V EDRAN POLLARD'S HORSE REARED AS HE BROUGHT
his sword down hard on the infantryman to his right,
cleaving the man from the shoulder through the ribs. The
night sky was filled with torchlight and smoke as two forces
faced each other at the base of the Riven Mountains.

Pollard's mood was darker than usual. He lay about with his
sword, slicing his way through the motley assembly of army
survivors who had followed Niklas Theilsson home from the
Meroven front. They stood little chance against Pollard's contingent of nearly two hundred men, even if Lanyon Penhallow
had brought a dozen or more *talishte* with him.

The battleground stank of blood and offal. Few of Theilsson's men were mounted, which meant that Pollard's small cav-
alry was at a distinct advantage. Pollard led the charge against
the foot soldiers, with his own infantry closing ranks behind
him. Thanks to Reese, Pollard had *talishte* of his own in the
field, moving with deadly swiftness among the poorly armed
soldiers.

Hoofbeats sounded, coming hard and fast. Pollard's attention snapped to the man on horseback riding toward him with

single-minded focus, sword raised in challenge. His mood, already grim, grew blacker as he recognized Lanyon Penhallow.

While Penhallow lost the advantage of *talishte* speed for his attack astride a horse, he forfeited none of that edge in the series of sword blows he rained down on Pollard. "I've been looking forward to this," Penhallow said, bringing his sword down hard against Pollard's blade. "You've made yourself extremely inconvenient."

"So now you're McFadden's bodyguard?" Pollard returned, parrying the blow although it took his full strength to do so. Sparring with Reese had conditioned him to fighting a *talishte*, but it still required exceptional focus to track the faster-than-mortal movements, and despite his own skill as a swordsman, it put the odds against him.

"More like his vermin killer," Penhallow said, scoring a nasty gash in Pollard's shoulder. "Call your troops off. You won't win."

Pollard laughed and blocked another strike. "That outcome is very much up for debate."

Penhallow prepared for another onslaught, but just as he was about to strike, two of Reese's *talishte* warriors appeared behind Penhallow astride war steeds. They attacked in tandem, drawing off Penhallow, as Pollard carefully backed his horse away from the skirmish.

"I'll leave you to my friends, Lanyon. Of course, it's not too late to change sides," he added with a laugh.

Penhallow cursed, but whether it was intended for Pollard or for his new assailants, Pollard did not know and did not care. He spurred his horse in the other direction, intent on rejoining the fight.

Pollard spotted Nilo across the field and fought his way through the tangle of soldiers and horses to reach him. Nilo and a small contingent were battling a nearly equal number of

Theilsson's soldiers. What the enemy soldiers lacked in armor or supplies, they made up for with sheer determination, and they were giving Nilo and his men a fair fight. Pollard rode in, taking out his frustration at Penhallow on the soldiers in his way. Within minutes, the enemy soldiers had been killed or had fled for their lives. Nilo directed his men toward a new target and turned toward Pollard.

"Where in Raka are the additional troops?" Pollard demanded. "They should have been here before this."

Nilo shook his head. "Not here, that's for certain."

Pollard cursed. "I want to break through the line and get men into the pass. They can still pick up McFadden's trail."

Nilo looked at him askance. "You believe McFadden is actually going to find Valshoa?"

Pollard glowered. "I believe McFadden is going to find a place of power where he'll make an attempt to bring back magic, as he did at Mirdalur. And when he does, I want our men in place to capture him or kill him, if necessary. Whoever controls McFadden holds the fate of magic. That's the kind of bargaining chip I like."

Nilo's eyes narrowed as he looked out across the battlefield. For now, the fighting had shifted west. "We've got the advantage in numbers," he said. "I think we can break the enemy line if we use a wedge formation, drive at the center of the line, and use our *talishte* fighters on each flank. They don't have the resources to withstand that kind of concentrated assault."

"I like that," Pollard said, nodding. "Make it happen."

Nilo mustered his commanders and shouted orders, rallying his men. The enemy troops sensed a change, and Pollard could hear the sound of distant voices preparing for an assault. From his vantage point on a small rise, Pollard could see across the plain toward the mountains, where Theilsson massed his soldiers. Pollard had made certain to have enough *talishte* fighters to eliminate the danger that Penhallow's men would try their firebombing trick again.

Penhallow will be lucky to survive the battle, Pollard thought. *We'll sweep McFadden's pathetic little army out of the way and end this farce. Lord Reese will be very pleased, and we will be one step closer to our goal.*

Theilsson's army formed a line blocking the entrance to the mountain pass. Trumpets blared, and Pollard's army surged forward, hammering that line with brute force. Outnumbered, the enemy held firm, but even at a distance, Pollard could see that Theilsson's position was becoming untenable. When the line broke, Nilo's men ran for the pass and the trumpeters sounded their horns in victory as the enemy army retreated in disarray.

We'll have McFadden before the night is over, Pollard thought, smiling. *And when I'm through here, I'll make sure the backbone of any resistance movement McFadden was planning to lead is utterly broken.*

"Lord Pollard! Sir!" A voice shouted from behind him. Pollard turned his horse to see a runner coming from the direction of their camp.

"What is it?" Pollard snapped, unwilling to miss a moment of Nilo's glorious rout.

"Sir, there are troops coming from the rear. A large force, headed this way."

Pollard glowered. "Commander Britt is late. I assure you he'll pay for disobeying orders. He should have been here yesterday—"

"Sir!" the messenger interrupted, and Pollard looked down ill-humoredly at the interruption.

"What?"

"They're not our troops."

CHAPTER
THIRTY-SIX

W E'RE HERE AT THE INVITATION OF VIGUS
Quintrel," Blaine countered, defiant despite the leveled
crossbows. "Take us to him. He called us here."

The leader of the group stared in silence at Blaine for a
moment, deciding. "Surrender your weapons. We'll take you to
the Quorum, and they'll decide."

Blaine nodded for the others to lay down their weapons.
Given how well armed the group had been, this took a few
moments and was regarded with raised eyebrows by many in
the 'welcoming' group.

"You don't appear to come for peaceful reasons," the speaker
observed.

"We've got some powerful enemies," Blaine replied, his
mood dark. After losing Illarion and a grueling day cheating
the traps of the Guardians, he thought, being taken hostage
capped off a miserable journey.

"Bind their wrists," the speaker said. He returned his attention to Blaine as men from the mob went to do his bidding.
"Fight us, and we'll kill you without bothering with the Quorum. Many have tried to reach Valshoa and have lied about

their purpose. If you aren't who you claim to be, none of your group will leave this place."

"Heal my companion," Blaine demanded as one of the soldiers tied his wrists with rope.

The man looked down at him with grim amusement. "You're hardly in a position to give orders."

"Quintrel invited us here. We have a passage token from the Knights of Esthrane. What will they say when they learn you've murdered one of my companions?" Blaine challenged.

The commander stared at Blaine for a moment as if taking his measure. Finally, he turned. "Rillen," he called to one of the men who stood guarding Blaine's group. "Bind up the wound. We'll get him a healer when we reach the city."

"Who is your Quorum?" Blaine's voice was defiant. "It's Quintrel we're here to see and the Knights of Esthrane." Their captors did not bother to answer.

They waited while Rillen crossed to where Desya lay and broke off the quarrel, leaving a portion of the shaft embedded in his shoulder. Kestel and Zaryae reached for their packs to get to their medicinal herbs, but the guards warned them back. Blaine knew that withdrawing the arrow without proper preparation could make Desya bleed out, but the sight of the quarrel protruding from the skin still made his gut tighten. Rillen packed and bound the wound and then straightened. "That's all I can do for him here."

"Thank you," Blaine said, an undercurrent of anger still clear in his voice. "But it wasn't necessary to shoot him in the first place."

One of the men bent to lift Desya in his arms. He groaned. In the lantern light, Blaine could see a spreading stain where the quarrel had pierced Desya's shoulder.

"Just take us to Vigus Quintrel," Blaine said, tamping down his anger. "He's the one who brought us here."

It took another half a candlemark to reach the back of the canyon. They passed through a narrow cavern entrance and took a route through passageways so complicated that Blaine knew he could never find his way out unassisted. Their captors did not seem to need any markers to keep their bearings. Lanterns were the only light, and several in their group stumbled in the rough passageways.

Cooler air signaled that they were near an exit. Blaine's minders shoved him out of the cave and into the moonlight. Before them stretched a valley filled with a city of stone. Blaine could see the shadowed outlines of hundreds of buildings, and the ruins of many more. Valshoa had once been a city of the size of Castle Reach, and despite the devastation, it was possible to imagine its former grandeur. Lights glowed in only a fraction of the buildings, and Blaine wondered if the other structures were habitable, or if the Knights and mage-scholars who had sought refuge here had not yet reclaimed more of Valshoa's lost glory.

"This way," the leader said, heading down the slope toward the city.

Moonlight was sufficient to gain a better idea of the lost city as they drew closer. Many of the ruins lacked upper floors or roofs. Some were nothing more than the footprint of a foundation. Yet at least a third of the houses Blaine could see looked livable. They walked along what had once been a wide boulevard. Now, its paving stones were pocked by wear, and debris littered the gutters.

Their arrival drew attention, and as they made their way through the streets, a crowd followed. Bound and under guard, Blaine could not shake the memory of a similar walk, when he had left the dungeons of King Merrill and been paraded with the other criminals to the convict ship that would take him to

Edgeland. It was a memory he did not care to relive, and he hoped it was not an omen.

Finally, the leader stopped in front of one of the largest buildings still standing. It looked as if it had once been a place of official business, a court or royal office, with large columns and wide stairs leading up to massive wooden doors.

"In here," Blaine's captor said, giving him a push for emphasis.

Blaine glared but did not reply. Instead, he focused on their surroundings, trying to assess every detail for some clue as to their likelihood to survive. Inside the huge doors was a large gallery, and the walls were ringed by balconies on each of three stories. Whatever the building's original purpose, it was clear at a glance that it was now a library.

"You will wait," the man said, stopping midway across the gallery.

Blaine studied the room. The building was old and weathered, and the tiled stone floor had clearly seen a lot of traffic. Several bookshelves looked like recent additions, cobbled together out of necessity rather than crafted by cabinetmakers. Rough tables and chairs gave the impression that squatters had overrun an abandoned palace. *And to an extent, that's what happened*, Blaine thought. *First the Knights of Esthrane, then Quintrel and his followers. They moved in and made the best of it.*

A gray-cloaked figure approached from the back of the gallery. The figure stopped, and the leader of the men who had taken Blaine's group captive stepped forward.

"Scholar," he said. "These trespassers were found at the end of the fourth Guardian. One has been shot. What shall be done with them?"

Blaine shouldered forward, heedless of his keepers. "Vigus Quintrel called us here. I have a passage token from Nidhud of the Knights of Esthrane. I am the last Lord of the Blood, and we've come to see if magic can be restored."

The gray-cloaked figure lowered its hood to reveal a woman with the close-cropped red hair of a sworn scholar. "I know who you are."

For a moment, Blaine could not breathe. Despite the scholar's robes and the short hair, Blaine recognized her. Carensa, his onetime betrothed, thought lost in the wreckage of her father's manor at Rhystorp. He stared at her as if she were a ghost, and his mouth went dry. Before he could speak, Carensa turned to their captors.

"Cut their bonds, and take them to the gathering room. Get a healer for the wounded man, and next time, have a care about who you shoot," she said with a hard look at the commander, who bowed his head in acknowledgement of her censure. "See that they have food and drink. They're honored guests and have been expected." She gave Blaine an evaluating gaze that he could not decipher. "Master Vigus and I will join them shortly." With that, Carensa turned and strode back the way she came.

The soldiers cut the leather straps that bound their wrists. "This way," the leader said grudgingly.

The gathering room was only slightly smaller than the main gallery. It looked to be capable of holding a large crowd. A fire burned in the fireplace at one side of the room, and over the mantel Blaine saw a crest that by now had become familiar: the shield and diagonal blue stripe of the Knights of Esthrane. A man carried Desya to a small couch near the fire and laid him on the cushions.

"Our healer will be here very soon," he said, refusing to meet their gaze and looking more contrite than Blaine would have imagined possible. "We didn't shoot to kill."

Zaryae rushed to kneel beside the couch and fumbled for the herbs and potions she carried in her pack. She folded Desya's hand in hers. Borya stood behind her, a hand on her shoulder, but said nothing. Kestel took the herbs and conferred quietly with Zaryae, then moved to the table to begin preparing something to staunch the bleeding and ease Desya's pain.

"Who was the woman scholar?" Piran asked. "She looked at you as if she knew you."

"That was Carensa," Blaine said, still in shock.

Piran raised an eyebrow. "*Your* Carensa? Your betrothed?"

The others turned to look at Blaine. Kestel was watching him with an unreadable expression. Blaine felt his face redden. "After nearly seven years, she's no longer 'my' Carensa," he said. "I released her from the betrothal when I was exiled. Aunt Judith said she'd married and then disappeared in the Great Fire."

He paused. "Judith also said that Carensa rebelled against her father's wishes to study with the scholars. Her husband didn't seem to mind, and Judith said she seemed to have passion for little else." He grimaced. "Her husband and son died in the Great Fire. She's probably not the only one to take advantage of an opportunity to disappear and start over."

They turned as the door through which they had come opened. Several gray-robed scholars entered bearing platters with bread and meat and pitchers of water and wine. Another scholar went directly to where Desya lay and began to unpack potions and small bottles of elixir from a bag on her shoulder. Kestel and Zaryae offered their assistance, and the healer put them to work.

"Eat, and then the others will return to talk." The speaker was a man whom Blaine guessed to be in his late thirties, with dark hair and brown eyes. He had an intelligent look, although he seemed hesitant in their presence. The other scholars did not speak, but they eyed the newcomers with open curiosity.

"Were you mages?" Blaine asked. "The mages Quintrel helped to disappear?"

The man looked away. "I was both a scholar and a mage before the Cataclysm. Not long before the fires came, Master Quintrel persuaded me to leave the city and come to this sanctuary." He nodded toward the others. "That's true for all of us."

"And the Knights of Esthrane?" Pirran asked. "Are they here as well?"

The man looked uncomfortable. "The Knights keep to themselves, for the most part, but they allowed Master Quintrel to bring us here, and they protect what's left of the knowledge we were able to save from the fires."

Kestel gave the man her most winning smile. "You're so isolated. How do you feed yourselves?"

The man blushed at her attention. "The canyon entrance is deceiving. Behind the city is a valley good for farming and small herds. The Valshoans tended the lands until they died, and the Knights maintained the herds to give them a source of blood. Master Quintrel had been preparing for our arrival some time before the fires. The first to take refuge here replanted the gardens and tended the vineyards and orchards. There aren't many of us, so it doesn't take a lot to sustain us.

"Please," he said gesturing toward the food. "You've had a long journey. Refresh yourselves. Master Quintrel will be in to see you soon."

"How is Desya?" Kestel asked, looking toward the healer. Desya was pale, but his chest rose and fell in deep breaths, and he appeared to be sleeping.

"Your friend will live," the healer replied. She wiped Desya's blood from her hands on a towel from her bag. "It could have been far worse."

"It's plenty bad enough," Borya muttered.

"He'll need rest, and he won't pull a bow or wield a sword with that arm for a while, but there should be no permanent damage." She paused. "If I can convince one of our *talishte* to help, would you accept his healing to speed the recovery?"

"Of course," Zaryae replied.

"Thank you," Blaine said, meeting the healer's gaze.

The healer gave a wry smile. "We caused the damage. I've just put things right." She followed the other scholars from the room.

"Bit of a switch, isn't it?" Dawe remarked when the scholars had gone. "We got from 'We're going to kill you' to 'Have a bite and take a load off' within a candlemark."

Verran plopped down in a chair by the food. "I much prefer being fed to being killed," he said and took a roll and piece of meat. "And I have to say, after all this, I'm rather curious about this Quintrel fellow." He took a bite from the roasted meat and poured himself a cup of wine. "At least he's real. I'd have hated to come all this way to find out he was just a story someone made up."

"Oh, he's real enough," Connor muttered.

"Do you think you can raise the magic here?" Dawe asked and looked at Blaine.

Zaryae answered, "There was great power here, before the Fire. I can feel it." She shivered and wrapped her colorful shawls tightly around her. "Now the power is wild. If the magic can be harnessed at all, it could be bound here. I'm sure of it."

Blaine shrugged. "We're here, and we have the disks, the maps—and my blood. Let's hope it's enough."

They ate with little conversation, and Blaine guessed they felt the same grief and apprehension that gnawed at his stomach. Illarion's death cast a shadow over all of them. Borya especially was struggling, and Blaine guessed that he blamed himself for being the cause. Zaryae tried to comfort Borya and tend to Desya, but sorrow was clear in her face and she looked near collapse.

Kestel seemed to be purposefully keeping her distance and avoiding his gaze. *I let go of Carensa years ago—or thought I had. I never expected to see her again. But to have her show up, here of all places, like a ghost from the grave—it's a shock. Life's changed us both. It's easier to let someone go when she's dead and buried, or half a world away.*

Doors at the back of the room opened, and three figures entered. Blaine recognized Carensa immediately. One of the men wore a tunic with the symbol of the Knights of Esthrane. He was broad-shouldered with cropped dark hair and piercing black eyes, and by his pale coloring, Blaine guessed he was *talishte*.

The third man held Blaine's attention. He was in his middle years, and his bald head reflected the glow of the torches that lit the walls. Wire spectacles were perched on his nose. He had the undeniable look of a scholar about him.

"Welcome," the bald man said. "I'm Vigus Quintrel." He looked at the group and smiled when he saw Lowrey. "Treven. I'm pleased to see that you survived." He sought out Connor at the back of the group, where he stood with his arms crossed over his chest and a mistrustful expression on his face. "Bevin Connor," Quintrel said. "My intrepid messenger."

"Conscript is more like it," Connor muttered with a glare. His fists were balled.

Quintrel's gaze came to rest on Blaine. "Lord Blaine McFadden," he said. "I'm pleased that you responded to my invitation." He paused. "When I left clues for Penhallow, I wasn't sure who the survivors would be—or whether there would be any at all. For this, at least, your exile was most fortuitous."

"That wouldn't be the word I'd have chosen," Blaine replied. "You went to a great deal of trouble to leave a trail of bread crumbs to your door. Now that we're here, and the solstice is tomorrow, the question is: Can the magic be restored?"

Quintrel lost his jovial mien. "I chose Penhallow because he's a man of honor, and as a *talishte*, he would be most likely to survive the Cataclysm. Whether or not any of the Lords of the Blood would survive, I had no way to know. I don't know whether the magic can be restored," he said, "but if there's any chance of using the disks as has been done the last two times the magic was raised, you're the one to do it."

Quintrel waved them toward the chairs. "Have a seat. You've come a long way. We have much to discuss."

"This is Lady Carensa of Rhystorp," he said with a nod toward Carensa. "She was one of my best pupils before the Cataclysm. As you've guessed, I brought as many of my top mages and most talented scholars with me when I sensed danger, as well as all the books and materials we could salvage.

"And this is General Dolan of the Knights of Esthrane," Quintrel said, glancing toward the tall man in the gray tunic. "Our benefactor."

"The healer requested my help speeding your friend's recovery," Dolan said. "Since you were attacked while carrying a passage token from the Knights, I will do what I can for him." With a nod, he moved to where Desya lay. They watched in silence as he carefully drew back the bindings on the wound then spat into his palm and pressed his hand against the torn flesh. He replaced the dressing and stood. "He should be quite improved by morning," Dolan said. "He is in no danger."

"Thank you," Blaine said. He and the others returned their

attention to Quintrel. "You've been planning all this," he said with a gesture to indicate Valshoa.

"For a while," Piran said, an edge in his voice. "But you didn't bother to warn everyone else?"

Quintrel looked pained. "As the gods are my witnesses, I tried. King Merrill didn't want to hear me. The court mages saw me as a threat to their power. The army had no use for mages who didn't want to follow their orders. When I saw that I couldn't stop a magic strike, I did the only thing in my power: I saved a remnant and retreated to a place where we might survive."

"Why did you send your messages with me?" Connor's voice was sharp and Blaine could hear an edge of resentment. "All those months, because you blacked out my memory, I feared I had betrayed my master."

Quintrel grimaced. "I chose you because you served both Penhallow and Garnoc. I knew you had access to court, which Penhallow did not. And I had to flee the outside world to stay out of Reese's grasp sooner than I had intended. It was the only way I could think of to leave a message behind so that, when the time was right, the right people would know where to come. And you did brilliantly!"

Connor did not look pleased. "You made me think I'd lost my mind."

"And yet, clearly you have not," Quintrel replied, sweeping his arm in a circle to acknowledge their location.

From the look on Connor's face, Blaine guessed that the argument was not settled, but Connor said nothing more.

"What I want to know is, how did you find Valshoa in the first place?" Piran asked.

Quintrel drew a deep breath. "I followed the clues left by my ancestor, Archus. He's the one who stole Valtyr's maps—and the one who hid them. If it's any consolation, the first time I made the trip was before magic failed, so there was another level of protection you didn't have to deal with."

"And you just walked up to the front door and knocked?" Piran challenged.

Quintrel shrugged. "Something like that," he said, and a look passed between Quintrel and Dolan that gave Blaine to suspect it had not been quite so easy. "I made my case to the Knights. While they owed no allegiance to King Merrill because of his grandfather's betrayal, their loyalty to Donderath is still quite strong. I convinced them of the imminent danger, and they allowed me sanctuary for my Remnant."

"And you brought all your mages and scholars back and forth through the Guardians?" Piran pressed.

"How I got them here is no concern," Quintrel replied, growing impatient with Piran's questions. "What matters is that I succeeded in safeguarding their knowledge."

"What's required to work the ceremony?" Blaine asked. "And what must I do?" He laid out the twelve disks on the large table in the center of the room. "We have all of the disks but one."

"Wonderful!" Quintrel grinned and withdrew the thirteenth disk from beneath the folds of his robe. "I kept this disk to assure that the trail would lead you here."

"We nearly died at Mirdalur because your clues left a lot to interpretation," Blaine said.

Quintrel frowned. "I didn't expect that. I visited Mirdalur and hoped that you found the journal I left behind. To the best of my ability to determine, its power was scattered, harmless."

" 'Harmless' doesn't do it justice," Piran muttered.

Quintrel gave a sigh. "It was possible, at least, in theory, that you might have been able to raise the power somewhere other than Valshoa. Also unlikely. It requires a place of especially strong power, and few of those spots exist." He nodded toward the maps Kestel had placed on the table.

"My ancestor, Archus Quintrel, spent years trying to understand how magic works. He searched for Valtyr's maps, believing, as Valtyr did, that the null and power places played a crucial role. But even Valtyr didn't recognize how widely the power varied or how it waxes and wanes over time. Only a few places have the conditions necessary to raise the power at any given time, and even with the right physical conditions, the only way we know to raise the magic still requires a Lord of the Blood," Quintrel said.

"Why didn't the Great Fire destroy Valshoa, if it was so powerful?" Dawe asked skeptically.

"Valshoa was not one of the places that the Meroven mages targeted." Carensa met Dawe's gaze levelly. "And it had protections in place—both physical and magical—that kept it reasonably secure until the magic failed. Even so, the damage was considerable. When you see the valley in daytime, you'll be able to tell how much destruction was done by the Cataclysm."

Blaine rubbed his temples. He'd had a pounding headache since just before sundown, and a growing feeling of uneasiness. Unbidden, he thought of Penhallow and had a blurred image of steel and blood. The moment passed, and he looked at Connor. They met each other's gaze, and Connor nodded solemnly. *More than my imagination*, Blaine thought. *Is that the* kruvgaldur? *Just a glimpse, but I'd guess Niklas and Penhallow are under attack.* He looked back to Connor, wondering what he had seen.

"What has to happen tomorrow?" Blaine asked, knowing that if the images were from Penhallow, it was a warning. "We left an armed force outside the mountain pass, but if my suspicions are correct, they're under attack from Reese's soldiers. If they can't hold the pass, we could have company."

Quintrel gave a cold smile. "The Guardians have protected the pass for a long time. The Knights of Esthrane also protect it. That should be sufficient for us to work the ritual tomorrow evening. If you're successful, our magic will prevent Reese from reaching Valshoa, even if he breaches the valley's protections."

"Those are our friends out there," Piran snapped. "They're putting themselves in danger to buy time for Blaine to raise the magic. They're not disposable."

"I didn't mean to imply they were," Quintrel replied, "merely that we're unlikely to be interrupted with our effort." Piran glowered at Quintrel, unconvinced, but remained silent.

"What about the disks?" Kestel pressed. "Blaine had just one of the disks at Mirdalur, and the ritual failed. We've got all thirteen now, but still just one Lord of the Blood. Will it make a difference?"

"Technically, two Lords of the Blood, although only one with a body of his own," Zaryae remarked. "Connor carries a bond to the Wraith Lord."

Quintrel looked at Connor and his eyes gleamed. "Now that's something I did not expect. You can speak with the Wraith Lord?"

Connor looked uncomfortable. "At times. He possesses me when he sees fit. But he's already said that without blood, the ritual won't recognize him. He's more of an adviser than a participant."

"We'll see," Quintrel said, deep in thought. He roused himself and turned back to Kestel. "The disks? They were focal points, designed to draw—and trap—the wild magic so it could be harnessed."

"So you mean that the bloody disks we've been lugging all over the kingdom actually attract wild magic?" Piran asked, agape. "And here I thought we just had rotten luck with all the magic storms. Might as well have painted a bull's-eye on our camp."

Quintrel looked up quickly. "If you've been dogged by magic storms, that's a good sign. The disks have retained their ability."

"A good sign?" Piran repeated incredulously. "He says it's a good sign that we've nearly been torn limb from limb."

"I'm curious," Connor said, eyeing Quintrel warily. "Penhallow and I gathered more of the disks than Blaine did, but we weren't hit by an unusual number of storms."

Quintrel nodded. "Neither of you is a Lord of the Blood." He looked at Connor over his spectacles. "We have no idea how the presence of the Wraith Lord may affect the disks. No way to tell until we do the working."

Blaine's headache had dulled, and he gathered his thoughts. "The disks attract the wild magic. This place had more power than usual, so using the disks here will draw even more magic. But there were also symbols for each family of the Lords of the Blood. We saw them at Mirdalur. What of them?"

Quintrel looked as if he were about to begin a lecture to one of his classes at the university. "Over the centuries, people who had the ability to act as conduits for magic were drawn to the power and found workings to harness it—temporarily. At Mirdalur—and before then, at other places of power like Valshoa—mages layered working upon working to bind the magic permanently. The disks, the ritual, the symbols, and the blood of someone with a particular sensitivity to magic: Layer them together in a place of power at a time when magic is strongest. And the mages found a way to harness the magic for long periods of time.

"There are meridians, invisible lines of power that cross the world. The wells of power are places where the meridians intersect. The last time magic was harnessed, it drew upon the meridians that intersected at Mirdalur and anchored the magic at the manors of each of the Lords of the Blood—manors that were built on thirteen separate meridians."

"But binding the magic isn't really permanent, is it?" Kestel said, fingering one of the obsidian disks. "What's done can be undone." She met Quintrel's gaze. "So the ritual tomorrow, if it works, can still be broken. What's the new anchor?"

Quintrel sighed. "This valley is another place where meridians cross. Spots where thirteen lines intersect are quite rare, at least on any particular continent. This is one of the few on this continent."

"So if we can raise the magic—and that's not certain," Blaine said, "it's going to be more fragile than it was before, because it doesn't have as many anchors."

"A necessary risk." Everyone turned as General Dolan spoke. The Knight's voice was deep and resonant. "Given the unrest, it was impossible to find a better site. Prior to Mirdalur, magic had been unbound for a hundred years. There was time to build the manors on lines of power, making it possible to link them together. I doubt anyone would care to prolong the current situation while thirteen fortresses are rebuilt."

"So I'm the catalyst," Blaine said. "Without me, you could try to find a new group of promising 'conduits,' as you called them, but it would be trial and error."

"Yes."

And all the while, the misery goes on, thousands die needlessly, and civilization slips further beyond our grasp. "Tell me what I need to do," Blaine said. "And let's hope by all the great and little gods that it works."

Quintrel nodded. "Very well. Sundown on the solstice is the most powerful time to do the working. The Valshoans built a large shrine on the nexus of power with the ritual chamber belowground. Its upper building was leveled in the Old Destruction, before Mirdalur. The Great Fire scorched the ruins and opened the ritual chamber to the sky. We've removed the rubble, preparing for this opportunity."

"And?" Piran asked. "Mick just walks over there and hopes the magic doesn't kill him?"

"My people will ready the site. We will arrange the disks and symbols along the meridians. When Blaine takes his place, the power should be drawn to him. My people will speak the word of binding in that moment, and the magic will be harnessed once again," Quintrel said, clearly anticipating the event.

"Assuming everything goes as planned," Kestel said. "And Mick doesn't die."

"I don't like it." A candlemark later, Blaine and the others were together in the large room where they would spend the night. Kestel paced, too concerned to eat any of the meal that Quintrel's people had brought for them. "Mick's the one with all the risk, while Quintrel and the Knights sit back and watch."

"Not completely," Zaryae said. "Wild magic is unstable. There's some risk to those who are preparing the ritual space, since the disks and the symbols, in a place of great power, could trigger an unexpected reaction."

"All this risk, and if the magic is harnessed, it still won't be the way it was before," Dawe observed.

Verran sat with his chair tipped back against one wall, playing his flute. Piran and Borya played cards near the couch were Desya slept, and from the sounds coming from the game, Piran had met his match at sleight of hand. Zaryae, Kestel, and Dawe had been debating the merits and risks of the venture since dinner. Lowrey had left them before dinner with a mumbled comment about finding some of his former colleagues from the university. Connor stood at the other end of the room, staring out a window into the dark, empty streets. Blaine found that his thoughts were too jumbled to join the conversation, and so he drifted toward the windows.

"You feel it, too?" he asked quietly when he was beside Connor. "Penhallow?"

Connor nodded. "Probably more than you do, since the bond's been in place for longer. I remember when I first began serving Penhallow. The images were very faint, and I thought for a while I was imagining things. Over time, the bond grew stronger. The images became clearer, but still often chaotic." He sighed. "It's an imperfect way to communicate, that's for certain.

"Penhallow's worried," Connor said. "We'd best be about our business quickly, in case they can't hold out."

Blaine's expression hardened. "Quintrel didn't seem worried about Reese getting in, but I don't like how casually he dismissed the possibility." He paused. "Do you trust Quintrel?"

Connor gave a harsh laugh. "As much as I trust anyone who kidnaps me, plants memories in my brain without my permission, and then leaves big blank holes to worry me. In other words, no. But I don't see an alternative."

Blaine sighed. "I don't trust him, either. But I agree—he appears to be our best bet. Gods know, trying it without him didn't go well."

Blaine thought about Carr, taken by madness, and of Kata, killed by the gryps, and Illarion, lost to the Guardians. He remembered the ruined farms and deserted homesteads they had ridden past as they crossed Donderath, and the desolation that had claimed his homeland. *If I can bring back the magic, even if it's not what it used to be, even if it doesn't last hundreds of years—what choice do I have?*

The door burst open from the corridor, and Lowrey stood in the doorway. He scanned the room and brightened as he saw Blaine. "There you are. The scholars would like a word with you. Come with me."

With a sigh, Blaine let Lowrey lead him out of the room and down a long corridor. As they walked, Blaine got a better look at the Valshoan building. Built of blocks of stone that had been cut out of the canyon, the building was solid. The floor was tiled with smooth stones, and along the walls, empty niches and nooks undoubtedly once housed statues or decorations. Blaine had thought that Quillarth Castle and the lyceum seemed old, but the millennia weighed heavily on this building. The floors showed the wear of centuries, and the marble thresholds were marked by the footsteps of countless passersby. Valshoa had survived the Great Fire as well as magic storms and the cataclysms of old, but each had left scars that did not fade with time.

"Look around you!" Lowrey enthused. "Have you ever seen a more perfect example of early Donderan construction?" He did not wait for Blaine to answer before hurrying on. "There simply are no comparable sites that haven't gone to total ruin."

Lowrey rubbed his hands together gleefully. "Quintrel tells me that although the Knights have been here for quite some time, the original Valshoans died out long ago, and the scholars have had little time for studying the site. The only histories that exist are legends and stories passed down among the Valshoans' scattered descendants," he said. "Which means I could be the first to do a comprehensive history of the Valshoan civilization. Think of it!"

"But the university in Castle Reach is gone," Blaine protested. "Where would you share your findings—assuming we get out of here alive?"

"Get out of here? Who's planning to leave?" Lowrey snorted. "Vigus Quintrel assembled the best scholars and mages of our generation in the Remnant he saved. And he's invited me to stay as a part of their community!" Lowrey's pleasure at the compliment was so great, Blaine did not have the heart to suggest that the invitation was a pleasant form of captivity to assure the valley remained hidden.

Lowrey may have a reason to stay, but the rest of us intend to go home—if we survive, Blaine thought. *Let's hope Quintrel and the Knights don't have other plans.*

Lowrey ushered Blaine into a room where a dozen gray-robed scholars awaited them. They eyed Blaine as if he were a particularly interesting specimen to be studied. Blaine guessed this was the Quorum the guards had mentioned.

"May I present Lord Blaine McFadden, the last Lord of the Blood," Lowrey announced with proprietary pride.

One of the scholars, a man who looked a decade or more Lowrey's senior, looked over Blaine from head to toe. "Can't say I'm overly confident that the future of the kingdom rests on a McFadden," he said gruffly.

"I can't say I blame you," Blaine replied. If the scholar expected him to bristle at the slight against his family, he would be disappointed, Blaine thought. "My father certainly didn't inspire trust. I keep my word."

Another scholar eyed Blaine, a thin man whose face was so haggard it was difficult to determine age. "And a convict, no less. What was Quintrel thinking?"

"Quintrel had no idea who would survive the Cataclysm," Blaine replied, growing less patient. "It's just your lucky day that I'm the only Lord of the Blood still breathing, so you'll have to make do with what you've got."

"We've only got your word for that," replied a stocky man

who looked as if he liked his ale and supper as much as his books. "Vigus brought most of us here before the so-called Great Fire. I'm quite happy out of the intrigue of the palace city, but it's difficult to believe things are as bad as Vigus says."

Blaine's temper started a slow burn. "If you doubt the kingdom is in ruins, you're welcome to leave with us when the ritual is over. Of course, if you don't like what you see and you want to come back, you're on your own."

"It would be like Vigus to stretch the truth a bit if it served his purposes," the stocky man said. "I think he rather fancies having a captive audience here."

"Is that what you are? Captives?" Blaine asked, wondering if he and the others would find it difficult to leave the valley.

The stocky man shrugged. "Maybe. Haven't tried to leave, so I can't say for certain. Not sure I want to."

Blaine decided to take the offensive. "Quintrel chose you as his Remnant. Why? What's so special about you compared to all the scholars and mages who died?"

The older man turned his attention back to Blaine with a glint in his eyes that said he was reevaluating him. "In part, we were his loyal friends and supporters at the university and elsewhere. Maybe this is a surprise to you, but not everyone liked Vigus's opinions, or his tactics." The others chuckled, giving Blaine to know there was a long story behind the comments.

"And the fact is, we're good scholars and were good mages," the thin man added. "Maybe we weren't the best in the kingdom, but we were good enough to be able to train a new generation so the learning and the magic—if it returns—won't be entirely lost."

And if you weren't the best in the kingdom before the Great Fire, you are now, by virtue of the fact that you're still alive, Blaine thought.

"Why Valshoa?" Blaine asked. "I've seen Valtyr's map. There were many places of power—maybe some just as strong. You could have hidden in a null space and not worried about the Great Fire or the magic storms. Why here?"

The older mage-scholar looked at Blaine for a moment and blinked, resembling an ancient tortoise. "Treven tells me you were acquainted with Quillarth Castle and with the Lyceum of Tobar. Is that correct?" he asked in a gravelly voice. Blaine nodded.

"Both were built on places of great power, and both had powerful wards and protections built into their very foundations, added layer upon layer over many years. The protections are older here, stronger. The Valshoans survived their own version of the Cataclysm, as well as the destruction of magic before it was raised at Mirdalur—and who knows what else. Vigus believed we would be safest here, even if the worst happened. And it did."

"What happens after we work the ritual tomorrow night?" Blaine asked. "Assuming we survive. Are we free to leave?"

The stout man chuckled. "We're not the ones to ask, and honestly, I don't think Vigus is either." He leveled a glance at Blaine. "The ones who have the biggest stake in keeping this valley a secret are the Knights of Esthrane. Whether or not you leave will be up to them."

For the next candlemark, the scholars asked Blaine about the devastation he had witnessed, both in Donderath and in Edgeland. He recounted what he had seen at the lyceum and in Castle Reach and gave an account of the fall of Velant. They quizzed him about Valtyr's maps and the disks and were especially interested in Connor, both as the pawn in Quintrel's game of clues and as the unwilling host to the Wraith Lord. Blaine answered cautiously, aware that he had no assurance either the mages or Quintrel was truly his ally.

The door to the chamber opened to reveal another gray-robed visitor carrying a lantern. "Vigus asked me to bring Lord McFadden to him," Carensa said, focusing her gaze on Lowrey and the older mage and completely avoiding Blaine's eyes.

"Forgive us," the older man said. "We've monopolized our guest. We're always hungry for news." He gave Blaine a smile that did not completely reach his eyes. "Thank you for your information. I wish you success with the ritual, for all our sakes."

Carensa turned and led Blaine from the room without a word or a backward glance. The corridors were deserted, although Blaine guessed that it had as much to do with the sparse population as the late hour. He was unsure whether to speak and what to say, and so he followed in silence for a while. Carensa turned down an unfamiliar corridor and stopped in front of one of the rooms.

Carensa's lantern barely illuminated the chamber, but Blaine could see it was a sparsely furnished sitting room. The fireplace at one end was dark, and the rough furnishings looked as if they had been salvaged or built from scraps.

All the years in Velant and Edgeland, I thought I knew what I would say if I ever saw Carensa again, and now I'm tongue-tied, Blaine thought. *Where do I even begin?*

"I lied about Vigus wanting to see you," Carensa said. "But I needed an excuse to rescue you from the Quorum." They were both silent for a few awkward moments. "I'm glad you're alive," Carensa said, breaking the silence. She kept the distance between them one might keep with a casual acquaintance, neither expecting nor inviting an embrace. "I feared the worst."

Blaine drew a deep breath and slowly exhaled, hoping his voice would not convey his nervousness. "I heard nothing from you or Judith all those years, and now I know that you both wrote to me, but Prokief confiscated the letters," he said. "As time went on, I hoped you built a life for yourself and that you were happy."

Carensa turned so he could not meet her gaze. "I survived. Father finally arranged a marriage for me, to a man who was decent and kind, but love was never part of the bargain. I gave him a son, and I loved our son, but I buried them both after the Great Fire."

"I asked after you when I came back. Judith told me that you were presumed dead," Blaine said.

Carensa let out a long breath. "I had a chance to leave behind all of the grief and memories—of you, of the years after you went away, of my son. I took it."

"I came back from exile, and you went into it," Blaine observed with a mirthless chuckle.

Carensa nodded. "Perhaps. Father despaired of me after you were sent away. He feared I would waste away, and I guess I hoped I would. To draw me out, he hired tutors. When I proved to be a good pupil, he was so happy to see me care about something that he brought a parade of scholars to the manor, never dreaming I would want to become one myself."

"Judith said he forbade you to go to the university."

Carensa sighed. "He felt that private instruction more befitted a lady. But the tutors told Quintrel about me, and when I advanced, he became my tutor. I confided in him, and after the Great Fire, I went looking for anyone who might be able to find him."

She shrugged. "Word reached him, and he sent for me." Carensa looked down. "I stole Father's disk. I don't think Father even knew what it was. It was the only thing Vigus asked of me, and so I brought it with me when I ran away." She raised her head and gave Blaine a defiant glare as if she expected him to disapprove. "I've been here ever since."

"Are you happy?" Blaine was surprised how much the answer mattered, even after all this time.

"Yes, I guess so." She met his gaze with a sad smile. "Perhaps not as I would have been if we'd married, or if my husband and son had lived, but it's enough."

They fell silent for a moment. Finally, she looked to Blaine. "What about you?"

Blaine looked away. "Velant was as bad as its reputation. I survived by sheer luck, and the fact that Merrill put a note in my file forbidding Prokief to kill me. When I earned my Ticket of Leave, my friends and I built a homestead. I made a hand-fasting with a girl who'd been sent away for thieving. We were happy enough, but then the fever took her."

"I'm sorry," Carensa said. She paused. "The woman in your group—"

"Kestel."

"Is she yours?"

Blaine chuckled. "I'm not sure Kestel belongs to anyone but Kestel. But yes, we're more than just friends—much more, I hope."

Carensa smiled. "You always had a thing for redheads."

Blaine returned the smile. "Maybe so." Though they stood only a few feet apart, the gulf that separated them was as wide as years and as far as the cold shores of Edgeland. "What will you do after the solstice?"

"Vigus hoped that no matter how great the damage, at least one of the Lords of the Blood would survive," she said. "If he suspected that you were the likely survivor because you were in Edgeland, he didn't tell me." She sighed. "If you're able to bring back the magic, Vigus and the others will have quite a task ahead, restoring what's been lost. They'll need helpers." Carensa paused for a moment. "Regardless of what happens to the magic, this is my home."

"So you're staying here?"

Carensa nodded. "There's nothing for me back there," she said. "What about you? Are you staying in Donderath—or going back to Edgeland?"

"I gave Aunt Judith my word that I would go back to Glenreith," Blaine said. "There's a lot of work to be done. And there are some powerful people who have tried very hard to keep the magic from coming back. They won't be happy—and I have the feeling they won't give up."

He paused. "Will Quintrel and the Knights let us leave?"

Carensa met his gaze. "I don't know. I wanted to warn you. I owe Vigus a great deal, but he uses people to get what he wants. Like he used your friend."

"Connor," Blaine supplied. "He's had rather a bad go of it."

Carensa nodded. "Vigus likes that the valley is so hard to reach. And the Knights have kept their hiding place here a secret for a long time. You and your friends know how to best the Guardians. That's dangerous knowledge."

"But with the kings dead, the Knights have nothing to fear," Blaine pointed out. "And if magic can be restored—even if it's not quite the same as before—surely Quintrel and the mages can use it to set a new group of traps for unwanted visitors if they want to remain in seclusion." He spread his hands, palms up. "None of us are mages of any power. Lowrey's the only scholar, and he intends to stay. We'd be a drain on your scarce resources, with nothing to show for it."

Carensa's gaze was sorrowful. "I don't think Vigus is worried about it," she said quietly. "The only value you and your friends have is working the ritual. I'm afraid he's expecting it to kill you."

CHAPTER
THIRTY-SEVEN

F ALL BACK!" NIKLAS THEILSSON SHOUTED ABOVE
the din of battle. The foothills at the base of the Riven
Mountains were thick with torch smoke. The cries of men and
the clang of swords reverberated from the high rock mountain
walls. "Fall back!" he shouted again, eyeing the onslaught of
Pollard's troops.

Across the way, he could hear Ayers giving a similar command, allowing the line to break that they had fought so hard
to hold across the mountain pass. Niklas grimaced. The ground
was littered with bodies, many of them his soldiers. It was bitter to watch as Pollard's troops whooped in victory while thirty
men poured into the cleft in the mountains. The others took
up the position that Niklas's army had just vacated.

Bitter, but not unexpected. He and Penhallow had been of
one accord on strategy. They would hold Pollard back to give
Blaine the longest possible lead. And if necessary, to reduce
casualties, they would fall back. Pollard, as Penhallow pre-
dicted, sent his men to seize the victory.

But Niklas knew it wasn't quite over yet.

"Rally here!" Niklas shouted, hearing his call repeated down the line. He gave a silent prayer for the souls of the dead and an apology to their spirits for the cost of the ruse he was now about to reveal.

"They're getting through, Captain!" one of his men complained, and it was obvious he felt the defeat keenly.

Niklas nodded. "For now, soldier. For now."

When they had withdrawn far enough to give Pollard's troops full access to the pass and remove his men from danger, Niklas scanned the horizon. He could see Nidhud's Knights and Penhallow's *talishte* maneuvering into position as Ayers got his own men situated.

"Formation!" Niklas shouted. "There's the line!" He indicated with his head where the other troops had gathered. "Find your place."

"You *want* the blighters to go into the pass?" one of the soldiers replied. "I thought we were trying to keep them out of the pass!"

Niklas chuckled. "Yep. Line up. You'll see."

He heard the muttering and saw the questioning glances as his men followed orders, and he sympathized. They had lost friends in the battle to hold the pass, and they had fought with all their might to keep Pollard away from the mountain.

And if that would have done the trick, we could all go home now, Niklas thought with a sigh. *But Penhallow and Nidhud and I knew it wouldn't be. So I hope Nidhud's fall-back plan is as good as it sounds.*

"Sir!" A *talishte* scout seemed to appear out of nowhere in front of Niklas, making Niklas's horse step back a pace and rear.

"Report."

"A large contingent is heading our way." He grinned, showing his fangs. "Voss's men."

Niklas sighed. "I wouldn't have minded having them arrive sooner, but better now than never."

"Aye," the *talishte* replied. "Best he hurry. It's only a few candlemarks until dawn."

Niklas could already hear the sound of hoofbeats pounding, testimony that a sizable force was heading their way. *I'm glad they're on our side*, he thought. *Or as much as Voss ever is.*

A cheer went up from Niklas's men when they spotted the flag of Voss's mercenary company and realized that reinforcements had arrived. Niklas rode to where Penhallow, Ayers, and Nidhud had gathered. Voss shouted orders to his men to position them, then rode to meet the commanders.

"You took your time," Penhallow said, raising an eyebrow.

Unlike most of the other soldiers, Voss was astride a true warhorse. His armor—and the armor on his horse—was expensive and richly detailed. Voss grinned. "Just making certain none of Pollard's reinforcements showed up," he said. "Left nothing to chance. Just a wake of dead men."

"I see you found a way to end the siege, Traher," Penhallow said.

Voss chuckled. "You know me, Lanyon. I don't stay penned up long. Gave Pollard a surprise, we did. That whole plain in front of the fortress was honeycombed with caves. My engineers diverted that underground river to flood the caves, then drained them. Made the ground drop out from under his feet," he said, chuckling harder.

"We put on a show for them," Voss said, grinning broadly. "The rooftops of my fortress are stone, so I put a thin coat of oil on them and set them afire, just for effect. Then I rigged up a hinged metal puppet and made it look as if I were dancing in the flames." He guffawed. "The best touch was the kite we made with an effigy of Vessa, designed to burn slowly as it flew in the air." He slapped his thigh and tears glistened in the corners of his eyes. "Pollard's men not only ran away, but I'm betting they soiled themselves!"

"Time later to celebrate your cleverness," Nidhud said dryly. "We're not done here."

Voss looked at Penhallow skeptically. "Now what?"

"Connor and the others made it through," Penhallow said. "I sense it in the bond." He paused. "From the images I can make out from Connor, the pass has four traps set by the Knights." Nidhud and the others listened as Penhallow recounted what he learned from the bond.

Nidhud nodded. "What you've seen matches the fragments the legends tell about the Guardians." He gave a predatory smile. "Our plan should work. We'll drive Pollard's men right into the traps and let them take care of his forces for us."

Niklas looked at him askance. "Isn't that risky? What if some make it through?"

Nidhud's gaze was hard. "If any survive the traps, my fellow Knights await them. And if the magic is restored, Quintrel's mages—and the Knights—will be quite able to defend themselves."

Niklas and the other commanders dispersed down the line and were soon assembled in front of the army. "They wanted to get into the pass!" Niklas shouted to his men. "So we gave them what they wanted. But we're not going to let them out. They will not leave the mountains alive!"

Nidhud, positioned in the center of the forces, raised his sword, the signal to charge. With a roar, the soldiers ran forward, swords at the ready. Pollard's soldiers braced for the attack. Niklas's men, heartened by reinforcements, plunged toward the enemy line. Pollard's troops had their backs against the mountain, unable to retreat in large numbers into the narrow entrance to the pass.

Voss's soldiers killed with precision, and Niklas's men took out their frustration over their forced retreat. Thanks to Voss, the numbers now favored Niklas's side, and before long, those troops of Pollard's that had not reached the pass either lay dead or knelt in surrender.

Niklas turned to Nidhud when they had secured the mouth of the pass. "Now what?"

"I need a mortal volunteer, someone who isn't afraid of fire," Nidhud replied.

"I'll go, Captain," Ayers responded. "I'd let Torven take my soul if we could send Pollard's men straight to Raka."

Niklas met Nidhud's gaze. "Is this a suicide mission?"

Nidhud shook his head. "That's not my intent. I can't guarantee safety. This is war, after all. But I have every intention of coming back intact."

Niklas nodded to Ayers. "Go. But plan on coming back."

"Yes, sir."

Nidhud gestured to his Knights, and a group of seven broke away from their fellow soldiers to follow him, folding Ayer into their company. Niklas watched them go and turned to Penhallow. "What now?" he asked.

"We wait," Penhallow replied. "My men destroyed Pollard's *talishte* fighters. Nidhud won't need to worry about them."

Niklas peered into the darkness of the canyon, but he saw nothing but shadows. Time passed, and he felt the tension, wary of attack.

A sudden explosion roared through the canyon, and flames flashed high into the night sky. Niklas's men fell back several paces, ready for treachery.

"I'd say Nidhud achieved his objectives," Penhallow said with a cold smile.

Not long after the explosion, Nidhud and the Knights came walking out of the canyon, along with Ayers.

"You made better time coming out than going in," Penhallow observed as Nidhud joined them and Niklas's troops cheered.

Nidhud shrugged. "We were wary of overtaking the enemy on the way in, as they were mortal, and slow," he said.

"What happened?" Niklas asked, eyeing the plume of smoke that rose from deep inside the canyon.

Nidhud chuckled. "One of the Guardians is a cave that is treacherous to navigate. The real danger is the bad air inside the cave. We concealed our presence until they were just about to enter, and then pushed them so that they hurried. When most had entered, Ayers was kind enough to lob a few lit torches inside to light their way."

"And blew them all sky-high," Ayers finished with a satisfied grin.

Nidhud shrugged. "Perhaps not all of them," he conceded. "But they have no way to return the way they came, and between the remaining Guardians and the Knights that await them in Valshoa, I believe we have a rout."

Niklas watched the smoke ascend. "Now it's up to Blaine."

CHAPTER
THIRTY-EIGHT

THE DAY DAWNED WITH AN OVERCAST SKY THAT threatened snow. Blaine's sleep had been fitful, and because of the heavy burden of the task that lay ahead of him, he could not rest.

He walked to the window and looked out over the valley that sprawled from the city to the horizon. He tried not to think about the ritual that evening, tried not to dwell on the idea that this might be the last dawn he would see.

Blaine was so deep in thought that he did not hear Kestel approach. "I'm happy for you that Carensa is alive," Kestel said quietly.

Blaine turned. Kestel was far too adept at politics to let her feelings show in her face, but Blaine could read the expression in her eyes. "I'm glad she survived," he replied. "When she lost everything else, Quintrel gave her a place to go and a reason to go on." He paused, knowing what Kestel was waiting to hear.

"I told her that you and I were together," Blaine said. "What was between Carensa and me happened a long time ago, when we were different people. She plans to stay here with the scholars permanently. I have other plans."

Blaine moved a step toward Kestel and took her in his arms. She leaned her head against his chest and sighed. "I hope we have a chance to make plans."

Blaine looked down to meet her gaze. "I have every intention of living through this," he said. "I'm not a martyr. We'll go back to Glenreith, get down to the business of making the homestead—manor—self-sustaining again. With Niklas's help, maybe we can restore the rule of law, at least in the area we can protect."

He smoothed a hand back through her hair. "There's one more thing I want to do when we go home. I want to marry you."

Kestel looked at him skeptically. "Are you sure?"

"I know what I want, Kestel. And I want you. What do you say?"

"Yes," she murmured. "Now we just have to live long enough to make it happen."

Blaine bent to kiss her and drew her closer. She returned the kiss with passion. The kiss lingered until they heard the sound of applause.

"It took you two long enough," Dawe said with a grin.

Kestel laughed. "Maybe you haven't noticed, but we've been busy."

Reluctantly Blaine let her go, and Kestel stepped away. The others were waking, and a knock at the door signaled the arrival of several scholars laden with trays of food and pitchers of *fet*. Blaine and the others waited to talk until their hosts had left the room.

"What's the plan?" Piran demanded as he reached for two of the warm rolls and a handful of dried fruit.

"Not sure," Blaine said, taking a piece of sausage and some bread, as well as a tin cup to hold the hot *fet*. "I get the distinct feeling the scholars—or the Knights—don't want us wandering around." Briefly he recounted his conversation with Lowrey and the scholars, and his concerns about their ability to leave the valley once the ritual was complete. "We need an alternate plan."

Blaine swung a leg over the bench and sat down facing them. He swallowed a mouthful of *fet*, made a face at the bitter taste, and set his cup aside. "All right. Everyone at this table, except Piran, has some kind of magic, right?" They nodded. "If the ritual works, and the magic can be controlled, we may need to be ready to defend ourselves the moment the magic rises."

"We'll be ready," Kestel promised. "You raise the magic, and we'll take care of the rest."

As the day wore on, Blaine could feel the group's tension rising. Thanks to the healer, Desya was awake and able to stand, although he would not be able to hold his own in a fight. Zaryae, Borya, and Desya spent much of the morning huddled together, and Blaine guessed that they were taking what comfort they could mourning Illarion.

Kestel asked the scholars for candles and made a small shrine to the gods. Zaryae joined her, and as the hours passed, everyone except Piran made a stop at the shrine to ask for protection or make their peace with the gods.

I'm not sure whether you're real, Blaine thought as he addressed the gods, *and if you're there, I'm not sure you're listening, but in case you are... Please get my friends home safely, and if possible, I'd like to live through this.*

Blaine sighed and figured that if style and wording made the gods heed prayers, he was doomed. *Kestel would say that it's the thought that counts. I guess at this point, I'll take all the help I can get.*

Dinner came early so that they could be ready for the ritual at sundown. Blaine forced himself to eat, remembering how badly the botched working at Mirdalur had drained him, but he tasted nothing. By the look of it, the others had little appetite either.

A knock at the door startled them. Blaine opened it and found Carensa and another woman standing in the hallway, each carrying a large basket of what appeared to be dirty clothing. "Let us in—quickly!" Carensa said.

Blaine stepped aside and frowned as he heard the clink of metal against metal as the two women moved. When the door was shut, Carensa and her friend lowered their baskets and skimmed the clothing off the top. Inside the baskets were their weapons.

"Be quick! We managed to get into the storeroom, but Vigus doesn't know we took your weapons," Carensa said. "You were right, Blaine. Vigus and the Knights don't want you to leave. Take your weapons with you to the working. Tomorrow, be ready. Once you've had a chance to recover from the ritual, I can get you out."

"How?"

"The valley path with the Guardians isn't the only way," Carensa said, glancing nervously behind her as if the door might open at any second. "The Knights had another route, but it's well hidden and dangerous. I'll show you where to go if they won't."

"Thank you," Blaine said, laying a hand on Carensa's shoulder.

She gave a wan smile. "You've spent enough time as a prisoner." She paused. "There's another piece of news—and it's not good. Our watchers say there's a large force moving toward the Guardians. For the first time in a thousand years, Valshoa is under attack."

Blaine and Piran exchanged glances. "That means Pollard's men got past Penhallow and Niklas," Blaine said. "It doesn't bode well."

"I don't like it, not one little bit," Piran replied. "Fix the magic, and we might have a chance."

"I've got to go," Carensa said. "Despite his faults, I owe Vigus a lot, and I still intend to stay here," she said, stretching up to kiss Blaine on the cheek. "Now go—and be careful."

A few minutes after Carensa left, the door opened once more and Quintrel himself entered the room, followed by a handful of mages. He eyed their weapons immediately. "Where did you get those?"

"I was out for a walk this morning to stretch my legs, and I saw an open door," Piran lied. "Found these in a heap and figured, with all that's going on, you forgot to get them back to us. So I spared you the bother."

"I see," Quintrel said, unconvinced. "Where you're going tonight, swords will do you no good."

"We'll need them on the journey home," Blaine said pointedly, meeting Quintrel's gaze. "We mean to leave as soon as possible."

"We're in no hurry for you and your friends to depart," Quintrel said amiably. "Treven Lowrey has chosen to become a permanent member here. Your group would be welcome to stay as well. Depending on how things go, you may need time to recuperate." His expression darkened. "And leaving may not be advisable. Our scouts tell us that there's an army headed this way, up the pass."

Piran gave a snort. "I'd like to see them manage the Guardians."

Quintrel gave him a mirthless look. "I'd rather not see that, thank you." He paused. "If you're successful in restoring the magic, we should be quite capable of handling the threat. If not—"

"If not, we'll come up with something else," Blaine replied testily. He was feeling the strain of the long afternoon of waiting.

"The ritual area has been prepared," Quintrel said. "All of the disks except for the one you wear have been placed along the lines of power, as have the symbols of the thirteen houses. Lowrey and Connor have done a good job piecing together what we believe is the chant used in the Mirdalur ritual, thanks to the help of the Wraith Lord," he said and inclined his head toward Connor. "My people will be in attendance to chant and lend their energy to the working, and, should you succeed, to help contain the magic." He paused. "All that is missing is you—and your blood."

"The space you'll be using is the most sacred in all of Valshoa," Quintrel continued. "The Valshoans esteemed it so highly that their women gave birth there, because they believed the powerful magic protected both mother and child from harm."

"So it's steeped in blood and birth," Zaryae said, looking up from where she sat, surrounded by her divination tools. She had cast her cards and sought the guidance of her crystals, and now she nodded. "A very auspicious sign," she said. Blaine did not feel any less worried.

"We're as ready as we'll ever be," Blaine said.

"That's why I've come," Quintrel replied. "It is time."

Quintrel led them through the heart of the city, past once-beautiful buildings with façades carved with scenes from the everyday life of their long-vanished culture. Perhaps under other circumstances, Blaine might have had the impulse to linger, but now his mind was far too preoccupied.

When they reached the center of the city, Quintrel left the roadway and walked up the debris-littered steps of a large, stately building. The pillars that had once graced its entrance lay broken and the roof was gone, but its former grandeur could still be glimpsed in the carved walls and elaborate mosaics visible on the floor. It reminded Blaine of the large customs house at the Castle Reach waterfront, and the king's public court.

Kestel walked briskly beside him, with Piran on the other side and Zaryae just behind them. Connor and Dawe were next. Verran and the twins walked farther back, sizing up Quintrel's contingent of mage-scholars and counting the Knights who escorted the group like an honor guard. Blaine eyed the Knights warily, wondering how vigorously they would defend Valshoa's secrets.

The corridor opened into an ornate gate flanked with pillars. Torches around the walls lit the huge room. The room opened to the sky. Most of the rubble from the roof's collapse had been cleaned away, exposing a beautiful floor tiled with smooth-cut stone laid out in winding, interlocking patterns, and in the room's center, Blaine saw a stone-pattern maze that reminded him of the concentric circles at Mirdalur.

Blaine paused as they entered to survey the area. Quintrel had, indeed, prepared the space for the working. The smell of sage hung in the air, purifying the room of negative energies. Along the wall, he could see a series of small shrines built beneath the figures of Charrot, Esthrane, and Torven. Candles burned at each shrine, along with gifts of grain, wine, and fresh loaves of bread, all intended to invoke a blessing from the gods. Toward the center of the room, in the maze, Blaine saw twelve pillar candles and twined around each one, the strap holding an obsidian disk.

"Let's have your friends stand inside the protective circle," Quintrel said, guiding Blaine by the shoulder. "Step over the line so you don't smudge it and break the warding." He pointed to a reddish line as thick as a man's finger that had been marked around the room. Zaryae bent down and touched a finger to the line, then tasted the red mark on her fingertip.

"It's a mixture of salt and several other protective herbs," she murmured.

Quintrel fixed her with a look. "Did you think we would leave the area unwarded?"

"What good is it until the magic returns?" Piran asked.

"We don't know how wild the power will be when the ritual calls to it," Quintrel said. "We've tried to create baffles to slow the rush of magic, to give Blaine a better chance to live through the working."

"Much obliged," Blaine muttered.

Just within the warding line Quintrel's mage-scholars stood shoulder to shoulder. They parted as Quintrel and Blaine made their way toward the center of the room.

Magic might have slipped from mortal grasp, but power still resonated in this place. Blaine could feel it humming, just out of reach. The obsidian disk that had been handed down through his family hung on a strap around his neck. Outside, in the canyon, Pollard's army was heading this way, and Blaine wondered what would happen if the city came under attack before the ritual could be completed.

Could the Guardians stop a full army? he wondered. *It's sundown. Will Reese and his* talishte *beat the Guardians' protections, or have the Knights prepared other defenses designed for them?*

Another thought occurred to him. *If the ritual works and it*

*draws the wild magic the way it did at Mirdalur, what does that
mean for everyone in the canyon pass—friend and foe?*

Kestel touched his shoulder, then followed the others to
where Quintrel indicated. Dawe, Piran, and Verran met
Blaine's gaze, and Piran gave him a mock salute. Zaryae made
a gesture of blessing, while the twins left him with a shallow
bow. Connor was the last to leave.

"Be careful," Connor said quietly. In a lower voice, loud
enough for only Blaine to hear, he added, "They're fighting
outside the canyon. Penhallow feels...optimistic."

Blaine nodded. Although his bond through the *kruvgaldur* was much newer than Connor's, and he lacked experience
interpreting its messages, he had received the impression that
Penhallow had not yet given up hope. *So we may not be overrun
in the next few minutes at least*, Blaine thought. *It's not much,
but it's something.*

Distantly, Blaine heard a bell tolling.

"That's the signal," Quintrel said. "We're almost at the
moment of solstice. When it tolls again, you must be at the
center of the maze, because the solstice will be upon us. When
you're in position, my people will lend their support."

He paused. "The maze pattern is designed to concentrate the
power. That's why you—and you alone—may enter it to work
the ritual. Don't step off the stone path. The magic will be
drawn by your blood and the disk, and your movement through
the maze will wind the power tighter and tighter around you
while my people speak the binding ritual." He paused again,
then met Blaine's gaze. "Good luck."

Quintrel stepped back into the circle of people surrounding
the ritual area. Blaine took a deep breath and pulled the disk
out of the neckline of his shirt. He began to follow the pattern in the stones. Behind him, Quintrel's people started a low

chant, and though he was listening intently, Blaine could not make out the words.

He reached the first of the maze's turns and found a lit candle, a disk, and a symbol he recognized as the mark of the Garnoc family. He moved forward cautiously, noting that as the maze twisted, the path spiraled in on itself, with the turns growing closer together so the candles seemed to blaze brighter the nearer he got to the center.

Concentrate the power, he thought as he followed the gray stone pathway. At the next turn, another candle and disk, and the mark Kestel had translated as belonging to Lord Corrender's ancestors. Blaine thought it was his imagination, but the disk around his neck felt heavier, as if it were tugging at him, pulling him toward the center.

A few more steps, another candle and disk, and Blaine had a growing feeling that power was rising around him. His own breath was coming faster, and his heart was thudding. The chant of the mage-scholars had grown louder. Their voices were pitched deep, so the chant echoed in the chamber like a bass horn, rich and resonant.

Two more turns, and the air began to stir. Through the *kruvgaldur* Blaine felt a flicker of concern, and he remembered that the bond went both ways. *I wonder what Penhallow makes of what I'm seeing, or how much he can read from me*, Blaine thought. A more disturbing thought followed. *If the magic kills me, as it tried to do at Mirdalur, Penhallow will surely know through the bond—but will it damage or destroy a* talishte?

Blaine wound through several more turns, mindful that the moment of solstice was just a few breaths away, and that the working would be at its strongest if he stood in the center of the maze at the very instant of the solstice. He passed the candle, disk, and symbol that Penhallow had identified as belonging to Pollard's family, and then, a few steps later, the disk that had been King Merrill's inheritance.

At each step, the disk's presence grew in Blaine's mind until he could think of little else. The mage-scholars' chants echoed in the stone chamber, and the disk seemed to draw him along.

Another step, and as Blaine watched, the air around him began to glisten, as if ice crystals hung suspended. "It looks like this is drawing a storm!" he called back across the maze.

"Keep your mind on what you're doing!" Quintrel snapped. "We'll deal with the rest."

Blaine continued to move toward the center of the maze. By now he had stopped trying to remember which symbol went with which of the thirteen original families. His head was beginning to pound, and the air shimmered like snow in the candlelight. The chanting had grown faster, and it echoed through the chamber. Overhead, the stars were bright in the night sky, and the wind was bitter cold.

It felt to Blaine that his heart beat in time with the chant, that the glistening air burned his lungs. The disk that hung on his chest felt as if it were eager to get to the center, anxious to play its part in the night's work. Just a few more steps, a few more turns, and Blaine would be at the center of the maze.

In the distance, the bells began to toll once more. Blaine quickened his step, careful to heed Quintrel's warning and stay on the stone path. The maze twisted so tightly back on itself that it taxed Blaine's balance to follow the path without falling, without disturbing the last three candles. From where he stood, he was completely surrounded by the candle flames, and the glittering particles swirled as the pain in Blaine's head grew so sharp that it hurt to keep his eyes open and the sound of the chanters made him wince.

Only four steps left to go . . . three . . . two . . . one.

Blaine stood at the center of the maze, and the power around him churned like a mirrored vortex, reflecting the candlelight in its glowing particles, leaving the flames untouched. Blaine knew that it was magic, not air, that stirred around him, robbing him of breath, searing through his mind. The Valshoans had created a place to harness magic, and Quintrel's people had strengthened it. All it needed was his presence, his disk, his blood to make it happen.

A faint green glow rose, suffusing the central circle with light. Blaine felt the growing energy crackle around him, building as the glow spread from one twist of the maze to the next.

Energy rose from the soles of his feet, spreading upward rapidly. The tingle grew in intensity until it burned, and Blaine couldn't move. His legs refused to obey his mind, and within seconds, his arms and hands were numb. The disk on its strap began to glow, pressing against his chest with cold fire that burned and froze. The green glow swirled around him, enveloping him. As it rose, Blaine felt as if bands of steel encircled his chest, hindering his breathing, and he fought panic. As the energy around him and the pain grew, he felt a scream build in his throat, yet he could not draw the air to cry out.

Blaine felt the energy shift. The bands of power became needles coursing through his blood, burning along his nerves. Caught in the unbreakable grip of the energy, Blaine writhed. Without air, his vision was growing blurry, and pinpricks of light danced in front of him. Against the power of the energy, his strength meant nothing, and his struggle to break free seemed to intensify his pain. Blinding light flashed through the chamber like trapped lightning.

The pressure on his chest eased, and Blaine gasped for breath, drinking in gulps of cold air. Energy still surged through his body, wracking him with pain, and a scream tore from his throat. The green glow that had started as a faint phosphorescent fog now rose in pillars of emerald fire streaking skyward from each of the candles. The twists of the maze pulsed with their own radiance, as if lit from within. All of the power of the meridians coursed through him until Blaine felt as if he were being burned alive. The pendant grew hot, and the black disk seared his chest.

The mage-scholars kept chanting, and it sounded as if drummers had joined their number, pounding out a relentless rhythm. The light formed a green dome over the entire ritual space with walls of coruscating energy that pulsed and crackled. With every tortured breath, Blaine expected to be burned alive, yet the pain did not abate and he did not die.

When pain threatened to black him out, a jolt of energy coursed through him, setting every muscle and nerve atremble. He heard a distant roar, and then the ground beneath his feet shook.

Blaine fell to his knees, holding his temples in both hands, eyes tightly closed, heaving for breath. Magic coursed through him and his blood felt like fire, burning with the untamed energy. *Too much. I can't hang on*, Blaine thought as the power blazed through him.

Just when the coursing magic seemed as if it would sweep him away in its current, Blaine felt a slender tether anchoring him to his body. He saw Penhallow's image clearly in his mind and felt the compulsion that had brought him back from the brink of death. That same compulsion bound him in its power, linking him to Penhallow through the *kruvgaldur*.

With all his waning consciousness, Blaine dove toward the bond that linked him to Penhallow. He grasped it and caught hold, feeling as if he were being plucked from deep water by strong hands and held fast in the swift current.

The chants became screams and the drumming abruptly stopped. Blaine felt as if the magic lifted him out of his body, so that his essence was contained in the glowing crystals that swirled around him. He could feel the magic changing, shifting, losing the wild peaks of its energy. And as it did, the gossamer fabric of shimmering light stretched thinner and thinner until it dissipated completely.

Blaine fell face-first onto the stone, gasping. As abruptly as it came, the pain left him, but the bond remained, then gradually loosened until it slipped beyond Blaine's ability to sense. He lay still, struggling for breath, utterly spent, and realized that for the first time in many months, he felt the flicker of magic kindled within him.

It worked, he thought, stunned. *It worked and I'm alive.*

Blaine slowly rose to his feet and looked out over the chamber. The candles had been extinguished. He raised a hand to touch the disk that hung at his chest, and it burned his fingers. When he glanced down, he saw that the disk was glowing, and as he watched it dimmed from yellow to orange to red. As the red faded, the disk shone black once more, and the symbols and runes that marked its surface pulsed with an inner, golden light.

The chanting resumed, weak at first but then its tone and rhythm shifted to a song of victory as the voices gained strength, and the drums offered up a triumphant rhythm. Blaine did not understand the language of the chant, but the spirit of rejoicing did not require translation. *Thank the gods—and Penhallow.*

He took one staggering step and then another back the way he had come. Now that the glittering light was gone, Blaine could see across the room. Even the Knights of Esthrane looked shaken by the wave of power that had shot through the room.

The mage-scholars looked pale and unsteady, but they had managed to sit or stand after being felled by the burst of magic.

Quintrel spared Blaine a glance to assure he was still alive and gave a signal for the chanters to fall silent.

"Now you know why we warded the chamber," Quintrel said. "The warding triggered the first tendrils of harnessed magic, limiting the damage of the wild power. Without the warding, we might all have died in the attempt."

Blaine searched for his friends. Kestel was just being helped to her feet by Dawe, who looked ashen and wide-eyed. Borya supported Desya. Verran knelt next to Zaryae. Piran was leaning heavily against the wall. He looked angry, and Blaine remembered that when the magic died, Piran had felt the pain of the shift even though he possessed no magic of his own.

Connor stood apart from the others, his posture rigid, and his expression was one of total concentration. *He's channeling the Wraith Lord*, Blaine thought as he made his way back through the darkened maze.

Quintrel met Blaine at the entrance to the maze. "I can feel magic again," Blaine said, his voice dry.

"How, exactly, the magic returned will take a while to figure out," Quintrel replied. "According to the old documents, when it comes back it's not quite the same as before. We shall see. But yes," he said, clapping Blaine on the shoulder, "you did it."

General Dolan left his post by the wall to join them, mindful even now not to break the red warding line. "You were successful," he said, eyeing Blaine as if reevaluating him.

"Apparently so." Blaine felt as bone-weary and sore as if he had just returned from battle. The aching in his head was gone, but the rest of his body felt as if he had been beaten. He gathered his remaining strength to stand tall. "Once my group has rested, we'll be ready to leave the valley."

Dolan frowned. "I'm afraid we can't allow that. We've guarded the secrets of this valley for far too long to risk exposure."

Exhaustion wore Blaine's temper thin. "There's an army headed this way through the pass," Blaine snapped. "You're already exposed, and you can thank Reese and Pollard for it."

"The army has been dealt with." Connor spoke with the certainty of the Wraith Lord.

"What happened to them?" Blaine asked.

"I called to the spirits of the third Guardian, the souls of those in the crypts," the Wraith Lord said. "They drove the vanguard back into the blades of the maze. Nidhud's man waited until Reese's soldiers were in the cavern, and then he threw down burning brands. Many died in the explosion."

So I really did hear an explosion as the magic turned itself inside out, Blaine thought.

"Those who survived the attack have been destroyed by your friends. It is over," the Wraith Lord said.

Blaine eyed Connor with respect tinged with fear. He did not envy him the burden of playing host to the Wraith Lord's powerful spirit. "You helped save us," Blaine said.

Connor inclined his head. "I made a promise to Penhallow to do so, if it was within my power," the Wraith Lord replied.

"Thank you."

Connor nodded, then turned to regard the general. "Dolan," the deep voice of the Wraith Lord said, "do you know who I am?"

Dolan straightened, but Blaine caught a glimpse of irritation in his eyes before the general's expression shifted into an unreadable mask. "You are Kierken Vandholt. You are the Wraith Lord."

"When I walked among the Knights, I was your patron and your protector," the Wraith Lord said. "Do not allow the youth of my host body to delude you. I am as powerful as I ever was, and with the return of magic, even stronger than before." Possessed by the Wraith Lord, Connor turned an imperious glance toward Dolan, and his features seemed older, unforgiving.

"Hear me. This is an order, binding on you and upon all the Knights. You will not hinder Lord McFadden and his party from leaving. You will assist them so they reach the lowlands safely, and you will permit them to go on their way."

"Yes, sir," Dolan replied, though he did not look happy with the command.

"I find this body quite compatible," the Wraith Lord continued. "And the mortal who possesses this form has asked only one boon of me, despite how hard I have used him. I grant that favor." He turned to meet Dolan's gaze. "You and all the Knights will cause no harm to befall McFadden and his companions, and insofar as you are able, you will lend him your protection when he requires it. Am I understood?"

Dolan's jaw was tight, but he gave a curt nod. "Yes, sir."

The Wraith Lord turned to Blaine. "You have done well, Lord McFadden, but your part is not yet over. I was able to help destroy the army that sought you, but there will be others. You are the last Lord of the Blood. You may find that this means you are in more danger now than ever before, since you are bound to the fragile new magic."

"I brought back the magic. I'm done," Blaine said, meeting the Wraith Lord's gaze levelly and finding that the soul that looked back at him with Connor's eyes was ancient.

"So you believe. This land has need of you. When I can, I will assist you."

Though the Wraith Lord's voice never wavered, Blaine could see that Connor was growing pale. "I will consider what you've said," Blaine replied cautiously. "But you must let go of Connor. He's weakening."

"Remember my words," the Wraith Lord replied.

Connor collapsed like a severed marionette and would have fallen had not Blaine and Dolan caught him. Blaine eased Connor to the ground and met Dolan's gaze.

"First, we're going to get a healer for Connor, and food, drink, and rest for my people. Then we're leaving," Blaine said.

"I know my orders," Dolan growled.

Blaine turned to Quintrel. "I hope you've kept our rooms for us, because I think we're all going to sleep well tonight." He looked Quintrel in the eye. "And we're leaving at dusk tomorrow."

Quintrel chuckled. "You don't have to convince me further," he said. "I'm not one to question the Wraith Lord, especially when it comes to standing in the way of destiny."

CHAPTER
THIRTY-NINE

"CAN YOU FEEL IT?" KESTEL LOOKED FROM BLAINE to Dawe to Verran.

"No, obviously I can't," Piran remarked, "since I never had magic to begin with. The question is—can you?"

They had returned to their room inside the large Valshoan building, reluctantly aware that even with their concerns over Quintrel's questionable hospitality, the night's working had taken too high a toll on Blaine to contemplate leaving the valley without rest. Blaine and Connor were hardest hit from the efforts, but the others looked exhausted as well.

Despite a generous dinner and ample wine set out by the mage-scholars, Blaine felt completely spent. His only consolation was that Connor looked worse. They had kept their weapons, although after the Wraith Lord's announcement, Blaine doubted they would have further difficulty from Dolan and the Knights. Still, he remained wary of Quintrel's reach now that the magic had been restored.

Zaryae also looked tired, and she had eaten little. The twins were quiet. "My offer still stands for you to come back to Glenreith with us," Blaine said. "Stay as long as you like."

Zaryae and the twins exchanged a look, and Borya nodded in agreement. "We would be grateful. We can earn our keep. Thank you."

Kestel sidled up to Blaine. "I don't really have anyone to test my magic on except the likes of you," she said with a grin, "so it's difficult to know whether or not it works." She paused, and her expression was contemplative. "It feels different...But I can't put my finger on why."

"I would agree," Dawe said, "although I won't have much in the way of proof until I'm back in a forge. There's something odd, and I can't quite figure out what it is. If you pressed me, I'd say that the magic feels slippery, the way it did right before it disappeared, like it comes and goes."

Blaine frowned. "Do you think that means it's temporary?" He sighed. "I hate to think we've gone through all this and the magic won't last."

Verran chuckled. "Take me to a tavern, and I'll test my magic." He played a ditty on his flute. "If the tavern master buys me dinner and a drink for my efforts, it's my own skill. If the entire bar buys me drinks for the night and the trollops fight over me, the magic is back."

"Would those be the blind trollops or the deaf trollops?" Piran asked blandly.

The door to their room burst open and they rose to their feet, weapons at the ready. Treven Lowrey bustled in, oblivious to the raised swords. He rushed to where Blaine stood and threw his arms around him.

"Wonderful! You did it! I never doubted you for a minute!" Lowrey enthused, as the others chuckled and Blaine struggled free.

"So your magic is back?" Kestel asked. Lowrey had been among the mage-scholars chanting in the ritual chamber, but he looked no worse for the experience. Or perhaps, Blaine thought, it was difficult to tell, since Lowrey usually looked as if he'd just been roused from bed with no time to tame his wild gray hair.

"It's back!" Lowrey agreed and gave Kestel a bear hug, swinging her in a circle and planting a kiss on her forehead. "I can't begin to tell you how wonderful it feels." He peered over his spectacles at her. "Your magic returned as well?"

Kestel nodded and gestured toward the others. "To an extent. We were wondering—did you and the other mages receive the same abilities and strength as before?"

Lowrey shrugged. "I'm happy enough to have any magic at all that I don't see the point in quibbling. But now that you ask, no, it's not exactly the same as before. It's... crackly, if that makes any sense. Brittle." He sighed. "I'm not sure what that means. It's too soon to tell if it will last. According to Quintrel's notes, every time the magic has been restored it's wobbly for a while, as if the power takes time to stabilize." He shook his head. "All the documents I found said there would be changes. I suppose it will take time to sort it all out."

Blaine stifled a yawn. "As long as the magic can be controlled again, I'm just happy to be done with it."

Connor had said little throughout dinner. Now, although he sat with the others, he seemed lost in thought, and Blaine wondered if he had fully recovered from the Wraith Lord's appearance during the ritual. Lowrey turned to him.

"Commendable effort, m'boy," Lowrey said, grinning. "Penhallow will be quite proud of you. I always knew you had it in you, Conroy."

Connor sighed. "It's Connor, and as I recall, you had your doubts."

Lowrey brushed the comment aside. "It's said that the mark

of a great scholar is the ability to change his mind." He sobered. "So you'll be leaving the valley?"

"Tomorrow at dusk," Piran said, in a tone that indicated they could not leave soon enough.

"Where will you go?"

Connor did not reply right away, so Blaine stepped in. "As far as I'm concerned, they're all welcome at Glenreith for as long as they want to stay." He met Kestel's gaze, and she smiled. "Permanently, I hope."

"Where I go depends on Penhallow," Connor said. There was no hiding the weariness in his voice. "I suspect there will be loose ends to tie up." He looked at a bit of a loss, now that the adventure was at its end. "At least, I'm assuming I have a place with him."

Kestel laid a hand on his shoulder. "I don't doubt it, but you're always welcome with us if you change your mind. Maybe you'd like a little peace and quiet before you go adventuring again. I think you could use it." Connor smiled wanly.

Blaine looked at Lowrey. "Did you hear anything about the attackers in the pass?"

Lowrey gave a cold chuckle. "Between the Wraith Lord, the Guardians, the magic storm, and the return of magic, there wasn't much left."

Kestel met Blaine's gaze. "Do you think that puts an end to Reese and Pollard?"

Blaine sighed. "Doubtful. I don't think they're the type to give up easily."

"We'll find out the details soon enough," Dawe said, pouring a fresh cup of wine for all of them and raising his in a toast. "Right now, I'm happy we've lived to tell the tale."

"I'm just hoping that someone kept track of our horses," Piran muttered. "I've got no desire to walk back to Glenreith."

*　　*　　*

"Here you are, as promised." Dolan gestured toward the end of a narrow passageway that led to the plains beyond the mountains.

"Thank you for leading us out," Blaine said, eyeing the starlit sky at the end of the passage.

"We are in your debt," Dolan said. "Without magic, the Knights were mere warriors. Now we are whole once more."

"What will become of the Knights, now that there's no need for exile?" Kestel asked.

Dolan looked thoughtful. "A good question, m'lady. We serve no purpose hiding in the valley now that there is no king to hunt us. Perhaps, after all these years, we can return to our true purpose as protectors." He scratched his beard. "It will require discussion, but we may see you again."

They neared the entrance, and a shadow crossed the opening, blocking the stars from view. At the front of the group, Blaine, Piran, and Connor drew their swords.

"Be at peace. I mean you no harm." The figure stepped away from the opening, but it was still too dark to make out a face. "It's Nidhud," the shadowed form said. "Penhallow sent me to bring you to the camp."

Just a few steps more, and the group stood on the open plain at the foot of the mountain. Nidhud and a half dozen of his Knights waited for them.

"Hail, brothers!" Dolan greeted his fellow Knights. He and Nidhud clasped forearms.

"It's good to see you again." Nidhud greeted him with a grin that revealed his long eyeteeth. "So it's true. Some of the Knights did make it to Valshoa."

"And it's true, I see, that some of our brother Knights survived exile," Dolan replied. "I'm happy you're among the survivors."

"That's one of the reasons I asked Penhallow to send us as their honor guard," Nidhud said with a nod toward Blaine and the others. "I was hoping that, if your band of Knights still existed, we might regroup to consider our place in this new Donderath."

Dolan nodded. "When Lord McFadden spoke of your Knights, I hoped for the same thing. Yes, by all means, see to your task, and then return with your men. Our brothers in the valley will be happy to greet you and to hear your news."

Nidhud shook his head. "I have no happy news of late to share, but we will speak of what we have seen." He looked up at the shadowed peaks of the mountains. "Perhaps the Knights will find a role in the reawakening of this kingdom."

"Personally, I think that's an excellent idea," Blaine said. "But don't stay hidden away too long. I have a feeling the hard work is just beginning."

Blaine and the others followed Nidhud down through the foothills to where the army camp sprawled on the flatland. Campfires blazed among the tents and lean-tos, and as Blaine got nearer the encampment he could see that it stretched much farther than before the battle.

"We seem to have picked up reinforcements along the way," Piran remarked.

"Voss's troops, most likely," Blaine replied. "None of Nidhud's men would use tents."

"You are correct," Nidhud answered from far enough ahead that Blaine had not expected him to be listening. "Traher Voss and his soldiers arrived in time to turn the tide." He chuckled. "I must admit, despite Penhallow's confidence, some of us were skeptical until Voss actually arrived."

"I understand that completely," Connor muttered.

As they drew closer to camp, they could hear the sound

of drummers and pipers playing familiar tavern songs. With Nidhud's escort, they were waved through by the sentries and found themselves in the thick of postbattle celebration.

Nidhud motioned to a passing soldier. "Find Captain Niklas and Lord Penhallow. Tell them I'm bringing our guests to the captain's tent. Then go to the cook and bring enough food and drink for our guests." The soldier went to do as he was bid, while Blaine and the others followed Nidhud as he wound through the camp. One glance at Verran showed that he was eager to go join the musicians, and that Piran was already sizing up the opportunities to lift a pint or two.

"It's not going to take all of us to brief Penhallow," Blaine said with a tired grin. "I can tell Piran wants to head into the thick of things. Go ahead. Connor and I can make the report." He chuckled. "Besides, I figure you'll gather as much information as I will, and we can fill each other in later."

"I'll stay with you," Kestel announced, slipping her arm through his.

"I want to hear what happened while we were in Valshoa," Dawe said.

"So do I," Verran added. "We can catch up with Piran later—won't be hard, he'll be where there's ale."

"Frankly, if we're not needed, I think we would rather rest," Borya said, and the others nodded.

Nidhud nodded. "I can arrange that." He spoke to another soldier, who nodded quickly and motioned for Zaryae and the twins to follow him.

Blaine and the others struggled to keep up with Nidhud's pace as they wound through the camp. The night air was cold and smelled of smoke, ale, leather, and unwashed bodies. *Not too different from Edgeland*, Blaine thought.

Nidhud ushered them into Niklas's tent and bade them sit.

They found places near the small brazier that heated the tent. "Rest. Warm yourselves," Nidhud invited. "The soldier should be here soon with your dinner. Niklas and Penhallow won't be long."

"Actually, I'm here," Niklas said, grinning as Nidhud stepped aside to let him enter. Blaine and the others stood, and Niklas embraced Blaine in a bear hug, then shook hands with Connor, Dawe, and Verran and made a courtly bow to Kestel that drew a chuckle. He turned his attention back to Blaine.

"Damn! I'm glad to see you in one piece!" Niklas gestured for them to sit down. He looked to Nidhud. "Did you send for food and drink?"

Nidhud nodded. "Aye."

Niklas gave Blaine and the others a measuring gaze. "You made it back alive," he said. "And the magic is restored. Our healers knew the instant it changed. That's how we were sure you'd succeeded." He met Blaine's gaze. "Without the healing magic, we would have lost a lot more men. Thank you."

Blaine shrugged. "Restored, at least in part, and at least for now."

"A partial victory is still a victory," Niklas replied.

Nidhud returned with Penhallow and a stocky man Blaine did not recognize. "May I present Traher Voss," Nidhud said, and the man nodded in acknowledgement. In the lantern light, Blaine took a good look at the four men. Nidhud and Penhallow had no visible injuries, but Blaine knew how quickly *talishte* healed. Niklas sported fresh gashes and bruises and his left eye was purpled.

"How bad was it?" Blaine asked, meeting Niklas's gaze.

Niklas paused as two soldiers brought a pot of stew, trenchers of bread, and buckets of ale and the newcomers helped themselves. "Could have been worse," he said, accepting a cup of ale that Kestel poured for him. "Would have been a lot worse if Voss's men hadn't shown up when they did."

"Leave it to Traher to make a dramatic entrance," Penhallow observed, but there was a note of affection in his voice.

Voss harrumphed and downed a cup of ale. "That's the thanks I get for clearing your trail all the way back to Castle Reach. Made damn sure we weren't going to get attacked from the rear once we got here." Blaine could see a number of new cuts and scrapes on Voss's hands. Thin, pink lines showed where deeper wounds had been treated by healers now that magic worked again.

"Makes me think there may still be some money in the mercenary business after all," Voss said, leaning back in his chair. "If Reese and Pollard are set on consolidating their power, there will be others who want protection." He grinned. "We can provide that—for a price."

"We heard the short version of the battle for the pass from Dolan and Quintrel," Blaine said. "Maybe later, you can give us all the details. I, for one, would like to hear it. But the one thing they couldn't tell us was what became of Reese and Pollard."

"Reese was present at the beginning of the battle," Penhallow said. "My guess is that he was overconfident and wanted to be here for the victory—and find the so-called treasures of Valshoa."

Kestel cleared her throat. "Speaking of which," she said and elbowed Verran, who produced a sack from beneath his tunic. He dumped the contents out onto the floor in front of him. Thirteen obsidian disks glittered in the light of the lantern.

"You stole the disks?" Blaine asked, his gaze darting from Verran to Kestel.

"I think 'stole' is a bit harsh," Verran said with exaggerated dignity. "After all, one of them already belonged to you. Penhallow gathered the others for you to use, so technically, we only stole the one that Quintrel had—which he had because Carensa stole it from her father."

"Why did you take them?" Dawe asked, frowning at the pile of disks. "They're more trouble than they're worth. Besides, the magic is back. They're useless now."

Kestel's eyes gleamed. "Think of it as insurance. These disks have been part of raising the magic for at least a thousand years. I'd rather have them in Blaine's hands than in Quintrel's—just in case." She returned them to the sack. "Consider them in protective custody."

Blaine turned toward Penhallow. "Was Reese destroyed?" he asked, leaning forward with interest.

Penhallow shook his head. "Reese managed to escape, although I believe he was badly injured even by *talishte* standards."

"And Pollard?"

Niklas gave a potent curse. "We thought we'd boxed him in at the canyon, but he had a double with identical armor to draw us off. My bet is that he slipped away before we drove them into the canyon, outfitted as a common soldier, and left his double to die for him."

"Sounds like the Pollard I knew," Blaine remarked. "You gave them a solid drubbing. That's going to put both Reese and Pollard in the mood for revenge."

"Most likely," Penhallow said. "Battles almost always create as many new enemies as they settle old scores. But that's a fight for another day." He turned his attention to Blaine.

"You brought the magic back," he said with an approving look. "Congratulations."

Blaine looked away. "But not the same as it was before.

There's no way to know yet whether or not this magic is as strong or as controllable."

Penhallow's expression was surprisingly nonchalant. "No, there isn't, until everything plays out as it will. But the point is, magic can be harnessed once more. The magic storms will grow fewer and less violent. The madness will end. Monsters like the gryps will be destroyed, and new ones won't come through the damaged places. The kingdom can begin to rebuild. Your people owe you a debt of gratitude."

Blaine sighed. "Frankly, I'm just going to be happy to go home." He paused. "And I hope that with the return of magic, Carr will recover." He was quiet again for a moment or two.

"When I was in the ritual chamber and the magic was coursing through me, I thought I was going to die. Then I felt the bond through the *kruvgaldur*." He met Penhallow's gaze. "Thank you."

Penhallow inclined his head. "You are most welcome." He turned his attention to Connor. "The Wraith Lord was pleased with you. Once more, I fear playing host to him has taken a toll. Are you damaged?"

Connor hesitated before answering, and Blaine could guess that the other man was searching for the right answer. "He's learned to pull back before he nearly kills me," Connor replied with a trace of bitterness. "And he got us past the Guardians and out of a few tricky spots. But frankly, I'm rather tired of toting him around."

Penhallow nodded. "Now that the extraordinary events of the past few weeks are over, he assures me he does not intend to make a habit of having you 'tote him around,' as you put it." Blaine thought he saw a quirk at the corner of Penhallow's lips at the phrase.

Penhallow grew serious. "After all these centuries, Kierken is well aware of the temptation that a suitable body presents," he said. "He believes it best if he does not test his resolve."

"I find myself still in need of a good assistant," Penhallow continued, looking at Connor. "I'm certainly not Lord Garnoc. But I think you would find me a decent master. I would provide for your needs. You would remain under my protection, and I can train you to fight." He paused. "I suspect our help will be needed by Lord McFadden and his companions from time to time. You could remain a part of that. The job is yours, if you want it."

"I would be honored to continue," Connor replied. "Although—"

"Yes?"

"Do you think we could go a while—a week or so, at least—without someone trying to kill me? It would be a nice change."

Penhallow chuckled. "I will do what I can to make that happen." He looked back to Blaine. "Will you stay in Donderath? Or return to Edgeland?"

"I'm looking forward to going back to Glenreith, making the manor self-sustaining again and trying to bring some kind of order, if I can, to the lands around it," Blaine replied, knowing just what a task he was laying out for himself.

Niklas cleared his throat. "About that..." he said, and his voice drifted off.

"What?" Blaine asked.

"I think I mentioned that we've been attracting volunteers," Niklas replied. "Turns out we weren't the last stragglers home from the war with Meroven. After we made camp at Arengarte, a man came to the camp by night with a group of about thirty soldiers. Then another man showed up, right before we headed here, and he says he has another seventy or more men who made their way home only to find their villages had been destroyed and their families killed."

He drew a deep breath and let it out. "So I told them they were welcome with us. They weren't fit to rally in time for this battle, but they'll settle in with us at Arengarte—and I suspect they'll bring their friends. That more than makes up for the men we lost in the fight, and I think more men will find us as time goes on. It creates a sizable force owing its allegiance to you, Blaine." He managed a tired grin. "Congratulations. You're a warlord."

Blaine hesitated then nodded. "I've been a lord, a convict, and an exile. Maybe it's a step up."

Kestel took his hand and laced her fingers with his. "Donderath is a blank slate. We've got the chance to make it whatever we dare to dream."

Reclaiming that kingdom would be as daunting as any challenge they had faced in Velant or on Edgeland, Blaine knew. Reese and Pollard would be back for vengeance. Glenreith was still impoverished, and his claim to being a lord—let alone a warlord—was likely to be challenged in the days to come. But for now, he thought as he finished a cup of ale, it was reward enough to have survived.

"We're free. We're alive. We're headed home," Blaine said. "That's good enough for me."

ACKNOWLEDGEMENTS

Once again, it takes a village to create a book. Thanks first to my wonderful family, who never knew they would become permanent beta readers, but do it very well. Special thanks to my husband, Larry, who plays a very important role as first editor, proofreader, and plot brainstormer. Thanks always to Ethan Ellenberg, my agent, for his wisdom and perspective. Of course, thanks to the Orbit crew who work their magic and turn a computer file into a beautiful book and get those books to all the places they are supposed to go. A big thank-you to all my author friends for their help and encouragement, and the biggest thank-you of all to my readers, who give these stories a home in their hearts.

extras

orbit

meet the author

Donna Jernigan

GAIL Z. MARTIN discovered her passion for science fiction, fantasy, and ghost stories in elementary school. The first story she wrote—at age five—was about a vampire. Her favorite TV show as a preschooler was *Dark Shadows*. At age fourteen she decided to become a writer. She enjoys attending science fiction/ fantasy conventions, Renaissance fairs, and living-history sites. She is married and has three children, a Himalayan cat, and two dogs: a Golden Retriever and a Maltese.

introducing

If you enjoyed
REIGN OF ASH,
look out for

WAR OF SHADOWS

Book Three of the Ascendant Kingdoms Saga

by Gail Z. Martin

"Tell me again why we left a perfectly good army back at the camp," Piran Rowse grumbled as the small group followed their guide on a rocky trail to the foothills behind Quillarth Castle.

"For the same reason we left most of the mages behind," Blaine McFadden replied. "The fewer people who know, the better." He paused. "Besides, the soldiers needed time to secure the perimeter and spring any nasty traps Reese and Pollard left behind."

Blaine knew that Piran's real complaint was being out in the open without cover from the soldiers. It had taken half a candlemark's argument to point out that stealth with a contingent of twenty soldiers was impossible. Their goal was to find where the Knights of Esthrane had left magical items for safekeeping, items that might help the mages begin to reverse the damage of the last two years. And bringing a large force was sure to tip their hand and complicate any attempt to find and retrieve the items.

"It's here somewhere," Dillon, their guide, muttered as he moved inch by inch down what appeared to be the solid rock face of the cliff. The wind ruffled Dillon's short-cropped, dark hair. To Blaine's eye, Dillon looked as if he belonged in a countinghouse, and before the Cataclysm, that was exactly where he had been. It made him an unlikely adventurer. Dillon's hands played over the rough stone, lightly skimming the surface.

"It's a big cliff, mate. I hope you remember where the door is," Piran said.

"We're close," Dillon said, paying scant attention to Piran. "Just a little farther—here!"

He pressed his fingers against the rock with his hands held in an unnatural position, and what had appeared a moment earlier to be solid stone shifted enough to allow careful passage inside.

"When was the last time you went in there?" Blaine asked. At a few inches over six feet tall, Blaine stood taller than both Dillon and Piran. Blaine's dark chestnut hair was tied back, and his sea-blue eyes glinted with intelligence. He was tall and rangy, but years of hard labor had built both muscle and resolve, and months of nearly constant skirmishing had further honed his swordsmanship.

Dillon chuckled. "Me? Never. Sir Alrik showed me the entrance and told me that if I went in, I'd never come out."

"That's comforting," Piran grumbled.

Dillon looked at Piran with exasperation. "I took his meaning straightaway. He meant that the items weren't for me. In fact, he gave strict instructions that I was to tell no one except Blaine McFadden or Lanyon Penhallow what I knew, and then he sent me away and told me to stay away until the war was decided, one way or the other."

"Alrik must have suspected that Reese and Pollard would come calling," Blaine said grimly. "You were his inside man."

"Let's see what Alrik thought was so important," Piran said. He stepped in front of Blaine. "Sorry, mate. Niklas made me promise to go first. Thick skull, tough skin," he said with a grin that made it clear he relished courting trouble.

Their group was small but hardly defenseless. Piran was a soldier, and a damned good one before his court-martial. Prison and exile had given him skills far beyond what the king's army had taught him. Blaine McFadden, the disgraced lord of Glenreith, had learned a thing or two about combat fighting to survive in the brutal Velant prison colony where he, Piran, and Kestel had been exiled for their crimes. Kestel Falke had earned her exile as a spy and assassin, though her looks and wit made her best remembered as one of the most popular courtesans at court. She, Blaine, and Piran had forged their friendship watching each other's backs long before they returned to their ruined homeland, and it was an old habit that still served them well.

Zaryae, a seer, had been part of a traveling troupe that had joined in Blaine's quest. Dillon was the assistant to the king's exchequer, back when such things as kings, kingdoms, and exchequers still existed. In the ruins of what remained, those days seemed a distant memory, or perhaps a half-forgotten dream. Xaffert and Dagur had been mages at the university before the Great Fire and before the kingdom fell, when the magic worked as it should. As a group, they were a most unusual delegation to be heading into the tombs of the ancient kings to steal back the keys to the future.

Now in darkness, they moved toward what Blaine hoped might help them rebuild the kingdom. They had restored the magic that was broken in the war or at least made a semblance of the power able to be harnessed once more. The Cataclysm that had leveled the castle and killed the rulers had left the kingdom in chaos and anarchy. Blaine believed it would be much easier to rebuild if they could bend the power of the artifacts made before the Cataclysm to their will—assuming that the restored magic could be harnessed as it had before.

"By my reckoning, we're moving back toward the castle, and given the steep angle, we could end up underneath it before too long," Blaine murmured. They had each brought lanterns, making it possible to move through the dark and winding passageway.

Kestel held her lantern in one hand and a knife in the other. "Obviously this wasn't supposed to be the main entrance," she said. "Too bad so much of the castle collapsed. It would have been much easier to get there from inside, but there's too much rubble in the way."

They walked in silence, knives drawn, expecting ambush at every turn. Suddenly, Piran stopped and held up a hand in warning. "Do you hear that?"

Blaine listened carefully. "Voices. Up ahead."

"We're the only living things down here," Zaryae said, breaking her silence.

"But the voices—" Piran protested.

Zaryae shook her head. "Not alive. But very strong."

Blaine fingered the two amulets that hung on a leather strap around his neck. One was the inscribed obsidian disk that had helped him return magic to the control of men. The other was a passage token given to him by a long-dead soldier, one of the *talishte* Knights of Esthrane. These amulets were not for luck. For those with power, either among mages or the undead *talishte*, they were validation of Blaine's identity and safe passage among powerful friends.

The passageway ended in a solid wall of rock. Piran swore under his breath and began to feel his way along the stone surface as Dillon had done outside. Suddenly, a section of the rock swung away, opening into darkness.

"I didn't do that," Piran said, taking a step back. "I swear I didn't do that."

Blaine could feel magic all around them. Before the Cataclysm, magic gave him an added edge in a fight, a minor ability. Old magic, and another power he could not name, flowed around him now.

Zaryae placed a warning hand on Blaine's arm. "The spirits are strong here—can you sense it? Old and powerful. We must be very careful." Her dark hair framed angular features and large dark eyes, reminding Blaine of a raven.

"I think you'd better let me go first," Blaine said, edging past Piran. "Let's hope between the disk and the Knights' token that I pass muster."

He stepped out into a tomb. The lantern's flickering light revealed walls covered in an elaborate mural that told the story of the rise and fall of the mage-warrior Knights of Esthrane. One wall was blank, leaving the end of the story incomplete.

In the center of the tomb was a catafalque. Blaine held his lantern aloft and stepped closer for a better look. It was the bier of a warrior, clad in battle armor. The pediment and bier were austere, bearing only a name, Torsten Almstedt.

Piran gave Xaffert a shove to move him forward out of the relative safety of the passageway. Dagur followed cautiously, gesturing to Kestel and Zaryae that it was safe to step out. Kestel began to walk slowly around the room, taking in the story of the mural. On the other side of the room was a door, and beyond that, Blaine guessed, lay passageways that led farther beneath the castle.

"Knight Alrik had us hide the items down here right after Penhallow and his servant Connor left," Dillon said, glancing around as if afraid someone might overhear. "The Knight said Penhallow had already been through some of the items belowground and figured out which ones were most important. Alrik had us bring down any magic items that were left above."

"Where did you put them?" Piran asked, looking around the room that was bare except for the catafalque.

"There's a library down the hall that's outside that door," Dillon said nervously and pointed to the closed door on the other side of the tomb.

"So the Knights had already hidden the big stuff before Reese captured Lynge," Blaine mused. "Do you think Lynge betrayed them before Reese killed him?"

Dillon drew a long breath. "No. Lynge didn't know what the Knights had done. Reese and Pollard destroyed a lot of the castle, but that closed off the inside passageways to the crypts underneath. When I fled the castle, I kept a watch on the cliff-side passageway we just came through. I never saw Reese or Pollard or any of their men near it."

"From what's here, I'd say that Almstedt must have founded the Knights of Esthrane," Kestel said. "But from the mural, it looks as if he died before they were betrayed."

"Don't touch anything," Zaryae warned. "Our host is watching, deciding what to make of us."

"Our host?" Piran questioned.

Zaryae nodded and inclined her head toward the catafalque. "Torsten Almstedt."

The room grew suddenly cold. Outside the door, Blaine heard the low rumble of voices and the clatter of boot steps. He reached for his sword, sure they had been betrayed.

"Your sword is no use here," Dagur said. He lifted his face to the magic like a hound scenting his quarry. "Not against the dead."

A fine mist appeared from nothing, coalescing between the catafalque and the door to the hallway into the translucent image of a man dressed like the figure atop the bier. The ghost was a man in his middle years with the bearing and stance of a warrior. Almstedt's form may have appeared insubstantial, but here in the crypts, in his place of power, Blaine was certain the ghost could be dangerous. He was just as sure that the sword in Almstedt's hand would be as deadly as any blade in the world of the living.

"We've come to reclaim the items Seneschal Lynge left here for safekeeping," Blaine said, stepping forward.

Almstedt's sword swung through the air, narrowly missing Blaine. The blade barred Blaine from moving closer to the door. Almstedt's gaze swept over him, and his gaze lingered on the two amulets at Blaine's throat, the disk and the passage token.

"My name is Blaine McFadden, Lord of Glenreith," Blaine said, willing himself to meet the ghost's gaze. "Nidhud, one of the Knights of Esthrane, is our ally. He gave me this token when I traveled to Valshoa to bring back the magic. Some of the Knights took sanctuary there."

Almstedt listened without showing emotion. *He died long before King Merrill's ancestor betrayed the Knights. In his time, the Knights were the left hand of the king. They had no need of sanctuary*, Blaine thought. *If he exists as a ghost, does he know what's happened in the world he left behind?*

"Tell him why you've come," Zaryae urged.

"We brought the magic back—almost," Blaine told the ghost. "It's not the way it was before the war. The magic that returned can be harnessed, but it's brittle . . . not quite right."

"I fail to see what's causing the delay," Xaffert fussed. He was a sallow-looking man with thinning brown hair and a monocle, and right now he was indignant. "Alrik was the rightful owner of the pieces, and we're acting in his stead." He moved as if to go around Almstedt's sword, but the ghost shifted to block his path.

"I think it would be best to wait until our host wants us to proceed," Dagur cautioned. "And from the sound of it, the corridor's not a healthy place to be right now." Shouts and footsteps echoed from the rock, as well as the clang of swords.

"I thought you said no one else can get in down here," Piran whispered. "It sounds like there's a battle going on just outside the door."

"There is," Dillon replied. "The ghosts of the people buried down here are restless. They relive the battles and the betrayals that killed them. Alrik told me that's how Geddy, Lynge's assistant, was killed."

"Now you tell us this?" Piran said, eyes wide.

Dillon's expression was somber. "The ghosts don't reenact their battles all the time," he replied, keeping one eye on the ghost who blocked their path. "When we brought the pieces down here, Lynge was constantly fussing about the time. He must have known when the ghosts were likely to be active. Maybe he figured the ghosts could protect the items better than we could."

By the sound of it, the ghostly battle beyond the door was drawing to a close, and in a few moments, the tomb was silent. Almstedt lifted his sword and gestured toward the entranceway, gliding effortlessly through the door.

"I guess he's going with us," Blaine commented.

They moved into the cool, dark passageway. Despite the sounds of pitched battle they had heard just moments ago, nothing in the corridor suggested that anyone had passed this way for quite a while. Almstedt's ghost stood in a hall to their left.

"He knows the way," Dillon directed. "And keep your wits about you. There are ghosts aplenty. I'm glad I never knew that when I lived in the castle up above. I might not have slept well, knowing what goes on down here."

Wide passageways carved into rock led in several directions, and it seemed to Blaine he had entered an underground city. As they passed the entrances to other chambers, Blaine glimpsed rooms filled with catafalques, but other, larger areas where it looked as if rooms from the castle above, and even whole sections of the city of Castle Reach, had been re-created.

"Alrik told me that the kings and nobles weren't sure they would pass on to the Sea of Souls, given their deeds," Dillon whispered to Blaine. "So they made sure their accommodations here were comfortable and familiar—just in case."

"Can you imagine the secrets buried here?" Kestel murmured, her green eyes shining. She pushed a strand of red hair back into the braid that kept it out of her way. "I wish we could explore."

"The library's just ahead," Dillon said.

"Let's be quick about this," Piran said. "I don't like this place. The sooner we're done and out of here, the better."

"In here," Dillon indicated, using a key from his satchel and opening the door to a room not far from Almstedt's crypt. A warren of corridors led off into darkness. Blaine looked at the flickering light in his lantern and shuddered at the thought of being lost in those dark passageways among warring and treacherous ghosts. He did not mention it, but his sentiments echoed Piran's.

"Let us handle this," Xaffert said as they walked into the room. Xaffert was dressed in clothing that had seen better days. The richly woven brocade of his tunic was badly worn and snagged, stained in places, and his trews were mended awkwardly. Whether the clothing was what remained of his scholarly belongings or, more likely, something he had looted from a deserted villa, Blaine did not know. Xaffert wore his motley outfit with strained dignity, as if the loss of their status and the university itself was almost too much to bear.

Their lanterns illuminated a relatively large room with shelves lining the walls and a worktable with a few chairs. From the way the books were stacked on the tables and around the room, it was clear someone had already mined the library for information. On one table lay several cloth sacks filled to the brim.

"Lynge and Geddy brought Connor and Penhallow down here to help you find what you needed to bring back the magic," Dillon said with a look toward Blaine. "I'm not sure what they took with them, or whether it was helpful, but I'll bet those sacks are full of the items they wanted to come back for."

Blaine could guess. He suspected that Penhallow had found some of the obsidian disks hidden in the crypts, disks that had been used by the ancient lords to bind the magic long ago to the will of men. Perhaps they had taken books and scrolls as well, Blaine thought, looking around. Rogue mage Vigus Quintrel had hidden memories deep in Connor's mind, then left a trail of clues to help them find what they needed to restore the magic.

"Let's see what we have," Xaffert said, pushing past Blaine toward a cloth bundle on the nearest table.

"These crypts are full of old power," Dagur said. "Perhaps since the magic remains rather brittle, we might be safest handling the items as little as possible." Balding and thin, perhaps in his fourth decade, Dagur looked more like a tavern master than a scholar, clad in a serviceable woolen jacket, homespun trews, and sturdy boots.

Xaffert fixed his colleague with a glare. "I'm not going to let a few ghosts send me screaming," he said with a sniff. "We're better served knowing what the seneschal thought valuable enough to hide down here. That way, if we run into difficulties on the way back, we know what tools are at our disposal."

"I agree with Dagur," Zaryae said. "Even if the artifacts still work as they were intended, using them down here might attract unwanted attention."

Xaffert's contempt was clear in his face. "That's probably prudent for you. What magic you have is untrained. Dagur and I are scholars and adepts, formally educated in the magic arts by the most powerful mages of our era. We're quite well prepared to handle whatever arises."

Blaine was not so sure that Dagur agreed with the older mage. Dagur remained a pace back from the table and seemed happy to allow Xaffert to take the items out of the sacks in which Lynge and Dillon had brought them. He ignored the items Penhallow had set aside.

"Take a look if you have to, but don't spend all day doing it," Piran grumbled. "I want to get aboveground."

Xaffert examined the items from one of the sacks. Blaine stayed back a bit, as did the others, but from what he could see, the magical artifacts did not appear unusual. Half a dozen pieces now lay on the table: a silver chalice, a flat piece of burnished wood carved with sigils, a white-handled boline knife with a curved blade, a dark scrying mirror, a lavishly engraved bell, and a stone censor with carvings.

"I find nothing wrong with these pieces, nothing at all," Xaffert announced after a few moments. "In fact, I suspect that such basic tools cannot be subverted even by broken magic. It will be a pleasure to have these fine items in our study."

637

"Just put the bloody things back in the sack and let's get going," Piran said. "We've been down here long enough already."

Zaryae hung back. "The items may have been altered," she said. "We must be careful."

Dagur carefully gathered up the few small items that had spilled from the sacks. Even with the minor amount of magic Blaine possessed, he could feel the jangle of power from the items in the sacks. Yet to him, the magic felt... off-kilter, like a painting hung askew. Piran, with no magic at all, kept his knife and sword at the ready, watching the door to the hallway.

It seemed to Blaine that the shadows crowded more closely around them as they retreated to the corridor. Several times, out of the corner of his eye, he caught a glimpse of motion, only to find nothing when he looked again. The others also seemed to be on edge, and Blaine wondered if they felt the same tingle in the air that he sensed. The temperature in the corridor was now ice-cold. The sound of running feet echoed from every direction, yet what they saw hurtling past them down the corridor were blue-green orbs of light, bouncing and bobbing and moving at great speed. Almstedt moved to stand in the doorway and beckoned them to come.

As they watched, the orbs began to cluster, expanding and shifting until the forms of men appeared. Blaine and his group stared down the corridor to see opposing spectral armies facing off against each other in the wide chamber, blocking their path back to Almstedt's crypt.

Battle cries echoed from the stone walls as the two sides rushed toward each other and again Almsteadt's ghost stopped, barring the group from going farther toward the commotion. Almstedt raised his sword toward the spectral fighters, clearly intending to stand his ground while they got clear.

"I was afraid of this," Piran muttered. "Now what?"

"Dillon, any chance the entrance you and Alrik used to bring the items here is still open?" Blain asked.

"The upper level where we entered has completely collapsed."

"There's got to be another way out," Blaine said. He looked to Kestel. "How about you? You're the spy. Any great ideas?"

"I heard rumors about secret passageways to the crypts, but I never found any," she replied. "I didn't know about the one we used to enter, and even if we found other openings, are they passable, given how badly the castle was damaged?"

Those questions had plagued Blaine as well, but since they were cut off from their only known exit, as well as the spirit who might have protected them, he found no point in dwelling on the negative. "Let's find one and then worry about the rest. Gather up as many of the bags as you can carry and let's get moving," he replied.

They had reached a large chamber filled with catafalques, some ancient and some much newer. With a gasp, Kestel turned her lantern to illuminate the figure that lay carved in marble, eternally at rest upon his tomb. "Look," she whispered, pointing. "It's King Merrill."

Merrill had been the king since before Blaine and the others were born, and it was he who had exiled them. But Merrill had probably never imagined that he would be the last king of Donderath, or that in his reign the kingdom would burn, its magic would fail, and the people of an entire Continent would be reduced to desperate subsistence. Now, seeing his figure still and silent atop the catafalque, Blaine felt a flash of grief for all that was lost, despite the danger of their situation.

"We've got company," Piran said in a low voice.

Blaine looked up to see a young man standing just beyond the torchlight. The man beckoned urgently even as the sounds of battle seemed to close in. Xaffert and Dagur started forward, but Blaine threw out a warning arm to halt them. "Wait. We don't know that he's really on our side."

Dillon maneuvered forward. "Yes, we do," he said triumphantly. "That's Geddy. Thank the gods, it's Geddy."

Blaine met Piran's gaze and shrugged. Caught between threatening specters and the possibility of a benign ghostly guide, they had little choice. "Let's hope he knows where we're going, because the soldiers are getting closer," Blaine said. "Follow Geddy."

Geddy's ghost moved so quickly they were forced to run to keep him in sight. Blaine had rarely been to the castle before his exile. He barely remembered the seneschal, and it was likely that Geddy had not been in Lynge's employ when Blaine earned his exile. The ghost was tall and angular, with lank dark hair, all slender arms and legs. Blaine hoped that their unlikely guide could actually get them to safety.

The ghost led them down one corridor and then another, and Blaine struggled to remember their course in case it turned out to be a trap. But it seemed to him that the ground was rising under their feet, and instinct told him they were moving in the right direction to be inside the castle, or at least the bailey walls. They had divided the sacks of magical items up among themselves, but even so, the packs made it difficult to move quickly and quietly.

Finally, Geddy's ghost stopped beside a catafalque and pointed toward the raised marble tomb. He pantomimed moving its heavy carved lid aside.

"What's he want us to do, climb inside?" Piran's skepticism was clear in his voice.

"I think that's exactly what he means," Kestel said. "Come on, get to it."

extras

Blaine, Piran, and Dillon set their shoulders to the heavy marble, and Blaine was surprised when it moved much more easily than he had expected. He lifted his lantern and peered inside, expecting to see dry bones and rotted finery. Instead, he found stairs descending into deeper darkness.

"In we go," he said, stepping aside to allow Kestel and Zaryae to enter first.

"You expect me to climb into a crypt?" Xaffert huffed.

Dillon grabbed the bags of items out of his hands. "You can do what you want. I'm saving my skin."

Even Dagur moved quickly toward the escape route. "I don't have a problem with it, actually," he said, less worried about annoying his master than dying in the darkness. "Honestly, Xaffert, come along."

"We're not waiting on you," Blaine said brusquely. "Are you coming?"

Muttering, Xaffert followed the others. Piran waved Blaine on ahead of him. Blaine paused in front of Geddy's spirit.

Up close, he could see the dark stains on the young man's clothing where a sword had dealt a deathblow. "Thank you," he said. Geddy inclined his head, then gestured toward the catafalque. Blaine climbed inside and hurried down the narrow steps with Piran right behind him. Moving the lid back into place from the inside was also easier than he expected, as there were handles carved into the marble.

As the lid began to swing shut behind them, Blaine heard the door to the outer corridor slam open and the thud of boots on the stone floor of the crypt. A blue-white light flared as the panel sealed closed.

"Did anyone notice that Geddy didn't come down with us?" Piran asked as they moved through the darkness. The cata-falque steps led down to a narrow passage just wide enough to move single file. A little maneuvering had allowed Piran and Blaine to go first, with the mages taking up the rear.

Dillon, just behind Blaine, held his lantern aloft. "I think I know where this leads," he said. "And besides, there's only one way to go."

Blaine and his friends ran along the passageway, stumbling on the uneven floor. The sacks of artifacts seemed more an encumbrance than ever, and Blaine feared the ghosts would follow them. He ran, expecting any moment to feel a knife between his shoulder blades. But the sound of battle receded, replaced by the echo of their labored breathing in the narrow passageway.

After a few hundred steps, the passage came to an abrupt end, facing a stone wall with jutting stones offering a ladder of sorts upward. "Do you know where we'll come out?" Blaine asked.

Dillon looked uncertain. "Maybe. Once when I was moving about late at night, I saw Sir Alrik going down the hallway by the exchequer's office. I had to go in the same direction, and I expected to have to explain myself when he saw me, but when I turned the corner, he was gone. The corridor led to a work-room, and there was no one anywhere to be seen. I think there's a panel, somewhere in that corridor, that might open into a hidden passage."

"Yeah, but there's no telling whether it's *this* hidden passage," Piran said.

"Or whether we're coming up under a portion of the castle that's collapsed," Blaine added.

"We'll know soon enough," Kestel said from behind him. "Just climb."

In a few moments, they reached a dark landing that ended in another blank wall. This time, the wall felt like wood. Blaine and Piran edged aside to allow Dillon to step ahead of them, and he began to run his hands over the wood. A quiet *snick* brought a smile of triumph. "Got it," he said.

Dillon pushed on the door only to find it stuck. "Give me a hand," he said. Blaine and Piran edged up and put their shoulders against the door, shoving it open. On the other side of the wood, they could hear a heavy object sliding across a wooden floor. They stepped out into a dark room, and Blaine lifted a lantern.

"I think we're in a butler's closet," he said, looking around at the shelves that had once held neat stacks of linens and other items needed by the housekeeping servants. He turned to see a wooden crate behind them in the middle of the floor, the obstacle that had hindered their escape. The closet was now a ransacked mess.

"A lot of manors have hiding places—even whole hidden rooms—in case of attack," Kestel said. "Some have secret passageways leading out into the countryside."

Dillon nodded. "This is where I lost sight of Sir Alrik that night," he said. "I had no idea this was here, and with what a mess it is, I doubt Reese and Pollard ever suspected." He smiled. "What do you know? Geddy got us out."

Blaine offered another silent thanks to the young man's ghost, then turned to help the others onto the landing. He and Piran began clearing rubble to make their exit. While the storeroom was in an area still somewhat intact, it took several candlemarks to make their way out and back to their camp. Kestel seemed to take it all in stride and dusted herself off matter-of-factly, while Zaryae murmured a prayer to the gods. Dagur looked pale and flustered by the ordeal. Xaffert still seemed miffed over something, but at the moment, discovering what had gotten the mage out of sorts was not a priority for Blaine.

"We're here just for tonight, then we need to keep moving," Blaine said, addressing Xaffert and Dagur. "Call the rest of your mages together and let's get an idea of just what—if anything—those items Alrik thought were so important can do. Reese thought something left behind was worth killing for. I just want to know whether or not they still work and whether they're safe to take back to Glenreith. I should go check in with Niklas and see what they've found."

"Is there a particular reason we must work with them immediately?" Dagur asked. "My books and scrolls are at Glenreith. I'd feel safer taking our time and working on them there."

"How many times do I have to tell you that, for a mage of power, these items simply pose no danger, even with the new magic?" Xaffert said, exasperation edging his voice. He snatched the bag he had been carrying back from Dillon and thrust his hand inside, coming up with the dark scrying mirror.

"I really don't think—" Dagur began.

"Take this, for example." Xaffert brandished the mirror like a trophy. "Perhaps you'd like to know whether our road will be clear. Let me have a look."

Zaryae looked stricken, and she tried to move past Kestel to intervene. "Don't! I can feel the power—it's all wrong."

"Nonsense," Xaffert said with a dismissive gesture. "That's like saying that a hammer doesn't work the way it used to. These are mere tools. What matters is the skill of the user."

"The items may be damaged," Zaryae cautioned. "There's no way to know what will happen when they're used."

Xaffert regarded Zaryae before speaking. "I would recommend caution for you as well. But my colleagues and I have mastered all manner of magical items at the university. I'm quite certain that we can handle the pieces safely, even if the changing magic has altered them."

"Perhaps we should take this slowly," Dagur cautioned. "We could take them to Glenreith and set a warded circle for protection."

"I'm quite certain that such things are not necessary," Xaffert replied. He held the dark mirror in front of him in both hands, and his lips began to move silently. Blaine could feel power begin to coalesce around the mage, but it felt more like the wild magic storms. The air itself began to crackle and spark around Xaffert, who stared deeply into the mirror. He began to laugh, and then as the mirror's images changed, his laughter grew fraught with tension and became heaving breaths.

The mirror's surface began to glow, illuminating Xaffert's face caught in an expression of absolute horror. Blood streamed from his nose, mouth, and ears and he started to scream. Before anyone had a chance to move, Xaffert fell to the ground, the mirror still clutched in his hand.

Dagur and Zaryae rushed over to Xaffert, while Piran grabbed a wooden chair and used its leg to knock the mirror from Xaffert's fingers. "Is he dead?" Blaine asked, keeping a worried eye on the mirror, which now lay dim and inert beside the mage.

Dagur took a cloth from his pack and covered Xaffert's face. "Most definitely—his eyes and everything behind appear to be burned out."

"Let me make something very clear," Blaine said, fixing Dagur with a look. "I'm willing to give you and your mages sanctuary in exchange for your expertise. But I need to be able to trust you—and that means that you'd better be right when you give me your word on something."

Dagur pulled himself up to his full height. "Unlike Xaffert, when I give you my word, you can stake your life on it."

"That's the point," Blaine replied. "I am. We all are. And you'd damn well better be right."